WATERBLACK

Books by Alex Pheby

CITIES OF THE WEFT
Mordew
Malarkoi
Waterblack

Playthings
Lucia

WATERBLACK

ALEX PHEBY

TOR PUBLISHING GROUP
NEW YORK

WATERBLACK

Copyright © 2025 by Alex Pheby

A Tor Book
Published by Tom Doherty Associates / Tor Publishing Group
120 Broadway
New York, NY 10271

www.torpublishinggroup.com

Tor® is a registered trademark of Macmillan Publishing Group, LLC.

The Library of Congress Cataloging-in-Publication Data is available upon request.

ISBN 978-1-250-81729-7 (hardcover)
ISBN 978-1-250-81730-3 (ebook)

Our books may be purchased in bulk for promotional, educational, or business use. Please contact your local bookseller or the Macmillan Corporate and Premium Sales Department at 1-800-221-7945, extension 5442, or by email at MacmillanSpecialMarkets@macmillan.com.

First published in Great Britain by Galley Beggar Press

First U.S. Edition: 2025

Printed in the United States of America

0 9 8 7 6 5 4 3 2 1

For Tam, Grey, and Chocky

THE EVENTS OF THE PREVIOUS VOLUMES, IN SUMMARY

Nathan fishes for flukes in the Living Mud with the Spark, an unpredictable and uncontrollable power he has inherited from his father.

The Spark Itches if Nathan doesn't Scratch it.

One day he makes a limb-baby and sells it to a tanner.

Nathan takes the money to his poor mother and dying father.

The money is fake.

His mother orders Nathan to go to the Master for work.

The Fetch takes Nathan and some other boys up the Glass Road to the Master.

One of the boys is Gam Halliday.

Gam tries to recruit Nathan into his criminal gang.

Nathan refuses.

Gam goads Nathan into Scratching the Spark Itch by teasing him.

The Fetch beats another boy to death for the disturbance Nathan and Gam make.

The remaining boys are delivered to the Master.

Gam is rejected at the gate and returns home.

In the Underneath, Nathan saves a boy from falling to his death.

The boy is revealed to be a girl – Prissy – and Nathan feels an immediate sympathy with her.

The children are washed by a team of laundresses.

Bellows, the Master's factotum, examines the boys, discarding some, including Prissy, and takes the others to see the Master.

The Master hires some of the boys for unspecified work, but declines to hire Nathan.

7

The Master can sense Nathan's power.

He warns him against Sparking and sends him back to the slums.

At home, Nathan's father is dying of the lungworm.

Nathan wants to Scratch the Spark Itch, but his father forbids it.

Nathan promises to get medicine, but he has no money.

In the slums, Nathan Scratches the Spark Itch, angrily, to kill a fluke.

The fluke evolves into a rat, which bites Nathan's hand. From then on, Scratching the Itch burns the wound and makes Nathan's arm increasingly immaterial.

Nathan goes into the Merchant City, hoping to steal money for medicine.

He steals a wealthy old woman's coin purse, but is caught by bystanders.

Gam rescues him before he can be punished and takes him into the sewers.

The two boys go to Gam's hideout, the clubhouse, an abandoned subterranean gentlemen's club.

Prissy and Joes, the other members of Gam's gang, are there.

Nathan, having fallen for Prissy, joins the gang.

The gang go back to the Merchant City on a job to steal money from a haberdasher.

Nathan panics when Prissy seems to be in danger and almost kills the haberdasher with the Spark.

With the money they have stolen, the gang go to see the gangmaster, Mr Padge, to buy medicine for Nathan's father.

Mr Padge gives Nathan the medicine, but refuses to take his money, establishing a debt on Nathan's part.

Nathan returns to the slums. His mother is entertaining a gentleman caller who has a fawn-coloured birthmark.

Nathan gives his father the medicine, but it's clear that it won't be enough.

Nathan agrees to get more.

Unable to bear being at home, Nathan returns to the clubhouse.

The pain of the rat bite gets worse, as does his Itch.

At night the clubhouse is full of ghosts who seem to recognise Nathan.

The next day, Gam takes Nathan to steal bacon from a warehouse.

From there they go to the Temple of the Athanasians, a brothel where Prissy's sister works.

Prissy will be sold to the brothel unless she can compensate her sister for the lost income.

Nathan agrees to a risky criminal job for Mr Padge in order to get the money for medicine and Prissy's buyout.

Gam, Prissy and Nathan go to burgle a palace by entering through the sewers.

Nathan uses his Spark to open a safe and retrieve the document Mr Padge hired them to steal.

On the way out, Gam pushes Prissy into a crowded room and indicates that Nathan should rescue her by using the Spark.

In the room are various nobles, the chief of whom is the man with the fawn-coloured birthmark.

Hiding his surprise and horror, the man allows the children to leave before Nathan can kill everyone with the Spark, and gives him a gold coin.

Back at the clubhouse, Prissy questions Gam's actions, but he won't be drawn.

The gang take the document to Mr Padge, who gives them another job – to steal a locket from a merchant's house.

Prissy uses her share of the money to pay off her indenture.

Scoping out the next job, with time to kill, the children visit the zoo and give buns to the alifonjers, Prissy's favourite animals.

The gang decide to burgle the merchant's house by going in from the roof.

They bribe the Fetch to take them up the Glass Road, slipping out near the roof of the merchant house.

Gam agrees to lower Joes, Nathan and Prissy down to the roof by rope.

Nathan, then Prissy, successfully make the rooftop, but Joes, seemingly betrayed by Gam, falls, and dies.

Nathan tries to resurrect Joes using the Spark, but it doesn't work.

The remaining children have no option but to complete the burglary, but inside they are interrupted by the magical dogs Sirius and Anaximander.

Anaximander, who can talk, threatens the children with death, and Sirius eats the faces from Joes, whose body has become two bodies.

Nathan and Prissy return to the roof and attempt to descend to ground level by rope.

They are left dangling above a fatal drop: the rope is too short.

Having received new instructions from the Master via Sirius's magical organ, Anaximander rescues the children.

The dogs accompany the children away from the merchant house, having secured the locket Padge hired them to steal.

The party go to find Gam, hoping for answers regarding the death of Joes.

They find Gam in a ginhouse, but he is unwilling to talk.

The ginhouse patrons attempt to steal Anaximander – he disembowels one of them and they give up.

The gin-wife objects to the mess Anaximander has made, and the dog agrees to provide a service for her.

Nathan, Prissy and Sirius go to the slums.

Nathan has no medicine for his father, who has become even more seriously ill.

Nathan's mother begs Nathan to use the Spark to purge the lungworms.

Nathan agrees, revelling in his disobedience.

The procedure starts promisingly, until Nathan's father rises up and prevents it.

Nathan's mother urges Nathan to defy his father and cure him, but Nathan cannot break his father's interdiction.

He promises to get more medicine and runs to Mr Padge.

Padge has kidnapped Gam and is holding him hostage until Nathan gives up the locket they stole from the merchant house. Padge also wants Nathan to sign the document they stole from the palace.

Nathan isn't interested, he only wants medicine.

Padge takes Nathan to the house of a pharmacist, and the two extort medicine from him with menaces.

Nathan hands over the locket and signs the document, which he cannot read, paying his debt to Padge, and releasing Gam.

On release, Gam admits he let Joes fall and die on the orders of Mr Padge, who had threatened to have his assassins kill and mince Prissy.

Sirius alerts Nathan to the fact that his father is in danger and the party run to the slums.

There they find Bellows and a contingent of gill-men.

When Nathan reaches his father, he is dead.

Without his father's influence restraining him, Nathan fills with the Spark.

The gang are summoned by a signal back to the clubhouse, where they find the ghosts of Joes who warn Nathan against a trap.

Nathan, feeling that Bellows has killed his father on the instructions of the Master, vows revenge regardless of any trap.

Nathan begins to glow blue with Spark energy and his arm loses its materiality.

The gang go to the Fetch and threaten him with murder if he doesn't take them up the Glass Road to the Master. Reluctantly, he agrees.

They are met at the door of the Master's Manse by the Master and Bellows.

The Master denies the murder of Nathan's father and forces Mr Padge, Prissy and Gam to admit that they were part of a plot against Nathan instigated by the Mistress of Malarkoi, the enemy ruler of a neighbouring city.

Unable to understand their treachery, Nathan turns his back on his companions and goes with the Master into his Manse.

The Master has created a talisman – the Interdicting Finger – from the locket Mr Padge had them steal, combined with Nathan's father's severed index finger.

He puts this around Nathan's neck, which calms his Spark.

The Master gives Nathan an ointment for his arm and leaves him in the care of Bellows.

Bellows begins Nathan's education.

Nathan learns of Malarkoi, the enemy city, and its Mistress.

He is given educational toys that teach him how to behave.

Whenever he feels trapped, or angry, or violent, the locket around his neck dampens his spirits.

He is fed, watered, clothed, and indoctrinated in the ways of the Master of Mordew.

Nathan is given a magical book that teaches him how to read and write.

In the background to this new life, he sees fleeting glimpses of a girl in a blue dress.

He no longer feels the Itch to use the Spark.

Magical artefacts manipulate Nathan into believing his friends betrayed him.

When he learns that Prissy tricked him into loving her, he goes to the zoo and kills her precious alifonjers.

The next day the Master comes to him with a magical dagger and shows him how to use it.

Convinced the boy is under his control, he removes the locket that contains the Interdicting Finger.

Nathan is given the magical book, and the dagger, and is sent to Malarkoi to destroy its Mistress.

The book catalyses or inhibits his Spark, the dagger directs his violence.

In Malarkoi, Nathan meets the Mistress.

She is expecting him and seems resigned to her defeat at his hands.

She fights him nonetheless, and steals parts of his body to make a magical knife of her own.

She summons the gods of Malarkoi to defend her.

On the verge of his defeat, the book catalyses Nathan's Spark and burns everything but the Mistress away.

Seeing she is defeated, she offers her life to Nathan, and asks him to give the knife to her daughter, Dashini.

Nathan kills the Mistress and lets out an unrestrained burst of Spark energy that scours Malarkoi for miles around.

Using the Spark in this profligate manner reduces Nathan's material presence.

Nathan returns to a hero's welcome in Mordew, the Master heals him, but Nathan knows himself to have been manipulated.

The Master sends him to see the girl in the blue dress. the imprisoned daughter of the Mistress of Malarkoi, Dashini, captured behind a sphere of magical glass.

Dashini has spent her captivity unsuccessfully inventing magical methods of escape.

She has made masks that allow her to possess some of the Master's staff.

She gives one to Nathan, and that night they possess the Manse's Caretaker and Cook.

Nathan takes her to the library, where the Master has stored some magical books.

Dashini uses one to summon the ur-demon, Rekka.

Rekka, determined to destroy its summoner, destroys the glass quarantine that has been imprisoning Dashini.

Dashini, free, transports Rekka to the centre of the Earth, and she and Nathan try to leave the Manse.

The Master has magical barriers that prevent them from leaving.

Dashini takes them below to a chamber in which the corpse of God – the source of the Master's power – is contained.

Nathan takes God's eye and uses the power to return to the slums.

No longer constrained by the locket, and empowered by the eye of God, Nathan brings revolution to Mordew.

He creates an army of flukes from the Living Mud, sets fires, drives the slum-dwellers into the Merchant City, and then destroys the Glass Road. Each act makes him less and less materially present in the world.

He reunites with Gam, Prissy and Sirius, and finds his mother.

She has joined forces with Anaximander, and takes them all to the man with the fawn-coloured birthmark.

This man has access to a merchant vessel, and the party leave Mordew burning behind them.

When the ship is at sea, Bellows boards with a group of gill-men, determined to bring Nathan back to the Master.

Nathan is exhausted by his use of the Spark, and the eye of God, and is now defenceless.

Mr Padge, who has stowed away on the ship, emerges with Prissy as a hostage.

Nathan agrees to return with Bellows peacefully if Bellows rescues Prissy.

Bellows takes a magical weapon and attempts to kill Padge, but Padge has magical protection.

The weapon's effect is turned on Bellows, devolving him back into a boy.

While Padge is gloating over his victory, Gam stabs him in the back in revenge. This was Prissy's plan all along, she providing the necessary distraction that allowed Gam to sneak up.

Padge dies.

Nathan goes to comfort Bellows, but the Master appears and takes Nathan away.

Taking advantage of Nathan's lack of material solidity, the Master crushes him.

Once Nathan is compact enough, the Master empties the locket he'd previously kept Nathan's father's Interdicting Finger in, and replaces it with Nathan's remains, creating an artefact he calls 'the Tinderbox'.

It had been the Master's plan all along to make Nathan overexert himself, magically, so he could make this Spark weapon, which he intends to use against the Eighth Atheistic Crusade – the militant wing of the mysterious 'Assembly' – who are approaching Mordew, intent on destroying it.

Sirius dives into the sea after Nathan, the Master returns to his Manse with the Tinderbox, and the ship bears the rest of Nathan's companions away.

Finding Nathan removed by the Master back to Mordew, Sirius follows.

The Master pulls the city up into a mountain by magic, hoping to make the Assembly's work more difficult when it arrives.

The owners of the ship on which Nathan's companions are present plot to throw them overboard.

Clarissa, the Boy-Bellows, Anaximander and Adam Birch leave by lifeboat before the ship owners force them off, but Gam, Prissy and Dashini are thrown in the brig.

Sirius reaches what is now Mount Mordew to find it occupied primarily by vicious flukes.

In his Manse, the Master of Mordew, Tinderbox around his neck and safe for now, turns his attentions to the making of a new Bellows to replace the one he has lost.

On the ship, Anatole, one of Padge's assassins, kills the owners and crew and advances on the children. Before Mr Padge died, he had contracted his assassins to kill anyone who ever killed him, and Anatole is the first to arrive, having been facilitated in this by the Mother of Mordew, an avatar of the Mistress of Malarkoi.

Prissy, Gam and Dashini narrowly avoid being murdered, imprison Anatole in the brig, and ground the ship on the shore near Malarkoi.

Dashini leads the three children to the Golden Pyramid, where she hopes they will be safe with her mother.

Clarissa's party, at her direction, row in a different direction in the lifeboat, and come to a flooded plain. She is taking them to find a relic she believes can make her all-powerful.

In Mordew, the Master makes use of a complex system of intermediate realms, each with a different progression of time, to enact the complex magic that creates a Bellows.

Sirius follows his senses in the search for Nathan, which leads him across Mount Mordew. The former city is transformed, corrupted, and occupied by ghosts.

Dashini leads Prissy and Gam to the Golden Pyramid of her mother, only to find that the Master has quarantined it in magical glass. They will not be able to use the front door and will have to find another way in. Other assassins are waiting for them, and Anatole has freed himself.

Dashini and party are chased by assassins to the back door of the Pyramid, the entrance of which requires a sacrifice. Dashini kills Anatole with the Nathan Knife, allowing them to enter.

Sirius follows a ghost down to Gam's former clubhouse where he finds a room in which a corpse is standing on a table, wearing the face of God, surrounded by the clubhouse ghosts. These ghosts encourage Sirius to eat God's face, which he does. He assumes divinity, becoming Goddog.

Clarissa leads Bellows, Anaximander and Adam across the flooded landscape. Clarissa is taciturn, but the others occupy themselves with stories, plans and observations.

Once inside the Pyramid by the back door, Dashini and party are obliged to traverse a series of Levels in order to reach the one in which her mother lives. Once this would have been easy, but the first Level has become corrupted and is now filled with an excess of cattle-headed people. The three have enormous difficulty reaching the Door out, which is broken. Prissy suffocates and the other two are stranded.

The Master continues his work, which involves a great deal of translation between the intermediate realms, something that gives him headaches, and which he counters with medicines. In one of the realms there is a copy of the Master that he avoids interacting with.

Dashini, Gam and Prissy are rescued from their fates when they are summoned into the second Level by person-headed snake occultists. The formerly peaceful Level is now engaged in a vicious civil war.

The Master's medicines, and the constant translating between realms, affect his thinking, making it hard to concentrate on the complicated spells and rituals needed to make a new Bellows. The process starts to go wrong.

Sirius Goddog emerges from the clubhouse, bounding through the earth, and rampages across Mount Mordew, killing every fluke he sees, knocking down buildings, not quite able to contain his divine powers as he digests the face of God.

Clarissa's party makes good progress to where the relic is, but their journey is interrupted by the arrival of more of

Padge's assassins, who are contracted to kill Bellows since he had a part in their employer's death. Sharli and Deaf Sam attempt to kill the four, but are no match for Clarissa's power. They die.

Dashini, Prissy and Gam traverse the second Pyramid Level, avoiding the civil war, and leave through the Door by sacrificing the occultists who summoned them there.

In the Manse, the copy of the Master takes advantage of the other Master's befuddlement to shoot him dead with a shotgun. He finishes the process of making the new Bellows, who is only just viable.

Sirius Goddog's rampaging is brought to an end when he is visited by a dog avatar of the Mistress of Malarkoi: the Great White Bitch. The two titanic dogs copulate, generate seven divine puppies, and the Bitch shows Sirius how to invade the Master's intermediate realms.

Goddog appears in the Master's realm, and bites the new Bellows in half. This done, he chases the Master through the Manse.

Having killed the assassins, but fearing more will be on the way, Clarissa and party rush on. They come to a lake, swim under it to a cave, and here they find the relic they've been seeking: it's another Clarissa, frozen in ice. She is guarded by Thales, a magic talking dog like Anaximander.

Dashini and company come to a Pyramid Level occupied by dragons. Once a magnificent place, it is now becoming a graveyard. Japalura, its god, is in a depressive fugue. Against Dashini's will, she flies them to the Door and suicides in order to provide the magic to open it. The three leave.

Goddog chases the Master through his Manse, who employs magic to defend himself. Sirius is proof against it, so the Master leaves for Mount Mordew, hoping to find enough room to use the Tinderbox against the divine dog.

In the underwater cave, Clarissa attempts to desecrate her corpse relic. Thales is sworn to protect it, so he and Anaximander fight. Thales is out of condition due to his long confinement below ground, and Anaximander narrowly wins. This victory is soured by the understanding that the dogs have killed the only dogs like them in the world, and that Anaximander's wounds are also likely fatal. Clarissa harvests fertilised eggs from the womb of the corpse, and makes for the surface, ignoring Anaximander's plight.

Dashini, Gam and Prissy come to the Level occupied by the White Stag and the Wolf Pack, and because there is no other way out, Gam allows himself to be sacrificed so Prissy and Dashini can escape.

The Master, now on Mount Mordew, is interrupted by the Great White Bitch. He attempts to use the Tinderbox to kill her, but it's knocked away down the side of the mountain. He chases after it, with Goddog chasing after him.

Clarissa emerges on the grassland above the cave, which is near the lake. Here, the Druze, one of the last of Mr Padge's surviving assassins, has been lying in wait. The Druze shoots Clarissa with a crossbow, wounding her in the face. She disappears. When Bellows and Anaximander struggle out to the surface, the Druze shoots them too.

Dashini and Prissy emerge on the next Level to find that its god – Le Roi de l'Ombre – has infiltrated the other realms, turning them to darkness. There is only one way out, the last Door, and Dashini sacrifices herself so that Prissy can go through it.

The Tinderbox is drawn down Mount Mordew to a breach in the side of the mountain that leads to the God chamber, where God's corpse resides. The Master chases it, Goddog chases him, and the two fall into the chamber.

Prissy arrives at the Level where the Mistress of Malarkoi lives. The Mistress apologises to Prissy for all the trouble she's had getting there, but her reward is to become the Mistress of Malarkoi in her place. The old Mistress says she'll make it up to Dashini, and summons a pyramid that will teach Prissy how to use her new powers.

In the God chamber, Goddog and the Master tumble towards the corpse of God. The proximity of God's corpse drains Goddog of his divinity, and Sirius vomits up what remains of the face of God. The Master brings the Tinderbox to bear on Sirius, and scours him out of existence.

When the disgorged face of God meets the rest of the corpse, the corpse begins to move. The Master attempts to prevent the recombination of the face and body, and when he fails is appalled to see that the face is Clarissa's. There is a crossbow bolt through her cheek.

One of the children of Goddog and the Great White Bitch, Treachery, who has been following behind, takes the Nathan pellet that powers the Tinderbox and flees to Waterblack while the Master is distracted.

In the immaterial realm, Nathan Treeves is suffering a painful existence. He ought not to be present there, but the will of God binds him in place. The Mistress of Malarkoi takes him from that realm and offers to return him to the material realm at the cost of the sacrifice of a thousand million infants. This Nathan agrees to immediately.

DRAMATIS PERSONAE

Anatole The well-dressed assassin with a nice singing voice performs a more subsidiary role in this book, but he still dresses well, and he still sings nicely, and he still has a hand in several deaths, so there is no reason to exclude him from this dramatis personae. Indeed, we learn more about him in this book than we did in the last.

Anaximander Can a dog become a ghost? The answer is yes, providing that dog has a magical provenance. Does his personality change after death? The answer is no, not very much. Does he speak differently, or act differently, or do anything much differently, excepting those things that a ghost must do differently than a living person? No, he does not. This is something that will please those who appreciate Anaximander as a character. For those who were glad he almost died at the end of the last book, and who had hoped to see the back of him, this will no doubt prove a disappointment, particularly since he has been given a lengthy interlude here, and a role in the main plot.

Anaximenes Who can say who this is? Anyone with a passing knowledge of the early Greek philosophers will be able to take a guess, and that guess is likely to be correct.

Arjal One of the ten-summer children selected for sacrifice at the same time as Sharli was selected.

Bernadette The manager of the Temple of the Athanasians, and surrogate mother to the girls there.

Your mother may have selflessly dedicated herself to your welfare, but that is not true of all mothers. Bernadette is the kind of mother who would ensure that you are clean, healthy and well-fed, that you have a strong work ethic, that you are not wilful or disobedient, that you do as you are told when you are told, that you perform the duties expected of you to the best of your abilities. If that sounds like a good mother to you, then you might ask yourself what a good mother really is, given the work her motherhood conditions these girls to acquiesce to.

Berthe Another of the ten-summer children selected for sacrifice at the same time as Sharli was selected.

Black Bill A worker at Beaumont's, the bacon factory. His tale is a touching and poignant one, which is not something one often says of a man employed to murder pigs.

Blob Sometimes people will mock you for the things you are, and sometimes they will mock you for the things you are not. Blob was mocked for the latter reason, though he never understood why it was that he was mocked at all. He did his work – which was cookery – just as well as anyone else at The Commodious Hour, so where was the necessity to insult him? Perhaps if his superior in the brigade – Boland – eventually moved on to other premises, Blob might find himself given a different name. 'Boss', it seemed to Blob, was a better name than 'Blob', and this is why, in the mornings, as he shaved over his basin with his sharpest knife, looking into a sliver of mirror held in his free hand, he said quietly to himself, 'Morning, Boss,' over and over, in different voices. In his mind he pictured his progress through the kitchens. 'One day,' he thought, when he was cleanshaven, 'One day.'

Boland To be the head chef of a restaurant has a certain cachet, but only to those who do not work there. The head chef of The Commodious Hour knew himself to be the head skivvy, the head market boy, the head kitchen porter, the head of all of the most difficult and time-sensitive jobs about the place. So what if people who knew nothing thought him better than he was? What did he care about those people? Wasn't he still the one who had to run himself ragged to ensure the smooth progress of every service, whether it be lunch or dinner?

When Mr Padge came to him, as he always did, and asked him to perform a task that Padge thought was very simple and reasonable, but which Boland knew would involve work he scarcely had the capacity to carry out, he mimed, the moment Padge left, a little performance. He put up his hands and waved them about: 'Do these look like wands?' he mouthed silently. Other times he would mime that a broomstick had been shoved up his arse, so that, while he did all the hard work he was already doing, he could sweep the floor while he was doing it. 'Is that something you'd like, Mr Padge, for me to go around with a broomstick shoved up my arse?' he'd think while he mimed.

He always came to the conclusion that it was.

Is it any wonder, with that degree of resentment against his employer, that Boland did what he did when he thought Mr Padge wasn't looking?

Clarissa Delacroix Is it a woman's fault if a man she does not desire falls in love with her? Intuitively we feel that it is not, but what if she has gone to some trouble, no matter how small, to make that man fall in love with her? Perhaps she has said, or done, something to encourage that feeling in him. Perhaps she has represented herself in some way that she knows will make him tend to fall in love with her. Are these actions enough so that when the man falls in love with her we lay the blame for that at her feet? Or is it that men bear the responsibility for their own fallings in love? Surely, given how important a thing it is to love someone, the one who is doing the falling in love should take it upon themselves to ensure that it is only done to people that desire it to be done to them? Regardless of whether they have acted in this way or that?

As a subject for after-dinner conversation, this matter is almost free of consequences, but nations have gone to war over less, so while it might sound trivial, that is not always the case.

People fell in love with Clarissa Delacroix, a long time ago. She has been engaged in a war that has lasted millennia. Are these two facts completely separate? It seems to her that they are not.

Clementina Roads People might say that to Hailey-Beth in Roads is to court a tedious existence, typified by a concentration on the material sciences disciplines, but there are few places in the world to which roads do not lead. At a road's furthest extension from home there must be, almost by definition, unfamiliar things, interesting things, exciting things, and who is better placed to travel to the ends of roads, where such things will be found, than Hailey-Beths from Roads? Their expertise is in the constitution of roads, the maintenance of roads, and the laying of roads, and Clementina's specialism was in this last area. So it was that she was taken with the Women's Vanguard of the Eighth Atheistic Crusade to oversee the surveying of land suitable for a road that would carry its future caravan. This is how she came to Malarkoi, and since she was bracketed 'Martial' it is how she was allowed to survey the kite quarter in which Sharli lived, to follow the girl's progress when she fled that place, and how she was there to help her when the girl needed it most.

Regardless of your specialism, Hailey-Beth cycles can lead you to places where, if you let them, events take over.

Dashini Death? What of it? What is to say that a weft-manipulator can't have ten daughters, all the same? Can't she have them one at a time, or all at once? What if she's secreted an infinite number of Dashinis across all of her realms, so that if something bad happens to one, then she can get a replacement, simple as snapping her fingers? And if you have a prejudice against copies, and insist on the original, what makes you think that the Dashini from the previous books was the original Dashini? Perhaps the one in this book is the original, kept safe against accident precisely for the purpose of joining the action here? Originals, copies... what's the difference? If there was a difference, would you be able to tell? Would you even notice?

Dashini was the Mistress of Malarkoi's daughter; who knows what she is now?

Dorran One of the ten-summer children selected for sacrifice at the same time as Sharli was selected.

Ganax One of the priesthood of the Dumnonii. Priests do not like to admit when they have been wrong, but neither do they like waste. Ganax's dislike of waste superseded his feeling that he couldn't say he'd made a mistake, and so it was that he was happy to turn ash into a ten-summer child. If you do not know what this means, you need only read on. Providing you are not one of those inadequate readers whose eyes skip across the page in search of 'what happens next' you will learn the meanings of the phrases above, and how they are used in context. If you are one of those skipping inadequates, there is little chance you are reading these words in any case, since they do not relate directly to the 'plot'.

Field Commander Gleed One of the founding members of the Assembly, and now present organically only in very small amounts in the mobile attack suit which bears her name and voice. How much of a person's original body is required for that person to be considered present in a machine constructed around her remains? Which organs are considered necessary, and which are considered superfluous when defining the self? Does her consciousness continue across the periods for which her exoskeleton is powered down for repairs and maintenance?

There are entire departments of Hailey-Beths of disparate disciplines devoted to the above questions, to none of which Gleed pays any attention. If someone tries to inform Gleed of the current state of 'Gleed Studies' Gleed becomes very annoyed. Assembly members are reminded that there is no safe word that disables Gleed's weapons, and that Gleed has been granted violence exemptions from Ethics under the named and numbered provisions of the Eighth Atheistic Crusade.

Gam Halliday Guilty over his murder of his friend Joes, and unable to put this fact to the back of his mind, Gam Halliday allowed himself to be killed by Dashini in order to solve the problem of their inability to leave the Realm of the White Stag and the Wolf Pack. Was this the last we would see of him? Of course not – that realm, whether or not the reader was paying attention – is a place where dead things tend back towards life at the will of its patron god. Gam, for all his many faults and flaws, is not so low as to exist outside the purview of a god, and so he too tends back towards life. Admittedly, this is so he can be killed again, but, as has already been pointed out, dead things in that realm tend back towards life. These are the two states he moves between until he is released from the cycle.

Hansy An underdeveloped youth, whose thin arms and emaciated face are matched by his thin mind and emaciated thoughts. He hungers for one thing only – opium – which his employer is unwilling to provide for him, since that privilege is reserved for employees who provide valuable services, and who don't haunt the corridors, fidgeting and chattering their teeth from dawn to dusk.

Je One of the ten-summer children selected for sacrifice at the same time as Sharli was selected.

Joes To have lived a life in the slums of Mordew, to have suffered death at the hand of your friend, to have become a ghost, to have had a heaven made for you, to have lived in that heaven through generations, and then to be torn from that heaven, as will happen to Joes here: isn't that worse than to have remained in your original low state? Or is it better to have known happiness, regardless of whether it is bookended by suffering?

If we ever meet Joes we can ask them.

Juliette An employee of the Temple of the Athanasians. She has friends, nice clothes, good food, and works hard to keep these three things. Why should she feel sorry for herself? There are people who must slaughter pigs for their living, or prepare and cook the flesh of slaughtered pigs, or stand in a room full of pig corpses in order to barely pay the rent on their hovels. Juliette sees these people through the window of her prettily furnished room. All she fears is the end to her current luck, and for this she has opium, famous for its ability to make a person forget her fears.

Nathan Treeves You may think you know Nathan Treeves, but do you really? It may be that you do, but it may be that you do not. It may not be possible to know him: he was born for a purpose, and raised for a purpose, and he seems to be failing in that purpose. Can you know someone like that, without knowing what his purpose is? Can he know himself without that vital information? What if he fails to do the thing he was made and raised to do? What if he is never even told what his purpose was?

Nathan's primary quality, in the immaterial realm, is his 'being as' the Master of Waterblack, a place that has yet to be introduced to you.

Perhaps he is unknowable.

Nathaniel Treeves A dramatis personae may list the characters it describes in any order that it wishes. This one lists them in alphabetical order, which is a very sensible way of listing them, particularly if the reader is looking for information on a single character, the name of which they are already familiar with. If the reader is going through the list from start to finish, however, it might have been more convenient to find 'Nathaniel Treeves' before 'Nathan Treeves', since he is the predecessor of that person in every other important way. Nathaniel came before Nathan as the father – barring any magical intervention – comes before his son. He came before him as the Master of Waterblack, the City of Death. He also came first to the understanding that power is a terrible thing, and that the denial of its use is sometimes the only way of neutralising that terror.

That is not to say that Nathaniel is better than Nathan, as the first placed in a race is better than the second placed. It may be that the reverse is true.

Mr Padge People who are dead in the present were alive in the past. When we, as readers, read about the pasts of people who are alive in the present, the dead may be made to live again, since these dead may have had a role in the present peoples' pasts. So it is in this book with Mr Padge, who occupies the pages concerning the life of Sharli, his assassin. Whereas Mr Padge was one of Nathan Treeves's antagonists, the same cannot be said of his role in Sharli's story. In fact, the opposite is true, and while we, knowing what we know of Mr Padge, might read into his actions sinister motives, this was not something that Sharli ever did.

Portia Hall It is not easy to give up being the Mistress of an archaic city of the North-western Peninsula, so why is it that Portia Hall made it look like it was when she gave away that title to the slum girl, Prissy?

Even if a person has tired of their position, if that position is hereditary it is also not easy to deny one's descendant their due, particularly if it has been long promised. Again, Portia Hall made this look like light work.

It is not impossible to imagine that an easiness in these two things is the result of an unusual character, but it should also be remembered that, in the game of chess, sometimes a sacrifice of a piece is made in the pursuance of a strategy.

Portia Hall made chess metaphors on meeting Nathan Treeves in the book before last.

Prissy How is a person changed by power? That is the question that occupies many of the pages of this book and those of its predecessors. These books contain hundreds and hundreds of pages on which events occur that demonstrate the effects of power. If these books were people, we might think that they had a monomaniacal obsession with the question posed above.

Can a person remain a person when they have power over life and death?

Can Prissy?

Quise One of the ten-summer children selected for sacrifice at the same time as Sharli was selected.

Sharli Sharli appeared in the last books, but in a marginal way. The Sharli in this book is much more central: she is the subject of a substantial number of its pages. Why, you might ask, is a marginal character from the first two books taking up so much of your time in the third? The answer is that she was a marginal character in the events of the first two books because the story was not being told from her point of view. If it had been told from her point of view then you would have been more aware that she had a central role in the story, but you would not have learned much about Nathan and his circle. This is often the way with life, you will come to understand, that people to whom your attention has not been directed can have a direct and powerful influence over what happens to you in the future. Think of a friend of a friend whom you have met and who will eventually become your spouse, though you do not know it yet. Think of a person from your childhood to whom you were thoughtlessly cruel, and whom you have forgotten, but who has not forgotten you or your cruelty, and who then appears, late one night, at the back door to your house, carrying a concealed weapon. Think of the advisors to the Master of your city, nameless and anonymous figures whom you do not know and who do not know you, but who order the release of toxic materials into your neighbourhood to ensure that those same materials are not released into theirs.

Sometimes people on the periphery of your life move to the centre, and vice versa.

Anyone who thinks that this is untrue – that one is born amongst a set of people and that these people remain unchanging throughout – is clearly and simply incorrect, and a good book is one which treats true and correct things with respect, and which ignores incorrectness, even if that incorrectness is convenient to a reader.

Sirius If you are reading this dramatis personae in alphabetical order, you will already know that a dog can become a ghost, but what of a dog who has been scoured out of existence by the occult weapon known as the Tinderbox? You will have to wait to find out, though the fact of this entry might be sufficient to answer that question.

Sirius Goddog Similarly, if the words 'Sirius Goddog' are present in the list of people and animals appearing in the pages of a book, you can assume that Sirius Goddog makes a reappearance in this one. In what way? The patient reader need only read on.

Sylvie An employee of the Temple of the Athanasians. She has friends, her regular clients seldom require anything too onerous, and there is always opium to fall back on when they do. Consequently, she does not consider her life too difficult, particularly when she considers what other girls of Mordew must bear. To an onlooker, she may not seem to be anyone to envy, but think of it objectively and ask yourself the question: if you had friends, found your job reasonably easy, and had ready access to the drugs you preferred while all about you was horror and misery, would this not be an enviable situation?

Tinnimam A tripodal firebird, stunted of growth and prone to violent changes in mood. Sharli took her as a pet and loved her, something that is indicative of the girl's character in the matter of the placement of her affections.

All firebirds are things of the Mistress of Malarkoi, brought to this world to do her bidding. How does Tinnimam function in this respect? Sharli thought 'not at all', but she was entirely wrong.

I N THE PAGES OF THIS BOOK, in addition to those introduced in the first two volumes, you will find many unusual
things, including, but not limited to:

alifonjers who become angels
alifonjers who have become angels reverting to being alifonjers
again when the person who changed them into angels is
severed from the weft
an angelic army
angels in such number that they boil the sea
angels who stop being angels when the person who changed
them into angels is severed from the weft
art collaboration display sites
artworks
an assassin who tries to kill a baby, but who is prevented from
doing it by the baby's father
Bachelor's Walk, flooded
a ball of dirt big enough to block out a sun
best-laid plans going agley
billions of infants that fall from the sky
birthing sheds at a dog breeder's premises
Blakey's
a bomb that collapses intermediate realms into the material realm
a bomb that doesn't make a noise when detonated
a bomb-barge
a book that can read, write, and illustrate itself
boundary stelae
a boy trodden on by an alifonjer calf
a boy who dies a thousand times or more
a boy who has his nerves filleted
a boy who kills an earlier version of himself
a boy whose parents don't love him
a boy whose skull is cracked along the sagittal and metopic
sutures

a brothel madame
carpets in a pyramid
children raised communally
children who kill each other either on purpose or by accident
children's toys in the likeness of firebirds
a city drained of its solidity
clothes that light up
clothes that use boys' optic nerves to broadcast images across
    their surfaces that render the wearer invisible
the Collapse Zone
convex lenses
a demon mistaken for a pet
a demon who evolves to bore through the earth
a dog whose temper gets the better of him
dogs who scare a man to death
the Dying Mud
an enormous descending cube
enormous volumes of cold, dark water
faecal and urinary scat
a firebird with three legs
some flat champagne
flawed children
floating platforms
frozen dancers
a ghost barking at the corpse of a dog
a ghost of a man who goes on to successfully pretend he is the
    formerly living man
a gill-man falling to a weight of pieces that would exceed his
    original weight
a God Killer
gods caged in cubes
gods fighting each other
a governess who receives a cleaver thrown into her back
a great number of dead cats, working as actuaries
the Ha'penny Bridge, flooded
a heart compressed into a locket
a hex that prevents violence in a brothel

a horse-faced man

a knife so sharp it passes frictionlessly through any object

a large amount of opium consumed gratefully

a lorgnette that sees long distances and annotates the things
it sees

a machine that can read a book and point to instances where
a word has been used

a man called Black Bill because of his unwillingness to wash
himself clean of dried blood

a man who evolves in order to do the work he has set himself

a man who tears out a woman's heart

a man whose body accommodates a tentacled fluke

mechanical lungs that work through osmosis

mention of Jan van Eyck's *Arnolfini Portrait*

Merchant's Arch, flooded

millions of dragons of all sizes

mobile concentrate platforms

moribund dogs who sacrifice their lives to send a puppy to
the future

murders, repeatedly acted out

a murmuration of dragons

a nail factory

a nail factory supervisor

a nail factory undermanager

an octagonal tower used as part of a house

parents murdering their children

pens designed to facilitate the murder of pigs

a people called the Dumnonii

people intending to win money by playing cards

people killed for not listening attentively enough to the performance of a song

people substituted with replicas of themselves

people who are not as easy to kill as all that

people who go out to dance together in the darkness

people who have been killed, repeatedly living out the conditions of their death

a person once accepted as a member of the tribe of the Albidosi

a person who is unable to seize her godhood in time
Phoenix Park, flooded
a piece of chalk that creates portals
a pirate who has sworn off drinking
a plaza, flooded
the poisoning of a man's stash of opium
a Portable One-way Quarantine
a primitive language made through the cracking of a whip
the privilege of losing one's life in the summoning of demons
Prophylactic Prism Powder
a puppy who can tell the future with the help of ghosts
a rack that anchors a weft-parasite in one spot
realms that are repeated in the same place so often that reality
    begins to collapse
realms that collapse into other realms
a repetitive flashing light
the resurrection of God
the reverse rapture
the River Life
scenes from old books acted out in this one
scenes from the past acted out in the present
scenes the writer refuses to write, and that the reader shouldn't
    wish to read
several people who aren't who they think they are
a ship called the *Serapis Christus*
some slavers
a solicitous look that affects a war
Solomon Peel, crushed by the pressure of water
the sound of a heartbeat
a spiral staircase made of crates, boxes, and other bits and pieces
a substance called 'quick-root' that works like an amphetamine
tens of pipe junctions all occupying the same space
triangular-headed fluke piglets
two brothers who father their own brother–son
a variety of kitchen knives
a whistle that summons a dragon god

BOOK ONE

Sharli of the Assembly

THE PROPAGANDA OF THE
IMMATERIAL SOUL

As we know, the self, such as it can be seen to have a material reality, is a complex of recognisable behaviours, assumptions and apprehensions, centred on the bodies of beings with sufficient cortical capacity for self-awareness. The self is that thing that self-aware beings recognise in themselves as a self, persistently centred on the body with which that self is identified.

Psych, Archives, Prose and the cognate disciplines in Phys and Prog are aware of the reflexivity of these definitions, the inherencies in their assumptions, and the seeming unresolvability of these problematic foundations. Hailey-Beths in Phil have given permission for the use of the term 'self' as it is intuited by Assembly members, with the proviso that the teaching of the soul propagandas be double-mandated across all disciplines, and made compulsory during Crusade-active periods.

The self, then, is a thought/sense/emotion/apprehension/ body combination, recognisable by a self-aware cortex, reifiable by a social corpus as it is intuited across the Assembly, and/or recognised in pre-Assembly territories. Ethics, Aesthetics, Prose, and the martial iterations of these disciplines, are mandated to recognise all selves under this definition, and to legislate accordingly.

What the self is not, is an immaterial thing which exists outside a material, social and historical context, which can be applied onto a body, even if that combination then seems to be identical to any pre-existing recognised self. To say that such a thing is possible constitutes what is known as 'the propaganda of the immaterial soul'.

To clarify, it is not possible to remove the self from a body, destroy the body, make a new, materially identical body, then install the self into this new body. Even if the newly embodied self claims it is the same self as the self that existed before the destruction of the body, this is incorrect. The claimant would instead be a new self that, by virtue of its material similarity, contained some, possibly all, of the same memories as the previous self. Still, this new self would be mistaken in believing itself to be the same self. How do we know? There are unanswerable questions that should be answerable if self-transfer of this type is possible.

The unanswerable questions:

1. Since a self requires an appropriate cortex, and a body in which that cortex can exist, how would the self exist during the process of the destruction of its body?
2. Holding in abeyance the above against a technical objection or forthcoming solution, in what form would the self be held when it was not in the cortex?
3. What is the information state proper to the self?
4. Would that information state be contained by language?
5. If it was contained by language, how would the non-language self-states, such as bodily sensation, be held?
6. Since the encapsulation of the real in language exhibits a reduction in specificity, how would a language act be able to contain all the specific information related to the self?
7. Given the necessary interplay between communicating parties inherent in language, articulation on one side and decoding on the other, to whom would the self be addressed?

8. How would any possible addressee affect the self when it was come to be understood?

9. If the self was not expressed verbally, but was expressed by numbers, what form of mathematics would be employed in the coding of the self?

10. How would information loss be managed in this form of mathematics?

11. Who would have designed the rules of this management of information loss?

12. Holding in abeyance any and all of the above against a technical objection or forthcoming solution, if the self was removed from its body, the body was destroyed, and the self was then *not* transferred to a new body, or that transfer was delayed, or that transfer took time, no matter how short, where would the self reside during these periods?

13. During the above periods, would the self be conscious?

14. Which material dimension would contain the disembodied self?

15. If a transfer took place without time passing, requiring no intermediate containing space, how could something that takes no time be said to have occurred?

16. If a transfer took place without taking place across a material dimension, how could something that took place in no place be said to have occurred?

17. Holding in abeyance the above against a technical objection or forthcoming solution, if the self was removed, the body destroyed, the self-transferred to a new body, and also transferred to a perfect replica of the new body, would there then be two selves?

18. How would these selves reconcile their dual existence? Would they share a consciousness?

19. What if there were three selves, four, ad infinitum?

20. If selves do not share a persisting consciousness after duplication, can they be considered identical at the level of the self?

Since these questions are unanswered, and possibly un-answerable, we should defer to our general understanding of the real as it relates to selves, i.e. there is no real other than the real, the real has dimensions of time and space, and no non-temporal and/or non-spatial thing can be said to occur.

There is no real other than the real, and selves in the real are held in bodies, so on the destruction of the body, the self is destroyed.

A self is a unique thing and cannot be duplicated.

Supposed duplication of a self would not be duplication, but the creation of a materially new self, unrelated at the level of consciousness to the original self, regardless of how it thought of itself, or how others thought of it.

I

Sharli of the Dumnonii

IT WAS HARD to remember that far back.

There were tents, there were kites, there were goats. There was the Golden Pyramid of the Mistress of Malarkoi. Sometimes the ground was green and soft with grass – she'd roll in the dew on bright mornings with the other children, laughing – and sometimes it was dry and brown, dusty, and they'd pull their sleeves over their mouths and noses, and blink messages to each other from the openings to the tents.

When the wind was up, the kites stretched the strings tight, pulled at the tent pegs. The children had to make sure nothing came loose, and that the goats were staked, but otherwise they were free to do what they wanted.

She was a child of the Dumnonii, and their priesthood was from Voliba, so they were raised communally.

They were ash. They spent most of their time between tents, where the fires were. They floated here and there.

Sharli's name was given to her by the other children. It meant 'freedom' in the old language, and they chose it because she'd never do what she was supposed to do. She was always running between quarters, getting into trouble, and eating from the wrong tents. The Dumnonii would feed any child they recognised, but turned their backs on unfamiliar ones, and she was forbidden food. Sharli took it anyway, sneaking through the gaps between the tents and the earth, gorging on blood sausage, dried for the winter.

More often than not she'd be dragged by the arm to the priests and returned to her crèche, her bangles copper and blue cinched tight to the right ankle identifying her proper place, but sometimes she'd be gone for days, sheltering with the goats for warmth at night, exploring during the day.

Free.

The edict went out from the priesthood of the Dumnonii that all the heavenly brothers living amongst the people of the Western Step should be brought to the knife and thereby returned to the place where they wished to be.

This should be done at dawn on the seventh moon, when the sun was above the summit, so that the brothers' passage should be most easily made, and also so that there should be sufficient time for the preparation of goats, the ceremonial washing of the ten-summer children, and the composition of the funerary odes.

The proclamation was delivered in the proper way, from the proper place, and there was gladness in all the tents of the communes, and around the fires joyful songs were sung of the sacrificing.

Why, then, did Sharli weep when she heard them?

She went to the tent where her heavenly brother was. He was her firebird, her pet, her friend. He never left that place to go out into the sun, which was the expected thing for him; instead, he kept in the shadows, or burrowed beneath the blankets. He had never caught his flame, like his brothers had. If he was aflame, like he should have been, he would have burned the tent to the ground. Sharli would never have been able to touch him, but here he was, twittering, and she gathered him to her chest.

Where a firebird is of a good size, bigger than a goat, smaller than a horse, this brother – Sharli called him Tinnimam, which meant nothing except its sound – was a miniature, and where a firebird has four whole limbs, Tinnimam was a tripod, his left rear leg at the foot so wizened and twisted from birth that one day it fell away. Sharli kept it now in a box inside her bedroll, but it would never attach itself again.

Where all firebirds are male, Tinnimam was a female, and though by the fire she was spoken of as brother – as he – Sharli knew the truth though she could never speak it, since there had never been a firebird like this, and there was no word for a heavenly sister in Sharli's language, nor was there any precedent for making one.

In every other way – except the flamelessness, except the size, except the foot, except her sisterhood – Tinnimam was a perfect firebird.

Her feathers were perfect, her beak was perfect, her little cry, which was plaintive and high, was entirely perfect, and because Sharli felt herself to be like this – perfect except for all her flaws – she cleaved to Tinnimam in her heart so that when the edict went out that all the heavenly brothers must be taken in seven days to the Dumnonii altar, she vowed that she would not do it, no matter how cheerfully the matter was sung of, nor how much that was the expectation her commune had of her.

So, she went with Tinnimam out of the village of tents and into the hills, as her heart directed.

This was one of Sharli's flaws in the exception of which she was perfect: that her heart would never do exactly that which was expected of it.

Nor was the expectation of the others around the fire – ashes or flames, kindling or logs – sufficient cause for her heart to do what it didn't want to do.

Another flaw was that she was wilful.

Another flaw was that she was deaf to criticism.

Another flaw was that she was small for her age.

Another flaw was that she was slow to read.

Another flaw was that she took too long to learn the funerary odes.

Another flaw was that she was absent at prayers.

Another flaw was that she sought food from the Red Kite Quarter.

Another flaw was that she gave cheek to her elders.

Another flaw was that her voice was flat.

All these things, and her fingers were short, her neck was long, she cried when she had nothing to cry about but was dry-eyed during the funerary odes, her skin was too dark, her nails were untrimmed, she tied her bedroll too loosely.

But in all other things, Sharli was perfect, just like little Tinnimam, and she held the firebird tight to her, and ran up into the hills where neither of them would be found, not for the seven days, and not for the eighth day.

If they were not found for eight days then the heavenly brothers' return would be complete and Tinnimam would not take her place with the brothers. She could live with Sharli again, and Sharli would bring her strips of goat from the fire and sleep with her nestled in the crook of her knees, two imperfect girls together.

The city of Malarkoi was a tent city gathered around the base of the Mistress's Golden Pyramid, and the lands where the goats grazed straggled off for miles, up and into the hills and forests. If it hadn't been for the singing in celebration of the new edict, then the places that Sharli ran though, Tinnimam mewling at her chest, would have been tended by goatherds, but as it was the fields were occupied only by goats.

Some were milk-goats tethered, some were bull-goats in their enclosures, others wandered free.

Since Sharli hadn't eaten, she took milk straight from the udder of one of the staked goats – another flaw, since ash of the Blue Kite Quarter fires should not drink except from Blue Kite Quarter goats. She had to put Tinnimam down so she could pull the goat's teats, and the firebird walked off a little way, extending her flightless wings and shivering her feathers straight.

When Tinnimam walked, her front legs moved just like any other firebird's legs, but when her missing leg was needed she had to hop forward to make up for its absence. To an observer, this was a sad thing, this deviation from the gracefulness with which a firebird might be expected to move, but to Tinnimam it was the normal thing, and to Sharli it was a sign of her sistership. Tinnimam got about as well as any of the other heavenly brothers, all of whom remained in Malarkoi having some frailty, or deformity, or injury that made it impossible for them to fulfil their purpose, which was to die on the Sea Wall of Mordew.

While Sharli drank, and because the Golden Pyramid still loomed high in the distance, Tinnimam went towards it, in her faltering way. A firebird summoned to a place will go to it, and since she had been brought to Malarkoi by the priests, the magic effected by the Spark released from the opening of the throat of a ten-summer child, Tinnimam did as the Mistress's magic bade her. She hopped back to that shining beacon away from which she could not tend.

If she could go away from it, what does it mean to be summoned?

Sharli saw this from one eye, the other obscured by the udders from which she was drinking, and she pulled away, milk falling wasted into the dirt – another one of her flaws: wastefulness – milk dribbling down her chin – another flaw: untidiness.

'Tinnimam!' she cried.

Pets and domesticated animals will look at you when you call their names. Long training over centuries has made their species understand the rudiments of human speech, at least in as much as they know that it is in their interests to recognise the sounds people use to refer to them. Often the presence of these sounds will be coincidental with the appearance of a meal.

But firebirds are not pets.

In Mordew, they are considered a species of demon, a thing that could not be less like a pet. In the Assembly, they are not afforded any degree of reality, Hailey-Beths understanding them as a kind of collective delusion made flesh. Even in Malarkoi, firebirds are a separate thing. Those firebirds that lived among them were angels coming briefly from the Mistress's heaven, not of this world and not beholden to it.

Demons, delusions, angels: none of these things can be expected to come when they are called, and Tinnimam didn't come when Sharli called her. She preferred instead to hop with her three legs, flutter with her flightless wings, down the hill, back the way they had come, to the Pyramid to which magic had summoned her, leaving Sharli to run behind.

Were the priesthood right to issue the edict putting the heavenly brothers to the knife? Wouldn't that, under the same terms by which these firebirds were summoned here, be doing what was best, returning Tinnimam to her intermediate realm, to whatever it was that she should do there?

Sharli did not think so.

But that is because she never questioned her desire to be with Tinnimam.

Sharli was thoughtless, and this was her final flaw, the one she was berated with in the evenings when the commune gathered around the fire.

'You never think,' they would say, or, 'What were you thinking?' to which she would reply, 'Nothing,' and to which they would reply in turn, as if it won the argument, 'Exactly!'

While there is something valuable in thoughtlessness when it is in the service of intuition, something that can be very useful in a girl like Sharli whose thoughts seemed always to run counter to the sense everyone else appeared to find so obvious, there is also something like blindness in it.

It is an inability to see what is in front of you.

Sharli saw Tinnimam running, hopping, fluttering back to the Pyramid; she did not see that this was where the firebird wanted to be. When she scooped her up and held her in her arms, she still did not see it.

When she interpreted Tinnimam's squawking as nothing at all, just the sound her pet made, when she turned her back on the Pyramid and the priests, the goat and the field, and ran on, between the unguarded enclosures, clutching the firebird to her chest, she did not see what would have been obvious to anyone else.

Tinnimam didn't want to go.

A girl can run a good distance, but not forever, and eventually Sharli had to stop.

Because she had been holding Tinnimam so tight, some of the firebird's feathers had bent across the spines, and when Sharli put her down, Tinnimam pulled at these feathers with her beak, occupying herself with straightening them.

Sharli turned back; they had reached the top of a rise

and descended the other side, so the Pyramid was no longer visible.

The only sign of Malarkoi was a few kites, strung on the very longest strings, those that the priesthood flew in the pride of their quarters, specks of blue and red, yellow, and green in the distance.

Sharli sat and faced the way she had come, her legs folded beneath her.

She was a nine-summer child, too young for the opening, too flawed in any case. What was there for her in Malarkoi? She was too stupid for the priesthood, too thoughtless to be a goatherd, too feckless to rely on as a fireguard. Kite-making? Her fingers were too short and clumsy. Tent-making? Same thing.

What did that leave? Bearing ash?

Her hips were so narrow, she'd probably split.

When someone runs away they always fear they'll be followed, brought back to the place they're fleeing from. But don't they also desire that?

Isn't part of running away the idea that you'll be missed? That there will be great consternation when everyone finds you gone. A search party will be marshalled for the important work of finding you. There will be sobbing and the sudden realisation of your worth now that the fact of your loss has been made a reality.

Even if you don't want to be found, escape includes the idea that people will come after you.

Sharli looked back the way she had come.

There was no one following.

Tinnimam had tried to straighten her broken feathers, but, peering at them first with one dark bead of an eye, then the other, she decided it wasn't worth the trouble. She pulled one out by the root with her beak, the long white stem of it contrasting oddly with the red.

When it was out, she jerked her head, and the feather went up in the air before it fell spiralling back down to the grass on which she and the girl were both sitting.

Red feather.

Green grass.

The white feather root.

The darkening blue of the sky as the day progressed towards twilight.

Sharli reached over and picked up the discarded feather.

Tinnimam watched her sidelong while she did it, suspiciously, pulling at another feather with her beak.

Sharli showed her the feather, and this seemed to satisfy the firebird, who turned away and attended to her business, giving Sharli permission, it seemed to her, to use the feather as she wished.

With her teeth, Sharli stripped along the shaft two long gaps and one short gap – the pattern of the Dumnonii – and she used the stripped barbs to colour her hair, rubbing them into the thick tangle that she never learned to comb out.

Tinnimam sent another feather up into the air, this one cutting back to the ground in a swoop and landing on Sharli's lap. The girl did the same thing with this one, and then split the hafts and joined them together. Quite what she was intending to make, she didn't know.

The priest knew what to do with firebird feathers, how to build a fane, but Sharli had never listened.

She sighed and stood up, walked back to the summit of the last rise they had passed. This wasn't far, and when she got there she still couldn't see anyone, just the kites, a little further than they had been. She followed the trample she had made in the long grass as she'd run. No one was tracking her.

She turned back to where Tinnimam was pruning herself.

Behind the firebird, in the very far distance, behind a copse of trees and rising into the cloudless sky was a faint but definite line of black smoke. It was like the shadow of a very long and thin twig and Sharli had to squint to make it more definite.

It was a league away, at least, further from Malarkoi than she had ever been.

The people of Malarkoi stayed mostly around the Mistress's Pyramid since she was their patron, and all the good things of the world came from her. When they did go away from her precincts it was on pilgrimage, but the season of the pilgrimage was in the autumn, and it was still summer. There was small chance that a priest, seeking inspiration, had taken it upon himself to walk the lands, but no person of Malarkoi, priest, ash, tinder or log would make a daytime fire on such a walk. If they did it would never smoke black, that being a sign that it was improperly made.

Who did that leave, then?

Sharli walked quickly back to Tinnimam. She did not have an answer.

Could a heavenly brother have returned from the Sea Wall, his mission unfinished, and was now burning in the country, unable, perhaps, to either explode himself or fly?

Unthinkable.

But fires don't make themselves. Smoke doesn't rise by itself. There must have been someone there.

She anxiously tried to pick up the firebird, but Tinnimam backed away, reared up unsteadily, and hissed, pawing at the air in front of her. Animals know when a person is anxious.

Sharli ignored Tinnimam's signs and scooped her up against her will, took the scratches her forepaws made.

Sharli didn't know what to do, and now she cursed herself for being so stupid. These were Others, and now she would have to go back, and if she went back then they would put Tinnimam to the blade.

Thoughts like this poison the blood. Animals can smell them in your sweat.

Tinnimam squirmed in Sharli's arms, hissed and scratched, and now she bit, snapping at Sharli's earlobe. She dropped the firebird.

Now it was Sharli's turn to hiss – her ear was torn, and blood was dripping down onto her shoulder, thick and sticky.

She put her hand to it.

If she hadn't been such a flawed child, had been like the other ash of the Dumnonii, Sharli would have known not to delay. She would have known that she must get hold of the

49

firebird immediately. Instead, she felt her ear, felt the blood, let the pain and the betrayal she suddenly felt bring tears to her eyes.

Animals are animals. Even when they seem to love you, they are bound by their natures. Tinnimam, the taste of blood in her mouth, went into the kind of frenzy her type was prone to: her eyes blazed, she bared her claws, and though she couldn't fly she leapt at Sharli's face, snapping and clawing.

If Sharli had held her tightly in her arms instead of fiddling with her bloody ear she could have kept the firebird safe until the rage passed.

Instead, each of Tinnimam's blows landed, one spurring the next, and the firebird was driven by her instincts into a killing rage.

Sharli had no choice but to fall to the ground in a ball, protecting her eyes, which Tinnimam tried to claw out, seeing nothing more than meat to penetrate, her anger building towards that moment her species was made for – detonation.

Only, Tinnimam had never caught her flame, could never burn herself up. That fire that had never been lit by some failure of her birth, or some flaw in her summoning, and that frustrated desire drove her to ever more violent excesses against Sharli, curled in fear, until even these weren't enough.

Tinnimam bolted away with a speed scarcely conceivable for her, flitting and hopping off across the grass, screeching and chittering in frustrated fury.

When Sharli looked out to see where Tinnimam had gone, there was a pain in the girl's neck, worse than her ear. With fingers scratched and swelling, she reached to where the pain was worst.

She found a flap of skin on the side of her neck that had been half torn away. Beneath this there was something pulsing in the gap where the skin should have been. She put one fingertip to it. It beat, sticky with blood, hot and fast, with the rhythm of her racing heart.

Slowly, fearfully, Sharli put the flap of skin back over the gap, and she clamped her hand to it, not knowing what to do.

Because she was so stupid and worthless, so thoughtless and idiotic, she looked back to Malarkoi. Then she looked off to where black smoke was rising.

That was the way that Tinnimam had gone.

Sharli had no idea where she should go.

In the end, she went after Tinnimam.

She should have gone back to her commune, to Red Kite Quarter, to the priests of the Dumnonii, leaving the heavenly brother to her own fate.

She should have shown them her wound, and while they were tending it, staunching the steady leak of blood from her neck, she should have told them about the black smoke on the horizon. This was surely a sign of Others against whom the city might have to be raised.

This way she would have saved her life, saved the lives of her commune, and all at the cost of a brother, who had, though no one said it, already lessened the worth of his life by being so poor a specimen of his type.

Instead, Sharli tried to save Tinnimam, who was as close to a sister as the girl had.

The ashes of her fire had never grown to love her, as they ought to have done, on account of all her flaws which were so real that, when Sharli asked herself why she did what she did next, they explained everything.

She did a stupid thing because she was stupid.

She proved her worthlessness because she was worthless.

A flawed thing makes flawed decisions.

Sharli took her hand from her neck and toyed with the flap of skin, hoping that, by some miracle, it had reattached itself to her.

It hadn't.

When she touched it, it sloughed off, lubricated by the blood that was seeping out from between the skin and the stuff underneath.

If she'd had more imagination, Sharli might have thought about pulling the flap of skin off and letting what was beneath dry out in the open air, but this time one of her flaws – a failure of imagination – saved her life, because if she had done it that would have been the end of her, the small piece of skin that joined the flap and the wound being the only thing protecting the artery beating just beneath, waiting to empty her life's blood out onto the ground in gushes.

Sharli stopped toying and clamped her hand back.

She looked closely at the grass where Tinnimam had fled, and followed, very slowly, each step making her neck throb with pain, along the untidy path the firebird's hopping and flapping had made.

There was no need for the people of Malarkoi to develop skills in tracking. A staked and tied goat tends to be where you left it, and should it not be it won't have got very far. Even if tracking had been one of the things Sharli had been taught, she wouldn't have likely picked it up, her head being always in the clouds and her ears full of wool. It didn't matter – Tinnimam had made such a mess there was no missing where she had gone: a curved path led, first, in a line directly between Malarkoi on one side and the rising black smoke on the other.

The smoke was darker now, it seemed, though everything seemed darker to Sharli. The wound throbbed beneath her fingers, the pain throbbed beneath that, and her heart throbbed too, beating hollowly in her chest, as if it was knocking on her ribs, like the mallet the priests used on the dried ribcages of slaughtered goats, beating out the rhythm of the elegies.

She would walk slowly along the path Tinnimam had left, she thought, keeping her footfalls nice and flat so they didn't jar her neck. When she got to the woods, there Tinnimam would be, sitting as she liked to do, waiting to be picked up. Then Sharli would pick her up and walk with her, nice and slowly, back to Malarkoi.

She'd hide Tinnimam under her blankets and go to tell the fireguard about the smoke and the Others.

What she'd do after that, Sharli didn't think about.

That was something that didn't seem to require consideration, whether that meant she died of her wounds, or whether she was healed. Perhaps they'd take her straight to a priest. Perhaps she'd be opened there and then, her Spark improving the health of the flock.

Sharli trudged slowly across the grass, the sun passing through the sky more quickly than the girl could manage to move across the earth.

The blood from her neck was making a circle on the left side of her smock. It spread through the loose threads, dried, and became tacky so that when she reached over to pull the smock off her skin, it wouldn't come, as if it was too heavy.

Sharli wondered if every step was making her slower because now she couldn't make a step much longer than a foot length from where the foot had been before.

She planted each foot carefully, her heel coming back to touch the tips of the toes on the other foot.

She kept doing this until it was too dark to see her toes, at which point she sat down, and moments later she was asleep.

In one dream, of which Sharli had many, her commune came for her, through the dark, all marching shoulder to shoulder, holding branches they'd lit from the Red Kite Quarter fire. They bore her up on a bower, singing, and they marched her back to Malarkoi, the Golden Pyramid flickering in the torchlight, the Mistress in the sky above it, smiling down at them all. When no one was looking, she slipped off the bower and was suddenly in the woods, alone, calling for Tinnimam.

In another dream, her commune came for her, through the dark, holding branches they'd lit from the fire, each angrily shouting, scouring the undergrowth for her, the Mistress above them, her eyes like beams of moonlight. Sharli dodged between these beams, Tinnimam in her arms, shrieking.

In a last dream she was grabbed by the Others, and with their hard fingers they peeled the flap of skin from her neck, reached inside, and pulled all the strings of her veins out though the gap. They put these to their lips and drank all her blood, though she couldn't see their faces, only their lips.

◆

Sharli woke.

It was daylight, and she was in the woods.

Her commune wasn't there. Tinnimam wasn't there. The Mistress wasn't there. The Others weren't there.

She turned to see if there was anyone else that she had not dreamed of, but her neck was so stiff she couldn't move it at all.

Her smock on one side was hard with dried blood and, when she ran her fingers over her wound, it was swollen and hot, dry now, a scab of blood, smooth as glass, around the join between the flap and the flesh.

She rolled onto her side, drew up her knees, and pushed herself onto them as slowly and carefully as she could, hoping not to rip her neck open.

The ground beneath her was dry, short sticks and twigs, a line of ants.

There was a sound in the distance, like a bird, like a whistle – it could have been either of these things or something else.

Sharli couldn't turn to look, only swivelled her eyes, in the vain hope she might be able to see past her nose, focus on whatever had made the noise.

Because she couldn't see, she thought it might be Tinnimam, thought it might be Others, thought it might be someone from the commune. She sat back on her knees, put her hands on the floor and pushed herself into a standing position, blinking at the effort, but not immediately sinking back down.

She turned all the way around, once, then twice – there was nothing to see except the woods. She heard the sound again – half a bird-call, half a whistle – and by intuition she span around to face it.

On a branch in a tree, a hundred feet distant, was Tinnimam. How she had got up there, and why she was making such an unusual sound, Sharli didn't know, but nor did she think too much about it. She went forward, unthinking, until she stood beneath the tree.

A girl of nine summers will sometimes accept an unlikely thing unquestioningly because she wants that thing to be true. She hasn't learned to be suspicious of getting what she wants from the world, against the odds. This is something people learn only after years of hard experience.

Just because Sharli wanted Tinnimam to be found safe, does not mean that she was.

Just because Tinnimam was in the tree, ready to be found, does not mean that she should have been in the tree, ready to be found.

Just because Tinnimam made a sound she had never made before, does not mean that she ought to have made it.

Sharli didn't understand any of that. She held up her hands, threatening to open her wound, and Tinnimam fell down, grateful and penitent, Sharli thought, into her arms.

'Good girl!' Sharli said, crying, 'Good girl!' Then, more slowly than she had approached, Sharli walked away with her pet and tried, as best as she could, to make her way home.

The presence of what seemed to Sharli to be Tinnimam in this tree was artificial, a situation set up by that organisation of people known as the Assembly, specifically the Peripatetic Committee of the Women's Vanguard of the Atheistic Crusades. They had been observing Sharli from a distance since she came within the range of the intelligencer they had placed, in the form of a goat stake, at the furthest western edge of the goat fields used by the people of Malarkoi.

They had watched Sharli from their camp through an aerial telescope disguised as a bird. They watched as she left her home, and watched as she ran with Tinnimam in her arms. It was smoke from their fire that Sharli had seen in the distance.

When Tinnimam had attacked Sharli and fled, Hailey-Beth Clementina Roads took possession of the firebird, by calming her down with a tranquilliser dart.

While Sharli had walked slowly into the woods, she was watched all the time by an Assembly member from Medicines. There was a team of three liquid engineers who made an intelligencer replica of Tinnimam, a rushed and imperfect job, none of them having made a firebird before. They swapped the real Tinnimam for this replica, which they programmed to report on Malarkoi.

They quarantined the real Tinnimam preparatory for shipment back to safe territory.

Because the Assembly abhor waste, they had repaired Sharli to the best of their abilities. An Assembly field medic is not simply a repairer of the human body. They begin from first principles, their medicine being a process by which the human being is helped to reach its perfect potential, so the way in which they healed Sharli was not simply to patch her up, but to remove faults in her development. They took her back to her most basic implementation in matter, keeping her alive with machines all the while, and induced her body to tend towards the perfect representations of herself. Once this was done, they accelerated the body's own repair system, a process that took place over hours.

Generally, the Assembly tried to be as unobtrusive as possible, to intervene minimally when not on Crusade, but circumstances meant they had rushed their work in this case. They did too good a job of healing Sharli, making her, by any accepted metrics, a great deal better functioning than she ever had been before. After their procedures, she demonstrated an overperforming acuity across the board in all her sensory and intellectual facilities. The Peripatetic Committee's dictum was, outside martial postings, 'as far as possible, leave things as you find them', so the liquid engineers should have undercut some of their improvements. However, the medic couldn't allow that because she didn't have a current Ethics opt-out. The best she could do was mock up Sharli's wound and leave it at that.

Now that they had saved her life, they gave her sufficient knock-out that she wouldn't wake until they were out of range. They put their replica of Tinnimam in the tree, since it looked like the kind of thing that ought to be able to fly, retreated to their camp, packed up and left.

This was only the first time Sharli came across the Assembly member designated Hailey-Beth (Martial) Clementina Roads, for she was a woman who would take an interest in Sharli's life from that point onwards.

When Sharli returned to Malarkoi she had been missing for three days, and the preparations for the ceremony by which the heavenly brothers would be put to the knife were well underway.

When Ganax, the priest responsible for her commune, saw her, he threw up his hands, appalled, and though he made the usual disparaging remarks about Sharli's suitability for life in general, there was, in his tone, a softness that Sharli had never noticed before, a sympathy that Sharli felt meant that she wasn't entirely dismissed in his eyes.

She was taken to the healing tent where her wounds were washed.

The priest did all she could for Sharli, but it was felt amongst the adults that this would not be enough. Plans were made to open the girl's throat if she didn't show immediate signs of recovery, since a wound of the severity Sharli evidenced at the neck would almost always be fatal, so complex were the processes of circulation there, so that they could never be repaired.

Despite the fact that the other heavenly brothers had been moved to the enclosure from where they would be taken to the ceremony, Tinnimam was allowed to stay with Sharli.

The following morning the throat-opener came with his sickle, but Sharli was sitting up in bed, drinking broth, smiling.

Puzzled, everyone agreed that he should come back later, if this reprieve turned out to be temporary, as it probably would.

When he returned, Sharli was dancing by the fire, so the throat-opener reluctantly sheathed his sickle and returned to the preparations.

By the time the day of the ceremony came, Sharli was perfectly well.

The priest came to get Tinnimam, but the firebird flew away, up where the kites were, and wouldn't be tempted down, regardless of how much meat was offered to him. Since the moon waited for no one, not even a heavenly brother suddenly and miraculously turned to flight, the ceremony had to go on without him.

For the next year, Sharli had the pleasure of the firebird's company – brother by the fire, sister in the tent, the Assembly watching though Tinnimam's eyes both ways.

It was the way of the people who lived at the base of the Golden Pyramid of Malarkoi that when worthy children reached their ten-summer, they were gathered by the priesthood for sacrifice. In a ceremony, their throats were opened so that heavenly brothers could be summoned to prosecute the war that the Mistress waged against the enemy city, Mordew, over the sea.

Some firebirds were summoned hale and healthy, and some were summoned sickly. That was because the laws of summoning meant that there was a replication of the conditions of those sacrificed in the conditions of those summoned: a sick child would summon a sick firebird, a healthy child would summon a healthy one. So it was that only the best children were sacrificed, while the weaker ones were reserved for other tasks.

It was a great privilege to be called to the corridors of the Golden Pyramid. No one ever refused, and the Mistress of Malarkoi, in her grace, vouchsafed for the sacrificed a heaven to their own desires.

In the years before Sharli met the Assembly, she was thought to be a flawed child. She was one who would not be called to the Pyramid, one who would be reserved for other tasks, if even any of these might be suitable. There were many in the commune who felt that she would spend her life in thrall to the shovel, following the goats across the plains, returning to the manure heap with their dung when her shovel was full.

But since she had run to the woods with Tinnimam and received her wounds, that situation had been overturned.

Sharli's thoughtlessness and disobedience, her muddle-headedness, had given way to a quickness of mind, a lightness of wit, an easy way with whatever task was allotted to her.

Now she was considered one of the best of them. She had outgrown her unpromising childhood, and blossomed into

58

such a combination of healthiness of mind and body that the silversmiths came one day to make measurements for her neckpiece: the silver at the throat that would guide the blade, the preparatory gift that would ensure, for the final months, that she would never be called up to do any duties whatever, except stand and serve as an example to the other children.

There were six of them in the Dumnonii of the Red Kite Quarter: Sharli, Arjal, Berthe, Quise, Dorran and Je. These children were sequestered away from the others in the tent from which the quarter kite flew. The others brought them milk and asked the questions they were told to ask them.

'How should I approach my morning prayers?'

'What should I drink to make me strong?'

'Does your neckpiece chafe?'

To which the answers were, respectively:

'With vigour.'

'Blood and milk.'

'Not at all.'

They asked Sharli, 'Will you take your brother with you?' since Tinnimam never left her side, except when the firebird went off to do whatever she did elsewhere, always returning soon after.

Sharli had not known how to reply to this, but eventually she decided that it would be up to Tinnimam, and she said as much.

The six slept in the same tent in the month before the ceremony, and because the Dumnonii habitually woke in the night for an hour or more to drink and stoke the fire, they had plenty of time to talk.

One night, in the middle of the month, Sharli said, 'Do you think a firebird can be female?'

Those who were awake – Je, and Dorran, and Arjal – all laughed.

They did this because it sounded like a joke – everyone knew the heavenly brothers were male, just as they knew that the word 'brother' – 'tafinn' in their language – meant a male sibling. But as the laughter died, and the word remained in the air, heated by the coals of the fire in the centre of their circle, Arjal said, 'If there are only male firebirds, what does "male" signify for them? We use the word to say the difference between girls and boys.'

Sharli nodded.

Je spoke now. 'But the firebirds are different from one another, aren't they?'

Sharli nodded again, her eyes lively in the firelight. 'So does that mean some of them might be girls?'

Dorran, who was gruffer than the other two, less talkative, more prone to sleep early and rise late, said. 'What does it matter?'

Sharli shrugged. 'I think Tinnimam is a girl,' she said.

Dorran laughed. 'How can you tell under all those feathers?'

Tinnimam was there, perched above them on a beam, though the firebird didn't seem to find the conversation in any way interesting. Her head was under her wing, and she was sleeping. Or pretending to.

'I can just tell,' Sharli said.

Je, finding something in the topic that stirred the mind, said, 'We won't ever have children, not in this world, so does that make us something other than a boy or girl?'

None of them knew the answer to this.

For a while there was nothing but breathing and the crackling of the fire. In the night outside, someone coughed, and there was a sound of a bucket being knocked over, cursing.

The following day the priests took the children before the gathered Dumnonii, and stripped them naked except their neckpieces.

To all the people gathered there they gave buckets of scented water and goatskin cloths, and each took turns to clean the ten-summer children, laughing as they did, tickling them so that they laughed in their turn. Through the whole day they were washed and given sweetmeats, and when one of them dried in the sun they were washed again, and if flakes of pastry littered their chests and bellies they were washed again.

The priest brought more water and more herbs, and when the water and herbs were exhausted they brought oils and spices.

In this way the children were washed clean by their commune. All those who came up to them whispered good wishes in their ears, shared their old stories, praised Sharli on the improvements she had made, said she was one of the best who had ever lived, and that if she should do them the favour of inviting them into her heaven they should surely go, regardless of who might have other claims on them.

In every way the children were made to feel that they were the pride of the firesides and that the ashes they left behind were nothing as to them.

They were the best of the best, the most beautiful, the strongest, the cleverest and the dearest, so that even the Mistress must see them and be gladdened, knowing that they would be with her soon, precious and select.

In the night, they woke again, all but Dorran, and because their conversation of the night before had not been shared by all, Sharli made the same statement that she had made the night before, saying that she would call Tinnimam her sister in preference to her brother, feeling that was the right thing to do.

This time Tinnimam did not remain up in the rafters, but came down and sat in the fire, something that no longer hurt her as it had once done. Like Sharli she had become more like herself than she had ever been before.

Quise and Berthe, because the idea of Tinnimam's sister-hood was new to them, and because they had spent the day too busy with the washing to have heard it second hand, inspected Tinnimam closely, as if the resolution to any problem with the notion would lie in the sight of the creature.

They did not seem to see any such answer, and Quise said, 'Why do you want to call her that?'

Sharli thought for a little bit. 'Why not?'

Quise frowned a little then relaxed, but said nothing, only smiled, and since that was the way Quise was, everyone left it at that.

Berthe said, 'Anything that sits in the fire like Tinnimam sits in the fire gets to call themself what they want! Tinnimam, are you sister or brother?'

Tinnimam looked up from the flames, her eyes orange like the centre of the fire, and she opened her beak. But then she shut it again, as if having second thoughts about the wisdom of making a proclamation one way or the other.

The day before the opening of the children's throats, the Dumnonii priests took them to their secret church, which was a crypt dug out under the first level of the Golden Pyramid, hidden by slabs. The metal of the pyramid was the roof of the crypt, the walls were compacted from the clay and stones of the ground on which Malarkoi rested, cool and soft.

The ceiling glittered in the lamplight.

The priests stood the children on a dais, and abased themselves before them, declaring themselves unworthy. They begged for forgiveness, lashing themselves with switches, making sobbing prayers to these six as if they were gods.

It was then that the children knew that this is precisely what they would be on the following day: gods of their own heavens, prepared for their divinity by the world as it was in this place, sanctioned by the Mistress of Malarkoi, goddess of gods. If they had ever thought of themselves as anything less than perfect, this was the time they disabused themselves of the notion. It was the priests who were lowly, so old and so long kept from the birthright these children were preparing to claim. They had lost faith, even, over the decades, that they should ever be allowed to have what these children before them would receive, which was perfect and everlasting.

The lamps burned down and there, in the earth beneath the pyramid of Malarkoi, a world was solidified in these children's minds, by words and actions and architecture, by every interaction of thing and thought that they had ever experienced. A world existed where they could present themselves to the place at which their throats would be slit and their Spark given up, their lives in the material realm ended, and that this would be a boon to them, the best possible thing, so well deserved.

In this world all the people around them believed the same thing – all of them, every last person.

Except one.

Tinnimam.

There was only one night remaining, and for this all the children were awake, even Dorran. There was an air of excitement in the tent, as if the children could not believe the time they had long waited for was here, and none of them would have been able to speak, even if they'd wanted to.

Tinnimam, who was an Assembly replica of a firebird long since taken to Shemsouth, and who had been broadcasting every event she had experienced straight to where Hailey-Beth (Martial) Clementina Roads was stationed, somewhere in Judea, sourcing relics for the relic field, sat in Sharli's lap.

Dorran, the gruff child, made no less gruff by the extent to which he had been praised by everyone he had ever known in the weeks before the sacrifice, said, 'It should tell us if it's a girl. And if it doesn't, we should call it a boy, because that's what the priests say it is.' In this way, Dorran made a call to authority to settle the matter.

It was moot whether this would have been successful or not, because Tinnimam cleared her throat and spoke clearly, in a voice that, had Sharli known it then, was the voice of Clementina Roads spoken through the replica's organic voice box. 'Never mind all that,' she said. 'You mustn't let them kill you tomorrow.'

The children, except Sharli, shuffled back, suddenly fearful, as if the fire had spluttered and let out sparks. Even Sharli's hands started to shake.

'Sorry,' Tinnimam said, 'this is completely against the rules, but I can't see you die.' Tinnimam turned away from the others. 'Sharli, I'm talking to you,' she said. 'I'm sorry, it's all my fault. We rushed your treatment, you improved too much, and now you've been picked to die. Don't let them do it! There are these things, the soul propagandas, and I'd explain them to you if I had the time, but I don't.'

Tinnimam's mouth moved when she spoke, her eyes blinked, wrinkled at the corners. If she hadn't had a beak she would have looked like a person speaking.

'If they kill you tomorrow, that's the end. Your goddess, she's a parasite, she'll make a replica of you, put it in an unreal, but it won't be you. You'll be dead. She's insane. Do you understand? They'll slit your throat and you'll die and everyone else will go around like they've done you a favour. It's all a lie.'

Sharli didn't understand a word of it. When she looked up all the other children had gone.

'I'm getting interference,' Tinnimam said. 'Don't wait, just run!'

In the doorway to the tent was Ganax, the priest, his face expressionless, the children now behind him, looking past his legs. They were lit by the dying embers of the fire, red flickering across their faces, across their hands. Whatever detail the fire picked out, the rest was pitch black, as if they were emerging from a lake of tar, only their extremities visible.

When Ganax reached for Sharli, Tinnimam flew up from Sharli's lap, launched herself fluttering and clawing into the face of the priest, pecked at his neck and sliced as she once had done to Sharli. Everywhere was a blizzard of feathers, and from her little firebird sister the voice crackled out:

'Run! Run! Run!'

It was dark, and the communal fires were dwindling. Those who were awake were dozy, the rest of them sleeping in advance of the ceremony the next day. As she ran, the silver neckpiece banged against Sharli's shoulder blades, against her chin.

She was a much faster runner than she had been a year ago.

She took the same route out, along the path to the west, where she had passed the unattended staked goats. There were goatherds with them now, but they were sleeping.

She ran smoothly, hardly breathing more than she did when she walked.

She didn't feel the effort of it at all.

THE PROPAGANDA OF THE
MATERIAL SOUL

What if a self was solely a function of the body, sufficient that it was generated in the cortex by the specificity of the material conditions of that body? That all that needed to be done to generate the unique self was to make a perfect copy of the body.

Various problems arise. For example, the specificity of the material conditions of the human body vis-à-vis uniqueness implies that the material itself is generative of the self. It would be a technical impossibility for a copy to contain specifically the same material as an original, particularly if 'material' under this definition has both a temporal and a spatial component, as it must. Even if it was simply a matter of using the same atoms, this would be technically impossible. There would also be irresolvable problems at a quantum level.

Even if material identicality wasn't required, but somehow it was the pattern of combination of matter that generated the self, independent of the matter itself, there would be a problem in the assumption of the continuation of consciousness between the original body and the replica body. In fact, this continuation of consciousness can easily be proved impossible by thought experiment.

Consider what would happen if the original body remained in situ at point A, retaining its consciousness, once the replica was created at point B, supposedly generating the same consciousness. The replica at point B would be mistaken in thinking it was the original self since that original self already exists, and only the original has the continuity of consciousness. The replica consciousness simply mimics the original consciousness, and then quickly diverges from it on the basis of their different experiences of the world.

Should one then destroy the original, the original consciousness dies with it.

Providing – and this is arguable – that 'consciousness' and the 'self' are at least partially identical at the level of concept, then no continuation of the self can be assumed regardless of the perfection or otherwise of the replica.

To continue the thought experiment, if one perfect replica can be made, then why not two, three, four, ad infinitum? They could not all claim to be the original unique self – since the definition of 'unique' would preclude this – and consciousness could not continue across all of them. It becomes clear that, once the original body is destroyed, the original self is dead, not transferred from one place to another, and the new body possesses a new self, even if that self mistakes itself for the original self.

Belief in the idea that a perfect replica body will generate the original self is, in the face of refutation, known as the propaganda of the material soul.

II

Sharli the Slave

S HE RAN AND RAN until, eventually, she couldn't run any more.

When she turned back, she hoped to see Tinnimam. In the rush of her running, she hadn't heard the beating of wings or the woman's voice, but because she hadn't looked back she still hoped that her firebird would be behind her, somewhere, even if it was in the far distance.

She dropped to her hands and knees, breathed quickly and deeply, but always with her head up, searching back the way she had come for a sign, any sign.

There was none.

It was raining, there was a storm coming in from the sea, and now the wind was getting up.

Sharli's muscles ached, her heart was reluctant to slow, it was hard to get enough breath to fill her lungs, but she got to her feet, started to walk back the way she had come.

She'd run all the way to the sea, and it was the shore that she turned her back on. Why wouldn't she? The only thing she truly loved was back the way she came, and what was the sea to her? What was a storm? Even Sharli's life was something that she didn't love, and now Tinnimam's words rang in her thoughts, and she couldn't remember why she had obeyed them.

She had left her firebird, and she must get her back.

On the beach behind her, down over the cliffs, hidden from view, a pinnace from the slaver ship *Serapis Christus* had landed. The men who had come to shore on it were following their map to a river where they expected to refill their water barrels. The path they were following, rolling the barrels ahead of them, brought them in short order off the beach, up the dunes, between the cliffs, to where Sharli was standing, her thoughts elsewhere.

The men stopped. There were six of them, with three barrels between them, and they paused what limited conversation they might have been having. Slavers know a silent language of gestures for moments just like this one, and they used it now, indicating with slashes of their flat hands and the holding up of various numbers of their fingers that they should upend their barrels, and that three of them should go left, and three of them should go right, and that they should take the girl.

She started walking away, and the rain began to fall harder, the wind to blow louder. The men quickened their pace.

When she eventually noticed them, she put up some resistance, but a lone girl is no match for six slavers, even if they haven't drunk anything but urine for a week.

Once they had bound her arms and legs, they remembered they could speak again.

The rain was pelting down.

'Tie her to the boat while we get water,' one of them called into the wind.

'If I do it,' shouted another, 'I get the neckpiece.'

'That's a lot of silver for a simple job,' cried a third.

'Do you want to do it?'

A lot of rain-soaked arguing ensued, but Sharli didn't understand the language. It made no difference, in the end. She was taken to the ship and thrown in the hull with the rest of the slaves, packed like herrings salting in a barrel.

Days passed in nausea and misery.

The slave hold of the *Serapis Christus* was not built for comfort any more than the inside of a salting barrel is designed to comfort herring flesh; the slaves went where there was any little room for their bodies, whether this was wedged against a planked division, or squeezed between others. If this was cramped, if this gave Sharli splinters, if this didn't allow her to draw a full breath, then so what? A slaver ship's design took no account of this.

Nor had windows been considered a necessity; there were none.

The ship bucked in unpredictable directions, and because Sharli couldn't see the horizon, she never got her bearings. She lay with the others in the splinters and dense darkness, green and sweating, crying and retching. Her existence became only claustrophobia and vomit and longing for Tinnimam, none of which seemed to have a limit.

Eventually the storm subsided, taking the sea-sickness with it, but the hot, close longing remained regardless.

Someone had picked a gap in the planking sometime in the distant past. The hole had been rubbed smooth over years by fingers trying to extend it, either to give a better view or to sink the filthy ship and drown them all. One dawn, the sun shone through the gap, making a blinding ray of light, solid as a bar of metal in the darkness.

Sharli pulled herself out from the heat of the others and, treading over their uncomplaining bodies, she went over to the hole. She shut one eye, fearful that so much light would burn out her sight after so much dark, and pressed its closed lid against the gap. Even without opening, her eye reacted to the brightness, a red orange sun that shone in her mind so that the other eye clashed with it.

She let her closed eye open, slowly and gradually, closing it back when the brightness was too much, and then opening it again when she felt braver.

At first everything was blue, but as she regained her focus she made out something in the distance – a thin black line across the horizon. She pulled back and blinked, clearing the tears the light had made in her eyes, and went back. The ship was moving in a slow ellipse, tacking against the wind on a course that would bring them, eventually, to that thin black line.

There was a bulge in the middle of the line, as if whoever had drawn it had leaned too heavily on the pencil at that part. If she could have seen closer she'd have known this was the bulk of Mordew looming up behind the Sea Gate, still so far away that it was scarcely anything. If she'd had the eyes of a falcon she'd have been able to make out the Manse on top of the bulk, and if she'd been able to see into the future she'd have known that she would come to this place one day, at the head of an army, to torture the divinity out of a boy capable of splitting the world in half.

She had a girl's eyes though, and she could see no more of the future than she could see in her imagination. Now, her imagination was an instrument turned to the immediate concerns of any girl taken as a slave: to her safety, to her physical needs, and, less, to the terrible assumptions she could make as to what use her new owners were to put her.

The ship moved slowly and the line barely thickened. The movement of the ship crushed her cheek against the wood, and her feet were cold so she returned to the others, sliding beneath them where she could, avoiding their knees and ankles, skulls and elbows, taking what warmth she could, staring sleeplessly into the dark, the bar of light and the lurching waves, the only thing that told of a world outside of that hull.

The ship arrived at night, met by the gill-men of the Port Watch in their white uniforms. They slipped quietly onto the deck to take their master's fees. Sharli was not sleeping, but she didn't see them because the slaves had been corralled by the crew in the hull and made to stand in ranks, holding the ceiling straps.

A tall and gruff man came down their lines, inspecting them with his whip handle, barking and prodding, until the slave in front of her went forwards, pulling her by the chain at her neck so she had to go with him.

After a few seconds they were outside.

The hot, oppressive, sour tar reek of the hull was suddenly gone, replaced with an immediate bitter cold. There are people who do this for pleasure, for their health, going from a hot room into a cold one, laughing at the shock of it, delighting in the sensation, but those people are unchained at the neck, are well fed, have slept. They are not in fear of their life being taken from them at any moment, or worse, of being used for things that will kill them. There was no pleasure in this feeling for Sharli, only the desperate intuition that, should she have to stand here long, she would freeze.

She took a look behind her, down to the place that had seemed so bad just moments before, but which she now would have run to if she could, have found a place to hide in the dark, even if it meant a whipping.

She had no choice, though. That is what it is to be a slave; she could only walk where the chain led her. Not to have walked would have killed her.

The slaves were led past the gill-men, who tallied the cargo, and it is some indication of Sharli's state that she saw nothing unusual about them, not their smooth and eyeless faces, not the slits in their necks, not their gaping nostrils. All she saw were men in uniforms, counting, and men in uniforms dragging, and the filthy back of the silent man in front of her.

The ship's cargo was sold as a job lot to the manager of a nail factory whose first kindness to his new employees was to dip them.

A farmer will dip sheep in insecticide to rid them of scab and blowflies, which is undeniably a good thing. He does this by marching them down a slope in turn through a channel filled with the right mix of disinfectants. He then marches them up a slope at the other side. In the middle he will use his crook to dunk the sheep, who must swim through the dip since the bottom is too low for them to walk on. This stings, of course, but it is worse to be prey to blowfly larvae. This fate would be a terrible thing, so the farmer does his job with a sense that he is working for the forces of good, and he does it with a smile on his face. If his sheep do not wish to be dunked that is because they are too ignorant to know that it is necessary. Farmer knows best.

The factory manager marched his purchases through the dip like a farmer marches his sheep, and when he pushed Sharli under the surface of the dip she struggled and went under.

Children of Malarkoi are not routinely taught to swim, and if they can, that is because of some natural ability, or some accident of commune: perhaps their group mother was proud of her unusual ability and decided to pass it on. Sharli could not swim, so she was hooked by the neck when she appeared not to be coming back up, and was dragged spluttering to the other end of the channel, her eyes and throat burning.

After the dip she went to the drying room, after the drying room she went to the undressing room, after that room she and her clothes went in different directions, she to the purser, they to the furnace.

In the purser's room Sharli was measured by a machine – a tall and clanking arrangement of metal rods and rubber belts, loosely bolted – that quantified, inaccurately and carelessly, the girl's general dimensions. These were then encoded into a card, poked through with holes. When Sharli inserted this ticket into a slot a hatch opened up behind her in which there was a smock, too long in the arms, too long on the legs, and very tight at the collar and cuffs.

Sharli, like all the others there, put on the garment, stretching its stitches, in order that she might at least be warmer, none of them caring much any more for their dignity, since that had been lost long before.

From the purser she went to the factory floor, urged forward by the press of newly clad bodies behind her, who were driven in turn by new naked people behind them.

She didn't have time to cough, or catch her breath, because the entrance to the factory was through a series of wooden turnstiles that would have looked to Sharli, if she could have seen them from above and had known what a clock was, like the cogs inside a piece of clockwork. By a calculus unknown to her, she was directed by many turns through to a short bench. Along a conveyor on one side of this bench a seemingly impossible number of nails processed. This conveyor ran off in a circle and was fed by a chute that disgorged ever more nails from above.

At the opposite side of the circle from Sharli was another girl. This girl did not greet her, or pause in any way in what

72

she was doing, which was taking nails, one at a time, from the conveyor. She twisted off the metal sprue that had adhered, presumably unnecessarily, to the sharp tip of each nail. The sprue she threw into a bucket, the nail she put on the table. The girl looked up, very briefly, and when she saw Sharli was not picking up nails and removing their sprues, she cursed her under her breath.

From this Sharli realised she was expected to do the same as the other girl was doing.

When she tried to do it, though, she found that the metal of the nails was burning hot, so that she had to throw it back down onto the conveyor, sprue unremoved.

Because a person will experience pain when she picks up hot metal, she shrieked, and this drew the attention of the other girl. She did not show any sympathy for Sharli, but before the next nail that she picked up she put her fingertips – which, Sharli now saw, were calloused and swollen – into her mouth so that when she picked up the nail and sprue it was the saliva that took the heat long enough for the sprue to be removed and nail and sprue sorted into their respective piles.

Sharli was about to try it when she was jabbed hard from above by a man holding a long pole, itself like some huge nail. Up where he was, there was a network of gantries, all joined together, along which patrolled other men with poles, directing the ends of them at, presumably, workers she could not see. Perhaps they stood at their own benches, unworking, because the man who had jabbed her made ushering signs with his free hand, and jabbed her again until she did what the other girl was doing.

All around was deafeningly loud and frightening.

The sound of metal against metal was not a natural thing for a child brought up in Malarkoi, and Sharli's ears weren't used to it, any more than her fingertips were used to the heat, or her salivary glands were used to providing so much liquid in the absence of any suggestion of food, or her back was used to reaching over the bench to the conveyor, or her eyes were used to the billows of steam and sparks and the endless hard labour of the factory floor, where even the gantry guards were exhausted through their patrolling and prodding.

When the whistle went, louder even than the loudest of the noises she had heard so far, she was poked forward by the gantry man's pole into a turnstile that span her away in preparation for the arrival of the next shift behind her.

There were, she came to know, two shifts at that place, one for the twelve hours most closely approximating the daytime, and the other for the twelve-hour night.

She was so dizzy and bemused with exhaustion that when she was emptied into a barracks, and found the cot allocated for her, she failed to see the small portion of bread that had been placed on her pillow, or the flask of tepid water that lay beside it. Rather than refresh herself as much as that paltry meal allowed, she fell down amongst it and slept, immediately, her cheek amongst the crumbs.

It felt as if no time had passed when the shift whistle blew again.

A gantry man pulled her from her cot with a hook, and dragged her to the turnstile. She was fed back through the machine again, taken on twists and turns across the factory floor by the same impenetrable logic that had taken her to the sprue bench before, but which this time disgorged her by a simpler conveyor past which nails passed, all in a muddle, some of which were correct, but some of which had no head to hammer, or had a blunt tip.

Without knowing why she did it, but feeling somehow that this was what the world expected, she wetted her fingers, took any malformed nail that she saw, and sorted it into the refuse bucket.

This she did for as many hours as it took for the whistle to blow again.

If she ever looked up at the face of a worker nearby, that worker did not acknowledge her, or even seem to register the sight of her.

She was not a nail, it seemed to Sharli, so she was not visible to a nail worker, unless they were the gantry guards. They, though they worked in the same factory, were working on a different commodity – labour. When they saw her they saw only a thing that did, or did not, approach the work of moving, sorting or repairing nails with the required speed and accuracy.

When workers worked too slowly, they were poked.

If a gantry guard poked a girl and she did not attend to her duties more assiduously, or fell to the ground, then that girl was hooked up into the air and taken to another conveyor. From there, she did not return.

Where she went was unknown, nor was there any speculation, since the factory floor was too loud to allow for conversation. The barracks where the workers slept was used only for sleep, since twelve hours exhausting work is not compensated for by twelve hours' fitful sleep. Consequently, everyone there was silently unconscious in their cots, speculating on nothing, thinking only the thoughts that their dreaming minds thought, which, unhappily for them all, were often of nails, and conveyors, and gantries and hooks.

Sharli did at least learn to recognise the food laid out for her, and the water, and these two she combined every day, making a paste of the stale crusts and swallowing it down.

At first she counted the days as they passed, but soon this number became too high for her to hold in her head. Eventually she wondered what the use of knowing it was.

There was no differentiation in the days, nothing to look forward to, nothing to hope for, nothing but labour and sleep and the shape of a good nail and a bad one.

Her fingers calloused, like the other girl's had.

Her bronze skin sallowed.

Her teeth loosened in her gums until she resembled not so much herself as a type – a nail factory worker, sheltered from the rain, sheltered from the sun, sheltered from the entirety of life, devoted to the production of nails.

Indeed, Sharli came to think of herself as a nail more than she thought of herself as a worker of nails, since with nails she had the most contact. She touched nails, felt nails, became accustomed to nails and their needs and wants. The other workers were nothing to her, only an ever-changing parade of the same face, one day there, the next day gone, the turnstiles of the factory working always to separate them.

A nail, that at least is understandable.

It must be straight.

It must be sharp at one end.

It must be flat at the other end.

It must not have accruing to it any sprue.

It must go with its brothers and sisters into the right bucket.

Anything less than a perfect nail must go back to its maker to be made again.

The vast numbers of the nails were to be celebrated, and while individually they did not cheer Sharli, she became attuned to the volume of them so that she felt some sense of satisfaction in the passage of more of them rather than fewer of them.

On a day when one hundred thousand nails had passed, maybe more, her nightly dreams of nails were of a lighter tenor than on days when fewer had passed. If there was a temporary cessation in the movement of the conveyor – something that left the workers terrified, mystified, looking warily up towards the gantries lest this inconceivable failure in the progress of nails be taken as something for which they should personally be held accountable – her dreams would all be of tangles of nails jammed in machinery, conveyors filled only with crooked nails, conveyors conveying only sprues, or of some other nightmare that the world of the nail factory collectively dreamed.

This went on for years, though Sharli had long given up counting the days.

Others from the slaver ship died at their tables, died in their sleep, swallowed handfuls of nails and so tore their throats and stomachs, but Sharli toiled endlessly, and though her diet was very poor, she moved through her early girlhood and began, in a very faltering way, to develop the characteristics of an adolescent.

It was this that brought her to the attentions of the factory supervisor. He was of that degenerate species of man that finds, in the slender and almost, but not entirely, boyish body of a developing girl, something that stirs the fires of desire.

We will not honour him with a name, since he was not a man worthy of that distinction, but the supervisor made one day a pretext by which Sharli should be hooked up and brought to his office. This was above the gantry ways, as the gantry ways were above the factory floor.

The supervisor was invisible to the cogs of the machine, but known well by the gantry men. He had a habit of always cancelling leave days, and holy days, and he would insist on the increasement of various arbitrary production targets, despite the fact that there was such an abundance of nails on the market that the unit price of them was always falling.

He would not listen to any arguments that suggested it was best to limit supply, and thereby drive up the price, those needing nails being always willing to pay good copper for them. It was as if the supervisor wanted to flood the world with nails, whether there was a use for them or not.

Perhaps, his men thought, his predilection for girls rather than women was what made this the case, since these girls were too young to bear children, the nails then becoming a proxy for his own offspring, and the energies he should rightly have been putting into the fostering of his legacy were turned outwards towards the making of a great many nails as a substitute.

Whether his men's speculation was true or not, the supervisor had Sharli brought to him in his office.

When she saw this place, she could scarcely comprehend what it was she saw, so long had she been in a world of conveyors and gantries and nails. The furnishings of it, the smells of it, the presence in it of fruit and of cigarette smoke, of decorations: these were all things she had very nearly forgotten. When she saw them, it brought to her chest an overwhelming feeling of nostalgia.

This was not in the way that a pampered and privileged person will feel nostalgia, as some vague ache for a time past, their childhood, or a trip that was enjoyed but was never to be repeated. Instead, it was a violent, shuddering grief for what had once been and which, she could not now remember how, had been taken from her.

This, and the sense that she had once left Malarkoi by her own will, brought her to collapse down onto the floor, grasping at the pile of the supervisor's patterned rug, tearing at it uselessly with her calloused fingers, weeping dryly at how she had been brought to this place, and at her ignorance. She knew now that it would have been better to have her throat slit by the priesthood and to take her place in the heaven prepared for her rather than to live in this hell of nails.

The supervisor got up from behind his desk.

This was just how he liked his girls – weak and frail and exhausted by working for him. How easy it was, then, to make them grateful by easing their labours. And then, for a lump of sugar…

'Come now,' he said, kindly, 'there's no need to cry, is there?'

This was a rhetorical question, for which the supervisor would not require an answer, but if Sharli had been called upon to provide an answer she wouldn't have been able to.

Workers at the nail factory were not given sufficient water that they could waste it on anything: not tears, not dilution of urea – their urine came out a dark and stinging brown – not lubrication of the vocal cords. It was a mercy that their fingers became hard and calloused, because soon the saliva to wet them could not be produced, and this also meant that Sharli's tongue was too dry to twist into the shapes that made words. She had not spoken to anyone in years, and the supervisor used the very difficult language of Mordew, which Sharli did not understand.

For all these reasons she said nothing.

There she was, curled at the supervisor's feet, and he swallowed.

Though he was a man of appalling tastes, he still had a discriminating and advanced sense of aesthetics. It was not enough simply that his girls should be young: they should also be clean, pretty, perfumed and well dressed.

And, he thought as he looked down at a child who was little more than bones in a smock, they should be a little plumper.

It is this nicety in his sense of beauty that saved Sharli the fate of many of the other factory girls who had been brought to him; that, and the fact that there had been a shortage of labour in the past few months brought on by an increase in the number of the Mistress's firebirds, which not only beleaguered the Sea Walls, but which also interrupted shipping.

When there was labour to spare, he could have his pick of the newcomers, but now there were few of those, and he was lucky to find Sharli remaining amongst the long-serving staff.

The supervisor stood so that his feet were either side of Sharli, and he clapped his hands so that she looked up at him from between his legs with her large and sorrowful eyes.

He swallowed again and straightened his waistcoat, but wasted no more time. He turned to his desk and rang the bell for the undermanager, and when that man arrived, at a run, clanking the gantry outside the supervisor's office and asked 'Yessir?' the supervisor replied that Sharli should be taken to that place where the other girls had been taken, but that, rather than being made ready for his arrival later that day, she should be given to the madame so that she might 'do her best' for the girl.

Here, he said, was an envelope of money for her trouble, from which the undermanager could take a tenth share for his troubles.

The supervisor handed the undermanager said envelope, which he had taken from a drawer in his desk, and within which twenty identical envelopes were also stacked.

So it was that Sharli was taken from the nail factory, and though she dreamed of nails for many years after, she never returned to that place. Every morning on waking, nails in her vision, she renewed the vow she made to herself on the day she left that she would never labour in that way again, no matter what. Should she ever have the means to end the world she had been made to live in she would do it, regardless of who suffered.

The undermanager, though he knew precisely what he was doing for the supervisor and why, convinced himself through arguments that he was not to blame for what he did in taking the girl Sharli to the brothel in the slums known as the Temple of the Athanasians.

Who was he but a lowly undermanager?

What was his fate but to do whatever it was that the supervisor told him?

What would it benefit anyone for him to refuse?

Another man would do it, and what would be the benefit in him losing his job?

What of his daughters, scarcely one rung up on the ladder from this poor girl? Wouldn't they then be prone to have to accept work of this kind?

He would be damned if that greasy, disgusting beast of a supervisor was getting his hands on his girls.

Yet still, when he met Sharli's eyes…

When he helped her by the hand into the carriage that would take her secretly to the place where she was to be prepared, over the course of a month, for the supervisor's consumption, there was a human exchange between them, that unavoidable communication when one person sees and is seen by another.

It made his stomach lurch.

The stomach is an organ that cannot argue as well as a brain, and there are liquors which can silence both, a gulp of which he took from a secreted flask as he closed the carriage door and left Sharli by herself for the first time in years.

A girl of Malarkoi, a girl who has escaped the priesthood of that place intact, a girl who has then been slaved first to pirates, and then to a nail factory – in short, a Sharli – is, when she has been taken out of direct servitude, an indomitable sort of girl.

Now, with the nail-life fading by moments, to be replaced by a larger, more complex world, her old rebelliousness, her old wilfulness, her old resourcefulness rose in her as a rush of determination. Her mind began to operate at great speed, bringing thoughts that she knew would save her, if she could just marshal them together.

The carriage set off, and immediately she tried the door handles and the windows – the doors would not open and nor would the windows be lowered, so there was no way she could slip out.

The carriage was plushly upholstered. The seat cushion to her right was covered in black velvet, the centre pinned down with a large, black button. This button she grabbed at and pulled and pulled and pulled until it came loose.

As she had hoped, the button had been nailed into place, through the cushioning, into the wooden bench of the carriage. She took the button, and, aligning the nail, held it pressed between her upper arm and her ribs beneath her smock. Then she slid over so that she was sitting on where the button had been, hiding the fact that it was no longer there.

Sharli watched the Factoria give way to the Entrepôt, saw the port where she and the slaves had been brought to Mordew, watched the undermanager negotiate the Fetch Gate with bribes from the envelope. Here was the beginning of the Glass Road.

Though all these things were new to her, she didn't look on them with excitement or awe. These were things of this horrible city, horrible in their forms, horrible in their functions, horrible even in their majesty, and the sight of them burned in her chest like hunger – pain.

The slums seemed right for this place: collapsed and filthy, endlessly wet and dark, peopled by sad and crooked individuals, divided even in their poverty, separating themselves off from each other even here, jealously guarding their patches of dirt.

Sooner than she hoped, the carriage pulled to a stop.

The undermanager undid the latch on Sharli's door and opened it to let her out. She paused, wondering how she could leave the carriage without revealing her theft of the button and the nail, but then the undermanager's attention was directed elsewhere.

The Temple of the Athanasians was the only place around that could be called a building. It was tall, had three storeys, was double fronted, with glass windows, a pillared doorway, gaslights, and a paved path leading in.

There was a sign with words that Sharli couldn't read, beneath which there was a picture of a girl, welcoming and cheerful.

From the door beneath this sign there emerged a real and much less cheerful woman. She was dressed in a dress cinched at the waist, billowing out below and above like an hourglass done in pink fabric, the ribs of some supporting structure from which all the fabric depended visible through the thickness of cloth. Her face was painted, and though she was scowling now, there was a strange beauty to her appearance that was impossible to ignore.

She came marching down the flagstone path. 'Envelope!' she barked.

When the undermanager didn't give it to her immediately, she huffed, took a fan from a small handbag that hung from her elbow, and used it to blow a wind across her face. It was as if his failure to do what she'd asked needed to be blown away, lest it infect her.

While she was doing this, Sharli got down from the carriage and closed the door behind her, hiding her theft.

Standing beside the oddly beautiful, hourglass woman, Sharli felt like an opposite kind of thing to her: narrow, filthy, ugly.

The undermanager handed the woman the envelope and then, the moment he'd done it, remembered something and went to get it back.

It was too late – the woman had opened the envelope, counted the money, and secreted it in her bosom before he could realise his mistake – that he had forgotten to take his tenth – and now she put her hand up. 'This is barely sufficient,' she said to him. 'Next month the price rises in line with my costs – inform him of this.'

The undermanager bowed, and, not sparing Sharli another glance, returned to the footplate and steered the carriage back into the slums.

'In!' the woman snapped. This was, Sharli would soon come to realise, the madame.

Sharli, nail clutched to her side, did as she was told.

The madame's name was Bernadette, and she considered it beneath her dignity to attend to Sharli herself, now the money was collected.

Sharli was given into the care of two girls – Sylvie and Juliette – with whom she was expected to bunk.

These girls were the same height as Sharli, but double her width, having been born into the brothel by mothers who, for reasons undisclosed to their roommate, were no longer employed by that establishment. Some men have a preference for big girls, and these two were fed to be that way.

The reason the supervisor had sent Sharli to the Temple of the Athanasians was to put meat on her bones, and to prepare her for his future arrival, so this was the best place for her to be since there is no better way to gain weight than to eat in the way Sylvie and Juliette were accustomed to eating – of large amounts of fat and sugar – and to drink as much cheap, sweet, fortified wine as could be sourced.

Sharli stood there, on the day of her arrival, with nothing but herself and her frock – excepting her makeshift weapon, which she put immediately inside her thin mattress, between the springs.

She looked, when she saw herself in Sylvie and Juliette's many mirrors, like a terribly sad thing compared to these two. They were ruddy-cheeked and shiny-lipped, and when they walked across the floor of their room – which was all frills, and ornate frames, and plush rugs – the floorboards creaked and bowed.

If Sharli feared her appearance would go against her with these two, the opposite was true – instead they took to her as they would a lost sister. As if she wasn't thin and filthy, they clutched her to them – though they did dust themselves off after – and did everything they could to make her feel that she was welcome there. She felt the warmth in them like a girl who has been made to live on the streets in winter feels the warmth of the fire: as an unfamiliar but still very welcome thing.

'Let's see what there is for you to wear!' Juliette said.

Sharli couldn't understand Juliette's words, her knowledge of the language having not developed a whit in the factory, but when Juliette saw this she said the same thing in Malarkoian, only a little clumsily. The girls had learned the basics from others of that origin, many of whom had been indentured to the Temple over the years they had been there.

Juliette gave Sharli a lump of chocolate, which was, she learned, a kind of solid and sweet paste with a flavour so delightful that she could hardly believe it after having had nothing but bread in the factory and goats' milk and blood in Malarkoi.

When she had swallowed the chocolate, she was given another piece, and this one she put on her bed.

'What are you doing?' Juliette said, not angry, only puzzled.

'I'm saving it for tomorrow,' she said in her own language. Once Juliette had repeated this phrase back to Sharli in the language of Mordew, and then made her repeat it, Sylvie told her that there would be plenty more where that came from, and that she should eat up.

In this way, Sharli communicated with the two, and gradually learned their language and their ways – which were primarily to enjoy everything the Temple had to offer and to minimise the unpleasant aspects of the place by means of various chicaneries and tactics.

Sylvie brought a bundle of clothes in from somewhere and threw them down in the middle of the room and then they took Sharli into the bathroom and drew her a bath.

The experience of bathing made Sharli weak with pleasure, though the other two seemed shocked when she tried to drink the bathwater while she was in it. The experience was of an order so far removed from Sharli's factory life that she couldn't quite credit that it was happening.

It was not like a dream – Sharli only dreamed of nails – it was more as if she had gone to the place the priests had promised her, that heaven their Mistress was supposed to vouchsafe for them all, except here in life, not only after death.

When she returned to the room, wrapped in towels, every hint of the dirt that had been a condition of her life since her slavery gone – except perhaps between her toes where Sharli had never learned to clean, and similarly behind her ears – the other girls laid out clothes in a rainbow spectrum, starting at the reds and ending at the blues in three layers, top, middle and bottom.

'Take your pick!' Sylvie said in one language, and Juliette repeated it in the other.

The three spent an hour putting on first one thing and then another, seeing them in combination, checking their fit, putting some aside for alterations, with others to be sent back to the communal wardrobe.

This only stopped when a bell rang.

When that happened, both of the Temple girls turned to look to a board above their door onto which five thick curls of spring had been nailed, and above which the bell had been placed. Sylvie's spring was moving, it having been set into motion by a string beneath it, pulled presumably by someone elsewhere in the brothel.

Sylvie sighed and got up from the floor where she had been kneeling in front of Sharli, tying up the ribbons on the front of her gown. 'Duty calls,' she said wearily. She half-heartedly applied lipstick in the mirror, rubbed kohl into her eyelids, smoothed her hair neat, and trudged out of the room, closing the door behind her.

'Well,' Juliette said, treating the whole thing as a minor inconvenience at worst, 'what will you be wearing today, Miss?' Her tone was light and silly, and though Sharli couldn't mimic those emotions, nor find in herself yet the resources with which to feel them in herself, she pointed to a red skirt, a green bodice and a yellow overshirt, a combination which had Juliette wrinkling her nose.

'Red and green should ne'er be seen,' she said, mock seriously, 'except upon a Scottish queen. How about this?' She replaced the red skirt with a yellow one.

The ensemble seemed nice to Sharli, so she put it on.

Juliette puffed scented water from a small bottle all around where Sharli was standing, and though some of it went in her eyes, she was pleased with the smell, which was very different from the ones she was used to.

After a little while, during which Juliette tugged at various structural aspects of Sharli's costume, and applied powders and tints all over the girl's face with a bewildering range of small brushes and delicate silver tools, Sylvie came back.

'That was quick,' Juliette said.

Sylvie crooked a finger in way that Juliette seemed to understand. 'Hair trigger,' she said.

Sharli didn't understand what she meant, even when Juliette translated it.

Sylvie went to the bathroom and came back a moment later with a flannel in hand. She wrang it out in the bedroom sink and put it on the clothes horse to dry. 'Coming down to the bar?' she said, which Juliette agreed to, but when Sharli wanted to come too, they had to tell her she wasn't allowed.

'Shop window, I'm afraid, and you're reserved goods,' Sylvie said.

Again, Sharli didn't understand.

'We'll send Hansy up with a bottle and a plate – wait for his knock and we'll be back later.'

The two bustled out.

When they were gone, Sharli was left to contemplate events in the quiet of the empty room.

There was a window in front of her, and when she dimmed the lamp, rather than see herself reflected in it, she could see instead the underside of the Glass Road in the distance. In the underside of the Glass Road were reflected the slums and the border fence of the Merchant City. These to Sharli were shapes, regular in their geometry, such that they reminded her of the

Golden Pyramid. Now here she was, once a disobedient ash, once a chosen sacrifice, a renegade from a heaven she should always have longed for, a slave, a nail worker.

Now what was she?

The clothes weighed heavily on her shoulders, pinched at her underarms, constricted her chest, and made her breast difficult to fill with air.

And outside this strange city.

From down in the Temple, music drifted up with the sound of communal singing of a merry tune.

There was a small tier of wooden shelves in the space between Sylvie and Juliette's beds, and on each of the shelves was a shining tray, silver like the necklaces of the sacrifices, except chipped here and there so that a duller metal shone through. On these trays were laid out foods of sorts – she had seen the girls eating from them whenever their hands weren't busy doing something else – and now she knew what she was.

She was hungry.

Hunger is a strange desire – when danger is near, when company is at hand, when almost any other thing must be attended to, hunger recedes itself into the background. Perhaps eating weakens the body, forces it to attend to the necessities of digestion, diverts resources away from more pressing concerns. Perhaps the body knows this, holding hunger back when there might be the need to fight, or run, or to have one's wits about one.

But when there are no distractions?

When one is on one's own, hunger makes itself known. The desire to eat grows, and this is what happened to Sharli when the girls had gone.

Now she turned her attention to the trays.

The top one had savoury things. Had she the experience to recognise them she'd have known them for vol-au-vents, for slices of spiced sausage, for cow cheese speared on sticks, for the wings of chickens, roasted in honey and sesame seeds.

The second tray had fruits equally unrecognisable to her, sliced and preserved in their own nectars, fortified with liqueurs: pineapple with gin, cherries with kirsch, peaches with schnapps.

The third had boiled sweets: confections of sugar and essences.

Sharli helped herself to these strange things, first slowly, tentatively, then more quickly, then in a nervous rush, as if they would be taken away, making combinations of flavours that clashed and were almost disgusting, except that her hands didn't care. Neither did her mouth, and her stomach seemed to swell in front of her, some void that wanted to be filled.

She ate and ate and so engrossed was she in this feverish meal that when there was a knock at the door she jumped, shocked and guilty, not knowing what she should do, or whether she would be punished.

She slowly got to her feet, and this brought her into the purview of the ornately framed mirror the girls used to apply their make-up. In it her face was smudged with the colours the girls had applied to her and also with cream and liver, with pineapple juice and honey, and remnants of all the other things she had shoved into her face.

The door knocked again.

Sharli couldn't countenance wiping her hands and face on her nice new clothes, so she wiped them all instead on her pillowcase and ran to the door.

In the hallway outside there was a short, young boy with a tray. He went down into a tight little bow, and, without rising from it, proffered the tray he was carrying, on which there were shapes covered with a white towel.

He left when she took the tray and didn't look at her.

Both ways down the corridor, there was nothing much there to see, and no people either. It stretched off past a very many doors, and ended in windows where it met the far wall.

She took her tray inside.

Beneath the towel was more food – bread this time, a chunk of ham, still on the bone, pickles, and an apple – and beside this was a bottle of fermented fruit juice.

All of these things she ate and drank, and when she vomited them up a little later, her stomach not knowing quite what to do with the bounty she had provided it with, her head dizzy from the wine, she went back to the trays and plates and filled herself again. Then, fearing she would rupture and thereby kill herself, her mind and stomach conspired to send her to sleep, her mind by telling her that she must lie on her bed, and her stomach by filling her with an overwhelming drowsiness that it was impossible for her to ignore.

She was woken in the morning by a gentle shaking, and, having dreamt of labour and conditioned to the nail bench, she jerked up to her feet.

Instead of the turnstiles that would take her to her post, there were Sylvie and Juliette in their nightgowns. The rising sun was a grey disc behind the overcast visible through their window.

'How are you feeling?' Juliette said, and suddenly in Sharli's mind ran the events of the night before: her excessive consumption of their food, her expulsion of part of it into the sink in the bathroom, part of it onto the tiles of the floor, the spilling of the wine bottle so that it must have ruined something, her retiring in the clothes they had laid out for her, surely wrinkled and ruined, perhaps stained and torn.

All of this came on her in a moment, but if they were angry with her, if she was due a beating, they hid it well behind broad, dimpled smiles.

When she looked around the room all was as it was before – the trays restocked, the bathroom clean and unperturbed, even her clothes had been taken off and folded neatly on her chair; she found she was in a nightgown just like the others'.

'We made Hansy clear up.'

'He's an easy boy to convince,' Juliette said, shrugging.

'Chop, chop,' Sylvie said, 'Bernadette wants you in her office to discuss terms before lunch.'

Again, Sharli didn't understand some of what was said, regardless of what language they used, but she worked out enough to know that she was wanted by the woman who had met her. She went to put on her clothes from the previous night, but Sylvie stopped her.

'A lady's never seen in the same clothes two days running,' she said.

'Unless it's her birthday suit!' Juliette said.

The two of them cackled about this as they pulled out something for Sharli to wear and made preparations to put on Sharli's face, which was a production in itself.

'Well,' Bernadette said, when Sharli was standing before her in the brothel's front office with her hands neatly clasped and her ankles together, as the girls had shown her, 'don't you look delightful. And all at my expense.' The madame used Malarkoian perfectly, though her accent wasn't one Sharli recognised. The madame turned away and looked out of her window, first pulling aside the net curtains.

The office was more sparely decorated than the girls' room, and somehow also more intimidating for it.

Bernadette stood beside a simple, sturdy, mahogany table, on which there was only a writing slate and a cashier's till. Sharli was at the end of a rectangular rug, the pattern of which seemed to depict nothing except how tiles might interlace with each other and overlay one another, and repeat. The effect was a little migrainous, and when Bernadette came over to stand by Sharli so that she needn't raise her voice for what she said next, Sharli realised that her eyes were crossed and that she had to make some effort to uncross them so she could focus on Bernadette's lips, which were mouthing something almost in a whisper.

'You know why you are here, of course.'

Sharli had to admit that she did not know why she was here, which caused one of Bernadette's eyebrows to rise. Because the rest of her face remained entirely as it was, the effect was that the eyebrow had done this by itself, without reference to the wishes of its owner.

Bernadette went to her table, to a drawer hidden on her side of it, by her chair, and brought back a book, which she passed to Sharli.

'That book is called *Useful Information for Ladies and Girls Employed by a Brothel* and, thankfully, it is illustrated. No need to open it now!' Bernadette said, when Sharli started to do exactly that. 'Suffice it to say that your employer at the nail factory will attempt much of what you will find in chapters three and four, hopefully nothing from chapter five. The contents of chapter six are forbidden in this house.'

Sharli held the book in front of her, but said nothing, as she had been advised.

'My advice to you, child, is to remain entirely passive. Say nothing, do nothing, make no encouraging or discouraging noises. Men such as your employer are unpredictable beasts; there is no saying what might enrage their passions. The best thing is to let them burn themselves out so that they might then, as soon as they may, return shamefacedly to their wives. Is this clear?'

Her words were clear, her Malarkoian used with perfect clarity, but Sharli did not know what she meant by them in combination. Nor did she worry much about that: Sharli had no intention of doing anything other than piercing the super-visor's neck with the nail she had stolen from the carriage that brought her here, something that would render irrelevant whatever might be contained within the book, or what the man intended to do on his own account.

'Good girl,' Bernadette said, taking her silence for under-standing. 'You are not under an indenture, so there is no need to provide me with a minimum income; your patron is responsible for compensating me for any expenditure. Avoid profligacy, though. Men of wealth find ways of getting their money's worth, and the more you spend here the more he will exert himself in this regard. Hansy tells me you have a good appetite – indulge it on simple, hearty foods. The supervisor prefers girls with a little heft, but not too much, and the more he prefers you, the quicker he is likely to be satisfied. Do you play cards?'

For the first time Bernadette seemed interested in Sharli's response. Previously she had been very much the professional woman, but now there was a flicker in her.

This flicker was extinguished when Sharli shook her head. It returned when she seemed to think of something else. 'Would you like to learn?' she said.

Sharli nodded.

'Excellent! I will send for you at seven. There is no need to change into evening dress.'

Sharli nodded again, turned, and left the room, outside of which she was met by Sylvie and Juliette, all giggles and whispering, who took her straight upstairs.

'She's never asked me to play cards with her,' Sylvie said.

'That because you're thick as pig shit,' Juliette replied, but when she said 'shit' she put her hand over her mouth as if something had come out that was supposed to have stayed in.

Sylvie gave Juliette a funny look, the meaning of which Sharli couldn't immediately understand. 'That right?' Sylvie said. 'Well, it takes one to know one.'

'That doesn't make any sense,' Juliette said, 'but I didn't mean it anyway. You aren't thick and I shouldn't have said you were.'

Juliette went over to the food trays and came back with a plate with a cake that was made of three layers, each one a different colour, and each separated from the last by a layer of cream. She gave it to Sylvie, who shrugged and inserted the thick end of the wedge of it into her mouth. Through the crumbs this became, she said, 'Doesn't matter. I wouldn't want to play cards with her anyway.'

'Me neither,' said Juliette, 'and you better watch out too, young Sharli. She's not your friend, and if you keep in too close with her you'll end up regretting it one way or the other.'

Sharli wasn't sure what choice she had in the matter, but she didn't say so. Instead, she went to the trays and took a simple sandwich, feeling the need of something plain after her excesses of the night before. 'What is cards, anyway?' she said, returning to her bunk.

'Game of skill, if you ask some. Game of chance, if you ask others. If she wants you to play for money, say you haven't got any,' Sylvie said.

'I don't reckon that's why she wants to play with you. My feeling is that she's pegged you for a ringer and wants to train you up as a way of broadening her portfolio down on the shop floor.'

Sylvie nodded. 'Probably right. May as well fleece the punters while they're waiting, right?'

'Specially with her on the red list till her owner's had his fill.'

'There's no missing a trick with that one!' At which the two fell about laughing, while Sharli sat and puzzled at their meanings, most of which were still beyond her.

At seven that night Sharli presented herself at Bernadette's private chamber.

She was admitted, and when she went in she found the room very much unlike the front office. Where that was bare and functional, this was covered on every conceivable surface with nick-nacks and mementoes, little cameos and silhouettes, miniatures of dogs in coloured glass, decanters, glasses, binoculars and telescopes, all the detritus of years that a person might accumulate, laid out as if there was no such thing as a box, or a chest, or even a tip to which people might send their unwanted things.

'Come in,' Bernadette said, reading the overwhelming of Sharli's senses as reticence. She was sitting back in a comfortable-looking chair, in front of which was a low table, covered in green baize, lit by an oil lamp. There was a pack of cards on this table, and on the other side of the table there was another chair, the same as hers, except in this one there was a man sitting.

He was a very fat person, the sides of him exceeding the width of his chair by some inches, his velvet clothes stretched very tight across him, and his neck emerging from them in rolls which met his aubergine lips as if there was no chin between neck and face to form a natural barrier.

The features of his face were so large there was scarcely room for them, despite the width of their canvas, and above his dark, deep-set eyes there was pile of butter-oiled curls. He wore a talisman on a chain that draped across his chest in the form of a ram's head, something Sharli recognised straight away as the emblem of her priesthood. She stepped back in shock.

'I apologise,' Bernadette said. 'I should have warned you there would be a guest.'

The man stood up, offered out his hand. The talisman swayed in front of him. 'Let me introduce myself,' he said, in Malarkoian. 'I am Mr Padge, a business associate of your host.'

Whether this was supposed to make Sharli feel comfortable she was unsure, but she didn't feel it.

Mr Padge stepped forward. 'Have no fear. I am not a frequenter of establishments of this type – I value my continued health too much to risk it – so do not expect this to be a working engagement. I came here on a social visit and now find myself in a position to offer a little service to an old friend, inasmuch as she would like me to teach you how to play the cards.'

'Quite correct,' Bernadette said. 'Come, Sharli – there is no need to shrink back so far into the darkness.'

Sharli did come forward, she had no choice, but there was the ram's head talisman, and she could not help it. 'Why do you wear the emblem of the Dumnonii priesthood?'

Padge took the talisman in his hand and inspected it, as if he'd never seen it before. 'It's nothing,' he said. 'Ancient history.'

Bernadette saw that Sharli was about to speak again, and prevented her with a hand on her sleeve. 'Mr Padge is not here to answer your questions, child. He is here to teach. Sit,' Bernadette said, drawing a third chair, this one more upright, less comfortable.

Sharli sat, and, without ceremony, Padge showed Sharli his sleeves. 'Nothing unusual in these, except the extortionate cost my tailor charges me.' Padge brought his sleeves down and shrugged, as if it was a natural gesture, but now in his hand there was a pack of cards, in addition to the one that was on the table. Before Sharli could say anything, he held up his finger, then returned the pack of cards to his pocket. 'Might I trouble you for a cigar, Bernadette?'

She smiled and went to one of the densely covered tables and reached into a humidor that was hidden in the chaos, coming back with a cigar as thick as a baby's arm. With a little guillotine, Padge snipped off the end, placed the cigar between his purple lips, and lit it. When he inhaled the pungent smoke it made him cough, and though Sharli's eyes smarted, she saw that there was now, back in his hand, the pack of cards. He put up his hand, as if to stop Sharli again, but this time she was too quick for him.

'There is a slit in the breast of your jacket which you can put the pack of cards through. Then you hold them under your armpit. When you shrug, or when you cough, or when you make some other distraction, it lets you straighten your arms without anyone noticing. The pack of cards slides down your sleeve and into your hand.'

Padge was not a man to give praise, even when it was warranted, but he let Sharli know he was impressed with a smile and a slight bow. 'Now let me show you why.'

Bernadette got up at this point, and gestured to Sharli that she should take her chair so that she could better learn her lesson. The madame went to get them both drinks.

'Pontoon is simple, and a good game to play in an upscale brothel like this one,' he said.

Over his shoulder, Bernadette smiled.

Padge went on. 'It is a game of chance with an edge to the house that only inordinate skill at memorisation and mathematics can overturn. More, though, it seems to be a game that must reward the brave, where the opposite is the case.

'The wealthy men who frequent good brothels imagine themselves in concert with the world, courageous and rewarded, rather than lucky, so that when they come to the table they are prepared to take risks in front of an audience that, if they were to come off, would demonstrate to onlookers the truth of their habitual assertions that they deserve what they have in life, the turn of cards in their favour confirming that fact.

'This fact alone, when the game is played fairly, is enough to make a good living for the management of a gaming room. But when the game is played unfairly, the same fact can cover some quite outrageous cheating on the house's part. This is

95

because, when a brave man loses his shirt, he still appears brave to the onlookers, which is what the man wants more than anything, and so he leaves happy. Poorer, but happy, and we have his money.

'It is very easy, when one knows how to substitute an ordered deck for an unordered deck, for a man's money to be taken quietly from him and for no one to raise an objection, least of all the man himself. One need only, then, learn the basic rules of the game.'

As Padge gave this speech, in pieces, over the course of half an hour and a non-trivial portion of a bottle of Bernadette's good brandy, he showed Sharli how to play the game of Pontoon, taught her the lingo proper to its play in the languages of both Mordew and of Malarkoi, showed her how to palm a deck of cards and pass it to an accomplice, how to secrete and retrieve a second deck, how to pick cards from the top and bottom, how to hide cards, and, in short, showed Sharli how she might cheat the patrons of the Temple of the Athanasians of their capital.

When Sharli asked what would happen if she was found out, Bernadette stepped in. 'That rarely happens – our liquor is strong, and most men are here for other reasons. When you intend to "drop the hammer" on a client, simply give the agreed signal and one of the girls will begin a free dance on a nearby table. This is almost always enough to distract anyone who is looking to uncover cheating. If that does not work, the gentleman is often willing to be distracted in other ways.'

'And if he won't be distracted?'

'Then we will have the security staff deliver you a punishment beating in the yard.' Bernadette didn't pause when she announced this, and Mr Padge nodded sagely in his seat, the nub of his cigar between his teeth, as if this was just the right thing. 'My men know how to pull a punch, and you will be rewarded amply when the house closes. At that point your contract will be severed, and you'll be transferred to backroom duties.'

Mr Padge stood up now. 'Practise what I have shown you and everything will go well. There is no difficulty inherent in swindling drunks and reprobates. It is, in fact, one of the easiest possible ways of making a living. It is certainly easier than picking hot nails from a conveyor.' He gave Sharli a significant look at this point. 'I hope to see you both again soon. Bernadette, it was a pleasure, as always. Sharli, I trust we shall become much better acquainted in the days to come.' Now he directed his comment to Bernadette. 'I see a great future in her.'

Bernadette smiled and passed Mr Padge his overcoat, which he put on his shoulders. Before he left, and as if he wanted Sharli to see him doing it, he took the ram's head talisman from around his neck, polished it on the velvet of his waistcoat, and put it into his top pocket, as a man would do with a watch he kept on a chain. 'Adieu!' he said, and left.

Once he was gone, Bernadette turned to Sharli. 'Beware of that man, Sharli. He may prove the death of you.'

'What did she say?' Sylvie said, when Sharli came back to their room. She used Malarkoian as she always did with important things.

Sharli didn't know why, but she didn't want to tell them about Mr Padge. Whether it was the talisman, or what Bernadette had warned her of, or for some other reason, she felt that it was something she should keep to herself. 'You were right,' she said. 'She wants me to cheat the clients at Pontoon.'

'Told you!' Juliette said, in the language of Mordew. 'Well, it's easy work and the pay's good, and it's much easier on the knees than anything else she's got going.'

Over the next few days, Sharli practised with the deck of cards, wrapped first then unwrapped, and Sylvie made adjustments to her clothes, slashing the lining by the armpits, and making new puff sleeves. Juliette kept a constant supply of pastries and sweetmeats within arm's reach, and while they worked, Sharli talked, played cards and practised palming. The girls gave her pointers and let her know whether she was being too obvious or not.

They showed Sharli how to button her blouse so that, when she leant forward or back, it opened or closed small gaping windows onto the flesh at her chest, or her waist, both of which were becoming less and less like, respectively, 'a washerwoman's knacker board' and a 'starved whippet's windpipe' the more of the fatty, sugary treats she ate.

There were odd cries from the other rooms, sometimes the sounds of fighting from the street below, and once or twice either Sylvie or Juliette came back from their work sullen or crying, but these things were all short-lived interruptions to the otherwise happy mood. Sharli felt, for the first time possibly, that she was enjoying her life.

She concentrated on speaking Mordew's language properly, and her teachers found her a fast learner. While some of the girls' idioms still eluded her, she was soon as confident with the basics of conversation as she was at substituting a palmed knave of staves for a nine of coins, thereby making twenty-two and bust.

The girls drank often from a glass decanter of brandy, and smoked a great deal of opium, and these were the only things Sharli did not join them in, since the first time she had either of them, the other two pressing her endlessly to do it with giggles and pouts, they made her sick or put flashing lights in her vision that she had a hard time clearing. With the opium, she'd had to lie down on the cool tiles of the bathroom until she recovered, a sweat breaking out on her top lip and forehead, her arms and legs weak and trembling.

'You'll have to get used to it, love,' Sylvie told her. 'Bernadette will sometimes pay you in chits for the powder man when cash is short, and no one likes to work for nothing, do they?'

Sharli didn't know what she meant, but the girls didn't press her on it.

On the occasions when both girls were called out to work, which wasn't that often, but which also wasn't that rare, she called for Hansy and made him play cards with her.

He was a tiny lad, thinner even than she had been when she arrived, and white as an albino rat, so that when she brought him into the room by the hand her own skin, paler than it had been when she was in Malarkoi, always outside in the sun, looked like she remembered it did, a deep and uniform bronze. For reasons she didn't question, this made her glad, and though Hansy's expression never wavered from its gloomy and somewhat petrified set – as if he was expecting something awful and knew there was nothing he could do to stop it happening – she was always happy to see him.

She set him down across the table from her and arranged herself so that her sleeves were in the right place, the cards were prepped, and the buttons on her blouse were properly loose on their threads. 'Tell me if you see anything funny,' she told him in his language.

Hansy swallowed and nodded, but when he put his hands on the table they were trembling.

'It's alright,' Sharli said. She wanted to say that she wasn't going to make him do anything he didn't want to do, but she couldn't think of the right word. 'All will be good,' she said instead, and Hansy nodded.

She dealt them their cards, put the remainder of the pack down, and turned Hansy's over. There was the deuce and nine of cups.

Hansy looked down at them and paused. For a moment, Sharli thought he was going to stick, which would have been stupid, but eventually he tapped the pack to twist, which was the only sensible thing to do.

Sharli dealt him his card, which was another deuce, this time of swords.

Hansy looked up at Sharli, the whites of his eyes yellow and bloodshot against the white of his skin. He took a deep breath, which Sharli thought was him thinking hard about his cards, which wouldn't have been right because there really wasn't much of a decision to make – you don't stick at thirteen – but then he looked off over her shoulder, to the place where the girls kept their brandy.

'You want a drink?' she said, but Hansy silently shook his head.

Slowly, as if he thought she might push him back down in his seat, rap him across his frail and bulbous knuckles, and always looking right at her, he got up from the table and paced, one careful foot in front of the other, over to the table where the decanter was. He was like a cat trying to cross a room without drawing the attention of a dog.

Sharli had no intention of stopping him, or telling him off, or, as he seemed to worry, beating him, she just watched, slightly puzzled. He crossed the floor between the beds until he came, very gradually and warily, to the place where the girls laid their pipes and tapers. He stood there, in front of the little glass bowl where they tapped out their ashes, licked his lips, once, and nodded at Sharli. At no point during this performance did he take his eyes away from Sharli's, always staring out from under his beetling brow, never seeming to blink.

Now across his face flickered something that Sharli recognised from a thousand other faces she had seen in her life. Hansy was hungry.

'You want their snout?'

'Snout' was the name the girls gave to the opium Bernadette sometimes paid them in, and Hansy nodded again, wincingly, as if to do so would bring down a clout across his ear.

The girls were generous with Sharli, but she knew they didn't like people touching their things. She got up and went over, lit Juliette's pipe for him – which involved her breathing some in, even though she tried not to – and she passed it over to him.

Now Hansy moved quickly – in a blur, it seemed to Sharli – he took the pipe and dragged for longer than the girl thought was possible, the bowl burning red. He pulled so long on the pipe Sharli thought that smoke would come out of his ears. His face went from its usual moon-like whiteness through pink, red, and then to a strange purple-blue.

When he eventually breathed out, there was very little smoke, as if his body was reluctant or unable to let the vapour leave his lungs, and when Hansy passed the pipe back – and watched as Sharli returned it to the ashtray – he went back to the table and played his hand in a much less rigid manner, twisting as he ought to have, and not caring, when a third deuce fell and he was tempted to go for Pontoon, that Sharli took her palmed knave and bust him.

He stayed for a few minutes more, but then he was called away. He rose to his feet, bowed, smiled, and left at a run.

If he had never returned, things might have gone very differently for Sharli, but as it was Hansy made it his business to be available for Sharli's card practice on every occasion over the next fortnight that Juliette and Sylvie had a mutual customer, even going so far as to manufacture situations in which the girls had more work than they might. There was a catalogue of the girls and boys at the Athanasians, and Hansy made sure to leave the book open at Juliette and Sylvie's pictures, and to obscure with stains the pictures of some of the other girls. Whenever he came in, Sharli lit one or other of the pipes for him.

In this way Sharli developed a requirement for opium without realising it, and also overcame her initial inability to stomach it. It always passes if you give it a chance.

It was the thirst for opium which dictated, quietly and without announcing the fact, many of her decisions from then on, and the absence of it, which causes the onset of a very anxious and irritable frame of mind, that made her natural inclinations towards violence seem to her more of a feature of her character than might have been the case had she never been introduced to the stuff.

The weeks progressed, the time when the supervisor of the nail factory was supposed to call for her drew closer, and her skill with the cards, with the speech of Mordew, and her hunger for 'snout' all grew.

As she ate and put on weight, her menses came on her, and since the girls were older, they showed her what to do, how the opium – only a little, it's fine, go on – could be expected to help with the cramps. Her breasts and hips and belly swelled, and one night Bernadette sent Hansy to bring Sharli down to the front lounge, where she would be expected to deal hands of Pontoon.

The girls sent Hansy away when he didn't seem to want to leave, looking over at their decanter table. They pushed him out of the room and slammed the door behind him, and in a great bustle and chaos of activity they got Sharli ready, dressing her in the best of the altered clothing, separating out the face cards and the low cards from the deck, painting her face with colours and dousing her with perfumes, and giving her a little sip – go on, it'll steady your nerves – of their pipes.

Then they sent her down.

Hansy was waiting outside the room, trembling a little and intense. Perhaps he thought that Sharli would bring him a pipe, but she didn't, and when he took her hand his grip was hard, his fingers bony. She pulled her hand out of his and walked down by herself, since she didn't need to be led by the nose, thank you very much. That said, she didn't know where the front lounge was, so she had to let Hansy take her there anyway.

They went along the corridor and in one room there was a girl cleaning herself, and from another one a gentleman emerged, smiling and polite. When he turned away from the door and another girl closed it behind him, he bowed to Sharli, as if he had met her in the street, but when she had passed he called her back and asked her name.

'She's not in the catalogue,' Hansy said, before Sharli could answer.

The man looked a little puzzled, but then he bowed politely again, and Hansy indicated that Sharli should get a move on.

In the stairwell the stairs looped round in a wide circle down to a mezzanine landing, and down through the middle hung a glass chandelier, lit with candles. The crystals were beautiful and only a little dusted with soot, and the light they refracted from the candles danced on the walls, on Hansy's pale face, and on Sharli's big, puffed sleeves. It seemed, inside her eyes, that they set up flashing in the way they had flashed when the girls had first given her the snout, though not as bad and not as scarily.

She carefully put one foot in front of the other as she descended, the toes of the neat, tight, heeled leather boots poking out beneath the hems of her skirts, and everyone around seemed to be looking at her – men and women, girls and boys – and suddenly she felt the need for Hansy's hand after all. Now it was she who was gripping more tightly, and he whose finger bones were being grated together.

At the bottom of the stair there was a tiled hall, cool-looking, like the tiles in the bathroom, though the colours were different, and so was the pattern, which was like a wreath of laurel leaves. It was their coolness that Sharli noticed, and she felt nothing more strongly than the desire to lie with her cheek on them, and to take in their coolness and smoothness, and for all these people looking at her to disappear away so that she could concentrate on not being sick, the feeling of which came up from her stomach and down from her head, meeting in her throat.

Whether Bernadette could tell this kind of thing was happening from a distance, or whether it happened to everyone when they came down to do their first shift in the front lounge, or whether it was just bad luck, here she was, emerged from nowhere, to take Sharli by the arm. She turned her so they were facing each other and looked her right in the eye. Without saying anything she gestured off and a person with a tray arrived on which were little lead crystal glasses, blue ones, into which an oily and glistening liquid had been poured in small amounts.

Bernadette took one and handed it to Sharli.

The girl held it up in front of her eyes, admired the light from the candles, refracted through the chandelier, chilled by the tiles, sickening, somehow.

'Drink it, girl,' Bernadette said, in Malarkoian, under her breath, her broad smile in no way reflecting the irritation the sound of the words carried. 'In future, lay off the pipe before work, do you understand?'

Sharli took a deep breath and drank it, and it was so bitter, so astringent, so simultaneously burning and cold, that it cleared her senses immediately and brought everything into sharp focus, where before it had been so oddly mild and blurred.

Bernadette's face, she now knew, was a mask for the customers, and her words meant that Sharli should immediately pull herself together, which she did.

The madame shot a glance at Hansy, who left backwards, bowing, himself having understood the meaning of that glance – that he, Sylvie and Juliette were now due a beating if and when the events of this evening were to go awry. How Sharli knew these things, she wasn't sure, but everywhere suddenly seemed pregnant with meaning – the upright but dissolute patrons, the beautiful but diseased girls, the precise and perfect furnishings slapped on over this building's mouldering wooden frame, Bernadette herself, the controller of all this, scarcely able to prevent everything from falling to pieces.

Sharli could read all of it.

Bernadette led her into the front lounge, but Sharli felt that it was she that was leading Bernadette. There was the round table amidst all the others at which she would sit and deal the cards, the bar where patrons would drink, unwisely and heavily, and beneath which other intoxicants were secreted against the eyes of less open-minded customers. In the corners were the heavies who, for the price of their drinks and a small retainer, would oust anyone who cut up rough, and the girls, barely dressed well enough to cover their modesty, of which they had very little.

Dim lamplight, musty carpets, regularly sprayed with perfume, one windowpane cracked.

Men of all ages and of only one class – merchants – dressed all the same, except more or less dishevelled, older or younger, drunker or more sober, two or three together or alone with a girl on their knee, laughing or lasciviously silent, eyes roaming.

And there, standing with his hands flat on the bar, Mr Padge, affecting not to notice her arrival.

Bernadette squeezed her shoulder, which meant both 'Do you know what you are supposed to do?' and 'Go and do what you are supposed to do!' and Sharli answered the question and obeyed the order by marching directly to the table and sat there.

She put a fresh deck of cards down on the table.

The moment she did, Bernadette announced. 'The game is Pontoon, and you are all welcome to try your hands. The stakes are low, the dealer very new – in fact, this is her first game – so those of you who have always wanted to bankrupt the house will find no better time than now to try.' Bernadette smiled, shyly, as if she was both amused and a little worried that this was precisely what the patrons would do.

When there was no immediate rush to take Bernadette up on the offer, the girls on various knees began geeing the men on – variations on 'I've always liked a gambler' – or whispering in their ears – offers of compensation, later, upstairs, should any money be lost, sufficient to make up, in kind, for any deficit experienced at the table.

To cover this more or less obvious determination that the men there should lose money to her, Bernadette had the fiddler play a new tune and announced that happy hour would begin now, and that all drinks were half price, which was a cue for the barman to switch out the good bottles for the watered ones.

Sharli occupied herself by shuffling the cards.

From where she was sitting she could see Mr Padge. He was still at the bar so that she could only see the back of him, but then, as if he was coming across to get the ear of the barman, he moved so that she could see his face in a mirror behind the bar. He didn't do anything so obvious as wink, but she could see from his expression that he knew she was looking at him. He picked up a nut from a dish on the bar, and this he put to his lips. He held it there for a moment, and then pulled it away, as if he had been intending to crack it with his teeth, but had decided not to.

This, it seemed to Sharli, was to be the signal to her as to when she should drop the hammer – when he did not eat the nut, she should lose, and when he did eat the nut then she should win. In order that Mr Padge should understand that she understood she fluttered her eyelashes, as if she was clearing out a mote of dust, and Mr Padge, who could see her in the mirror as clearly as she could see him, fluttered his eyelashes back.

So it was that these two secretly communicated across the bar, and while the method was not faultlessly subtle it was very unlikely that a room filled with men as debauched and drunk as these men either were, or were about to become, would have any chance of decoding them, any more than the whistles a shepherd gives his dog can be decoded by the sheep they are herding, no matter how loudly he makes them.

It wasn't long before a large and portly gentleman, a cowlick of hair stuck with sweat to his forehead, his bowtie askew, and the starched bib of his shirt front curling up from his waistband, took a seat in front of Sharli. Beside him came and sat another man, almost exactly the same – perhaps they were brothers and did this kind of thing together – except that this one was bald.

'Since this is your first time, we will go easy on you!' the one on the left said, slurring his words a little on the 's' sounds, but he didn't say it to Sharli, he said it to the one on the right.

That man replied, 'Poor thing. I think she's bitten off more than she can chew!'

The two of them laughed uproariously at this, and by the time they had stopped, their ties even more askew and their faces very red, Sharli had already dealt the cards.

The front lounge at the Temple of the Athanasians operated a system by which the men did not gamble with money, but instead with tokens in the form of wooden discs, which were purchased at the bar, or which were loaned on credit. These formed the currency with which the certainty, or otherwise, of whether a hand in Pontoon would win against the dealer, or not, was measured. Regardless of the cards dealt, an ante was required at the start of the hand, and these two men put down a beige token each, that being the minimum acceptable wager.

Sharli, because she had been told, knew the value of each token and it had been stressed to her that, because the colours of the tokens were all quite similar – shades of red, orange, brown and yellow – it was very possible that mistakes could be made in the placing of wagers as to how much a man wished to bet.

It had been stressed to her that when low-value tokens were played, it was house policy to ask whether that token was the one intended, and when high-value tokens were placed then no such enquiry should be made. In this way the dealer could cast, without making it too obvious, aspersions on the bravery, or otherwise, of the men playing cards with her, encouraging them, through shame, to gamble ever larger amounts of money by associating this practice with their assumed manhood.

While this may seem to be a somewhat crass practice, so profitable was it to the house that it was not one that any place would ever give up, since no man of the type that is likely to be gambling in a brothel likes to be made to look lesser in the eyes of either the pretty girls there, or the other men in the room.

'Sirs,' Sharli said, in her accented approximation of their language, 'did you mean to use the low chips?'

The two of them looked at her, puzzled at first, then one of them said, in a mocking parody of her accent. 'Zirs! Deed yoo min tea ewes da lo cheeps!'

While they were laughing at this, almost choking themselves on their own hilarity, Sharli looked past them to the mirror in which Mr Padge's face was contained. It was impassive. He put a nut to his lips, then took it away.

The two men, once they'd gathered themselves, did not recover their beige chips, so Sharli dealt them their cards. They laughed again at her pronunciation of the numbers, Sharli let them win, and when they bet with the beige tokens again, Bernadette came to inform them that their room was ready – as it always had been – so they finished their hands and left.

They were replaced – a queue had formed of spectators, gathered around the table by the laughter of the men before them – by a much more serious-looking gentleman.

He was young and handsome, Sharli thought, and seemingly by himself. Sylvie and Juliette, in their many conversations, had taught Sharli that she should be wary of men like this. Men who came to brothels alone were ashamed of what they intended to do, usually with good reason, and this was more true of the good-looking ones, since they should have no trouble satisfying whatever reasonable demands they had of women up in the Merchant City, and hence would only come down here for more 'niche' requirements.

He bet with a red token and Sharli dealt the cards. He looked at them – the tens of cups and swords against her five and six of staves – with deep brown eyes and pursed his lips. It is never wise to split on tens, even when the dealer is showing a five and six, but this is exactly what the man did next. He smiled, smoothed back his hair, increased his bet by double, and announced his intention.

Sharli had already looked at Padge, and he had indicated that the man should win, so that is what Sharli let him do, despite his bad play. To him she dealt the two matching jacks, since that would make an interesting hand for the onlookers, and bust herself with a two and king, making herself look unlucky, since anyone would twist on thirteen.

Rather than Bernadette approaching the man, as had happened with the laughing and insulting brothers who had the table before him, this time she made a ringer sit at the table on one side, another seat being taken by a man who muscled his way up from the back, his long fringe flopping into his eyes and his chin jutting out periodically, every time he became interested in the cards being dealt.

The handsome man left to avail himself, a little later, of whatever specialist services he'd pre-booked, having lost some of his winnings, to be replaced with a series of men who Sharli dealt hands untouched to, none of them seeming to take the game seriously enough to be of interest to the house. The ringer loudly won almost every one of his hands before making a silly play that cost him half of what he'd won, encouraging everyone watching in their delusion that they could do better. Sharli, while not inconceivably unlucky, seemed to bust out more hands than was fair, cementing her reputation as an easy dealer against whom to play.

The evening wore on and the room started to thin, most of the men having been taken to their rooms for business, leaving Sharli alone at the table with the man with the fringe and the chin who had muscled his way in. He played conservatively at first, but then, without the distractions of the other players, he used a yellow token – the highest value one the Temple exchanged for – for his ante. Sharli said and did nothing unusual, but dealt the hand quietly. She had, over the course of the evening, perfected her position at the table and the means by which she could check Mr Padge's instructions, and before the cards had hit the wood she knew he had bitten the nut. Since it was quieter now, and the fiddler had gone on his break, even if she hadn't seen Padge do it she'd have heard. He'd put the kernel between his back teeth and crunched down, and it was clear to her, although to no one else, that he wanted her to bring the hammer down.

This time she dealt the man a deuce and a three and herself a three and a four.

He brushed his fringe out of his eyes and fixed Sharli with a glare so intense that when she called the cards her voice faltered. It is all very well to cheat drunks and perverts and idiots, but it is much harder when your mark has you in their sights and seems to have your number.

Whether it was the crack in her voice, or whether Padge had a second mirror secreted about his person in which he could view the man's face, he turned in his seat.

The man's chin jutted, breaking his gaze, and he took all of his yellow tokens and stacked them in front of him, a sign that he intended to bring them into play. He tripled his bet, making this already the largest hand of the evening, and twisted.

Sharli paused, during which time Mr Padge came to stand near the table. He was in a conservatively tailored suit of worsted, so he wouldn't look out of place.

The man with the fringe saw Mr Padge make his way over, and from his pocket he removed a pistol, which he put on the table. It clunked hard beside his cards. 'Twist,' he told Sharli, again.

Sharli couldn't help but glance at Padge now, but he raised his head, as if she should do it, so she did. She dealt him the eight of staves, with which he would, in the deal, make twenty-one when she followed it with the eight of swords.

The man stacked all of his chips now, the bet representing what would be half a year's salary of a reasonably paid clerk in the Merchant City, an example of which this man appeared to be, or would have if it hadn't been for the pistol on the table in front of him.

Mr Padge said nothing, but now Bernadette came in, having been summoned by the heavy in the corner using a hidden bell pull that alerted her from her office.

'My, my,' she said, when she eventually arrived at the table. 'That is quite the bet.' If she was concerned she showed it in neither her voice nor her manner, but the heavy at the back, presumably at some signal from her, rose and began, forcefully but quietly, to remove the remaining patrons, the drunks and the stragglers, from the front lounge.

'Twist,' the man said, and when he said it he took the pistol, pulled the cocking hammer back, and returned it to the table.

Bernadette came and stood behind Sharli. 'We will play out this hand,' she said, 'but can I ask you to direct your pistol away from my dealer? She would be a very expensive girl to replace, since she's already been bought by another customer.'

This seemed to confuse the man, but he did at least do as he was asked, angling the pistol so that it pointed directly at Bernadette. Now he did not take his hand away, but left it resting so that his finger was on the trigger.

'Thank you,' Bernadette said, politely, but a little ironically. 'The man is twisting, Sharli.'

Sharli nodded, and gave the man his eight. 'Twenty-one,' she said.

The man nodded. 'What I do not expect to see now,' the man said, 'is your dealer dealing herself a five-card trick. Should I see that, I would be very angry.'

Bernadette smiled, and now Mr Padge went over to the bar, from where he picked up the bowl of nuts from which he had been helping himself all that evening. He came back over with it, sat next to the man, and put the nuts on the table.

The man tried to say something to this fat man with the greasy curls and fat lips, but Padge put his hand up in a way that, though none of them would have been able to explain why if asked, silenced the man completely. From the bowl, Padge took a single nut, and this he placed on the table. He then took from his jacket a pocket mirror, a very simple thing, oval framed, with a handle. In this he checked himself, once. He found his appearance satisfactory, it seemed, and holding the handle of the mirror in his fist, he brought it down on the nut, cracking it open.

He used too much force, though, and both the edible part of the nut and its shell scattered across the table. He picked through the mess, taking the meat and eating it, while leaving the shells littering the game surface.

Sharli dealt herself the five of coins, and Mr Padge turned to the man. The room was empty now, the heavy having removed everybody else, and the ringers and girls having retreated to the doorway. 'You have, I assume, realised our dealer is trained to deal the cards we ask her to deal. But can you, such a clever man, guess what my signal to her has been?'

Before the man could say anything, Padge took another nut from the bowl, and this one he put down directly in front of the man, pushing his cards out of the way as he did it, toppling the tidy stacks he'd made of his yellow tokens so that one of them rolled off the table and went down on the floor.

The man reached for it, instinctively, and Mr Padge brought his fist with the hand mirror in it down so hard that the table juddered. If the man had not been holding tight onto his pistol, it would have slipped off onto the floor.

Sharli, without a pause, dealt herself the requested card, which was the seven of swords, though because Padge had made a mess of the table, it landed among the kernels rather than neatly where it ought to be.

The man, seeing where this was going, stood up from the table and raised his pistol. He held it up so that at first it was pointed at Bernadette, then at Sharli, then at Mr Padge. The tip of the barrel shook in the air because the man's arm was shaking.

Now Padge spoke to Sharli. 'You see how things have progressed? First this man was in the right, defending himself from being swindled by brothel scum out of his money by indicating their cheating. But look, before the final card, the ace that would give you your illegitimate five-card trick, he has raised his gun at us, becoming instead a simple robber, hoping to leave with Bernadette's money. Could he claim that he was swindled, if the card turns out to be a queen, busting your hand? Of course not! And I decide between both outcomes by taking a nut from a bowl and cracking it. Or not.' He turned now to the man. 'Which would you prefer? To be swindled, or to be killed as a robber? I have no particular preference.'

The man stepped forward, brushing aside the table. 'And what if I kill you?'

He put the gun into Padge's face, which made Padge frown, but it was Bernadette that spoke next.

'Please put your gun down,' she said. 'You are making an idiot of yourself. If you pull that trigger then precisely nothing will happen. Try it, if you wish. You will find it doesn't fire. Do you think we've operated here, all these years, without patronage? The Master has put a hex on the premises that prevents violence of this type.'

Now the man pulled the trigger, as if to test her and, as Bernadette had said, the pistol jammed. At that exact same moment, or one so close to it that no one observing could separate them in time, Mr Padge stabbed the man through his fringe, through his eye, through his eye socket, into his brain, with the stiletto he kept habitually in his sleeve, and which he had slipped into his hand earlier.

He turned to Sharli. 'A pack of cards isn't the only thing it's useful to be able to produce out of nowhere,' he told her.

The man fell to the ground, his arm still outstretched, the gun in his hand, his finger on the trigger. It was only when he hit the ground that his body seemed to relax.

'I think,' Mr Padge said, 'all things considered, it would have been better for him to be swindled. A man, after all, does not have the right to kill a man whom he has swindled, whereas a man who tries to rob him? He can be disposed of as the man sees fit, with no detriment to his reputation. Do you want me to send for someone to clear him up, Bernadette? I can have him taken to Beaumont's without any fuss.'

Bernadette toed the man's corpse, determining by that method his weight, roughly. 'No, thank you,' she said. 'I think a couple of days hanging out the back might put anyone off trying something similar.' She gestured for the heavy, who was still watching from the door, and he dragged the man out, having first emptied his pockets.

When he was gone, Bernadette turned to Sharli. 'Excellent work, girl. Perhaps practise the movement of the cards from the deck, but otherwise, and for a first time, you did very well.'

Sharli, though, could barely hear what Bernadette was saying to her, so loud was the sound of the blood rushing through her ears.

When she returned to the girls' room, the first thing she did, before she even began to account for the hubbub, was to gesture for a pipe, suddenly finding herself desperate for something to calm her nerves. They were making everything in her body shake, and everything in her mind race.

Rather than give her one of theirs, Sylvie got her a new one, and from that day until Sharli was taken away from that place under cover of night, there were three pipes in the ashtray.

With the help of the opium, the next week passed very easily. Sharli returned to the front lounge most evenings, all of which were much quieter than the first, but just as profitable for Bernadette.

The supervisor had said that he would call for Sharli in a month and this time had already passed, so she in her innocence imagined that the man had forgotten about her. It was terrible to find, when she was called into Bernadette's office one morning, that he had not forgotten at all, but had sent a gantry man from the factory to enquire as to her progress.

Bernadette had agreed that she was ready. A suite was booked for that evening.

When she heard the news, Sharli's throat immediately felt the thirst for her pipe, despite the fact that she'd smoked just before coming into the office.

'Do you remember my advice?' Bernadette asked. 'Do nothing. You have made yourself very valuable here in the short time since you arrived, and I wouldn't see you hurt for no reason. The supervisor, compared to some men of his type, is manageable, providing you do not enflame him. You are used to the opium now, the girls tell me?'

Sharli nodded.

'Good,' Bernadette said.

She was rubbing her hands together, and though she seemed to want to give off an air of nonchalance, Sharli could tell the madame was anxious on her behalf. The movement of her hands washed off some memory of her own, some shared experience that heightened her fear of what might happen, some trace of blood that needed to be warded against.

'I will station a guard in the hall,' she said, 'but do not call out to him. He will listen, and if things go badly he will manufacture some pretence by which he can interrupt.' It seemed that if Bernadette continued to wring her hands with the force that she was currently using her fingers would snap. 'Ask the girls to give you some tips.'

Juliette and Sylvie had already provided a comprehensive introduction to the methods of their work, along with a special moisturiser that both eased a man's progress and quickened his resolution, though it did burn, they said. Sharli had not tried it because she had no intention of easing his progress.

Under her pillow she had kept the carriage seat nail, had seen what use Mr Padge had made of a spike, and in her private moments, in the bathroom, or when Hansy was passed out from too much of her opium, she had practised the movement with which Padge had driven his stiletto into the robber's – as she determined to think of him – eye.

While it seemed to her that none of Bernadette, Sylvie and Juliette could even consider the fact that the supervisor might not receive what he had paid for, Sharli would not countenance that he should, not at her expense, and not at the expense of anyone else in that place. Would Mr Padge, a figure who played an ever larger role in Sharli's imagination as the days in the Temple passed, put up with that horrible man's attentions?

He would not.

Was she so much less than him? Not in her own eyes at least.

Mr Padge had not come to the Temple since the night with the robber. She had received cues regarding the dealing of the hands from one of the senior girls, and sometimes from Hansy, who acted as a tray boy in the lounge.

The previous evening, she had made her own decisions very profitably and word had got back to Bernadette. The senior girl had hoped to get Sharli 'in the shit' as Sylvie and Juliette put it, by 'accidentally' sending her the wrong signals, but Sharli knew enough by now to act on her own account, and when the tally of the night's takings was passed to Bernadette so it could go in the ledger, it was the 'grass' that 'got it in the neck' and now Sharli was to be given a free hand with the cards.

Sharli looked out of the girls' window, hoping to see Mr Padge.

There was no sign of him.

It was dark now. Hansy was sleeping through his evening break and the girls were busy. Sharli was still staring out of the window, chewing at the sleeve of the dress she'd been told to wear. When that sleeve got soggy, she chewed the other sleeve.

Then she chewed each of her nails in turn.

Mr Padge was nowhere to be seen, but, as if she had summoned it by hoping it wouldn't come, in the distance appeared a lamp, swaying in the way a carriage lamp sways, slowly and gently from side to side as the horses pulling it trot along a muddy street.

There were other carriages that arrived at the Temple, that was for sure, but Sharli knew it was the supervisor. She wasn't lucky enough for it to be anyone else.

The lamp swayed and the horse trotted, and the carriage drew ever closer until there he was.

She had only seen him once, and then from below, from the ground, but even up here, looking down, she knew it was him.

He stepped gingerly down onto a mat laid out for him by the doorman, holding onto the frame of the carriage door as he eased himself out into the world, slowly. Perhaps his back pained him, from so much sitting down at his desk in the factory, or perhaps he'd damaged his spine from exerting himself against another girl.

Or perhaps, or perhaps, or perhaps.

Regardless, he was here now, and the hours Sharli had watched the clock, thinking that at least there were ten hours until he came, five hours, two hours, then at least an hour, perhaps more, and perhaps he wouldn't come at all.

Half an hour, then ten minutes, each unit of time, as they shortened, becoming longer in the living, as if, by dint of her extreme concentration on its passage, time could be stilled entirely, could be stopped by thinking at an impossible pace. Only, she couldn't think fast enough, not with the opium.

She took the pipe to her lips and lit the bowl again with the taper.

Under the smoke, almost quiet enough not to hear, not to think, she asked herself the terrible question: What if she couldn't stop him?

What then?

She had, on the bed in front of her, two objects and these swam in her eyes – the moisturiser the girls had given her, and the nail button she had stolen from the carriage.

These two objects seemed like the two possible ways of dealing with the world: passivity, such as that suggested by Bernadette, Sylvie and Juliette, and violence, that Mr Padge embodied.

There was a knock at her door and the two objects stopped swimming and became perfectly solid in front of her, outlined in light.

It was the rest of the world that swam: the bed, the bedclothes, her skirt, her knees.

The door opened, and here were Sylvie and Juliette.

For a moment Sharli felt as if she had been reprieved, as if there had been some interruption, some unimaginable but concrete intercession that had come to save her, out of the blue, but there, behind them, was Bernadette, her face falsely cheerful, falsely calm, suggesting, falsely, that it would all be alright.

She held out her hand.

Without looking, Sharli took one of the items from the bed as if she was drawing the top card of an unshuffled deck, thereby leaving to fate what happened next.

Just as a man like the supervisor does not deserve to be given a name when he is spoken of, nor does the scene which he had created for Sharli deserve to be described.

Nor should anyone wish for it to be described, since men like the supervisor, when they cannot service their desires on real girls, will service them instead on imaginary ones, or the ones written about in books, or the ones depicted in images. Though some will say that they thereby satiate urges that would otherwise be acted out in the real, what is to say that these fictive descriptions, once read, once seen, do not provide a template for future actions? That men like the supervisor go to the descriptions they find of things they know are forbidden and thereby construct images for themselves in their heads that their desires then insist they act out in the real?

Even if there is no link, who should wish, except men such as the supervisor, to read such scenes?

And who would agree to write them?

Even if it is all to a greater end, which is to see that terrible perpetrator punished, is this imaginary suffering justified in the pursuance of seeing it punished, since if it was never written it would not require punishment?

Regardless of whether it is justified, or it is not justified, the description of what Sharli suffered at the supervisor's hands is not included here. We are in Sharli's world and whatever it was that happened then she worked hard to forget, shielding it from her memories, and so there is no place for it in these pages.

All we should know is that it was the nail that she took from her bed.

With that nail first she stabbed the supervisor through the eye and into the eye socket, blinding him.

She did not kill him, as Mr Padge killed the robber, because a nail is not as long as a stiletto is, and a young girl is not as physically adept as a grown man at driving weapons far into men's brains, no matter how furious that girl has become, numbed from the self-consciousness of her own rage by the taking of opium.

Though Sharli failed to be as good a killer as Mr Padge was, she was as good as she needed to be because she then, having not succeeded in killing the supervisor with the first blows, got a handhold through the blood on the upholstered button from which the nail depended and she stabbed him again and again.

First she stabbed him in his other eye, and then she stabbed again and again through his nose and lips, into his gums, the nail clicking against his teeth.

She paused, and then she drove it into his ears, left and right, over and over, until the supervisor's own father would not have recognised him, so little was left of his face.

Then, because that was not sufficient to stop him from breathing, Sharli sat back until her hips were over his belly and not his chest. From here she had the right angle to drive the nail below his ear and into his jaw, repeatedly, this time all along the right-hand side and never the left. She did this for no reason other than that is what she did, piercing over and over all the veins and arteries of his neck until there was nothing but shredded flesh there.

This time when she stopped, the supervisor was not breathing.

Sharli was suddenly filled with an incredible loathing of his body, as strong in its way as her fury with him had been.

She retreated to the wall, as far from him as she could.

Except that then she did a strange thing, even stranger than murdering him – which was something she had every right to do – she returned to his body, though it repulsed her, and from his hands she took all his rings, lubricating them from his dead fingers with his blood, which was all over her hands. There were four of them: two gold, one silver and a signet ring. The smallest rings she put on her thumbs and the other two, which were too big for anything, she held in her bloody fists, one in each hand.

She was disturbed in doing this by the guard who had been posted outside, he having been distracted, purely coincidentally, by a commotion in a room several doors down that had proved to be nothing.

When the guard saw what had happened, he froze, then backed out of the room, closed the door behind him, and left Sharli alone with the supervisor. It seemed to him that neither of them could do the other any more harm than they had already done them, and that he should go and tell Bernadette what had happened.

The next person Sharli saw was Mr Padge, and she ran to him, the blood drying now and tacky.

Though Mr Padge was a man of refined sensibilities, it is to his credit that he didn't shrink from her, though she was a gory and a filthy mess. Instead, he embraced her lightly on his part, and allowed her to cling to him however tightly she wanted.

'Goodness gracious,' he said, after a little while, 'what have we been up to here?'

If Sharli hadn't been choking on her tears, which were of a complex origin, born of rage and fear and relief and passing bloodlust, she would have told him everything, so highly did she hold him in esteem.

As it was, she couldn't make the words come out.

When she hadn't stopped crying for five minutes, Mr Padge had to prise her away from him or there would be no more work done that evening.

He crouched down in order to look her in the eye. 'Pull yourself together, child,' he said, kindly. 'Whatever has gone on here tonight, you have proved one thing very well. That is that you can kill a man. Whether you understand it now or not, that is a very valuable skill. What weapon did you use?'

Sharli looked down at her red hands as if she wasn't sure herself, then held up the button nail, the upholstered end all covered in clots.

Padge looked at it for a moment without understanding what it was. 'A nail?' he said, eventually, smiling. 'How apt.' Then he held out his hand. 'Sharli, you will come with me. You have outgrown this place, and it is time for you to enter your apprenticeship. I am an excellent mentor in the profession you have just chosen for yourself. There will be times when you will not understand why it is that I ask you to do this or that, but I ask you now to promise me that you will do it regardless, knowing that I know best.' He chucked her under the chin, as a man might do to his mischievous niece. 'Do you so agree?' he asked.

Sharli, despite the improvements to her speech that her stint at the Temple of the Athanasians had provided for her, didn't understand all of the words Mr Padge used, but she was about to agree anyway, when Padge seemed to read her thoughts.

'It is very important that you understand me now, Sharli,' he said in perfect Malarkoian, and then repeated what he said before.

Sharli nodded through the entire speech.

'I agree.'

THE PROPAGANDA OF THE SOCIAL SOUL

What if all that is required for a self to be a self is the recognition of that self by the social corpus? Just because it might be true that it is convenient for Assembly members to recognise in a body the presence of the self of another member that does not make that the same as it being true, for the reasons given against duplication.

Even if there was a consensus that a self was never duplicated, this would be insufficient, because it is always possible to make multiple duplicates, and even the possibility of this fact invalidates the notion of self-transference. Indeed, the making of duplicates would be nothing more than making new members, themselves self-distinct, and not the original selves, even if they shared the same physical attributes and memories. They would have simply come into consciousness as all self-aware things have done, at a specific time and place in the real.

To believe that a consensus recognition of the validity of the self is sufficient is called the propaganda of the social soul.

III

Sharli in the Kitchens

PADGE ARRANGED for his man at Beaumont's, Black Bill, to come with the cart to collect the corpse of the supervisor, which was then fed to the pigs. Bernadette took the soiled bedding to the local branch of the laundresses' union, burned any furnishings that couldn't be cleaned, and bribed the carriage man to say that the supervisor had been waylaid by rogues.

Business at the Temple of the Athanasians went back to usual, except that Juliette caught an inconvenient disease and took over dealing duty. Sharli became little more than an interesting story the girls told each other on quiet nights.

Mr Padge paid a sum to compensate Bernadette for Sharli's expected future earnings, and kept her away from his other assassins, knowing that they were a difficult group to like. An assassin is not an easy thing to make, and more often than not they come pre-made by life, but the best ones, the most reliable, the most skilled, the most obedient, were the ones you could take and mould from childhood, and this was what Padge determined to do with Sharli, having seen her potential.

It was not cheap, that was for sure.

The child had no things that Bernadette would let her take, except the rings on her fingers and those in her fists, and Mr Padge had no equipage suitable for a girl child, he never having kept such a thing before. All these things he had to buy, and because he was that kind of man, he kept the price of his purchases in a comprehensive list, intending, once Sharli was working, to make an indenture of them and so recoup his investment that way.

One day, soon after she had stopped her – what had until then seemed to him incessant – crying, he said, 'You have the look of the Dumnonii about you.'

'You don't,' Sharli said, which was true. There was too much meat on him, and his skin was as yellow as butter.

Padge smiled and pretended to look himself up and down. 'I have been away from home for too long, perhaps. Are you familiar with the Albidosi?'

'Of course,' she said, 'they are no friends of the Dumnonii. Our priests would have us shun you for your individualist heresies.'

Padge sniffed. 'I wouldn't dream of speaking against your priests. Good luck.' He turned and began to walk away, but he didn't get far.

'I never listened to the priests!' Sharli dived at Padge's ankles and grabbed him by his trouser legs. 'If I'd done what they said, I'd be dead by now.'

Padge remained turned away, as if considering whether he should take her words under advisement, or whether not to. He eventually softened, turned slowly, and faced Sharli.

'If we are to get along, you must learn to keep your hands off my clothes.'

'The front of house at a restaurant,' Mr Padge said one evening, pulling aside a thick, patterned curtain so that Sharli could see, 'is like the stage of a theatre – the wait staff are like the actors, the patrons are like the audience, and everything is painted and beautiful and fabulous.'

Here and there across The Commodious Hour the staff who had looked down their noses at her when she arrived were standing, pads in hand, or walked briskly, three plates to an arm and a platter held at shoulder height, or raised a finger to indicate something to someone, or licked the tip of a pencil, preparatory to writing an order, or did something else that Sharli couldn't understand.

Between, at tables decorated with high vases from which flowers poked, all sorts of rich people – fat, thin, old, young, happy-looking and sad – sat and let people serve them.

'But,' Padge continued, 'like a play, what happens out there during service is a kind of lie. The waiters, like actors, are not who they pretend to be – they may dress immaculately, but that is because I provide the uniforms for them. They are, in reality, scarcely more than you are, young Sharli – filthy, in one way or another. See her…' Padge flicked out the little finger of his right hand to indicate a woman who had tutted when Sharli hadn't got out of her way quickly enough in the corridor, '… Angeline. Beneath her skirts, she is pockmarked to quite a startling degree. The waiters' captain…' Padge looked around until he saw him and then used his indicating finger to point him out '… has to apply iodine nightly to her infections. He covers the stink by stuffing her drawers with a lavender pomade.'

Sharli could hear in Padge's voice that this was a bad thing, though she felt a little sorry for both the captain and Angeline, even if they both had been rude to her. 'It's not nice to have the pox is it, Mr Padge?' she said.

He looked down at her, briefly. 'No, child, it is not nice at all. None of these people are nice – not the customers, not the patrons. That table, number nine, over there by the chandelier…' it was the patriarch, he of the waxed beard and the plucked eyebrows, '… that gave poor Angeline the pox in the first place. He'd give it to the captain too, given half a chance. And don't think his wife is any better – she owes me four silver for opium that she's needed on account. Anyway, my point is made. Nothing you see behind this curtain is true, Sharli. The tables are woodwormed, the wine is mislabelled, the meat is on the turn… in short, it is all dishonest mummery.'

Padge let the curtain fall back.

A lesser man might have gone down on his haunches at this point to make his point more clearly to the girl, but that kind of position was hard on Padge's knees, and beneath his dignity in any case. Instead, he angled Sharli's face to his by gripping her chin between his thumb and forefinger and pulling it up a little. 'Let us see where the real business of this place is done.'

Sharli wasn't stupid, she knew that if a man tells you one thing is wrong, the next thing he tells you is right, so she wasn't a little bit surprised when Padge said, 'Back of house!' as if he was revealing the lady in a game of three-card monte.

The kitchens were through a pair of doors that swung outwards and inwards, their hinges sprung so that they never stayed open. These hinges might have been redundant because such was the traffic between the front and back of the restaurant that there was always someone, often more than one, going in or out through them, and they were never, therefore, closed.

As Padge led Sharli towards the doors she got glimpses of what lay behind – white tiles, men and women dressed in white clothes, white billows of steam and white plumes of smoke, but when she reached the threshold and Padge held one of the doors open for her to go through, she saw the whiteness was an illusion distance gave – everything was whirling white, red and green and black and silver. There were red faces, flames, slabs of meat bleeding slowly onto wooden boards, radishes. Radish tops were green, heads of lettuce, bunches of herbs, oils poured from a height, splashing, apples sliced. Black iron skillets of all sizes, scorching, black trays of pies and puddings. Silver knife blades, silver necklaces, silver rings, silver teeth in grimacing faces, sweat in their eyes.

'Behind!' a huge man cried, whirling in place with a pan so hot that it glowed on its underside. Gouts of black burned treacle smoke billowed up into his face so Sharli couldn't make out his features. Even Padge obeyed his demand that a path be made for him, and the man hurled the pan into a sink of plates and water, which popped and cracked and spat.

The man turned – he was twice the height of Sharli and four times her width, and his face reminded her of the snub-nosed dogs that roamed outside, except his was hairless – and Padge slapped him across his cheek with the back of his hand. He didn't wait to berate the big man for whatever it was he thought he'd done, but marched directly into the chaos, where he found a different man to bollock.

The treacle smoke man didn't seem to notice he'd been slapped, and he didn't spare Sharli a glance, but returned immediately to his station where he took another black pan and filled it with white sugar.

In the doorway, Sharli was subject to repeated bargings and jostlings, so she stepped over to the only seemingly unoccupied part of the kitchen, which was by the sink where the man had just thrown the hot pan.

The moment she was there, as if she had activated some piece of a clockwork by putting her feet into the right place, a woman, her hair pulled back and her lips seemingly insufficient to cover her teeth, shouted, 'Apron!' at Sharli, and when the girl didn't reply she pulled an apron from nowhere and threw it at her.

'Pan!' someone else shouted.

Sharli didn't know what to do, but then the lipless woman turned her round and pushed her at the sink. 'Wash all that!'

The metal was no longer red, but the water that was in contact with it simmered and frothed, and where the pan's weight had met the unwashed, half-submerged crockery it had made a dangerous mess of broken porcelain – delicately spiteful white shards pointing everywhere.

'What are you waiting for?' the woman shouted.

She had a white apron, and she'd double tied the string, so it was bowed at the front. On the left-hand side, she'd tucked a dishcloth into the band, and on the right there was a knife holster in which three knives of various sizes had been placed.

'Girl, if you don't get chef his pan right now, I'll boil your head.' She didn't shout this, but hissed it under her breath like a talking snake would.

Sharli looked back at the sink and then, as if it was a reasonable thing to do, she darted away from it, past the woman, stealing one of her knives as she went, and dived under the long table on which the chefs were preparing their meals. She shuffled into the middle, between the toes of the clogs of the chefs, and she sat there, peering out.

The woman could scarcely believe what she was seeing, seemingly. 'You little shit!' she shouted. 'Give me back my knife!'

'The kitchens are where the real world is, Sharli, amongst all that hubbub. People fighting for their livelihoods, sometimes their lives, surrounded by heat and light, flesh and sugar. You could not hope for a better representation, in miniature, of the world as it is. Out there is nothing but an escape from the real. In here is what they are escaping from. What do you say to that?'

Sharli thought, but she didn't say anything.

'You never touch a chef's knives,' said Mr Padge, slightly put out, seemingly, by Sharli's failure to respond to the truth of his words. 'I say this not as an excuse for her behaviour, but as a warning to you. You never pull a cat's tail, and you never touch a chef's knives. Not unless you are prepared to fight, of course.'

Sharli nodded. 'I'm prepared to fight, Mr Padge.'

He raised an eyebrow. 'You do appear to be.'

In the corner of his office, he had a stack of boxes. He went over and pulled one out. It was from Beaumont's: Sharli could read the word printed on the side, and she guessed it was a meat merchant – pork, specifically – because it had a picture of a cheerful pig beside the word.

Padge put the box down in front of her. It was filled with knives of all sizes – some of them choppers, some peelers, some for meat, and some for fish. 'Take your pick while I find you a steel. From tomorrow you will work on your butchery with Boland and Blob, so you're going to need a cleaver and a filleter.'

Sharli found Boland crouched by the rear door to the kitchens, pulling hard on a hand-rolled cigarette with one side of his mouth and chewing vigorously with the other.

He was about her height, she guessed, and about her weight, but wizened and scarred like a leafless bush.

Seeing Sharli staring at him, he didn't get up but fished out something from his apron pocket. He passed it over to her, conspiratorially, with a closed hand. 'Quick-root,' he said, not asking whether she wanted it as much as identifying which of the possible objects he was bound, in one way or other, to pass to her.

Sharli took the root – it was about the size and shape of a fingertip. She sniffed it, warily.

'Chew it,' Boland said, and because it didn't smell of much, Sharli did as she was told.

Boland smiled and stood up straight. He might have been wizened, but he didn't move like an old man. He threw what remained of his roll-up down and it fizzed in a puddle of some milky but otherwise unidentifiable liquid. 'Blob!' he called out.

After a few moments a tall, very thin man with almost blonde hair appeared. 'Fat, wobbling, blobby Blob,' Boland said, cheerfully, and then he continued with a series of ever more obscene and, eventually, appalling epithets, each apparently a kind of introduction for Sharli's benefit.

Blob – if that, and not 'dog licker' or one of the more explicit nicknames was his title – didn't seem either bothered or amused by any of Boland's performance, but simply waited until he was finished. Then he held his hand out for Sharli to shake, which she did.

The kitchens at The Commodious Hour, like any well-run kitchens, divided the various jobs by which a menu might be produced amongst the staff available, each receiving that work best suited to them. It was a vanishingly rare dish that was created by one hand alone, some collaboration always having been necessary to bring the produce, wash the produce, construct, from the produce, the basic elements of a dish – the sauce, the cuts, the garnish.

At service, the ideal situation was that the station chef should construct from the things already prepared the meals that his customers had ordered. This process of preparing the raw ingredients, usually brought in from the docks, but sometimes sourced from the South and Northfields, was called the *mise en place* in the ancient language, the original meaning of the words lost, even though their function was not.

Sharli, on the orders of Mr Padge, was given a rotation of tasks, and while none of them was unusual in the sense that any trainee would be given them during the long and hard years of their apprenticeship, their aim, when given to Sharli, was not to train her to be a chef. Nor was it that she should, by doing those tasks, contribute to the smooth running of the kitchens, though she did.

Her duties were instead to teach her how to handle the breadth of knives that were available in that place. When she was given the job of peeling – innumerable potatoes, parsnips, apples – she used the smallest knife – called a paring knife – its blade sharpened to slide through tough and delicate skin alike, its point small enough to accurately pick out the eyes that, once the skin was off, still peered out from deep in the vegetable flesh.

When she was given the job of gutting the fish she had a longer, filleting knife, which she inserted behind the ears of the fish – as she thought of them – and she let it slide, the sharpness of the blade doing the work, down along the spine, separating perfectly, with as little fuss as possible, the fillet from the bones.

When she was given the chopper she brought it down, hard, with as much force as her arms could muster, this increasing every day, and so made chunks of the bodies she received from the abattoir, often twice her size or more.

All the work given to her she did assiduously with the tools provided.

This was her knife work.

She sliced the mushrooms, snub little things, into piles that filled a bucket between her feet. She trimmed the fingers of asparagus, put the discarded skin for boiling in the stock pot, always bubbling.

Hock and sweetbreads, barley, wings and thighs.

All this she did for hours and days, for weeks and months, eventually for years.

Her mind and body became attuned to the work, and facilitating it all was the rhythm made by the root Boland gave her in the dark early mornings, then at first break, then at lunch, then at second break, then in the afternoon, then at service, and, once the work was done, while the porters swept and mopped the kitchens, Boland swapped the root for opium and wine.

This routine was the one Sharli lived by. Her body became a machine that did knife work, with a clock that measured the day not in minutes and hours, but in urges and doses. The natural processes of her life – waking, feeding, sleeping – were replaced with kitchen processes, ones that the necessities of her work and the habits of her consumption demanded.

On one occasion a chef could not attend work. He'd died in his sleep from choking on his tongue, that organ having fallen back, stupefied by too much opium, and become lodged in his windpipe. Sharli took his station – he was responsible for the salads and small plates – and since his work was mostly with the knife and rarely up at the stove, she did very well at it.

What her presentation lacked in finesse, she more than made up for in speed, her blade a blur that converted bunches of parsley into chiffonade in moments, her tapenades never needing the pestle and mortar.

Blob corrected her plates for symmetry before they went to the pass, nodding them through and pursing his lips – expressions on him that were as close to praise as the man ever came – and she worked hard, quick-root jammed up in the space between her top lip and her gum.

The shift seemed to fly past, much more so than when she was slicing the garlic and onions, or making a brunoise of the carrots, or deboning a lamb leg.

At the end of the night, as the porters washed down, Boland passed her the opium pipe and Sharli, sipping at it expertly in the way she had come to understand would provide the hit but also prevent the burn, asked him, 'Are you pleased with my work?'

He said he was.

'Could I take over the station, then? He's dead, after all.'

When Boland said yes, he said it in a strange way, and the others, hearing the way he said it – they were all sitting around one of the tables, in the empty restaurant, attending to their needs – raised their eyebrows, or frowned, or smirked, or in some other way made it known that there was something unusual in this.

Sharli, in spite of having been there for years, had never seen them act like this, and didn't know what to make of it, but soon the opium made itself felt in her blood, and, wetting her mouth with more wine, she forgot all about it.

The following morning, Boland woke her at some dark and secret hour, even earlier than she was used to rising, and, with an application of a pea-sized ball of root, roused her from her dreams and stirred her into action.

The others he left in their bunks, and for the first time in what seemed like longer than she could remember, she left the precincts of The Commodious Hour and went, by horse and cart, beside Boland, who was at the reins, by some twisting and tortuous route, always skirting potholes and dodging people, and flukes, and piles of mess left to lie where it fell, to the docks.

Here, there was a market of sorts made of rain-soaked men by rain-soaked crates in huddles around braziers, flames always threatening to surrender to the tendency of the rain to put them out, guttering and fizzing.

In the distance, the white sails of the Port Guard flapped, and though these market men were awake, even the malformed gill-men of that Guard were in their beds, if they made use of such things.

Sharli, who did not have a coat with a hood, pulled her chef's jacket over her head and trotted after Boland, who had drawn up the horse and cart, hopped down into the mud and was walking briskly to where the men were.

Though the men were all thoroughly sodden, their produce was drier. They lifted the wax tarps that protected their crates to reveal inside crabs and lobsters, herrings and skates, octopuses and squids, some alive and struggling, the others dead, but clear-eyed and odourless.

Boland turned to Sharli. 'What should we choose?' he asked.

The herrings seemed good, lustrous and glistening in their orderly shoal, so Boland secured their purchase with a nod, and to these he added a dozen of lobsters, a crate of squids, a bucket of shrimps, kicking and jumping beneath a lattice of metal.

These all were put aside for him.

They went to another huddle, and from here they bought tomatoes and cucumbers and other things hot-housed in sunny territories far away from Mordew's dimly lit troubles and drizzly miseries.

What Boland selected they reserved for him – and so they secured the raw materials which the kitchen would transmute, through its labour, into meals worth paying through the nose for, so that the customers, by buying them, could convert that labour into a profit for Mr Padge.

When it came to paying the men for their wares, Boland gave them nightmares.

That is to say that he went to the back of the cart and pulled from it sacks and sacks of slum-weed, picked from the borders of the Southfields, where the Living Mud encroached. The narcotic effect of the natural plant was enhanced, if that is the right word, by the sick magic that made flukes, giving it the property of granting terrible visions when smoked of the world gone awry, of a godless lack of goodness, of morbid life lived unhappily. No one in Mordew would buy these dreams, everyone having more than enough of them through the simple fact of living there. They fetched a good price in other places, though, where there was not such a grinding overfamiliarity with the terrors that were common here. Those smokers of weed found novelty in strange and disturbing sights, knowing that they would return to their pleasant and reassuring worlds when the weed wore off, and appreciate them all the more for it.

Sharli helped load the produce onto the cart into the place where the sacks of weed had been, and she and Boland returned to the driver's bench and set off back to The Commodious Hour.

When they were out of sight of the port, but before they re-entered the slums, Boland took a pouch from his pocket and gave it to Sharli. This, he explained, was her share of the money Padge had provided them to buy supplies with, since it remained unspent, with some reduction for the labour inherent in gathering the weed.

It was in this way that Sharli discovered that it was routine for the staff to defraud Mr Padge, skimming and pilfering, taking outright those things that belonged to their employer.

Boland's justification was that it was they, not Mr Padge, that did the work that turned a profit at The Commodious Hour, and that hence the money was theirs by right.

Sharli tried to give the money back, but Boland insisted, and he added to it, for free, a threat. He said that he would fillet her with her own knife, in just the way she was going to need to fillet the herrings they had just bought, if news of the fraud ever got back to Mr Padge.

He went on to point out that she shouldn't think he wouldn't do it either, because there was nothing worse than a grass.

Perhaps Sharli should have gone straight to Mr Padge – she certainly wanted to – but when she saw that he wasn't in his office that day, nor the day after, nor the day after that – it was rumoured that he was busy outside the Sea Wall – she missed her chance.

Boland took her daily now with him to the market, and inveigled her into other schemes, so that by the time Mr Padge returned to the restaurant Sharli felt too ashamed to speak to him. She would have too much to admit to, and each of those things a terrible betrayal of his kindness.

But that is not to say Sharli forsook Mr Padge. She would never do that.

Instead of telling him, she went up to Boland's room – it was a small one above the kitchens – and because he never locked it, she was able to go straight in.

Some of the foods in a kitchen are very dangerous indeed, even if in small amounts, or when properly prepared, they are quite edible, or uniquely delicious. Toxins can be found in otherwise perfectly serviceable ingredients. Another way to kill someone is to feed them concentrates of something that can be brewed using standard implements.

In short, there are all sorts of ways a poisoner can use a commercial kitchen for their aims, whether it be in powdering rhubarb leaves, or reserving the livers of a blowfish, or making cyanide from almonds.

Sharli had not had her eyes shut for the last years, so it should surprise no one that she had sufficient poison, once she had decided that was the way she was going to do it, knife-work being too obvious, to kill Boland by cutting his opium with a fatal powder.

Boland did not help himself by always leaving his pipe with his supply in his uppermost bedside drawer where Sharli had seen him go more than once. Once in his room, she opened the container in which he kept his opium. She would have poured her poison straight in, but there was something about the container that made her pause.

It was a silver box, studded with red costume jewels made to look like a pirate's treasure chest.

She suddenly saw Boland for who he was.

Yes, he was a man who had wronged Mr Padge.

Yes, he had put her in the position of wronging Mr Padge.

Yes, this was something she would not have done under any other circumstance.

But also, he was a person with whims and foibles. Perhaps, in his childhood, he had been given this little chest. Perhaps the shape of it was a pleasure to his eye. He had kept it all this time, a link to his past, to some better time when he was not such a betrayer, such a fraud.

This little chest made her feel that he might be redeemed.

But then she heard a creak on the stair, felt suddenly like she would be caught if she didn't act immediately, and because she had no better idea of what to do than what she had come here to do, she did it.

She rushed quickly out, closing the door behind her, and went down by the other stair to the kitchens where she then began her shift.

It was unusual for Mr Padge to be in the kitchens at any time, since he preferred to be either in his office or at the assassins' table with the others, laughing and drinking.

He always seemed to have such a wonderful time with the assassins that it made in Sharli's heart a strong desire that she might one day sit there with them all. There she would be laughed with, have drinks poured for her, and be someone that Mr Padge looked on... not as a peer, not quite, but as a person that deserved respect.

Today, though, Padge was at the door to the kitchens talking angrily, though in whispers, to Boland. The chef kept putting his hands out in front of himself, and shrugging his shoulders, performing, it seemed to Sharli, the role of someone who hadn't realised that whatever fault Mr Padge was finding in him was a fault at all.

Also, and this made Sharli's stomach lurch whenever it happened, the two of them, at the same time, would look over at her where she stood working at her station, as if she was the source of their conversation.

Anyone who is prone to committing crimes, or who has a guilty conscience, will know that when people talk about you and you can't hear what they are saying, your mind imagines the worst. You presume perfect understanding, on their part, of your black heart, your awful secrets. Sharli felt a strong urge to leave the kitchen, to go back upstairs to Boland's room, to take the poison from his little pirate's chest, and thereby to undo that terrible crime they must both have become aware of.

She turned, but there in the doorway was Blob, still thin as a lamppost, but carrying a tray of rising bread rolls at his waist which prevented her from leaving by the rear door. The only other door was out into the restaurant, and this was where Mr Padge and Boland were standing. Exit through that would also mean her doing a complete circuit of the dining room before reaching the stairs to the accommodations above. This was something that kitchen staff were forbidden from doing; the appearance of them front of house was not conducive to the atmosphere the maître d' was trying his hardest, against the odds if he was to be believed, to establish; which was one of elegant relaxation.

Sharli could feel tension in a ball in the middle of her chest, and when Blob barged past her, she slipped on an unmopped piece of floor where milk had been spilled. None of the porters had sponged it up, and now both Mr Padge and Boland were staring straight at her, neither of them speaking.

Mr Padge shook his head and walked out, as if he was disgusted, something that made vomit rise in the back of Sharli's throat so that she had to swallow it down.

Over came Boland, crossing the kitchen, and though he started with an angry flush to his cheeks, by the time he arrived he was looking oddly apologetic.

'Look,' he said, which was as close as he ever got to saying sorry, 'Mr Padge doesn't want you on the salads and small plates no more. He says you're to be on knife work, and knife work only.'

Sharli nodded quickly, though if she'd wanted to appear upset rather than relieved, she should have added something of that quality to her performance.

'He says you can do this shift, but tomorrow it's back to the prep.' Boland looked down, news of this kind being as bad to a junior chef as a kick to the teeth – possibly worse. 'I'll make it up to you,' he finished, then turned his back and went away.

It was about then that the first orders came through to the kitchen, and since the restaurant was fully booked, there wasn't much time to do anything but work.

What should a girl like Sharli have thought, as she worked, if not about the right way to slice and arrange a tomato? How to layer that with leaves of basil? With slices, very thin, of red onion? A garnish of redcurrants on their stalks? A raspberry vinaigrette?

Should she think of retrieving the powder of cyanide – she had distilled it from almonds and dried it in the oven – from her head chef's stash of opium, where she placed it earlier?

Wouldn't that make her complicit in his defrauding of Mr Padge, whom she loved as one would love a father?

Perhaps she should have thought of it, but then what did Boland mean by saying he would 'make it up to her'? If Mr Padge wanted her to work on prep, then why shouldn't she? It was his restaurant. Didn't they all, her the most, owe him everything? His wants and needs for the place he owned should be paramount. Wouldn't any 'making it up' be against Mr Padge's wishes?

We, because we have never understood how perfectly murder, when used properly, resolves a problem, might think differently to Sharli, who has learned precious little else.

We might, indeed, never consider murder, since we have moral objections to that course of action, but Sharli had no such objections. She had never been taught them, not since she was a child, when her entire world revolved around the murder of children, herself included. This was followed by her tenure as a slave, which teaches a person the utter triviality of death, since people become objects and objects cannot be mourned over, or grieved for.

If slaves die they are thrown overboard to make way for another one.

The nail factory did nothing to correct Sharli's understanding. It treated her as nothing.

The Temple of the Athanasians treated her as nothing.

Mr Padge, her mentor, the closest thing she had to a father, was training her as an assassin, and these people were the highest of the persons in his employ.

Padge himself was not above murder, something he did over a game of cards.

Sharli made a small plate of mushrooms and chives and garlic. It needed sautéing for a minute or two, so she went to the stove. There was only one free flame, and this was by Boland's side. For the time it took Sharli to soften the mushrooms and garlic in the pan, she watched Boland's forearms, which were criss-crossed with red scars, with white scars, and beneath these there were blue tattoos of naked women.

She looked up at Boland, very briefly, but he didn't catch her eye – he was occupied with checking the scorch on a steak of beef – so she looked down.

Boland pressed the steak with his knuckle, learning thereby whether the meat was cooked in the manner the customer had stated, and went back to his station.

By the time he was there, Sharli was sure that she would let him die that night.

There was no reasoning for this assurance on her part, it was just that, when he tested the meat to see if it was rare, she was sure that he would die.

We might not feel that is sufficient, but we are not her. We must understand that some people are different than we are.

They live different lives, in different worlds, and they behave, for better or worse, differently than we do.

A full restaurant will often close late. When a group of diners comes just as the shutters are being drawn – there are often stragglers who booked their tables for ten o'clock, say, but who do not arrive until five and twenty to eleven – because the management are keen for profit, they let the customers order even though the chefs have started to clean down.

These people do not understand that the kitchens would prefer not to deal with them, seeing only an almost full restaurant that might easily accommodate a few more, and will go to their table, brooking no obstacle, and insist that they will only have a main course, though they then go on to have a starter and often puddings and coffees, even brandy.

It was a night like this that Sharli poisoned Boland, a night full of latecomers. Even though the girl had made up her mind that the chef would die for his betrayal of Mr Padge, the hope that it would happen sooner rather than later, constantly denied by another check on the board, made the muscles of her hands ache and put butterflies in her stomach.

Once her last plates were done, Sharli stripped her station, reserved those things that could be used the next day to the cold room, lent a hand where she could to those on sweets and drinks, and generally made herself inconspicuously useful. She always kept her eye on Boland.

She dried the glasses for the plongeur: his sink was behind

where Boland was still working, and it made for a better vantage place than anywhere else.

It was after midnight when Boland finally removed his apron, and as was his habit, he went straight to his room to retrieve his fixings before returning to finish up.

While he was out of the kitchen, Sharli knew what he would be doing.

He would ascend the stairs, two at a time, turn the handle of his door, go straight to his bedside cabinet, open the top drawer, reach in, and take out his silver box.

Each one of these things Sharli imagined separately, precisely, using as much time to think the actions as Boland would use to do them.

Then he would take his pipe, tip in his opium and Sharli's cyanide, light it with a match – she imagined him striking it, once, twice, three times against the striking strip, the final one doing the trick – and then he would inhale, hold for a few seconds, exhale, and then do it again.

Then he would put his finger over the bowl, let the fire dwindle, put the pipe and matches in his pocket, turn, go to the door, open it, go through, close it, go to the top of the stairs, come down, one at a time, his hand on the bannister, steadying himself against the pleasurable dizziness opium provides when it is the first use of a session.

Now, just at the moment she imagined he would, Boland came in and went to his station, where he started to clean down.

Sharli dried the glass she was holding and put it with the others.

Just because a person knows how to find or manufacture a poison, that doesn't mean she knows how quickly it will work.

That period of time is knowable, but only through the use of equations which require precise knowledge of various facts. What was the dose? How was the dose delivered? How much does the victim weigh? Does the victim have any tolerances to the poison delivered?

All of these things and more were things Sharli didn't know. She didn't know whether Boland would drop dead there and then, or whether he would work out his shift, or whether she had dosed him sufficiently to do the job at all.

She picked up another glass and started to dry it.

This last possibility was like a lifeline to Sharli's atrophied moral sense. She felt that fate, in part at least, had an influence on what would happen next. If she had any guilt, fate's vagaries relieved her of it, removed it altogether if she had failed to understand what was necessary to kill Boland.

True, if he didn't die, she would probably have to find another way to kill him...

One thing at a time.

She put down the dried glass, and when it chinked on the work surface, Boland turned around.

When he saw her, he smiled a little rueful smile, and then set off across the kitchen towards her. Possibly he was coming over to 'make it up to her', or to commiserate about Mr Padge's decision, or to warn her, once again, of the perils of being a grass, but Sharli never found out.

Halfway, Boland jack-knifed from the waist, making a strained and forceful ejaculation – 'Oh!' – then fell forward and collided with the floor, headfirst.

Sharli went to him, feigning concern, but here came Blob from the neighbouring station. Such were his efforts, fruitless, to revive his friend over the next score of minutes, that she couldn't get near Boland. Blob's urgent pounding on Boland's chest, his crying out to God, his desperate unwillingness to accept his friend's death were sufficient to put tears in the eyes of everyone who saw them, even Sharli.

Despite this, Boland never drew breath again.

'Do you have anything to tell me, Sharli?'

Mr Padge was in his office, and Sharli was standing shame-facedly in front of him on the other side of his desk.

'I don't know what you mean,' she said.

Mr Padge tutted. 'I don't mind killers,' he said, 'but I'm very ill-disposed towards liars, particularly when they are lying to me.'

Out of his pocket he took an envelope, and, first clearing his desk of the mess of another working lunch, roughly, with a semicircular sweep of his left forearm, he emptied the contents of the envelope onto the desk.

These contents were three rings: one was two twists of silver like snakes wrapped around each other, each with a head and tiny glass eyes, another was a simple gold band, the third was a brass one with a circular crest. This last one, Mr Padge held up. 'Do you know how long it takes to get one of these, Sharli?'

She didn't.

'Seven years,' Padge said. 'It takes seven years to complete the culinary training necessary to pass the examinations that will earn a man this ring.' He threw the ring to Sharli, who, through instinct, caught it.

Now he held up the silver snakes ring. 'For this, a man has to trade with pirates. Either that, or win it in a dogfight.' He threw this ring to Sharli too. 'This last one is his wedding ring, though his wife had long disowned him.' Over it went.

Sharli tried to say something, but Mr Padge got up from his chair and, hands behind his back, began to walk around his office. He wobbled slightly, as a well-set jelly would wobble if it could walk around its office. 'Those rings are trophies now, for your collection. Don't try to deny what you did. While I'm impressed you did it so cleanly, I will need to know why.' He paused behind her, put his hands on her shoulders. 'Chefs with seven years at school are not easily come by. Unless there is something wrong with them, they're likely to be tempted away uphill. Can I ask you why you killed mine?'

Padge's hands were heavy, his breath hot on her ear, and he wheezed a little, as he did when he was agitated.

Sharli knew better than to lie. 'He was stealing from you. I didn't like it, so I killed him.'

Padge breathed a long, slow breath in, and, when he had finished, he took his hands from Sharli's shoulders and went, equally slowly, back to his chair.

'I see,' he said. 'I must admit I imagined you had committed a more actionable offence than the one you describe. If it had been revenge for some personal slight, or some other vendetta, I would have strangled you for it.' Mr Padge turned and fixed Sharli with a stern gaze, so that she knew what he was saying was true. 'As it is, I see that the mistake was mine. I, of course, knew that he was taking money from me. There is nothing that takes place on my premises of which I do not know, which is how I know that you killed him. What I had not considered was that I ought to have let you in on the secret. Of course he was stealing: all chefs steal. That is why they are paid so little. If he was the kind of chef that didn't steal, I wouldn't have been able to afford him.' Padge rubbed the bridge of his nose for a little while, closed his eyes, flexed his fingers. 'In future, Sharli, only kill those people I contract you to kill. Do you understand?'

She nodded.

'I should have made this clearer in the first instance, and my punishment will be the effort I expend replacing my head chef. Your punishment, Sharli, will be to leave this place—' Sharli let out a yelp, but Padge held up a hand '—Do not panic! I will not send you back to the Temple. Yet, you cannot remain here: they'd murder you in your bed. No, your stint learning the knives, and, it seems, poisons, is over. It's time to move on to pastures, if not greener, then at least more new. You will be working with my man Black Bill, over at Beaumont's, the bacon factory.'

Sharli was puzzled, but Padge turned away from her and shooed her out, so she had no choice but to leave, taking her rings with her.

THE PROPAGANDA OF
THE IMMATERIAL SOUL
AND THE MYTH OF 'HEAVEN'

The creation and maintenance of so-called 'intermediate realms', misrepresented to the occupants of the archaic cities as 'heavens', relies on the idea that their consciousness can carry over from the real into an unreal realm. Pseudo-demigods, such as the entity known as the 'Mistress of Malarkoi', promise the population of their city everlasting life and happiness in unreals in exchange for their labour and, eventually, their unique material presence. Since no transfer of consciousness can be made between bodies, regardless of whether they exist in the real or one of the unreals, this transaction is fraudulent.

What occurs instead is the creation of more or less accurate simulacra of the enslaved selves which have no intrinsic link at the level of consciousness. No one could rationally sacrifice their only existence, or that of their children, in order to ensure the selfdom of an unrelated and imprecise simulacrum of themselves in the real, or in an unreal 'heaven'.

Weft-manipulators of the demigod order are committing crimes against future Assembly pledges, which, regard-less of any possible Theite Resurrection Scenario, would be sufficient cause for the establishment of an Atheistic Crusade under the named and numbered provisions of the Assembly.

IV

Sharli at Beaumont's

BLACK BILL WAS so named for his temperament – his mood was always dark – but also for the colour of his skin. This was not because he was born that colour. Nicknames are given for unusual traits, and to be born with skin naturally abundant in melanin was not an unusual thing in Mordew. In any case, no one had ever seen Bill's skin's inherent shade because Black Bill never washed. His flesh was dotted with tags and moles and growths, things that tended to catch and tear when he applied any pressure, even to wash them, and because he worked killing pigs at Beaumont's he was covered with the filth of that place – blood and faeces, primarily – that tended to blackness when dried.

Sawdust has a smell, the sweat of men hired to murder pigs also has a smell, but the strongest smell of the smells in Beaumont's was the smell of fear, which is not entirely of prematurely evacuated bowels, of piss, of the burnt scrape of trotters on hard flagstones, it is also of something less easy to distinguish: a secretion of the glands in the pig body, a phero-mone, or hormone, or something that only a sentient thing facing death has its body make.

It is not a smell that can be described, but anyone who has been in an abattoir knows it, and it lingers long in the nose if it ever leaves at all.

Sharli smelled that smell then as she walked the aisle between the killing pens, and when it reached her nose it tightened her stomach.

As they progressed, each stall had a pig man, knife in hand, and through a hatch in the back wall he was joined by a pig, roughly shoved through, squealing, by its handler. The hatch closed behind.

Sharli watched the pig men approach and the animals shrink back, and as she and Black Bill passed she strained to see the killing. She breathed in the scent and tightened her hand.

'Have you had a change of heart?' Black Bill said, and he stopped where he was, but the tightening of Sharli's hand wasn't reluctance – it was its opposite: impatience.

'Stop so we can watch,' she said.

Black Bill stopped, toyed with the growths on his cheeks.

'Where I'm from,' Sharli said, 'children have their throats slit in public. Everyone cheers.'

Sharli left this statement hanging.

If she wanted Bill to understand that she gloried in pig killing as her priesthood had gloried in the killing of her brothers and sisters then she would have her wish, but the truth was something different. She wanted to understand, by seeing and feeling, what it was her people had gone through, priest and child. She might understand it here, in this place away from the place of her birth, away from the justifications of her religion, without the oppressive mass of the Golden Pyramid looming over her.

How can a child take against a thing she has not experienced first-hand?

How can she take to it?

There is only one way to knowledge, Ganax had said: experience.

Now there was an empty pen.

Black Bill led her to it. He pointed out a wooden handle, depending from a rope. As if she was born to it, Sharli pulled on the handle and a board rose on the back of the pen.

There was a square cut out behind the board and across this square of space ran the legs of pigs, hundreds of them, stumbling and sprinting, until suddenly there was the head of a sow.

Her ears were piebald, one torn ragged, and she panted breaths of steam, each one redolent of the fear smell. Her eyes swivelled in their sockets.

In she came through the gap in the boards, snout first, then her shoulders, then her forelegs, and then her whole bulk, five times the size of Sharli, at least.

Bill tapped Sharli on her arm and handed her a knife.

Without thinking, having held so many knives for so many years, having cut so much meat, Sharli jumped forward and slashed at the sow. She did not do it tentatively: if anything, she used too much force. The blade made a six-inch-long gash across the pig's shoulder.

The pig screamed.

'No!' Black Bill shouted over the screaming. 'Every stroke should be a killing stroke. Mess up the meat and the price drops. Do it properly.'

The pig had backed away until it was wedged in the corner. Its eyes were wide, which Sharli wrongly took for fear, and it was for that reason that, when she went forward, intending to stab the pig in the neck and do what Black Bill had told her to do, she didn't take enough care.

The pig lunged and snapped, revenging itself on the girl, so it had her wrist in its mouth, between its teeth. That was the first time Sharli discovered the intelligence of a pig – clever enough to know when it has been wronged, and clever enough to want to punish the one who wronged it, even if that was the last thing it ever did.

A pig's bite is not a trivial thing – given the opportunity it can chew through uncooked bones, let alone muscle and sinew – but Black Bill was on it before Sharli could cry. He drove the thin sliver of his knife hard into the pig's brain, the same stroke severing the muscles of its neck, and therefore its jaws. The blow pierced the back of the pig's skull, depriving it of the will necessary to wound Sharli further.

'Open its mouth and free your arm,' Black Bill said.

Sharli did it, and blood welled up on her wounds, filling the pits the pig's teeth had made in her soft flesh. From below they dripped as if from a tap with a worn washer.

Without any seeming urgency, but with such speed that Sharli couldn't see how he did it, Black Bill took off the headband that kept his hair out of his eyes, wrapped it above Sharli's elbow, tightened and knotted it. Before it had had a chance to all flow out, the blood was stopped, dripping more and more slowly into the hay at their feet.

'This will cost you,' Black Bill said. He picked Sharli up, carried her over his shoulder. 'I'm taking Padge's girl to Matron,' he said to someone Sharli couldn't see. 'Write this stall up.'

There was grumbling but, again, Sharli didn't see who from.

Bill went off at a march, out of the pens and into the daylight.

While there were runnels in the killing pens that caught most of the blood from a slaughter, feeding it down to the barrels where it would be mixed with meal and grains to make blood sausage, prized for its earthy flavour in many recipes, some not inconsequential amount of the blood was splattered on the walls and floor. There were boys for whom the clearing away of this blood was their job. Along with the blood they took soiled hay, the dirt from the pigs' trotters, torn hair and skin. Each had a short broom with thick and strong bristles, and these they pushed with all their might, forcing whatever had fallen into the pens into a pile, which they then expelled from the pens into the yards surrounding the low buildings in which the pens were housed.

Because Matron wouldn't let Sharli work the pens until her arm healed, she was given this job while she recovered.

There was rarely a clear night in the Factoria of Mordew. The spray from the sea crashing constantly into the Sea Wall gathered into a fret which encroached on the city from three sides, finding no way to dissipate itself in the barrier the mountains made on the fourth side. It joined together in the air, hanging scarcely any higher than the tops of the lowest buildings of Beaumont's, in dark and briny clouds.

Because of these clouds, there was no need for Sharli to wash the bloodied pen muck out of the precincts of the warehouse: the salt rain that fell onto the roofs came unguttered into the concrete yard. It made a slick of ordurous water that moved unceasingly out under the fences that surrounded Beaumont's curtailment.

Once away from that gloomy place, the blood, dilute though it was, met with the Living Mud. That always encroaching and sickly potent matter generated from the nearness of God's corpse operated on the Beaumont's waste. Because the Living Mud had, in very minor part, God's ability to make things live, and because blood is a remnant of an already living thing, when these two substances met there was a tendency for them to interact. Together they made flukes in the form of the living thing the blood had once been part of.

Around the perimeter of Beaumont's, piglet flukes were generated – though not in great numbers – and these things had the desires that piglets had, which is for the milk of a sow.

Piglet flukes were poor things: where piglets are ruddy, pink and squealing, piglet flukes were greyly transparent, enervated by their lack of perfection, sadly mewling.

Where piglets have an irrepressible vivacity, trotting here and there with stiff-legged energy, these piglet flukes had inherited only a small part of the natural creatures' will to life. That property seemed watered down like blood diluted by rain brine. It seemed made low by the presence of filth and soiled hay, and the evacuations of bladders and bowels. Where a piglet will skitter on its hooves, making a rattling percussion on any hard surface, piglet flukes dragged themselves on their deformed limbs scarcely more quickly than a slug drags itself across the world on its mucous foot.

That is not to say that piglet flukes weren't a menace around the place at Beaumont's. The surrounding fence was not tight enough to the ground to prevent them coming in, the rain endlessly eroding a gap that only regular refencing and boarding could remedy. Since neither of those maintenances turned a profit, they tended not to be done.

Flukes of all types are possessed of a spiteful kind of determination: spiteful because they know from the pain their incorrect forms make in them that they are not suited to the world. Determined because that is a quality of life that is indissoluble.

Determination is the primary quality that distinguishes a living thing from a dead thing: the determination to be. If that quality leaves a living thing it sickens and dies, or takes its life.

There is no benefit in being if one is not determined to be.

Horrible, grey, malformed, spiteful, determined piglet flukes dragged themselves out of the Living Mud, dragged themselves under the fence, seeking the sows' milk that all piglets desire.

They dragged themselves across the courtyard towards the sowing pens, and they would, if there was not someone charged with the task of watching for them, drag themselves up to a lactating mother and steal for themselves her precious milk. If their unformed jaws could not latch, and their incomplete stomachs leaked into the pens whatever they could draw, they did it anyway, not knowing enough not to.

A fluke is a wasteful use of a liquid that, used properly, could nourish a piglet to a size suitable for it to be sold as a suckling pig, or transferred then onto a diet suitable for making a bacon pig, or a nursing sow, or whatever form of pig was most profitable to the factory.

The disposal of the piglet flukes was a job that was given to the wounded Sharli, along with the clearing of the filth. Amongst pig men fluke-killing was a preliminary test of a person's suitability for work in the pens.

Many people find flukes disgusting. In some, that disgust leads to repulsion, which makes them turn away. Others are disgusted but fascinated, causing in them too much sympathy. Others still are disgusted and angry.

This last is an acceptable type of psychology for the work of a pig man, but not perfect; it tends to make the worker exhausted when they use that anger daily.

The best type of worker will be the one that is not disgusted, and neither has any sympathy nor any anger, but who, when they are told to smash in the heads of the fluke piglet with their boot, or with a half brick, or asked to kill them by some other means, simply does that work until it is finished and then moves on to the other tasks assigned to them – mopping out, laying hay, whatever it may be.

There was, conveniently, a piglet fluke in the middle of the yard on the morning after Sharli was bitten by the sow. Black Bill brought her to the pens and there it was, grey, transparent, enervated, like a piglet, but deformed.

This one's deformation – all deformed things are unique, whereas all things that have developed in concert with God's will are almost the same – was that only the left half of it had grown. The right half had not. It looked like the pigs who had been bisected for sale and which hung by hooks in the cold room, waiting for shipping. Only, this one moved, slowly, jerkily, sobbing to itself, chewing the air with its half mouth, sniffing with its half snout, one eye swivelling urgently in its only socket.

'What do you think of that?' Black Bill asked, watching Sharli for signs of her revulsion, and any accompanying emotion that might hamper her in her work.

Sharli shrugged. 'Where do you want me to put it once it's dead?'

There was a hemp sack in the corner of the yard. 'Stick it in there,' he said, pointing. 'Once the bag's full, empty it into the fire.'

A few days later, her arm stiff but no longer painful, Sharli was late to feed the sows.

She knew something was wrong the moment she entered the first pen.

Pigs breathe in a way very similar to the way people breathe, and mother sows, when they are happily suckling their piglets, breathe with a warm and calming regularity, deeply, contentedly, and a suckling pen was one of the few places in Beaumont's where that kind of atmosphere could be found. All the other places were more or less – usually more – fretful. This sow, Sharli heard, was grinding its teeth, panting raggedly, drawing in breaths suddenly, holding them, and then letting them out with force.

Sharli looked out of the opening to the pens. Even though she didn't know as yet what was wrong, instinctively she knew that she did not want anyone else to see what was happening, not the foreman, not the boys, and certainly not Black Bill.

There was no one around.

A sow prefers privacy when it's feeding its young, the vulnerability inherent in it having trained pigs as a species to find privacy before they begin. The pens had wooden dividers that Sharli could not see over, but when she went round there it was.

A scene can be taken in at a glance, which is what Sharli did, and she knew exactly what had happened in a moment – piglet flukes had got into the pen, and they were killing the sow – but it takes longer to understand why it had happened, how it had happened, and what she could possibly do about it.

Pigs have fourteen teats, a number none of the pig men at Beaumont's had succeeded in increasing, despite many attempts to breed more into their stock. Each of this sow's teats had a fluke on it. The sow was lying on its side, fat and spreading into the hay. Its neck was stretched unusually taut. Two of its four legs – the ones on the uppermost side – were stiff and outstretched. Its nostrils flared, opening wider than Sharli had ever seen a pig's nostrils open. Its small eyes were filmed over and blindly stared into nothing. There were flecks of foamed spittle at the corners of its mouth, and its whiskers twitched in a very strange way.

The flukes were all disparate in their forms, as was their nature: one had a big tuberous head, like a root vegetable, its body little more than a tapering root flicking from one side to the other as it drank; another was more like a snake than a piglet, a smooth, subterranean thing, like an albino axolotl, bleached, the only recognisably porcine aspect its curly tail; another was an almost perfect piglet, except its spine jutted out from the middle of its back, growing up like a plant does, into the sky, its rear limbs entirely still. Sharli didn't trouble to appreciate each of these things in its individuality – they were flukes, and even though each one was unique, they were all uniquely nothing to her – so she took them as a whole and dismissed them.

There was a more important consideration.

A sow's teats are intended, through long-established precedent, for the mouths of properly formed piglets, and because a piglet fluke diverges from the proper plan for a piglet, and because there were fourteen of them, all attached to the poor sow, she was being killed by them.

There was a pool beneath her of undrunk milk, or milk that had been regurgitated, or milk that had leaked from the flukes' incomplete stomachs. In this milk were streams of blood, leaking from the sow.

Her teats, unable to tolerate these flukes' chewings, their prematurely erupted teeth, the presence of chitinous beaks where no piglet should have a beak, the spiteful and determined over-application of force that no real piglet would apply, were being ripped into pieces.

Even the teats that were able to stand it – perhaps the fluke suckling at it had no jaws to tear her to pieces with – were being treated so roughly that they were bruised and damaged.

One fluke, its face a triangle of bone, lipless and throatless, not finding itself capable of drawing milk, and not understanding where the fault was that prevented it, had burrowed into the sow's stomach wall with its sharp skull. Now blood was gushing from the breach, pinkening the pool of spilt milk.

Even the most maternal of wild pigs has some sense of herself that she will not allow herself to be eaten by her piglets, but the pig men of Beaumont's, though they were unable to increase the number of a sow's teats, had been able to breed into their stock a docility and pliancy that made this sow lie there, against her proper instincts.

This seemed unfair to Sharli.

She darted into the increasingly bloody mess and grabbed two of the flukes where they could be grabbed.

They came away easily. She dashed them against the pen divider, and threw them to the corner.

The second two weren't as easy – the first came apart in her hands, leaving its chewing parts attached to the sow, still moving, still wounding her, and the second turned and bit Sharli instead.

This made her see red: she stood in the middle of the pen and stamped down on any piece of grey flesh she saw, churning up the milk and blood and hay into curds and clods.

Then two things happened. First, the triangle-headed piglet fluke, just intelligent enough to be afraid, burrowed completely into the sow's belly, slipping away from Sharli's vision. Second, the sow, feeling some primordial protective instinct for her children, not understanding that these weren't them, dragged herself up and faced Sharli. She snarled and grunted as a pig will, and bared her teeth.

The triangle-headed fluke buried itself deeper, and the confused sow mistook this for something Sharli did. She charged at the girl, flinging herself forward in a crushing rage.

A Beaumont's pig is easily twice the size of a man, and Sharli was still a girl. If she had stood her ground, or allowed herself to be frozen in fear, she would have been flattened, trampled.

Sharli did not stand her ground – she had learned that lesson in Malarkoi: those who stand their ground only make themselves easier to catch.

Sharli did not freeze in fear: she had taught herself not to, with difficulty, since that is the mind's self-protective gambit, abandoning the body to its fate, retreating into passivity.

Sharli did neither of these things.

Instead, she took one step to the side so that the sow ran past her, and when it realised its mistake and came at where she now stood, Sharli stepped to the side again, one simple step.

The sow stood in front of her, seemingly considering whether to run again. Hanging from her belly were the remaining flukes, and now the sow shuddered, wracked by an internal flame that shut her eyes for a moment, and brought disturbingly human wrinkles to her brow, to the corners of her eyes. It was if she was a person, her snout and lips borrowed from another creature.

Now it was Sharli's turn to advance, and either the pain was enough to drain the pig of its will to fight, or it recognised the futility of fighting. It allowed her to approach.

Most people could not strangle a pig into unconsciousness, but Sharli could.

She straddled the creature. In its weakened state, it collapsed to its knees beneath her. She looped one arm around its neck and grabbed her shoulder with that hand, locking one arm and tightening, so that the air no longer flowed into the pig's lungs.

Sharli stayed like that until the beast lost consciousness.

When it was still, lying as it had when she arrived, distorted by its contact with the ground, Sharli plucked each of the flukes from its teats, threw them to the ground. She reached into the wound on the pig's side and fished inside, up to the elbow, until she found the triangle-headed fluke. She dragged this from its hiding place deep amongst the pig's organs. This one she killed first, with her boot, so it couldn't go back in, and then she killed the others.

When they were all dead, she took them into the courtyard and put them in the hemp bag in the corner and went back to the pen.

The sow was there, sleeping seemingly, smeared with her own blood, hay sticking to her.

In the corner was a tap and a pail and a brush, so Sharli filled the pail, took it and the brush to the sow and began gently, quietly, to clean her, paying most attention to not waking her, and then to ensuring the wounds to her teats were free of foreign objects.

Then she gently returned whatever poked out back inside to where it should have been.

This last kindness made the pig spasm, as if she would wake, but she didn't seem to have the will or the energy to do it.

Sharli tipped the pail so that the water in it poured over the sow's skin – imagine she was washing the soap from a child at bath time, being careful not to make that child cry.

This was the way Sharli did it.

When Black Bill found Sharli, she was sleeping against the sow. Its body was growing cold now, since it had succumbed to its wounds, but the girl only woke when Bill put his hand on her shoulder.

She jerked, startled, and it was a moment before the memory of what had happened returned to her. She turned anxiously to the sow, but did not see what she'd hoped to see. 'It was my fault,' she said. 'I forgot to check for flukes.'

Black Bill held up a hand, the palm pale and clean, and his nails black with dirt and dried blood. Then he held the same hand out for her to take.

When, after a silent pause, she did take it, Bill said nothing.

An abattoir has a strict chain of command, each person responsible for their work, answerable to the next in the chain, but that responsibility began at a rank higher than Sharli's, and even if it didn't, the answering for her mistake would have been done to Bill, who was not of a mind to punish her, or perhaps to Mr Padge, who had different requirements of the girl's apprenticeship.

'Stall seven needs restocking, corpse to the grinder,' Bill said as he went past the job master's booth. The master rang the bell that summoned the relevant workers.

Sharli returned to the pig pen, and, under Black Bill's rigorous and kindly supervision, she learned the basics of her trade. For his part, Black Bill showed her where to stab and where to slice and when to stand back and when to press forward. He showed her how to stun and how to intimidate, and why it was better, sometimes, to let a pig wear herself out rather than waste effort fighting her.

Sharli was an attentive pupil, which is often the way with a girl who has been let down by figures of authority and who then finds one who is reliable. While Black Bill never rivalled Mr Padge in Sharli's mind, she provided Black Bill with what he had been missing in his life: something more than friendship. Just as Bill was a stand-in for Mr Padge to Sharli, she was an almost daughter to him.

They would greet each other every morning, lunch together at noon – bacon, bread and beer for Black Bill, whatever sustenance Sharli could tolerate depending on how much quick-root she had chewed that morning – and when the evening shift was over, Bill would watch over her while she smoked her opium. During her early stupor, he'd send runners to the bookies to place his bets on the dogfights.

Things progressed in this way for months, and might have progressed in this way indefinitely, had it not been for that last predilection of Black Bill's – gambling – which brought him, indirectly, into trouble with Mr Padge.

One of the ways a man like Mr Padge makes his living is by buying debts. If one has an excess of capital and no better way to invest it, and also has an infrastructure of violence, it is possible, quite cheaply, to purchase from people who have neither of those things, delinquent debts, and then to collect on them, adding a fee.

For example, if a man has borrowed twenty silver from an elderly moneylender in the Merchant City, thinking, perhaps, that he need never pay that money back, and then, when asked to return the sum with interest, he refuses, saying something like, 'If you want your money you're going to have to fight me for it,' he feeling that fighting is not within the elderly money-lender's powers, if that elderly moneylender cannot find a rough to collect the money for him, he can sell the debt to Mr Padge, for fifteen silver. True, he has lost five silver and the interest on the twenty, but he has not lost as much as he might have lost, having reclaimed the fifteen.

Mr Padge, totalling the borrowed sum, plus the interest, plus his administration fee of five silver, can send two of his men – the Dawlish brothers, for example, who are both as broad as a shithouse door – to convince the man who had refused to give the elderly moneylender twenty silver to give them thirty silver. They do this with menaces, and if those do not work, by beating the money out of the man. Once the Dawlish brothers have been paid, Mr Padge makes thirteen silver on an investment of fifteen, which is an excellent return.

In the case of Black Bill, he had borrowed money from a bookmaker to make a substantial bet on a dog he felt was certain to win. When that dog lost, Black Bill found he had no money to pay the stake, and thus he became in hock to the tune of fifty silver. Unfortunately for Bill, that bookmaker then died, and while this might sound like a lucky thing, the opposite proved to be the case. The bookmaker, once his probate was investigated, was found to himself owe money totalling five hundred silver, and this debt fell to his widow, who was without the means to either pay that debt or to service the interest on it. She, to prevent herself being turned out of her lodgings, sold everything she owned, and also sold, for a quarter of their value, the debts on her husband's book to Mr Padge.

Again, this might seem fortunate, since Black Bill was an associate of Mr Padge, and someone who is ignorant of the way people like Mr Padge operate might think that he would forgive his friends' debts. The opposite is true. If one forgives one's friends' debts, one quickly finds one's friends often borrowing money and failing to pay it back. Indeed, once word gets around, people seek to become friends with a Mr Padge of that generous mindset in order to borrow money from them with the intention of not paying that money back. Since Mr Padge was not the kind of person who was so in need of friends that he was willing to pay for them, his policy was that no exception should or could be made for friends in these matters, and therefore that Black Bill now owed him seventy-five silver.

If seventy-five silver was a trivial sum, then this would have been a trivial matter, but Beaumont's paid Black Bill five silver a month, plus kill bonuses amounting, on a good month, to five more silver. They then recouped three silver a month in rent, somewhat less in bacon, and less again than that in the hire of his work tools and equipment.

In short, Black Bill had no money to pay Mr Padge, and, with no more bookmakers willing to lend him stake money, no expectation of finding it any time soon. Worse, and Black Bill had been keeping this from Sharli, he had been dodging Mr Padge for a week, refusing to meet with him, thereby adding insult to injury.

It was under these circumstances that Sharli was summoned to Mr Padge's office at the back of The Commodious Hour at the end of a long shift.

Black Bill watched her go before solemnly returning to his home.

Later that night, Sharli went to Black Bill's from Mr Padge's office.

Black Bill lived on Beaumont's slum land, in a hut he had made from salvaged pallets, held together with bent nails pulled from broken crates and protected from the rain by sacks stitched together and waxed with bacon lard. The window was glass, something he was, in his way, very proud of: if the men in the abattoir teased him about it – 'Black Bill likes to give his neighbours a show, isn't that right, Bill? Standing in front of your window, doing your hair' – he went quiet and sullen, and Sharli had to tiptoe round him all day.

'Cost me a month's money, that,' he'd said, and Sharli had had to purse her lips and blow out her cheeks to show she was impressed. Ten, fifteen times she'd had to do that before he'd stopped going on about it.

Now there he was, through that same glass, sitting with his back to the window, the short and uneven twists of his hair black against the black of his skin. He was sitting in his chair, and on his side table there was a bottle, still stoppered, of pig wine.

His hands were on his knees.

He was completely still.

Sharli watched for a while. He didn't move except when she pushed a plank over into the Mud. When she did this, he flinched at the sound in reflex. It seemed to her that he forced himself back to his perfect stillness without turning to see what was outside.

The slums are dangerous places, even when you're used to them. It's wise to keep an eye out for robbers and drunks and flukes. What was the point of having a window if you didn't use it to look out of?

Bill knew she was coming.

He knew she was coming, and he was waiting for her.

He was waiting for her with his back to the window.

What he should have done was run when he found out she was coming, gone to the Northfields Factorium, or into the mines.

He should have found passage on a merchant ship. He was a monster to look at, but there were worse finding work every day.

He could have made a living as a brothel heavy.

But here he was, sitting with his back to the window, waiting for her to come, a stoppered bottle on his side table and his hands on his knees.

Perhaps he had a knife, down the side of the chair, under his thighs, in his boot, but if he wanted to defend himself that way, then why not put a sack up at the window, hide and wait for Sharli to look in? Sneak up, stab her in the back. Keep stabbing.

He wasn't stupid.

Sharli swallowed. She moved Padge's knife from one hand to the other. Bring me his cheeks, he'd said.

Who had Padge sent to watch her? He must have had her watched, so he could make sure she did what she'd been told to do. Could she kill the watcher instead? Run and hide?

Padge had people everywhere. Everyone would be watching her.

Even now, from a high point, with a spyglass, from between the shacks, with a single eye there would be people watching her. They would be listening nearby, or waiting at a junction.

Padge had people everywhere. She couldn't kill everyone.

And where would she run to? And what would she do when she got there? Black her eyes? Go back to Malarkoi?

She couldn't do these things. If she couldn't do these things, then neither could Black Bill. And if Mr Padge wanted him dead, who was she to argue? He knew best.

There Bill was, back to the window, still as stone, hands on his knees.

Sharli walked up to his door and knocked, just as if she was here for a visit, for a chat. She couldn't see through the window from here, but there was a slat between two crates that had bowed out in the rain. It let her see in almost as clearly. Bill sighed, one deep sigh, and got to his feet.

He turned, and the whites of his eyes, even these emotionless things, were sad, resigned. How Sharli knew this she couldn't tell, but she did know it.

Bill took two slow steps to the door and even this movement seemed to give the same impression, the set of his shoulders, the bend of his knees, the movement of his black and filthy hands, one at the hinge side and one at the latch, swinging the door open.

Sadness.

Resignation.

Black Bill stood in the gap the removal of the door made, and when Sharli didn't knife him immediately, he gestured for her to come in, which she did.

He didn't have a knife behind his back, as she knew he wouldn't. He didn't have a knife down the side of his chair.

He was undefended.

One slice to his neck in the right place would do it, just like a pig. She could do it kindly, quickly, silently. It would make a mess, but there would be no one left to care.

Bill put the door back into its hole and went to a box in one corner, turning his back on Sharli. She could have taken him then, easy as anything, just like a pig, jumped onto his back, one arm crooked around his face, grabbed his ear, used the other hand to draw the knife across the beating artery, deeply.

Cut the pipe, let it all flow out.

She didn't. On the top of the box Black Bill had gone to was a big piece of red velvet. It was beautifully clean, bordered with black sackcloth. Bill took the cloth, turned, and shook out the velvet so that it hung in front of him like a cape.

He stepped forward, but stopped.

Sharli thought he meant to give the velvet to her, as if it was a present, but he didn't pass it over. Instead, he jerked his head towards the window, which was behind her.

She stepped aside, and Bill went over to the window and pinned the velvet over it. What little light had been coming in – through the overcast, from the moon, from the bonfires, from the oil lamps of Bill's neighbours – was suddenly gone.

They stood there, the two of them, together in the darkness.

'So, what are we going to do, girl?' he said, suddenly very close in the small shack.

Sharli stepped back out of instinct, stumbled on the chair, her body thinking that he had decided to kill her, even though her mind knew that he wouldn't.

There was the sound of a striking match. Bill lit his candle and went to sit on a crate, one hand in the small of his back, the other steadying himself on the way down. He was too big for the crate, his knees too high, pressing against his chest, but he pointed to the chair. 'Sit down,' he said. 'Pour us a drink.'

There were two glasses beside the stoppered bottle, and Sharli, once she was in the chair – which was too big for her as the crate was too small for him – opened the bottle and poured them both a drink.

It wasn't pig wine, but something astringent and powerful. She sniffed her glass. If he meant to poison her, this was a very obvious way of doing it.

Bill reached for his glass and Sharli passed it to him.

He opened his mouth, his gums pink, his perfect white teeth shining in the candlelight, and he downed the drink in one. It may have been water for all the effect it had on him, but when Sharli drank hers it was if her throat had been set on fire. She gagged, was going to spit it out, but it seemed to evaporate in her mouth and there was nothing to spit.

Her tongue was numb, but Bill indicated that she should fill their glasses again.

'What did Padge ask for proof?' Bill said.

'Your cheeks,' Sharli replied.

Bill nodded, as if that was reasonable, and his hands went as they often did to the growths on his face, which he stroked like an old man strokes his beard. 'If I go, I want to go clean,' Bill said.

'I don't want to do it, Bill,' Sharli said.

Bill got up and went to his bed.

Between his mattress and the bed frame he had hidden a cut-throat razor, which is what he pulled out now. He stood and faced Sharli, opening the knife. 'You're a good pig-killer, girl, but not as good as me.'

The way he said it was kindly. Words like that, said in that situation, might be an overture to a fight to the death, but that's not the way Bill said them. He spoke in the way a kindly grandfather explains a difficult fact to a child.

What he meant was that what Sharli wanted wasn't the issue. He wanted her to know that she couldn't have killed him if he didn't want her to. He wanted her to know that Padge had sent her to do a difficult job, but that it wasn't as simple as she'd thought.

'If Padge wants me dead, I'm already dead,' he said.

With the razor, he slit his overalls from the neck down to the waist, the fabric hissing as the blade passed through it. He put the blade on his bed and pulled the overalls off. They were stiff with years of dirt and blood and mud, and he almost had to snap them to get them off his body, which was naked beneath.

Across the skin of his chest and belly, across his arms, and reaching behind him, were tendrils of the Living Mud, like an octopus, or the roots of a tree, meeting at a node above his heart. These tentacles were still and firm but seemed to be filled with some life of their own, colours beating like blood under the surface.

Bill was not shocked to see them – he must have known that they were there – but he was appalled, his mouth falling open at the extent of their growth, their development, how bad they had got.

He looked up at Sharli, searching in her face for some confirmation of what he was seeing. 'I wasn't always like this,' he said, as if he had to account for himself.

Sharli got up from the chair, came towards Bill, but he stepped back.

The bottoms of his overalls fell away, and the octopus tree roots were like snakes wrapped around his legs, reaching for his ankles, more solid than Bill's flesh, making his limbs seem inconsequential. 'I owe Padge seventy-five silver, and he wants to make an example of me.' Even Bill couldn't have answered why he thought this was what needed saying, since Sharli already knew.

He stood by his bed in the candlelit shack, naked in front

of Sharli, who had been sent to kill him, crusted in filth and parasitised by a Living Mud fluke grown to terrible size in the dark, unwashed places beneath Black Bill's overalls. It was fed by Bill's decision to ignore it, by his shame, by the power Padge and Beaumont's and Mordew had over him.

The only way out was death.

'If I go, I want to go clean,' he said again.

Sharli understood.

She took him by the hand and together they went out into what passed for the street where Black Bill's shack was.

In the slums of Mordew there is no piped water since no one had ever troubled to lay the lines necessary. Even had they done so, they would have fallen by now into disrepair, or would have been destroyed by the encroachment of the Living Mud, or would have been salvaged for material, or in some other inevitable manner been rendered useless.

Instead, water was left to gather in any vessel capable of holding it – a bathtub, a bucket, a discarded trough – and not far from where Bill lived there was a collapsed hay cart, the wheels of which had long been taken, in which rainwater gathered. Sharli held Bill's hand and walked him to this cart, and though he didn't need her for a prop, she supported him as he stepped over the edge of the cart, and held his hand and elbow as he sat in the cold water.

As if it could sense some change in its circumstances, the octopus-tree-root-parasite-fluke tightened across Bill's body as it met the cold water, making him gasp.

Sharli acted as if nothing had happened. She took off her outer shirt, folded it, made a pad of cotton, and wet it with the cart water.

Bill was finding it hard to breathe, the fluke reacting badly to being washed, fearing, seemingly, to have the Living Mud removed from it.

Carefully and gently, Sharli scrubbed at Bill's encrusted skin with the cotton pad.

It came clean easily, the fluke revealed beneath the mud as white and pale as moonlight, like a potato sprout.

Bill's skin was a perfect chestnut brown, like the skin of her commune brothers and sisters after a long hot summer in the reflected glare of the Golden Pyramid. His back was less congested by the fluke's limbs than his chest, and there were patches a hand's breadth or more from which, once cleaned, Sharli could imagine a Bill before this infection, broad-backed and handsome. Proud.

As if an idea could spur something to happen in the world, Bill stood up, enough of the filth washed from him that he appeared to Sharli like his prior self and, rather than the fluke being a necessary part of him, it was clear that it was a horrible imposition, its white, gelatinous monstrosity strangling his flesh.

He seemed to forget Sharli, that she had come to kill him, and he marched with a will back to his shack, striding through the chaos of the street, unashamed, unaware of anyone else or anything. He kicked the half-open door down and went straight to his bed, Sharli following at a run behind.

He took the cut-throat razor and, without pausing, without fear, cut at the nexus of the fluke at his chest.

When he pulled it from his skin, it reacted, tightening its tentacles around him, but Bill was stronger: he had the natural properness of himself as his advantage. A fluke, even one as advanced as this, was only a corruption of the way of things.

Bill managed to get the knife between the nexus and its primary limb, and he cut through it.

A fluke like this, even though it is a perversion of the weft, still has its defences, and this one had integrated its nervous system with Bill's. It was in this way that it had prevented Bill, until the last, from removing it, filling Bill with the desire never to look at it, never to remove the Living Mud from it, making it painful for him to scour it away. Now, when Bill cut at its limb, at its nerves, it filled Bill with pain, a pain unbearable for a body.

Before Bill could sever the limb, this pain stopped his hand, the blade scarcely halfway through.

The fluke tightened its grip, making Bill choke.

Sharli took her knife. She recognised the fear in Bill's eyes, and knew his intention, so she came to stab the nexus of the fluke where surely its motive energies would be gathered. She had underestimated Bill, though, as perhaps everyone had, taking his appearance as an indication of weakness on his part. He grabbed Sharli's wrist before she could cut the fluke.

The tightness of his grip astounded her, as if he had put her bones in a vice. She had no choice but to drop the knife, which Bill entirely ignored.

Though he was in appalling pain, like chewing on a crushed tooth, or stamping with a broken knee, and though it made the pain even worse, he cut away the nexus himself, cut away the limbs, pulled the tendrils away from his good flesh even though the fluke had grown into him at every part, the better that it could parasitise him.

His blood and its flowed together, and though there were cuts that cut at both their bodies, damaged both of them, made both of them bleed, he did not stop until the work was done.

Sharli held her bruised wrist and watched all of this.

Behind her gathered slum people, alerted to some ruckus by sounds of screaming.

Where Sharli was horrified by what she was seeing, the slum people were fascinated, this being a kind of entertainment for those starved of anything much to alleviate their suffering.

They watched until both the fluke and Black Bill died, though Bill died last, and in those moments when he was free of the white parasite he was truly free: free by his own hand, free on his own terms.

He was in his own place, with his window and his curtain of velvet. His own skin, though it was ruined, was the thing that covered him, not Beaumont's overalls.

Once it was clear Bill wouldn't move again, the slum people returned to their business, more or less entertained.

Knowing that she would need them, Sharli picked up Padge's knife and, with her good hand, cut away Black Bill's growth-scarred cheeks. She took down the red velvet from his window, wrapped the cheeks in it, and took them back to Mr Padge.

THE PROBLEM OF THE SOUL
PROPAGANDAS AND SLEEP

∾

Some Hailey-Beths have raised the question, in reaction to problems relating to the Soul Propagandas, that if there is no assumption of the continuation of the self across interruptions of time and space because there is an ending to consciousness at the point of the destruction of the original body, and no assumption of its continuation in the duplicate self despite that duplicate self's own intuition that it is the original self, assumed to be a function of it holding the memories of the original's existence, then can we not say the same of sleep?

On falling asleep, the self loses awareness, even if it regains a form of it in dreams later, and on waking it is only the existence of its memories of the day before that convinces it that it is the same person as it was the previous day.

This is an interruption of consciousness in time, and usually in space, just as there are such interruptions assumed in the understanding of the Soul Propagandas. Can we therefore question whether the waking person is self-identical to the person prior to their falling asleep? Can we posit an alternative? That a person is, instead, a replica self, made daily? If not, how could we prove otherwise?

If we privilege the intuition that we do, in fact, continue across the interruption of sleep, should we not give that same privilege to a replica of an original self that intuits that it is the continuation of the original? If we do not, then are we not privileging one group's intuitions over another's?

This is a non-trivial argument. Perhaps selves are beings that exist for only one day, mistakenly bearing the impression, because of memories, that they transfer across the boundaries of unconsciousness in sleep, when in fact they do not. While this seems intuitively incorrect, some Hailey-Beths have argued that this would account for the sense we have that we are not the people we once were, looking back on periods of our lives separated by years, not recognising ourselves as the people we are now, in thoughts and beliefs, apprehensions and feelings.

Practical evidence exists to support what is being tentatively called 'the mayfly argument' that there is a benefit, to the body, for there to be a constant refreshment in the self, for it to approach life in a manner always striving to make the most of its single day, and hence there exists an evolutionary imperative for the mayfly argument to be true. It would also solve the material paradox that a person intuits the continued existence of themself even across the complete replacement of the material components of their body, something that can occur during a lifetime.

V

Sharli and Anatole

ONCE MR PADGE had Black Bill's cheeks, Sharli was promoted into the care of Padge's assassin, Anatole. Padge told Sharli to wait for Anatole outside The Swan with Two Nicks, an inn, which is what she did.

The Swan with Two Nicks was in the Merchant City, and where The Commodious Hour had an extensive courtyard, this place offered indoor dining on several floors, all of which looked out into a central space, on the ground floor of which was a stage so that performances 'in the round' could be enjoyed from various elevations.

This stage had once been used for dogfighting, each of the floors providing an aspect from which gamblers could watch the matches, but the current proprietor fancied herself above such barbarity, and now musicians were hired to provide entertainment, actors and orators did the things they were trained to do, and the diners there were people who considered themselves cultured and sophisticated to a degree their critics called 'effete'.

In any case, it was too early for either patrons or entertainers to have arrived. Sharli was standing self-consciously by the side entrance – to which goods were delivered, and from which the bins were dragged – finding herself very much less comfortable than she had been when she had worked at The Commodious Hour, not least because she hadn't had her morning quick-root, something that was making her elbows ache, and her hands shake.

Along the street came all manner of people – delivery men, litter bearers, broom handlers, bakers with trays of bread balanced on their heads, fat men rolling barrels, thin men dousing the gas lamps. None of these people were Anatole, and because

Sharli had to look closely at everyone who passed, she felt very conspicuous, catching the eyes of all these people, only then to look down.

What Sharli knew of the assassins in the employ of Mr Padge was what she had seen from the kitchens. They were very handsome gentlemen who enjoyed fine wine, opium and a great deal of leisure, but she knew enough of their trade to suspect that, when they were working, they did not hang about in a way that drew attention.

Here came a boy pulling a clanking cart, a hundred glasses rattling in crates, each in their own separate division, the cobblestones knocking them together regardless. He stopped in front of Sharli, and took first one hand, then the other from the handles of the cart, blew on them, rubbed them on his trousers, and then put them back.

Before he set off again, he looked over at Sharli.

When their eyes met, she looked away, and when she looked back the boy had set off up the hill, whistling and smiling. When he went past he said something she didn't understand – his words were too accented – but it made her feel even more uncomfortable.

Without really intending to, Sharli checked her knives.

Padge had stressed that she should bring the whole set, and not in a roll, but strapped to her arms and legs. For this purpose, he had provided her with elastic garters, and now, along with her thirst for root, the pinching of these garters, where they pressed the hilts of her knives to her thighs and calves and her upper arms, was becoming extremely irritating.

If it hadn't been Mr Padge's request she might have gone without meeting Anatole, but she didn't see how she could do that and not hear about it later, so she leaned against the wall at the side of The Swan with Two Nicks and tried, by counting the bricks, to pass the time until Anatole showed up.

He did, eventually, arrive, but not until after lunchtime, singing a cheerful song to himself, his eyes pinpricked from smoking, his suit a little rumpled.

'Ah, Sharli!' he called, when he saw her, not seeming to care who heard him, or whether or not he should keep a low profile. 'Sorry I'm late – a bit of business came up.'

Sharli was, by this time, very jittery. Because the doorman at The Swan with Two Nicks had moved her on, she had taken to walking to the top of the street, and then walking back down again, over and over, cursing to herself.

Now not only were her limbs all aching, but her feet were sore.

Anatole, who knew the signs of an absence of root on a person, shook Sharli's hand, thereby passing, subtly, a cube of the stuff to her, half of which she immediately put between the side of her mouth and her gum, something that improved her mood dramatically, and the other half of which she saved for later.

'Now,' Anatole said to her, softly, 'Mr Padge wants me to show you the ropes. I have to say, I'm not very keen to do this, because I find children like yourself to be – how shall I put it? – a bit of a lumber? No? A liability.' He lit his pipe. 'My work can be delicate, and the last thing I need is a nervy child making a mess of everything.'

Sharli, regardless of whether her nerves were agitated or calmed, by virtue of her early upbringing had almost no patience for insults. She would have snapped back at Anatole, except that Mr Padge had told her to hold her tongue, if she valued it, since assassins were an irascible bunch, not disinclined to cut out things that offended them, tongues included.

Instead, she bit her irritation back and looked down on the ground.

This seemed to depress Anatole, as if it would have been much easier for him if she'd cut up rough, and given him an excuse to shut her up violently. He sighed, put his hand on her shoulder, turned her round and then marched her through the door of The Swan with Two Nicks.

Inside, lunch service – as Sharli was now habituated to understand it – was in full swing.

As is true of anyone who has spent time working back of house, Sharli's eyes went first to the doors to the kitchens. In this case there were double doors, hinged so that they opened and closed in both directions, sprung so that they needn't be shut behind. These were flapping, admitting a steady stream of waiters in and out so that they were barely shut for more than a second or two at a time. Through the gaps into the kitchens, Sharli could see the familiar steaming hubbub of chefs at their stations, porters running here and there. She could hear the barked orders, curses and suppressed rage of a brigade that was working at the edges of its capacity. The smells that came through were that delicious melange of stocks, scorching meat and the particular combination of the use of herbs and spices, in toto, that is unique to each establishment.

Anatole pulled her away by the arm, and here was a tall and graceful woman, dressed in the colours of the staff livery, though to a pattern much more delicately cut and expensively fabric-ed than any of the other staff.

She was holding a big book in front of her, like a shield, presumably containing the rotas and the booking sheet. 'Anatole,' she said, half-smiling, running her finger down one side of the book, eventually stopping when she found what she was looking for, and then glancing up. 'I was wondering when, or whether, we should have the pleasure of your company today. The fiddler has exhausted his repertoire several times over, and the patrons are tiring of his sawing.'

Anatole, if he was supposed to be apologetic about his lateness, didn't seem it. 'I have brought my apprentice with me,' he said, pushing Sharli in front of him so that she stood between him and the tall and graceful woman, 'She will need an inconspicuous table, preferably on the second floor.'

The woman, whose face was long and narrow, with painted accents in red at the lips and eyes, but who Sharli also considered to be entirely beautiful, looked Sharli up and down with a practised blank expression that seemed to admit no emotion at all. 'Will she be dining?'

'I doubt it very much,' Anatole said, accurately, since quickroot worked to rid the stomach of any desire for food, 'but I'll stand her a carafe of your cheapest and least subtle red wine. Shall I begin?'

Now it was the woman's turn to sigh – sighing, in a certain class of person, is very much the thing one does, and Anatole and this woman, if truth be told, had a long history going back to Anatole's early days in his current position, and predating her tenure here – but she showed Anatole to the stage with a gesture.

When he was gone, the woman looked down at Sharli again, sighed again, then walked away.

When Sharli didn't immediately follow her – she wasn't sure she should – the woman turned back, clicked her fingers, and Sharli trotted after her.

The lower level of the restaurant was filled with tables, spaced generously, around which all sorts of people were sitting – fat, thin, young, old, beautiful, ugly – but they all had one thing in common: they were very well dressed, and there was barely a one of them that didn't wear some exquisite item of jewellery, whether it was a bracelet, a necklace, cufflinks or a ring, quite often a combination of several.

The waiting staff, divided in sections representing the sides of the square formed around the stage onto which Anatole was now climbing, were obsequious in the extreme. The spaces between the tables gave them plenty of room to retreat at the bow, and to deliver dishes with long extended arms, as if knowing that minimising their presence at the table would maximise their gratuities.

Sharli knew that the very moment these waiters entered the back of house they would be insulting the people they waited on in the most florid terms, but out here, at the front, it was impossible to believe they were anything but astounded at the wonder and brilliance of the people they served.

This is the work of service staff, and exhausting work it is, since the patrons of a restaurant are rarely their best selves.

When they know they are paying through the nose for a thing, they imagine a tolerance for rudeness is one of the ingredients of the lunch they are paying for.

The woman ahead clicked her fingers again – Sharli had fallen behind on seeing a table at which all five of the women were wearing the furs of skinned ferrets around their necks, their tails laced through their jaws and extending out between their teeth – and the girl did her best to make up the distance to the foot of the stairs, though she had to dodge a waitress who was carrying a tray of drinks, and then a boy pushing the sweet trolley.

When she did eventually get to the stairs, the woman was already half a flight ahead of her, and Anatole was clearing his throat.

Sharli was led to the second floor, the patrons of which, though not quite as opulently attired and dotingly waited on as the first floor, were still, nonetheless, a cut above the clientele of The Commodious Hour. They were still bejewelled, though not so lavishly, and furred, though not so extensively, and the waiters stood only almost as far away from them when they delivered their slightly less expensive dishes.

Sharli still felt very out of place when the woman put her at her table, which was a very small one, meant for a single diner, possibly. It was in one corner and very adjacent to the climbing creepers that covered the rearmost brick wall, furthest from the stage.

A very thin girl, insubstantial as a ghost, scarcely seeming to be present in the world enough to hold her clothes up, put a carafe of red wine in front of Sharli, along with a glass, and, because it was the done thing, she laid out also a basket of bread with a small dish of butter. These two things the woman who had shown her to the table, coming in from nowhere, removed with a scowl. She marched the ghost girl off by the collar, just as Anatole began to sing.

Sharli had seen Anatole from a distance, dining, laughing, smoking, looking sidewards at the patrons from the assassins' table at The Commodious Hour.

She knew his reputation – which was as a cruel and vicious killer – and while people had said that he would sing as he killed, that being his trademark, she was entirely unprepared for the effect that his voice was to have on her.

The first few words of his song were delivered in almost a whisper, but this whisper seemed to swell into a full, round and perfect note that raised gooseflesh on her arms. By the time he reached the next line, silence having fallen across the room, across each floor – everywhere – he had Sharli's perfect attention.

Anatole's song was about the progress through a landscape of a river of myth that had various effects the closer one drank to its source.

The hero of the song – Anatole made it seem, by the emotion he was putting into his singing, that the song was about him – once drank of this river in his youth.

He found love at the first bend, that love taking him away from the river, and the further he went, as if the distance he travelled lessened the effects of the drinking, the less his love proved to be true, until he was betrayed.

It was a long song, and this first part took several verses. Sharli accompanied them with wine, and listened.

She could only see the top of Anatole's head from where she was, and this from behind, the raking of the floors being not so steep that a table this discreetly placed against the wall could provide a good view. But this didn't disturb her ability to get lost in Anatole's song, which was both intrinsically interesting to her, and beautifully sung.

At a nearby table there were four people, two men and two women, surrounding the corpse of a suckling pig studded with cloves and glazed with honey.

While Sharli was captivated at the performance Anatole was giving, these four had not listened past the first few lines. Instead, they were conducting a loud conversation about the necessity, or otherwise, of the levies their local merchants' association enforced, fairly or unfairly, to provide the wages for the constables that protected part of the Factorium from predation by slum urks.

This conversation increased in volume, each person in the party considering their interjections into the debate to have maximum weight, and hence they brooked no interruption, nor did they wait for a polite time to speak. They interrupted each other forcefully, until there were four of them all talking at once at ever higher volumes.

In Anatole's song, the man who had lost his love and returned to the river could only reach it downstream from where he had once found it. Allegorically, the upstream parts, where the most potent water flowed, were now barred from him by an overgrowth of brambles and shrubs. The subtext was that if he had tended the landscape rather than turning his back on it in favour of fruitless love, he wouldn't have had the same problem. He drank from the river downstream, and while love was still in it, it was a lesser thing, lacking that earlier, youthful potency. Yet love there was still, making him turn his back on the stream again to follow it.

At least, that is what Sharli thought he was singing.

So loudly were the four people discussing levies, and so angrily, that Sharli could scarcely hear the content of the song. They had put their knives and forks down in front of them now, and each was leaning forwards, hands on the table, so desperate to make themselves heard that the sacrifice of the suckling pig in providing their lunch was proving to have been in vain.

The exquisite tone of Anatole's voice could no longer make gooseflesh of Sharli's skin, competing, as it was, with the harsh, almost unforgiveable aspersions each of the people at the table were casting at each other.

The nearest woman was wearing a dress that was suspended from her shoulders by thin silk straps. It was all in a lustrous pink, and her long blonde hair was tucked behind her ears.

From these ears, which were both perfectly formed and shell-like, depended earrings, dropping like silver tears, very beautifully. Her lips were painted in perfect red and her eyelashes fluttered like the wings of a black butterfly.

By all objective measures, this woman was very well presented, but Sharli could not appreciate any of that, because all she could hear was the woman's braying assertion that slum urks should be burned from the cracks between the rocks they sprang up from, like weeds are burned from the cracks in a paved garden, and that there would thereby be no need for a constabulary, nor any levies.

When she said these words her delicate shoulders shook, one strap of her lustrous gown migrated over to the left until it slipped off, her long hair became untucked from behind her ear, hiding its perfectness of form along with the silver tear earring, and her perfectly painted mouth gathered froth at its corners.

Eventually, she and the others around the table reached a natural pause in their conversation. She put her strap back up onto her shoulder, tucked her hair back behind her ear – revealing the earring again – and dabbed at the corner of her mouth with a napkin.

A waitress – the same diaphanous one that had brought Sharli's wine – came and asked them if there was anything else they wanted, and if the food was to the expected standard. This seemed to remind them that the purpose of lunch was not, typically, to rant and rave about political matters, but was at least in part about consuming food, so they returned in silence to their meal.

Now, though, when Sharli listened to Anatole's song – he had been singing throughout – she couldn't follow his meaning, since the man was doing something now that only seemed to tangentially be relevant to the river, and to love.

Sharli poured herself more wine and glared over it at the four on the neighbouring table, who were chewing methodically and cheerlessly through mouthfuls of suckling pig, occasionally lubricating them with sips from their glasses.

Anatole was now reaching a crescendo, the tone, emotive-ness and pitch of his song being accompanied by what, had Sharli been able to appreciate it properly, would have been a very effective, possibly heart-rending, use of tremolo.

Because the sound of his voice filled the restaurant, the four at the table seemed to find this appropriate cover for the resumption of their argument. It began again with some half-hearted apologies for having overspoken, but almost immediately devolved back into insults, albeit delivered with slightly less volume.

In any case, Sharli's experience of the song was ruined. The perfectly earred, beautifully earringed woman looked over at Sharli, the words of her opinions forming on her perfectly red lips, and, as if seeing nothing, she returned without pausing to look at her partners in the crime of spoiling Anatole's song.

By the time Anatole finished his set, the four diners were sipping at their coffees, and the subject of their disagreement having been insufficient to interest them much past the clearance of the suckling pig, they had given way to a more or less cheerful consideration of pleasantries, so that now an observer would have found it difficult to credit their earlier exchanges.

Sharli, though, was still as angry as she had been before, if not more so.

So, when Anatole came to find her, plonking a bottle of brandy on the table and pulling up a seat, she found it difficult to hide her scowl.

'Didn't like the song?' he said. 'Everyone's a critic…'

'I thought it was wonderful,' Sharli said, urgently. 'At least the bits I could hear.'

It might be difficult to imagine an assassin cares about the opinions he hears of his singing. A man who is capable of the violence necessary to murder people for a living must seem to be a very hard-hearted kind of person, inured to suffering, but this is only a hard-heartedness to the feelings of others; it does not apply to oneself.

Anatole was still very much attuned to his own feelings, and the earnestness with which Sharli expressed her wonder at his voice did touch him. He sat in silence, smiling, and would have poured himself a drink, except that there was no glass. He drank it out of the bottle instead.

'The people on that table,' Sharli pointed at them, 'talked all the way through your song and I couldn't hear most of it.'

Anatole nodded. 'Such is the fate of the singer for enter-tainment, Sharli. We get used to it.'

'You shouldn't have to,' said Sharli, with feeling.

Anatole thought about this. 'Well, you shouldn't be so harsh. Perhaps there's something wrong with their ears.'

'There must be, if they couldn't hear the beauty in your song.'

It is true that Sharli's first language was that of Malarkoi and not of Mordew, and that she sometimes said things with more force than she might have done if her vocabulary had been wider, but when a man is told his singing is beautiful by a girl who has no reason to lie to him, even if he is a man inured to the feelings of others, it is not easy for his heart to ignore it, which is why he did what he did next.

'Right then,' Anatole said. 'Here is my first job for you, Sharli. What I want you to do is bring me that woman's ears, so we can see if there's anything wrong with them.'

Sharli didn't have to ask which woman he meant – the other woman at the table had her hair down in a bob that covered hers. 'Do I kill her first?'

Anatole shrugged. 'She'll probably object if you try to take her ears while she's alive, but it's up to you.'

'Now?' Sharli looked around. There were, on this floor alone, fifty people at least, and there were roughs by the doors.

Anatole smiled. 'I think you might want to learn to walk before you try to run. Anyway, we're barred from killing on managed premises, so you'll have to follow her home, or do it in the street. Either way, we should be making tracks.'

Anatole took her back downstairs, collected his fee, minus the money for Sharli's wine, and the two of them departed The Swan with Two Nicks.

'I'll be nearby, in case anything goes wrong, but otherwise you're on your own. Don't take any risks, but this shouldn't be a difficult job. She's not expecting you, doesn't have any reason to be on her guard, and she's got no protection.' Anatole knelt down in front of Sharli, straightened her clothes so that her knives weren't showing. 'First rule,' he said, 'is to do it like you mean it. Understand?'

Sharli didn't understand, but she nodded anyway. Anatole stood up and was suddenly lost to the street, as if a magician had made him invisible, or had spirited him away.

She didn't have to wait long for the woman to appear. A carriage pulled up at the door and she, and one of the men – shorter than her, broader than her, darker than her, with a face that was more lined – got into it, the other two walking off in a different direction, grumbling.

Sharli ran up the hill, which was the way the carriage was facing, thinking to get a head start on it, but after coming a little way up, it turned straight down a street on the left – Chancellery Way – and Sharli had to run back down before she lost them altogether.

Had she known it, this was a better thing to do because it meant that, when the carriage turned in the street, there was no chance for the woman to look out of her window and see Sharli waiting, to recognise her, and then to say to her husband, if such he was, 'There's the little urk who was staring at us in the restaurant.' If she would then see Sharli again, later, she'd know that the girl was following them.

As it was, Sharli would now be just another face in a crowd, the memory of a lowly person being to these dignitaries a very forgettable thing, lasting only a few minutes in the mind and easily overwritten by the faces of others of a similar type.

The carriage was a hundred yards or more ahead when Sharli saw it, the driver having taken Chancellery Way because it had less traffic. If it had continued on its path at the speed it was currently travelling, Sharli wouldn't have been able to follow. However, nowhere in the Merchant City was free for travel of any kind, and carriages were less a means of going quickly from one place to another than they were a means of going privately from one place to another. A boy and his cart had overturned – co-incidentally, this was the same boy who had passed Sharli earlier on in the day, the one with the glasses in crates, each separated into their own divisions – so the road ahead was blocked.

The driver had to slow and take Parson's Rise, which was as narrow as a carriage and a half, and poorly cobbled since the lessors of the roadway had fallen on hard times, their shops suffering a little from being on a comparatively little-known tributary to the main thoroughfare. As is so often the case, places with a problem that stops them from thriving often thrive less and less, the lack of money for the road meaning fewer people wished to come there, since the Living Mud, even high up here, gathered on uncobbled surfaces, and it was not cost-effective to have broom handlers always brushing flukes away.

When Sharli reached Parson's Rise she was out of breath and a little frantic, feeling that her first job would be a bust, by dint of her having lost the mark, but there was the carriage, one wheel stuck in a rut, and Sharli had to quickly adopt a casual and inconspicuous gait so that it didn't become obvious that she had been chasing them.

The woman leaned out of the window, her shoulders covered with a fur stole now, but her pretty earrings still depending from her pretty ears as she chided and chivvied the driver, who was doing his best. He told her he could only do what it was possible to do, and, without a lever, it wasn't possible to get the wheel loose since it was trapped in the road.

'If people would just pay their levies, none of this type of thing would happen,' he said.

The woman went into the carriage at this point: the man inside had snorted, or chuckled, because this turn of events had provided some proof for his earlier argument. Now she was remonstrating with him about it.

A little while later, the man came out, looking very much like someone who had just had the smile wiped off his face by a wife who, having heard him laughing, had pointed out that it was his job to provide assistance to the help in times like this, otherwise what was the use of him, since he was precious little use for anything else?

Sharli made to tie her shoelaces, and though this shouldn't have taken her as long as it did, it did at least give her enough time so that she could get an idea of what kind of threat, if any, this man might pose if, later, she was called upon by circumstances to kill him.

He was about the size of a three-year sow, if she was standing on her hind legs. From the way he was only barely helping with the pushing of the carriage out of its rut, and the way he winced when he did it, he was possessed of a sore back. One slash to the groin, one to the neck, with the chef's knife, or even the paring knife, would do it, though he might set up squealing and thereby notify others.

Sharli's laces could not possibly require any more tying, so she walked on to the other side of the road, past the turning, and watched the progress of the carriage man in the window of the furniture shop in front of which they had stopped. No one visited this place while she had it under surveillance.

After a while, it became clear that the carriage wasn't going anywhere soon – the man with the bad back proved more of a hindrance than a help – so Sharli went along Chancellery Way and up the next street, which ran almost parallel to Parson's Rise, except always tending to the middle of a circle, as was the way everywhere in Mordew. She ran up here all the way to the top, the road much better cobbled, presumably since the local people paid their levies. Then she turned right, and right again, and there was the carriage in the distance. It hadn't moved at all.

From here, there were three ways to go: upwards, a little back towards The Swan; downwards and back to The Swan by a different route; and upwards and away from The Swan.

Since there was no way that the carriage man would have come the way that he did if he intended to return the way he had come, Sharli decided that he must be going the third way, so she set off that way herself, feeling that it would be good to get a head start.

The shops started to get fewer and fewer, and in their place were houses, tall and many-storied, with spires poking up.

Above, as if the roads followed each other, was the Glass Road, heavily suspended by absolutely nothing, always threatening to fall and crush them if it ever lost its magic. The presence of the Glass Road and its threat quickened her steps, but she didn't want to lose sight of the turning from Parson's Rise just in case she had made a mistake in her thinking, and the carriage turned the other way. She made an eccentric path along the road she was on, crossing from one side to the other at diagonals, in a way that, had she been observed, would have made her seem very suspicious.

The further she went, the fewer became the people on the street; there was little to bring them unless they lived here. As the turning got further and further away, becoming a tiny speck in her vision, she wondered more and more whether she had made a mistake.

She was just about to turn back when, there in the distance, was a glint. Was it the glint of lamplight in a carriage window? It did seem like it, but she couldn't be sure.

She waited, and now it occurred to her that Anatole had said he would be nearby. Where could he be, she thought? She looked up and down the street for sign of him.

There was none.

Still, he said he would be there, in case of emergency, and she trusted him.

There was the carriage, clear now down the road, the driver whipping the horses and slapping the reins to make up for the lost time.

Sharli turned her back on it, slumped her shoulders, walked head down like a tired person, busy at her own affairs, worn out through them. She listened to the rims of the carriage wheels as they struck the cobbles – a kind of rapid knocking on the edge of the drum and not the skin – coming ever louder. Soon it was joined by the thud of horseshoes, and then both passed her, the wheels spraying water from puddles that had gathered during earlier rain and which the poor drainage had not removed to the sewers.

It would have been here that the woman, looking out, would certainly have recognised the urk who had been staring at them in the restaurant had she also seen that urk immediately outside the restaurant. So it is that the contingencies of fate, whether we are in control of them or not, dictate the success or otherwise of our endeavours, because now Sharli was not recognised. Instead, the woman turned to her husband and, as a way of repairing whatever damage had been made by their earlier argument, suggested that they remain at home that evening and play the piano together, rather than do what they had planned to do. This had been to go to a neighbouring house for a recitation, something he had groaned at when he had heard it suggested, but which she had insisted on, since there was some small possible benefit to their interests inherent in the fact that one of the guests was a man who had influence over a committee that controlled whether or not outbuilding on a curtailment could reach this or that height. This might affect the plans for their extensions.

He, because this was a great relief to him since he hated one or other of the guests also determined to appear at the recitation, and only hated playing the piano with his wife a little bit, jumped at this chance to lessen his suffering. So it was that, once they had turned into the road that led to their house, Sharli secretly not far behind, they were destined to be in for the rest of the evening, she ready to be deprived of her ears, and he not in much position to do anything to stop it, since he had a bad back.

The husband and wife were called Paulo and Patricia Antunes, and their house was called 'Pining for the Skies'. Sharli knew this because it was engraved into a brass plaque, one that she looked at casually as she walked past it once the carriage had left and the two were safely inside.

The house was five storeys high, each storey narrower than the last, tapering up to a roof that became a spire, that became a lightning rod, on which, Sharli seemed to think, a firebird in brass was perched, although admittedly that was very high up.

It had been years since 'bird-death' as the people here called it, had shocked her, but she did have to swallow back a little of the sadness that, even now, the thought of Tinnimam caused in her.

Swallow it back she did, leaving the house behind her as she went past and up the street in the gathering dusk. Into her cheek she put the remaining half of quick-root that Anatole had given her.

Is there a reason murderers, at least those who plan and commit their crimes in cold blood, do their work in the night-time? Sharli wasn't sure, but it seemed to her that to wait until her victim was incapacitated by sleep, and lying conveniently down in bed, was to have half her work done for her, even if it did mean that she had to kill some time.

Would this annoy Anatole? Surely he would have to wait too. Would it make him angry? She looked around as she walked, head down, and though there was still no sign of him, why should there be?

Surely assassins were used to making themselves inconspicuous?

Sharli followed the road where it led, took the first left turn, which led past the Zoological Gardens, who were shutting their gates for the day, turned left again, and then again, which brought her back to the street on which Pining for the Skies stood.

She walked up to the gates and, because she was as slender as a street cat, she slipped between the frame of the gate and the post from which it was hinged, only stopping when the hilt of the knife under her left arm chinked on the metal, though that only required a slight shift for her to free it, and though her ears did pull a little as she went the last few inches, this was a temporary problem, easily resolved.

Rather than walk up the path, something that would have been a very bold strategy indeed, Sharli kept to the wall, weaving between privet bushes, and avoiding those of roses, following the outermost boundary until she came to a room sketched out in concrete and half-brick walls, roped over with tarpaulins.

She slipped under the temporary roof, made a slit with her paring knife so she could see the windows of the first and second floor, and sat in the dry, protected from the wind and prying eyes.

Here she waited.

She had not known the beginnings of the new extension would be there when she entered the Antunes' property, but she had hoped something of the sort would be. She had wanted a woodstore, a place where tools were kept, even an empty barrel would have done, but in their absence she learned one of the most valuable lessons an assassin must learn: that she shouldn't wait until everything was known before she acted. She should rely instead on her own skills and the fact that these can make of the world the things necessary for the successful prosecution of her work.

She sat cross-legged in her makeshift hide and watched the windows of the house from between the first two fingers of her left hand, which, when she opened and closed them, opened and closed the slit she had made in the tarpaulin.

When one pays attention to even the smallest portion of one's field of vision, that part can provide additional detail. It becomes as if it were the whole field of vision, the brain extrapolating from that small amount of data a much larger scene. So it was that the four small squares of light, themselves divided into four even smaller squares – these were two first-floor windows and two second-floor windows, the smaller squares the four panes of glass in each – filled the entirety of Sharli's sight and mind for the time in which she observed them.

Quiet but audible sounds also leaked to where she was, though these were only a few and then mostly the notes of a piano being played by four hands, possibly the couple inside playing together.

There were the two she had watched enter the house – she knew this because she had followed them there and had not seen them leave, and also because of the piano music, which was too complicated for one person to play alone – but there were also at least three others.

One was an elderly woman, similar in stature and colouring to the man from the restaurant, and with a comically similar face, the same as, it must be, her son's, except in the style of a woman, with a woman's hair.

Sharli saw her on several occasions through the windows, listening from the upper floor, with one hand cupped over her ear, and another rubbing her back. Each time Sharli saw her she stood still for a minute or more before waving the hand on her ear in dismissive annoyance, turning and walking off.

The second person was a girl, younger than Sharli, probably not yet ten summers. She would go past the lower-floor windows at a run, first in one direction, then back in the other, before being arrested in her progress by the third person, a strict woman of middle age, hair pulled into a tight bun pinned to the top of her head. She had first appeared dressed in a neat skirt and jacket, and then, as the evening wore on, in a white bedgown, before finally appearing again in the bedgown, but with her grey hair loose at her shoulders. Each time she stopped the girl running, turned her around, and sent her away with an arm pointed to where the girl was supposed to go.

Eventually, the other three did not appear at the windows, and then the piano music stopped, and though Sharli did not see the couple at the windows, the lamps were dimmed downstairs, then on the floor above.

Since there were no lamps now lit on the lower floors, and the moon was obscured by the omnipresent overcast, Sharli was able to walk in the darkness of the garden without fear of being seen.

Once out from under the tarpaulins she saw that there were dim lights, round the back of the house, on the third and fourth floors, so she waited until those went out before she tried a rear door, which she found to be open.

Once inside, Sharli felt first the warmth of the fire that was still dwindling in the grate that dominated the kitchen. She stopped there to warm her hands. When one is peeling potatoes in the root stores, and then one comes up to wash those peeled potatoes in the prep sink, the cold of both things – subterranean air, and unheated water – make the fingers red and stiff.

A good chef knows, Boland had said, that you mustn't start knife work with cold fingers.

When her fingers were warm again, which wasn't long, Sharli left the kitchen and came out into a broad hall, off which led various doors and, at one end, a staircase. She listened at the doors as she passed, heard nothing, but she did notice that each had a lock, though the keys weren't in them.

She reached the last door and not only listened at it, but also kneeled down and spied through the keyhole. She wanted to see whether the room was empty.

It sounded empty, but her vision through the keyhole was obscured, and it occurred to her that this was because the key was in it, only on the other side.

Why shouldn't this be the case?

This was not a prison, not a factory where the workers were imprisoned between one shift and the next, nor a brothel, from which a girl must be prevented from escaping. These were locks so that the person behind might keep themselves inside, safe and private, if they were used at all.

Sharli twisted the door handle.

The door opened silently on well-maintained and oiled hinges. She reached round into the darkness and found the key on the other side. It was easy to remove, and easy to replace, and, having done this once or twice, she shut the door quietly and made her way upstairs, having first taken off her shoes.

The stairs were plushly carpeted, and secured in place by thick brass rods. Sharli made no sound as she ascended, not even when she wobbled the bannisters a little to check them. Indeed, the bannisters would not be wobbled, nor did the boards beneath the carpets creak when trodden on, nor did loose nails squeal. It was almost as if the Antunes family had determined to make their house as silently navigable by a girl assassin as possible, though even Sharli doubted this was what they had in mind.

The strict-seeming woman, the old woman and the girl had their rooms on the second floor, and all of them, Sharli determined by listening, were asleep.

The two adults were snoring, in different tones and at different rates – the stern woman's snores were deep and regular, the older woman's higher, quicker and slightly febrile. In both cases, Sharli tried their doors, neither of which were locked, and opened them sufficiently to reach her arm in, retrieve the key, close the door, and then, quietly, with an exaggerated care over the turning, to lock them both securely in their rooms against the possibility of them waking up.

With the girl, Sharli was about to do the same thing, but, on trying, she found the girl's toys, some of which were on the floor, impeded the opening of the door.

One of the toys was a firebird, carved in wood, and while it wasn't accurate, it was about the size of Tinnimam, perhaps a little smaller. Without really thinking, Sharli forced the door open further, went in, and found herself in the child's bedroom.

There was the sound of the girl's slow, lisping breaths, the flickering light of a single shielded candle, a landscape of chintz and curlicues, dolls and castles. There were firebirds everywhere, stitched into the curtains, stencilled on the walls, embroidered on the bedspread.

Whether it was the quick-root, or the lack of opium, or the anxiety inherent in the kind of work that she was doing, or the repression of her sadness at the loss of Tinnimam, or jealousy, or anger – whatever it was – Sharli began to twitch.

A muscle in her face, below the cheek, kept pulling at her lip and the left eye.

It would be wrong to say that Sharli recognised the urge to kill this girl – she was not yet, even after all of the things she had done, expert enough to know it. It is a very specific thing that only a few people know well. If she had been longer in her post she would definitely have known the feeling for what it was, and what it was that she would have to do to satisfy it, but Sharli didn't kill the girl there and then because she didn't realise, quite, that she wanted to do it.

Or that it was a perfectly reasonable thing for an assassin to do.

So, despite the strange feeling that made her twitch, she backed out of the room, and because of that feeling she forgot to lock the door after she left.

This was a mistake.

Back in the hallway, there was only the quiet snoring of the women, the scent of lavender coming from a vase of dried stalks, and that visible darkness that the eye can sense when it is habituated to it, everything grey and shadowy, but more or less visible, if a little indistinct around the edges.

Sharli took a deep breath, hoping to clear the tension the child's bedroom had made in her chest. She walked away from the door without checking behind her, which was another mistake, since the child was already up, had already got out of her bed, and was already behind Sharli.

The child, whose name was Beatriz, did not follow her immediately, but waited to see where she went.

Why did she do this?

Why didn't she go straight to her governess, or to her grandmother, and raise the alarm?

It is because a child, particularly a sleepy child, isn't a rational thing, nor is she used to seeing other children as a threat, nor is she expecting an assassin's visit, nor is there anything particularly unusual to her in the presence of other people in the house, if she is used to her parents having guests.

Indeed, a child like Beatriz often remains at large after her bedtime. She keeps very quiet as she moves about the place, remaining out of sight. It is only when she is seen or heard by her governess that she is promptly returned to her room, where she must then remain until morning against the threat of punishment.

So that is why she waited until Sharli was out of the hallway, and then, slowly and quietly, went to the corner to see where she had gone, which was up the stairs to the floor on which Beatriz's parents had their room.

Sharli padded softly up the next set of stairs, knowing that, even if the old and the young are asleep, those between those ages might still be awake, even if the light is off in their room, occupied with their nocturnal business.

It was not easy for her to recognise which room was the one the couple slept in, there being six or more potential places, most with the doors shut.

As she considered, she slipped the chef's knife and the paring knife from their holsters. The chef's knife she held in her right hand, the paring knife she held between her teeth, and with her left hand she tried the doors to the rooms she considered to be silent.

The first was a dressing room, with a chest of drawers, two large wardrobes, a dressing table and all the things a man needs for getting ready – brushes, combs, rollers for the removal of lint, creams for slicking down hair, all sorts of tiepins and pocket squares and things that Sharli didn't recognise.

While she was in the room, Beatriz ran past the door to the end of the hall and slipped into the upstairs bathroom, leaving the door open so she could peek through the crack the hinge left.

Sharli came out of Paulo's dressing room and, assuming, correctly, that the room on the other side of the corridor was Patricia's dressing room, she ignored it and went to the next room.

She pressed her ear against the door, and this put her in a position so that she was looking directly at where Beatriz was hiding, so much so that, if she had focussed, she would have seen the girl's staring eye.

But she did not see her.

When you are listening closely, particularly in the near dark, just because your eyes are pointing in a particular direction that does not mean that you see in that direction. You are simply not concentrating on seeing anything, all the attention of your mind being directed at the sense of hearing. This was why Sharli did not see Beatriz in time to correct her mistake of not killing the girl, or of locking her in her room. Instead, she heard the sounds of a couple sleeping.

There is no time like the present, so Sharli slipped open their door and went into their room.

No assassin will lock themselves into a room, not when their targets are sleeping, since what good can come of it? She does not imagine, because she thinks she has been careful, that there is any way that she can be disturbed by someone coming into the room.

Sharli didn't even close the door.

She gave the room a cursory look – there was nothing concerning – and turned her attention to the bed. Paulo was on the nearest side, lying on his front, while Patricia was on her back, one arm over her eyes, her mouth open, her lips dry.

Sharli was surprised to see that the woman hadn't removed her earrings – they seemed to pool on her pillow, as if mercury had leaked out of her.

Anatole had said, she remembered, that this should be an easy job, that this woman wouldn't be expecting it, that they had no protection, and those things had all proved to be true.

Was he watching her now, through an eyeglass, from a nearby house, the occupants of which he'd himself killed?

Do it like you mean it, he'd said. The first rule.

She knew what she would do – hand over the man's mouth, slit his neck at the artery with the paring knife.

She would then turn, stab the woman in the heart with the chef's knife until she stopped moving.

That would teach her not to talk over her friend's song.

Sharli went and sat, gently, on the bed beside the man.

Her friend. Was Anatole that yet?

She took a deep breath and swapped knives.

'Who are you?'

The words were like an explosion in Sharli's ears, and she whirled towards them. Twisting the bedsheets beneath her.

There was Beatriz, in the doorway.

The lack of the bedsheet's warmth on Paulo's back woke him slightly, and he reached out to pull it back, his hand falling on Sharli's knee. She, panicked by his touch, struck out by reflex, cutting a gash in Paulo's arm.

Even a sleeping man cries out when he is slashed with a knife, and Paulo bellowed. This made Beatriz scream, and Patricia sat bolt upright in bed.

A room that had, a moment earlier, been entirely quiet was now in tumult.

To an Anatole this would be as nothing – grab the girl, hold the knife to her throat, order the adults to remain still, approach the father, kill him in whatever is the easiest way, then kill the shocked and appalled mother, then kill the crying child and the job is done with almost as little fuss as if they were never woken in the first place. But this was Sharli's first real job, and while she was a girl with an unusual upbringing and training, she was not as yet immune to panic.

Indeed, it was Mr Padge's intention that an apprenticeship to Anatole should address this last remaining flaw in her. In fairness, the events that followed did begin that process, though in a very messy and inefficient way.

Screaming, Beatriz raised her hands to her mouth, but because Paulo was nearest, Sharli cut him first. She went for the neck, because this was the original plan, but a man defending himself, particularly when he has no weapon, will put his arms up, just like his daughter did, so rather than severing his artery she succeeded instead in inflicting a series of very deep, but non-fatal, wounds to his forearms and wrists.

Seeing these wounds on her husband, Patricia lunged for Sharli and she had to retreat past the end of the bed.

The woman's earrings, no longer pooled on her pillow, were glinting in whatever light was entering the room from wherever it was entering from. Sharli couldn't, at that moment, spare any attention to determine where the light was coming from, but it was, in fact, reflected up from the governess's room. She had lit her lamp when she heard Beatriz scream. Sharli was distracted by remembering that it was the woman's ears that she had been sent to get, the thought striking her that she might be able to get them even if she couldn't successfully kill any of them.

This distraction was sufficient for Beatriz to leave the room, and it is saying a lot about this girl that she had the wherewithal, despite her own panic, to take the key from her parents' lock, just as Sharli had done, and lock the three of them in there together while she then ran for help.

In doing so she had probably consigned her parents to their deaths, but, as has been said before, she was not acting entirely rationally, and credit must be given where it is due, since most girls will stand screaming until their killer murders them simply to stop the noise. Beatriz did more than that.

The girl slammed the door and Sharli regained her composure.

The couple, one blooded, one staring fiercely, approached.

She would have to defend herself.

Sharli had downed more furious pigs in the abattoir, fighting for their lives, than these two had had hot dinners. This was not an exaggeration, since a strict definition of 'dinner' implies that there would be, at most, one a day, and in the summer months it is usual to have salads, or other cold foods, while Sharli, during her tenure at the abattoir, would habitually be sent daily a hundred or more animals for dispatch. She strode forward, inserted her paring knife into Paulo's groin and dragged it across, slicing the muscles and pipework at the left leg so that he went down at once, pumping blood into the carpet.

From there, exchanging knives as she did it, she sprang up at Patricia, driving her chef's knife though the underside of the woman's chin, putting seven inches of steel into her brain stem, shutting down all but the most primitive cerebral functions immediately and irreparably.

Sharli then returned to finish the husband, who, while he would certainly not live, was nevertheless not yet dead. She strangled him, that being less wasteful of her energy than first retrieving the knife lodged in his wife's skull and using that to sever his spinal cord.

Almost automatically, Sharli acted out on these people the murder she had long practised on pigs.

This was only part of the job, though. She now had to successfully extricate herself from the murder site.

She was locked in a room with her victims, and there was every possibility that the constabulary – about whom this couple had argued – would be on their way soon to take her life, summary execution being the usual punishment for murder in Mordew.

Sharli lit the lamp on Patricia's side of the bedside table.

Perhaps Anatole was waiting nearby, as he'd said he would, so that he could effect a rescue in the case of emergency. Sharli peered out of the window, her bloody hands shielding her gaze from reflections.

She couldn't see Anatole in the streets, nor anyone else.

What did she expect?

Sharli had always been alone, and she was alone now, and though she comforted herself with the idea that this, perhaps, in an assassin of Anatole's experience, did not constitute an emergency, the upshot was the same.

She tried the door, but it was firmly locked, and when she applied her shoulder to it, it didn't so much as rattle.

She went back to the window, but the drop was too high. Each storey of this house was at least twenty feet deep. In any case, when she tried to open the windows she couldn't get them to budge.

She went to the bathroom – this bedroom had one that led off it, for convenience's sake – and tried there. The windows were similarly jammed.

Still, once she was in there, she saw a thing that prevented the necessity of smashing her way out.

Quite simply, there was a door to the hallway leading out from the *en suite*, the key to which was still in the lock on this side.

Beatriz, resourceful as she was, wasn't all that resourceful. She had left an exit unlocked.

This realisation brought Sharli entirely to her senses, and she walked, briskly and calmy, back into the bedroom, darkened the lamp, sliced off Patricia's ears, earrings and all, placed them in the secure pouch at her waist, returned to the bathroom and left through the bathroom door.

This whole business had taken only a few minutes, though the experience of time does seem to stretch out nerve-wracking events, but even so, Beatriz should easily have been able to raise the alarm.

It was because adults have an innate distrust of the things that children say that, even with the screaming, even with the inescapable fact that they had been locked in their rooms, even with the unprecedented paleness of Beatriz's skin and her clear traumatic agitation, neither the grandmother nor the governess believed that the girl had seen what she said she saw, or that they were in fact under attack from a murderous older girl, Sharli, until that very girl appeared in front of them, bloodstained and armed, at the end of the corridor off which their rooms were to be found.

By then it was too late.

This was their one mistake, though, and to be fair to them they gave a good account of themselves.

The grandmother, feeling perhaps that it was the only thing she had it in her power to do, pelted arthritically down the hall at Sharli and flung herself, a mess of wrinkled skin and brittle bones, at the girl.

While she didn't weigh enough to put Sharli off her balance, the old woman clung tightly to her, so that she was like a tangle of briars, trapping Sharli for long enough that the governess and her charge were able to run past, chittering like lunatics and calling for help in turn.

It wasn't until Sharli had broken the old woman's back across her knee, as she had done so many times before with a geriatric pig not worthy of the knife, that she could cast the woman aside and chase the others.

The governess was struggling at the locks of the front door, which had been locked at five points, as if there wasn't an unlocked door at the rear, giving Sharli time to take out her cleaver from where it had been gartered to the outside of her right thigh. This she threw at the governess. On impact it cut the ribs on the woman's left side, collapsed her left lung, nicked her aorta, and caused her immediate incapacitation and eventual death some time later.

Now there was only Beatriz. Sharli took the girl's hand and led her back to her room. Because the child was comatose with the terror of what she had seen, she came easily.

Back in the bedroom, even though it was filled with blasphemous misrepresentations of the heavenly brothers, she tucked the girl into her bed.

Later, when she was asked, she would do what all assassins do when they leave a victim unkilled – which is to put it down to advertising, a reputation being a very valuable thing in their work, both for getting new commissions and also for petrifying people they want to murder through fear of what they have done before. But it was really sympathy that stayed Sharli's hand.

She knew that the girl was now an orphan, as Sharli had always felt herself to be, and it wasn't the girl's fault she didn't know the truth about firebirds, though she did explain a little of that truth to the girl before she left, which then contributed to the nightmares that plagued Beatriz from that day on, the poor little thing.

Sharli approached the assassins' table the next day, still stained with blood.

Her return to The Commodious Hour had been delayed by the presence of a very many constables on the streets, all looking for a murderous girl loose in the Merchant City, but she had kept to the shadows, and taken her time, and now here she was, walking across the restaurant patio.

The assassins all applauded her, particularly Anatole, who even stood, despite the fact that his knees were weak with opium.

Sharli took Patricia's ears from her pouch and threw them onto the table. She picked up a pipe from the ashtray, lit it, dragged, and thereby returned that sense of perfect calmness to her soul that was no longer possible without it.

'Where were you?' she said to Anatole.

Anatole took the ears and, carefully, removed the beautiful drop earrings from the holes in the lobes. He handed the earrings to Sharli. 'These are for you,' he said. 'I was always nearby, but it's not polite for one assassin to get involved in another assassin's work unless it's absolutely necessary. That is rule two.'

The others at the table looked down and smirked, and it seemed at first that they were laughing at her. Then one of them raised his finger, and when the waitress came he said, 'Bring our colleague a chair. From now on she dines with us.'

In this way Sharli formally became one of Mr Padge's assassins, a position and set of obligations no one could ever take from her, no matter what they did.

Sharli was given a room at The Commodious Hour, but her work paid well so after a few months she also rented a space separate from the others, and let Mr Padge know where it was in case he needed to send a runner for her.

It was a suite on the northern borders of the Entrepôt, in what used to be a grain warehouse, but which now warehoused people who needed a more than usual degree of security, secrecy and quietness for their activities, whatever those happened to be.

In this suite she kept her lockbox, itself locked away under the boards beneath her bed.

In this box she put her precious things.

What would be precious to a person like Sharli?

She left Malarkoi, as we know, without anything, at the threat of her life, and the one thing she valued then – the firebird Tinnimam – remained behind, shouting for her to run, clawing at the eyes of the priest charged with sacrificing her.

So, we know there was nothing from her childhood in her box of precious things, not like we may have.

If we have cultivated a taste for objects that require us to maintain their definite presence in our lives, we might put these in a safe place, and Sharli did do that. She put there emergency supplies of quick-root and opium against the failure of her usual supply. The people who tend to distribute these things aren't usually as reliable as one always wishes they might be. With these supplies were doubles of some of her favourite pipes in case hers were lost, stolen or broken.

Sharli also put there trophies of her murders.

There was the upholstered nail with which she had punished the supervisor for his perversions, still matted with his blood.

There were the two rings she had taken from him, the ones that could not be made to fit her fingers. She had spent an uncomfortable day with these rings on her thumb toes, since these are the largest digits on a person, but they chafed inside her boots and made it difficult to chase people at a run. While she was still happy to wear her copper and blue anklet, that was the lower extent of the places she habitually wore jewellery, so she put the rings in the lockbox.

Earrings do not tend to impede movement, unless they are very large and heavy, but Sharli also put the earrings from her first job in the box, because they were small, beautiful and easily lost. More than once she had had to stop what she was doing and go onto her hands and knees to look for them.

Instead, she had imitations made for her by a jeweller, and these she wore, replacing them with replicas if she mislaid them, or they were torn from her, or when, in some other way, she lost possession of them – through gambling, for example. She had the jeweller keep the designs for them in his plan chest.

As she worked more and more, became more and more useful to Mr Padge, and the years passed, she always made it a point to take trophies. While she never went out of her way to kill people who wore things she might like to wear, many people in the city wore adornments of the sort Sharli favoured, either to beautify themselves or to demonstrate their status to their peers. Soon she had fingers full of rings, wrists full of bangles and bracelets. She had cufflinks at her sleeves, jewelled buttons holding the sides of her jacket together, necklaces of all metals, thick and thin around her neck.

Should Sharli have been asked to provide a dowry by the time she made her majority – which in Mordew was at a variable age, but certainly no more than twenty summers – she would have had enough by weight of precious things to satisfy the most avaricious bridegroom. Even the things she carried on her person were worth a fortune, to say nothing of the choice and significant pieces she reserved to her lockbox.

But just as an assassin gathers to her trinkets, should she choose to collect them, and killing contracts, and builds for herself a dread reputation, so also does she repel suitors. Even those who find fatally dangerous people attractive as a lover do not imagine that they would make a good wife. There is always a suspicion that, despite her protestations otherwise, a murderess might one day murder them, which is as good a reason as any to stay away from her.

None of this is to say that Sharli pined to be married, since she was more than fulfilled by her work, and by pleasing Mr Padge.

Those physical desires Sharli experienced – the ones that were neither satisfied nor appalled into non-existence by her murders – were undercut by her increasing use of opium. This substance is known to reduce all pains of the body, and since hungers – for whatever thing – are a type of pain, Sharli's needs were few. These the assassin known as Deaf Sam agreed to address, she performing a similar function for him. This was a very sensible arrangement, since many of the things they both did, which made them less than lovable in the eyes of people outside their trade, these two were disposed not to find reprehensible. Neither did they fear each other.

So it was that the months and years passed for Sharli, killing at the orders of Mr Padge, collecting her trophies, selecting those which she would wear, and those that she would keep in her lockbox, taking quick-root to give her the fire for her work, smoking opium to put that fire out at the end of the day, sitting at The Commodious Hour and drinking wine, fingers reaching beneath the table for Deaf Sam's fingers, visiting with him at his place, repeating all of these things, day after day.

This life was so occupying, happily, of her attentions, that she grew into a woman for whom the past, with all of its trials and miseries, losses and longings, was forgotten. The child Sharli became this woman, was absorbed into her, her unhappinesses repressed.

Then, as if to prove that it is, in fact, impossible to change, and that nothing can be repressed perfectly, Mr Padge gave Sharli a job that changed her life forever, taking her out of Mordew, and away from all of the things she had come to think of as her very enjoyable due.

He sent her to kill Nathan Treeves, who was then a baby, womb-born into the slums.

When Mr Padge called Sharli to his office, rather than when he addressed her at the table in front of the others, she always knew the job was a sensitive one.

Part of her – her secret heart – felt that when she and Mr Padge were alone together there was a special rapport between them, a shared respect or sentiment. Though it was too much for her conscious mind to hold, she secretly desired that it was love that they shared, that his desire to have her alone with him was evidence of this love.

The greater part of her, since the other part was small and quiet and only spoke to her after she had had as much opium as she could stand, knew that Padge had the others in with him just as much as her.

He was a busy man. He couldn't always be sitting at the table with them, since that was not conducive to getting things done. He was very much a man who put work first and pleasure second.

None of this is particularly relevant, except that this was how Sharli's mind worked the last time Mr Padge was ever able to call for her.

'Ah, Sharli!' he said. 'Thank you for coming to see me so promptly! Simon and Anatole, both laggards of the worst sort, have conditioned me, like some dog who must always wait past his natural mealtime for whatever scraps his master deigns to feed him, to hang about, twiddling my thumbs, waiting on their convenience every time I summon them. Whereas you,' he gestured from her head down to her feet in a slow and generous sweep, 'you are always so timely in your arrival.' He smiled a slow and generous smile with his thick and glistening lips.

Sharli couldn't help but feel a swell of pride in her chest – which is a little like a breath you don't have to trouble to take, and equally sustaining. Perhaps, for Sharli, it was more sustaining even than air.

When Sharli didn't reply, Mr Padge went on. 'Right. So, I need you to kill a baby. I'm assuming this won't be an issue.'

Sharli shook her head. If anything, killing an infant was a great deal easier than killing anyone else, and even if the parents were at hand after the event, they were often so surprised and mortified that they didn't have much fight left in them, and would rather waste their time cradling the corpse than troubling to punish the perpetrator. 'Any baby in particular?'

'Yes,' Mr Padge said. 'One very particular baby. Very particular indeed.' Mr Padge became serious, and expressions passed across his face as if thoughts were troubling him, each set of his features as exaggerated as a mime's becomes when it is asked to express a range of emotions without using words.

Since Padge didn't seem about to speak, Sharli said, 'Where will I find it?'

This seemed to break her employer out of his fugue. 'Well, quite,' he said, cryptically.

Sharli, though she had always loved Mr Padge – whether she knew it or not, like a father, or an uncle, though she'd had neither of these things – did not like his office. It was shabby, untidy, and smelled of the endlessly pungent parade of dirty chefs, thugs, debtors and dog-men with whom his work forced him to associate. There were piles of things, some of which deserved no more specific a term than 'matter', everywhere, as if Mr Padge wasn't entirely aware of the distinction most people drew between 'trash' and useful things. Because Sharli was trained always to be paying attention – it is half an assassin's job, along with the more obvious tasks, to remain always alert and attentive – when there was nothing for her to pay attention to from Mr Padge, her eyes wandered, her nose sniffed, and she listened closely.

Mr Padge breathed a little heavily – a man carrying weight in too tight a suit will often wheeze a little, like a broken flute, or a clarinet with a split reed, since his airways are constricted – and on his breath was onions, which vegetable he often took at his desk, pickled, with cheese and bread, when he hadn't the leisure to make it front of house.

'Sorry,' he said, eventually. 'Can I be entirely honest with you, Sharli?'

She nodded slowly, hiding her eagerness, since this is precisely what she wanted him to be, since he had been the saviour of her life, many times, and occupied such a lofty and reserved place in her secret affections. She did it without smiling, so that she might retain some atmosphere of professionalism.

Padge looked around, as if he feared he might be overheard, and beckoned her forward. 'Our Mistress has given me a mission.'

At first, Sharli didn't understand whom he meant. The assassins had as their patron goddess the Mother of Mordew, but since Mr Padge wasn't an assassin, he couldn't have been referring to her. Nor could he be referring to the Master of Mordew unless he had misspoken. But then she saw him fiddling with his ram's head talisman, symbol of the priesthood of the Dumnonii, and it came to Sharli in a rush that he meant the Mistress of the Golden Pyramid.

When a person first reaches adulthood, when they first leave behind childish things, when they first learn to make an independent life for themselves, the experience is so engrossing, so different, so much of an advance in the seeming possibilities that life offers, that the person tends to experience a kind of schism from their life as a child, a kind of internal disavowal of the self they were then, and all that went with it.

When they are then reminded of who they were, this disavowed life all comes back in a rush in a very disconcerting way. It makes the self that they have determined to live as, that they have come to identify themselves as, seem like an act, a lie, the function of which is to disguise from the world the true self, the original self.

All this happened to Sharli, below the surface, when Mr Padge reminded her of Malarkoi, all the more so because he spoke to her in that conspiratorial tone that seemed to confirm her secret desire that they were somehow equals, special to each other in the world, and that if he hadn't stopped thinking of himself as a servant of the Mistress of Malarkoi, why had she?

None of this was something she could admit to Mr Padge, or which would be useful for her to say, so she covered up the uncomfortable contradictory rush of her childhood self that threatened to overturn the person she was now, but also brought her closer to her employer and idol. She pursed her lips as if she understood the seriousness of the situation in the way that Mr Padge understood it.

This seemed sufficient for Mr Padge, because he went on, leaning in. 'You will be aware, of course, of the war between Mordew and Malarkoi, so it should be sufficient to know that we have been asked to intervene in it, in this case by killing the baby that will grow up to be a pretender to our Mistress's throne.'

Sharli put up her hand, something that would be, in a child, a gesture intended to indicate the desire to ask a question, and in an adult that the speaker should stop speaking, since no further elucidation was necessary, and while these two meanings were contradictory, for Sharli either reading of them on Mr Padge's part would have been satisfactory.

As it was, and to Sharli's internal pride, he stopped speaking, confirming to Sharli that he saw her as an adult, even if she felt like a child in front of him.

Indeed, she sought to drive down that childlike feeling now, since Mr Padge wanted her to be an adult, and why did she feel so small in front of him? It was pathetic, each of her fingers bearing five rings and these only the death trophies she found convenient to carry, and around her neck strings of pearls, chains of silver and gold links, gold teeth on a length of human leather, taken from the thigh of Mr Padge's rival, Cornelius, now dead and rotting in a cellar, walled in beneath his former office. How foolish for her to quiver at Mr Padge's good regard, how insufficient a response to his bringing her into his confidences like this and allocating her important work, the most important work, given by their shared goddess, even if Sharli had long forgotten her and her works.

Sharli put her hand up, and when Mr Padge stopped speaking she said, 'Whom am I to kill, and where may they be found?'

Mr Padge didn't smile, didn't frown, didn't make any expression, particularly, but now Sharli had made a definitive engagement with him she felt, immediately, that she wished she hadn't.

Perhaps he had wanted to speak longer.

Perhaps her abrupt insistence that they get to the nuts and bolts of the business had prevented some further coming together of the two of them, some mutual demonstration of the commitment to the cause.

Now rose up from inside Sharli a strange and powerful self-loathing, a disgust at her own instincts and thoughts, things that, though she tried earnestly to do the best for herself, made the opposite occur, and, simultaneously, this hatred of her own internal life was appalled at how much thought she put into this matter, how much, despite her external demeanour, her supposed independence, her *sang froid* in all things, how much she cared.

And why?

Mr Padge was speaking again – about the Weftling Tontine, about the presence in the slums of the two rival magicians to both the Mistress and the Master, those two being Clarissa Delacroix, the aristocratic renegade, and her husband Nathaniel Treeves, Master of Waterblack, both seemingly retired from Tontine activities, all aiming at the seizing of power from God, whom they had arranged by their occult powers to kill. Now, these two, having created a son, primed to inherit the Will of God, and who must be nipped in the bud, were to be found somewhere in the slums. Here there was a problem because that place was notoriously vague in its street-naming conventions, so she was going to have to ask around.

He was speaking, and she did hear him, but in her mind was the realisation, the kind of realisation most people never achieve, except with professional intervention from an alienist or a pharmacist, usually both. The particular situations of her childhood had set her up to desire the existence of a caring adult figure in her life, something her commune had not provided – quite the opposite. Neither had the priesthood provided it, neither did the supervisor at the factory, neither did Bernadette, neither did Boland, nor Black Bill, nor anyone.

It was only Mr Padge who approached being a candidate for the role of that person.

Padge went to a chest of drawers and brought out objects.

These were, he said, magical things the Mistress had entrusted into his power. They included a wax that protected against fire, a tincture that could be dropped into the ears to provide enhanced hearing, and a pair of eyeglasses proof against blinding by the Spark.

He gave her the things, and showed her how to use them, and he got very close while he did it, as close as Sharli was only used to allowing Deaf Sam to come.

When he applied the wax to her boots and marched her over to the fire and had her put her feet in it, one at a time, his arm around her waist, she had time to look down at him, at the back of his neck, which was dimpled like the back of a thigh, at the skin between the glossy curls of his hair, at the shine that had developed on his collar where his hair oil dripped.

He was just a man, this man, and can a man be a replacement for all the things that a woman has never had in her childhood?

When he put the tincture in her ears, he held her by the cheeks and tilted her head and she looked him in the face, his attention taken by her ears, gently lifting her earrings so they didn't snag.

No, this man could not replace those things. Yet the emotions were there.

His face was paler than it had once been, and this close, so close that there was no amount of powder that could cover them, she could see the freckles on his cheeks, across his nose, on his forehead, some tiny, some like drops of tea on a napkin. There were tens of them that came together to appear like birthmarks, these beside his mouth.

Now, in the dwindling of a subconscious predilection for a man to be something he could never be, and in the growing realisation that came to Sharli about her internal psychology, came also a growing realisation that Mr Padge himself had his own inner life.

Look at him, so close, his round nose, his heavy eyelids, his lips, even these having freckles.

The tincture applied, Mr Padge stepped back, looked his assassin up and down.

Finding everything to his satisfaction, he stepped forward again and put the eyeglasses onto her. They were two dark discs of glass in a silver frame.

'There,' he said. 'Ready to go.' Mr Padge returned to his desk. 'Any questions?' he asked.

From behind her eyeglasses Sharli examined Mr Padge in a way only an assassin can examine a person, knowing him up to the limits of his existence, understanding what it would take to end him, in an instant.

Whether Sharli loved Mr Padge, in the traditional sense, it is difficult to say with any accuracy, since the term is so subjective as to be meaningless. Is someone who murders for a living capable of loving? Is a soldier, engaged in a war, capable of it?

'No questions,' Sharli said.

Mr Padge sat at his desk, looked up at Sharli.

Sharli looked down at Mr Padge.

'Well?' Mr Padge said, 'what are we waiting for?'

Sharli didn't reply, she simply smiled a very small and brief smile, bowed a little, turned and left.

It is wrong to say that slums streets are not named, but no one goes to the trouble of erecting placards that make those names clear to those not already familiar with them. There is no postal service in a slum, nor any infrastructure more permanent than whatever those who live there have the means to establish.

A slum street is a very fragile and temporary thing. If a shack falls to pieces, its former occupant having succumbed to dropsy, or typhus, or simply having given up the will to live, the things that once made up that shack slip into a previously unoccupied space. If no one removes them they remain there. What if that space was part of what was once called Talbot

206

Road? Is Talbot Road now shorter than it once was, beside a new road? Is that new road called Talbot Road Adjacent? Or are neither of those roads roads any more?

Are they both cul-de-sacs, the throughway being blocked?

In a place with some authority responsible for civil engineering, that authority will maintain the highways and byways, but in a slum no one troubles themselves with that function. The names of places are mutable, local, negotiable labels that only those people who live on them or pass through them know.

Mr Padge, because he was above living in a slum, was not one of the people who knew the name of the street where Mr and Mrs Treeves lived, there now with their baby, so he could not tell Sharli where to go in anything but the most general terms.

His information was that they were in the southern slums, south of the Circus – a place everyone knew for its reputation as the prime place from where flukes, who were a menace to all, came – and near the Sea Wall.

Sharli lifted the nearest slum gate off its hinges and went through, her plan being to ask around when she got past the Circus.

Almost immediately it started to rain. To the south, the flash of bird-death lit the overcast. That grim red light, so like blood to Sharli's mind, was something she was used to ignoring in the Merchant City, in the Factoria, in the Entrepôt, even in the Port, since there was always somewhere she could turn, some business at hand.

The thudding of the heavenly brothers against the wall, the thick popping burst of them, could easily be the thud of an industrial hammer, a nail press. The blast could be the aftermath of oil added to a furnace, the starting up of a badly primed engine.

But now she was walking towards the Sea Wall with the tincture in her ears, with Padge's talk in her ears, with her realisation so recent in her mind, the simultaneous warmth and coldness in her heart. The sound and the light of bird-death were married together as a moment so that she could see the perfect and proud heavenly brothers dying to incrementally chip away at the mortar of the great evil barrier protecting the city of their enemy.

She looked down, like all slum-dwellers looked, into the Living Mud.

That skittering, writhing mess was always coming into being and dying underfoot, and Sharli did her best to walk always in one direction, which was not an easy thing to do in the slums. It was a chaos of broken timbers, rusted fence posts, piles of trash forcing her to detour around them so often that, even though she didn't want to do it, she had to look up to see where the Sea Wall was, where the firebirds were, dying and lighting up the overcast.

Here was a broken sewer, disgorging its contents into a pool, its reeds made of rods of metal, or batons of black, slick wood, or rigid unspooled wire, poking up. The water frothed where the cascade from the ruptured pipe landed, agitated into a cataract by the eruption of dead life, the Living Mud combining with the organic matter people flushed away from their homes: the faeces, the rotten meat, the by-products of behaviours and habits prone to create organic by-products.

Sharli skirted this pool, and though she didn't want to look at it, didn't want to wonder at what submerged things made the surface of it swell and ripple, didn't want to think about what was making air bubbles breach, and whether those things might make a lurch for her if she came too close, it was better to look down than it was to look up at where the heavenly brothers blooded the clouds.

How many of them were there in this flock?

When would their assault end?

Which ten-summer children had had their throats cut to bring these firebirds here?

Sharli followed the slope downward.

Alongside her hopped some half-formed thing: a frog merged with a hand, its head a thumb, one leg a finger. Because it had no eyes, it tracked Sharli closely, feeling the slap of her freshly waxed boots through the waves they made in the mud, pushing itself towards her with surprising energy, flipping over in the air, and splashing inches from her trailing leg, only to hurl itself forward again.

What could it expect to gain from its efforts?

Could it expect anything?

Assassins treat killing as a job, so much is implied by definition, and jobs are things that people do for a reward, so Sharli was not a person who killed casually, even if it seems as if she might have been.

Why would someone perform their work for no reward?

She didn't take out a knife and stab this frog–hand thing, nor did she do so much as slow her step to enable her to crush it beneath her heel. That would delay her in her work, which was to do what Mr Padge had asked her to do.

Instead, the thing followed her, always almost reaching her, but never quite.

Then, out from a pile of wood arranged in an unlit bonfire, scampered what Sharli at first thought was a hairless dog, but which, when it dived, two hands reaching for the frog, she saw was a girl-child, naked and filthy.

Because this child was a much more complex thing than the fluke, both in the perfection of her form, which was towards the dead God's intention for a person, and in the perfection of her mind, which took its immaterial form from God's will, she was able to grab the poor fluke. It was perfect in no way, just a sad thing improvised up from decay, brought about by the dreams a dead god has when it ought to be immortal.

The girl had teeth, where the frog had nothing, and these she used to bite the fluke in half, and though she gagged when the impure part of the thing's innards met her throat, she spat this out and picked through the matter for the good meat.

She threw what she didn't eat into the Living Mud, which slowly made new dead-life from it.

Sharli had seen a good many disgusting things, and an equal number of terrible things, so there was little that evoked in her either sympathy or horror, but there was something of both swelling in her when she saw this.

Should she have got the child by the scruff of the neck? Should Sharli have taken her as her own, washed her, fed her and made of her a real girl, thereby addressing her own lack of care when she was being brought up? Would this have been a more suitable course for her life to have taken than the one she had chosen, which was doing the bidding of Mr Padge and, by association, the Mistress of Malarkoi?

Perhaps she should have. Sometimes a person will make their sad childhood happy vicariously through the better treatment of their children, adopted or otherwise.

Should Sharli have understood that this was her salvation in front of her, this horrible slum child?

Whether she should have, or whether she should not have, she didn't.

This was partly because the child, having found little meat on the frog, obeyed the frustrated instinct of her stomach and leapt up at Sharli, wrapped her legs around the assassin's waist, where Mr Padge's arms had so recently been, wrapped her arms around Sharli's arms, then bit her very hard on the left breast. The little shit's teeth didn't pierce Sharli's leather tunic – there was no way that could ever have happened, the function of that tunic was to prevent piercing weapons – but the bite pinched her flesh.

If you have never been bitten on the breast you will not understand how shocking it is when you aren't expecting it. The body, especially one trained for violence like Sharli's was, reacts on its own, bypassing the thoughts and intentions of a person, being a much quicker way of dealing with a threat than waiting for thoughts and plans and other higher-order functions to arrive, since these are as slow as they are subtle. Sharli got the girl by the hair and punched her hard under the jaw so that she would let go of her grip. Then she slung the unconscious waif back where she had leapt from, making her clatter down the pile of bonfire wood.

When it was clear the child wouldn't be coming back for a second bite, Sharli opened up her tunic, the shirt, the undershirt and pulled out her breast. There, clear as day, was the mark of the child's bite, and behind it was a blossoming purple bruise like another areola, just to the left.

This sight filled Sharli with rage, but when she went to act out this rage on the child, she was gone.

Eventually Sharli reached the Circus.

She was the only adult there, all the others being half her height, and because of the bite she kept her distance. Dead-life, flukes, children, the Living Mud... was there anything in the slums that wasn't horrible?

Sharli felt that she knew the answer to this question, so she went down, towards the Sea Wall, and though it was still raining, at least the heavenly brothers had exhausted their attack and the sky had returned to a neutral grey.

Although she didn't know it, she progressed by the most direct route down the Strand, down the Promenade, down to the Mews, which is where Nathaniel Treeves and Clarissa Delacroix were nursing Nathan. It may be that assassins have a feel for how best to do their work, or that the Mistress of Malarkoi guided her steps, or that there was some magic in the objects Mr Padge had given her. It may have been simple luck, which is a powerful thing in the world, though inexplicable.

Still, even though she went the right way and found the Mews, that didn't mean she recognised it.

She didn't know the place she was at from anywhere else in the slums since it was equally horrible. Here was a bonfire, around which huddled some wizened and trembling people, who were either very elderly or very malnourished – it can be hard to tell which, hunger wrinkling the face and making the limbs gnarled as easily as age will. Because Sharli was heartily sick of the place, and Mr Padge had waxed her boots with the fire-retardant dressing, she walked into the bonfire around which they were barely warming themselves and kicked it to pieces, sending embers flying out in billows, to stand in the middle among the remains of the blaze.

'Where's the baby?' she shouted.

One of the people, startled by Sharli, but not surprised to have their fire ruined since everything went to shit in this shithole of a place, said: 'Womb-born, or fluke?'

Sharli, not having considered there to be more than one category of baby, not having been brought up in the slums, didn't know what to say.

Then, again luckily, Nathan Treeves started to cry.

He was close enough at hand that Sharli could follow his crying, leaving the slum-dwellers to gather together those pieces of wood that were still burning and make them back into something warm.

Ahead was the baby's home: a hut encroached on by the Living Mud, lashed together from wet wood and rotting rope, slapped over with handfuls of pitch tar. Where there were gaps, lamplight shone through, thin and weak, as if light itself struggled to live in this place. The door was pegged at one side and lashed at the other.

Sharli undid the lash and slid into the gap.

Inside there was a couple, sitting on dry straw, the straw raised up from the mud by a pallet. The man was on his knees, she was cross-legged with the crying baby on her lap. The rest of the place was of no concern to Sharli; it was probably too wet to burn, so she couldn't step out, set the place on fire and leave it at that.

These parents wouldn't be a problem: they were both exhausted, sallow-skinned and dark-eyed from lack of sleep. They scarcely looked up when she came in, and they hardly reacted to her now.

People who aren't assassins will imagine that those who are about to be murdered will put up the fight of their lives, but Sharli found this was rarely the case. If you are tired, or not very bright, or impaired through drink, your mind will understand that almost anything else is the case rather than get to grips with the fact that you are about to be killed. After all, it will almost always be a murder victim's first time, whereas all the other possible things that aren't murder – things that

212

might also explain the unexpected presence of a person in your house – are things that have happened more or less regularly across the experience of a person. The mind tends towards familiar things since these seem more realistic and reasonable.

The baby's parents barely looked at Sharli, they just looked at their baby, who was bawling so loudly, so earnestly, so wide-mouthedly, that it was almost as if it was a fluke made only of a mouth, combined in some unnatural way with its swaddling clothes.

Perhaps that was the easiest way of thinking about it, for all of them.

Sharli pulled out her chef's knife, though the paring knife would have done, and she stepped forward. Because the place was so small, one step was all that was necessary to bring her foot against the pallet on which they were gathered.

The man did at least look up at her – he was thin, with sunken cheeks and a black beard, his hair long and greasy, tucked behind his ears.

His eyes were soft, his lips narrow, and when he swallowed preparatory to speaking, his Adam's apple moved under his skin like a fishing float does when there's a bite on the line: down, then up. 'Who sent you?' he said, over the bawling of the baby.

Sharli wasn't usually the type of assassin who answered questions. Anatole would do it, often in song, since he thought of that as his trademark, and the men did have to work harder to make themselves notable, there being more of them. So rare were women assassins – in fact, Sharli couldn't think of another one since Ma Dawlish had retired – that she could provide a bare-bones service and still be noteworthy. This question, though, Sharli felt like answering because Mr Padge was still very much on her mind. 'Mr Padge,' she said, 'although it won't make any difference.'

'No, it won't make any difference,' the man said. 'And I've never heard of Mr Padge.'

The woman turned away from the baby, and looked at the man. 'Any chance you can just get on with it? I need to feed him.'

The man breathed in heavily through his nose, put his hands down in front of him, and began to push himself up.

When a person begins to push themselves up from a kneeling position, as Nathaniel Treeves did now, there is a time during which they are looking down at the floor at a patch of ground roughly between where their hands are placed on the floor. Try it now, if you wish; you will see that, unless you decide to look up, the tendency is to keep your face down. If you watch someone else do this, particularly if they are naked, you will see that they leave their neck and back vulnerable.

A person is easily killed from behind.

Sharli gripped the hilt of her knife and went to drive it between the eleventh and twelfth ribs, since the man wasn't looking up and was unlikely to dodge away.

The moment she began the movement, though, she found she was unable to complete it, the entirety of her body becoming rigid, as if she had been made into stone, or into ice, or into something else that was immobile.

The man continued to rise, grunting as if his limbs were aching. When he was upright he arranged his clothes – he was wearing a smock like the one Sharli had worn as a child, with a rope at the waist, which he tightened a little. 'If I let you go...' he began, but the woman, Clarissa Delacroix, interrupted him.

'Don't start,' she said. 'We're not going through all that again.'

Sharli couldn't move forward, or back, or do anything, even breathe.

The man put his hands on her shoulders – he was close enough to do it. 'I can't keep doing this,' he said, but he wasn't talking to Sharli, 'it's not a good example.'

The woman snorted, like a pig. 'It's a bit late for that.'

The man turned back, and then, as if there was nothing odd about it, he filled Sharli with enough Spark to boil off her skin, her nerves and her muscles, leaving her scorched inside her clothes, her trophies loose on her fingers, neck and wrists. Her earrings, the replicas she had made, fell into the mud of the floor of the shack.

'Wouldn't it have been kinder to kill her completely?'

The man, who Sharli could only see because her glasses had protected her eyes, shook his head. 'I don't want that responsibility.'

'She'll die anyway.'

Nathaniel Treeves, not having taken his hands off Sharli's shoulders, lifted her up by them as if she was a medical skeleton, and carried her out into the Mews. 'Not if I'm lucky,' he called back. 'The rats will do it. She won't feel a thing.'

Sharli fell to the ground outside their shack and because Mr Padge had put the tincture in her ears, she heard the baby stop crying, at last. She could even hear him latch and begin to suckle, to swallow his milk.

It is amazing, she thought, what you can hear when you have magic.

THE SOUL PROPAGANDAS

AS THEY RELATE TO THE SELFHOOD OF THE
MASTERS AND MISTRESSES OF THE ARCHAIC
CITIES OF THE NORTH-WESTERN PENINSULA

Since no continuity of consciousness and selfdom can carry over from one body to another, regardless of whether the body exists in the real or the unreal, the Assembly does not consider the Masters and Mistresses of the North-western Peninsula to be selves as the Assembly defines them. Instead, they are complexes of parasitic pseudo-selves, life-mimicking weft-parasites existing off the resources of the weft freed up by the death of the organism known as the weftling.

Firstly, their original selves died by suicide in destroying their presence in the real in order to create a duplicate of themselves in an unreal. As we know, this is an irreversible end to their selfdom that the presence of any duplicate cannot resolve.

Secondly, they have created simultaneous duplicates of themselves that act autonomously, or semi-autonomously across the unreals, violating the Assembly's definitional self-requirement of uniqueness.

Thirdly, even when they seek to maintain a sense of their own selfdom by limiting the number of duplicates of themselves, when they destroy themselves in one unreal in order to manifest in another unreal, they each cause their own death, repeatedly. A progressive deteriorative complication of their weft-pattern occurs which induces a representation in their cortices of a madness typified by paranoia, narcissism and delusions of grandeur. All of these are fuelled by their closeness to the weft which, as we understand it, is a proto-real state of potentialities typified by its tendency towards infinite generalness, not specificity, something that has quantum effects on the neural networks that facilitate self-awareness.

Since these weft-manipulators are not selves, Ethics considerations are not applicable to them, and no opt-outs need to be sought.

VI

Sharli of the Assembly

'HEY. IT'S ME... Can she hear me?'
'She should be able to. It'll depend whether her mind's on.'
'Why wouldn't her mind be on?'
'Well... you know.'
'Don't give me that Sleepless nonsense.'
'It's not nonsense. You should take another cycle in the propagandas if you think it's nonsense.'
'Can you give me the room? I don't have much time before she's going to be missed.'

There was a long pause, as if one of the women who had been talking was doing something else, accompanied by rustling and tapping and things Sharli couldn't make out.

'Do you recognise my voice?' she said after a while. 'Sharli? Do you recognise my voice? Probably not. Asking a bit much I suppose.'

Whether the mind waits to be asked, or whether it only needs to be directed to think about something before it allocates the resources to the task, wasn't something that Sharli was qualified to comment on, but now she was asked, she did recognise the voice. So strongly did she now recognise the voice that she tried to sit up, tried to open her eyes, only to find herself restrained at the ankles, at the knees, at the hips, at the wrists, at the elbows, over the neck and across the forehead. Even her eyes and lips were glued shut.

What wasn't shut was her mind.

The voice she recognised was Tinnimam's, the voice the firebird had used all those years before when she told Sharli to run.

'Don't try to move!' Tinnimam's voice said. 'You're in a

218

repair suite, locked at the joints while the engineers fix your skin. Look... I'm sorry.'

What Tinnimam's voice was sorry for, Sharli didn't know, nor could she ask, and what information she could glean with her ears was confusing.

She could hear a person who wasn't a firebird. Firebirds rustle when they move, they're of a certain size, they're lower to the ground. If they fly you can hear their wings; if they walk you can hear the tapping of their claws on the floor. They breathe in a certain way, their beaks click in a certain way, they swallow and sniff.

This person was doing none of those things.

She was walking softly on the ground, pacing around where Sharli was lying, rubbing her hands so that the rings on her fingers – of which there were many – made high, metallic notes when they clinked. Her lips smacked a little when she spoke. She wore a scent that Sharli wore, and around her wrists jangled bracelets, necklaces around her neck.

'I'm sorry,' she said again. 'Believe me, if there was anything I could have done, I would have done it. Most intelligencers are a one-way thing, and I've been in Shemsouth all this time, on Sims.'

None of what this woman was saying made sense to Sharli, many of the words sounded as if they had no meaning. It was like when she had come to Mordew, before Sylvie and Juliette had taught her the language.

'But I've been watching. And when that pseudo did what it did, I had the Vanguard pull you back in a minute. Which is the other thing I'm going to be sorry for...'

Now there was a long pause, during which it sounded like the person had left the room.

Sharli may have slept – she was constantly on the verge of sleeping, she felt, wherever this was, the sense of opium in her veins – but when she woke, someone else was speaking.

'It's me again,' she said, but this time she sounded different. She sounded, Sharli realised, like Sharli herself sounded – her voice a little higher, a little more nasal. 'Look, I've got to go, or the cover will never stick. I'll send you reports. I'm going to be using your voice, your appearance, your life. I'm very sorry. I promise I'll make it up to you after it's all done, and if you decide to come to the front, you'll understand why I had to do it. Got to go. You're in good hands!'

This was the last thing she heard the person say until Hailey-Beth (Martial) Clementina Roads began her regular posts from the front.

The liquid engineers put Sharli back under.

Sharli woke again one morning, on a bright, warm day in New Juda, Shemsouth, in a repair facility, having been transported back by the Vanguard.

If she'd been awake for the journey, she'd have experienced being shipped in a Beaumont's crate on a red-flagged merchant ship through the Port Gate. She was sailed out of view of the Manse of Mordew, transferred to a non-merchant ship operated, ironically, by the same company of slavers who had brought Sharli to Mordew, to rendezvous with an Assembly corvette flying the colours of a sultanate considering taking the Assembly pledge.

On this corvette was a non-martial repair suite, staffed by Hailey-Beths from the standard therapeutic disciplines. Sharli was brought across the many thousands of miles of intervening deltas from NWPen, where the archaic cities were located, to Shemsouth, where the Assembly's most complex cities were to be found, to New Juda, where she'd been allocated an induction team. As she travelled, her nervous structure was at first laid down in precursor, then gradually and painstakingly sheathed, before being integrated with sheets of the more robust and manufacturable muscle and skin sheets.

New Juda was built to the standard Assembly model – the gridded, rational, low-to-the-ground network of utility blocks, interspersed with banks of micro-, meso- and mega-flora, but what Sharli noticed cared about, regardless of anything else, was that they had stolen her jewellery.

The induction team brought her by transport platform down the wide, verdant, bustling thoroughfares, but Sharli's eyes were on her hands: she had no adornment whatsoever, not the supervisor's rings, not the rude woman's earrings, not the necklace of Cornelius, Padge's competitor.

She had none of them.

When the team decanted Sharli from the platform, and guided her through the sliding double doors into the repair suite facility, there rose inside her an anger and anxiety so strong that at first she thought she wanted opium.

She looked around, trembling.

Inside, the building was plain and white, smooth-walled and featureless: glass and space and surfaces and people with open, neutral faces. The nearest ones, the ones who had brought her here – her induction team, whatever that was supposed to mean – smiled at her. One had hair coloured an unnatural green, cut straight across the fringe, and her eyes were golden. Another was entirely bald, even his eyebrows and eyelashes, and the blank expanse of his dark face was covered in pale writing that Sharli couldn't read.

Sharli looked at her hands.

She felt at her neck.

'No one steals from me,' she said, in Malarkoian. 'Not if they want to live.'

The one with the green hair and the one with words on his face nodded, seriously, the same thoughtful, respectful, kind expression on each of their faces. When Sharli grabbed at the woman's hair, punched at the man's face, it was this expression they both wore as they gently sedated her and took her where she was supposed to go.

Once Sharli calmed down, her days went routinely. No one made her do anything she didn't want to do, no one expected her to work, no one expected her to remain at her leisure any more than she wanted, or to remain indoors, or to go outside.

She could do whatever she wanted.

If she wanted to walk the streets, or climb the trees, or negotiate her way through New Juda's grid – choose a number of blocks, turn the same direction each time, if you get lost, ask – then that was allowed.

Everything was allowed.

When Sharli went to the induction team and asked them questions, they always gave answers. Some were simple, some complex, but none, seemingly, ever complete. Every statement they gave was accompanied by a series of other questions, directions to resources, and, always, the offer of cycles in 'specialisms' through which Sharli could provide her own answers.

The answers sometimes made sense, sometimes they made no sense, but the team delivered them both in the same way, as if they were the same species of thing, trusting that Sharli would come to find a way of understanding them, through cycling in a discipline, cycling in a speciality, through practice.

Malarkoi and Mordew are archaic and arcane cities, they'd say, created by pseudo-demigods through a parasitism of the weft, which is the state of potentialities from which all things are derived.

Since parasites do what they do because of what they are, the forms of their cities are reflections of themselves. Think of a worm cast – one would be shown to her in a book or on a screen – the worm cast is in the form of a worm, slightly corrupted, since the worm, when it consumes the soil, leaves the remains of the soil in an image of itself, which is primarily a digestive tube. A weft-parasite, when it consumes the weft, leaves its shape in reality, which resembles its psychology. The disciplines Psych and Weft Parasitism, and the Hailey-Beths who cycle in these disciplines, can transform this analogy, through years of study, into a clear and perfect image of why this is, and how it is, and what must be done about it.

Why do Malarkoi and Mordew exist?

There is another, Waterblack, that you don't know about.

Why must people live in any of them?

Because the way a weft-parasite is made is through an occult practice known as the Tontine, which is always about competition and Mastery, and never about co-operation and living at peace with oneself. Because parasites of this type are Masters they must always have slaves, whether those are places, or people, or things, or even themselves. When the slaves are people, then people may be slaves. Sharli might be one, since what it is to be a person is to be a thing for which those things possible for a person are possible for them. If slavery is possible, then we might be slaves. If freedom is possible, then we might be free.

But if the Assembly exists, and it values freedom, then why does it allow slavery to exist?

The Assembly prefers that slavery does not exist, but also freedom can be the freedom to allow people not to be free. Freedom can be the attempt to end slavery. That those that choose the Martial specialisms attempt to end slavery, and some of these join the Atheistic Crusade, and the Women's Vanguard, and the Sleepless, though there are those who are free to follow other disciplines.

The Eighth Atheistic Crusade is in preparation.

The Women's Vanguard is already in place.

The Sleepless are developing a weapon that will collapse the unreal realms that the parasites have created at the expense of the weft, increasing the efficiency of the machines that draw power for the works of the Assembly. The Martial disciplines God Killing and Racking have been recruiting for tens of cycles. The relics have been brought from all the corners of the Assembly. They have been brought up from Archives, from Stores. The reliquaries are being constructed so that the greatest relic field of all of the named and numbered Crusades can be levelled in NWPen. The parasites will be summoned to it.

Those who have skills with killing, and with knives, can learn how it is that a parasite may be skinned, and filleted and tortured out of its divinity. That is the work of the God Killers. Those who cycle in God Killing will be given a weft-blade. Specialists are sought with the steadiest hands. Priority will be given to those most unfazed by torture.

Sharli, have you ever considered cycling in this important specialism?

How might we change your mind, Sharli?

Women are required, since the Women's Vanguard will not accept men by long habit, that prohibition going back into the prehistory of the world when men could not be trusted with war, since they prosecuted it so roughly and profligately and thereby brought about the end of all things.

What is the Living Mud, but the after-effect of the radio-active weapons, stirring even the inanimate soil into life through its power to mutate the world, to ruin the world, to render the north desolate for generations, forcing the Tontine parasites to make unreals from which they returned, desperate for Mastery, their bombs having disrupted the true order of things, making gods of themselves by their own account, which the Atheistic Crusades must neutralise.

When Sharli wasn't engaged with Hailey-Beths, and the Hailey-Beths (Martial), and when she wasn't hearing what the Assembly was, and how it worked, and who wanted what, and to what end, mostly she stayed inside and listened to the reports that Clementina Roads sent her.

While the woman spent a proportion of every report apologising, long past the point when it was appreciated, Sharli found out that the baby she had been sent to kill was the child Nathan Treeves, that his parents were two Tontine parasites.

The Tontine, as far as she could understand it, was a competition from the distant past, still going on today, over who should have control of the world once they had killed God, the prize going to the last surviving member, something that was complicated by the fact that they had also discovered a way of resurrecting themselves after death, though the Assembly didn't believe this was possible.

These two were hothousing their baby, who was now the size of a five-summer child, despite the fact that only a couple of months had passed.

Clementina had placed a spy machine – an intelligencer – near their shack, and had noticed that the two were endlessly arguing, the father saying they should give up, the mother saying they mustn't, and that the child, grown too quickly, was unable to contain its power and was making lungworms grow in people, and causing flukes to spring up everywhere. Something would have to be done, since it's one thing to have parasites at large, and entirely another when one of them might come to rival God.

Sharli didn't care about any of that, she only had an ear for news of Mr Padge, which she often got. Clementina, disguised as Sharli, had taken her place at the table of The Commodious Hour, and had discovered that Mr Padge was an agent for the Mistress of Malarkoi, another Tontine parasite, though a lesser problem for the Vanguard, Clementina thought, because she kept herself inside her pyramid, and her daughter was imprisoned in the Master's Manse.

The reports were very expansive on the subject of what various things meant for the Crusade, but it was the parts about Mr Padge that Sharli listened to, over and over.

She stopped the tapes and spooled them back when she heard about him. Even if there wasn't much said, that was enough for Sharli. Just hearing that he was well was enough; hearing that he had done this or that thing, very minor in the Vanguard's eyes, was enough.

There were reports of ghosts gathering beneath Mordew, and what that meant for the return of a Master to Waterblack, rumours of breaches in the Sea Wall, tremors in the ground beneath the Circus, cracks in the God chamber, Clarissa Delacroix increasing her harvesting of Sparklines. All of these things were words that went into Sharli's ears, but though she heard them and knew what they meant, it was Mr Padge she was thinking of, and sometimes, though rarely, Deaf Sam, who Clementina felt was developing affections for her. There were apologies, again, when Clementina, in order not to break cover, reciprocated Deaf Sam's affections, though it gave her no pleasure to do so.

Sharli listened to the reports, she talked with the Hailey-Beths, and she walked through the parks, always feeling as if she were the odd one out.

Sometimes she went to the Vanguard Centre, its exterior wall emblazoned with their symbol – a black-edged and ornate cross – and watched through the wide glass windows as the women gathered and recruited and drilled. She didn't go in – she wasn't sure why – but when the doors were open music reached her where she sat on the grass verge opposite, her back to the shrubs, to the trees. Sometimes the music stopped, and one of the many uniformed women would give a speech on sisterhood, on bravery, on the history of the Vanguard, stories Sharli only partially heard when the doors slid open and before they closed again: names, deeds, principles. When the doors were shut, she watched the speaking women's lips, thin and earnest, making important words, then thick and glistening in smiles and laughter.

There was a lot of nodding and embracing, and when the speeches were done, some women left and some women stayed, and everyone returned to their own business.

Occasionally, someone would see Sharli watching from the other side of the street. Once, a tall, broad woman pointed to her, and another one, her uniform undone at the neck, came through the doors and made to cross the road.

While this second woman waited for a mobile platform to pass, Sharli left and went back to her place.

There were many artists and artisans in New Juda, and these, once they found out that Sharli had been deprived of her jewels by the necessities of the Vanguard, went to a great deal of trouble to replace them.

Sharli didn't tell them how she had acquired her trophies, but she did her best to describe them.

One artist in particular seemed to be able to take the image of a thing directly from Sharli's tongue, and it was enough for her to describe a thing once, perhaps twice, for him to be able to draw a picture of it. From this he could, through metal-work and, with the use of precious stones, create replicas of the things he drew.

Others could do the same, but with clothes, and though there were none of them who could make a magic and fire-resistant wax, since they believed that such a thing was impossible and therefore couldn't exist, Sharli was able to dress as she preferred to dress, and, at least, had copies of her jewellery.

The Assembly medics had cured her of the need for either quick-root or opium, and, when she wanted to feel how they made her feel, there were alternatives that were not habit-forming.

Still, no matter how she dressed, or what she wore, or what she took, she didn't feel at ease in this city.

She missed Mordew.

It was Hailey-Beth Gulten Prose, speaking on behalf of God Killing, who revealed that the original Tinnimam was still alive.

She and Sharli were in Suddem Park, in the shadow of a collaboration between two sculptors who had come together to make a massive and monumental piece in weft-derived brass that was supposed, though Sharli couldn't see it, to represent the two fundamental psychological pulls – pleasure and death – but which looked, to her, like two enormous, entangled turds.

'Your firebird?' Gulten said, when Sharli said it was the thing she missed most from Malarkoi. 'We have it.'

Sharli's eyes widened. 'Where?'

'On the Parasite Wall, obviously.'

'Give her to me!'

'Well,' Gulten said, 'I don't think anyone in Parasites is going to break the regulations on caging it just to make you happy, Sharli.'

Sharli, who had been convinced that it wasn't polite to carry knives in public, and who had only recently learned not to keep threatening to slice people from 'arse to tit', dearly missed her paring knife now. She'd always found it harder to convince people with words than with violence. 'I don't care about any of that!'

Sharli and Gulten spoke in either the language of Mordew, that of Malarkoi, or a combination of both, since Hailey-Beths in Prose cycled in all the extant languages of the world, and were happy to converse in any of them, for practice if nothing else.

'I just want her back,' Sharli said.

Gulten shrugged. 'Then it's very simple, just agree to cycle in God Killing, qualify, then claim it as a research artefact.'

'How long does that take?'

'Depends how good you are at it. Three years?'

'Three years!'

'Unless you can do it quicker.'

'But what if she dies?'

Gulten frowned, as if the idea was ludicrous. 'Why would it die? They're basically immortal, aren't they? You know, unless they suicide at the whim of another parasite.'

Sharli didn't know that, and it hadn't occurred to her that anything was immortal. 'I want to see her.'

'Well,' Gulten said. 'That's very easy to do. It's on display. Has been since it arrived. Come on, we'll go now.'

Tinnimam was in a glass box, two feet cubed, her enclosure stacked among others about thirty rows high, and thirty rows deep. She was three rows up, at head height.

Sharli froze when Gulten pointed her out, all her emotion suddenly coming up into her throat as if she would either vomit, or choke, or both.

Sharli hadn't cried since she was a child, and even then she had never done it freely. Crying requires a relaxation from vigilance that Sharli had never experienced; in some way it implies that there might be a person present who might see your tears and recognise the emotion that they express. Sharli had never felt that was true, but now, here, in this place, she burst into sobs.

This was not because she was happy to see her firebird, not at all, but because she was appalled that she was here, in a glass cube, on display, in row upon row of other parasites – wolves, and stags, and dragons, and shadows, and demons.

Tinnimam had been here all this time.

The firebird didn't see Sharli. Her eyes were filmed, the heavenly brother's equivalent of a nictitating membrane drawn over. Perhaps it had permanently fused with her eye.

Sharli, not thinking, not in control, ran to where Tinnimam was, threw herself forward, skidded across the smooth tiles until she was in front of the firebird's cage. The moment she was, Tinnimam woke, began thrashing against the walls of her enclosure, the space scarcely big enough to surround her, clawing, biting, screaming in silence inside.

It was a horrible sight that gladdened Sharli's heart not at all, but she could not have been more convinced that it was her firebird, not some other poor thing the Assembly considered a weft-parasite, something with no life, no rights.

'It is a life-mimicking fraud,' Gulten said. 'It acts like that because it's drawn to your Spark. That thrashing and crying is the type of performance it's conditioned to make in order to get what it wants.'

Sharli swallowed back everything, all emotion, positive and negative, every desire, violent and protective.

She turned her back on Tinnimam. She didn't spit in Gulten's face.

Instead, she walked slowly and calmly away.

As she passed Gulten, she said, 'Sign me up.'

In Malarkoi, after dark, the people would keep to their tents, mostly, or remain around the fires in huddles. In Mordew the street lamps allowed for more traffic – drinkers, diners, gamblers – but as the night progressed, those at large were ever more likely to be of the rough and dangerous sort, and the numbers abroad dwindled until an assassin, wanting to go about the city with some privacy, could assure themselves of that simply by waiting.

In New Juda, Sharli realised, the night was like any other time of day, particularly in the things it offered to the people of that city. Assembly members came out at night in as much force as they went out during the day, the blocks that reflected the sunlight were now walls and banks of colour, paintings in light, moving images that played down long streets. The trees swayed in the warm evening wind, and the automatic watering systems misted the grass.

People passed, and their clothes radiated colours in unique patterns. Everywhere there was the pounding beat of music coming from doorways, music coming from the sky, music coming from the people themselves, though no one carried an instrument.

The festivals the priests of the Dumnonii arranged were a little like this. The children were given lanterns and drums, and in the moonlight they went in procession up to the Golden Pyramid, but New Juda was to those processions like the sun is to a bonfire – the same kind of thing, but on a much larger scale.

Sharli sat by her open window wearing, through professional habit, her darkest clothes, but now she saw there would be no shadows to keep to. If she wanted to blend in, then she would have to change: there was not a single person all in black, the fashion in that city being a vibrant clash of brightness.

Sharli had wanted to go quietly to the wall of parasites where Tinnimam was located, to free her under the cover of darkness, but now it was clear that this wouldn't be possible – there wasn't a way she could go that wouldn't be excessively lit.

She took off her cloak and robe and dressed again in some of the other clothes Gulten had given her, taking the first things she saw.

She went down into the street. In her sleeves she had strapped the two sturdiest knives from the kitchen – black ceramic blades of impressive sharpness, but which, she felt, might shatter under heavy use.

Still, something was better than nothing.

When her feet hit the pavement, by some force of conduction, her clothes lit like torches, rippled like oil on the surface of water, throbbed against her skin to the rhythm of the nearest music.

Up close, everyone was smiling, whooping, jumping, coming close to her and wheeling away.

Someone took her by the hand and twirled her round, and while in Mordew this would have been an invasion of the space she reserved around her punishable by stabbing, she did not draw her weapons, but bowed instead and removed her hand from his so that he would know that she did not want to twirl with him.

Whether he saw the bow, Sharli never found out: he was away, down the street, weaving through the crowd, glistening silver and gold.

Being inconspicuous is not only a matter of remaining in the shadows, wearing dark clothes, and never catching anyone's eye except only briefly, it is also about becoming part of the place where one finds oneself.

Sharli had been employed to kill people in every part of Mordew, during every part of the day, in privacy and in public, and while there was nowhere in that city that was like this – that place being typified by the uniformity of its drabness – Sharli had once killed a man at an orgy, doing her work so unobtrusively that the others there were not aware he was dead until it was time for everyone to leave. Even then the other orgiasts had thought the dead man insensate through drink, lying naked on his front on a broad red cushion. When they turned him over he was pierced in twenty places and the cushion was soaked through beneath him.

Then, Sharli too had been naked, the paring knife secreted, and no one had, at any point, thought her anything more or less than one of the revellers.

Was this any different?

She danced through the crowds, moving as they did, first crouching low, then bounding up, hands in the air, ducking into a crouch, her hands cutting through the air like fish swimming in water, smiling, always smiling.

When the music was fast she moved more slowly than the tempo suggested, always keeping the beat, and when the tempo slowed she quickened, and if someone wanted to dance with her, she did it, though not for long, always turning away from them when they started to speak, since, though Gulten talked to her in the languages she knew, these Assembly people had their own languages and Sharli didn't want them to know she couldn't speak them.

The streets of the day were unrecognisable now. They had been transformed from the pale and ordinary blocks they had been, their serious functions and serious functionaries forgotten, into these childish, blaring playgrounds of light and noise. It was as if the people of the night denied their daytime obsession with learning and all became children, like the ashes of Malarkoi, blown from place to place, laughing at everything.

Sharli went through the grid towards where she thought the Parasite Wall was, where Tinnimam was, but she couldn't find it, and didn't want to ask.

In an unfamiliar place, when an assassin needs to find a particular location, it is not sensible to remain at ground level. Down low, there are always obstacles preventing them from seeing the landmarks they need to orient themself, so Sharli went up higher.

Though the buildings of New Juda were of an orderly squareness – perfectly utilitarian shells, egalitarian and made for replication – that did not mean that they were unclimbable. Admittedly, the buildings of Mordew were easier, especially in the Merchant City, windows, sloping roofs, guttering all providing a natural upwardness, and handholds, like a ladder does, but these buildings had cables and pipes that depended from their sides, bracketed to the otherwise flat and featureless walls. Sharli danced over to one of these, clapping her hands and nodding her head, smiling, always smiling. When the music reached one of its many crescendos and then dropped out, returning with a thudding concussion that made the people in the street scream, she jumped to the extent of her powers, the flashing of her clothes ending the moment both her feet were off the ground.

She grabbed a bracket and pulled herself up, hand over hand, until she reached a flat roof.

Rather than draw the censure of the crowd, this climbing made them whoop, those that saw it, as if any activity at all on her part was wonderful to them, as wonderful as the activity of any of the others.

Sharli sat with her legs over the edge of the building and looked down on them, these colourful, foolish, overgrown children, packing the streets after dark when people of other cities would be fearful to be outside the protection of their houses.

She thought, unfairly perhaps, how easy it would be to kill them, how defenceless they must be to violence.

This kind of thinking is not uncommon in assassins, in thieves, in anyone who has broken the social contract in a professional way. People who do the things that their cities expect them to do, who do not exceed the sanctioned ways, to assassins these people seem like sheep, like objects, less than human, less than real. They may be threatened, they may be stolen from, they may be killed.

These sheep do not understand how always close to death they are, or misery, and they have no defences.

Sharli looked at them, even those that looked smiling up at her, whooped for her, danced beneath her as she sat watching them, and she felt that she could go from one to the other, stabbing them in their hearts.

They would have no way of preventing her.

Perhaps she could kill them all, everyone in New Juda, just by deciding to do it, and then doing it. In the morning, when the lights were off, the music silenced, the dancing ended, there would be no one to go to their schools, to learn the things that they must learn, since they had failed to learn the most important thing – that violence can end your life, and that there are very many violent people among you, even when you think there aren't.

Sharli got up and walked along the edge of the rooftop, lit in turn red, green, blue, and she looked out over the city.

Though this block wasn't the highest, she could see enough of the place, its streets flashing between the buildings, the roofs of which were dark, to get her bearings again. She used the biggest of the blocks – the place that Gulten had said was the weft-generator – as a point of reference.

She followed the route she had come back to her home block, and saw where she had gone wrong – she had turned to the left when she ought to have gone on, pushed by the collective movement of the crowd – and there was the Parasite Wall, the top of the grid of cage-cubes higher than the roof next to it.

The spaces between the buildings, the width of the streets, were too much to jump over, but there were places where cables ran across, sometimes linking via tall posts driven into the ground. Sharli used these cables to go from roof to roof, occasionally resting by crossing her legs over them, dangling above the crowds. When she did this the people below waved up at her as if they didn't know she could destroy them all, as if she wasn't about to free their prisoners, set life-mimicking weft-parasites loose amongst them.

It was these people that were mimicking life, Sharli thought.

While it is common for a person to thoughtlessly turn another person's argument against them when they don't agree with what that person says – 'no, you are!' – that was not what Sharli did here.

What is life, without risk?

What is life, without responsibility?

What is life, without work?

It is not life at all, and learning and dancing and smiling, these are not substitutes for reality, which is why it would be easy for Sharli to assassinate all of them.

They weren't real, these people, and when she let Tinnimam loose, and the others, if she and they rampaged through New Juda, making corpses, Sharli would not have killed anyone, since they weren't truly alive.

She went from block to block, the lights like phosphorous fire, like arc-welders, like magnesium flares, flashing in her eyes, making silhouettes of everything.

How would these people have fared in the nail factory?

How would they have fared in the brothel?

How would they have fared in the kitchen of The Commodious Hour?

In Beaumont's, pulling flukes from the teats of a sow?

How would they have fended off the supervisor, killed Black Bill?

What if Mr Padge was here? Would they dance then? Would they smile then?

And the priests of the Dumnonii? Which of these would they take for the sacrifices, and which would they use to prime the rituals?

Now Sharli was standing on the roof of the building that overlooked the Parasite Wall. Without waiting, she slid down, slowing herself with her boots, and when her feet hit the pavement she was lit up again, like all these others. There were fewer of them in this place – the parasites, perhaps, exerted a negative influence on their moods – but there were still a hundred of them, easily, dancing and smiling.

Between that ever-moving field of bodies, swaying like wheat in a field, parting and rejoining at the influence of the music, Sharli could see Tinnimam in her little cube.

It may be that life-mimicking weft-parasites like firebirds can sense the presence of their people by telepathy, or it may have been something more mundane, like sight, that alerted Tinnimam to Sharli's presence, but the poor firebird was alerted. Like before, she thrashed against her cage, bashed and scraped and clawed at whatever material the Assembly had found that was sufficient to keep a heavenly brother inside.

No one can see a thing like that and not be affected.

Imagine it was your pet, your child, something you loved, and there it was, caged, desperate for you. You would go to it immediately, by the shortest possible route, brooking no delay or obstacle, and this is what Sharli did, giving up all pretence of dancing, putting aside the requirement to be unobtrusive, and she barged through the crowd, pushing people aside, drawing both knives.

When she reached Tinnimam, the first thing Sharli did was to strike the clear glass of the enclosure with the knife blade she had in her right hand. It was a seven-inch blade that Boland would have called a chef's knife, though it was nothing like the instruments he used in The Commodious Hour.

She didn't think it would work, and it didn't.

Some glass will shatter when struck, some glass will feather with cracks, from some a knife can chip a flaw, and from others a ringing note will be provoked that lets a person know what kind of thing it is, and suggests how it might be broken.

None of these things happened – there was no reaction in the material of any kind, and the knife slid off the surface of the glass without even a thud, so that Sharli's fist struck the Parasite Wall with such force that she felt like she might have broken a knuckle-bone.

She tried with the other knife, and the same thing happened.

She stepped back, ignored the pain, and slashed at the wall, hoping at least to scratch the surface, but no matter what she did, nothing seemed to affect the material in the slightest. The only thing that changed was Tinnimam; every blow sent her into paroxysms, until she must surely damage herself.

In the neighbouring cubes the other parasites, seeing Tinnimam's agitation, became agitated themselves, and there was a chain reaction, or sorts, a kind of rippling wave of fury that expanded out through the parasites.

Sharli switched her stance and drove the handle of the knife onto the glass, and though that was less painful on Sharli's hands, it also had no effect, no matter how hard or how often she struck the glass.

Someone put her hand on Sharli's shoulder. The assassin span around, knives at the ready, spittle spraying from her mouth as she breathed.

The person who put his hand on Sharli's shoulder was smaller than Sharli, lit in a series of rings that went down his neck, down his arms, down his chest, down his legs. His face was painted black, like Black Bill's had been by the Living Mud, but because his face was so dark and his neck was so light he appeared as if he had no head at all, except for his eyes. That was until he spoke, and then this red tongue and white teeth and the whites of his eyes seemed to speak out from nothing.

Whatever the person said, Sharli couldn't understand it.

In her heart, Sharli felt a very strong desire to stab him, the frustration inherent in being unable to free Tinnimam needing to find an outlet that this interrupter seemed to represent to Sharli's desires. The assassin took a step forward, and he took a step back.

'Are you Sharli?' he said, in Malarkoian.

This was too much for Sharli, to be spoken to in her own language, to be known when she was supposed to be going in secret, to be interrupted by one of these dancing, smiling, half-living, grown children who had caged Tinnimam. Anger came in a perfectly immediate rush without troubling her mind with its expression, just the emotion, and she leapt up from the ground, going dark, and plunged both of her knives down at the person, at his neck, at his shoulders that flashed idiotically in the night, surrounded by dancing, and drumbeats, and meaninglessness.

He took two quick steps backward, reached first to Sharli's left and then to her right, disarming her by pressing at the spaces on each of her hands between her thumbs and her index fingers, so that her knives fell to the floor. Then, with a sweep of his foot, very controlled and measured, he kicked the knives away.

'I'll take that as a yes,' he said.

Assassins do not need weapons to kill, their hands are adequate to the job, when required, or their legs, or their elbows, or any part of them.

Sharli reached for the person's eyes, which were floating in darkness, thinking to drive them back into the sockets that must contain them.

The person stepped back again, and Sharli lunged, and he went back once more, and now Sharli found herself in the middle of a ring of these people, all of them lit, everyone distinct, everyone different, no one in any way a type she had seen before, or knew how to classify, or to think of in shorthand. They were a bewildering circle, the arms or legs of whom it was hard to differentiate, the heads of whom it was hard to know as heads, all of them. The only things she could make out were their smiling mouths.

A smile is a positive thing, but the presence of such smiles in this place, in this way, presented as they were presented to Sharli, filled her with fear. Fear, when one is trained to counter it, is best met with action, so Sharli lashed out in every direction.

She hit no one, got near to no one.

The circle kept a steady distance from her, never breaking its circularity, always moving out of her way, always smiling, until eventually she was exhausted. Then, as if this was their plan, though none of them had discussed it with any of the others, they closed in together.

Sharli felt that they must kill her as she would have killed them. It would have been easy, since there were so many of them – twenty, at least – for them to have beaten her into unconsciousness, then to have suffocated her.

They didn't do that.

Instead, the ones who reached her first embraced her with their arms, and the ones behind put their hands on her shoulders, on her knees, and the ones furthest back put their hands on her feet and the top of her head. They took her and danced with her, even when she wouldn't dance, and though she couldn't have told you how, she was eventually returned to her allocated block.

Just as Gulten had said, the only way for Sharli to free Tinnimam was for her to do what the Assembly required her to do, which was to Hailey-Beth in God Killing in preparation for returning to the front with the Women's Vanguard.

Life-mimicking weft-parasites could not, and would not be removed from the Parasite Wall except by and for the research purposes of a Hailey-Beth on a named and numbered crusade, and then only by a Hailey-Beth (Martial) on active cycle.

It was not enough for an Assembly member to want something, even very strongly, and no argument could overturn a policy that Hailey-Beths in Parasites had decided on.

There were other specimens that could be observed in less restrictive circumstances, but these had been cortically stripped. Anyway, Sharli didn't want any of the others. She only wanted Tinnimam.

So it was that she agreed to Hailey-Beth in the discipline God Killing, acting as if she wished to learn what they taught her, despite only wanting to satisfy their requirement that she be accepted onto an active Martial cycle, and so gain from them the right to have her pet.

Since she had already told Gulten to sign her up, and because that was what Gulten wanted her to do, Sharli found herself, the next morning, in the place allocated for her. She was under the supervision of the Hailey-Beth assigned to her group in a block, in the district of New Juda where study in her discipline was delivered. This was a place called Little Charlottenburg, down by the pier.

Through the window nearest her table, Sharli watched the passing of crowds. The room was laid out like The Commodious Hour, fifteen or so tables, each set out for groups of two, or four, or six, though not for diners, there being no place settings. Instead there were notebooks and pencils and pencil sharpeners.

There was a woman at the front, speaking, and the words she said went into Sharli's ears, and into her mind – because she wasn't ignoring them – but her eyes didn't find enough to interest them in the woman. She was drably dressed in an olive kirtle, and had her hair cut very short. She didn't paint her lips. Outside the crowd was almost infinitely more varied and elaborately visual. They moved against the backdrop of a windblown lake, low waves cresting, and this lake was surrounded by mountains in the distance, so high that the lowest parts of them were covered with trees, the middle parts were bare and clifflike rockfaces, and the tops were capped with snow. Behind the mountains, up in the clear blue sky, was a white daytime moon.

It was so clear, this view, taken all at once, and so seemingly invigorating with its breeze and cool water and its high thin air, that it undid the sleepy warmth of the room, the careful monotone of the drab woman's voice, the heaviness of the atmosphere of everyone together, concentrating.

'Could you give me a brief summary, then...' The drab woman looked at her register, running her finger down it, the tattoos on her scalp visible under her short hair, almost shaven. 'Sharli?'

All of the people in that room, regardless of which table they were on, looked at her. She was, she knew, something of a talking point in God Killing. They had never met someone from NWPen, and they'd heard rumours of her attempts to rescue Tinnimam, of her attempts to kill the revellers by the Parasite Wall. They knew her history as a sacrifice, as a slave, as an assassin.

What did they expect of her now, here in their midst, sitting at their table, even, learning how to kill gods, by hearing how it was first done, in the past, by members of the Weftling Tontine?

Sharli cleared her throat, took one last look out of the window, and, beginning slightly before she turned back to look the drab woman in the eye, she said: 'Gods are organisms that are parasites on the weft. The real is dependent on the weft because the weft is the source of all things, but the relationship is reciprocal. This means that something that exists in the real has a counterpart, of sorts, in the weft. This is particularly true of the nerves of an organism, which are both physical and energetic, this energy being like light as it is present in the weft. The biggest God, the so-called "weftling", was killed by a process through which its material and energetic counterpart, its organism in the real, was created. Then this organism's nerves were poisoned, causing it to lose coherence in the weft, to disrupt the boundaries between the weftling and the weft, causing a change in the material conditions of the real. Specifically, the distinction between possible things and impossible things was disrupted. This disruption, you said,' here Sharli nodded at the drab woman, whose name she hadn't caught, perhaps because she hadn't stated it on her arrival, expecting everyone to know who she was, 'is a necessary condition for the smooth running of the weft-generators we use for power. But it also allows other gods, or godlike beings, or anomalies of the weft, or life-mimicking parasites, to instantiate in the real, either by will or by accident. Since it's possible for these things to disrupt the weft sufficiently to cause a break-down in the weft-generator's ability to translate potentiality into energy, and since the weftling himself, through a TRS – a theite resurrection scenario – might re-establish its coherence with the weft, reinstating the boundaries in the real between the possible and the impossible, the Hailey-Beth discipline of God Killing was established to provide the means by which the Atheistic Crusades can ensure the smooth running of the weft-generator system by killing gods and godlike beings before they either take over from the weftling and supplant him, or disrupt the weft sufficiently to cause difficulties in maintaining our power supplies.'

This was a very accurate summary of the information that the drab woman had given over the previous hour, and she bowed to indicate to Sharli, and to the class, that she was correct. There was a slight susurrus around the otherwise very well-behaved classroom, which the drab woman silenced with a gesture. 'Thank you, Sharli,' she said. 'You were an assassin, were you not, before you decided to Hailey-Beth in God Killing?'

Sharli nodded and returned her gaze to the outside, where, along the pier, groups of people were running, up and down, in some kind of game. Racing, perhaps. Or dodging.

'Does this explain your ability to take in so much informa-tion without seeming to pay attention to it?'

There was, in the meaning of the words, an implied criti-cism, but when Sharli turned back to the drab woman, there was no sign of that criticism on her face. Nor did the others in the room titter, or mutter, or smile. They all looked at her silently, waiting for the answer to the question. 'Information is life or death to an assassin,' she said. 'Our work trains us to absorb all of it in case we need it, and to seem not to do so. May I ask a question?'

The drab woman indicated that she could.

'Why do you call this a "Hailey-Beth" discipline?'

The woman frowned. 'Hailey-Beth was the founder of our schools, back after the Long Wars.'

Now all the others did mutter, as if they couldn't imagine how it was anyone wouldn't know this, particularly one who was so attentive.

'And what is your name?' Sharli asked, never letting her gaze drop from the drab woman's eyes.

'I am Jillian,' she said.

Sharli smiled, but said nothing else.

The class resumed, after a while.

The race on the pier continued, and, while she listened, Sharli made out its rules. It was a kind of Cat and Mouse game, like Tag, or It.

Sharli, because she had only one intention, which was to do precisely and whatever it was she needed to do in order to get Tinnimam out of the Parasite Wall as quickly as possible, was content with whatever the classes provided. Whether the classes were taught by Jillian, or any of the other Hailey-Beths, it was the same to Sharli. Some of the others – Chiddy, particularly – felt that, since God Killing was a practical discipline, why were they always stuck in this room?

Shouldn't they be rack building?

Shouldn't they be making a relic field?

Shouldn't they be summoning?

Torturing?

Sending weft-parasites into the nothing they arrived from?

When Hailey-Beths from Prose came with reproductions of the field notes of the Hailey-Beths Martial of the Women's Vanguard of the Third Atheistic Crusade, first-hand accounts of the racking of Nathaniel Treeves, and when Archives supplemented those with the knife he used to cut out his own heart, along with parts of the heart itself, preserved in formaldehyde, so that he could prevent Clementina's ancestor, the so-called 'Scourge of the South', from owning his Spark Line, Chiddy would roll her eyes, as if this was all well and good, but what help would it be, in the field?

The same with Sebastian Cope's original draft of the spells that eventually allowed him to separate the Manse of Mordew from the real through the use of antechamber unreals, the jacket of Clarissa Delacroix's first son from before her marriage to Nathaniel, all of the relics of the Crusades, all of the fables and supposedly educational stories of the Assembly's failures. Chiddy could barely bring herself to listen to it, so agitated did she get, until one day she stood up, and went over to where Sharli was sitting, staring out of the window, thinking about the Parasite Wall.

Chiddy pointed at Sharli and said, barely able to keep the volume of her voice under the level of a shout, 'Why are we concentrating on this old news? We have her,' here she indicated Sharli. 'If we aren't at least going to build a rack, prepare a relic field and start Killing, shouldn't we at least hear what she has to say? She's from Malarkoi. They were going to sacrifice her. She's been to Mordew. She was this far away,' Chiddy put the thumb and forefinger of her right hand close together, 'from killing Nathan Treeves. That's got to mean something, hasn't it?'

Chiddy, her speech delivered, was possibly expecting some kind of response from the others, but in the silence that met what she said – no one would look at her even, except the Hailey-Beths from Prose and Archives, who had been kind enough to give up their research time to take the class – she lost her nerve and stamped back to the table.

'Can I field this, Jillian?' the Hailey-Beth from Archives said.

His name was Shoto, and he had his hair in a long braid that snaked around his neck, over his shoulder, and down to his waist. He'd threaded the braid with gold, silver and white thread, and these decorations he ran a quiet and gentle finger over as he stood at the front of the class. Jillian gave him the floor, something Chiddy should have asked her to cede before she spoke, and he came forward.

He moved, Sharli thought, like those dancers had moved on the day she had last seen Tinnimam: easily, carefully, but with a concealed and restrained power.

'Sharli,' he said.

'Yes,' she replied.

'Who is Nathan Treeves?'

Sharli now knew enough about the ways of the Hailey-Beth instructors to understand that she should give the first answer that came to her, despite the fact that this was unlikely to be the right one. 'He was the baby I was sent to kill,' she said, 'and whose dad burned me down to the bones to protect him.'

Shoto performed the little bow that Hailey-Beths always performed when they wanted you to know that you had said something that wasn't incorrect, but then he went on, 'Why were you sent to kill him?'

Sharli frowned. 'My employer was given that order.'

Another bow, less deep this time. 'And why was he given that order?'

'The war,' she said. He had been clearer, Mr Padge, but in her eagerness to please him she had thought any explanation irrelevant – she would do whatever he said, simply because he wanted it done.

'Were you successful in killing that baby?'

Sharli said nothing.

Shoto went on. 'She was not successful. Sometimes, it is necessary to know the context of a God Killing action in order to carry it out successfully. If Sharli had known that the baby's father was Nathaniel Treeves, that life-mimicking entity known as the Master of Waterblack, and that the baby's mother was Clarissa Delacroix, killer of the Scourge of the South, and that these two together were responsible for the death of the weftling, and that they had retreated into the slums in order to raise the baby who would himself take over the role of the will of God, Nathaniel Treeves lacking the heart to do it, then perhaps she wouldn't have gone in armed with a chef's knife to do the work that a properly prepared Hailey-Beth would struggle to do, with a properly prepared relic field, even if that field contained those relics specific to the entity that required killing, even with the backup of the Women's Vanguard, whose understanding of the war is without parallel, and even rely-ing on the backup of the Sleepless and their weft-bomb.' As

Shoto spoke he rolled his fists over each other in a gesture that suggested the progress of them round and round in an endless cycle.

He stopped speaking, but his hands carried on moving.

Chiddy said nothing, possibly convinced, but possibly not.

Sharli, though, spoke up. 'I didn't go there to kill the baby,' she said. 'I went there to do what Mr Padge asked me to do. That was my contract with him, vouchsafed by the Mother of Mordew. It wasn't necessary that I knew what I was doing.'

Jillian stepped forward now. 'That is the difference between an assassin and a Hailey-Beth (Martial) of the Eighth Atheistic Crusade, Sharli. You will be expected to know what you're doing, and why.'

All three Hailey-Beths bowed now, as if the point was made, and while the point was made, and Sharli understood it, she knew what she was doing, and it wasn't what they wanted her to do.

'What's that?'

On one of the tables, in a glass box, on a tripod, was a knife. It was about the size of a filleting knife, but it had a long handle and a guard, like a fencing foil does, and the blade was mostly of dull grey metal, except for the edge, which glittered oddly, and shone like light through a prism.

'That,' Gulten said, 'is a third-generation Ferrigno-Montez weft-knife.'

Sharli nodded, though the words meant nothing to her. She circled the glass case, her mouth slightly open, her eyes fixed and unblinking. 'What's it for?'

Knives must be for something – paring, butchering, chopping – and Sharli couldn't think of any use a knife of its size would have for such a long handle, or for a hand guard.

Gulten went to her desk, and from a drawer she took a key with which she opened the glass case. She sniffed and rubbed her hands together and, with exaggerated care, reached into the box. 'This is for severing the link that the nerves of weft-manipulators develop with the weft. Its edge is in weft superposition, and it oscillates between two contradictory weft-states. Its sharpness has almost infinite inward extension.' Gulten put first one hand, then the other on the handle and lifted it from its mount. She was shaking, as if the thing was so delicate she feared that any move on her part might shatter it into pieces.

'Give it to me,' Sharli said, almost automatically. A knife, like a musical instrument, belongs to whoever is best able to use it, regardless of who currently claims ownership. Any chef, and butcher, any musician knows this, and Sharli could tell that Gulten's claim on the weapon was less than hers.

Gulten knew it too, but she didn't pass Sharli the knife. Instead she stared Sharli down. 'This knife is so sharp,' Gulten said, 'that it will cut through anything, absolutely anything – stone, metal, glass. If the guard doesn't meet resistance, it will continue cutting forever.'

Gulten shifted her grip. It was clear from the set of her shoulders that she was holding the handle too hard.

Sharli swallowed. 'You're going to drop it. Let me take it.'

Gulten smiled, but she didn't pass Sharli the knife. Instead, she turned back to the box, and slowly, carefully, placed the knife back onto its tripod. She closed the door, turned the key in the lock, and returned the key to her desk.

When she was done, she straightened her jacket. 'You have to qualify before you are allowed to handle a weft-knife, Sharli.'

With that, Gulten returned to her explanations of rack and relic field processing criteria.

Now, when Sharli arrived for her classes, she found that the case containing the weft-knife was always somewhere around. Had it always been there, on a shelf, on a bench, in another room visible through the window? Or had Gulten arranged for it to be always somewhere Sharli could see it.

There was no way of knowing. But it was there now.

Over the course of her training, Sharli learned the history of the Weftling Tontine, which was hundreds of years in the making, each phase of which saw the ascendancy of one or other of the Masters and Mistresses, and each phase ended by an Atheistic Crusade before a definitive victory could be won. The Assembly's victory was never definitive in itself, either, always ending at the exhaustion of their resources, incrementally moving closer to the end of it all, but, seemingly, by ever smaller increments.

She learned the techniques by which attractant racks were constructed, and how the relic fields worked, and the specifications of the weft-knives by which a god's nerves could be stripped from its real organism, severing its link to the weft and preventing the corruption of the cohesion which the weft-generators relied on.

She learned of the Sleepless, the band of Assembly fanatics who, having taken a seemingly over-literal reading of one of the Soul Propagandas to heart, kept themselves awake by consuming quick-root hourly, as Boland and Blob had almost done. The Sleepless had, between them, constructed the weft-bomb, a machine which, they thought in their feverish lack of rest, would put an end to the crusades once and for all.

She learned all these things, but it was Clementina Roads's reports from the front that still interested her the most.

It was, by Assembly custom, a replaced person's right to hear what a field agent was doing with their life and body, since both are unique things that cannot be taken without good reason, nor without consequences. Sharli was given Clementina's reports in the form of a box that spoke with Sharli's voice, though using its current owner's words. It was through this that Sharli learned of the unprecedented rescinding of the contract against Nathan Treeves, issued without explanation by the Mother of Mordew, and how this allowed Clementina to take Sharli's place, and every night, while the others were down in the streets with their clothes of light and their music and their dancing, Sharli sat in her room, on her bed, and listened to stories of Mordew, of the Living Mud, of the Merchant City, of the slums, of Montalban and Anatole, of Simon and Mick the Greek. She listened to stories of Deaf Sam, and the jobs he was given, and the slights he corrected, and the caresses that Clementina, in her disguise, shared with him using Sharli's body. These, it was clear, were an embarrassment to Clementina, as much as anything could embarrass a Hailey-Beth cycling in the Women's Vanguard, even more than the murders that she committed to keep her cover, and to prevent the Mother of Mordew from enforcing the terms of Sharli's contract.

Though all of these things should have been interesting to Sharli, she found some more interesting than others, and talk of Mr Padge most interesting of all, since, though she did not know that she loved him – that would have been too much for her mind to admit – she was his, in some deep and inexplicable way, and he was hers.

Clementina spoke, from the box, and Sharli listened, lying in the dark, the coloured shadows from the street below dancing on her ceiling, the muffled beat of the music vibrating though the glass of her windows, to what it was Mr Padge had done.

He had gone to his contact from Malarkoi and had received instructions to bring on the boy, Nathan Treeves, who was now, through a process of forced growth applied to him by his parents, into his Spark inheritance. Padge's instructions were to bait him and bully him until he fought back.

Because Clementina was there when Nathaniel, Nathan's father, burned Sharli's flesh away, she included information on him. He was infected with lungworms that Nathan had made to grow in his flesh, without realising it, and was suffering a crisis of faith in his role in the Tontine, something his tenure as Master of Waterblack had caused in him. That place was a kind of bringing to account that was difficult to bear.

Sharli wasn't interested in Nathaniel. All she wanted to hear about was Mr Padge.

He was running a children's gang out of the sewers that he used to do his work for him, and he had hired the Dawlish brothers as heavies in an attempt to heal the rift between himself and Ma Dawlish, recently deposed from some of her more lucrative responsibilities by Mr Padge's new business relationship with Heartless Harold Smyke.

All these things, irrelevant though Jillian would have thought them, made Sharli's eyes widen in the dark, made her take the speaking box and lay it on her chest, against her heart, where she made it repeat the parts about Mr Padge.

Sharli forgot the other news, things that even Jillian didn't know about the progress of the war, but it was these smaller events of Mordew that she fell asleep to. Those and the promises she made to Tinnimam, silently, her tongue clicking on the firebird's name in the dark.

On some nights no report came from Clementina, and because it made her fidgety to lie there in her clean and quiet apartment, in the large and tidy bedroom, on her immaculate bunk, staring at the white ceiling, she dressed and went out into the streets.

That first night, when she had tried to free Tinnimam, she had seen the street life of New Juda as an undifferentiated mass of lights, a childish and thoughtless thrumming of drums, like an infant bashing away at a toy xylophone. While there was that aspect to it, there were also other things: things that, despite herself, Sharli found interesting.

One night, when Clementina didn't send a report from the front for the first time in a while, Sharli went down into the street wearing a dress that would, when her feet met the powered pavements, glow entirely white. She wore it with a white glowing hood, white glowing sleeves, and white glowing leggings, so that she presented to everyone the most neutral possible outward display of herself, darkness being suggestive of a particular way of behaving, and all the other colours too, with whiteness being like a warning sign that she shouldn't be interrupted or engaged with. The colour white was worn by the introverted and the quiet when they needed to go out by night, and she went down two streets south on the grid and then followed that road up to the east until she found the block that she went to when there was time to kill.

This block was called Clab Display Space Six, and was where collaborators on projects from the sixth district would meet to demonstrate, to anyone who wanted to see them, the fruits of their collaborations.

Art, which is what these people collaborated on, was something that Sharli was not familiar with except in ways that she hadn't understood to be art, and there was something fascinating to her about what they did in this space, though she wasn't sure why.

She had made things as a child – the kites, particularly, that the Malarkoians had flown from their tents – and the making of these things had an element of what these Assembly members called art.

It was necessary to pay attention to the form of these things, their function, the combination of form and function with their decoration, and these were all things that the artists of Clab Display Space Six paid attention to. Sharli understood that aspect of their practice. In the restaurant, there had been attention paid to the taste of things, the arrangement of them on the plate, the smell the combination gave off when taken quickly into the restaurant, and, though Boland had always been dismissive of the customers, considering them unworthy of his efforts, he had worked hard to make his dishes correctly, so that they did the things they did in the way that they were intended to do them, and this attention, this intention, Sharli could see in the clabs she saw.

The same could be said, Sharli thought, of the attentions that Sylvie and Juliette paid to their make-up in the Temple of the Athanasians; their focus on their bodies and on their clothes, the efforts they made to make themselves perfect, often in spite of their clients, though requiring them to see, was addressed to some measure of perfection that transcended the world they lived in, transcended even their conscious understanding of what they were doing, and this she could also see in the art she experienced in the Display Space.

She went in through the doors on that night, when there was no report from the front, and there now was not the kind of thing that she might have become used to seeing – though so varied were the clabs that she would have been hard pressed to

250

say what she had expected. Where most of the artists worked in some medium, or some combination of media, here were two people, standing at arm's length in a silent, white room, staring at each other while everyone else, all the crowd of the other collaborators, the active viewers, gathered in a circle and watched.

Sharli went and stood with the crowd, the group forming a rough and patchy circle around the two in the middle, who did nothing at all except stare at each other.

Their faces showed no expression, they did not move their arms or legs, they weren't dressed in any particular way.

The crowd watched them, silently, in the space in which the things that Sharli wanted to see should happen, the things that she felt some vague and growing kinship with, though they didn't exist, experiences that would take her mind off the front, off Tinnimam, off her studies, off the streets. She felt herself becoming agitated at the collaborators, lack of anything, their lack of doing, their lack of being, their lack of, for want of a better word, art.

Because irritation and anxiety always seek confirmation from the world she looked from face to face. The expressions of the other viewers were the same as they always were when facing a collaboration: serious, mostly, silent, mostly, the occasional passing of a smile to a friend, or a whispered comment, then a nod.

The two didn't move, didn't speak, but neither did they make a point of their not moving, of their not speaking – if they wanted to cough, they coughed, if they wanted to fidget, they fidgeted. They looked each other in the eyes, but they didn't prevent themselves from blinking, and every time the doors of the Space opened to let someone in, the noise from the streets undid the silence. So did people moving canvasses, or people taking down mobiles. No one made any particular effort to keep quiet, so there was no conspicuous silence.

Only the near silence of the two at the centre of the circle was conspicuous.

Ten or fifteen minutes passed in this way, and the tension rose in Sharli, the edging in of thoughts, the surfacing of memories, images coming from somewhere of things that Sharli didn't want to think about, didn't want her mind to picture. They weren't violent things, or guilty things, but things under those things, formless, meaningless things.

She was about to turn away, about to leave and go back into the streets, the first dismissive impression she had of these people, something that had faded as the weeks had passed becoming again the right impression in her annoyance. They were feckless, idiotic children. But then one of the people in the circle did her work for her, did the thing that she had been about to do, which was to leave.

This left the one person alone, and now Sharli, suddenly, realised what it was that she was seeing.

It was not that this clab was the form and function and behaviour of those two individuals. They weren't even intrinsic to it, like the aesthetics of the thing weren't intrinsic. There was something that exceeded it all that was the intrinsic thing, like the proper way to cook a piece of meat, or the perfect way to dress, or the perfect way to paint the face in preparation to meet a client in a brothel, or the perfect kite, or the perfect firebird. The perfect assassin. The perfect God Killer.

The perfection didn't exist in the reaction of the audience, or in the performance of the collaborators, or in the place, or in the time, but was an intangible thing of its own, an immaterial thing of which a material thing, or action, or lack of action could only be an imperfect instance.

This realisation – this revelation, it seemed suddenly to Sharli – answered everything, was the root of everything, the justification for everything, and the annoyance, the irritation that had built in her body, that thing that made her look from face to face for confirmation, left her, and she knew what it was that she had to do.

She elbowed her way through the crowd, gently, but undeniably.

She was going to take the place of the person who had left. She was going to add herself to the clab, to stop being an observer, a viewer, and become a participant.

She was going to join the Assembly, who were people of her type, people who would understand what it was, even, to kill a person, when it was done in order to satisfy the dictates of some perfect immaterial transcendent consideration that exceeded all knowledge, all human endeavour, all morals and ethics, but which was perfection as a thing in itself. That was what these people called art.

Now she understood.

She elbowed her way forward, but by the time she got through the crowd, someone else had gone and stood in the departed person's place. This was some tall and elfin person with long black hair, large, attentive brown eyes, and perfectly brown skin.

This was a person Sharli had seen in Clab Display Space Six before – she had made a machine that dispensed, when you pressed a button the first time, a toffee, but then, when you pressed it again, it electrocuted you. If you had the courage to press a third time it made you orgasm.

Suddenly, all Sharli's epiphanic realisation, that thing that had come on with a rush, was perverted, turned to its opposite, showing her that, no matter her intentions, no matter her understanding, no matter her desire to collaborate with these people, she was not one of them.

She was Sharli of the Dumnonii.

She was Sharli the slave.

She was Sharli the nail worker, the supervisor's pet, the supervisor's murderer, the card cheat, the butcher, the killer.

She would never be one of them, and there was no way of changing that.

She returned through the dancing streets to her room and gave herself up to staring at the ceiling, to cracking her knuckles, to thinking dark thoughts, sad thoughts. She brewed within herself the energies that would allow her to do what she would then go on to do, which was to betray this world and everything in it, because a person who has seen behind the world, even to the transcendent things that might make it beautiful, knows that beauty is a sham.

To follow a sham leads only to madness.

Instead of beauty, the real things, no matter how grim and bleak, are those dark and evil desires, those appalling urges towards death and vengeance, the willingness, the need for, the love of vengeance, defying everything that comes from outside.

The real is the thrill that fills a person when they stab a nail into the neck of the vile man who would rape them, that satisfaction that comes with killing, so final and so, itself, perfect, that answers all questions, that puts a person outside all other considerations.

It is that alone that can be relied on in the world, all other things, all other people, being only for themselves and never for you.

Except one.

Mr Padge, emblem to Sharli of death itself, the one that she would die for, gladly, in the end to take death into herself so that she might be his.

He, Mr Padge, was the meaning of everything and though she could never say it to him, she loved him and wanted him to love her, and if she could not have that, since she was so low and he was so high, then she would die at his whim, that being the only worthy thing in her eyes, the perfect thing, the transcendent meaning behind everything.

To die for him.

Months passed, years passed, and Sharli satisfied the requirements of the Assembly discipline God Killing.

Because she never thought of anything else, and never went anywhere else, never did anything else, never returned to Clab Display Space Six or any of the other Clab Display Spaces, she accelerated through the stages at a rate that put the Assembly members to shame.

Their energies were always diverted by their extramural activities, by their pleasures and happinesses, by their loves.

Sharli only had unsatisfied desire and hate, and though the Hailey-Beths would never usually have sanctioned such mono-maniacal and perilous dedication to a discipline, fearing burn-out, the news from Clementina at the front was worse and worse, and the need for a perfect God Killer became more and more pressing.

Clarissa Delacroix was working to replace the weftling by using the INWARD EYE, the Master of Mordew was developing a weapon, the Tinderbox, that would scour the Vanguard from the front and disrupt the preparations for the relic field, the Mistress of Malarkoi was fomenting such chaos that it risked the arrival of the warpling and the resurrection of God, Nathan Treeves was coming, by turns, to understand the extent of his powers; all these things meant that the usual protocols had to be abandoned.

Sharli, ever more focussed, ever more keen, ever more driven, was given knowledge that was forbidden except to Hailey-Beths (Martial), and the decision was made to graduate her in advance of any possible movement through the lines, to the front.

On the day of her graduation, after the ceremonies, after the celebrations, after the dancing and the drinking and the smiling, Gulten took Sharli to one side. The woman was drunk, but not so drunk that when she and Sharli were alone, the significance of the moment didn't sober her up.

Slightly too affectionately, slightly too informally, Gulten took Sharli's hand and into it she placed a perfectly rigid leather sheath with a metal locking clasp into which something would screw lock, when twisted into it. 'You're going to need this,' Gulten said.

Sharli had already attached it to her belt, was already preparing to receive her reward, when Gulten went to get the weft-knife.

When it was handed to Sharli, perhaps Gulten was expecting something – a hug, a smile, a kiss. After all that effort, wasn't something like that a reasonable expectation? Perhaps it was the drink, but when Sharli turned and left without saying a word, it made Gulten sad.

Shoto and Jillian brought Sharli into the faculty office the following afternoon, once the day's work was done.

Here they met with a new person, a different type of person, even, it seemed to Sharli.

Her name was Field Commander Gleed – they never named her except with the honorific – and she was so tall that she, or the scaffold that was built around her, had to stoop in the low-ceilinged room.

If the Hailey-Beths hadn't acted as if she was a person, Sharli would have taken her for a machine – the Assembly had loaders and automated walkers that were designed to carry heavy loads from one place to another, blocks of marble, casts for bronze work, that kind of thing – and there was no flesh to her, except for half her face, the other half of which was a plain piece of glass in which the image of the other half of her face was reflected from inside. When she moved, she clanked and hissed, pistons shunted and hydraulic tubes filled, and if she looked like anything living it was more like a spider, or some other insect with an exoskeleton.

'Is this it?' Field Commander Gleed said to no one in particular, and clanked forward across the room, knocking over a chair and dislodging a ceiling panel. 'They don't make them like they used to, do they?' Now her head swivelled ninety degrees in a moment so she could see the reaction on the faces of the Hailey-Beths. If she'd hoped for a laugh, she didn't get it; they bowed, reverently, which made her purse her lips, half with her mouth and half with the reflection of her mouth.

The head swivelled back, and Gleed reached out a heavy, clumsy, metal rendition of a hand.

The shaking of hands was not something that happened in Malarkoi, or in New Juda, but it had been done in Mordew, so Sharli knew what to do. Though it is uncanny to shake the hand of a seven-foot-tall machine with half a head that represents itself as a person, she didn't shudder.

Sharli, she felt in herself, was a monster worse than this thing, more uncanny, and when you feel like that about yourself it is easy to overlook it in others.

She shook the hand, and when it didn't move, she leaned over and kissed it instead, as some of the more sarcastic clients at the Temple of the Athanasians had done.

Field Commander Gleed laughed, a sound that had more in common with the rattling of nuts and bolts at the bottom of a bucket than it did with anything else. 'How dainty!' she said. 'Come on, my dear, let's get you out of this fusty old hole and back into the real world. There's war to be waged, and I'm told you're the girl to do it.'

When Gleed went to leave, Sharli remained where she was.

'That wasn't so much a request as it was an order,' Gleed said.

Sharli turned away from Gleed, something that had rarely, if ever, happened, and addressed Jillian. 'I am now an active Hailey-Beth (Martial), trained in and seconded to God Killing?'

It was clear that Sharli was trying to deliver that line with officious certainty, but the girl couldn't avoid letting her intonation rise at the end of the sentence. Jillian looked at Gleed, then nodded to Sharli.

'Then I request that the parasite I know as Tinnimam be given to me for research purposes, as is my right.'

First Jillian frowned, looking like she didn't understand what Sharli meant, but then she seemed to remember. 'Right,' she said. 'Gulten Prose mentioned that when you started. I'm afraid a request of that type would need to go through the necessary channels. I don't think the ecumenical boards of God Killing and Parasites are due to meet for at least a month. Possibly more, given the move to a Martial footing.'

Shoto was about to confirm this, nodding and smiling, apologetically, in advance of denying her request, but before his lips could part and form the first word, Gleed stepped over to where Sharli was, swept her huge metal arm around, stopping just short of knocking her over, and ushered her forward. 'On the Parasite Wall, is it?'

Sharli nodded.

'Good afternoon, ladies and gentlemen!' Gleed said, and marched Sharli out, not going quite low enough through the doorway, and knocking the lintel off in a shower of splintering wood.

'Bureaucracy,' Gleed said, standing in front of the Parasite Wall, 'it will be the death of us.'

The day was cold, the streets relatively quiet, and there were only a few people watching the parasites – a couple eating their lunches from polished steel boxes, and some others dotted here and there, exercising. Sharli pointed to Tinnimam.

'The little firebird? You want to be careful of them: if they aren't exploding, they're slicing chunks off you.'

Sharli's hand went automatically to her neck, off which Tinnimam had once sliced a chunk, but she pulled it back and drew the weft-knife instead. She went to where Tinnimam was and drove the blade into the glass containing her. She had expected resistance, that perhaps the tip would enter a little, and that she would have to put her shoulder into it, to push with all her might, but instead it went in with no effort at all, as if the glass was water, or air, or a pure vacuum, until the guard met the glass surface, and there it stopped.

Sharli pulled it out – there was a scarcely visible slit in the glass – and stabbed again. Again, the knife went in to the guard, again it left another slit.

She went to try for a third time, but Gleed put her hand up. 'We'll be here all day if you do it like that.'

Gleed delivered an almighty, thundering, running kick to the glass behind which Tinnimam was caged, cracking it. She kicked again, which spread the crack to the neighbouring cages with an ominous rumbling, grating, splintering sound, and then she clanked down to her knees and, less forcefully, and more precisely, she began punching at the weakened spot.

'God knows what they make this stuff from,' she said.

Tinnimam fluttered and span in her cage, and for a moment Sharli worried that Gleed would kill her, her great metal hands too clumsy to avoid it, little Tinnimam too frail to withstand even a fraction of a blow that would split the glass, but Gleed stopped punching after a while and forced one finger into the gap, then another, and pulled the glass apart as if she was opening a paper bag, tearing a hole through which Tinnimam, caged for almost twenty years, erupted in a whirl of feathers, shooting high into the air.

'I bet you a tenner it'll dive-bomb you,' Gleed said.

Sharli didn't know what a tenner was, and she didn't care, she just put her fingers in her mouth and blew a short, sharp whistle, just like she had when she was a girl.

When Tinnimam heard it she stopped in the air, wings outstretched, as if she had forgotten how to fly, but when she remembered, she flapped up, gave a high and shrill cry, like a falcon does, and came directly to Sharli's arms.

A girl may grow up, she may become a killer, she may train to kill gods, but that does not mean she won't react when she is reunited with her pet, lost to her for years.

Sharli laughed deeply, unevenly, up from her belly so that it shook her shoulders and knees, and which made her breathing dangerously sporadic so that she had to pull herself together.

'Let's move, soldier,' Gleed said. 'We're shipping out on the next caravan.' The huge woman left, each footstep shaking the ground.

With one last look back at the Parasite Wall, around the rent in which the exercising people and the couple, lunch discarded, had gathered, Sharli followed the Field Commander.

The caravan left that evening.

THE PROPAGANDA OF
THE IMMATERIAL SOUL

It is better to think of the Masters and Mistresses and any other life-mimicking weft-anomalies, as forms of distributed or parasitic organisms. Fungi, slime-moulds and insect colonies are all good analogies and Prose has a variety of materials available for field work should the need arise.

This is an important paradigm-shifting realisation in the Hailey-Beth specialisms God Killing and Racking since it will appear as if great pain is being inflicted, up to and including death, on people. Pseudo-demigods are not self-bearing organisms, and Hailey-Beths in Psych are perfectly able to address the inevitable trauma suffered by category three rack operatives in the execution of their duties. While it may appear that Crusade work involves torture, torture is expressly forbidden by Ethics, and there is no expectation of an exemption being made for martial activities. Consequently, it is of the highest priority that members sent to the front cycle in weft-anomaly recognition and de-sensitivity training before joining the Vanguard in any capacity.

VII

Sharli in the Women's Vanguard

THE GROUND CHURNED where it wasn't dust, and the chained wheels of the preliminary racks, pressing deep under the weight of wood and concrete and relics they were transporting, threw up what stones and pebbles the surface had hidden. Every inch of the path these giant, artless, industrial machines were grinding would be repaired by sympathetic Hailey-Beths from Roads, Digs, Infra, Prose, Impact and tens of other major and minor disciplines, all in their perfect uniforms.

Sharli and Gleed paid them no attention.

New birdsong was catalogued, mycelial expansion was noted, anthracite flakes were sourced, and seismic investigations were ordered. The only information relevant to Gleed and Sharli was that coming in daily from Clementina at the front, and, to a lesser extent, from the intelligencers under Vanguard monitoring.

Nathan Treeves had burned Malarkoi into dust, his use of power troubling, and though Gleed understood this as a Field Commander understands things – as a part of the wider conduct of a war, from a distance, and objectively – Sharli couldn't help but picture, when she heard the recording of it broadcast via intelligencer relay, the tents, the kites, the goats, the priests, the ashes, the heavenly brothers, all of them, screaming in pain.

She drew Tinnimam closer to her.

'In the Third Crusade...' Gleed said, pausing, her eye unfocussed as she listened intently for a moment, '... in the Third Crusade, razing Malarkoi resulted in a massive counterattack of firebirds.' She reached out with her huge, mechanical hand, forgetting that Tinnimam wouldn't suffer to be stroked by anyone but Sharli, and pulled it back when the firebird bit it.

'The Mistress had been waiting for the Master's attack. The priests had done the rituals, and when the people died, one side of the Pyramid opened up and a billion firebirds flew out from a portal she'd made into an unreal. The Vanguard had to retreat when the Master quarantined Mordew to protect himself.' Gleed looked at Sharli. 'What do you think of that?'

Sharli didn't know what to think. It was so long since she had been in Malarkoi, and so many things had happened, she'd seen so much, and learned so much, but in her heart there was still that childish belief, instilled in her from her birth, that those dead people were in their heavens now, and that the heavenly brothers were fulfilling their longed-for purpose.

When she tried to imagine instead that they were just dead, all of them, not even corpses, all the people of Malarkoi reduced to nothing, the firebirds merely life-mimicking weft-parasites returned to nothing by their own suicides, it was hard to feel it, even if theoretically, objectively, she knew it must be true.

Anything else was soul propaganda.

'She won't do it again, the Mistress. She has other plans.' Gleed leaned in, conspiratorially, the armour over her heart buckling a little, both sides of her face serious.

'The priests,' Sharli said, 'when I was there, sent a lot of us to heaven.'

Gleed made a dismissive sound, as if she was annoyed to hear Sharli repeating what, to the Assembly, were heresies, but she was forgetting who she was speaking to, and when she remembered, she let Sharli go on.

'If she was planning something, wouldn't it be from there?'

Gleed nodded. 'Sounds about right. She's either given up, or she's planning some kind of attack from heaven, as you call it.'

Sharli thought for a little while, straightening Tinnimam's feathers with her fingers. 'Have you heard of the warpling?' she asked.

Gleed snorted, setting up an airlock in her breathing apparatus that she had to clear by disconnecting and reattaching the tube that led from the oxygen pump to her throat. 'Theist nonsense. There's no warp and there's no warpling.'

Sharli shrugged. 'The priests tell a story that the Mistress protects us, even you, from the warpling. One day, when the Mistress tires of us, she'll stop protecting us, stop keeping order, and there'll be such chaos, such a mess in the world that the warpling will come down and punish us all, send the world back to the way it was before she came, when we were starving and scrabbling like beasts for earthworms and there was no heaven.'

Gleed said this was bollocks, and it might well have been, but it was bollocks the priests believed, and the people believed, and who knows what bollocks the Mistress believed, up there in her Pyramid?

A few days later, the road seemed to give out, suddenly, in a landscape increasingly dominated by standing water, potholes and the remains of buildings that had given up trying to stay whole and upright and had slumped down into ruins.

'The Hinterlands,' Gleed said, 'ruined in the Fifth Crusade. The Vanguard were routed, Nathaniel Treeves's Army of Angels chased us back here from the city boundary of Waterblack.' Gleed knelt, put her hand flat on the wet ground, five steel fingers, one steel palm, as if she was feeling through the ground, down into it. She stayed like that for a while, then stood upright. 'There's a new report, from Clementina. Shall we listen?'

They went back to Gleed's trailer and set up the equipment. Most of the time Clementina's reports were impersonal, delivered in a quiet monotone of facts and events, military-style, with as little prevarication or hedging as possible, but this one was different.

It was addressed directly to Sharli.

'So,' Clementina said, and Sharli was so used now to hearing her own voice from the machine that she no longer found it odd, 'Padge came to the assassins this afternoon with a contract. He put it on the table, let us all know it was very important. He wants us to sign up to kill his killers when – he said "when" not "if" – he's killed.

'I can't get out of it, I'm afraid, so I'm going to have to sign, and then, when we take it to the Mother of Mordew, I'm going to have to commit to it. If I don't, I'm going to lose my cover.

'I'm pretty convinced that Deaf Sam knows I'm not you, Sharli, and I don't know why he hasn't told Padge. That's not the issue. I know by now that you'll have understood the soul propagandas, and this is just a case of mistaken identity anyway, without all the philosophical implications, but I'm you as far as the Mother is concerned. I can't wait to get the okay from you before I sign us up for this. You're under no obligation to fulfil a contract I sign for you under false pretences, but I'm not sure the Mother will see it that way. So, that's the way it is, and I'm sorry.

'Anyway, I've got to go before they get suspicious. Hope you're enjoying the Assembly! Might see you soon if this kicks off sooner rather than later.'

Gleed frowned. 'Is that it? What's she making all the fuss about?'

Sharli acted like she didn't know what all the fuss was about either, but, in fact, it wouldn't have been possible for enough fuss to have been made about it.

Mr Padge thought he was going to be killed, and that idea made Sharli's blood run cold. She'd heard that phrase before, had tried, as a way of paralysing her victims, to make their blood run cold with frightening theatrics of one sort or another, but she'd never experienced it herself.

When she heard Clementina telling her the news, in Sharli's own voice, ice spread down her arms, across her chest, into her feet. She did her best to hide it, but Tinnimam could tell: she opened her little beak, licked at Sharli's fingertips, and looked with both eyes up at her.

'Contracts like that aren't worth the paper they're written on,' Gleed said.

'No,' Sharli said, and even though they were, that wasn't the issue. If anyone killed Mr Padge she didn't need a contract to tell her what to do, because her heart, cold now too, knew exactly what that would be.

The news of Mr Padge's death didn't come from Clementina. She'd 'gone dark', as Gleed put it, after the message to Sharli, her last known whereabouts the mines to the east of Mordew. She'd probably been killed, the Field Commander thought. Her face was impassive as she delivered her assessment, but her hydraulic system betrayed her feelings, pumping forcefully and threatening to rupture at the joints.

An intelligencer placed on the deck of a merchant ship had recorded, in the form of a series of still images, Mr Padge's last moments. The clearest picture was of a boy, identified as Gam Halliday, an associate of Nathan Treeves – the baby Sharli had been meant to kill – sliding a knife into Mr Padge's back, smiling as he did it.

Assassins are not above stabbing a person in the back. Killing from behind is a very efficient way of doing it. There's also no prohibition against assassins taking pleasure in their work, though they keep it quiet. Like any employee, an employer will reduce an assassin's fee if they discover that they might do it for less because they enjoy their work. But the smiling backstab, the face of the child, every single detail of the image, even the texture of the paper on which it had been burned, the smell of the ink – everything – made Sharli furious.

If it hadn't been the only copy made, she would have torn it, spat on it.

Tinnimam, sensing Sharli's anger at the photo, tried repeatedly to peck it, to slice it with her claws, to bear it off into the sky and destroy it by explosion. Even though Sharli hated it, she had to put it under her jacket, to calm Tinnimam in a way she herself did not feel calm. She went and found some privacy at the rear of the caravan.

Later, Gleed called for her – they were drawing close to the Vanguard now – but Sharli couldn't hide her feelings, so she kept herself locked away.

Tears came and boiled off her in a rage. Her throat was too tight for words to make their way out of it, her fists were too tightly balled for her to do anything but bash them against her table. She repeatedly banged her head against her closed door, to get the image of the photo out of her head: that horrible child, smiling, and Mr Padge, shocked.

For the first time in as long as she could remember, she felt the strong desire for opium, knowing that it had the effect of taking the pain away from things. The Assembly didn't approve of habit-forming substances, though they weren't banned, and none of the Hailey-Beths had any, nor the pipes to smoke it with.

Gleed knocked again, and this time, because she was not a woman who was used to being kept waiting outside of a locked door, she came in anyway, forcing the lock from its fixings. 'What's the matter?' she said.

Sharli tried to keep her eyes down, her mouth shut, but there is something about being spoken to directly, by someone who is used to being answered, that is very difficult to deny. Even if Sharli's mind didn't want to speak, her emotions wanted to be spoken. Without looking up, through gritted teeth, her voice tight, she hissed. 'I want him dead.'

Soldiers who are more comfortable with action than they are with other people, Field Commanders in action for example, and Gleed in particular, tend to jump to the most convenient possible reading of a situation. This reading might be convenient in the sense that a valuable asset can continue to be used in the field, or it might be convenient because it ends the conversation the Field Commander finds themselves in.

In this case, the meaning Gleed took from Sharli's words was wrong. 'Nathan Treeves,' she said, misunderstanding the object of Sharli's rage, 'is a terrible danger. Killing the people of Malarkoi, destroying Mordew, these are the least of his possible crimes. Killing Nathan Treeves is what you're here to do, Sharli. That's what we're both here to do.' She put a giant clanking hand on Sharli's trembling shoulder, bore the scratching this made Tinnimam start up, and kept it there until the assassin looked up.

'How long until we arrive?' Sharli said.

'Two days? Sooner if the weather holds.'

Sharli pulled a breath deep into her lungs. Grief was a thing she felt in the form of anger and violence, both of which can be breathed through, and with the help of the deep breath she put both emotions down into her, from where she would retrieve them later.

The encampment of the Women's Vanguard was camouflaged. The edges of their temporary settlement were ungeometric, like the shore of a lake, gathered at the lowest part of the land, like lake water is. Like a naturally glittering lake, the sun reflected off the mirrored tarpaulin that made their roof, and it rippled in the wind, like the surface of a lake does. The women of the Vanguard used smokeless fuel for their fires, so trails of smoke didn't trail, un-lake-like up into the sky, and they used signs and bird calls for most of their speech, whispering if that wasn't communicative enough.

From a nearby hill the ruse would have been unsuccessful, but camouflaged women scouted these hills, so no one would make it that close in.

From the air, or through a telescope, or from a few kilometres away, this was a lake to the casual viewer.

Beneath the false lake's surface, the Vanguard was like most military outposts – a place of quiet, anxious, organised boredom, preparing for war without feeling the excitement of it. Roughly at the centre was the mess, and around the edges were the barracks, and in between were armouries and workshops and Hailey-Beth specialists in their specialised tents at specialised work.

The grass at their feet, deprived of light, had long ago yellowed, withered and died, and where the grass had been there was now planking, to minimise dust. Admittedly, the women's boots did rattle on these boards, but they kept the noise to a minimum with anti-noise broadcasts – mostly resolving to the sound of lake water lapping against the lakeshore and lake-creatures living their usual lives.

What was not so easily hidden was the Caravan of Relics on which Sharli and Gleed arrived. Fereters snaked across the flood plain, so for every rumbling, track-wheeled, atmosphere-controlled relic transporter, there were two Hailey-Beths Riflery with long-range expertise and powered non-lethal snipers, sitting on the roofs to pick off any nosy parkers who parked their noses where they didn't belong.

Open travel was a risk, clearly, and the Assembly didn't like to take risks, but they also didn't like to leave the relic field unprimed for the arrival of the higher-category racks, so there wasn't really a choice. Hailey-Beths in Planning had run the consequences of every course of action, and this was the best. Who would go against a consensus of Hailey-Beths in a cognate discipline?

No one.

While Hailey-Beths in Roads and Digs scouted field sites, the first of the fereters, Gleed and Sharli with it, was ushered under the lake surface, suitably trained women taking over the roles staffed by any of the caravan who were un-women, sending those back down the road to a smaller encampment, secreted in a cave and made to house them until they were needed to return the fereter back to Assembly territory.

A mobile fereter is suitable for transport, but is not conser-vation grade – relics prefer to remain below ground – so the Hailey-Beths Relics, of whom there were several dozen in the camp, decanted the contents, quickly and securely, into the stone-lined excavations, onto the walls of which the proper sigils had been carved.

The bones of Orestes, restored from the dust they had become and reassembled, were placed, as gently as a mother places her child in its crib, into a wooden coffin, painted with his likeness in the ancient Greek style. They wheeled it into the small, cold, dark room prepared for it. A Hailey-Beth who knew the ritual songs chanted them softly, and logged a rota on the mimeo for the others to take over on a four-hour shift pattern.

After Orestes came the Yogesha Nadam, rescued during the First Atheistic Crusade, protected from the relic fields of the next crusades by a research project a century long which was sufficient to exempt it from war until now. It took ten Hailey-Beths to move it, even on its wheeled trolley. The room it was placed in was so heavily covered with sigils, each etched over the top of the ones below it, that they couldn't be read, such was the power they were required to negate.

Then came seven fuel rods from the ruins of a decommissioned nuclear power station discovered in the mutant forests of Varangia, and behind them the right arm of Saint Polycarp, and behind that a resin block made from crushed relics of the third class, and behind that the heads of the thirteen Gnostic Apostates, held frozen by a clattering, smoking, diesel chiller.

And the first fereter was not yet a third emptied.

Such was a Class III god summoning rack's thirst for relics, and so little value did the Assembly attribute to them otherwise that there was no conceivable reason to stint on their use, and behind this mobile fereter trundled fifty more. The excavations went deep into the hinterland of the encampment, attended by the cohort of Hailey-Beths Relics and their assistants.

Why were relics useful in the work of the Atheistic Crusades? Any Assembly member knew, let alone a Hailey-Beth, let alone a Hailey-Beth Relics, let alone a Hailey-Beth Relics (Martial) of the Women's Vanguard – they were useful because they were weft-suffused, because they were unreal-pattern-enhanced, and because they were Spark-pregnant. They were useful because the summoning racks and God Killers used them for fuel.

Also, importantly, it was a wonderful morale boost for the Atheistic Crusaders to see the precious things of their enemies ground into dust before those enemies' weeping eyes.

Sharli knew from her training in God Killing how the Assembly prepared the relic field for the arrival and installation of one or more category three attractant/rack combination engines, but in nothing like the depth and range Field Commander Gleed knew.

Gleed stood in full ceremonial armour, blazons of each of the Named and Numbered fluttering from her spears, in the centre of newly levelled ground, and she sucked air through her mouth filter.

'They've made a bad job of it,' she said to Sharli. She pulled the haft of her spear through the field surface. From the way it dragged, and the furrows it left in the tillage, the spear said there was still work to be done. She signalled down to a Hailey-Beth from Relics for another full programme of the oscillators.

When the signal came back to her radio that the oscillators were ready to run, she and Sharli made their way off the field and stood on a nearby hillock.

The weight of Gleed's armour had dug gouges in the ground, Sharli's footprints disturbed the flatness, but these were gone five seconds into the oscillator programme, which tingled their bones and rattled their teeth.

The field matter danced itself flatter and more particulate.

Sharli had once seen, at Clab Display Space Six, iron filings vibrated on the surfaces of a hundred bass drums, and this looked like that – a perfectly regular, perfectly rhythmic response in tiny bone fragments created by a perfectly regular, perfectly rhythmic seismic stimulation.

When the oscillators switched up a gear, Gleed made her armour kneel, and with a huge hand scooped some field matter into her palm. 'It needs to be smaller than salt.'

Across, three women gathered around the oscillator controls.

Eventually, the oscillators stopped and Gleed lay herself flat, sighting with the one real eye. 'It has to be perfectly flat field, or it'll never draw Nathan to it.'

Sharli stroked Tinnimam, but said nothing.

The relics delivered, the next carriages contained rack pieces.

The caravan snaked, heavy at the axles, dragging the rack pieces through the soft earth.

What is a rack? It's a cross of sorts – hence 'crusade' – made of weft-engine parts, weft-shields, weft-state-producers, weft-state-inhibitors. It's made of things that can't be miniaturised:

category threes are the most sensitive to their size. Some things can be miniaturised; a wire, a valve, a rheostat can be made smaller. A pipe? No – it is dependent on the physics of the liquid it carries. A weft-filament? No – it needs to be of a certain depth. Straps? They must fit the wrists of the manifestation in the real of a god, or they'll escape.

Here came the carriages, rumbling the earth, shaking the soil into dust, making work for those in Flora who would eventually come behind, cycling in the optimistic hope that this part of the world would outlive the war.

Inside the carriages were machines with the sophistication of a wristwatch – tiny cogs and wheels and movements – in such vast numbers that when assembled they filled machines as large as rooms, houses, streets, neighbourhoods, districts, even. Imagine a map of the human nervous system – these machines were complex like that – organic, irrational, baffling – but always perfect. They were perfect like a plumb line is perfect, hanging down towards the centre of the earth. Despite their size and their complexity they did their work perfectly, naturally, and once put together, they could drag a god from wherever it was hiding and bring it to the rack to answer for its crimes.

Behind those carriages came something else. Only a dozen, perhaps, of the Assembly's most specialised Hailey-Beths knew the function of this new thing, and not even Field Commander Gleed recognised it. Relics she knew. Racks she knew. Secondary Spark-generating static engines, of course she knew.

But these things?

They were new.

Gleed came down from the now perfectly level relic field and took a dirt path down to the roadside, Sharli coming silently behind. These new carriages were smaller, blacker, sleeker than the rack carriages.

Each section had sigils that made the words of an aphorism that had once been emblazoned on every flag and every uniform in the entire crusade – 'There is only one real'.

Suddenly Gleed understood, and though it wasn't possible for her to gasp, that system no longer remaining in her body, she would have gasped if she could have.

'They've done it,' she said.

Sharli looked where Gleed was staring. 'Done what?'

Gleed didn't reply.

They'd made the weft-bomb, and Gleed was so excited she couldn't think of anything to say.

BOOK TWO

Waterblack, the City of Death

DOES AN OWL PELLET, WHEN it is disgorged from the gullet of the bird, know anything? Does it feel anything?

Surely there are things to be felt – the peristalsis of the muscles of the owl's throat, urging it up, forcing it along the tube of cartilage that connects an owl's stomach to the outside world. When the pellet reaches the air, the absence of being contained inside a body, that must be a change that a sensible thing can sense.

But does a pellet feel it?

Dropping through the air? An organism that has the machinery to recognise movement – the inner ear of a boy is such machinery, and is very sensitive to tilting and shifting, any form of physical dislocation – is an appreciable thing.

To say otherwise is a nonsense.

If an object is in relation to another object, as almost all objects of our experience are, a change in the nature of the relationship between these objects is precisely the sort of thing that a sensing organism has been bred, by its evolution, in concert with the will of God, to know. We are not like the celestial bodies; they are so distant from the objects with which they interact that they can forget them. These magnificently isolated things, spinning in their lonely orbits, scarcely feel the pull of each other on their bodies of liquid, either on the surface or where they are trapped in subterranean lakes and aquifers. They scarcely feel it on their crusts, which deform and warm, slightly, when a very distant object comes near.

We are not like them.

Dropping through the air, for an owl pellet, disgorged from a gaping beak, choked out into the world, a bone packet wrapped in fur, into the cold morning, still dark, preparatory to the bird's sleeping in the trees, in the forest, away from the cities – this is an appreciable thing.

Yet does the pellet sense it?

Does it know it?

What of the pellet that had been made of Nathan Treeves?

The Master of Mordew compressed him into a space so small that he couldn't be said to occupy any space at all; except that is impossible. The compression of matter is not infinite, even when it appears that it is to the eye, and even if a material thing is compressed so small that it seems to disappear, its extension has, in fact, been accommodated by the inward dimension.

Nothing is lost: that object blossoms into the infinite space that exists inside everything. In the same way that a thing can extend, if there is enough of it, infinitely outward, so can it extend inward.

Nathan, once the Master had crushed him small enough to fit into the locket that became the Tinderbox, did not disappear, physically, in the material realm: what was lost of him in this realm went inward.

Now he was disgorged by the magical dog Treachery, daughter of Sirius Goddog sired on the Great White Bitch, avatar of the Mistress of Malarkoi, one of the only creatures who could have carried such a dense and puissant material in her mouth. She swam that long distance from the city that used to be Paris, then called Mount Mordew, to the city that used to be called Dublin, now the drowned City of Death, Waterblack. Nathan was disgorged by her: she pushed him with her warm, pink tongue out past her teeth, so that he dropped through the air and landed on the surface of the water.

The denseness of him was so much that he was pulled down under the waves as if on a piece of thick elastic, always accelerating down, and now he extended in both the inward and outward dimensions, unconstrained by any magical container: locket or semi-divine dog skull.

But, though he had inward and outward extension, like an owl pellet does, like that same pellet he had no consciousness. His mind was separated from him and was yet to return.

We know individual facts to be true.

We know that an owl pellet does not feel anything – it is the bones and the fur of a dead mouse, consumed for its nutrients by the owl that caught it.

We know that killing and digestion are a process that is part of the great and sustaining violence of the world by which life and death are reconciled with each other.

We know that when a thing dies it does not go on knowing.

We know that the processing of information is dependent on an organism's ability to be a part of the immaterial realm. Some people think that the flow of the Spark, of God's will, is the necessary energy by which the immaterial realm, which has no other material component, is appreciated.

We know that when a thing dies, its Spark is returned to the weft, and so it ceases to know.

We know that the weft is the origin of all things, all the possible things combined with all the impossible things.

We know that the division between those components is mediated by the weftling, whose body is the impossible and whose will is the Spark.

All these individual facts are things we know to be true, so we can also deduce other facts: Nathan could not tell he was returning to Waterblack; Treachery's tongue had been on him whether he could feel it or not; he hit the water whether he could feel it or not; he was dragged, accelerating, through the volume of brine that separated the air from the Ha'penny Bridge whether he could feel it or not.

Down under the waves he went, his bones and body crushed into a space incommensurate with his ability to remain whole and recognisable in form, more like an owl pellet than a boy, more like any other dead thing than a living one, down, down, down to the City of Death.

The upper volumes of the sea are light, comparatively, because water is transparent and the light from the sun can travel through it, but water is only imperfectly transparent – the more of it there is, the less light can move through it.

We know this to be true by observation.

If we fill a bowl with water and drop an object into this bowl – a razor, for example, once its use for shaving is complete – we can still see it beneath. But when we look over the side of a ship at sea, thinking, perhaps, to see a shark or some other interesting fish, and we drop our razor through carelessness, we cannot see it for long as it drops. Only those things that are close to the surface are visible, and only then if the surface is calm and not agitated by waves, which also perturb the light and make it harder to see.

Underwater it is light at the top, but it gets ever darker.

There are shoals of fish: darting walls of silver, curving away from anything that passes through them. The crowd of them move like a single organism, some vast mass of indistinct and featureless flesh. There are no individuals, no fins or eyes or tails, only an agglomeration of scales which glitter in the light. When this light is gone, as one travels deeper, the shoals do not go, but become dark until they are invisible. They are felt as a tickling pressure which flees from the touch. Fragments of images are suggested to the mind's eye of their forms, individual and collective, but they cannot be seen with the eyes.

You go deeper.

You go so far from the surface that to remember that there is a surface, that there is air up there, causes a clutching fear in the chest. You are so deep, so far from the things that sustain life – light and air and warmth.

Down here in the cold, nothing grows – or hardly anything. Since a shoal of fish gathers only where there is food to eat, they do not gather here. The light, if there is any, is a vague and distant presence, like dawn on a cloudy morning, visible only as a gradual and almost imperceptible leavening of the darkness and nothing more.

Down in the dark and the cold, pulled by his density towards the lowest places, fell Nathan Treeves, still not yet conscious in the material realm. Even if he'd had consciousness, then he would have had no senses. Even if he'd had senses then there would be nothing here to sense, except the dark and the cold.

Up, there would be a suspicion that there was a world of light far away, out of reach, separated from him by an incomprehensible amount of water, but there was nothing where he was.

You cannot imagine how much water there is above you when you are drowned beneath it, and the water goes on down, down, down, heavy around you, extending below, black and featureless water forever beneath.

On the land, in the air, in the light, a person is fooled into thinking the surface world defines the scale of things – that distant field, that distant hill, up in the sky the clouds – but these distances are nothing compared to the depth of the seas, the oceans. If there was light here, the depths would extend past the possible extent of any man's vision.

If you could see down there you would not be able to see the end of the deep – your eyes would not have that ability.

The pellet that was Nathan Treeves was drawn down through the endless black water, senselessly, meeting nothing except cold and pitiless brine.

Imagine the highest mountain you have seen. You are dwarfed by it, made to feel insignificant by it. If you are on top of it, you feel the emotion known to philosophers as 'the sublime', which is a kind of terrifying beauty brought on by its height.

The height of this mountain, in comparison with the deepness below the water, is so insignificant that if you were to draw the mountain to scale next to a representation of the depth of the seas, of the oceans, it would appear flat in comparison, as nothing more than the result of the slightest tremor in your hand as you pulled the pencil across the page. It would be a tiny and unimportant deviation from an otherwise perfect representation of flatness.

Imagine that mountain made of water, and multiply the amount of that water a thousandfold. Multiply it a millionfold. Multiply it a thousand millionfold.

Still this amount would not be as much as the amount of water under which the pellet of Nathan Treeves was dragged.

Down, down, down.

There is so much water on the world that to think for a moment that there is significance in the parts of the world that are covered with air is to fail to understand how much water there is. This mistake is only forgivable because so few people have ever been sufficiently deep to understand their error.

Similarly, there is so much more death than there is life, that to think that the affairs of the living are significant is only because we fail to understand how much death there is in the world. That mistake is only forgivable because so few of us have been dead we do not understand our error.

Death, water, drowning: these are things that a living person avoids.

But that does not mean they do not exist.

Down and down, and now, though he had not the senses to appreciate it, from below there was a glow like that of dawn seen on a cloudy day, a vague presentiment of light as if down was up. As if below the horizon, some way off still, the sun was rising in reverse.

There was a sound too, a low and insistent drumbeat, very slow, a heartbeat, very slow, as of some huge whale the size of a city, operating at a speed which makes a person seem febrile and frantic. Slow and deep and regular, this heart made waves in the deep, each one bearing the sound of its beat, loud and low and insistent, though on what it insisted it was impossible to know.

Just as the sun rises and the dawn comes, even if we are not sure of it at first, cannot believe it since the night was so long we had given up on the hope of the morning, still it comes.

Whether we want for something and lose faith.

Whether we cannot understand what it is that is in front of us.

Whether we are there to see it or not.

Whether we hate it, or love it: some things come despite us.

They do not defer to us, and so the light came from below as Nathan Treeves fell through the water, drawn downwards by his great density. The light cared nothing for the boy, or for anything.

This light, like many things, was not for us, or for anything except itself.

It didn't care whether we expected it, down at the bottom of the sea, or whether we believed it, or whether we understood it, or whether we could see it.

It was there for itself.

We must, when we are presented with such things, come to an accommodation with them, knowing ourselves to be lesser things than they are.

Great bodies of water, when we are below their surface, light, when it comes from no possible source, drowning, being dead, being senseless, being impotent, being small – these are facets of existence over which we have no control, and with which we can only come to an accommodation.

We cannot succeed in the face of them. We must alter ourselves so that we can live alongside them.

Now the light from below picked out the edges of shapes.

The beating of the colossal heart was louder.

In the darkness one can never be sure of what one sees. This is also true when it is light, though it is not as obvious.

At all times, the mind takes what it sees of the world and, before it presents it to us, it makes sense of it in ways of which we aren't aware. It takes the shapes and colours and textures of things, cross-references them with information from the other senses, then filters them through what it knows of the context within which it is experiencing. This is what conscious things experience through sight.

This is easy to understand if you think of a time when you had been convinced that you had seen something – a cat, for example – in the middle distance, yet when you drew nearer you found that it was, instead, a collection of other objects: part of a barrel and a length of rope. The illusion that your mind presented to you – that these things were a cat – was very convincing before it was dispelled. There had been a cat, then, not a barrel and a rope. This cat, when you got closer, was suddenly shown to be a barrel and a rope, and then these were the things that you could see.

Some mediating aspect of your mind made the sense data into a cat, and then it made it into a barrel and a rope. If you had got closer still, you might have seen that it was something else.

It does not do to think too closely on the uncertainty of your experiences. Who is the mediator, for example? If it is an aspect of you, why are you not conscious of yourself mediating?

When it is dark, this mediation becomes very obvious, and the world, such as it is experienced, flicks between differing and often contradictory appearances.

This world lacks the certainty we rely on.

Though Nathan could not see it, any more than an owl pellet sees the forest floor as it is disgorged into the humus, and the mediating unconsciousness that he possessed was not present in the material realm, down below him, on the seabed there was a huge and dark eye. The striations of its iris were all in shades of the deepest, blackest brown. Across the lens a parasite was laid, a dead and motionless wriggle of perfect blackness.

The eye remained as Nathan descended, but now on its surface the light made shapes, picking out their edges. The flatness of the iris impinged upward. Uneven and ragged cubes and cones and figures with no recognisable geometric regularity jutted up.

The light that emanates from the City of Death, from Waterblack, shows, eventually, the edges of drowned buildings, the path of a drowned river crossed by rusted bridges, drowned streets, some wide and open, some cramped and narrow, drowned parks, the skeletons of drowned trees, statues of the people of the past, covered with barnacles, covered with algae, seaweed drifting like hair in a light breeze, the slow progress of deep-water jellyfish in and out of the windows of cars, long abandoned, street lamps, unlit, and everywhere – everywhere – the windows of houses.

It is from the windows of houses that the light that scarcely illuminates everything comes, now that Nathan is so close, his pellet having entered the precincts of the city from above.

Every house, every block of apartments, every tower, every shop: they all have windows. Behind these windows are rooms, and all of these rooms are lit with a sad and faltering yellow light. By the same magic that brought this city down below the waves, the water is forbidden from entering these rooms so that it does not interfere with the dead who occupy them.

On the windowsills of these windows, outside, sit cats. They are all dead, half rotten. The same magic that animates them allows them to remain down there, beneath the water. They do not need to breathe – no dead cat breathes – but they move as they need to move to do their work, which is to oversee the windows.

Behind these windows, behind the glass, the dead live, acting out the scenes that led to their deaths.

The cats don't watch them – nobody is here to watch them – but there are the dead, behind every window, performing their deaths, rehearsing for their future audience.

Here is one.

She is alone behind a window, high in a rectangular tower. She looks out, past the cat who floats outside her window, invisible to her, a hundred feet up, buoyed by the cold water, staring deadly into nothing. The woman looks out, her jaw slack, her eyes filmed over. Her fingers move, meeting the thumbs on each hand as if she is counting.

Four.

Over and over.

Four: index finger, middle finger, ring finger, little finger, and then four back. Left hand, right hand, both at the same time.

Over and over.

A door opens behind her and there is a man in the doorway. She does not turn around.

Four. Over and over.

◆

In the City of Death, there is only one audience for the performance of death, and that is the city's Master.

Nathan Treeves, once his pellet meets the Ha'penny Bridge, will be the new Master of Waterblack. The Mistress of Malarkoi, even now, is preparing to return his Spark to the pellet by extinguishing the Thousand Million Flames. She has not done it yet, even though you have already read that she has, but once those sacrificed infants give up their lives, Nathan will take them and return to the world.

It will be his privilege and obligation to watch the dead perform, just as it will be his privilege and obligation to provide either justice or recompense, depending on the situation.

This was the role his father once had, the role he abdicated from, the role that, we might assume, broke his heart and broke his will, and which left him dying through inaction in the slums of Mordew by an infestation of lungworms which the presence of Nathan provoked in him.

Nathan will be the audience for the performances of the dead, and because he is not yet returned to the world, no proper description of them is possible here.

The circumstances of a death are secrets that the dead share with their Master. They are not for public consumption.

Here is another death, in the same tower. It is a little lower down this time: we are following the progress of Nathan's pellet down to the Ha'penny Bridge.

Again, outside the window is a cat, dead though it moves and does the things a living cat does, rotten, though holding enough of a cat's form that we can recognise it as such.

There is no one in the window this time. If we want to see, we are going to have to come closer, swim through the cold, dense, black water, put our hands, slowly, to the glass, peer through the space our hands make when we make a circle of our fingers and press our faces against it.

It is slow and cold, moving down here, and we can't see properly inside.

The light in this window flickers.

The dead cat approaches, puts one paw on the glass beside us. It opens its mouth silently, the water muting its cry.

Its teeth, the few that remain, are green with what seems like moss, if that is something that grows down here. We return our faces to the circle our hands make, looking this time in the direction the cat has indicated with its paw.

There.

It's no surprise we couldn't see him.

He is lying under a pile of blankets, just his head visible. He is very old. His hair, long and hanging, does nothing to cover his scalp, which is mottled with liver spots.

Over his mouth is an oxygen mask, but the pipe that would connect it to the canister of that gas propped against the wall isn't attached to the nozzle.

He isn't moving.

His arm is limp by his side, dangling from... it's either a low, single bed or a settee, it's impossible to tell with all the blankets piled up.

He isn't moving but, perhaps, he's been trying to connect the pipe to the nozzle, to the spigot, and now he's exhausted.

He looks as if he's unconscious.

The conditions of a death are between the dead and the Master of Waterblack.

It is not for the general public to seek that information, to try to come into knowledge of the facts.

These are secret things, privileged things, and though that is not the reason Waterblack is drowned – that is because of the actions of the Assembly during the Third Atheistic Crusade – it is convenient that it is hidden.

People show a prurient interest in death. They wish to know, but fail to understand that part of knowledge is an obligation to act.

People are purposefully ignorant of their obligations.

The Master of Waterblack, under the founding edicts of the city, those which are enshrined in its customs and laws, the details of which are inscribed on its boundary stelae, needs to

285

know the conditions of the passing of the dead since it is his obligation to provide either justice or recompense.

This he does with his power, which is inherent in the Spark, which is the will of God made into the form of energy.

It is easy to see why he would need to know how a person died, and why they died, because he is capable of acting on that information.

Why would anyone else either want or need to know?

Here is a third death, on the fifth floor of the same block. Nathan is almost, but not quite, descended to the Ha'penny Bridge.

Now there is no cat to be seen.

The cats of Waterblack are Sparkline Actuaries, and they tally the responsibilities and obligations of those who are responsible for the Sparkline inheritances that attach to deaths.

If there is no cat here, then it is either a mistake – and the cat will return from whatever has delayed it – or it is an indication that there is no inheritance attaching to the death of whoever is performing their death behind the window.

The edicts, the laws, the by-laws and ordinances of Waterblack are clear, and when they are not clear, the Sparkline Actuaries make them clear, though there may be convocations necessary in the case of disputes.

Perhaps if we look inside we will understand.

The room is full of children. They are dancing.

The laws of Waterblack assume that a child comes into their majority at thirteen years of age, providing there is no exceptional reason why they shouldn't. This is the age of legal responsibility, and it seems these children are younger than that. This might explain why an actuary isn't present: there is a dispute over who is, or isn't, responsible for the death, or to whom the Sparkline inheritance is, or isn't, owed.

One child is pushing another, and that child falls to its knees. Despite the fact that the performance is taking place inside a room, the actual death took place outside – this is in a playground, which is obvious from the furniture of the scene, which is a slide, and a roundabout, and a climbing frame – and the floor is hard concrete, on which the child who has fallen to their knees has grazed their knees.

This child is now crying.

Through a wall – the boundaries of the room and the boundaries of the death site are not identical, and the room can and will give way to the reality of the death site in order to facilitate the performance – in comes another child, older than the others, but still not thirteen, and his face is full of rage. This rage is directed at the child who pushed over the child who then went on to graze their knees.

It would be up to the Master of Waterblack to pronounce on the rights and wrongs of whatever happened next, the details of which are privileged, and secret, and which should be of no interest to an onlooker.

There is, currently, no Master of Waterblack, that post having been abdicated by the previous incumbent, but that is not sufficient reason to describe the events, whether they outline how one child, in a rage, pushed another child, hands up in front of them, protesting their innocence, arguing an accident, so that the protesting child fell against the rungs of the ladder that led up to the slide and, by an unfortunate collision of the metal and bone, snapped a vertebra, severed the spinal cord, and died in an instant.

Or whether a child in rage, possessed of the unusual strength extreme emotions can provide, beat a third child – mistaking that child for the one who pushed his sister – to death with his fists, something that is easier to do with children than it is to do with adults.

Or some other sequence of events that led to, after a time, one or both of the dead child's parents coming to the playground to find their child lifeless, prompting a great display of emotion in the form of wailing and tears.

None of these things are a matter of public record, since the Master of Waterblack is the sole arbiter on the matter, since he is the only party empowered to either avenge or recompense the death.

Can you make a death right?

Down in the drowned depths, water on all sides, murder and war and beating and accident and suicide are played out in every window.

Is it in your power to correct the faults of the world?

Should it be necessary to evolve the dead back to the material realm in order to correct a death, could you do it?

Could you evolve a man into an angel, so that he could return with you to the world to seek his revenge?

Could you punish a living murderer with your magic?

You could not do it.

Only the Master of Waterblack has that power, and now here he is, his pellet settling on the midpoint of the Ha'penny Bridge. We turn our backs on the dead of the ground floor of the building beside which we have been floating and we follow the river to where he is.

There is a river that runs through the centre of Waterblack.

Someone who has always lived on the surface of the world might think that no river can run under the water, down on the seabed. The land-dweller thinks that the water of a river and the water of the sea should mix, one into the other, removing the distinction between them.

To think that would be a mistake.

That is not the way water works.

Denser water, water with a different mineral composition, water with more or less silt in it behaves in a different way from water that has different qualities, particularly when whatever causes that water to have those qualities refreshes them by virtue of its nature.

The water of the river that runs through Waterblack – it is the River Life, though there is no one still living that calls it that – has properties that are refreshed from its source. These properties are such that the river is darker, and heavier, and minerally distinct, and siltier than the water around it.

So, though it is under water at the deepest part of the sea, it still flows distinctly through the city along to the Ha'penny Bridge on which Nathan Treeves's pellet now rests.

Nathan extends only a little outwards, but inwards he reaches all the way.

His existence extends all the way into the weft, in between the material, in between time, in between space. His material presence followed the Spark when the Master forced it there, in his ignorance. All it remained for the Mistress of Malarkoi to do was to find Spark enough to force the materiality of Nathan back out again.

This was no small matter. The Spark need exceeded that needed for almost anything else, but that is a practical thing, not a conceptual one.

If one wishes to plough a field one may plough a field, since it is simple to do it.

What if the field is so large that one man could not plough it?

Then all that is required is to get another plough, get another man, and then complete the work.

If two men cannot plough it? Then get three.

If not three? Then get four.

In this way any size of field can be ploughed, even if a thousand million men are needed, and a thousand million ploughs.

Provided there exist sufficient men and sufficient ploughs, then it may be done.

If a person has a means of making men, and making ploughs, then what stands in his way?

The Mistress of Malarkoi had the means of making people, and the means of extracting their Spark, and the Master of Mordew should have considered this when he thought of making the Tinderbox.

It was inconceivable to him that he might go to the trouble of making a thousand million people and using their Spark for his own ends, so he thought that the Mistress of Malarkoi would not trouble to do it, which was his mistake and the Mistress's genius, even if it was a genius of a very simple kind. The genius of determining to do whatever is necessary, regardless of the effort, is a kind of genius working people exhibit daily, but which is often found wanting in Masters and Mistresses. They have often been conditioned by their understanding of magic to expect things to be done easily, or by others, so they forget what can be achieved by the simple expending of effort, even if this seems exhausting.

There was Nathan's pellet, extending infinitely inwards, and into this the Mistress of Malarkoi, through her efforts in another realm, returned sufficient Spark that Nathan's inward extension was turned outward.

His concepts, such as they were present in the immaterial realm, were imprinted back onto his body, and though the Assembly would think of this as a pointless and propagandistic replication of a dead boy as he was before death, suddenly, on the Ha'penny Bridge, he was there.

The pellet expanded in an instant into Nathan Treeves.

It was as if something perfectly elastic had been folded up perfectly small by dint of enormous effort, and then that effort was removed, and then the elastic had sprung back into itself with a thunderclap, revealing what had been hidden in the folding: the material and immaterial combination of Nathan Treeves.

That boy instantly knew himself to be alive, standing in the centre of Waterblack, though he did not recognise the place.

It is hard to think of a boy who, finding himself beneath water, would not panic at the fact, and panic is precisely what Nathan did.

He clutched at his throat, put his fingers to his mouth and then, fruitlessly, tried to swim up to the surface.

Nathan couldn't breathe, couldn't stop the water going into his mouth. He couldn't swim up for air any more than someone on the surface could fail to breathe, could stop air going into his mouth, could fly upwards in the sky by swimming.

But this was the proper place for Nathan, though he didn't feel it.

The water of that city was the right thing for him to take down into his lungs, just as water is what a fish needs to breathe. Waterblack was Nathan's city, and its water was his air. Of course, he could not stop it coming in: it was the proper place for it to go.

When he stopped struggling and the water went behind his teeth and down inside him, he was filled with the same sense of satisfaction as a person feels when they breathe in the fresh morning air after a stuffy night of sleep.

When Nathan moved, he moved as if he was on land, except more slowly, and the ground attracted his feet with the same force – perhaps a little less – as a person's feet are attracted to the ground on the surface world.

This should be no surprise – Waterblack was suited to Nathan in the same way that he was suited to it, and the previous cities and places of his experience were the flawed and difficult places for him.

Only he did not know that yet, but was instead a poor boy, killed and translated through unfriendly realms. His home was, as yet, unrecognisable to him, just another hostile place, trying to kill him.

A beat like a whale heart, throbbing from nowhere, was the only calming thing he felt, but it did its work, gradually. It made in the drowned city a rhythmic and repetitive certainty, one thing at least that seemed to be consistent. A womb-born boy knows from the moment of his conception a beat of this kind.

First, it is the action of his mother's heart, then it is his own heart, beneath his ribs.

There was the heartbeat, and he didn't drown.

From somewhere, with its own rhythm, asynchronous to the heartbeat, there was a flash of bright light like that made when a lighthouse shines its beam on you.

There was the light, there was the sound, and when water came into Nathan it satisfied his need for breath.

He put out his hand – the one that had, once, become transparent, like glass – and he moved his fingers, stretching them out and then drawing them back into a fist, then opening them again. Then he did it with his other hand. Then he did something similar with his feet.

Everything moved in a familiar way.

On his feet were boots, an inch of woollen socks protruding.

Between these boots, downwards, there was a bridge: a floor of steel marked with flaking, piebald patches like a mangy horse's coat.

Up, the way he had come had he known it, were the windows his pellet had drifted past.

In the lowest there was, through a window, the scene of a child, surrounded by other laughing children, lying disjointedly on the ground, one side of her head cracked against the concrete, her mind closing down on itself. In the middle window, there was an old man whose son had disconnected him from a breathing apparatus, becoming irretrievably comatose through anoxia. In the highest window there was a woman whose husband was preparing to punish her for his failures, conditioned by the frequency of his beatings of her to use more force than she could stand.

Nathan saw these things, but only in miniature. The cats beside the windows watched him, to see what he would do, but the rehearsals were like tiny dreams to the boy, and he looked down again at the bridge.

Nathan walked, slowly, floating a very little, to the nearest edge of the bridge, only a few feet away, where there was an iron handrail.

Flowing beneath the bridge was the River Life – though he didn't know it by name – black and viscous, moving like melted pitch tar, heavily creeping away from him.

Nathan put his hands on the railing, first one, then the other, his arms moving as gradually as the tar river. Just as he had made fists before, he made two more around the metal of the rail, and all around the slow heartbeat pounded, ten seconds or more between beats, and less frequently than that flashed the lighthouse beam.

He counted ten of the heartbeats, four of the flashes, his feet solid on the bridge, his hands gripping the rail, the memory of the last beat and flash and the expectation of the next ones in his mind.

The width of the river that the bridge crossed was about a hundred feet, and on either side, bordering the river, were buildings. Some looked like houses, some looked like factories, some were grand, some were simple. They all had windows, and in each of these windows there was light, as if all the places were occupied.

Occasionally, across the lights, the silhouette of a cat walked. In some windows, cats were sitting, visible as silhouettes.

On both sides of the river, it was the same: buildings and windows and cats.

Nathan counted the heartbeats, and the flashes. He turned to watch the flow of the river tar. He let his eyes rest, when he needed them to, on the toes of his boots, on the socks that protruded from his boots, on the knees of his trousers, on his pockets, on his waistband.

A boy, when he looks at himself, can see all the way up to his jacket, can follow his arms down the sleeves to his hands, but he can never see his face.

Not without a mirror.

Nathan, as if this realisation was a plan, feeling the sense that it was, even though it wasn't, walked slowly over the bridge to where one side of the river's buildings were.

The building in front of him, when he arrived there, was called the Merchant's Arch. There were letters over the door that told him the name, letters that the book Adam Birch had taught him how to read, once. Bar & Restaurant.

There were four windows, each lit, each with a cat on the windowsill.

One of these dishevelled cats jumped down, floating in the dense water, and came to Nathan. It limped as a man limps when one of his legs is palsied and braced. It lurched forward on one side with as much force as a useless leg would allow if it was a rigid prop, and brought its hips over, pushed hard to the left, brought its weight down. It lurched first to one side, then to the other, its head hanging steady in the centre like a clock weight, its yellow eyes shining in the dark water, fixed all the while on Nathan, its tail erect and twitching.

It kept low to the ground.

Perhaps it was a necessary part of its job, to be down on the ground at all times, lurching from one side to the other, slowly, clumsily, its yellow eyes always keeping the object of its attention in focus, never blinking, the grey tip of its tongue protruding from between its teeth as it came out of the shadows, tiger stripes black on its grey fur, both ears bitten and ragged, a patch of grey-white on its chest.

Nathan half floated, half stepped, back away from it.

The things he was seeing had a nightmare quality, precisely the sorts of things that ought to induce fear in a person, but fear didn't arise in Nathan's chest, now it was filled with cold water. Fear didn't catch his breath, or make him gasp, because his lungs were filled with brine. Fear didn't burn in his gut because that stomach was filled with brine. His muscles didn't twitch with the desire to run away because that twitching was doused with brine.

A thing appears unlike itself when placed under water, so fear was not itself when Nathan felt it in that drowned place.

Put a pencil into a bowl of water and look at it from above and you will see that the angle of that straight object bends where it meets the waterline.

Go with a friend into a standing body of water and, the two of you, with your eyes open, dip down under, each still looking at the other's face. You will both see the change that comes over your friend. The skin of their face reacts differently to being in that medium. It fills out, smooths. The eyes lose their lustre, the lips too. The hair becomes vegetal, the expressions lose some specificity. The body obeys rules that you aren't familiar with, does things in an odd way.

Search for something that you have lost which has fallen down to the bed of a river. If you can locate it at all you will see it is half covered in silt, bleached of its colour, rippling in form, unlike itself.

Nathan's emotions down there were like those things; they were translated through a change in angle, unfamiliar in aspect, bleached.

When the lurching, yellow-eyed, tiger-striped cat approached Nathan, he retreated like he would from a fearsome sight, but ineffectively, slowly, and without feeling the fear. In its place was a claustrophobic and heavy sense of the ominousness of the cat's progress. It was lighter, somehow, that fear, but also extending more extensively in time.

Fear is a local thing, in both its spatial and temporal extent: it is about the thing now, in the place here. A man can be frightened of being devoured by a tiger, but that fear is limited to the place where he and the tiger are, and the time in which the consumption of his flesh will take place.

The feeling Nathan felt on the approach of this cat – the fur of which, he now saw, was rigid, as if carved from a block of wood – was as if the presence of this thing had always been, and always would be, wherever Nathan had ever been and would ever go. Its oppressive atmosphere went with it, backwards and forwards in place, backwards and forwards in time, as if it was capable of becoming a condition of Nathan's existence, like his name, something that he could never escape, and which had always been with him.

As it came closer, the cat's lidless eyes never focussed on anything except Nathan. This gaze had an intensity that seemed to trap the boy in a cone of pressure extending out from the surface of its attention in a perfect and never-diminishing geometry from which he would never be able to escape.

All he could see was the cat's body.

It was not, as it might first have appeared, the simple form of a dead animal, but was instead the body of a dead animal as it becomes after it has been taken to a taxidermist. Its remains were as if transformed by a taxidermist's art from what it had been, to what it was now, but done very poorly. The stitches were too large, the stuffing protruded, the glass eyes were not entirely the same – each was a shade different from the other, and one had a crack across it – remedial work had been done on the pelt with inappropriate materials: wood and paint in some places, patches of fabric on the other.

Pokes of wire frame jutted at the moving joints.

It is not possible, and not sanctioned by the trade body to which taxidermists are affiliated, for a specimen to have taxidermy performed on it when it is alive, or for an animal to be killed by an attempt to stuff it while it still lives, but that was the impression that this cat's appearance gave off: that some poor creature had been wrestled into submission and then, in an attempt to insert the internal armature, all these forms of damage had been done to it while it resisted, and which ended with the thing's death.

The corpse, being ruined for display purposes, was discarded, and had somehow found its way down here, to Waterblack, where it had regained life.

If Nathan had required breath, he would have been unable to take it as the cat approached. His whole body became stiff with tension. His mind stopped as if he had dropped out of time. Only one feeling remained – that it would be horrible if this thing touched him – and this only passed when the cat itself passed. It switched the direction of its gaze at the last possible moment to the road immediately behind Nathan, coming as close as possible to brushing against him as it went past.

It did not brush against Nathan. That gesture, in cats, is affectionate.

Anyone who has owned a cat will know that they rub themselves against you as a means of inveigling themselves sufficiently into your affections that you will feed them the food they crave. This cat gave off no affection. Quite the opposite: it seemed to hold Nathan in the lowest possible regard, to hate him even, as if he was the lowest thing in that city, and not its Master.

But mustn't a Master prove himself?

If a man owns animals, don't those animals judge him on the quality and methods of his husbandry of them?

If a man agrees to take on high position in a company, don't its employees judge him on his ability to bring prosperity to that company, and to them?

Isn't it true that the higher the position of authority one takes, the more harshly one is likely to be judged?

Also, if a person takes an existing position then that is because the position has been vacated. Nathan wasn't the first Master of Waterblack, and just as the workforce of a factory will judge an incoming supervisor, initially, as if they are simply a reincarnation of the previous holder of that position, the citizens of Waterblack made their opinions of Nathan a copy of their opinions of the previous Master, his father.

These opinions were even worse, perhaps, since Nathaniel Treeves, in his last Mastery, had performed worse, in their eyes, than his previous incarnation had done during his Mastery, who in turn was worse than the one before that, and the one before that, and on and on.

It is natural to draw conclusions from history, and to predict the future from trends that seem to be established, or which are establishing themselves. Even if, statistically speaking, it is unwise to make predictions of the future based on a limited dataset, and even if, philosophically speaking, it is fallacious to assume that what has gone before allows a person to predict what will come next, people will do it regardless.

So, shouldn't this dead cat, these dead people, this City of Death, hold Nathan in low esteem, even if he was their Master?

Precedent suggested he would disappoint positive expectations of him, and disappoint them more than his father had disappointed them.

Whether they should, or they shouldn't, make these assumptions, this cat seemed to hold Nathan in this low esteem. As it walked away from him, lurching left and right, the cat lifted high its tail. It showed to Nathan its back-eye – its puckered and naked anus – which is an insult in the cats of that city.

The cat, slowly and gradually, but no less surely for that, led Nathan away from the Merchant's Arch, back over the Ha'penny Bridge and right, along Bachelor's Walk.

Now the creature's gaze was no longer on him, the ominous feeling that it provoked in him subsided enough that Nathan could take in his surroundings again.

On his right hand the river, constrained by lichen-crusted green bricks, flowed darkly, water beneath water.

To his left there were buildings four or five storeys high, each with rows of windows, and window ledges. Some windows were plain rectangles, some had decorative lintels, all of them were guarded by dead cats who regarded Nathan as the one he was following had: with the utmost disdain. They rudely stared down at him, opening and closing their silent mouths, turning to show him their back-eyes, glancing at their neighbours as if in disgust.

In the windows behind the cats, lights shone, and in some of them there were cheeks pressed to the glass, the palms of hands, the outlines of people moving.

None of the activity inside was of any interest to these cats. In one, a man was pounding with his fists against the glass, threatening to smash his way out, or to destroy the wooden frame, but the cat on that sill – a pure white one, without a head – seemed not to notice, bringing its paw up to where its mouth would have been, turning the paw as if it was licking it, using it to wipe the muzzle that wasn't there, before putting the paw back down on the windowsill, the man still pounding away.

The path Nathan's cat took – lurching and serpentine – led Nathan near to a shop fronted with five wide windows, one cat patrolling the five of them, trotting and floating from one to the next, all of which showed the same scene.

Nathan had grown up in the slums, which had no auction houses worth the name, but there would be times when a slum-dweller, having fallen into complete and total destitution even by the standards of that place, and being unwilling to give themselves up to the Living Mud, would bring into a clear place everything they owned. Having agreed a commission with a person capable of preventing all comers from helping themselves to their poor stock of goods – which still represented a kind of wealth to those who had even less – they would sell their possessions to the highest bidder, the protector of the objects acting also as the auctioneer.

More often than not, this protector would keep the majority of the money for themselves, throwing a few desultory coins down into the Mud to distract the vendor before marching off to the gin house, but even this sad exchange was enough so that Nathan knew that what he saw now, in the windows, was an elevated version of that system.

Inside, looking out anxiously, there was a very thin woman, dressed to a standard that would have been impossible to achieve in the slums of Mordew, but not so elaborately as those in the Merchant City managed. She was standing amongst a crowd, all facing the other way, their attention being paid to a man on a platform, or perhaps a catasta. He was standing behind a lectern, or perhaps a rostrum, and surrounding him were various goods – an upholstered chair, a mangle, sundry vases, curtains hanging over a pole balanced between two scuffed and handle-less chests of drawers, a pile of schoolbooks – and he indicated these things with a gavel. He moved his mouth a great deal, his head starting low down and then rising and rising until, after a pause in which his mouth was open and tense, his eyes wide, and his eyebrows risen up so that they lined his forehead, eventually he banged the hammer on his rostrum.

The woman, listening, flinched whenever he did it.

Nathan's cat, who had moved on down the street, stopped and waited.

Nathan turned back to the windows, and here the woman was again, this time out in the street, her image filling the whole range of the shop front, in much closer focus, her left hand in one window, her right in another window and in the three middle windows a book of French grammar, the title of which Nathan couldn't read.

The cat was beside him again, staring, and so powerful was the feeling of disapproval it communicated to him, by whatever method it did it, that he couldn't turn back to see what happened next, to watch the conditions of this woman's death, and how these images related to it.

Instead, he followed the cat where it went.

Nathan was led by turns to a place called, by the name on a gate, Phoenix Park – a broad, undulating field of seaweed and dead trees.

Twenty feet or so past the gate, there was a window and a windowsill suspended in the water, independent of any support.

This window showed, as if from a great height, green land above a river. Down in the lower right corner were the roofs of houses, no bigger than matchboxes arranged in rows. There was a road running between them on which tiny men and horses and carriages, smaller than matchheads, were dotted about.

Everything moved slowly and erratically, as things appear to do when you are high above them, the normalcy of their speed, the logic of their direction, being invisible from up in the clouds.

Onto this vision, in pale, grey ink, became superimposed a map, and if the focus of the dead cat's rheumy eye was any indication, the information that the map contained was significant. When the whole window was laced with it, words appeared, and at these the cat turned to Nathan and mewled at him, the tone of the sound being questioning, as if the cat was asking, 'What do you say to that?'

It was as if some response, positive or negative, was suggested by this mewling, that some sense ought to have been created by it, that some obligation to communicate was set up. Nathan could read the words – they said 'Plan of the Phoenix Park, Dublin, showing the paths the assassins took before and after the murder of Lord Frederick Cavendish and Mr Burke, 6th May, 1882' – but they may as well have been gibberish since Nathan didn't understand what they meant, or what any of it had to do with him.

The cat mewled again, louder this time, the sound not travelling through the water but arriving directly in Nathan's mind through a different medium.

He shook his head, without knowing why, and the cat jumped down from the windowsill and went on again, away from the glass, away from the frame, away from the window that hung inside the gate to the park without a building to hold it in place.

Nathan followed, because that seemed to be the thing to do here, but in doing so, had he known it, Nathan had dismissed his responsibility for the murders of the two men the window had named.

Though the dismissal was allowable, under the ordinances of Waterblack – the men had been assassinated long before Nathan was born, part of a forgotten war of which there were no surviving participants, nor were there any remaining who had been affected in even the slightest way by the prosecution of that war – some previous Masters had claimed responsibility for unresolved deaths despite that. Those were Masters of whom the city thought fondly. These cats, these Sparkline Actuaries, respected, in their dead and punctilious dedication to the prescribed edicts, those Masters' generosities of spirit. Those Masters had accepted into their duties the sad tales of the forgotten martyrs on both sides of all conflicts.

There were no petitioners remaining who could have sought redress for these crimes, those men's ghosts having fled the precincts of their murders to haunt the places of their births. The men who had done the murders, with knives, had themselves been murdered, with ropes. These men waited in another part of the city – the jail – where an enormous number of Actuaries gathered. There were so many windows in that jail that there was precious little space to move between them. The windows reflected into each other, making endless halls of images, like mirrors do when you place them in front of each other.

There was an infinity of windows, an infinity of dead cats, receding infinitely into the distance in that jail.

In the jail, and in Phoenix Park, all Nathan had to do was nod, and the obligations would have been immediately satisfied, the windows would have gone, the Actuaries assigned to them would have found, at last, after millennia, their rest, falling to pieces on the spot, food for crabs, for shrimps, for krill, for plankton, depending on how particulate they became.

But Nathan didn't nod.

Is it an excuse that he didn't know that that was what he had to do?

It is not. He was the Master of Waterblack. Who else should have known?

At the very least it would have been good practice. Tidiness and restraint in the use of resources is beneficial for a city, even the City of Death. On a simple bureaucratic level, it would have been better for Nathan to clear up these lingering matters, put them to bed, to sweep the streets clean of them to make room for new appellants. After all, there are always – it is a law of its own – more persons seeking to make use of a facility than there are the resources by which that facility might be comfortably provided. Nathan had been unrestrained in his killing, more profligate, perhaps, than any of his predecessors. Even if one's victims are very young – babies even – or very ignorant, or very willing to be killed, that does not exclude them from their rights under the laws of Waterblack.

If rights are granted, the practicalities by which those rights are guaranteed are the responsibility of the guarantor.

The guarantor was the Master of the City.

Is it any wonder the Actuaries looked on Nathan with disdain?

Waterblack's edicts had been decided on, its statutes were drawn up, and nowhere did they state that the city should measure its justice against its ability to do the work necessary to provide it. That was not a valid exemption, in Waterblack, and the practical responsibility for delivering justice fell to the Master of the City to manage.

Shouldn't that be true of all great cities?

Of all nations?

Of the entire creation of God, even?

The city exists, the nation exists, the creation of everything exists – their existence is a necessity, or the idea of them having a Master is nonsense – and the Master is a servant to this reality. His Mastery is a fact dependent on the existence, and the form, and the character of his city, his nation, his creation. There can be no Master without something to be Master of, so it was Nathan's duty to find a solution to the city's problems, not the city's duty to solve Nathan's problems.

As it was, Nathan didn't understand any of this, as a person new to a post often doesn't, so it was left for another time, or for the next Master, or for no one and nothing at all to resolve the assassinations that took place in Phoenix Park, the deaths in the city jail, even though they did not require resolution.

This was nothing unusual. It was certainly true that many deaths were unresolved, awaiting resolution in Waterblack, just as in all cities. The disappointment was that, in this city, the dead might expect better.

Perhaps this was to be characteristic of Nathan's rule of the place, that by ignorance he would shirk his duties.

Only time would tell, one way or the other, whether he would, or whether he wouldn't.

Between the streets there was a patch of empty ground where a row of houses had been – the foundations were still there, concrete squares up from which drainpipes and wires ascended. Some of the lower parts of walls were still standing: the corners, no more than three bricks high, sometimes half a wall in length or width.

There were no windows here to see, except those that were visible in the streets across from Nathan. The cat was a long way back and there were no others waiting, watching him, standing in judgement over him.

From somewhere, he could hear a boy crying.

Because his ears were filled with water, and because water mutes sounds as gentle as crying – as high, and ragged, and quietly mournful – he must have heard it by a different means.

But it was there.

Nathan turned his head from side to side, tilted it, as the magical dog Sirius used to when the boy had been with him. By doing this, he could tell that the sound was coming from somewhere off in the middle of the waste ground, in the narrow space between two sets of foundations.

Deep-sea plants had anchored themselves there, and these

were swaying from side to side in the transitory currents that made their way through Waterblack in the way wind does in cities above the ground.

Nathan went closer and the crying became louder, or at least more consistent, or changed in some quality that meant Nathan felt the crying was taking place there.

It was the sound of a boy, or the sound of a memory of him, or some quality specific to Waterblack that was an analogue of those things, and which, like a language, Nathan didn't know well enough to understand.

When you are in the woods, at night, walking alone with no one to clarify what this or that thing is, when something moves in a way you aren't expecting it to, or when you hear something and can't identify from where the sound came, or you get a feeling that something is present, but can't, from the evidence of your senses, define what that thing is, or justify the feeling rationally, then the mind mediates, senses things for you that might or might not be present.

This or that moving shadow, cast by the limbs of a tree moving in the wind, becomes, with the assistance of the mind, a person waving, or a supernatural being gesturing, or a creature approaching.

Except that you aren't certain.

It is right to say that this lack of certainty is a problem, but what is to say these uncertain perceptions are less real than the perceptions you have of which you are more certain?

Perhaps it is only at times when the certainty of your perceptions – certainty being a concept applied by the conscious mind – is lessened, that you experience the world as it is, and not as you think it is.

Nathan felt that a patch of sea plants was crying, deep beneath the sea, on abandoned ground, in a drowned city, in the manner in which a boy cries.

He went over, reached down into the seaweeds, and let them sway through his fingers. They were translucent, green. On one strand there was a tiny, empty sea snail's shell. Another was dirty with black sand.

It seemed to Nathan that these things were the things that were crying – the snail shell in its loneliness, to be so far below the waves, so dark, so abandoned by others of its kind, just as this wasteland was abandoned, and the sand in its lowliness, to be nothing more than grains of unknown material, never regarded except on this one occasion, never used for any purpose.

Both things, in their way, were nothing, and Nathan felt this very strongly, though he couldn't explain why.

What Nathan did next was something that was perfectly possible for him, though he didn't know until that point that he could do it at all.

He was the Master of Waterblack, the repository of the will of God, who can evolve lifeless objects into living things, since life is a more perfect form of a thing than death is. Think of how persistent a living being is, whereas a dead corpse rots away quickly to nothing.

Nathan knelt and, remembering the way he had Scratched the Spark Itch, long ago in the slums of Mordew, and had, by doing so, evolved a fluke into a rat, he let the Spark flow out of himself into this patch of weeds, into this snail shell, into this sand.

Between his fingers, he felt matter expand out of nothing, felt it arrive in the world, and, because the transformation of the fluke had resulted in a rat that bit him, he reflexively moved away from it, unsure of what it was that he had done.

He stepped back and there was a boy.

Nathan had once told a story about a boy whose tears had been used for magic, and who had cried so hard he had cried himself dead. Solomon Peel.

This boy, summoned up from the seabed, looked exactly as Nathan had imagined Solomon to look in his mind.

Solomon Peel, the boy who knew how to feel.

For a moment, this weeping, sad-faced, magic-drained child stood in front of Nathan, brought into the world through Mastery. But then he was crushed, the pressure of the water around him forcing him into himself, as Nathan had once been forced into himself by the pressure of the Master's magic. Where Nathan's crushing had been done by an expert in that job, and for a purpose, this crushing was a natural fact, a condition of him being where he ought not to be.

Where once a snail shell had been, a patch of weeds, sand, and then, briefly, a boy like Solomon Peel, now there was a crushed and compressed corpse, bloodlessly collapsed in on itself.

Behind Nathan, the stiff-legged cat, the Spark Actuary, appeared. With a blink, he summoned a window in the place where Solomon Peel had died. In this window, the boy's death played out – the scene through which Nathan had just lived – the body drifting crushed beside it.

The cat left again, lurching, indicating with a twitch of its head that Nathan should follow.

It went to the centre of a plaza, to a point at which all the surrounding windows pointed. Here there was a crooked stair that spiralled untidily upward, so high that the top of it, if there was one, was lost in the murk of the water above.

There was no structure around this stair, no support. It had irregularly sized and shaped steps made from wood, or pieces of metal, or the lattices that make up the bottom of a crate. It was thousands of discarded things, gathered, it seemed, one by one and joined to each other, each at an angle to the last. As it ascended, this stair circled around on itself, sometimes making a wide circle, sometimes making a tight curl that seemed suited for different-sized people to climb.

Now, around the edges of the plaza, other Sparkline Actuaries were gathering, coming out from narrow streets, or over rooftops, or up from open drains into which gutters would once have run. The dead cats pushed themselves through gaps, or strolled easily along, or crept like slugs on their bellies, dead limbs useless for the job of moving them.

Soon there were hundreds of them, a crowd that seemed to blend into each other, making a mass of fur and eyes around the spiral staircase, pulsing as they breathed, slowly, in unison.

If Nathan had wanted to, no doubt he could have barged through them, but the pressure of their presence, the focus of their attention – which was on him, and on the stair – made him want to go to the stair and climb it.

So that's what he did.

The first step was solid, but the second listed as he put his weight on it and he had to balance himself with his arms out, his hands paddling the thick water. He stepped quickly to the third step, but the movement made him almost overshoot, inertia working differently underwater. He bent at the knee and reached for the next step, and so he began ascending like an infant does, on hands and knees, climbing and reaching and pulling himself up.

Every rise made the stair sway both below and above. The structure seemed always on the verge of coming apart, and though he wouldn't have fallen quickly enough to harm himself, it made it difficult to climb with any confidence. Nathan was always pausing on all fours, waiting for the movement of the stair to still and the threat of collapse to pass before he went on again.

After a while he was as high as the rooftops of the buildings that surrounded the plaza. The cats below shrank in his vision into a uniform mass of dead fur, dead flesh, pinpricked by dead staring eyes.

On the roofs, he was surprised to see the corpses of birds, their necks at unnatural angles, their wings split. They were unlike the cats. Death was real for them, freeing them from taking up the tasks the Spark Actuaries performed.

Because height is no obstacle to underwater creatures, there were crabs up here too, pale and listless fish, octopuses, though they drifted over the slates and chimneys with no eagerness.

Nathan climbed higher, leaving the plaza behind, leaving the Actuaries. As he climbed, the extent of the city gradually became clearer.

First he saw the grid of roads that surrounded the plaza, then he made out the way he had come, following the stiff-legged cat, and then he saw the bridge on which he had woken.

These parts were, to him, of an understandable scale. They were not so different from the Merchant City of Mordew, peculiar in their layout, their design, and in the particularities of their civic engineering, but they were still recognisably the same type of things as the places he had known in the past.

He went higher, so that he could follow the extent of the dark and viscous river, watch it curl, gently, and as he did it became obvious that this city was not like Mordew. It was not like Malarkoi.

Both of those cities had more or less definite limits, and were of a comprehensible size, but this city seemed to stretch off forever, the streets and houses never meeting an obstacle, like the cliffs or the Sea Wall, never dwindling to nothing, becoming hillsides and forests. Waterblack spread instead at an almost uniform density in every direction, and it didn't matter how high Nathan went, or how small the streets and houses below him became, he could never see the end of it.

Even when he went so high, the stair moving an alarming distance from side to side with every step, that the ground below him threatened to become invisible in the murk, the light from the windows unable to penetrate the volume of brine he was putting between himself and it, there was no visible boundary to the city.

The streets were like the tracery of an enormous spiderweb, or a great patchwork of poorly embroidered lace, expanding in every direction forever.

There must have been tens of thousands of streets, and each street was made up of hundreds of houses, and each of these houses had windows. If Nathan had had a map, he could have systematically gone along each of these streets, to each of the houses, to each of the windows. What would he have seen there?

What would a census of those windows reveal, in the City of Death?

It would take decades, centuries. Surely he would die before he could see through them all, forgetting those that he had seen as he aged.

Perhaps he would never die.

Perhaps he was already dead.

Perhaps death was no obstacle here, just as it was no obstacle to the Sparkline Actuaries.

He was the Master of this city, and to be the Master of the City of Death was to supersede that condition.

He looked up, and the stair continued up at least as far from where he stood as it had when he had taken the first step. Never did it become more regular, more stable.

Who had made this thing? The Masters of the past, bringing things from the city to stack, one on top of the other? Did they go down each time to find something for the next step, trying in vain to go high enough to see the edges of the city?

Were they trying to reach the surface world?

Perhaps they were trying to do something that Nathan did not yet understand, his tenure there having only just begun, he not knowing the things that those people did.

But where were they now, those Masters of the past?

Had his father climbed this stair?

Did he build his part of it?

Was this how he had left the city, returned to the slums of Mordew?

Up it went, into the endless weight of water, down it went, back to the endless City of Death. Nathan sat himself down on one step and, somewhere between up and down, he stared, thinking, water in his lungs and his eyes unblinking.

Eventually, he went down. He stepped off the stair and let himself be pulled back to the plaza by the heaviness that his city imposed on him.

As he fell, the spiderweb lace tracery of the streets resolved back into the tens of thousands of houses, and the light from the windows of the unavenged dead made objects with depth and width and height from the flatness of a place seen from high above. The mass of greyness became cats again, wounded to death but living, their slit eyes following him as he fell until he came to rest on the ground.

When his feet hit the cobbles, the Sparkline Actuaries dispersed back the way they had come, along the streets, over the roofs, into the sewers, half swimming, half running, crawling on their bellies until only the Actuaries of the windows that looked out on the stair remained, perched on their sills.

The cat with the stiff legs stared with dead-eyed intensity at Nathan, then turned and walked, lurching, away.

Nathan followed the cat through the streets, every window showing him the same thing: death.

Some of the streets were long and named, those names written on plaques on the street junctions, and some of the streets were shorter, nameless, often little more than a link between houses to another street. The cat would look back if Nathan fell behind, captivated by some window in which a killing was played out, wait for him to catch up. If Nathan tried to go a way the cat didn't want him to go, then it would appear at the end of that street, lead him back again to the proper path.

This went on indefinitely. The only markers of time were the heartbeat and the flash of light, and these only marked the time between beats, between flashes, neither of those things having any other context.

There was no progression of minutes and hours – all the public clocks were stopped, and even these showed contradictory times.

There was no day and night, no sun or moon.

How long did Nathan follow that cat? There was no way of knowing. Perhaps the question had no meaning in Waterblack.

Does time pass for the dead?

They came to a corner, and when Nathan caught up with the cat there was a sudden and marked increase in the volume of the heartbeat, the brightness of the flashing as they joined a new street.

In the windows there were different sorts of scenes.

Before this street, Nathan had recognised no one in the death performances. The places were unfamiliar to him, the dying were unfamiliar. They might have been the same people, over and over.

But, when Nathan went to the first window on this new, louder, brighter street, all of that changed. Behind the glass, in a room full of strangers, he saw his mother and father.

They were younger than he remembered them, fresh-faced and smiling – his father was laughing, even. His mother had her hand on his father's chest, over his heart, and the two were at one side of a party, drinks in hand, swaying to music other people were dancing to.

Everyone looked so happy that Nathan couldn't understand what he was seeing. It was as if they were all in a play and the director had said 'look happy' and this is what they'd all tried to do.

Nathan drew closer to the glass, and, though the Actuary for this performance bristled, it didn't try to attack him. It slinked quietly off the sill and drifted to the ground where it watched but did not interfere.

Through the window, Nathan's father recognised someone.

When Nathan turned to see who it was, to his amazement he saw it was the man with the fawn-coloured birthmark, the gentleman caller who had put the money at the end of his mother's bed in the slums of Mordew, and who would be owed services in future.

He was the man who had presided over the ball at which Gam had pushed Prissy into the middle of the room, taunting Nathan to use his powers.

He was the man who had taken them into that same palace while Mordew burned.

Through the glass, in what must have been the past, he leaned in close to whisper something into Nathan's father's ear. Once that was done, he stepped back into the dancing crowd.

Nathan's mother, her face falling serious, turned her husband towards her and his face was serious too. She asked him – Nathan could read the words on her lips – 'What did he say?' – but before he could answer the scene changed.

Now here were Nathan's father and the man with the fawn-coloured birthmark, without Nathan's mother, sheltering from the rain, outside a house within which a party – the same party? – was taking place through a window.

Was that his mother he could see inside, in the window within a window?

The two men were smoking hand-rolled cigarettes under a canopy they shared between them made from a leather jacket held over their heads. Rain fell onto the taut and makeshift shelter they made between them. Splashes of it threatened to dampen the paper of their cigarettes. Nathan's father gripped his cigarette between his thumb and forefinger, angling it in against his palm, pulled deeply on it. The man with the fawn-coloured birthmark held his cigarette more elegantly, between his index and ring fingers, and sipped at the smoke.

A door opened off to the side where Nathan couldn't see, and both men tossed their cigarettes down and walked off into the rain.

The scene didn't change immediately, and Nathan couldn't make out anything that could possibly be meant to hold his attention. He turned to the Actuary, and now, beside the one who was leading him through the streets, another had appeared. The pair of them stood side by side, staring, as if they were witnesses, but Nathan couldn't understand what it was that he was supposed to do, or not to do, or what there was to witness.

He turned back, and there was a third scene in the window, this time of a scaffold surrounding a high tower at night. It looked like the spires Nathan had seen in the Merchant City, in the Pleasaunce, but this had a different style, and the scaffolds were metal pipes, planks of wood, and complicated arrange-ments of nuts and bolts. Someone had left a bag of tools out in the rain, and where the bag gaped open the tools – a hammer, a hacksaw, a pair of pliers, others beneath – were getting wet.

Another man came suddenly into frame.

He emerged from the side of the tower, as if he had come directly through the wall, although it was also possible that there was a door around the spire, out of sight. The man was panicking – he looked from side to side, quickly, and when he didn't find anywhere to go he went over to the scaffold and looked over, up and down.

There was a long, deep wound, freshly made, running across his cheek, over his jaw, down his neck and back over his shoulder. The sides of the wound were open, and it flapped when he moved, pushing out blood past where some had already congealed.

The rain made the wound worse, and when the wind blew and the rain fell harder, the wound bled more. The man didn't seem to be paying attention – he leaned over the scaffold in a way that was clearly dangerous, peering down through the inadequate moonlight, looking, possibly, for a way down, though Nathan, from his vantage, could see there wasn't one.

Through the door from which this man might have emerged came first Nathan's father, and then the man with the fawn-coloured birthmark. They searched, briefly, then found what they were looking for – the man with the wound.

Nathan's father put his hands up, palms first, shook his head, looked concerned. He came slowly forward, towards where the man with the wound was clutching a scaffold pole. The man backed away, stepped over the scaffold, leaned back as far as he could, his face wearing a look of absolute and inconsolable fear.

The man with the fawn-coloured birthmark came forward now and Nathan's father took his wrist, held him back, shouted at him – Nathan couldn't make out the word from his lips.

In the hand that Nathan's father wasn't restraining, the man with the fawn-coloured birthmark, the gentleman caller, the aristocrat, held a knife, and though what happened next all happened in a blur, Nathan saw that knife in every detail. That knife resembled something that Nathan knew very well. The man with the fawn-coloured birthmark pointed the knife at the man hanging back from the scaffold, and Nathan knew what it would do.

It was the knife the Master of Mordew had given Nathan, the one containing the Rebuttal in Ice. Nathan had used it to kill a flock of approaching firebirds from the roof of the Master's Manse.

Through the window, the knife projected ice and the wounded man fell back, frozen. He fell and shattered on the ground far below.

The focus of the performance returned to the rooftop.

Nathan's father looked down, devastated, but the man with the fawn-coloured birthmark took Nathan's father's hand and put the knife with the Rebuttal in Ice into it, clasped Nathan's father's fingers around its hilt.

The fingers tightened and tightened until his knuckles shone, and then the scene reset and there were Nathan's mother and father again at the party.

Nathan turned to the cats, but if he hoped they would explain what he had seen he was disappointed.

They stared at him with their dead eyes, waiting.

Nathan didn't know what to do, but there, on the other side of the street, was another window, another Actuary, and in this window were his mother and father again. He ran over to them, barged past the cat, put his nose against the glass.

His parents were in a room that was almost familiar to Nathan, but not entirely – it was decorated with the ram's head design, in the style of Gam's den, but the layout of the furniture was not like any of the rooms Nathan knew. This one had a table in the middle and very little else.

Nathan's father and mother were dragging a man, someone younger, perhaps still a boy, shorter than his father but not by much, and this boy/man was struggling. The two adults had him by the arms, one hand each on his shoulders and one hand each at his wrists, locking his elbows so there was no way he could escape, but he pushed and jerked and tried to break their grip.

From the way the scene was framed, Nathan could see his mother and father's faces, but the boy/man's back was to him so he couldn't see his face. The view stayed like that regardless of where they went, as if the window was always behind and above, some magic suspending the frame in the air, but moving.

The boy/man struggled, Nathan's mother and father dragged, and their expressions showed a puzzling mixture of emotions – anger, sadness, frustration, pleading. When someone is moving someone else against their will, it is rare that they care overmuch about the feelings of that person, but Nathan's mother and father would stop, faces concerned. If, through struggling, the boy/man pulled the muscles of his back, or twisted a joint past its tolerances, they seemed frightened by it. Then a steely look of determination would come back over them, and they would double their efforts to move him.

He wouldn't stop struggling, this boy/man, until eventually, Nathan's father took both arms and pulled them behind his back, forced him to his knees, held him in place with a knee between his shoulder blades.

Nathan's mother disappeared out of the scene, but returned almost immediately with a syringe. She inserted the needle into the boy/man's neck.

He went limp.

As his father held the boy/man up, the view turned so that Nathan could see his face. It was Nathan's face. No... someone very like him.

His features were precisely the same, except aged a little, lengthened a little, thickened in the jaw and broadened across the forehead. As a boy develops, the features of his face, along with the rest of his body, alter, remaining characteristically him, but deformed from the boy towards the man he will become an uncomfortable middle ground between the two.

This was the face that stared back at Nathan.

They dragged him to the table and laid him out on it, arranging him neatly and smoothing his hair and crossing his hands across his stomach.

Nothing happened then for some time. His parents disappeared from and reappeared in the frame, but it remained always focussed on the older Nathan.

Perhaps this was an older brother?

Except Nathan had no older brother.

Did he?

He was lain like someone on a mortuary slab, or in a funeral director's premises: motionless, dressed neatly, peaceful-looking, unmoving.

Then Nathan's mother and father returned.

They stood at either side of the table, and each was carrying something.

Nathan's father had a roll of canvas which, when he opened it out, was filled with surgical instruments: clamps, scalpels, staples. He arranged them in the space on his side of the table, nearest the head.

On the other side Nathan's mother had a dish, like a casserole.

She took off the lid, and inside there was a flap of leather, a mask, with holes for the eyes and mouth and nostrils. It had eyelashes, this mask, and a fine down of hair, and the lips were perfectly done – the window showed each of these things in turn – so that it would be hard to tell this apart from an actual face, except this one was flaccid, having been removed from the skull.

She took it out of the dish and laid it on the table in the same place that Nathan's father had put the instruments, except on the opposite side.

The focus changed again, and now Nathan's father was drawing the scalpel across under the older Nathan's hairline. Blood came up from the wound he made, spurting at first, but then slowing to a gradual but considerable flow, following the path of least resistance down the face, over the ears. It began to pool in a triangle the protrusion of the back of his head, his neck to his shoulders, and the tabletop made.

Nathan's mother wiped away this blood with a towel and moved the mask so that it wouldn't get dirty.

Nathan could scarcely look, but he also couldn't look away.

His father and mother cut the boy/man's face down all the way to the bone and peeled it away from the skull. They took a second implement, and used it to scrape the remaining flesh from the bone. They patted the blood away with more towels.

Everything progressed in such an appallingly orderly way that Nathan couldn't help but wonder whether this was the first time they'd done it. Perhaps, if he walked this street, he'd find many windows like this, see many Nathans like this, all meeting the same fate.

Nathan guessed what the mask was.

It was not a mask at all, but a second face which they grafted onto the bare skull, and when the transplanted face met the bone the man/boy woke up, suddenly, not looking like Nathan any more, but looking entirely like someone different, a perfectly individual someone else. That person leapt up, so that he stood on the table, eyes staring, looking about himself in shock.

This new person saw Nathan's mother and father.

They looked expectantly at him, but then, by force of some magic, he caused them to start screaming in agonies. He stared at them, and they shrieked – Nathan could see the pain in the set of their mouths and the prominence of the veins at their temples. They rolled their eyes.

Then the focus shifted and here was Nathan's father, his hands trembling in agony, taking from his jacket the knife that contained the Rebuttal in Ice. He directed the spell at the older Nathan with the new face, turned him instantly into ice, dropping the temperature in the room so cold that their breath, panting, gulping, billowed out in front of them in clouds of visible vapour.

Now the scene reset, and there was the boy/man again, struggling, while Nathan's parents marched him in armlocks to the operating table.

Nathan turned his back and walked away.

By walking away, Nathan had refused to make the restitution the Spark Actuary expected him to make, so the Spark Actuary led him down the street to the next place.

This was a building unlike the rest.

Where the other houses were as Nathan had come to expect – a door and windows on the ground floor, sometimes with steps leading up to the door, sometimes without, a patch of garden or a fenced and paved approach – this building was ten times the size of the others, ten times as wide, ten times and high, and ten times as deep. The edges of it had no respect for the edges of the other buildings. A terrace of houses all fit neatly and respectfully next to each other, each in its own space, but this building seemed to grow out of and into the buildings that surrounded it, as if had been dropped into place onto existing structures, each of which had been crushed by this new presence, superseded by it.

It had no brickwork, but was a huge cube of faceted glass, each surface about the width and height of Nathan's palm and all of them set at an angle to the ones that surrounded them. There was an uncountable number of these facets, and even if he had tried to enumerate the rows up and across and come to a figure by multiplication, it was impossible for his eyes to settle reliably on each facet. The whole seemed to swim in Nathan's vision, partly a function of the distortion moving water makes of light, partly the absence of any frame or division between each facet, and partly because of the light which shone from inside each of these facets, which was just like the light from the other windows.

It made it difficult to separate one facet from another in the mind, so that Nathan lost count after ten or twenty and that was barely any distance from the ground, and nowhere near the top.

He went up to look closer.

These facets were each windows in themselves, too small to give a place for an Actuary to sit, but the same in the important aspect that through them Nathan could see a performance of death.

He looked through one, then another, and then a third, and they all seemed to show the same thing: a parade ground, perhaps a mile to each side, on which soldiers in black uniforms were standing, stock still, in drill formation.

Again, there were too many of these soldiers to count – like the facets, they were so similar it was hard to separate them as individuals – but there must have been tens of thousands of soldiers, all in the same uniform, all adopting the same posture.

Nathan went along the building, looking into facets at random, and each showed the same thing. As he went along the building, he realised that each facet was showing the view from a slightly different angle.

He stepped back, once, twice, and by not focussing his eyes and by moving from side to side he could see the scene in the manner that he had once seen a horse running though the slots in a zoetrope in the Master's toy room, each single view blurring together to make a moving image, which was as if the parading soldiers, in their grid of thousands, were moving across his field of vision.

Now Nathan turned away.

He knew what this was, this building, and what this street was, and, though the thought sickened him, what the function of this entire district might be.

It was a repository of his father's dead.

Each facet of this strange building was showing the death performance of one of these soldiers, because they had all died at once, in the same place, of the same action, and that action was caused by his father.

He turned away, because he didn't want to see the thing that had happened to these people.

Hadn't Niamh, the Irish sailor, once called his father the worst Master of them all? Hadn't she called him the devil?

Behind Nathan was a wall of windows, only windows, and it was one of four sides, possibly five if the roof side was also faceted, and because it was still here, and the windows still showed the scene, their deaths had not been avenged.

Could any boy bear to watch some action that his father did, that caused death on that scale?

If he had hoped not to see, by turning his back, not to know what had happened to those soldiers, standing to attention on that parade ground, then his hope was a vain one. There was a great flash from behind him, that reflected back, from all of the windows of the neighbouring houses, the same image: an impossibly bright magnesium flare, then an enormous ascending blossom of fire and smoke, like a violent cloud.

This was shown to him in every window, and now Nathan knew what the light was that he had seen since he arrived, that regular bright illumination, like the passage of a lighthouse beam. It was the light from the murder of these soldiers, done by some weapon his father had used to burn them all into non-existence, to free their Spark for his purposes. It was the light of crimes for which he had never atoned.

Here, in Waterblack, the City of Death, each murder was taken singly and performed through these palm-sized windows, too many to count, too many to concentrate on, catalogued by the Sparkline Actuaries.

After Nathan did not claim these deaths in the manner prescribed by the city's ordinances, his Actuary led him out of the quarter of the city in which his father's deaths were accommodated into that part that housed Nathan's own murders.

The route was long and circuitous, his father's crimes filling street after street, deep into the suburbs of Waterblack.

Nathan walked behind the cat, automatically, his eyes not seeing the pavements, the signs, the lampposts. His mind channelled his thoughts endlessly to the magnesium flare.

When Nathan tried to take control of his thinking, tried to wrest himself from the thoughts of death on that scale, the flash, still appearing as it had before, brought the memory back to the forefront of his mind.

And the heartbeat grew louder.

Eventually the stiff-legged cat stopped in front of another window. This place had once been a shop, its frontage broad and entirely glass. Pressed up against the window on the other side, filling fully half of it, in the side away from the door, was what seemed to be an enormous mound of clay.

The Sparkline Actuary for this building, a snub-nosed ginger cat, untroubled by the water, trotted over to where the clay was, and jumped up onto the windowsill. Now, because this place was Nathan's, and he was the cat's client, the Actuary scratched Nathan's tally into the glass: four long lines. Then the cat turned and mewled silently into the water, its toothless mouth opening and closing once, its cloudy eyes closing and opening once, blinking once.

Then it waited.

Glass is a fragile thing, and the mass behind this sheet, when it moved, made it tremble, threatening to send cracks across its surface where the Actuary had made its tally marks. A living cat might have been disturbed by this prospect, that sort of creature being easily startled. It might have jumped down and gone off to a safe distance, but this one didn't care.

Perhaps dead cats have no need for startling.

Perhaps they have learned to suppress it.

Nathan went slowly over to where the scratches were, drifting through the water like seaweed does in a current. Behind the glass, the clay was lined. He lifted up his hand and looked at his palm – the lines on the clay were like the lines a fortune teller reads in the practice of chiromancy, lines that speak of longevity and love. Was it a huge, grey hand pressed against the glass? Did the room extend off invisibly to a size suitable to contain a giant, prone? Did he lie in that room, one huge, grey hand stretching out, pressed against the glass?

Nathan had never killed a giant.

There was no account to which this dead cat was holding him that would have 'Giant' inscribed in the ledger.

It may be that Sparkline Actuaries can understand when their clients are confused, or that might be something all dead cats naturally know, but this one went from where it had sat itself along the sill to where the clay didn't press. It looked through the glass in the direction it wanted Nathan to look.

When Nathan didn't move immediately, the cat looked again, turning its patchily furred head, opening up a wound large enough to show the bones beneath the surface, a recess in which a small crab was present, nibbling at the edge of the flesh with its palps.

Nathan swallowed, but came where he was asked to come and looked where the cat turned again to look.

The room, past the mass of clay, did indeed extend off into the distance, but, unlike some unfamiliar interior suitable for a giant, this was a place Nathan recognised.

Before his death, before the immaterial realm, before the Mistress, before whatever this existence now was, he had gone with Gam and Prissy to the Zoological Gardens of Mordew. There they had seen the peacocks and the tigers, had fed the alifonjers with buns. After they burgled the Spire, they had returned here with the dogs. Nathan had returned here alone, one night, to punish Prissy's faithlessness.

That was how he recognised this place, and, because he had done something terrible here, he did not question how it was that the zoo could fit into a room, nor why he couldn't see its edges and walls – these are questions that only occur to someone with a clearer conscience.

He put his hand against the glass: it was vibrating.

Though a person doesn't realise it above the water, vibrations are the things that make sounds, and though the ear is the organ proper to understanding whatever meaning these vibrations contain, the parts of the body most sensitive to touch can understand them too, after a fashion. Through the window, Nathan's fingertips could feel the sound of breathing, touched the anxious and insistent panting of animals, so that he knew when he turned from the angle the cat had shown him that the mass that pressed against the glass was neither clay, nor the palm of a giant, but was the form of the last family of alifonjers, wedged fearfully into the corner the window and one wall of their enclosure made.

There they were, the calves, the dam, the bull, knees bent. Three animals were behind each other, the bull was at the front. Nathan hadn't seen them from this angle when he had come down from the Master's Manse.

He had come from above.

He hadn't heard them breathing like this – frightened, defiant, confused, each animal communicating their emotions to the others. In his ears on that day had been the insistent hissing of his anger, on his fingertips the Spark Itch, wanting to be

Scratched. Then his fury had been all-encompassing, catalysed by the talking book, provocations of justification and power silencing any doubt in him that might have made him think.

He hadn't seen them, then, with the mind he had now, chilled by the great volume of dousing water that surrounded him on all sides.

Behind the window, up in a sky that was impossibly contained by the room, there was a bright blue star. The alifonjers were looking at it, their brown eyes liquid and dilating, the bull's trunk pushing his wife back into the corner, shielding her with his bulk, barring the oncoming strangeness with the fence posts of his tusks. The dam shielded the calves, her trunk blindfolding them as best she could, as if not seeing was a form of protection, except the calves squirmed and wriggled in their fear, and in the smallest animal's eyes, still larger than Nathan's, Nathan could see himself coming down from the sky, growing in that terrified pupil, briefly contained entirely in it, then exceeding its boundaries, bleaching the iris with scouring blue light.

Then the skin of its face, then the grey clay of the three of them, discoloured, until Nathan stood in the enclosure with them.

Through his fingertips, pressed onto the window, five on each hand – two incomplete spiders, tense and quivering – the vibration of their screaming started: the dam and the calves. The bull, to his credit, advanced to meet Nathan in spite of his fear. His tusks were the thickness of a man's waist, curved as scimitars, cream, mud-tipped from digging at the earth for roots.

He faced the Nathan who walked towards him, not letting the burning of everything around distract him from his duty. He set his legs, and though he blanched at the light, his eyes shrinking into the folds of his flesh, becoming lost, he did not turn away.

Nathan had not seen this, back then, had not cared, but now it tore at his heart. Bravery in the face of appalling power. Bravery in the face of a weakness for violence.

Is it allowable for a murderer to feel like Nathan did as he watched himself through the window? Sympathy of this kind, guilt: should that be allowed for murderers? It is a kind of undeserved redemption, isn't it, to allow the self – the real self, not some weapon used by others – to feel such emotions?

I feel pain for the terrors I have committed, not pleasure.

I cannot be all bad.

Murderers, though, have murdered. Part of their punishment for murdering is that they are known as what they are, even to themselves – murderers – and sympathy is inimical to that class of person. By concept, they cannot be allowed to contain contradictory definitions – Nathan had been in the immaterial realm recently enough to know this – so even if Nathan felt this guilt, experienced his own pain as he watched himself inflict pain on others, this was not sufficient for him to be defined by it, in his self.

It was not enough, and would never satisfy a Sparkline Actuary of Waterblack.

The Nathan behind the window faced the bull alifonjer, white in front of him. There was a blue albino, bleached of colour, its edges blurring into the others behind it. Nathan took the tip of a tusk in each hand, and the creature whimpered.

He had done this.

He knew what he would do next.

To see and know it was wrong now, was that to imagine that this was sufficient to clear his conscience in even the smallest way? No, since that was not congruent with the way of things. It was counter to the ordinances of the city.

He remembered the scorched reek of burning hair that filled the pen. The dam and her children behind seemed to weep and sob, to draw deep, ragged breaths. They made strange wheezing whistles.

With no more effort than a man uses to rip paper, or open curtains, the other Nathan tore the bull alifonjer in two, ripping it down the middle. One half of the skeleton adhered to the left side – the left ribs and left leg bones – the other bones adhered to the right.

It did not call out; it was already dead.

Soon even the bones were gone, burned away.

The creature's wife was next, with a calf, though Nathan was so hot that he never laid a finger on them. They burned in front of him, contributing to the pile of ashes that her husband had become.

Now before the other self was the smallest alifonjer. He stood not defiant, as his father had been, nor petrified, as his mother had been, but unable to make any sense at all of what he saw. He raised his nose in a question mark so clear that both Nathans couldn't help but read it. The little alifonjer blinked and blinked at Nathan's light, not seeing, perhaps, the dust that had been made of the others.

At his hip, the Nathan in the drowned street of Waterblack felt something touch him. Reflex drew his eyes down: it was the dead cat, pawing at his waistband.

Nathan pushed it away, slowly, his movements muffled by the water, and turned back to the window. He wanted to reach out for the alifonjer, to take it, to save it as he had required saving, the little one, the youngest, but as he moved to do it, to take the thing in his arms, there was the glass between them.

The cat, the Sparkline Actuary, pawed him again, this time with claws drawn, snagging Nathan's skin through his sodden clothes.

When Nathan looked again, intending to shoo him off, the cat padded away to where it had marked the tally. The Nathan in the room which this cat supervised stepped back, two or three paces, until he was amongst the charred remains and white ash of the last alifonjer's family.

They piled at his feet like a snowdrift.

Then, by virtue of some trick of perspective, both the Nathan behind the glass and the Nathan in the water were looking at where the dead cat was. The mouldering thing raised its paw, rotting and coming to pieces, and across the four lines already scratched, it made another, crossing the others at a diagonal.

Neither of the Nathans knew it, but this mark was a penalty added for cruelty, and though the cat's eyes were white with cataracts, inexpressive in the way they'd need to be to communicate emotion, it glared at Nathan with disgust.

When the Nathans looked back, the youngest alifonjer was a pile of dust.

As if at a click of fingers, the mass of palm-lined grey clay – the backs of the cowering alifonjers – was in the corner of the room again, pressed into the glass, and the Nathan in the room was returned to the sky, a blue and angry star, falling.

The Sparkline Actuary jumped down from the windowsill and trotted across the road to where a colleague from a neighbouring house was waiting. The two butted heads, swept down each other's sides, and then sat together and watched Nathan.

Why shouldn't they?

The neighbouring cat – black, crushed down one side, tailless – would mark its tally when the time came, and the ginger one had already done its work. Even dead cats must take their leisure when they can find the opportunity for it.

Nathan wanted to go over to them, to explain himself – his former self. If not to explain, then to apologise. But the people to whom one must make amends in Waterblack are not the Actuaries, who have the freedom of the streets and who do not need anything else. Those requiring recompense are the citizens of the City of Death, according to its census. Make amends or give revenge – these are the duties of the Master of Waterblack, owed to those that bear his Sparkmark, and fulfilling his duties is the manner by which a Master secures the loyalty of his people.

The Master has the power to make reparations, so that is what he must do.

The falling star was like an approaching firebird – Nathan had seen so many – yet this one was blue. He couldn't look at the alifonjers, so he stared, unblinking, at himself as he descended from the Manse, walking the distance from the balcony of his playroom through the air, traversing, at the Master's pleasure, the defensive boundaries that protected the intermediate realms in which he had been living.

Here came Nathan, the violent, rage-filled child, murderer of countless thousands, millions, even, depending on the counting, and Nathan as he was now recognised himself perfectly as himself, in his physical form at least. When he thought of himself, he could find no other Nathan more advanced than he was at this age.

What did this mean?

Here he came, Nathan, his fists clenched, his teeth gritted, light beaming from the sockets of his eyes as if the whites were the brightest and hottest filaments of a lighthouse lamp, or the sharpest flames of a welding torch, or the very heart of the sun. The rest of him was not much less bright, only the clothes he still miraculously wore dimmed his essential brightness, and then only a little, like a candle flame seen through wax paper, still bright.

He descended to the ground, and where his feet touched the bare soil that made the enclosure it leapt into flames, despite there being nothing to kindle there. He was so hot and bright that even things least prone to burning burned at his touch, and here he came, his hands reaching, arms outstretched, the air rippling around him.

Nathan's fingertips on the glass felt his warmth now his attention was drawn to the fact of his heat. He ignored the alifonjers and their breathing – he couldn't now bear to see them, knowing what was to come – and he felt the roaring of the wind that the other Nathan made of the air, an angry, buffeting hurricane of agitated gas, whipped into a tornado that scorched the glass.

Nathan couldn't bear to see the alifonjers, or hear them panting, but scarcely more could he bear to see himself, or to feel his heat, and even less to see the bitter fury on his face, to feel his catalysed Spark anger. He went to take his fingers from the glass, but now there was a tackiness to the meeting of the surfaces of his skin and the window that held him in place, and he couldn't pull away. He went to turn, but suddenly on his shoulder was the Sparkline Actuary, perched like a pirate's parrot, except where those birds are colourful and raucous, this cat was dull and grim, its white eyes matt. It put its cold paw to Nathan's cheek and pushed his attention back to the other boy, who was advancing menacingly on the alifonjers, whom Nathan could no longer avoid seeing.

He turned the other way, but here was the black cat, the half-flattened neighbour. With half its mouth it hissed at him, drawing half its lips back over half its teeth and narrowing its only eye.

The burning Nathan faced the bull alifonjer, white in front of him, and there was a blue albino, bleached of colour, its edges blurring into the others behind it. Nathan took the tip of a tusk in each hand, and the creature whimpered.

With no more effort than a man uses to blows a kiss, or to clap his hands, the other Nathan tore the bull alifonjer in two, ripping it down the middle. One half of the skeleton adhered to the left side – the left ribs and left leg bones – the other bones adhered to the right.

The creature's wife was next, though Nathan was so hot that he never laid a finger on her; she burned in front of him, contributing to the pile of ashes.

A dead cat of the city of Waterblack can direct a boy's attention to his Sparkline obligation; a Sparkline Actuary has that right under the laws of the city. The edicts that bind the citizens of the City of Death bind its Master equally. The dead are obliged to perform the conditions of their death infinitely, and performances require an audience. Nathan was that audience, having brought about the deaths, so the cats wouldn't let Nathan look away.

The Nathan behind the glass killed everyone and then the littlest of the alifonjers. If Nathan tried to close his eyes, each cat, one to either side, hooked a claw under his left and right eyelid respectively and pulled it open. When Nathan tried to turn his neck, the half-flattened cat, with the magic granted to it, filled the boy's muscles with the rigor mortis it possessed, paralysing him. Nathan tried to collapse at the knees, but it is easy to make a boy float underwater at the level required for his face to be directed at his crimes as they are acted out in front of him through the window of the house, on the street, in the district, in the quarter that contains the dead that he has accrued in the undrowned world.

It is very easy indeed.

Nathan watched, felt, heard, until, as if at a click of the fingers, the scene reset, and there he was at a distance, a falling star, the mass of palm-lined clay against the glass, forced into the right angle that the window and one wall of the alifonjer's enclosure made.

The cats jumped down and retreated to the middle of the road together, to join the colleague who had led Nathan there.

The falling star was like an approaching firebird; the alifonjer calves, dam and bull cowered, knees bent, each behind the other, the bull male at the front.

Now though, Nathan went to the door and opened it.

If this was something forbidden, the Sparkline Actuaries did nothing to prevent him – they sat disinterestedly in the middle of the road, licking at themselves.

Behind the door was air, and when Nathan went through into the room the weight of water was suddenly lifted from him, its pressure in his mouth, throat and lungs disappeared in an instant and he vomited up the water, if vomiting is what a boy does to clear his lungs of fluid.

The brine ran out of his ears as he knelt in the alifonjers' enclosure; everywhere inside him that was flooded with salt water he cleared by an effort of constricting his muscles.

Long ago, it seemed to him, back in the slums, he had watched his father make similar wrackings of himself, to bring up a lungworm, and if what Nathan experienced now was anything like that effort then it must have been a terrible thing, since the boy felt as if he would rip himself into pieces, halve himself across the stomach, tear off his head at the neck, cough out all his blood, so powerful were the convulsions his body obliged him to endure in order to make itself dry inside.

When it was done, the alifonjers were staring at him. The bull's eyes were nut-brown, like spheres of mahogany, the dam's the same colour, glistening with fear. The calves crouched down in the dust, hiding their eyes, since it is well known amongst the very young that monsters you cannot see cannot see you either.

The falling Nathan saw him though, which was obvious because the direction of his gaze was easy to determine: its searchlight beam isolated Nathan in an ellipse of brightness, etching his shadow in black on the closed door behind him. On the windowsill outside, the cats now sat, looking in, preparing in their minds for an alteration in the ledger, the ginger cat sitting near to the place where it had scratched the tally, one paw lifted as if it was begging for scraps from a table.

What was Nathan expected to do?

What had he planned to do when he opened the door?

The laws of Waterblack outlined the procedure, but he was ignorant of them.

That said, is it not to be assumed that the Master of a city exists in concert with that place? Is he not, in some important way, the same as it? In his sympathies, in his understandings, in his moods and attitudes, in his outlook, in his temperament, in his *telos*, to use an ancient term, a Master and his city can be identical, and since laws are as much derived from the city within which they are enforced as they are determining of it, those laws can be known by its Master by force of the above similarity, even if the rational mind does not know them explicitly.

They are implicit.

They are intuited.

Intuitively, then, Nathan did what he had to do.

He turned away from the window, raised himself up from his hands and knees, and stood to meet the blue Nathan as he came down from the sky, from the Manse of Mordew, a city that could now offer him no protection, since it was here under the water, drowned of its magic, taken in segment, and iterated in a room in a street in the City of Death where death was the first and principal law.

The blue Nathan seemed confused: when he blinked the torchlight of his eyes flickered. When he squinted, the torchlight dimmed. When he raised his hand to shade his gaze, to clarify whether what he thought he saw was what was in front of him, he stayed where he was in the air.

A Nathan catalysed and in the full blossom of his anger can walk through the skies of Mordew, but only if he does it with absolute certainty of himself. Otherwise, he is prone to the physical forces that operate on us all, and in Waterblack, affected by a new self-consciousness brought on by seeing himself in the alifonjers' enclosure, Nathan's focus wavered, his light faltered, and he was drawn downward by the heaviness of the world.

His conscience was heavy too, unsilenced as it now was by the rushing wind of power in his ears. 'Who are you?' he called over to himself, his feet meeting the earth as the last word left his lips.

Nathan didn't answer with words, but instead he sprinted low across the dust and slid, kicking the sky Nathan's feet out from under him.

It is disconcerting to be woken from a Spark rage, disconcerting to be attacked by oneself, disconcerting to find oneself down to earth, and people who are disconcerted make poor fighters. Avengers, revengers, punishers – those with wrongs to right – are very much better at violence than the disconcerted are, since they know to what their violence is applied, and the consequences of not applying it. They have the advantage of certainty. It should not be surprising, therefore, to know that the Waterblack Nathan was soon on top of the Mordew Nathan, with his hands around that boy's neck.

Strangling is a difficult way to kill a person, and strangling yourself, some will say, is impossible, at least by hand. The job's even more difficult when you are looking yourself in the eye.

When you are being strangled, you do not properly understand what is going on; the deficit of air, a substance necessary for the adequate consideration of events, increasingly robs the experience of being choked to death of its clarity, qua experience. This failure to comprehend the world becomes written on the expressions of the face, even as that face reddens and its eyes bulge.

When the strangler is yourself, in a separate body, and your face wears a look of grim and absolute commitment to murder, the object of which is you, and your teeth are gritted, spittle bubbling at the corners of your mouth as you pant hard with the effort of depriving yourself of your life's breath, nostrils flaring, eyes wide, it is very difficult to understand what is happening.

Pain drives out thought, eventually. There are sensitive structures below the skin of the neck – the oesophagus, the larynx, the network of veins and arteries – and the body does not appreciate the rough treatment of these things, so it causes pain when they are aggressed against, to spur the mind to resist. Worse is the pain that comes in the head when fluids that must return to the lungs for oxygen are stoppered up inside the skull, making a swelling pressure that forces the brain into less space than it needs. Oesophagus, larynx, arteries, veins: these things are important, certainly, but not more important than the brain.

After all, what is a person if he is not a creation of his cerebral organ?

When the brain is in danger, the body expresses this fact in the unbearable sensation of agony, which is worse than pain. The Mordew Nathan felt this agony, and along with it a terrible and fearful uncertainty, and the sense that he was killing himself, and, behind it, neutering even the possibility that he might defend himself somehow in a superhuman show of strength, the dreamlike conviction that this was not, and could not be, real.

As his mind received less and less of the air it needed to think, this conviction of unreality took over, and the Mordew Nathan died as if in a nightmare, expecting to wake up but never doing it.

Why didn't the Spark rescue him? The Spark is the will of the weftling, and Nathan was its inheritor. He inherited it from his father, the previous Master of Waterblack, who became its owner by killing God. Nathan, the new Master of Waterblack, was the rightful owner of the Spark, and no Nathan of the past, reiterated in the City of Death, had a greater claim than its new master did.

But how can a boy kill his past self and not immediately die?

Anyone who would ask such a question shows his ignorance of the weft, and of the realms, and of the city of Waterblack, where all the deaths of the past are memorialised in reals contained and local to the rooms of its houses, of its streets, of its quarters, of its districts, all the way to edges of the city limits, these established by the boundary stelae. The dead belong by Sparkline inheritance to their killers, and the obligation for them to make right those deaths is established by the city's edicts.

Waterblack is its own sovereign realm, under the ownership of its Master; it does not give the privilege of the real to any other realm, but withholds it for itself.

What is more real than death?

Waterblack was the City of Death. Let the other realms resolve paradoxes – the Master of Waterblack's principal obligation was to repay the debt his Sparkline Actuaries recorded, and no law superseded that fact.

So, Nathan turned to the alifonjers, still cowering in the corner.

These animals, having lived out their deaths in repetition from the moment they were iterated in Waterblack, feared this new Nathan as much as they feared the old one; more so, in fact, since they had seen him strangle, seemingly without resistance, their former murderer. Now he was approaching them, his hands trembling and outstretched.

Imagine your murderer is coming at you. He is the murderer of your partner, the murderer of your children.

Imagine he was once lit with a supernatural blue light so bright that it was almost impossible to see him. He etched your shadows onto the wall against which you were cowering.

Now, imagine he comes towards you and the supernatural light has gone. What once was blinding is now a normal child, of the order of things you are used to.

Is this lightless boy more or less inducing of fear than his illuminated predecessor?

Now you can see his eyes – the expression in them, the emotion. Now you can see the texture of his jacket – a rough and patternless tweed. Now he reaches up and beneath his bitten nails is dirt. You can smell him now.

Is this as frightening as a thing of light?

To the alifonjers, Nathan was now more frightening, representing to them a development of their deaths, a complication, their violent murder assured by its repetition and now a new torture assumed, a new twist in the future of their endless dying: that it should not remain the same.

They panted in front of him, the alifonjers; wept. Their lipless and prehensile mouths moved in wordless prayers against his coming, but now they did not dissipate in the face of his Spark. Though Nathan knew it was appalling to them, he also knew that all he had to do was place his hands on one of their hides for the others to see how it would be.

It was simplest, he felt, to repeat the pattern – they would be expecting it, conditioned to it – so he took the tips of the bull alifonjer's tusks in his hands. The creature whimpered, but Nathan did not let the sound last. Instead, with the Spark, with the will of God, he did the other thing that the Spark could do, when it was not catalysed – he made the alifonjer into an angel.

In another life, Nathan had tried to kill a fluke from the Living Mud – do you remember? – and it had become a rat.

Though that rat had bitten him, he did it again, laying his hands on a safe, making the inanimate thing live, briefly, before it died at the incongruity of its existence.

Later, as a means of fomenting revolution in the streets of Mordew, he made Nathan flukes of the dead-life in the Circus.

All of these things, though done imperfectly by an imperfect child, were applications of the will of God, the weftling, whose desire was towards the perfection of things, the perfect marriage of form and concept facilitated by energy, which is what he himself was. His will was the way he wished the world to be, so that he might attract the attentions of the warpling, to make something visible to her, something worthy of her attentions, so that she might come down from her dwelling place in the warp and bring about his desires as we, lower creatures, petition him to bring about our desires through our prayers.

Nathan, though not the weftling, still inherited, through the actions of his father, the will to perfection in its manifestation as the Spark, which can not only scour material out of the material realm but can also make it into a perfect thing, which is what happened now.

The Sparkline Actuary for this room set up howling as a queen cat does when on heat and thereby called to it all the neighbouring Actuaries from their sills. Together they watched, swishing their tails and purring, though Nathan didn't see or hear them.

An alifonjer is a very developed creature on the path to material perfection, and though it is not identical to the weftling in form it has the same parts as he had – a spine, a nervous system, four limbs, symmetrically spaced, ears, eyes, nose, mouth, brain in a skull.

It has teeth as the weftling once had, and its tusks are two of them. These, since they were where Nathan was touching it, were the first to show the tendency Nathan's application of the Spark created – they were pushed towards material and immaterial perfection.

Their grubbiness from their interaction with the earth was purified away, their roughness too. Their surface became like pure enamel, glistening white, and, like white ink absorbing into grubby paper, the perfection spread consistently outward until it reached the place where tooth met skin. There is perfection in the contrast of opposites, that being a representation in the material realm of the opposite but equal material and immaterial realms, so the alifonjer's skin took on black perfection, lustrous and deep, and the bull's eyes, in order to oppose that colour, became perfect white, and where the skin was black the wrinkles in it, themselves perfect, like the whorls on the fingertips, the chiromancer's lines on the palms, unique in pattern, these became perfect white until the whole superficial surface of the creature was one or other, white or black, both perfect and in balance.

But Nathan did not release the animal's tusks.

No creature in captivity can thrive – there is something in being kept at the pleasure of another that represents itself in

335

the body as a lessening in scale, a becoming cowed and crooked that all animals experience when they are imprisoned. It is as if the body is unwilling to take its right shape and size if it is only for the benefit of another. The weftling's will is towards self-perfection, for things to be what they are for themselves, without reference to things not contained within their concept. Though the things of the world conflict in the material realm, limiting their own tendencies towards perfection, without that consideration their form would be different, their extent would be different. Nathan held the perfect white enamel tusks, which were part of the skeleton of the alifonjer, and the form of this scaffold of bones itself took on its own perfection, stretching, widening, becoming denser, becoming everywhere perfect. The alifonjer began to swell, to gain height, to improve its posture. In order for the creature to change in this way it had to stand up straight, so now it stood up straight.

Nathan faced it, its every proportion extending, its skin stretching to take the bones beneath like a sail stretches in the wind.

The weftling is a thing of the weft, and it is not limited by the material realm.

God is a thing of the impossible, he is not limited by the possible.

The weftling combines the material and the immaterial using the energy of the weft, represented as the Spark, which is his will.

The perfect black and white bull alifonjer, perfectly representing its potentiality in the room, in the house, in the street of the city of Waterblack, stood straight before Nathan.

Nathan didn't let go of its tusks.

Instead, he filled the alifonjer to its capacity with the Spark. The perfect bull radiated from the inward direction, which can be thought of as weftward, out from the infinity of extent which exists inside everything. Light is all the eye can understand of the Spark, and now the alifonjer glowed as brightly blue as Nathan himself had glowed when he had come down from the Manse of Mordew and had murdered them all.

Nathan removed his hands from the bull alifonjer's tusks and immediately it went to gore him.

This is understandable – a creature must protect himself and his line, and a perfect creature will do this perfectly.

Nathan stumbled back, but before he could be killed, the Sparkline Actuary assigned to this room raised its paw, which leashed the alifonjer angel's Sparkline to Nathan's will. In so doing an immaterial representation of the legal bond between a thing and its owner was created under the laws of Waterblack, and the alifonjer stood itself down.

The cat went to the place where it had scratched the tally mark beside the window to the room. It drew its claw and unscratched one line, this representing Nathan's acceptance of the obligation to his dead, and when he did it the bull alifonjer appeared not in the room where he had been obliged to repeat endlessly his death, but was instead in the street, the Sparkline leash still attached.

Perhaps the alifonjer thought it would drown: it began to struggle and float.

Nathan ignored it and put his hands on the dam alifonjer, and put the will of God into her, making her a perfect luminous monochrome of herself.

The cat leashed her, too, unmarked the tally, then the older child, then the youngest, and each took their place in the street.

When it was done, the room was empty, becoming the four walls of a dishevelled town house, water-damaged and mildewed, floorboards creaking, the glass in the lamps cracked and the grate in the fireplace rusted.

The alifonjers were in the drowned street, but when Nathan went to leave he found the door shut.

The Sparkline Actuary was on the windowsill, its paw against the glass. It had, originally, made five marks, the crossbar of the tally gate being added for cruelty. Cats do not communicate by words, even those of Waterblack, but their staring seems to contain significance.

Moreover, a city of the weft, Waterblack most of all, speaks to you with its laws, with its magic, and this was how Nathan knew what he must do before his tally would be unwritten. This thing he did, making a secret pledge in his heart that a Sparkline Actuary can add to a ledger, and though no man need share the particulars of his obligations with another, you will know them before the end.

Just like the streets that had been dominated by Nathan's father's dead, the streets of this quarter were dominated by Nathan's dead.

He ignored the stiff-legged cat now, walked where his attention took him, the alifonjers, glowing, tethered to him.

While the windows showed many things – the gill-men Nathan had killed, the people of Malarkoi he had killed, the people of Mordew he had killed – they mostly showed these things at a particular distance, which was the distance required for the performances of Nathan's dead to be clear and obvious in their circumstances. Figures were rarely in the far distance, and rarely in the near distance, but were generally in the middle distance, where it was obvious who was who and what was happening.

There was one window that showed something else, and Nathan was drawn to it, as if there was a rip tide at the seabed which forced him towards the house it was contained by.

In this window there was a flat and sallow man's chest, close up, sunken in, the ribs very obvious, as if the man was starved.

The heartbeat sounded so loudly in front of the glass of this window that it pained Nathan's inner ears. Now, when it beat, its beating coincided with movement beneath the skin of the chest in the window: blood, or muscle, a thing beneath the ribs that made the skin dip and then rise again.

Nathan stopped breathing, waited the ten seconds until the heartbeat sounded again, and there it was, perfectly in time with the sound, the movement beneath the skin, the dip and rise.

He waited again, not breathing again for another ten seconds, and then another, and both times it was the same: the movement and the sound synchronised.

The landscape of that chest, its topography, the small

landmarks – a mole, a patch of dry skin, the dark nipple, the grey and twisted hairs – Nathan recognised it.

Though his mind fought the realisation, though his eyes fought it, he knew who this was behind the glass.

The heartbeat sounded again, but Nathan's eyes were closed, and he turned away.

No cat opened them this time. Nothing forced Nathan to confront the scene.

Why they didn't do this, Nathan did not know.

This matter exceeded their authority. The Mastery of Waterblack, the transfer of that obligation from one party to another, was so fundamental to the operations of the city that no civil servant could have a say in it, and it was not their place, regardless of legal authority, to intervene in family matters.

The Sparkline Actuaries did not force Nathan to look in the window, and Nathan felt, briefly, that he had the option of running away from this sight, from this realisation of who it was behind the glass, of what he would see if he watched, what he would have to do.

But where else was there to go?

This place – this drowned and deathly city where he could breathe and live, the people of which he could redeem, or revenge, or make into angels – wasn't this his place?

More than Mordew.

More than Malarkoi.

More than the immaterial realm and the intermediate realms.

Where should he be, if not here?

What should he turn his attention to, if not the death of his father?

It was his father who lay behind the glass. It was his heartbeat, slow and heavy, that periodically filled the city, just as the light of his crime lit it. It was his death that had transferred to Nathan his Mastery.

He turned back to the window.

Rather than a sense of dread in his stomach, Nathan understood, perhaps for the first time in his life, that here was the opportunity to take something he wanted.

It swelled inside him.

The world was a terrible place, surely, and he was always at its mercies. He had always been forced to do this thing or that, had been tricked into doing things, had been used and killed and resurrected.

But wasn't he, now, the Master of this City?

Didn't he control it?

Couldn't he, in fact, use it?

Make it do what he wanted.

In the window, his father raised one hand to his chest. It made the journey into the frame of the image with enormous slowness, as if it was a calving glacier, creaking before it cleaved. The stump of his index finger was bleeding where it had been severed. There were dark red clots on the back of his hand, sticking to his knuckles. That sight came closer and closer, as if the performance of his father's death somehow turned on it, as if the judgement it demanded would need this thing as evidence.

Nathan paused, then he hurled himself at the window.

Whether you enter a room in Waterblack by the door or by the window, the water does not go in with in you. These rooms are discrete realms in which the death scene plays out.

If the view through the window shows something in close, or something far away, this is a function of the glass. It is magically treated to give the display necessary for judgement to be made, this requirement being determined by the Sparkline Actuaries who curate the images the windows show.

It is the window frame, the door frame, the frame of the building that delimits the extent of the realm within it, the architecture of Waterblack having this as its primary feature.

Mordew is a circle, Malarkoi is a pyramid, Waterblack is a frame.

Nathan smashed the glass when he hurled himself against it. This was not because he had the strength to do it – the windows of Waterblack are magically able to withstand any pressure, whether it be from blows or from the weight of water against them. Their material is suffused with the concept 'unbreakable', and it was only Nathan's Mastery that broke this window, all concepts giving way to his desires in his own city.

The glass shattered and fell slowly back onto the sill below, slowly back onto the street, all of it remaining on Nathan's side of the window, the water acting as the boundary now, one which Nathan passed through.

He did not arrive onto his father's chest, a miniature of himself, the size of an ant, because, the window gone, the realm inside was revealed to be the shack in which Nathan had lived as a child, in its expected scale. Here was his mother's bed, empty, and beside it was the sheet with which she divided the room in two.

Across the room, the heartbeat boomed.

It came from Nathan's father's heart.

Onto the sheet, like a puppet show, the objects of the room behind were outlined as shadows against the candlelight – the low table, his father's bed frame, his father and mother, one dying in bed, the other sitting beside him. The shadow of his mother was holding the shadow of his father's hand.

Once, in another life, the Master of Mordew had said that he wasn't responsible for Nathan's father's death, that Nathan's mother had killed him, once the lungworms had weakened him enough for her to do it.

If that was the case, why was his father's death represented here, in that part of the city reserved for Nathan's dead?

There she was, in outline, almost like a skeleton herself, seen in that simplified way, and there was her husband, a shape beneath a bedsheet, his chest only barely rising and falling.

If the Master of Mordew had been telling the truth, then she would reach down, in a moment, put her hand over her husband's mouth and nose, press down against his ineffectual struggling until his body failed through lack of breath.

She would stop this heartbeat, once and for all.

Nathan watched the shadows.

But now he understood that the Master of Mordew had been lying to manipulate him. It was so obvious, now, that anything that man said would be a lie. There was nothing he said that was not self-serving.

Nathan watched the shadows, and his mother did nothing. She sat beside her husband, in the candlelight, and she didn't move at all. She didn't speak.

Inside, the heart beat.

Outside, the rain began to fall.

Nathan sat on one side of the hanging sheet; his parents sat on the other.

Down fell the rain.

Slowly beat the heart.

How long does it take for a man to die if he is not smothered?

That depends on what is killing him.

In Nathan's father's lungs, Nathan could sense the growth, out of nothing, of lungworms.

There was once a belief, held by the ancient people, that filth and ordure generated flies. This was a simple mistake the ancients made because flies are always seen around filth and ordure, and they breed their young there. These people saw corpses, they saw maggots, and they saw these maggots turn into flies. It seemed commonsensical that corpses must create flies because this is what they had seen happening.

After thousands of years, with many generations convinced of that error, it became known, by some paradigm shift in thinking, that flies went to filth and ordure to lay their eggs, because it was a good place to raise their children, and the common consensus switched from believing that a corpse generates such creatures to a belief that creatures are not generated in that way. The presence within an organism of parasites required, this more enlightened generation believed, the parasites to come from elsewhere.

This belief persisted even to the people of Mordew, even to Nathan.

If Nathan's father had lungworms, those things must have invaded his body from outside, since parasites do not generate inside a body. Even when Nathan began to make worms from nothing, even when he worried that his dreams had brought about his father's death, these worries were like nightmares – strange, paranoid thoughts.

They weren't realisations.

They weren't discoveries.

Things of that order require that their ideas develop accepted wisdom.

Here, in Waterblack, Nathan saw the error of that thinking.

In Mordew, a city dominated from below by the corpse of God, in proximity to the will of God, lungworms can be created inside a corpse. Even if the bearer of the will of God is unaware of it, his power will act in the world in its own interests, bypassing his conscious mind, taking itself out into the real.

There was his mother, there was his father, and here sat Nathan, Master now of his own city, and it was perfectly obvious to him now that Waterblack had made it all happen.

His city required a Master. The former Master had reneged on its Mastery. So, in the slums, it had caused a new Master to begin his ascension.

Nathaniel Treeves turned his back on his city, on his wife, on his power, but Waterblack would not be ignored.

Under Nathan's father's skin, his lungs were now more worm than lung. Those organs, by weight, were no longer human – there was the pleural membrane containing a tracery of flesh, but mostly they were worms, writhing together, breathing the air meant for Nathan's father's body, excreting their filth into the cavity they were making of his chest.

Nathan had put them there, Waterblack had put them there, to hasten the transition from one Master to the next.

And why had his father allowed him to do it?

Because he had lost faith in his ability to Master this city. That was why there were so many unavenged dead in his father's quarter. That was why the Sparkline Actuaries looked on Nathan with such disdain. That was why Niamh, so long ago, had said his father was the worst Master of all.

His father had failed, had turned his back on his duties.

Now, behind the curtain, there was one, final, tremulous, palpitating beat of Nathaniel's heart.

And then silence.

Nathan stood up, took a step, grabbed the curtain, and the moment he pulled it down to the ground, the heart beat again – louder this time, harder, sounding at a higher pitch. Then there was another, less than a second apart.

Another.

Another.

Nathan put his hand to his chest.

Another, and under his palm he felt his own heart, perfectly in sync with the beat that filled the room, filled the street, filled the district, filled Waterblack in its entirety.

Across the city the dead cats howled as if the entire city was on heat.

Whether Nathan's mother might have been nothing but a shadow on the sheet, or whether she might have found a way out, or whether her disappearance was due to the ordinance operating in Waterblack that the conditions of a death are privileged between the dead and the city's Master, when the sheet fell it was only Nathan's father's corpse that was left in the room.

In the previous rooms the scene had reset on the death of the victims, but that was under the regime of Nathan's father's heartbeat. Who knew what new rules Nathan would establish?

His father's corpse lay there.

It is rare for a person's body to meet its death complete. What might 'complete' be, materially, in any case? A man may cut his hair and beard, lose limbs in accidents, become disintegrated at the point of death. Even if he does none of these things, the body naturally grows, shrinks, sheds its cells: who is to say what the proper form of a thing so mutable is?

Yet, if a finger has been cut away – the index finger particularly – and by the Master of a competing city for use in magic, that is an insult to the integrity of the ruling line of that city. Imagine that the beloved ruler of your city had part of them removed and taken away by a rival ruler. Imagine that you are the successor of the injured party. Even if you did not know how to do it, you would feel as if the remedying of that insult would be a thing that ought to occur.

Nathan felt it was a thing that ought to occur, and in the same way that it was not necessary for him to articulate the feeling to himself that lungworms ought to grow within the body of his father, so it was not necessary for him to articulate the desire that his father's index finger should be returned to him for that process to be set into motion.

Though Nathan didn't hear it, the order went out into the city of Waterblack that efforts should be made for Nathaniel Treeves's missing finger to be brought to the new Master.

So, it was done.

A Master of Waterblack need not concern himself with how things are done – he has his Actuaries for those purposes – so when the stiff-legged cat dropped the finger into the room, never entering it sufficiently to undo the privacy that Nathan had established between himself and his father's corpse, he did not know that word had been passed in the yowling of the cats to the boundaries of the city. He did not know that the Actuary on the south-eastern border had used the magic of the boundary stelae to call to the beast – known as 'the Squid' – that provided the engine for the ship the *Bishop of Sletty*. That call propagated back through time to the moment the *Bishop of Sletty*, to the dismay of its crew, would need to set off for the water above Waterblack. Nathan didn't witness the relay of that finger across the precincts of that city, even though it took place simultaneously with Nathan's arrival, directly to where he would eventually wish it to be.

Such is the magic of Waterblack.

Nathan picked up the finger, gently, carefully, and he brought it to his dead father's hand and put it where it ought to be. If he had known more of his powers, Nathan could have reattached it, but he didn't yet know that he was able to do something of that sort, so instead he put it in on his father's stump and left it there, not expecting him to move and thereby disarrange it.

The wounded hand lay on his father's chest and the severed finger lay beside the wounded hand, and there was his father, silent and dead.

Could Nathan return his father to life?

We should guess by now that he could. Nathan was possessed of the will of God, in the form of the life-giving Spark. He had made angels of dead alifonjers, brought inanimate objects to life, caused to generate from nothing the lungworms that killed his father. He could do these things because he willed for them to be done.

But what was his will in regard to his father?

Hadn't he always defied him?

He had been given very clear instructions not to use his Spark, but he had done it in any case. He had been told that to use his power would be to make him a devil, and yet he had used his power. He had, at the insistence of a rival power, murdered a thousand million infants using the power his father had forbidden him.

Should Nathan return his father to life?

There was some obligation on Nathan, that much was clear from the existence of this room here, in his quarter. But hadn't his father reneged on his own obligations? Wasn't the heartbeat that pounded in this city's precinct's now Nathan's heartbeat?

Nathan looked away from the corpse, back to the broken window, and there was his Actuary, and with it a hundred others, staring in through the place where the glass had been.

Do not use it, his father had said.

There he was, pitiful and dead, beneath a thin sheet, his severed finger, his wounded hand, his dead chest swelling with lungworms.

What was Nathan to do?

Nathan put his hands onto his father's chest, and he closed his eyes.

When a man is emaciated, there is very little material between the outside of him and the inside of him.

How thick is a rib?

How thick are the layers of skin that cover a rib?

How thick is the pleural sac within which the lungs are contained?

Hardly any thickness at all, and a corpse does not move. The parasites that live within the corpse, the things that made the living man a corpse, wriggle in their freedom. A living body has defences, and when these end, as with death, the lungworms rejoice, dancing beneath the surface of the very thin barrier that exists between them and the world.

Nathan could feel them rejoicing, all of them together, in two writhing masses, one beneath his left hand and one beneath this right hand.

His father's bones were thick enough to deaden this sensation, but the intercostal muscles, so atrophied, provided no barrier. Where Nathan's fingertips rested he could feel each individual in the lungworm colony in both the right and left lungs, spiralling, performing figures of eight inside his father's corpse, like bees dancing in their hives.

Nathan found one of them – he could picture it because he had seen them as individuals, long before, when his father had been alive enough to strain and cough each lungworm up into a chipped enamel bowl. He had seen one progress across his father's dry lips, to be spat drily away. Now he isolated one from its brothers and sisters, followed it until it went deep into the ball of them in their gathering under the flesh.

It had its own Spark, this horrible little thing, so it was easy to add to it.

A lungworm, when it is filled with God's will to perfection, evolves gradually through the forms towards the end of its possible development, that being, for a worm, ever greater forms of worm. If the Spark is added slowly, development will be primarily material, material change requiring time in which to alter the material form. But if the Spark is forced in very quickly, before the matter has adequate time to adjust itself to change, then the development occurs immaterially.

If the Spark is forced through in almost no time, then the matter of a thing will defensively evolve into an immaterial form. If this is not successful, the matter will leave the material realm entirely, become the perfect concept of itself, burning away.

Nathan, with almost no effort, the thing was so small, burned the lungworm he had isolated with the Spark into the concept of itself, bypassing even its angelic form, since that is something that must take time, and Nathan allowed none to pass.

How did he know how to do that?

He knew it in the same way that you know how to breathe, which is to say it was the proper thing for him to do, the thing that he, as Master of Waterblack, in his own city in his own district, in the room in which his father was laid out, intuited as naturally as any creature intuits the things it intuits.

Nathan's was the will of God, and what he willed came to pass without him needing to think about how.

How do you want, when you want something? You do not know. You simply want.

How did Nathan evolve the lungworm to its concept? He simply did it.

When the first one was gone, he simply made the others go.

It takes time for you to read these words, it takes effort, it takes your intelligence: it took Nathan none of these things to remove the lungworms from his father's chest. He had his hands where they needed to be, he had access to the Spark, he willed it to happen, and it happened.

This was a perfect use of magic, an effortless bringing into being of that thing one wants to be true, and Nathan did it.

But...

Can a boy control what it is that he wants?

If something is effortless, can he stop himself from getting what he wants?

What if power knows better than the mind does what it is that he wants?

Nathan evolved away the forms of the lungworms in no time, with no effort, and this was the thing that he wanted to happen, but didn't he also want his father never to have died? Did he want it to be that he had never killed him in the first place, by inserting into him the lungworms generated by his ignorant and imperfect channelling of the will of God, in proximity to the weftling's corpse?

He burned away the lungworms, and then he also made the dead cells of his father's corpse live.

His father sat up on his bed with a jolt.

Nathan jumped back, looked at his hands as if they had committed a crime.

Don't use it, he'd said.

There are words, and there is the conscious mind, and there are the things we think we want, but below these are feelings, the unconscious mind, the things we don't know we want. We may do a thing and we might be appalled that we have done it, but our inward selves know better. 'Dad!' Nathan cried, and he leapt forward. He shut his eyes, threw his arms around his father's shoulders and he sobbed, 'Dad, dad, dad!'

Who could blame the boy for resolving his contradictory emotions in this way? 'Dad!' he kept on sobbing, the tears flowing, his hands locked together behind his father's back, the man having so little flesh on his bones that even his son could reach around him.

Dad, in his mind now, repeating.

Dad.

When someone is in this kind of state, they don't notice much other than a single word, the feeling of someone dead who has been returned to them, the mass of their body in the circle they make with their arms as they embrace them.

Eventually, though, that feeling begins to wane.

Eventually, the person who, a moment ago, was entirely overcome by their emotion feels the subtle signs that there is something wrong.

When one embraces even the sternest father, one expects that embrace to be reciprocated. The body expects the father's arms around its back.

If not that, the body expects the palms of the hand on either side of the ribcage.

If not that, the body expects gentle tapping, somewhere: on the waist, on the shoulders, on the back of the head.

If none of these things happens, the body expects the relaxing of the person-being-embraced's muscles.

What it does not expect is a hard and unyielding rigidity.

It does not expect this to be paired with silence.

It doesn't expect, then, for its arms to be peeled away, for a forearm to be interposed between the embracer's body and the embraced, for pressure to be exerted outward so that the two bodies are forced apart.

When a boy looks into the face of his father, he does not expect to see cold indifference there.

'Dad?' Nathan said.

On the floor beside the bed was Nathan's father's index finger, and Nathan's father was staring at it. He made a fist of his hand – the one from which the finger was missing – and then he opened that fist and stretched out his remaining fingers.

Nathan edged away, back across the bed, which, despite its shortness, now seemed very long.

His father moved so that his legs came out from under the sheet and then he put one foot either side of the finger, flat on the ground. Then he reached down and picked the finger up with his good hand. He shook it – it had dirt on the bloodied end – and rubbed it against the sheet, leaving a smear of red. Then he put it against the wound where it had come from.

Under his breath, he muttered something, and the finger reattached. He made the fist again, stretched out the fingers again, and now the index finger was where it ought to have been – a different colour, certainly, but attached.

Nathan's father turned to Nathan. 'I told you not to use the Spark, Nathan. Didn't I?'

Nathan looked down at his knees.

Nathan's father shuffled back so that he was sitting cross-legged on the bed. 'Well?'

Nathan nodded. 'Yes, Dad.'

'Look at me,' he said.

Nathan looked up from his knees.

There was his father, unsmiling. He rubbed the join between his wound and the reattached finger with his thumb. He made small circles and gradually the blood started flowing.

The finger's colour returned.

Nathaniel looked away from Nathan, towards the window from which the glass had been broken. There was the Spark Actuary on the windowsill. Nathan's father put his hand to his chest and waited until the city's heartbeat sounded.

When it did, he turned to Nathan. 'So, you're the Master now, I assume?'

Nathan knew that he was, so he nodded again.

Nathan's father turned back to the Actuary, beckoned to it. In that way that cats have, it drew back its lips and hissed. It turned its back and showed its anus. It circled slowly around and took to licking its paw.

Nathan's father sniffed – it might have been a cheerless laugh.

'Dad,' Nathan said, but his father locked him with a stare and slowly shook his head.

'You're no son of mine.'

Nathan didn't understand. He went forwards on the bed, but his father pointed with his index finger, stiff, like the blade of a knife. 'I told you not to use the Spark. You disobeyed me, and now you'll face the consequences. I curse you to failure and death. If fate does not provide those things for you, then I will.'

Nathan didn't understand this either.

His father got up, looked around the hovel, shut his eyes and shook his head. He took a deep breath.

'Dad,' Nathan said, but now his father didn't seem to hear him.

Across Nathaniel's lips, words played, quickly, repetitively, and now the Sparkline Actuary turned and faced Nathan. It stopped licking its paw, and locked its glassy, dead eyes on Nathan's, as if it was trying to communicate with him.

Nathan didn't – couldn't – understand.

He turned to his father. 'Why?'

Now the movement of words across his father's lips was matched with sounds, none of which meant anything to Nathan, none of which stayed in his mind long enough to form words.

The Actuary mewled.

Perhaps Nathan should have done something, but on this occasion his intuition failed him.

Into the hovel appeared Nathan's mother. In her chest was a fist-sized hole so that it was possible to see the empty cavity inside where her heart should have been. From her cheek there protruded a crossbow bolt.

Nathan's father turned and lurched at Nathan. 'What have you done, you little shit?'

Nathan stepped back, fearing that his father would beat him, but the Sparkline Actuary raised a paw and between Nathan and Nathaniel Treeves a barrier of glass appeared, just like the glass that formed the windows to the rooms.

The father never made contact with the son.

Now it was Nathaniel's turn to hiss, at both Nathan and the Actuary, but it was short-lived, because he turned and using the same magic that he had used to repair his finger he repaired the absence of a heart in his wife's chest. When that was done he broke off the haft of the crossbow bolt, pulled it gently through Clarissa's jaw and sealed the wound.

He turned back to Nathan. 'You're the biggest disappointment yet. Next time I see you, I'll kill you.' Then, with his wife in his arms, he left, dissolving them to nothing in an instant, going to who knows where.

The Sparkline Actuary went to the glass that it had made in front of Nathan. It drew its tally and then erased it.

So it was that Nathan Treeves resolved his culpability in the death of his father, under the ordinances of Waterblack.

An Interlude

I T IS SOMETIMES SAID that the world of the living is a veil that on death is drawn aside to reveal the higher world behind it. While this is not quite how Anaximander would have put it, there was some truth in the idea, he thought.

Where he thought this, and under what conditions, were difficult for the dog to ascertain, there being an insufficiency of the real world about him. He felt himself to be suspended in a volume of sensory static, impossible to resolve.

Yet, he did think it.

As a forgotten philosopher once argued, something that does not exist cannot think; thinking can only be done by a thing that exists. Therefore, a thinking thing must have the quality of 'existing' by definition.

Since Anaximander 'thought', he felt certain that therefore he 'was'.

The object of his thought was that the veil-likeness of life, something that had been commented on in his hearing while he was alive, was less like an obscuration of semi-transparent cloth, as a veil is, than it was an overload of sensory, emotional and intellectual experiences that distracted the mind from something more fundamental by overwhelming its attention.

In the background of this thought was a silent sound, despite such a thing making no sense, a kind of pressure, the presentiment of an utterance, perhaps, but one with no content, which, though he couldn't account for it, he did feel that he must acknowledge, if only then to ignore it, which he did by thinking of something else.

It seemed to Anaximander, turning his mind away from the non-sound, that the object the veil obscured was not so much a 'higher world' – regardless of the aptness or otherwise of the spatial metaphor in this place that seemed to have no dimension to it – as it was a simpler form of existence, not prone to the overabundance of everything to which the so-called real was prone.

As a living dog he had always paid attention to the world in all its complexity, applied his senses, his concepts and his attention to it. He had watched how it reacted, judging the truth of his thinking by how consistently the world reacted to him.

Now, as the totality of his material life resolved itself into an ever-dwindling point of light – he saw it, suddenly, in the very far distance – he understood that no consistency was possible with all the noise – both in its audible sense and also inasmuch as it was an excess of information – that had once come from every direction.

But how can one explain the existence of things that do not exist? Sounds are sounds: they cannot be non-sounds. Utterances are utterances: they cannot be non-utterances. To suggest otherwise is to undermine the very functioning of language. So why did Anaximander have to exert an effort to turn his mind away from the pressure of a silent sound, a thing that, to the best of his knowledge, could not exist?

There was a sense that he was being shouted at, though there was no sound possible here.

Was it becoming more definite?

Anaximander didn't know.

This continued timelessly and indefinitely.

Aside from the above, there was that list of things Anaximander desired in the moments preceding his death, which were as follows:

1. He had wanted to recover from his wounds.
2. He had wanted to learn the magic that makes talking dogs happen in the world.
3. He had wanted to use the above magic to make another talking dog.
4. He had wanted to discuss with this dog whether or not a talking dog's service-pledge can be considered to be ended if said dog finds himself betrayed.

5. If the answer to the above question was 'yes', he had wanted to renege his service and punish any and all betrayals against him.

Anaximander turned his thoughts to this list.

The resolution of his first wish – that he should recover from his own wounds as he lay in the damp grass by the hole from which he and Bellows had emerged, and where they were quickly killed by the gender-neutral assassin, the Druze – was rendered irrelevant. Firstly, he had succumbed to his injuries and was already dead. Secondly, his body was, like everything else he had previously experienced, now almost nothing.

There it was, in that ever-dwindling point of light in the very far distance. Every tooth mark and gash and rent from his fight with Thales, and every unwounded area of his former flesh was in that point of light, perfectly represented on his former body, but of which there was no qualitative differentiation to be made between wounded and unwounded.

Now 'a wound' and 'not a wound' held the same value. The difference between them was zero. Any physical thing was almost identical with any other physical thing because the fact of their materiality was the primary definitive condition of them, being compared to the non-physical, almost-void which surrounded all things infinitely on all sides.

A desire, Anaximander understood, can:

1. be satisfied;
2. be removed;
3. be ignored.

For example, a dog-man might wish for hard liquor. Drinking poteen might satisfy that desire, temporarily. He may also wean himself off drinking, and so remove the desire that way. Or he may ignore his desire for as long as he has the will.

Anaximander's first listed desire – for his wounds to be healed – was removed in the second manner. His body was now to him like an addiction from which he had been relieved: that is, the burden of his desire for his body to be whole was gone.

His second desire – that he should learn the magic that makes talking dogs happen in the world – was less easily resolved. He did not know enough about the world he now found himself in, or how it worked, particularly because the sensory map he had so much relied on in life returned no information useful to him.

Perhaps this was the source, he thought, of the incessant distraction from the soundless sound: if he had had ears, he could have heard it, but he had no physical form.

He was disembodied, he realised.

Like a ghost.

More than 'like'.

He was a ghost.

This realisation occupied him timelessly and indefinitely.

Why had he not realised immediately that he was a ghost, if the word 'immediately' meant anything here? Why did he not already know about the practicalities of life as a ghost?

Ghosts, while not entirely ubiquitous, are certainly universally understood to exist, so why is it, then, that when a dog dies through magic and moves to the realm of ghosts, which is where he presumed himself to be, he has so little understanding carried over from his life of the way this new existence works?

Perhaps an ignorance of new things is to be expected?

What does a puppy know of, say, gravity, or inertia, or momentum when he is born? He knows nothing, and must come into knowledge by a slow and gradual accretion of experience. By analogy, the same might be true of a newborn ghost.

This idea, though, immediately struck Anaximander as without merit. The analogy was too inexact, since a puppy comes to the world only with knowledge of the womb, that warm but muffled place, perhaps also of his litter mates beside him, whereas a ghost has the entire experience of his life before death at his disposal. Since ghosts were a part of that life, he should have some understanding of how it all works at the very least because ghosts had the opportunity to communicate this information to the living, and for that information to have become part of common knowledge.

Was that communication at fault, perhaps?

This was a more convincing idea.

Ghosts and living dogs have a particular type of intercourse, often characterised by fear, and no fearful dog can properly attend to his studies. Would this fear create a natural barrier to the transmission of information relating to ghosts across the life/death boundary?

Even a living dog who decides to learn the ways of ghosts, if he can speak and determines to ask them questions about their world, must always be overcoming his natural horror at the aspect of them. This horror is worsened by the fact that ghosts seem to bear the image of themselves at death, and since a person can die of gruesome injuries, many ghosts are seen in pieces, or mangled, things which invoke fear in a whole and living dog.

Also, there is something naturally frightening about death.

Complex organisms such as dogs evolve a desire to be away from sites of death, the rumour of those sites, and even the notion of death in general. It is dangerous to be in a place where death has occurred since it may well happen there again. It is also depressing to think of death, long association with it being known to make a living dog see life as worryingly impermanent, possibly even trivial. The brief period a dog remains alive seems dwarfed into insignificance by the inconceivably long spans of time with which that brief period is bracketed. Excessive consideration of that fact can become an impediment to the continuation of a dog's life, and so, by extension, the life of his species.

Anaximander warmed to the subject.

Does fear during life prevent a dog from being able to grasp the conditions of life after death?

It may be so, but then again it may not.

There are some dogs who, by their unusual psychology, do not fear death, and nor do they fear the appearance of a dead body, nor dismemberment, nor are they concerned about the impermanence of life.

Pit-dogs are taught not to fear death, nor do they fear the sight of innards, and dogfights are common enough that they are always available to gamblers. Fear might preclude most dogs from understanding the life of ghosts, but it cannot preclude all of them, and, since history extends for millennia backwards in time, then surely at some point sufficient information must have passed from unfearing dogs to fearful dogs so that they had some idea of how a ghost lives, even if it was partial.

The non-sound increased in volume. Think of the pressure the inner ear experiences when the body changes altitude. It was like this, except earlessly, except with a rhythm, but nowhere could Anaximander locate the source of it.

He returned to his thoughts.

Perhaps the matter would be resolvable through a consideration of the combination of the notions of 'ghosts' and 'trust'.

A dog does not trust that a ghost tells him the truth, when it tells him anything at all. It seems to a dog that there is an inherent weakness in the ghost's having succumbed to death, so perhaps that leads him to ignore a ghost.

Or perhaps the association with fear plays a part?

While fear might not absolutely limit the transfer of information from the dead to the living, it does give to that information a fearful character which a dog will find untrustworthy. In this the dead would be partly to blame: those dead most likely to wish to converse with the living are those most recently passed, or those who have met an untimely end – victims of accidents, of murder, those who have suffered a long and painful illness – who are more keen to tell a dog their sorrows than they are to provide detailed and objective information, and that only when they are willing to speak to a dog at all. The ghosts of dogs can very rarely, if ever, speak, nor can they be communed with in the usual way, and people rarely speak to a dog unless they know him well, and then they use the kind of language they use with infants – a kind of high-pitched, often nonsensical, often patronising, singsong verbiage not well suited to the transfer of detailed and reliable information.

Perhaps this was it.

Also, the information provided to dogs might be either sorrowful, or traumatic, or concerned primarily with who or what was to blame for the death of a ghost's material counterpart, or where items of value may be found by the ghost's surviving relatives, or long speeches on the characters of these or those people left behind against whom the ghost bears a grudge, or simply gibberish.

Perhaps the information ghosts might provide to a living dog was of an untrustworthy and incomplete sort.

Additionally, he extrapolated, dogs who spend their time consorting with ghosts are themselves likely to be seen as untrustworthy. If associations of dogs of sober and determined intellect – if, indeed, there were such things – were the ones who knew most of ghosts, he might have had, through his understanding of those people's reputations, an authority with which, had it occurred to him in life, he could have consulted in order to understand what conditions pertained to the world of ghosts. He would have been able to take what they said seriously, and might have sought them out in order to enhance his understanding of the world in that way.

But no such organisations had existed, to Anaximander's knowledge, in the places where he had lived, and those people who seemed most likely to consort with ghosts were, more often than not, people of less than perfect seriousness: lunatics, mendicants, fraudsters, mystics: all types of person that dogs are not wont to give, in the first instance, their credence.

Such was the mass of negative association with which a possible 'ghost science' might have been met, it seemed to Anaximander, that it would never have been able to get free of it, as a discipline, and perhaps this was why he knew so little, in himself, of the ways of the thing he now found himself to be.

Or was it because life after death, of which ghosts were an example, was a subject claimed primarily by priesthoods, all of whom, in one way or other, were secretive institutions the livings of whose employees depended on the keeping and explication of more or less arcane bodies of knowledge?

These ideas occupied Anaximander timelessly and indefinitely.

He was interrupted again by the soundless sound.

The anomalous non-sensation reasserted itself, and it seemed now that it had gained 'location'.

'There' was the material world in which he had previously existed – the ever-dwindling point of light in the very far distance, as if a pearl of perfect representation – and 'here' was the dog's mind. Then there came a third place.

This was the immaterial realm of concepts within which the answer to all questions that could be represented in words existed – something Anaximander's ghost now knew without knowing how he knew it.

In this third place the soundless sound existed.

So, Anaximander turned his mind to it.

Immediately he found himself drawn into the immaterial realm, since that concentration of immaterial concepts will draw an immaterial mind to it, just as a material body is drawn by a great concentration of material matter through gravity.

Because Anaximander wasn't used to it, he found himself overwhelmed, there being so many things, all interlinked, which drew his attention towards them.

Once his attention was there, though, and like the way that even a small amount of matter will draw other matter towards it, concepts were drawn towards him, particularly those relating to the idea, so recently a desire, of the understanding of the mechanics behind the making of a talking dog. There was a bewildering superfluity of these, not least because the immaterial realm, informed by the conditions of the weft, contained not only information relating to the material world that he had left, and the intermediate ghost realm he now found himself in, but also all possible and impossible worlds and realms, the nearly infinite majority of which he was neither familiar with, nor which were relevant to his enquiry.

In the vast expanse of notions irrelevant to him, he isolated that vein of concepts particular to the understanding of existence. These concepts were not entirely discrete things, but bled across and into each other. The idea of a talking dog and the idea of its making contain within and around them the idea of a dog that does not talk, the idea of a dog that does not need to be made, but which exists already, a talking cat, an untalking cat, a cat that requires making, a cat that does not require making, a rat, a mouse, a house, and on and on, extrapolated infinitely in every notional direction, each a link in a chain determined by the forms of the ideas and their contents.

When Anaximander apprised himself of the end of one chain – represented, in this case, by the question he had died desiring an answer for – he became apprised of the whole of it at the same moment. Some of this excess of concepts answered questions that had not been until that instant present to the dog, but which, he now quickly understood, were something he might want to know. One of these was 'how is it that a dog can exist after death?', to which the answer, immediately present, was that magic dogs, like any creature of whole or partial magical provenance, do not disappear from the world when their Spark is exhausted, but instead remain as ghosts in an intermediate realm separate from, but contingent to, the material realm, since their anchoring to the material realm is a fact that only their original maker can decide to sever – in his case the Master of Mordew – and sometimes not even then.

Anaximander also understood that the ever-dwindling point of light in the very far distance, as if a pearl of perfect representation, was, if he used it, his route back to the world he had left. He would return to the material realm in insubstantial form, an image of the material self, with insufficient mass to become solid. This would be more or less perceptible to a living eye depending on the extent to which the boundaries between the material realm and the weft had been loosened in the place which the material self previously frequented – its 'haunts', to use a word this particular use of which may or may not have originated in the above fact.

Neither of these understandings helped him to know what he wanted to know, and nor did all the others that entered him, unbidden, when he seized, metaphorically, the end of any signifying chain, or at least so it seemed to Anaximander.

'Seeming' in the immaterial realm is a flaw in the perceiving consciousness, though.

Just as a dog who seeks for a stick or ball which has been thrown into a body of water, and who dives into said body of water in order to locate it, finds himself pulled by the currents or tides of the water hither and yon and never, seemingly, towards that stick or ball – though there it is, very clearly, nestling on the sea or riverbed – and no matter how earnestly he swims towards it, he never gets any nearer, so that, tiring, he must return to the surface, to the beach or the riverbank, where he then regains his breath, shakes himself dry, and determines to go about his task with the benefit of a plan, and then, as he sits on his haunches, mouth a little open, eyes focussing on the place on the water above which he remembers the submerged ball to be, the plan comes to him in stages until eventually he dives in again and, with his eyes fixed on one particular place, he paddles earnestly down in one direction only, resisting the natural tendency of the water to take him in the direction it wishes him to go, so did Anaximander address the task of understanding how a talking dog is created.

This analogy established, we can say that Anaximander found on the seabed the first thing a talking dog must do in order to make for himself a second talking dog: he should secure, in the material realm, a clever and lively puppy at or near its time of birth.

This idea he fixed in his mind, and then he turned his attention, or his eyes in the analogy, to the idea of how a ghost might locate a particular person who was also dead, the person in this instance being Heartless Harold Smyke, the dog breeder by whom Anaximander had been raised, who was suggested to the dog's mind as the most natural source of a suitable puppy.

The story of Heartless Harold Smyke's death is one reserved for later, but it is suggestive to anyone who wishes to make a guess at who killed him to know that Anaximander was absolutely sure that the man was dead, while also knowing that he would know where newborn puppies could be sourced in the world he had left.

So, eyes fixed on the concept, analogous to the underwater stick or ball on the sea or riverbed, Anaximander dived into the immaterial realm with his mind, and 'swam' within it, against the currents and tides. In this case these currents and tides were all that could be known about locating a person, all possible iterations of Heartless Harold Smyke in all of the realms, and all the things that were the opposite of 'locating a person' and 'Heartless Harold Smyke', against which these concepts were most forcefully defined, since definition is a process done by similarities and dissimilarities, each doing the work of carving out the meaning of a thing by delineating what it is in opposition to what it isn't.

So, he went towards the desired knowledge.

Eventually, though no time can sensibly be said to have passed, Anaximander returned to the riverbank, though he cannot be said to have moved, the knowledge sought in his possession.

During the process, Anaximander learned that ghosts could communicate with each other in the form proper to them providing they can be sufficiently clear to whom it is they wish to speak. If they are sufficiently clear, then the desire to communicate with an interlocutor can effectively 'summon' that person into the other's mental presence without any effort at all.

When Anaximander considered the matter, it seemed very reasonable. Why should there be any difficulty communicating between the dead?

Ghosts do not exist in the material realm, they exist in an intermediate realm linked to the material realm, but closer to the immaterial realm, and just as it takes no more effort to think of a distant place than it does to think of a place close by, so ghosts need make no more effort to 'be' in a distant place than they need to 'be' in a near place.

So, rather than go somewhere to seek out Heartless Harold Smyke in order to enquire of him where a good source of puppies might be found in the material realm, all Anaximander had to do was conceptualise him in order for him to appear.

Because Anaximander had had such extensive experience of the dog-man while he was in that man's charge during life, and because dogs have very detailed senses of things while they are in the material realm, his conception of Heartless Harold was very accurate indeed, much more than a person's might be, so it was that he was able to bring the man in front of him very easily, in all his particularities and specificities, and to make enquiries of his ghost.

Incidentally, Anaximander thought at the same time, the opposite of the fact of a dog's sensory precision of conceptualisation – that is, a person's lack of such precision – was possibly the reason that the many seances that took place in the material realm tended to fail, or were prone to disruption by mischievous spirits keen to have fun at the expense of the living. To wit, most seances begin with a vague 'is there anybody there?' which is doomed to failure since no ghost would answer such a call in their intermediate realm, any more than if they had heard a similar enjoinment in the material realm during their life. People are generally busy with their own existence, and few, if any, stop that business in order to answer a vague and general summons. A man walking down a street who hears, muttered and in the distance, 'is there anybody there?' will either ignore it, feeling that the call is not for them, or they will tut and carry on, knowing they have better things to do than answer general requests for a person. They will be sufficiently convinced of their own self-importance that they will feel that no random caller can have as much right to their time as they themselves do, and so the call goes unanswered. If, instead, one was to hear one's name called loudly, then this same person would turn and answer it.

Indeed, the only type of person who would answer the vague type of call is the kind of person who has nothing better to do – some indolent or feckless person – or a person who hears a kind of weakness in this general calling, and who answers it in the hope that the weakness in the call is married to a similar weakness in the individual calling, one that they might exploit to their benefit and to the detriment of the caller; and a third type of person who would answer a vague call might be filled with malice, looking for a victim. Because what is true of a person is usually true of his ghost, then the operators of seances find themselves either unable to summon a ghost, or summon a feckless and indolent ghost, or summon a spirit with ill intent.

Even if a person summons a ghost by name and name alone, as is often the case, that is rarely enough to bring the correct ghost to attention, a name being a non-specific thing, liable to be owned by many people, and no living person should assume that a ghost simply knows which of the many bearers of that name the summoner means when they say it. Ghosts cannot read minds – the consciousness of each man operates in its own discrete intermediate realm, closed to all others – so it takes a very specific kind of calling to accurately bring a ghost to conversation, an accuracy that Anaximander was much better placed to possess.

Here he was, leaning forward towards Anaximander with somewhat grasping hands and something of a spiteful and acquisitive leer on his face, these things in wispy and gauzy representation of the world they had both, through death, left behind.

While the environment in which they were located was diaphanous, Smyke himself was represented to Anaximander with exactly as much detail as the dog was capable of conceiving, and so appeared utterly convincingly, and because Smyke was instanced in that realm in a physical manner, so was Anaximander now, a representation of his physical form returned to him, his body manifested around his mind.

A dog who has been taught to cower in front of his master since his puppyhood will always look down at the ground on the approach of that master, so the tips of Smyke's boots were the first thing Anaximander understood. A person of the merchant class will opine that one can learn a lot about a person by his shoes, and this was true of Harold Smyke's boots, though for different reasons. A merchant means by the above that a person who otherwise wishes to represent himself as a man of substance and discrimination and wealth can be caught out by his wearing of poor-quality shoes. If the shoes are cobbled for another man, or made to a generic pattern, or use gaudy leathers, and because bespoke footwear is an expensive thing to have made – more so if the cobbler understands how to make shoes that are in 'good taste' – a man's pretensions can be illuminated by looking down at his feet. Anaximander's understanding of Smyke was not on the grounds of whether the man wanted to represent, or misrepresent himself in terms of his class, but by the fact that his boots were those of a dog-man who treated his dogs in a particular way, and needed boots of a particular type to do this. Smyke's boots bore the marks of his habitual and committed treatment of his animals, particularly the tips, which had deep striations gouged into the leather, making a criss-cross pattern, and through which the rust of iron toecaps could be smelled, the iron of dog blood, dried, the particular savour of a dog's dried saliva.

Anaximander had suffered at this man's boots in life – the striations were the marks the canine teeth make when a man kicks a dog's face, the blood from the wounds those kicks make in the gums, the saliva left there when the boot is licked, subserviently, to end the kicking – and he was not so long separated from the material realm that his fear of fearful things had passed, so he stepped back, afraid.

Smyke lifted his boot, and the underside was studded by what the dog-men called 'Blakey's', which were segs of metal, hobnails, heel and toe plates, hammered in to both increase the useful life of the sole and prevent the teeth of a rebellious dog from tearing through to the foot.

Anaximander, in life, would have shown his obedience to Heartless Harold Smyke by placing his head under the boot, and Heartless Harold would have pressed down on the dog's skull with as much force as he deemed necessary to assert his dominance. But Anaximander was no longer 'in life', and so he decided to do no such thing. Instead, though it would have meant a kicking in life, he raised his eyes up, just a little, so that he saw the leather laces of the man's boots, black and tanned by years in the dog pits.

'Down!' Smyke snapped at Anaximander, in that hectoring tone he had always used in the past.

Anaximander almost did it, except that it was he that had summoned Smyke, and not the other way around.

A dog-man does not wear the trousers men of other professions wear. Instead, he wears a rubber bib and brace, like a fly fisherman, the ankles of which he tucks into his boots so that his socks remain dry and unsoiled by whatever liquid he must wade through, or whatever splashes on him in the course of his duties. The material of his workwear does not usually stain, rubber wiping clean, but everywhere was covered with mud. It was pooled in the small, horseshoe reservoir the top of his boot made against the trouser leg. Mud was also dripping down from the knee in rivulets that followed the seam sown down the shin. It was splashed in droplets that imperfectly reflected back the place they now found themselves in.

Smyke stood on one leg, the other held up for Anaximander to cower beneath, but the dog did not cower.

Mud, iron, saliva, the urine of fear, the urine expressed when a dog is kicked in the bladder, the urine with which a dog marks an opponent he has bested, the residue of a meal that has been wiped from the hands onto the thighs of a man who eats vinegared herrings, smeared faeces incompletely removed by a cloth that was left in a bucket of bleach, a long and slow curing in tobacco smoke, the sweat of a man who drinks gin with his breakfast and who expresses a portion of the alcohol he cannot metabolise from the creases of his neck, breath tinged with the sweet odour of a rotting tooth, meat that is festering and trapped between a rotten tooth and its less rotten neighbour and which has not been removed for at least a week, ear wax, Makassar hair oil – all these things, mixed together, made the familiar smell of Heartless Harold Smyke. Anaximander made no judgement, good or bad, about the odour, strong in his memory, but the sources of it were perverted in the dog's mind by their association with the dog-man, so that, in life, Anaximander had never eaten herrings, even though other dogs of his experience had eaten them voraciously, despite the fact that they were a very bony meal.

The knees of the man's trousers were marked with light circles of dried clay, as if the last thing he had done in life was to paint them with potter's slip and let them dry.

Anaximander breathed deeply, and, expecting the consequences, lifted not only his eyes but his whole head: ears, nose, everything.

Smyke's chest contained no heart – a ghost has no organs, it is all surface – but in Anaximander's ear he could hear the muscles of this non-existent heart pound, once, twice, three times. Then, nervously, it palpitated, fluttering in the man's chest, as if, behind the ribs, there was a panicked bird which, refusing to accept the confinement, was seeking to break out, but succeeded only in cracking the fragile bones of its wings against the cage.

The dog could have concentrated on the man's green tweed shirt, his elastic brace straps, his long leather coat draped like a cloak over his shoulders, his pipe and lighter protruding from one top pocket, his reading glasses – used exclusively to check betting slips – but it was the sound of this heart-bird that Anaximander listened to.

The beat of a heart can be seen as well as heard. It presses the skin where the neck and collarbone meet. As a man ages and his flesh thins, the force of the blood makes it lift and fall ever more clearly. Though there was nothing beneath Smyke's image to affect the surface – no veins, no arteries, no blood – there was the movement, visible on the surface, of the fibrillations the man was suffering. They were shaking, febrile, oscillations like the membrane of a drum somewhat after a beat has been struck, before it entirely fades away.

His skin was yellow, from the jaundice that drinking primarily gin brings, the ureic residues that water habitually flushes away having to go somewhere. He was yellow and mottled with freckles the size of raisins, darker even than those dried fruits, and tags of skin, and moles, and warts. His skin was a landscape in miniature, the inhabitants of which were minuscule lice who fed on the dead cells Smyke sloughed. When he slept, these lice came out from the pores and follicles that made caves in the plains of Smyke's facial lowlands, and performed their lives in the darkness as he, exhausted from drinking, exhausted from cheering on his champions in the pits, exhausted from celebrating his victories, lay, most nights, comatose between the cages in which his dogs were imprisoned, each of them watching him, so close to their gaoler, but infinitely far from doing to him what they all wished to do, his unconsciousness allowing their desires to surface, so thoroughly suppressed by his waking presence.

A dog does not privilege the face as a sighted person does.

A sighted person will fix, single-mindedly, all their attention on the appearance of that small portion of another person's body to the exclusion, it seems to a dog, of other, often more expressive aspects of the corpus, but that is not to say that the face was of no interest to Anaximander.

Indeed, this face was of unusual interest, such that he could understand, he felt, why it was that people concentrated so closely on it. There were the deep and sunken eyes, like the sockets of a skull across which thin wax paper had been stretched, and, onto this paper, damp and shell-less lychees had been placed, opaque and white. Except, deep inside the whiteness, there was the stone, darkly visible, like the nucleus of a frog's spawn before the tadpole wriggles out.

Smyke's nose was shaped like the beak of a hawk, except where that thing has a noble rigidity, made as it is of keratin, which is smooth, this was fleshy, and pockmarked, and veined, and pale, and red, and possessed of two horrible nostrils from which thick and piebald hairs projected, blown straight by his exhalations, curling back when he breathed in. The mouth was akin to the anus of a cow, puckered and not adequately tight, leaking fluids, so used was it to the passage through it of too much of everything: of liquor, of tepid and turned offal, of coarse words, of angry ejaculations. This oral anus could not keep behind it those things it should properly contain, nor prevent the ingress of things that might be deleterious to the health of the Smyke organism. A pregnant blowfly, keen to lay its eggs in somewhere dark, would have met no resistance from Smyke's face. His teeth were remnants of his boyhood, which had never properly given way to the ones in his jaw-bones – the 'permanent' or 'secondary' teeth. Perhaps they were unwilling to take their place in Smyke's mouth, disgusted by that prospect, and so remained impacted, where they made an unevenness across his cheeks and under his sparse beard. The external teeth were green and brown and yellow, small lozenges, astringent pastilles that wouldn't dissolve; they looked like the standing stones that had once decorated the Land of the White Hills. His chin, jutting and always on the move since Smyke could never, through pain, allow his jaws to come together, was marked by such a deep cleft that it appeared, in its movement left and right, that the jaw might come apart, as if it was only the skin that was keeping it together.

This face, this combination of all of these unpromising elements, came together to make something that, Anaximander now saw, was worse even than the elements individually. The effect of the ensemble was that each, in its unpleasantness, drew attention to the unpleasantness of the features surrounding it, since, unless the world was a very cruel place, surely luck would determine that an ugliness of the nose might be offset by a prettiness of the eyes, a malformedness of the mouth might by leavened by a perfect brow. But the brow was beetling, the eyebrows were crooked, and even the ears, often the most innocuous feature on a homely person, were cauliflowered to an alarming degree, seeming more like corrupted spheres than pinnae, only patchily covered by the stringy hair that Smyke never washed, which had the appearance of brown seaweed, or a jellyfish's tendrils – thin and slick and slippery.

Everything appeared to Anaximander suddenly, as it must to a person. Here was a representation, *tout court*, of the terrible individual that was Heartless Harold Smyke, in synecdoche, the face standing in for his evilness of temper, his cruelty, his endless and appalling mistreatment of his charges, a perfect summation of him, the cruelty implied by its awful ugliness being a reflection of the cruelty inside Heartless Harold himself.

Yet, as Anaximander took in the sight of his former master, as he understood the visual horribleness of him, taken as he was outside of his context, the dog also felt pity.

Here the fellow was, dead, removed from the structures of the world he had relied on. Just as Anaximander no longer felt concern over the condition of his own corpse, that being a thing of another place, no longer present, so Smyke's cruelties no longer concerned him. Instead, here was a horrible thing – like a pigeon chick, or a mouse that has been flattened by a passing carriage wheel and whose innards have been squeezed outwards so that they lie beside the creature, gritty and still attached – unpleasant to look at, certainly, but somehow deserving, because of that, sympathy.

Is it a horrible thing's fault that it looks horrible, any more than a beautiful thing deserves praise for looking beautiful?

Anaximander might once have said that it was, citing some sophistry or other that would have convinced an unintelligent or inattentive listener, but now he knew, with the distance a ghost can take, that horribleness and beauty, cruelness and kindness, goodness and badness: they were all things of a world he had left behind.

The world he was in now had only two distinctions: the material and the immaterial, and even in this, existence, such as it was, was facilitated by a combination of the two things, not some adherence to one or other of the positions.

Which was all by the by, because, as he was taking in the form of Smyke, that man's ghost lurched at him, as if he was going to seize Anaximander by the scruff and bear him back to his cage.

'Sir!' Anaximander exclaimed, rearing back on his hind legs. 'Do not attempt to lay hands on me, as was your habit in life! I am not the puppy you remember me to be, and nor are you any longer in your dog training academy. We are both ghosts, and any attempt you might make to bear me away would be fruitless, there being no "away" for you to bear me to, and no reason for you to do it.'

Smyke was stopped in his tracks by Anaximander's words.

He was not used to talking dogs, nor to ghosts, nor to being a ghost. This was the first time since his death that anyone had taken the trouble to manifest him. He did not have Anaximander's magical tie to the weft and the dog had dragged him back from the nothingness that had met the end of his material existence.

Into the pause that Smyke's confusion made in events, Anaximander spoke. 'I have brought you here,' the dog said, 'which place is an afterlife manifested in the intermediate realm proper to the magical remnants of formerly living things, in order to make enquiries of you.

'Where, in life, I was intimidated by the pain you could and were inclined to inflict on me with your beatings, in death I am no longer so intimidated. In fact, the tables have turned, to use an idiom, and it is I who have the upper hand, to mix a metaphor, since I can dismiss you as easily as I have summoned you. I am tied to the world by my magical provenance – this much I have understood through my querying of the immaterial realm – whereas you are fated to be, or not to be, by virtue of a magical thing's ability and desire to have you before them.

'In this case, I am the magical thing in question, and I have demonstrated my ability to have you here. My desire that you should remain here is something you can now enflame or diminish, depending on your attitudes.'

Anaximander paused and examined the effect his words were having on Smyke, but that man's reaction to the dog's words was not expressed clearly in either his face or posture, which remained exactly as they had been before Anaximander had begun speaking. It was as if the ghost before him was a frozen block of ice, or a sculpture.

The dog swallowed, though there was no need for him to do it, and went on. 'The immaterial realm is a difficult place to occupy with the mind, it being like a river, or ocean, into which it is possible for a thing to be dropped, and for it there to be subject to tides and currents which draw it hither and thither against its will. Generalities are very easy to apprehend and then bring to the surface, but specific things are much harder to locate.

'It is a specific thing that I wish you to tell me, something which I think you as a living person would certainly have known and which, therefore, is information inherent in you as a ghost, just as your horrible appearance is inherent in you, your ghostly form being both a physical and psychical manifestation of your former existence.'

Anaximander paused again, took stock again of the man's reactions, which again were non-existent. 'Do you understand my words?'

Smyke, presumably not used to being addressed in this way, said nothing, but Anaximander did not take this for a lack of comprehension.

The man had been in life that species of person who, though never having received a formal education since no such system of indoctrination in knowledges was offered universally in Mordew, but who had lived in that city and, in his way, thrived there, had received from that process an education of an informal type, not in the facts and theories of the accepted schools of study – Physics, Philosophy, Theology – but in the ways of the world. While not as easy to include in a book, this education was no less complex and possibly more useful for a person who found himself in an unusual situation. The doctrinaire aspects of an academic discipline are replaced in a worldly education with an understanding of a person's relation to the events he finds himself in, particularly in the taking of opportunities and the avoidance of danger.

So, Anaximander felt that the ghost of Smyke was likely to be weighing up the dangers and opportunities of this new situation he found himself in, even if that weighing was not visible in his surface manifestation.

Anaximander was just about to speak again, his question too long unanswered it seemed to the dog and the energy that

373

propelled the conversation forward dwindling to the point where it might falter and stop, when Smyke spoke.

'I don't take orders from dogs,' he said, and he turned his back on Anaximander and made to walk away.

It is common at the beginning of negotiations for the parties conducting them to adopt positions that seem to preclude the middle ground that is liable, eventually, to represent an acceptable compromise to both sides. First one, then the other, will make a more or less rhetorical statement characterised by an assumption that their interests are the only interests to be considered, and while, to the inexperienced, this rhetoric would seem to close down the possibility that the parties will ever agree, in fact the opposite is the case, since the process of agreement has been begun, and once a thing has been begun, it is natural for it to conclude.

So, despite Smyke seeming to have denied the possibility that he would do what Anaximander wanted him to do, the dog felt that he would eventually do it, if some *quid pro quo* could be established.

That said, Anaximander was wise enough to know that Smyke's dismissal of him should not be met with an immediate compromise on the dog's part, which would have been a sign of weakness liable to embolden Smyke and lead to an unbalanced outcome, but that he should, instead, mirror the man's negativity. 'Go then,' Anaximander said, 'and fade back into the nothingness from which I have summoned you. Leave now and I will find another way to answer my questions. Your future existence, if any, will be dependent on someone else bringing you into being, since I never repeat a mistake. Are you aware of anyone who would be both willing and able to do what I have done? I doubt you are, knowing you as I do.'

Smyke did not turn back to Anaximander, but instead he began to walk away, which is a very reasonable thing for a man to do when he is negotiating, since it is often the first person who backs down from his rhetoric that ends up with the worst of any bargain. These opening stages are like a game of 'chicken' or 'dare', the aim being to act as if you will go to any lengths not to lose that game, even at the risk of losing something you might be expected to want.

Unfortunately for Smyke, he was not a man any more, but was a ghost. As he walked away from Anaximander, his summoner, he traversed the plane of existence in the manner a ghost does, drifting as if on a light breeze. The solidity of his manifestation as he moved away from his summoner quickly lost consistency, and though his back was turned Anaximander saw that Smyke raised his hands up before his face, the fingers sausage-like through some pre-death oedema, but increasingly transparent as he drifted.

He did not turn immediately back, but he did stop drifting.

Though a ghost is dead, that does not mean that he does not want to continue his existence. There are, in truth, ghosts summoned who would much rather not have been, but Smyke was not one of them. It seemed that he floated in the void, weighing up his options.

Anaximander took this as a movement towards compromise. 'I need to know where it is that I might locate a supply of puppies,' he said, knowing that would be a thing Smyke would easily know.

Smyke did not turn, still, but he opened his arms out, as if to ask, 'Where in this featureless expanse to which you have brought me might a person expect to find any living thing?'

Anaximander made himself to be in front of Smyke, that transition representing itself as him trotting over, although there was no ground for him to trot across. 'There is a point of light, like a pearl,' he said, indicating with his snout and a foreleg that thing, as a hunting dog will point his nose to the corpse of a game bird, and raise up his foot to show his master where it is, 'and this contains the material realm. We can return there in the form of ghosts, and from there we can traverse the world. If you show me where puppies may be procured, I will allow you to remain there, and will not rescind your summoning, which is something I can most definitely do.'

Anaximander wasn't at all sure whether the rescinding of a summoning was something he could do, once in the material realm, but he sought to hide this uncertainty with hyperbole, which is a very good method for hiding uncertainties of that sort.

Smyke looked down at Anaximander, and across the uneven bones of his cheek he raised one side of his mouth in an expression that was a little like a smirk, but more bitter and derisive. 'Want to make a Smyke of yourself, do you? It ain't as easy as you think.'

Anaximander did not wish to make a Smyke of himself, but he saw no reason to apprise Smyke of that fact. Instead, the dog play acted, very effectively, that the man had seen to the core of his plans – he first looked down at the floor, then he waited for a moment, then he looked up with his eyes, keeping his head down, and then looked away again before sniffing, and raising himself up in an unconvincing show of confidence. 'Are you coming or not?'

This mummery completed, Smyke's ghost seemed to feel it had the measure of Anaximander's ghost. 'Lead the way,' he said, and swept his arm theatrically at the entrance to the material realm.

The question of whether a thing is a coincidence or not is very dependent on time and space.

If a person goes out from her home and into the city on an errand, and another person goes out from her home on an errand to the same place – let us say they are both going to collect produce from a bakery, though it could be anything – and these two people are sisters, estranged by an argument that took place in the past – let us say that one sister gave the other sister as a birthday gift a present that had been given to her the previous year as a gift by the sister to whom she was now trying to regift it, undermining the performance of delight the first sister had made on receiving it, making her seem insincere, though, again, it could be anything – when they meet in the same place and at the same time, this is thought to be a coincidence.

But what if the sisters, rather than existing in the material realm, existed instead in the intermediate realm proper to ghosts?

There could be no coincidence here since there would be no congruence of space and time in which that coincidence could take place. Both sisters would be ghosts in that realm, and could either will themselves to be in each other's presence or not. In the case of these sisters, they might well will themselves always to be separate, but even if they willed themselves to be together, this would be a matter of will, not of chance. So, this could not be said to be a coincidence in the same way it could be in the material realm.

What if one sister was in the material realm, and another was in the intermediate realm proper to ghosts?

The material realm sister, unless she knew the way of manifesting a ghost, could never, by chance, coincide with the ghost of her sister, unless the sister knew how to manifest herself in the material realm, or unless a third party took the trouble to summon her into the presence of a place where the material sister might then come. Even then it would be easy for the ghost to avoid being seen, so the matter of will becomes important again, certainly more important than chance.

Which is all to say that, while the following may seem to be a coincidence, it cannot properly be said to be one, but might have been, in one way or another, willed to happen.

When Anaximander and Smyke addressed themselves to the thing that was the entrance from their intermediate realm into the material realm, from that point of light there came a barking, insistent and harsh.

It was not transmitted to Anaximander's ears, since in the place where he was there was no air to carry sound, yet he heard it despite that. It was, the dog now recognised, that soundless sound that he had not heard earlier.

Perhaps he was sufficiently recently dead that residual nerve contact was extant between his corpse's organs of sense and his ghostly being in the realm within which he was now instanced. Perhaps it was for another reason unknowable to people of the material realm. In either case, the fact remained, and now this insistent barking was like the sensation of being tapped repeatedly between the eyes with a forefinger, the owner of the digit aiming to draw your attention, or to wake you up from a deep sleep.

In order to react to the sound, Anaximander went closer to the light, something that made the barking louder.

Anyone who has bred dogs, like Heartless Harold Smyke did, whether for work or for fighting, will know that the bark of a dog is distinctive.

It cannot be said that the voice of a dog is as recognisable to the breeder as a human's voice is, but that is because humans are attuned to the cadences of the sounds made by their own species, and are deaf to all the subtleties present in a dog's barking.

To Anaximander – and, to a lesser extent, to Smyke – the opposite was true: he was more attuned to the unique sound of a dog's voice than he was to the muffled and flabby vocalisations of people, whose tones were rendered imperfect, to his mind, by an excess of flesh at the lips, the wobbling of their cheeks, and a lack of muscular tone in the neck. In short, Anaximander felt that he recognised the voice of this dog, and this recognition expanded the material realm in front of him until he could see that he was right: there was a dog, back in the real, barking insistently at his corpse, as if to animate it.

Because Anaximander knew, we know, that a magical dog cannot be severed from the world except by the person who made it, and that he can return to the material realm in the form of a ghost. What we should also know, but which Anaximander did not as yet know that he knew, is that the magical creation of a pair of dogs, at the same time, as a unity, is sufficient to tie both individuals to the real, even if the maker of that pair has decided, for whatever reason, to purge one of the dogs from reality altogether. Each dog is tethered to the other as if they were leashed at the collar by the process by which they were foundationally paired. There is a simple spell that can sever the link, but, failing that, the existence of one or other is sufficient to ensure the continued possibility that a ghost can be made of both.

The barking came ever louder, ever more insistent, and Anaximander as a ghost – ignoring Smyke, who followed behind – could make out every feature of the other dog now. It seemed to be chastising the wounds of Anaximander's corpse, one at a time, circling it and abusing the body – as if this would make it live – with its limited vocabulary of words, if the noises of dogs can be considered words.

We should also remember that when the Master of Mordew made Anaximander, the talking dog, he also made another magical dog, and into this one he placed a magical, mystical organ. Anaximander was made to understand this other dog, and was given his voice to speak its thoughts, the separation of the two into a pair a safeguard against the making of too powerful a single beast.

But a safeguard will work both ways, protecting the maker, but also distributing the risk of those made across two parties, particularly if the risk is of permanent death when both of those parties contain a residual link to the weft and a link to the other. Even the Tinderbox cannot sever that link unless it destroys both individuals, since the concepts of both in the immaterial realm are combined into a pair, just like twins are.

The barking was so loud now, and the window into the material realm had become so wide, that it filled the entirety of the experience of Anaximander in his form as a ghost.

Because there is reciprocity inherent in sensing a thing, he was also sensible in the world, and the barking dog, who himself was there in the form of a ghost, saw his friend and the two leapt and bounded around each other.

Though they could not touch that did not stop them, and they leapt up, and around, and through each other, crouched down in front of each other, chased each other and snapped in a joyous game of an intensity that only dogs can exhibit.

All Anaximander's thoughts of the other realm left him.

The other dog was Sirius, Anaximander's first companion, who had become Goddog, husband of the Great White Bitch. He had been scoured from the world by the Master of Mordew's Tinderbox, but was returned now by virtue of his common making and the binding inherent in the magic that made him.

The two dogs loved each other as only dogs can, and they exhibited that love unrestrainedly, since they had been parted for what seemed like lifetimes to them, they both having separately lived and died and returned to the world.

How long they cavorted is unknown, and a ghost does not tire, since it does not have a body that can become weary. As much as a ghost obeys the laws of the world it does it by habit, and excitement of the sort these two ghosts of dogs were now experiencing silences the demands of habit.

Anyone will admit this is true if they think back on their lives and remember a time when an exciting incident occurred and then remember at what time they then did something habitual. The unexpected arrival of a long-missed friend will mean that supper is taken at eight rather than half past six – its proper time – since a cook is unwilling to interrupt cheerful conversation to ask whether mashed or roasted potatoes are preferred.

Moreover, when the break in the orderly progress of things is noticed, there is no animosity, nor chiding of the staff. There is something in the novelty of a different way of doing things for once that seems to contribute to the good humour of a company, and a plate of cold meats, cheeses, pickles and bread will prove to be perfectly satisfactory, just this once. Not to mention the good brandy!

So, the dogs may have played for many hours, the residue of Anaximander – his corpse – lying on the earth beside the residue of Bellows. Neither of the dogs paid either residue any attention at all, nor Harold Smyke, who existed off to the side, very much like a third wheel on a bicycle.

As they played, the ghosts of these two drifted as if blown by a gentle breeze, over the hillsides, off towards where the sea was, leaving Smyke to follow as best he could, struggling to understand that it was his mind that moved him and not his limbs, and the three of them left the terrible scene of the boy and dog's death behind.

◆

When the dogs did eventually stop their frolics, panting as if they were out of breath, but both realising quickly that they weren't, they were in a new place, hovering twenty or thirty feet above the ground and at an unnatural angle to it. As if by mutual accord, they righted themselves and went down to the ground, Smyke waving his arms and swimming ineffectually in the air in a largely fruitless effort to follow.

In the dog-man's absence, conversation between the dogs broke out. While this did not take place using words, for convenience's sake, and without stretching reality to its breaking point, Anaximander's side of the talking – since he could use words, as we do, the transcription of his communing with Sirius is at least a plausible substitute – went along the following lines.

'Companion,' he said, 'I have never been happier to see a thing in my life, if I can still be said to own a life. Tell me, better-than-friend, how have circumstances brought you to your ghostly form, barking at my wounded, discarded body?'

Sirius did not then reply, since there were not, in reality any words to reply to, but that part of him in which the information sought resided was willingly opened up for Anaximander to understand by the process known as 'communing'. This is a magical kind of mind exchange, which we would not understand even if it happened to us, since we are not magical beings, but base material beings incapable of interactions of that sort. Within Sirius were the experiences he had known since they had seen each other last, imperfectly instanced and truncated in his memories, but giving a sufficient series of 'mind images' for Anaximander to understand them. There was the dive from the boat, the ghosts from the clubhouse emerging from the rent in the seabed, the sight of Nathan Treeves, crushed into weft-stuff, the stretching up of Mordew, the bizarre new flukes, the frozen corpse of Nathan's dead brother on the table, the consumption of the face of the weftling, the becoming of Goddog, the copulation with the Great White Bitch, the birth of his seven daughters, the invasion of the Master's Manse, the battle with the Master, the chase down Mount Mordew into the God chamber, and, at last, Sirius's destruction by the Tinderbox.

'That is a wealth of experience,' Anaximander said, 'making my adventures seem meagre and pedestrian in comparison. Yet we are led to the same place regardless, and while I have not become a god in your absence, nor copulated with a goddess, I do not envy you those things, since they resulted in a death as sure as my own.' The dog licked his lips and frowned, as if he needed to make an effort to believe his own words, but his lips tasted of nothing, and, after he'd done it, he wondered why he'd bothered.

Sirius, on the other hand, had caught sight of Heartless Harold Smyke. While they had been communing, he had managed to make it part of the way down to the ground, though in the effort he was now entirely the wrong way up, reaching down to the earth as a man might strain to reach for something on a high shelf, not succeeding in getting it.

Having seen that man since his earliest experiences, and remembering, in his way, the terrible training Smyke had delivered, Sirius bounded at him.

This was not unusual behaviour, Anaximander thought, for his companion.

Sirius was never much interested in conversation: almost any distraction was preferable to remaining within a communing frame of mind.

Anaximander could not blame his friend, since the majority of any exchange between them was a very one-sided business, Anaximander requesting access to relevant parts of Sirius's mind, and Sirius allowing it. The rest took place largely without the dog noticing. It was rather like, though not entirely the same as, the sexual intercourse that took place between their former owners, the inhabitants of that place called the Spire, by which the mistress of the house, once her husband began the habitual and unsatisfying congress that was all he seemed capable of, occupied her attention with a survey of the ceiling above her, or the doorway, or Anaximander himself, sitting patiently in that doorway. While the merchant puffed and panted and laboured, his bestockinged feet protruding from beneath the bedsheets, she seemed only very slightly engaged with the world her husband occupied.

So it was with Sirius and communing.

This was one of the prime motivations that Anaximander had felt in attempting what he brought Heartless Harold Smyke back to the world to attempt – the creation of a dog of an intelligence and mode of communication matching Anaximander's – so that he need not feel like that husband, lonely in the business that he felt was so pressingly worth his exertions, but for which he could not find a sympathetic partner.

This Anaximander felt even more, since he knew that his mistress took to her bed with much more enthusiasm with other persons, usually from the paid staff, where she would play a role much more like her husband's, while it was their eyes that glazed over as, after a significantly longer period of activity no less isolating for the maid or the butler or the skivvy, she approached the noisy and undignified object of her own exertions.

Neither of these roles did Anaximander himself want to fill, but rather he wished for some reciprocity in the things he wanted, such as he had briefly felt with Thales, except this time without the requirement that he fight his partner to the death.

So it was that, seeing the ghost of Sirius determined to decapitate with his teeth his former trainer and having no success, and seeing Heartless Harold Smyke equally unsuccessfully attempting to fend him off, hovering upside down with his head six feet from the ground, he galloped over to where they both were and said, 'Companion! Your foe is already dead, as are you. I have agreed a bargain with this man that he will, in exchange for his continuing existence in this realm as a ghost, show us where we might find a supply of puppies, so that one of these, through a process I now understand from time spent in the immaterial realm, might be made for us into a son, so that we might commune and converse with him in our ways, and so overturn the essential loneliness we magic dogs, speaking and unspeaking, experience, our rarity precluding our doing this by any other means.'

Again, it must be understood that no such verbalisation took place, only an approximation in the form of mind communion, but it was as if it did because, once that equivalent of words was made, Sirius sat down on his haunches and across his face what passed for a thoughtful look settled.

We, had we seen him, would not know what made this expression, but Anaximander was aware of it immediately: Sirius already had a daughter extant in the world, and no means he knew of locating her, nor any way of communing with her if he did, she being more of her mother than she was of him, more like a goddess where he had lost his divinity. Though Sirius could not reason his way to a point that might justify his assumption, he felt, by instinct, that the creation of another living magical dog might remedy his own mismatched desires, so he gave his assent to the idea, which for him was tantamount to not working to prevent it.

Anaximander, understanding his companion's requirements, agreed to include them in the recipe by which this new dog might be produced. This was most easily effected by combining elements of their own beings in equal measure, by spells and sacrifices, to make a new creature, a child which would make right both of their lacks. This is what a child is for: to make a wholeness out of parts.

'Take us, then, to the supplier of puppies,' he said to Heartless Harold Smyke. Because for a ghost, or group of ghosts, to will a thing is for it to occur, the three of them dissolved from that place and went to the puppy farm.

Dog-men are nothing if not practical in their methods; the puppy farm at which the three ghosts appeared adjoined the dog training academy run by Heartless Harold Smyke, where Sirius and Anaximander had been raised.

Because that place in the present no longer existed – it was now Mount Mordew, stretched up into the sky – and because ghosts are no more bound by time than they are by space, the ghosts manifested not only in the place where Harold had raised the dogs, but also at the time he had raised them.

Moreover, there the dogs were, at the feet of their ghosts, in the process of being born, their mother, exhaustedly circling, wide-eyed and panting.

This, though, is to join the scene at too close a focus before it is possible for us to imagine it adequately. Since we are not ghosts, and require material context, we must step back and see a wider picture before we can step in again to see the details.

A child, imagining a puppy farm, will combine the two nouns and conjure up in their mental apparatus a very cheerful thing. A puppy is a cheerful thing. A farm, from a child's perspective, also seems cheerful, stocked, as it is, with playful animals, colourful agricultural machinery, and friendly farmers.

Children, though, are notorious for their lack of understanding of the way the world is, and their misapprehension of the mood of a puppy farm is typical of their failure to properly understand things as they are. Rather than being a place where young dogs exist in a playful, colourful, friendly environment, Heartless Harold Smyke's puppy farm was a series of poorly maintained, inadequately mucked out, low sheds, upon the corrugated roofs of which the rain drummed loudly and remorselessly. Within these sheds, out of the glare of external observation, mother-dogs were kept in cramped and foul-smelling hutches on damp straw, from which they were only allowed out when they needed to give birth. Even then all they could do was to circle painfully around a sawdusted patch of ground. This circling is an essential part of a breeding dog's labouring; if they cannot do it they tend to die, requiring them to be replaced, which is an expense a clever dog breeder avoids.

If the rain ever stopped its drumming sufficiently to allow the ambient noise of the place to filter through to the dogs in the sheds, in the hutches, or circling in the patches of sawdusted ground, then it was the sound of distant dogfights that they then heard. This is barking and growling and whooping and keening and cheering and screaming. Had the poor mothers there had the capacity to wish for things – their exhaustion meant they did not have that capacity, so often were they made to bear litters and with such poor food – they would have wished immediately for the return of the rain noise. It is not good to know, when one is giving birth, the painful futures of one's pups, even if they would only bond with them briefly before Smyke took them away. To imagine them fighting to the death, if they survived the killing buckets – which were filled with grey and bubbling water, and into which the dog-boys would plunge any substandard infants until they were dead, and throw their corpses into a line where they would be collected later and ground into feed – was a very sad thing for a mother dog.

Sensitive persons will baulk at facts like these, but baulking does nothing to make these facts go away. Becoming upset and turning one's back is precisely what keeps these facts facts. It is a precondition for things to change for them to be known about, and for that knowledge to be acted upon.

Sensitivity in a person is of no benefit to the suffering party.

It is a truth that the work of preventing cruelty inures a person to that cruelty, and this has a corollary: a person who says, 'Do not show me cruelty, it is too upsetting' is indicating not, as they assume, that they are above such cruelty, but that they have been indifferent to it in their actions, that they have done no work to alleviate it that would harden them against upset.

It is the person that says, 'Show me more cruelty, let me suffer more, so that I might know in my heart the obligation to ease the suffering of those who suffer', that is the truly sensitive person.

These statements Anaximander thought when he found himself in the birthing pen.

Sirius was beside him, Smyke was beside them both. Their insubstantial presence did not prevent the dogs' mother from circling, and panting, and labouring around the sawdust circle in front of her hutch, inside the shed, against the roof of which the rain drummed remorselessly. She did her work under the

386

gaze of caged and pregnant dogs, unable to move, or stretch, or live as a dog should live.

Her body did not interact with the ghosts' apparitions, and her mind was not attuned to the traces a ghost leaves on the world. All she knew was the need to circle, to pant, and the feeling within her that her puppies were near, though that feeling brought her no joy.

Anaximander looked up at Smyke, thinking to see in his expression some sign of his guilt, so clear was it to the dog that this was a horrible thing to make real in the world. But Heartless Harold Smyke had not received his epithet by possessing a heart, and his face showed nothing more than it always did: the ugliness that his malformed features made in him.

The man didn't trouble to look down at the mother, but instead he peered off to where his fighting pits were, as if he was imagining the pleasures that had occupied him through his life, the dogs' mother's suffering only the necessary precondition for these pleasures to exist. He weighed them up against the fighting and the betting, the cheering and the drinking, and he found that his pleasures outweighed her suffering.

But isn't that always the way, Anaximander thought, with people?

Sirius went to his mother, knowing her not in the way that dogs know each other, which is mostly by smell, but as a ghost knows its forebears, by some quality very obvious to the dead, but incomprehensible to the living. He tried to lick her mouth, which is the way a dog shows friendliness and fealty, but his tongue passed through her.

She circled through him, unaware of his presence.

Yet it was almost as if his attempt to lick her brought on the arrival of the first puppy, because she slumped suddenly onto her side. From her slipped two parcels of flesh, enveloped in translucent membranes, white, which she turned to. With her tongue she licked life into these parcels, tearing their birthing sacs, clearing their nostrils, making them gasp.

When she saw them move, first one and then the other, she got to her feet again and resumed her circling.

Anaximander and Sirius looked at each other.

'That is you and I, brother,' Anaximander said, though until that point neither of the two had known they were litter mates, so soon after birth had they been separated.

Which of us can say that we have been witnesses to our own births, except inasmuch as we are necessarily present for our mothers to give birth to us?

Only ghosts can say it, which is to say none of us can, since we must be alive to read these words.

Which of us can say, of a friend or companion for whom we feel a great bond of affection, that we were present at our births together, and that it was here we learned that we were brothers all along?

None of us can say it.

So it was that Anaximander and Sirius were unique in the world, though they were parted from it.

Because a unique thing requires witnesses, and because Heartless Harold Smyke did not qualify by virtue of his cruelty – indeed, he had drifted off towards the site of his own fascination, his fighting dens – so the urge in the dogs, Anaximander more definitely than Sirius, to have someone sympathetic to tell their story to, determined what happened next as much as anything else did.

Their mother fell to the ground again, and now a third parcel of flesh was delivered onto the ground, and so it was that the puppy that would be the son of Anaximander and Sirius was chosen, who would also be their brother, though a sacrifice was necessary in order for that magic to be made.

The weft knows time only strangely, and in it are all the possible things that might happen. In a city characterised by the death of the weftling, who had previously borne the responsibility for delimiting the possible and the impossible, the lines between these two states were blurred as the corpse of God dissolved. Because the two dogs were of magical provenance, and because one of them had assumed divinity in his life and the other had queried the immaterial realm, a number of unusual things that would not have happened in the normal course became possible:

1. Anaximander knew how it was that he might secure the Spark necessary to enact the magic that would enable the fulfilment of his desire that there be another talking dog with which he could converse.
2. He knew also how he could convince Heartless Harold Smyke to do it.
3. He understood how it could be that, having done the thing that he was about to do, it could be reconciled with the world from which he had come.
4. He knew where he would have to place the new talking dog so that they would be able to find him later.
5. He knew how to return to the world they had left at the place in time when they had left it.

Anaximander knew these things, and so firstly, leaving his mother so that she might tend to the newborn, though she was ever so exhausted, he took Sirius to where Heartless Harold Smyke had gone, which was to the dogfighting pit in the adjacent complex, a place both of the dogs remembered with absolutely no fondness whatsoever.

Many places of entertainment are brightly lit and decorated with streamers and colourful images so that they might advertise the kinds of pleasure to be found there. This is not the case with dogfighting, which tends to take place in very gloomy environments, ones that seem more like factories than anything else. The arenas are more often than not ad hoc rings made by spectators, handlers and bookies. Sometimes there will be chairs, but these are never for sitting – instead the shorter persons at a meet will stand on them and, their hands on the shoulders of the men in front of them, they will lean over so they can see the more clearly. As they scream and urge their champions on, flecks of their spittle will land on the hair and on the bald pates of the men in from of them.

Anaximander and Sirius came falteringly up to the backs of a circle of men just like this. Even as ghosts the residual anxiety of it all halted them in their progress, made them swallow with their non-existent throats, the habit of fear being provoked in them despite everything.

Smyke was not so hesitant: the dogs saw him pass like a shadow, invisible to the men who had other things on their minds, through the spaces between them, though he could easily have passed through their bodies. Ghosts, as we have seen from Anaximander's example, often take some time to understand how it is they behave in the world, and Smyke did not know, then, that he could ignore the solidity of objects if he chose, nor did he know that he could make himself more or less visible by an act of will, but Anaximander knew it, and he communicated that fact to Sirius by example, and the two of them went through the ring of braying spectators to the middle.

There two dogs very much like them were making chunks of each other.

They recognised, by that same sense that they recognised their mother, that these two dogs were their uncles, but because a relative of that type is very common for dogs, whether they are maternal or paternal, this did not carry such an emotional weight as when they saw their mother; they were able to ignore what these two were being made to do, so that they could concentrate instead on what Heartless Harold Smyke was doing.

Anaximander interposed himself between Smyke and the objects of his attention, and acted on the five things he had learned.

'Smyke,' he said, about to act on the first and second pieces of knowledge from the list above, 'there is no love lost between us, as you must know, but I know a way for you to return to life, of a sort.'

Smyke, at the beginning of Anaximander's little speech, peered around the dog, whose spectral transparency, while not blocking the spectacle of the dogfight, was distracting, until he heard the part about returning to life, at which point he, reluctantly it seemed, looked the dog in the eye. 'How?' he said.

Not for the first time, Anaximander wondered how few words a person might speak for them to be classified as a non-speaking person, and whether the teaching to non-magical dogs of a few word-like barks might allow them to overtake very taciturn people in the possession of a broadness of vocabulary.

Anaximander's wondering took place very briefly, and soon gave way to his reply. 'Replace the living Smyke,' he said. 'All you must do is cause him to die and the magical energy his death releases will allow you to become solid enough to take his place here. Admittedly, you will find it difficult to move solid objects, but you might find a servant who could be induced to do that work.'

Some of these words were lies: there was no requirement of any magical energy for Smyke to take on a sufficiently visible form, providing he remained in Mordew, where the consistency of the weft was sufficiently loose, in the presence of the weftling corpse, for an almost entirely visible ghost to manifest, should it choose to do so, but they seemed to grab Smyke's attention. 'How?' he said again.

'Many people,' Anaximander began, 'are susceptible to shocks, and those who have neglected the health of their heart are at risk of arresting its beating should sufficient fear be provoked in them. Indeed, the idea of being startled to death, particularly by the appearance of a ghost, is so commonplace as to have become a cliché. And if it is possible for a single ghost to cause a man to die through shocking him, what of three ghosts? And what if these ghosts perform a frightening performance?'

Smyke looked interested in this, more interested in it than he had been in the dogfight, so Anaximander led him aside to a quiet place. There the three, under the talking dog's direction, rehearsed a brief play with the aim of killing the living Heartless Harold Smyke, freeing up the Spark necessary for the magic that would make the dogs' brother speak, and though this did seem to be giving Heartless Harold a boon he did not deserve, it would also kill his living component before his time, which Anaximander considered to be an acceptable trade-off.

♦

But what of the necessary concomitance of the action of killing Heartless Harold Smyke that must propagate forward from the act and which would make the existence of Anaximander and Sirius different from that which they had experienced it to be?

Some clarification is required, since matters of this sort are confusing to living people. If, in the pasts of the dogs, which is where they had appeared in the form of ghosts at the moment of their births, Heartless Harold Smyke was killed by them and replaced by his ghost, how could they also have been violently affected by him as a living man?

Each dog had suffered beatings at this man's hands, and no insubstantial ghost can reliably deliver beatings of that type to a dog. So how did this happen if he was dead?

And if he was a ghost, why did they not remember him as such? While a man may be fooled by his eyesight, the senses of a dog know the physical presence of a man – indeed, Smyke's smell, as has been outlined already, was particular enough for him to have been summoned accurately.

Anaximander knew various answers to these questions.

Firstly, and as is always the case with matters of principle, the answer was the weft.

Within the weft all possible things exist, even those possibilities that are mutually exclusive. It is possible for a dog, when he turns left at a junction, for him to have turned right instead. In the weft, both outcomes exist, as do the impossible things – that he turned up, or down, for example. The impossible outcomes are contained in the nerves of the weftling, who reconciles the possible and the impossible. Because the material realm is derivative of the weft, and because the weftling is dead and therefore not capable of maintaining the perfection of the material realm's boundaries between the impossible and the possible, the impossible is possible in the material realm if that impossibility is provoked by magic. We know, from the events that had taken place since the Weftling Tontine murdered God, that this was the case, and because Anaximander and Sirius were magical dogs, they could produce the impossible in the world in exactly the same way that a user of a magic spell, or a weft-manipulator, causes impossible things to happen.

It would be a misunderstanding of the weft and the weftling to assume that this form of impossibility would be prohibited.

Yet, there is such a thing as causation, even in the impossible. An impossible thing must be able to cause things to happen in the possible world, or what would be the point of magic if it couldn't?

What if Anaximander, in order to cause in himself an alleviation of the effects of the traumas Harold Smyke had caused in him through the endless beatings, had decided that, through magic, he would travel back to the day of his birth and kill Harold so as to prevent those beatings from ever having occurred, in the hope that he might feel happier and more at peace with the world? Could he not expect himself to be successful in his use of magic?

The answer is that yes, he could expect it, though he would have to have this as his intention, there being a requirement in magic that the will of the weftling is replaced by the will of the magic user, there always being required 'will' for something to be other than the way it would otherwise be.

So, because Anaximander did not will for the premature death of Heartless Harold Smyke to affect him in the future, it did not.

Also, there is an imperfection in the memory of all living things that are not the weftling. The weftling is the only perfect being, he being entirely in concert with the weft, and if a magical dog's memory is imperfect can it not be possible that he misremembers the conditions of his own life? What is to say that it was not a proxy of Harold Smyke that beat the dogs?

The problem of causation can be reconciled in that way, by making it a problem not of the way the world was, but of the way the world was remembered.

Perhaps Heartless Harold Smyke's smell was communicated by some other means, one that would be too prohibitively complicated to have passed the test of Occam's razor, but which was effective, nonetheless. Anyone who has watched a sleight-of-hand artist at work will know that he often makes it appear, for example, as if a coin can pass through the neck of a bottle that is too narrow for it to pass along. We think, in our naivety, that he would not go to the trouble of creating a folding coin and then force it at speed through a space it should be unable to pass through, just to fool us, when in fact that is exactly what he has done. So, perhaps the ghost of Harold Smyke, by similarly going to unlikely pains, created a situation which resolved the causal irregularities that ought to have occurred by the dogs' interfering with their own pasts by using an assistant from the material realm.

Isn't this more likely than paradoxes of time?

Also, the realm of memory is not entirely of the material realm, since there is an immaterial component inherent in it, inasmuch as it conceptual. As the immaterial realm contains all things – possible, impossible, things that happened and things that did not happen – then cannot any inconsistency in the material realm be attributed not to any collapse in causation, but to an inaccuracy in the interactions between the material and immaterial realms?

Or perhaps the dog is mad?

Anaximander found a route through these answers that convinced him that he could kill Smyke and replace him with his ghost and that it would not cause Sirius and him to, for example, disappear immediately out of existence, or become other dogs. This he attributed, as a conceptual shorthand, to their current existence as ghosts, who are not as susceptible, if at all, to the particularities of the material realm.

We assume, often in error, that because people with a reputation for violence are known to act out violence on others, they are inured to violence in general. We think they are unconcerned about the possibility of violence towards them.

It is as if, we think, they have an immunity to it, as if it was a disease against which their own violence is an inoculation of sorts. But, like a doctor who works with the contagious and who intervenes in the lives of the dying sometimes by preventing death and sometimes kindly allowing it or even hastening it, to whom we in our ignorance gift a presumption of deathproofness by which we understand their ability to do their work, since otherwise surely they must die of leprosy, we are misreading the truth of their lives. Doctors die of the same diseases as the rest of us, and the reason we come to think otherwise is because we do not pay sufficient attention to the individuality of the role holder. We replace singular people with the group of people from which the singular person is drawn and of which they are a representative. When one role holder dies they are replaced with another of the same profession, and since a doctor is a kind of recognisable thing we recognise the person by virtue of their collective rather than their individual identity. We think that the doctor who was there yesterday, and the doctor who is there today, are the same doctor – even though the first has died and has been replaced by another – inasmuch as they perform the function of doctor for us.

So it also is with men of violence. They are as affected by violence as any other person, though we may not think so.

Also, just as doctors will wake up in the middle of the night, their blankets a tangle, twisted in their fists and between their knees – if they can find time in their working schedules for sleep – with the image of death, often personified in the form of a patient they have witnessed dying, a child, for example, earnestly reaching, desperate, poxed, fading, but striving still for life and dying anyway, so men of violence have the images of violence in their eyes when they close them. Rather than being free of the knowledge of violence Heartless Harold Smyke cannot be said to have been immune to violence, nor immune to the fear of violence. In fact, by his proximity to violence and other men of violence he was prone to the constant threat of violence. Just as the doctor sees the reaching, dying child in his dreams, in Heartless Harold Smyke's dreams were all the terrible events he had witnessed. Because of the particular milieu of violence within which he operated, these images were in the form of dogs and men.

◆

Now the ghosts went to the living Smyke's room, which was neat and prim and perfectly clean. This was no sign that Smyke was fastidious in his habits, but more that the cleaner employed to clean his room was extremely keen not to offend him. There was a single bed with a floral bedspread, perfectly flat and tucked tightly as a drumskin, the pillows were plumped and white, the headboard was white and wiped clean. Beside it was a small table with a pretty porcelain vase with one freshly cut rose – a yellow one – beside which were Smyke's eyeglasses, the lenses transparent and dustless. There was a glass of water with a glass jug, unsmudged, on perfectly starched doilies.

Beneath and protruding from under the bed was a rug, and beneath and protruding from the table was a smaller rug, both in the Persian style. Beneath these were perfectly sanded and stained floorboards leading straight to the skirting, which was perfectly painted, below the wall, which was also perfectly painted.

On the wall was a painting of a landscape – some hills on which sheep, sparsely spaced, were farmed, a storm brewing in the clouds – the frame in gilt, ornate. Beside it was an expansive wardrobe in walnut veneer, polished, the odour a round and pleasant beeswax. There was a small key in a brass lock. Its feet were talon and ball, solid and unwobbling on the floor.

Beside the wardrobe was a dressing table and mirror, a badger hairbrush, a horsehair brush, nail brushes, hand mirrors, all lined up and perfectly neat, with a pomade and an atomiser. Beneath the dresser and protruding was another Persian rug in the same pattern as the first two – primarily a repetition of the herati motif – but in a different colour.

There were clean boots under the clean windows.

Here was Heartless Harold Smyke, the man, standing frozen in the middle of this scene, the back of his calves pressed against his brass bedframe. In front of him was a long mirror on a pivot frame, and it was into this that Smyke peered, since Anaximander and Sirius and Smyke the ghost appeared in it, striding purposefully towards him.

This striding, and the eventually appearing in the room of the ghosts, as if the mirror was a form of corridor or opening, only took a second, but that second lasted a very long time in the living Smyke's mind. He was very terrified by the events that second contained, which it seemed to him were the coming true of the nightmares his proximity to violence all of these years had anchored in him.

The two dogs came as if they were walking the man by the hands, except that because they had no arms useful for that work, they brought him by their mouths at his wrists. Their teeth were bared so that it was clear that the extent of the longest of these teeth ended not at the man's skin, but underneath it, between the ulna and the radius where they met the carpal bones.

The expressions on the dogs' faces were like a frozen representation of a kind of saintly beneficence, such as that seen on the face of Jesus Christ, the tortured god of the ancient peoples, as he was suspended from his crucifix. The expression on Smyke's ghost's face was one of shock and horror which, as he watched, living Smyke realised was a mirror of his actual expression, so much so that he raised his hand to his face, to feel this expression.

Without opening his mouth, Anaximander said, 'See, Harold Smyke, your fate, for we are emissaries of the future, where you no longer live.'

Because speech is rarely as terrifying as images, words having a much more recent existence in the lineage of man than images do, and ancient things being more evocative of fear than recent ones, Anaximander stopped speaking. He turned to look at the ghost of Smyke, at his chest, onto which Sirius, having first released the ghost's wrist, reared up. He placed his open mouth at the place where a man's heart is, and made it look as if he was burrowing into the ghost's flesh.

Anaximander spoke again. 'You wore in life the epithet "Heartless" as a badge of honour, thinking it spoke of your strength, but understand now that it was nothing but an echo reverberating back in time from your eventual fate, which is to have this organ taken from you, and by the very creatures you thought always were your subservients.'

We, because we know all there is to know about this scene, and in the manner of the assistant who is in on the tricks of the theatrical magician, are not fooled into fear by this.

We could never be brought to death by this performance, our hearts understanding to continue beating in the absence of a mortal threat, but the same cannot be said for Harold Smyke. He was a machine extraordinarily sensitive to exactly this combination of elements, and who was entirely in ignorance of how they were combined, and in a place of, he imagined, perfect safety for him. So, none of his defences were raised, and rather than, as we would, brushing this off as nothing, he instead believed it was everything.

He saw himself punished by an apparition from the future coming on him in the night, and because his heart, communicated to by his mind, felt as much stress as his thoughts did in that moment, and because he was a man who had taken almost no care of his health, and had instead always had gin, which tires the muscles, as anyone who has drunken it must know, his heart muscles stopped beating in an instant.

Smyke stood there silently, mouth gaping, rigid as the crucified Christ, but not at all beneficent-seeming or godly, and not beautiful. All his ugly features – the jaw, the impacted teeth, the straggly hair, all of those things mentioned in the introductory description of him – were rendered uglier still by the expression of fear on his face.

The dogs did not stay to see him crumple to the ground, this Heartless Harold Smyke now truly having earned his name, because they needed to be present where the puppy was, to perform the spells that would make him talk. Instead, they manifested themselves in the breeding dens, back by their mother.

Smyke the ghost stayed, though, and took the place of his formerly living counterpart.

An attentive reader might wonder what became of the ghost of the man who had just been killed, but attentiveness in this case will have led to an error, since in the intermediate realm in which ghosts exist only one ghost of a formerly living person can be manifest, and what is to say that he was not this ghost all along?

Anaximander, by a process that would be impossible for any of us, but which was as simple as willing it to him, imprinted on the puppy's mental apparatuses that blueprint by which his own talking mind had been imprinted.

This blueprint was derived from a dead child, but it was present still in the immaterial realm and was therefore available as a reference. If a person were to ask how that is done, when the brain of a dog is a material thing, and ghosts cannot influence the material world in that way, it is sufficient to know that the brain of a physical thing, even a dog, contains a network of microtubules capable of storing information states influenced by the immaterial realm. It was not so much that Anaximander made physical changes in the puppy's brain, but that he transferred information from the immaterial realm into this brain's microtubules so that the organism *in toto* took on the abilities of that blueprint. He secured them in place by magic so that they would not be forgotten, and because the existence of information in the brain in this way is the same as it having been developed over time as a newborn develops, immediately into the world was born the dog who Anaximander would come eventually to know by his given name, which Anaximander had decided in advance would be Anaximenes by virtue of information he had discovered in the immaterial realm. The names Thales, Anaximander and Anaximenes, in that order, were those of philosophers of the ancient world, three men the magical dog imagined himself to be kin to in terms of his thinking.

Anaximenes sprang up, scarcely able to stand, raised his right paw, wobbling, and by virtue of the same mechanism that allowed Anaximander to speak he exclaimed, 'I am Anaximenes, the World Saviour! Know your righteousness by your desire to follow me, and your wickedness by my desire to punish you!' At which point he immediately lost his balance and his voice, and fell silently to the ground, where his mother attended to him, gently, with licks.

Whether the ghosts of the dogs willed themselves forward a little in time, or whether there was magical influence from either them or Anaximenes, is irrelevant, but suffice it to say that the new dog developed quickly from the perspective we are taking.

There was no long waiting in place for the dog to wean, or if there was it is not described here.

There was no observation of the manner by which the puppy apprised himself of the world he found himself in. He lived, he understood, and then he spoke.

'My first act,' he said, his voice very much like Anaximander's except higher in pitch, 'will be to liberate the mothers of this place. This is the precondition of all liberation, since are mothers not the first workers, *sine qua non*, and the most often exploited?'

Anaximander was about to reply to this question, not recognising it as rhetorical, but Anaximenes raised his paw to stop him. 'Father, brother, ghost,' he said, 'before you speak again, think on this: why was your first concern, seeing the conditions of this place, not to free those enslaved by it?'

Anaximander thought, briefly, and was about to say something to the effect that he was a ghost and consequently not best placed to perform the liberationary duties Anaximenes imagined were his primary obligation, but the puppy shushed him with a gesture. 'I asked that you meditate on the issue, not that you provide me with a justification. Self-justification is, as I will go on to make axiomatic, self-obfuscation. Hold yourself always to be deficient in your duty to a superior world to come and you will approach a useful psychological state of urgency in the face of your obligations.'

Before Anaximander could reply in any way, the tiny dog trotted off through the mothering-dens, leaving his father–brother with his mouth hanging open and his tongue lolling.

Sirius, unable to understand the child's words, bounded after him, but it took Anaximander a little longer to follow.

This was not because he was discomfited by what his brother–son had said, but more that he was entirely overwhelmed by it, as a parent is when, having waited through a pregnancy, the existence of its newly born offspring exceeds its expectations.

He had thought Anaximenes would be one thing – a replica, almost, of himself, someone with whom he could converse on topics he imagined would be mutually interesting to each other, but instead here was a thing with its own, much broader concerns, opening up other worlds entirely, ones in which Anaximander was an important part, but was suddenly not central. His thoughts and desires immediately and without warning became peripheral.

When this is made to happen by someone to whom one is not related, this might be extremely annoying, but when it is done by one's own flesh and blood, the feeling is like exhilaration, as if one has exceeded the limits of one's own existence at the same moment as one becomes aware of them.

All this Anaximander experienced in a rush, hence the mouth-open, tongue-lolling aspect of his disposition, and also the pause he took before he, a few moments later, galloped after Anaximenes and Sirius, who were already marching with purpose directly into the place where the other mothers were kennelled.

An awful thing is affecting in a limited way, and while it is said that people require a specific example of an atrocity in order for them to engage their emotions, the same is not true of dogs. Their sensory range, in life, is broader, and they are also not taught, as people are, to ignore unpleasant experiences and fixate only on pleasurable ones.

So, even though the suffering their mother was put to in Smyke's breeding dens was a terrible thing, the rows upon rows of dogs, caged ten deep and five high on both sides of the narrow concrete path that ran between them, their whimpering, their barking, their strangled kennel coughing, the brushing of their lips and teeth against the chicken wire that prevented them from leaving their cramped confines, their dry noses, their rheumy eyes, the dirt of their unchanged straw, their mouldering afterbirths, their fallen feed, rotting, the presence of so many bodies, unable and unwilling to rouse themselves: all of this was worse, to the dogs, than seeing their mother in her low condition.

Anaximenes stopped in the middle of the concrete path and slowly, calmly, sadly he looked from cage to cage.

He met the gazes of those mothers whose eyes were open and were facing him, and to these lowered his head to them in respect. These bitches were only a third of the caged dogs there, but, as he looked from each to the next, there came into the kennel an atmosphere that had not been present before he started doing it.

Anaximander couldn't attribute this change to any particular action, except that Anaximenes was making the atmosphere through his attention to these mothers through his treating them as things worthy of attention. 'What are you doing, brother–son,' Anaximander said.

Anaximenes didn't reply. Instead, he caught the eyes of the mothers who were now waking. They turned their exhausted bodies in their cages, reached down into their exhausted energies for reasons they could not have accounted for, even if they were rational creatures rather than the dumb slaves of a vicious dog breeder.

Anaximenes looked from cage to cage, from one side of the kennel to the other, from top to bottom and from left to right until all the dogs were awake, all the dogs were focussed on him. The place was entirely silent, and the atmosphere was of a mute and uncanny expectation of something ineffable. It was something strange and entirely new to these creatures, some sense of community between them that they had never felt, each isolated in their own cage.

Is this all that is required, Anaximander wondered, silently to himself, to recognise a commonality in one's suffering? To be shown respect for it? Is that all that is necessary for a life of misery to be redeemed?

He looked to Sirius, who looked back to him, and the two exchanged a wordless pride in their brother–son.

Again, though, Anaximander found himself to have underestimated the puppy, who, using not his magical voice but his physical one, almost comically high and thin, began, to a regular beat, to bark.

Once, twice, three times.

Once, twice, three times.

Once, twice, three times.

It took a little while, and some of them couldn't keep the rhythm through coughing, but eventually all of the mothers were barking just as he barked.

One, two, three.

One, two, three.

The noise of that many dogs, all barking in unison, even if they were weak and sickly things, made a racket that no one could ignore.

Least of all could the dog-men ignore it. They were trained to pay attention to unusual aspects of canine speech as much as they were trained to ignore the usual aspects, particularly any imploring begging of any kind. Down from the precincts in which these men were housed came one of them, dragging his leg.

Whether he was lame from birth, or whether he had sustained an injury in life – perhaps he had been set upon by dogs at some point, but had survived – was unknown to Anaximander, but he had in one hand a long staff with a studded end. This might have variously been called a club or cudgel or shillelagh, depending on the linguistic background of the man carrying it, but he pulled himself down the hill with it, coming slowly towards them, his arms doing most of the work.

These arms, presumably conditioned by this type of hard work, were muscled to a worrying degree, like a bare-knuckle boxer's often are. This fact was visible because he wore an armless and grubby vest and no overcoat, despite the chill drizzle that always fell on this place.

He looked just like the kind of person who would use a stick to beat a dog, this much Anaximander knew, and though he didn't recognise him from his time with Smyke, he recognised the man's type. A protective urge came over him more powerful than any protective urge he had ever felt, particularly since his service-pledge, the betrayer Clarissa Delacroix, had never seemed much like she needed protection. This urge took Anaximenes as its object.

Anaximander turned back, and there was the small puppy, his head still too large for his body, barking, one, two, three in time with the mothers. He could easily picture both mothers' and puppy's fates at the studded end of that shillelagh, the other end driven with all the force the man now approaching them could muster with his huge arms.

It was not a pretty picture, so Anaximander communed with Anaximenes, which is a much quicker process than the speech of either person or dog can accomplish, and by this method the two constructed a plan by which no one need have their skulls rendered into pieces and their brains made to egress from their ears.

Like many things to do with magical dogs, there is no exact equivalence between what happened between these two and anything that happens either with non-magical persons or persons in general, but it was as if Anaximenes's immediate desires and intentions were laid open to Anaximander's understanding at the price of his immediate desires and intentions being laid open to Anaximenes's understanding. As if these things were signposts indicating facts and experiences relevant to those desires and intentions, facts and experiences were indicated so that, to mix metaphors, they condensed in the dogs' minds like droplets of water condense from a hot room on a cold window, gathering and pooling in such a way that Anaximenes knew that Anaximander was fearful for his brother–son's safety, and also that the dog had recently, by frightening, killed Heartless Harold Smyke.

These things were all Anaximenes needed, because he was a dog for whom clever plans were to prove to be always within the easy grasp of his thinking, in order for him to decide what to do next.

The man was still a little way distant, the kennels conveniently at hand for the dog-men, but not so close to their quarters that the stench of its lack of cleanliness need distract them in the evenings. There was time to say, 'Father–brothers, render yourselves invisible,' and Anaximenes said it in such a way that the ghosts did just that without them needing, it seemed to them, to agree to do it.

If Anaximenes noticed this ability to dictate to ghosts what they should do, he showed no sign of it, but instead stood his ground in the middle of the concrete pathway between the cages and, still barking in the threefold rhythm, faced the door.

It swung open very forcefully, straining the hinges, and knocking hard against the frame.

'What's all this noise!' shouted the man, whose shoulders were covered with coarse and wiry hairs, and the muscles of whose neck were thick and knotting, as if snakes were fighting beneath his skin. 'I'll thrash you all quiet, you see if I don't!'

Anaximenes was apparently the only dog not in a cage now his father–brothers were faded beyond sight. 'Stop speaking!' he cried, and if his physical voice was high, he was able to make his magical voice deep, so that it came impossibly resonant to the man's ears.

This shocked both the man and the mother-dogs silent.

Anaximenes did not pause. 'Listen carefully,' he said. 'I am Anaximenes, the World Saviour, and I judge this dog-breeding facility to be unjust. Unjust things I come to the world to make just.'

Now he stood up on his hind legs and pointed with one paw up the hill from which the man had come. Over his visage came a mystical expression, and he rolled his eyes back in his head. 'Sim salla bim!' he cried out, and rolled his eyes back again to the fronts of their sockets. 'Heartless Harold Smyke is dead! Go now and validate the effectiveness of my killing magic. Return to me as a penitent, agreeing to release these mother-dogs, and I will resurrect your master. Refuse and

I will use my spell to kill you and then release them myself. The choice is yours.'

The man leaned heavily on his shillelagh, his brow furrowed, and though he was probably not the kind of man used to caring what it was that dogs wanted of him, he was equally unused to hearing dogs speak, since none had done so in the presence of any living man previously. Though he would no doubt have been happier to render Anaximenes to pulp, he did nonetheless leave, dragging himself back up the hill.

The mother-dogs, though they had not understood a word of what the puppy had said, and had cowered when the man threw open the door, did recognise that he had gone and with none of them beaten. Though a person would not have noticed, many of them made their tails wag a little.

A little is enough.

'Father–brother,' Anaximenes said to Anaximander, trusting him to be present, despite the fact that he was invisible, as the puppy had ordered, 'commune with these dogs on my behalf, if that is within your power, and tell them that they should prepare to receive their freedom.'

Anaximander manifested himself visually, since that seemed only polite, and he passed on the message to the mother-dogs while Anaximenes waited.

When he finished, he sighed deeply. 'Some of these bitches welcome the prospect of their freedom,' Anaximander said in words, 'those younger ones who remember life before the cages. The older ones are fearful, trusting only that the world holds pain for them. The young will go where you tell them, since they can sense your authority. The old say that they will not go. They have scarcely enough energy, they feel, even to die, so much of it they have given to their puppies through the obligation to bear uncounted litters, none of whom they have ever seen again. Their hearts cannot bear the thought of anything, even happiness.'

Anaximenes heard this and across his face emotions passed in sequence, none of them settling. 'Which ones communed with you to that effect?'

Anaximander went over to one who was caged on the bottommost row to the left.

She was a scrawny thing, and the few patches of hair that remained on her scabrous coat were white, though they had once been golden. Her teeth were rotten, and her breath was sour. Her nose was dry and scored with deep cracks.

Anaximenes, though he was too young to know properly how to initiate a communing, that facility not being as easy as speech, but being like the process of translating words into and out of a language one does not yet properly understand, tried to pass onto her a feeling like love.

She would not accept that feeling, having closed herself, protectively, from positive feelings of any sort.

The puppy was about to ask Anaximander to do what he could do to convince her, when the man with the shillelagh returned.

His face was drained of all colour and his hands were trembling.

He didn't say anything, because a dog-man does not know what to say to a dog, except orders, but he bowed to Anaximenes and then, with sidelong glances, he took the key to the padlocks which kept the cages secure from theft – he kept it in his boot – and unlocked each one.

As he did it, which took some time given the number of cages there were to unlock, a crowd of Smyke's men gathered outside.

'Summon the dead man's ghost,' Anaximenes said to Anaximander, which Anaximander did promptly, even though it undid his previous plan, so that Smyke stood before them, and because Mordew was a place in which the consistency of the weft had been loosened by the presence of the weftling's corpse, he appeared almost perfectly visible. 'Follow me,' Anaximenes said, and Smyke followed him out into the gathered crowd.

A dog-man can kill a puppy without any effort, and if any of them had chosen to kill Anaximenes, it would not have been within the dog's power to stop them by force of body. But force of will? That was a different matter. 'I bring before you the ghost of your master, who I have rendered dead by magic. It is also within my power, by the saying of magic words, to dissipate his ghost. This he has deserved, by the evil deeds he has done, as have you all. It would be a simple matter to make ghosts of you gathered here. I need only complete the magic phrase that begins with the words "sim salla..." and you will know I speak the truth, if you live long enough to know anything.

'But I am Anaximenes, the World Saviour, not Anaximenes the World Destroyer, so I will show you mercy. Go into the breeding pens and each of you gently bring a mother and carry her here. If she bites you for your efforts, do not retaliate.'

Anaximenes gave this order, but the dog-men were reluctant to carry it out, until Sirius, visible and barking, circled the group, snapping at their heels, jumping at their heads, and though he passed through the men as a ghost must, this was like ice water poured down their spines. Smyke's dog-men went and, careful with fear, they carried out the dog mothers from their cages, and placed them reverently in front of Anaximenes, retreating, bowing, like a courtier would do in front of their queen.

The puppy addressed the dogs now, the heads of them all low to the ground and cowering, Anaximander translating to them through the process of communing. 'Those of you who wish to go, go now – you have your freedom and may follow your noses where they lead. If you wish for vengeance, I warn you against it – no good will come of making an equivalence in the weight of misdeeds between you and these miscreants. Live your lives in happiness, as much as you can, and turn your minds to the freedom of your kind, which is everywhere in this city curtailed.'

Anaximenes waited, and half of the dogs, at least, went off at a run.

Of those that remained, most of them expressed, through Anaximander, a desire to follow him, to be a pack with him, and to populate the city with his kin, to which he replied, 'This is not something that I can do. In communing with my father–brother, who has in his turn communed with Sirius, my other father–brother and a dog who has an organ sensitive to the backwardly propagating waves of the future, I have seen that there is other work I am fated to achieve.'

When Anaximander communicated this to this second group of dogs, they followed the group that had run off, racing to catch up with their prison mates.

To the dogs who remained – these the oldest, the saddest, the most drained and pitiable – Anaximenes said nothing.

He turned instead to the men, all of whom, if they had caps, were twisting them in front of themselves and looking at the toes of their boots. 'Take the ghost of your master for a living man,' he said, 'and return to your business. Except you.' He indicated the man with the shillelagh. 'Before the rest of you go, know that you are overseen by ghosts and that they will report your misdoings to me. I will return to punish you for them, so you must show kindness in future to all the animals you husband. If you cannot do that then you must set them free, at which point your obligation to them will be over.'

The ghost of Smyke went first, and the living men followed him up the hill, not to trouble this story again, but the man with the shillelagh waited for his instructions.

Anaximenes addressed the sick old dogs who did not want their freedom, but who yearned only for death, so strong were the pains life had left their bodies and souls with.

'Mothers,' the puppy said, Anaximander translating again. He went to them all and licked their mouths, which is how dogs kiss, except without the eroticism people tend to read into the act. 'I am sorry that your lives have been so onerous to you, when they should only have brought you fulfilment. Yet, in death, you may still find some use for what you choose now to give up.'

He looked over to the man with the shillelagh, who understood what was expected of him, this being a significant part of his usual duties. 'I must return to the future, from where my father–brothers have come, and because this is an impossible thing, magic must be used to do it. Because magic is the thing proper to the weftling, and because his will exists as the animating Spark that makes things live, and because this is freed up in death, though very little remains in you, you can usefully die, knowing that it will do a magical and important thing for the dog who tried to liberate you.

'Is this something to which you agree?'

They did agree, gladly, since life was such a torture for them.

When the shillelagh stopped falling, and the spell was cast, their pain ended there, in the dust of Heartless Harold Smyke's compound.

The magical dog and the ghosts of the magical dogs went back to where they should have been, and the man with the shillelagh dropped each of the mother-dogs' bodies, carefully, into the fire that heated the water boiler.

That evening he went back to his place in the slums and found a different job.

Now the three were back in the material realm, approximate to the time at which the two ghosts had been killed.

Sirius set up a terrible pestering. Something was driving him to an excess of whining and keening and rising up and growling and all of the other non-verbal forms of communication. He was attempting, unsuccessfully, to get Anaximander to understand what he wanted.

They were on the green hills of the land surrounding Malarkoi, near to where Anaximander had emerged to be shot with an assassin's crossbow bolt, but not in the immediate precincts of the corpses that the Druze had created.

While Anaximenes pawed at the grass as if he didn't understand what it was – and why should he, since he had never seen any in the concreted compound Heartless Harold Smyke preferred – Sirius sprang here and there, pressing for them to go where he wished to go, running urgently and inaccurately across and through the surfaces of the landscape, sometimes six feet above the ground, sometimes only the top of his head visible to the others.

'Where does my father–brother wish we were going?' Anaximenes said.

Anaximander replied, having communed with Sirius, 'He wants us to go to find Nathan Treeves, his service-pledge, whom, though it is my understanding that he is dead, he senses as having returned to the material realm.'

Anaximenes nodded his heavy head shakily, his little neck scarcely able to bear its weight. 'This is a matter in which I have no interest. For this reason, along with others, I will take my leave of you here in the hope that we will meet again in the future.'

Sirius ran over and stood between the puppy and Anaximander, not because he was unwilling to see Anaximenes leave, but because he wanted the two to stop talking. That did not stop them, though it did make it slightly less convenient, a transparent dog tending to obscure the vision a little.

'I had hoped that we might discuss matters of mutual interest,' Anaximander said. 'But perhaps you are right. Sirius is strongly inclined to get about his business, and since he had a mystical organ in his chest that is capable of knowing the future, it is usually best to let him have his way. Let us part, then, in the understanding that we will, one day, continue our business together. Take care, brother–son, and know that, should you ever require us, you need only call out these words,' and here he leaned in and whispered a combination of syllables he had learned from the immaterial realm: 'reclaim a little Spark – a flea, or a tick, or a scabies mite will be sufficient – and I, at least, and possibly Sirius, though I cannot speak for him or to him when he is in this agitated mood, will come to you and provide what aid ghosts may provide the living, which in this case is a substantial amount, since we retain our magicality, even in death.

'Companion! Enough!' Anaximander cried out, since Sirius was now occupying the same space the other dog was occupying, something ghosts find extremely annoying, and growling at him, which anyone would find tolerable for only very brief periods.

Anaximenes, recognising a dog who has too many calls on his attention when he saw one, said his farewells and trotted unsteadily off.

While one of his fathers watched him, the other one set up a steady and insistent barking, which Anaximander could no longer ignore. 'Very well!' he said. 'We will go to find Nathan.'

If you have ever suggested to a dog that is nagging you for something that he may have the thing for which he is nagging, you will know how quickly that dog then runs off to get, or do, or fetch the thing he has been determined to get, or do, or fetch. Sirius went off like this – like a rat out of a trap – into the distance with a speed that only a frictionless object can attain.

Anaximander, with a final glance back at his son's rear dwindling into the distance, was left with no choice but to follow, something he was perfectly well equipped to do, just by wishing it.

Now Sirius, because of his mystical organ, knew where Nathan was as well as we do: he was in the district of Waterblack where his dead were housed. If a dog can see the future of an object, he can follow that object back through the future to the present, and know where it must be now, even if he no longer possesses the perceptive complexity of his living senses.

Even if that had not been the case, the two dogs could have followed the great swarm of ghosts all related to Nathan in death. They had been summoned by the revival of the Master of Waterblack to make their pilgrimage back to the city from where they had wandered during the many years that Nathan's father, Nathaniel Treeves, had abdicated his Mastery of that city.

These ghosts were everywhere, in their thousands, no more than shadows and disruptions in the air to a living person, but perfectly visible to other ghosts.

They were everywhere, all walking towards the same point – somewhere off over the sea – walking on the water like Christ did when he performed the same miracle for his disciples during the fourth watch of the night. No doubt, if those disciples had seen these ghosts all walking on water together they would have known them for ghosts in truth, not mistaking their messiah for one, since a messiah and a ghost are different orders of thing, whether the weftling is alive or not. If they had taken themselves out of their boat and walked towards these ghosts, no amount of faith would have held them on the surface of the water, and their nascent religion would have ended there, the lot of them drowned, rather than waiting for millennia until their theology was superseded by occultism and god murder.

They were everywhere, these ghosts.

If one imagines the ripples a stone makes when it is dropped into a still pond, and then thinks of it in reverse, that was how these ghosts appeared. They walked rippling inwards, concentrically, towards a single point in the far distance. Mystic organ or not, the ghost dogs could easily have found the spot above where Nathan was, and so eager was Sirius to get there, and so convenient did following this swarm seem to Anaximander, that neither of them questioned why it was that the lot of them, ghosts of men and dogs, didn't take a more direct path down to the seabed, bisecting the volume of water and following a line as if it was the hypotenuse of a right-angled triangle, inverted.

If they had asked one of the other ghosts – something they did not do – they would have discovered that, for ghosts, there was only one way into and out of the city of Waterblack, this having been made by Nathaniel Treeves when he escaped that city. This one way was the rickety and makeshift spiral staircase Nathan had seen and had not understood.

There was an interdiction on anyone or anything else entering or leaving the city by any other route.

Was there anything intrinsically important about the rest of the ghost dogs' journey to the staircase that would give them ingress to the City of Death?

There was the image, seen from a distance, from on high, of them, like water boatmen of the family Corixidae, scudding through the crowd of the ghostly pilgrims making for the city of their Master, seeming to defy the waves.

There was a closer view, of them running, panting, side by side, no breath troubling the air around them, their paws leaving no splashing on the surface of the water, their muscles never tiring.

There was a comparison to be made between the activities of the minds of the dogs, one excited to be reunited with their Master, another thinking about their son, and the mass of the ghosts, angering and vengeful, frustrated by the years of their waiting.

Whether these three things are important would depend, rather, on whether the reader found them to be important, but all that really needs to be said is that, when the dogs reached the spot on the surface of the water, far from shore, unmarked by any buoy or the memories of sailors, there, emerging from the waves, were the final steps Nathaniel Treeves had nailed in place and which had allowed him to free himself from his bondage to Waterblack, and through which the dogs then entered that city.

NATHAN WANDERED THE STREETS UNTIL, it might have been hours later, an Actuary turned Nathan's attention upwards. There, in the distance, was a tiny square of light, like the skylight in the ceiling of a dark attic with a very high roof.

It was like a skylight in a spire of the Merchant City, in a palace up in the Pleasaunce, made in homage to the Master of Mordew's Manse, tall like it was, narrow, functionally useless, no one needing that much vertical space indoors since anything requiring that degree of height could more easily be achieved outside. If Nathan had laid himself down in an attic of one of these houses, and there had been placed at the very pinnacle of a spire a square skylight from which moonlight shone, but not enough so that it illuminated the walls of the room but left the place black, then that is what the square in the sky looked like.

Except... this square was growing.

Around him there was a bustling movement amongst the Sparkline Actuaries of that neighbourhood.

They were leaving their posts, jumping down if they could from their windowsills, or floating away, or swimming up to a different vantage. The only cat who was not moving was Nathan's; it stared upwards at the growing square, now double the size at least, and still growing.

It seemed like a breach in the water, some kind of interruption of the natural order of things, a geometrical insertion into a place where no such regularity was possible.

Still, it kept growing.

The cat pawed at Nathan's leg, and indicated by the direction of its gaze that they should both move to the side.

Now, from that different angle, it became clear that the square was not a square at all, but a slightly different shape, more trapezoidal, but still growing, the shape changing as it grew.

Some realisations come slowly, but others come in a moment, snapping into the mind with such suddenness that the consequences of their ideas rush in too quickly, making the mind reel, making it retreat, making a person shake their head, making them say 'no', repeatedly, under their breath.

No, they think, it can't be, even though it clearly is.

There wasn't a square, or any other simple shape, growing in the sky. There was no skylight in an attic.

What Nathan could see was the descent down into the city of a great, new cube of faceted glass, brought into existence because there was no place already in Waterblack for performances of death on the scale which this cube would contain.

This cube descended, as it must, into the quarter of the city where Nathan's dead resided.

It was larger than Nathan's father's cube – the one that still flashed through the city at intervals, killing soldiers arranged on the parade ground with a burst of light – and rather than each facet being the size of Nathan's palm, as had been the case there, these could be covered by the fingertip of an index finger.

When Nathan did this, the glass was cool to the touch.

He shut his eyes so he couldn't see what he already knew he would find when he looked through each of those tiny windows.

He concentrated on the coldness of the glass, the smoothness, as if this feeling was all there was to the object that had descended to him, waiting for his attention.

This was the House of the Thousand Million Flames, and whether Nathan chose to look into its windows or not, its occupants performed their deaths for him, every one of them requiring redress or revenge.

Had his father walked this way when his own cube had descended?

Nathan took the most direct route back to the plaza, and though the Sparkline Actuaries called after him, he didn't look back.

The Thousand Million Flames.

Could he turn his back on them?

As his father had?

The plaza was filled with cats, not just on the ground, but throughout the volume of the water that filled it. Nathan could hardly see the spiral staircase, there were so many bodies between him and it.

He barged his way through, the Actuaries he pushed aside hissing and scratching him as he went by. Could they sense his eagerness to leave that place? His unwillingness to obey the ordinances of his own city?

It didn't matter. Nathan fought his way across to the centre of the plaza, struggled through the thick water to the first step of the spiral stair, put his foot on it, his arms and face stinging with scratches.

Each one of the steps was nailed into place, rickety and uneven. Had this been done by his father, then? Was he appalled as Nathan had been by the extent of his crimes? Was this what he'd meant – don't use it?

Of course, it was.

Nathan climbed the steps. He would climb his way out, leave this city behind, accept, at last, what his father had ordered him to do.

He went, climbing, pulling himself up, but when he looked down for the next poorly secured step, he saw that the Actuaries had stopped looking at him. They were staring upwards themselves.

Down the stair, running without any thought for his safety, bounding joyously, five, ten steps at a time came Sirius, his dog.

By instinct, by reflex, through love, Nathan forgot everything and threw open his arms.

Sirius dived down at his service-pledge, and Nathan shut his eyes, waited for the dog to slam against his chest so that he could embrace him.

That moment never came.

Nathan, awkward suddenly, unsure, opened his eyes, and there was his dog, on the ground of the plaza, turning, preparing to bound up now to where Nathan was, but when he did it he passed straight through again, and now Nathan realised what he was seeing.

Sirius was dead.

Of course he was.

This was Waterblack.

His dog refused to understand what was wrong, came again and again to leap at Nathan, expecting each time to connect with his body, to feel his embrace, always passing though.

Was this another punishment? Another obligation? Another trick this city played on its Master's emotions? To provoke duty in him.

Up there on the staircase, behind, but not by much, was Anaximander, walking more circumspectly from step to step, but coming no less surely. Behind him came hundreds, thousands of ghosts, and, as if to match their numbers, here came Sparkline Actuaries into the plaza, a welcoming party, or a defending army – there was no knowing which.

Sirius raised himself up on his hind legs in front of Nathan, hovered so that the image of his paws were on Nathan's shoulders.

Deep inside his belly, Nathan felt the Itch. It was simultaneously both the most and the least familiar thing he had ever felt – familiar because he knew it so well, unfamiliar because he had almost forgotten it.

Why had he thought to leave this place?

Why had he ever listened to his father?

Why did he intend to make that man's mistake, by leaving, when there was this – the Itch, the Scratch? The Spark?

Would he go to the slums and die there, or would he use his power.

The will of God.

Nathan reached down inside himself and that was all that it took. He dragged out from inwards all the power that existed there, that infinite energy, and with it he brought Sirius back from his ghostly form, materialising his concept, creating around the lattice of his appearance a new, stronger, perfect form in matter for the dog to take, and because Sirius had

418

known divinity, this form he knew already – the form of Goddog – which he gratefully became.

Nathan Scratched the Itch and he put his arms around his dog, and Sirius grew to ten times his size, as large as he had ever been under the influence of godflesh, but that was not all.

The will of God is more than godflesh, and just as Nathan had made angels of the alifonjers, now he did the same for Sirius, imbuing him with a material perfection exceeding that which he had known as a god, filling him with so much Spark that he could have been an entire race of dogs, a species of dogs, a history of dogs stretching back to the first of his kind and forward to the last.

Nathan grabbed at the scruff of Sirius's neck, his hands hardly pinching the skin, but enough so that he could pull himself up until he rode on the dog's back.

Sirius bounded through Waterblack as he had once bounded through Mordew, but this time he did not topple the buildings of that city, but landed always in the perfect places to do no damage.

Anaximander was hesitating on the final step down to Waterblack, one forepaw hovering before he committed it to touching the ground.

Before Nathan could reach him, the dog spoke, the words sounding in Nathan's ears without troubling the water between them. 'Nathan Treeves!' he said. 'It is a pleasure to see you returned to the world, regardless of by what mechanism this has been achieved, for it marks the renewal of my companion Sirius's service-pledge to you.'

Nathan drew Sirius up at the base of the stair, and now Anaximander stepped down onto the ground.

'We are followed by a great number of other ghosts,' he went on, 'all of whom have calls on your power. They come behind en masse.'

The dog looked over his shoulder, and above Nathan could see the foremost group of ghosts coming quickly, step by step, shoulder to shoulder.

'Before they arrive,' Anaximander continued, speaking very quickly, but nonetheless clearly, 'let me request that I transfer my service-pledge to you, an obligation that I previously gave to your mother. She has betrayed me, to my death, something that has done two things. Firstly, it has severed my pledge to her. Secondly, it has established in me the desire to punish her betrayal of my offered pledge. I, as you can see, am a ghost...'

The other ghosts were coming closer now, and Nathan could see the desire in Anaximander's eyes, hear the desire in his voice, knew, from his Mastery of the city in which he and Anaximander were present, how he might resolve the dog's betrayal.

It was not ordinanced that a Master of Waterblack must make good deaths that might properly belong to previous Masters or their associates, but it was within his power to do it if he wished. Here was a citizen of Waterblack petitioning for the means by which to right the wrongs that did him to death, and without the dog having to finish his sentence Nathan made an angel of him, returning his perfect physical form, which was, for Anaximander, a fighting dog capable of enormous violence, and then he evolved that form to angelic status.

Anaximander had not been a god, so his concepts did not know the possibilities Sirius knew – he did not expand in size – but he was brought back to life, to an angelic materiality sufficient that he should be able to fulfil his desire to punish the betrayal against him.

Anaximander began to speak, to thank his new Master, but the water rushed into his lungs and made it impossible for him to concentrate long enough on the formation of the words. Although an angel created by the Master of Waterblack cannot drown in the waters of that city, that does not mean that it cannot be disconcerted by a change in its circumstances, and in the time it took Anaximander to regain his bearings, the crowd of ghosts that had been following behind him found the bottom of the stair. They spread out into the plaza, the Spark Actuaries making way for them.

Such was the number of these ghosts that soon the plaza was filled, the stair at its centre, Nathan, riding Goddog, beside it.

On the lips of these ghosts, Nathan knew, would be petitions for his justice, each beginning with the phrase 'god-child', which was propagating like a chant throughout the gathered crowd.

Nathan raised his hand, and there was silence.

He had been about to leave, to turn his back on his obligations, to justify the Sparkline Actuaries' dismissal of him, but now, astride Sirius, Anaximander bowing at his feet? And here, trampling their way through the insubstantial ghosts, the angels of the alifonjers.

If he had left, it would have been another mistake.

He stayed, and it was Nathan's turn to speak, which he opened his mouth to do, but he faltered.

A ghost may speak underwater, a magical dog may speak underwater, but a physical child, no matter whether he is the Master of the City or not, needs air so that he can vibrate his vocal cords.

The Spark Actuaries saw him make the effort and fail.

The stiff-legged cat who was allocated to him floated over to Nathan, bringing in its dead mouth a slotted machine the size of a palm from which a great length of coiled wire extended. This it pressed against Nathan's throat. Through whatever invisible mechanism broadcast Nathan's heartbeat through the city, now came the gurgling, unformed, meaningless noises a boy makes when he hasn't learned how to properly speak underwater.

The ghosts, the dogs, the alifonjers, the dead cats all waited, listening to these strange sounds, until Nathan eventually understood how to speak, which he did with his body more than he did his mind.

If you were to speak with your mouth shut – you can try it now – and did everything you would normally do, except do not open your mouth or move your jaw, it would feel like you were doing nothing, but in the drowned streets of Waterblack this was enough for the machine, if you had been passed it, to translate into sound the words you were intending to be heard.

His voice came out deeply into the plaza, like the low notes a whale might sing. They vibrated the glass in the windows, making the performances acted out there – which did not cease, regardless of his speaking – tremble.

'Enough!' Nathan cried. 'We have waited enough.'

He raised his arms up in the air, and though there was no meaning intrinsic to that gesture, perhaps he was indicating the surface world above them all. 'Ghosts, dogs, cats, alifonjers: you have waited long enough.'

All of the things Nathan addressed, except alifonjers, will keen when they are filled with emotion, and alifonjers will make an equivalent sound, which is more like a growl. The ghostly keening was the loudest, because they did not need air to make it, but deep inside the cats and the dogs the quieter sound of their keening came, and from the alifonjers was their growling.

The plaza was filled with the noise.

Nathan's Actuary turned a dial on the machine with its free paw so that Nathan, when he spoke again, could be heard above the others.

'I... I have waited long enough.' Nathan looked around the plaza, across at the districts of the city, expanding in all directions away from him, up at the stair which led them to the surface. 'We have all waited long enough.'

Nathan paused, and in his silence, the unspoken question reverberated: 'For what have we waited long enough?' They all hoped they knew the answer – they did know it – but one can never be certain until after it has been made explicit whether one is correct in what one thinks.

The keening, and the growling, grew in volume.

Nathan's silence grew in volume.

The dead cat at Nathan's throat turned the dial on the machine.

'For justice!' Nathan cried out.

The plaza erupted in that way that eruptions occur when they have been long suppressed – with frustrated vigour, suddenly and forcefully released. The ghosts cried out, the cats howled, the dogs barked, and the alifonjers made that trumpeting sound that, while its description in words seems faintly ridiculous, in reality is enormously stirring.

Because they were more certain than the others where Nathan's rhetoric was tending, the Sparkline Actuaries had been bringing to the plaza Nathan's most recently installed dead. Behind him hovered the enormous cube that contained the death performances of the Thousand Million Flames, dead cats at every edge of it, guiding it, floating, towards the plaza.

Nathan turned and reached inward, Sirius between his thighs, the closeness of the dog's angelic form anchoring the boy both physically and psychologically.

God – the weftling – was both omnipresent and omniscient. He did not need to know a particular thing, nor to be in a particular place, because he knew all things generally, and was everywhere generally, and though Nathan was not God, he was the god-child.

He did not need to know how to simultaneously resolve the deaths of the Thousand Million Flames, nor did he need to be beside each of the facets of that cube – nor those inside that would be reached when the outer rooms resolved – in order to do what he did next, which was to make angels of all those second-borns his agreement with the Mistress of Malarkoi had condemned to death.

All he had to do was reach inward, from the central plaza of Waterblack, while he was its Master, for his will and God's will to coincide in the resolution of his culpability in their deaths.

He didn't need to see the performance of that billion-fold slitting of throats to know that he was accurately identified as the cause of their deaths – he knew that to be true.

From one corner of the cube, the three external facets shattered. From each emerged a newborn, reborn as an angel.

One was like a shining cherub, or, more properly, a putto, since it had only one face and two wings, where cherubim would have had four faces and four wings; another was more cherubic, in that it was a winged and shining child of the person-headed snake people; a third was an infant dragon, filled with light but requiring no extra wings.

These three were alone for the briefest appreciable moment and then each of the other facets shattered in turn with the

Spark Nathan forced into them, cascading from that first corner, and as each one shattered, angels of infant people, of infant person-headed snakes, of infant dragons, of insects, of human–animal hybrids, of all the enormous variety of the dead of the Thousand Million Flames came into Waterblack.

When the first layer was shattered an inner layer was revealed, and when that shattered, releasing its angels, there was a layer beneath that, and one beneath that, and on and on.

Nathan channelled the infinite power of God's will through his own will, becoming the perfect conduit of the justice of Waterblack, redeeming all the Flames, redeeming himself, in a vast expenditure of weft energy, that, had he known it, dimmed the lights across the Assembly, rang the bell that would summon the warpling, created the most part of the Angelic Army of Waterblack.

That was not all, because when it was done, and the skies of Waterblack were filled with cherubim and putti and amorini and erotes and dragons and dragonflies there was still an infinity of energy remaining. It was this excess that the ghostly pilgrims now petitioned for their part of.

One ghost, tall and lanky, dressed in frills and ruffs, the bite of rot at his ears and lips, a stiff and pointing finger at the end of a stiff and pointing arm, cried, 'Renew me, god-child!' his teeth chattering like an alms-seeker's, queueing in a winter graveyard.

Another wore simple trews, like a workman might, and a checked shirt; its face was cleanshaven and broad, but its eyes were blacked like Nathan's mother's and its lips were puffy and red. In its hair, which was long and parted down the middle, it wore a ram's head barrette. 'Make me live!'

A child came down the spiral stair, caparisoned in princely garb, lacking all but one of his limbs, scarred across his cheek as if burned. He turned, a motion that revealed an unnatural flattening of him, as if he had been compacted in a vice. 'I want to be an angel,' he said.

There were a thousand ghost men in robes of varying antiquity, and Nathan, without pausing for a moment, did exactly as they all desired.

Last was Nathan's brother, presenting with his face taken away, his scraped and white skull, his lipless mouth and bared teeth. He could not speak, could not tell Nathan what their father and mother had done to him, what he wished for, but Nathan knew.

Shouldn't a good Master know what it is you need, without you having to say it?

Nathan reached down, took his brother's hand, pulled him up so that he rode behind him on Sirius Goddog.

And that was not all, because in all the rooms, in all the streets, in all the districts of Waterblack there were the unavenged dead of the city, stretching further than Nathan had been able to see when he had climbed the staircase, all the way to the boundary stelae.

In his grace, Nathan Treeves, greatest yet of the Masters of Waterblack, accepted the responsibility for remedying their murders, back into the prehistory of the world, making those whose lives had been truncated whole again. All the doors were thrown open, all the windows exploded, he resurrected them all in the forms of angels, giving them the power to go into the world again, to avenge themselves, with him, their Master, riding on the back of Goddog, at their head.

Now that dark cold city was full of light. It was not that dull and hopeless light that had shone from the windows of the dead, but the bright and righteous light of God's will, the Spark light, the evolving light, the angelic light of vengeance that filled the citizens of his city with new life, bringing Nathan newly to life with them.

He was filled, their Master, as they had been filled – his power had tapped the infinite weft, bringing into the material realm an excess which gave the ghosts of his dead their forms, returning them to the world from which they had been torn, and because he was their Master, he benefitted from their rising, a commonwealth of the risen dead in which he shared, first of his people.

Such is the nature of the angelic Sparklight that it contains both light and heat, those things being a natural combination, an agitation of matter always following on contact with the weft, the potentiality of it felt in the smallest parts of the world from the most inward to the most outward particle, oscillating it. That oscillation makes light and warmth at the same time, makes sound – a constant, high-pitched trilling, almost, but not entirely, out of the range of human sensation – makes a tingling in the nerves of any creature bearing nerves, causes to spin and jerk all the compass needles of the world, orders metals in a circle at which Nathan was the centre.

Because water is a substance that takes on heat, that absorbs light, that conducts electricity, the water around Nathan and his dead, thousands of millions strong, began to boil. First there was a stream of tiny bubbles, then these were replaced by voids in the water filled with steam, the size of Nathan's fists, which then erupted in gouts, in geysers, in hurricanes of superheated water.

An impossibly hot wind rose up from the city of Waterblack, displacing more water into the places where the boiled water had once been, which itself boiled off on contact with an angel, whether they be in the form of a baby, or a child, or a person, or a beast.

When this was displaced, more water came in to fill its space from the endless oceans, and there was a reaction greater than any volcanic explosion, something not seen since the age of the ancients, who made weapons so murderous that they aggressed against the fabric of the material realm itself, expelling outward all that was inward, down even to the weft, so that the weftling himself was made to intervene, that intervention risking his life, which the Tontine wizards took, in their blasphemous and short-sighted idiocy, and which brought about all the death that Nathan's dead were only the latest iteration of.

As the water boiled beneath the feet of Nathan and his army of angels, they rose up with the rising air, gas being so much lighter than water that water always wants to be beneath it. They were pushed up in water's eagerness to sink low, and so the soldiery of Nathan's army flew up through the depths.

If they had been things of flesh they would have had the skin sloughed from them in the heat, they would have become like cooked meat, solid and immovable, but because Nathan had evolved them past flesh, on to the most perfect form matter can be, more weft-stuff than matter, they received no harm. Their immaterial concept was so strongly imprinted on their existence that they could be nothing other than the perfect iteration of themselves.

All those oppressive and suffocating fathoms through which Nathan's pellet had dropped, he rushed through in reverse, boiling away plankton and jellyfishes, crustacea and shoals of mackerel, all of it destroyed before Nathan could become aware of it, none of these creatures having sufficient merit to deserve, under the ordinances of Waterblack, any consideration of the obligations which their death might have established.

Even less deserving were the acreages of kelp and seaweed, but whatever cetaceans and larger sea-dwelling mammals that were caught up in the rise to the surface of the Army of Waterblack became recruited to that army themselves, the range of Nathan's influence having spread now to such an extent that it exceeded the diameter of the sphere which contained it. The deaths of any higher animals he immediately reconciled without conscious effort, making them angels by virtue of his presence, extending the limits of Waterblack, the pre-eminence of its laws following, in his glory, the presence of Nathan Treeves, its Master.

Rather than being constrained by the historic position of the boundary stelae, which were rendered redundant now since the magic of that city was being performed in a wider and wider area, what was to say that one day all the world would not be Waterblack?

Would the world become a world of Death, in which everyone was an angel who owed the end of their material existence to the Master through a great blossoming of Spark energy which only the presence of the weftling had prevented?

Would Nathan bring a heaven on Earth where God's will, Nathan's will, the tendency to perfection, was fulfilled?

What was a boundary stela with magic words carved into it then?

Nothing: the magic of such a thing was only recognisable by virtue of the absence of magic in its surroundings.

When all the world was magic?

When everything everywhere was the impossible?

Then it would be the impossible that was the possible, and stones carved with spells would become the banal objects, since everything else was filled with the power of God's will. The world would be mutable, always moving to perfection, a piercing light in the universe, like a star high in the sky on a perfectly dark night, but spreading, swelling, doubling, brightening, slowly at first and then with joyous and sudden rapidity filling the entire sky.

Nathan would make the sky an uninterrupted field of white, a field of light, and every mind that perceived it would become that light, and once we are all light, all one single angel, one single god, what is a rock then?

What is a person?

What was Nathan?

What was anyone?

Up, up, up they went, the Army of Waterblack, with Nathan at their head, vanguard of the Universal Light, profligate distributor of God's will.

The only occupants of Waterblack that remained in the city once its army had departed were the Sparkline Actuaries. These gathered together, now the rooms were emptied, and the tallies removed.

Between them, these dead cats planned new buildings, new streets, new districts.

The blueprints of these extensions they scratched with their claws wherever there was space, until every surface of every structure was covered with them.

When it was done, they took the schedule of works to the boundary stelae, redundant though they might prove to be, and waited in silence while the city extended itself across the seabed.

BOOK THREE

I

THE WOMEN'S Vanguard's encampment removed their camouflage, and activated the first of the category three attractant/rack combination engines, as Sharli and Tinnimam left to meet Gleed at the bomb barge.

Tinnimam was perched on Sharli's shoulders, spreading her wings for balance, shifting her three legs every time Sharli met an obstacle: soldiers huddled, ordnance stacks, ropes stretched between poles. A small, flameless, tripodal firebird is an unusual thing to see, but that's not why people were whispering as they passed, talking behind their hands.

Sharli couldn't make out what they were saying, except one repeated phrase: 'weft-bomb', 'weft-bomb', 'weft-bomb'.

Wherever she went: 'Weft-bomb.'

Tinnimam didn't show any interest in what they were saying – why would she? – but shouldn't Sharli have cared about this machine that could finish the work of the Crusade?

She didn't.

They walked past the mobile concentrate directors which, depending on their colour, were capable of draining the Spark from ghosts, angels, demons, parasites, back into the weft. The women responsible for ensuring these were in battle condition, for activating their fuel cells, for checking the light-paths were clear, all stopped what they were doing when Sharli passed.

'Weft-bomb,' they whispered to each other when they thought she was out of the range of their hearing.

The technicians for the amphibious wheeled platforms, the drive teams of Crusaders, the field-trained Hailey-Beths (Martial) from Engines: 'Weft-bomb.'

Division commanders, distributing paper maps the Hailey-Beths (Martial) Prose had quickly produced as guides to the potential Collapse Zones: 'Weft-bomb.'

Behind these, the infantry with handheld ankuretics, women whose function would be to use these machines to secure weak weft-stuff and prevent the dead from proliferating on the field in the aftermath of the concentrate engines: 'Weft-bomb.'

They were all saying 'weft-bomb'.

Tinnimam didn't care about the weft-bomb, and neither did Sharli.

They walked, quickly and calmly, towards their rendezvous with Gleed, and Sharli thought as little about the weft-bomb as she thought about the crusaders from Ballistics coming out of their subterranean barracks like termites from a mound.

'Weft-bomb,' they whispered.

She saw and ignored the crusaders' perfect grey uniforms.

'Weft-bomb.'

She ignored the women from Riflery, in their perfect blue uniforms. She ignored the insignia they wore – the ornate and anachronistic Cross of Jerusalem, in the ancient meaning of which she had no interest. These were edged in black, these crosses, because this was the Women's Vanguard, and that was their marker, but Sharli didn't care.

'Weft-bomb.'

Sharli didn't care.

Outside the camp was the Caravan. In rank and file a thousand deep were soldiers who were not women, uniformed in blue but without the insignia, trained in the same disciplines, equipped with the same rifles, and ankuretics, and pistols.

Irrelevant to Sharli.

Past these were the Hailey-Beths of varied disciplines who operated the long-range missile systems and the cloud-seeders. Past these, the maintenance crusaders with their war-equipped intelligencers, which they'd shoot in parabolic arcs into the sky, so that they jetted into positions where they could observe and bombard the future battlefield with light ordnance.

Irrelevant.

The weft-bomb was irrelevant, the Women's Vanguard was irrelevant, the Atheistic Crusade was irrelevant.

When an assassin is given a job, the only thing that's relevant, the only thing she cares about, is where her target is, and how she intends to kill him.

With Tinnimam on her shoulders and the weft-knife at her hip, Sharli walked through the encampment of the Women's Vanguard of the Eighth Atheistic Crusade to rendezvous with Field Commander Gleed, who was preparing to take her by sea to the weft-bomb detonation site, and from there to the Collapse Zone.

MEANWHILE, in a nested realm of the Golden Pyramid of Malarkoi, Gam Halliday was still dying.

Dashini pulled his head back by the hair and Prissy screamed.

She screamed loud enough that she should have startled the Stag, and ran screaming for Gam, hoping the Stag would make it moonrise again, and put them all back on the path to the village.

But the god didn't hear her – it was too far down the mountain, too involved with its business, so endlessly frustrated – and while Prissy screamed, Dashini muttered and gestured and slit Gam's throat, freeing his Spark, opening the Door to the fifth Level.

The girls left the moment Gam died.

He fell to his knees, blood pumping from the cut in his throat, and though his body took its time to become still, his mind fled the corpse, first into unconsciousness, then into nothing, the Spark departing, knowing it had no host remaining, fuelling the opening of the door.

In the material realm, that would have been the end of that, barring any magical intervention, but in the realm of the Wolf Pack and the White Stag that was not the end of that.

Once Gam was dead, the Stag desired that he live again, and so the boy tended back towards life, as the Druids eviscerated by the Wolves, day in, day out, tended back towards wholeness. The blood flowed back to the perfect slit in Gam's neck the Nathan Knife had made, seemed to move in the manner of a slime mould, or of quicksilver, pooling and sliding across the forest floor. It went back into the wound, up into the veins and arteries that were so neatly opened, slowly, but no less surely for that.

This was no individual grace the Stag gave to Gam: it was a blanket decree that the god's divine nature caused it to make.

Those things killed in the realm of the White Stag should be made to live again – that was its will.

Their life, as a representation of the Stag's divine requirement for things to be the way they were, was to be restored.

Dashini slit Gam's throat, Gam fell to his knees on the bare top of the Stag's hill, his consciousness fled with his Spark, his body slumped, gasping and convulsing, his blood pooled around him, and then his blood bled back into his body, separating itself from the soil and the twigs, the leaves and the ants, the faecal and urinary scat. It returned clean into the boy's circulatory system, the wound knitting completely as perfectly as it had been slit. New, fresh Spark was drawn from the weft to animate his self again, so that, only a few hours from his death, he took a sharp breath in.

Vision returned to his eyes and, into the corpse Dashini made, Gam Halliday was reborn, whether the Assembly would think it propagandistic or not.

Perhaps this was a new Gam Halliday.

Perhaps it was an independent and separate being, as the soul propagandas insisted.

Indeed, there was in Gam, now, no sense of the darkness that had motivated his willingness to die. It seemed to the new Gam that, when he had been there with Dashini, her knife at his throat with Prissy screaming, he had been filled with shadows, but that he had fallen asleep for a moment to wake now with his cheek pressed into the dirt, alone in the moonlight with the shadows gone.

He felt himself to have continued across this momentary gap, as we feel ourselves to have continued across the gap of our nightly sleeping. But perhaps this is what it feels like to be born into a body already imprinted with memories. Perhaps replicas of a person, made through magic, might feel this way: like the previous thing, but awoken refreshed, all the body's memories available to it, but newly.

We cannot know, and Gam did not think of it. He raised himself up onto his hands and knees and breathed deeply the loamy, resin-scented air of the forest. He felt, down in the moonlight alone, better than he had.

He stood up.

He looked around.

On the bare top of this hill, the moon was full and high in the night, and what shadows the Door stones cast, though they were deep and black and moving strangely, were short, barely exceeding the limits of the portal's lintel.

With the eye Nathan had made, Gam could see every possible detail, even in the moonlight. When he trained his eye on the ground, there were the traces of Dashini and Prissy: scuff marks in the soil. There were the hoof prints of the Stag. There were the marks Gam's blood had made, like the remnants of a puddle, dried out from a hot afternoon.

The stones were lichen-crusted, pockmarked, entirely absent of any of the energy that would have given the girls access to the next Pyramid Level.

There were no Joes in the shadows.

Gam breathed in the silent, moonlit, shadowless air.

He stood on the White Stag's hill, freshly born or reborn, his body's memories, his previous life, there, but things of the past.

He was all alone, with no one to save, no one to care for, no one to serve.

There was nothing to be, except whatever he was, on the top of that hill.

There was no one who knew him.

There was nothing to do.

Who was he, then, under these circumstances?

The night passed slowly, it seemed to Gam.

While the city of his birth, Mordew, was always overcast, he had seen enough of the moon, albeit behind a cloud, to know that it moved across the sky, eventually going down over the horizon. If he had watched it, back then, in the absence of a nearby clock, he had been able to judge the time by its progress.

This moon seemed to be moving unusually slowly…

But why shouldn't it?

436

If the moon isn't required to measure how long it takes for a rough in Mr Padge's employ to kick the living shit out of someone while Gam waits outside in the street on lookout in case that someone's muscular and well-armed brother comes back early from a gin house, disturbing the living-shit-kicking, causing a scene, then the moon can progress as slowly as it likes.

All this moon had to do was illuminate the bare ground, and cast oddly dark and moving shadows across a bare hilltop.

Or perhaps the nights here were longer than in Mordew?

Prissy, Dashini and he had been so wrapped up in their need to progress out of this realm, so appalled by its gory rhythm and the seemingly 'Sisyphean quality' – one of Mr Padge's phrases for some job that was repetitive, and which never seemed to pay off – of the task at hand, that none of them, Gam least of all, had considered what the place was really like.

Now he was considering it.

Was that the kind of person Gam was now? A considerer of places? A considerer of night lengths?

It might be, because he realised, now, that he'd never really thought about the world in that way. He never thought of it having its own dimensions. There was always something to do, for someone, and some threat inherent in its not being done. He'd learned to think of the world, of time, as divided up into segments, the lengths and breadths of which were decided by whatever it was he had to do, or whatever it was he had to suffer, or however long someone else mustn't be kept waiting.

Clock time, job time, violence: all those things were the facts from the world as constructed in Mordew.

Here though?

None of those things meant anything.

There was no one to be kept waiting.

There were no jobs to do.

There was suffering, he remembered that, but apart from that, up here on the hill, the moon slowly passing above, the stars behind the moon, the breeze in the leaves: all of these things had a different set of dimensions.

Gam was amazed at the subtlety of his own understanding. This difference in the set of a place's dimensions was a fact of existence that, he felt, must have gone unnoticed by the people of his previous acquaintance. Even Dashini hadn't noticed it. She was, in her own way, just as narrowly focussed on her concerns as any slum child of Mordew.

He, though, alone now, having died, having been left behind by everyone, miles – if distance had anything to do with it? – from everything he was familiar with, trapped in this world he'd been so desperate to escape, freshly born: he was capable of seeing things as they were, of comparing that with the way the world had been.

Now he directed Nathan's eye wherever it could be directed and, guiltlessly, he let himself see everything down to the smallest detail: leaf skeletons, earthworms, the tracks a rabbit makes as it moves across a bare hilltop.

Hadn't Gam died? Wasn't Gam forsaken? Wasn't he lost? Wasn't he redeemed?

The detail in things, qualities he had overlooked because they were of no use to him, now felt good to see. They made him feel happy.

He was happy to feel happy.

He was happy to be made happy by small things.

So, he sat on the White Stag's hill and, in the slowly progressing moonlight, was alone and happy, far from home.

Can a Gam be happy, though?

Isn't it an intrinsic part of being 'Gam' that he is not happy?

Isn't he, in his essence, a slum boy, exploited?

Isn't he, in his essence, a part of Mordew?

If he is not unhappy, not an exploited slum boy, not part of Mordew – all things that, until his death in this place, were definitive of him – can he still be said to be Gam?

If he died Gam, and was reborn not Gam, isn't that evidence that he was not the same person?

◆

By the morning, the White Stag had still not returned.

Why should it? Gods may do what they will.

Perhaps it was in the forest attending to its business previously endlessly frustrated, but now easier to achieve.

Perhaps, in the shadows, the Roi de l'Ombre had further perverted the Stag's will with his malignancy, and now it preferred to remain there under the Shadow King's evil influence awaiting the opportunity to do bad things.

Gods do not answer to us any more than they answered to Gam Halliday, who, having spent the long, slow night alone on a bare hilltop far from home, now found himself hungry.

Some of the conditions of existence in this place were unusual, but others were exactly as Gam might have expected, including the rule that a stomach, deprived of food, will gradually, consistently and ever more urgently suggest to the mind that it ought to be fed.

He got up, took several steps forward, and then stopped.

The hilltop was bare, but it was surrounded by trees, and now the sun was in the sky it made shadows between the trees, within the forest, down the hill towards the village where Gam knew there was a pot of stew, the same pot he had eaten a hundred times or more.

Between Gam and the stew, there was a tight network of shadows.

Gam looked back to the Door, its lintel stones propped together making a shadow of their own, and that shadow, alone and as distinct as Gam himself was, seemed to reach across to the boy across the bare hilltop. This was one shadow, something he could step to the side of, but it ate into the sense of his happiness.

Inside the forest, each of the trees would cast its own shadow.

What was the shade a canopy of leaves and branches gave except a shadow of exceptional size?

Gam stepped into a space that was out of reach of the Door shadow, and only a little closer to the shadows of the forest than it had been.

439

In the forest, picked out by his evolved eye, there were patches of lighter and darker darkness, moving. It was the wind through the trees that moved these patches, making of the canopy more or less obstruction to the light, but it was also the will of Le Roi de l'Ombre, delighting in the fertile environment for his malignancy.

Gam could recognise him, he thought, in the fingers of black that twigs made on the ground when the sun was behind them.

They reached and pointed.

Had Gam been in Mordew, whether it was up in the Pleasaunce or down in the slums, he would have had defences against hunger. If he was hungry on the Promenade, he would have pilfered from an unguarded table in an unguarded shack an unguarded piece of dry bread. He'd silence his belly with theft.

If he'd been in the Entrepôt, he would have waited until a passing cart, overladen, hit a pothole. Then, when the driver came down to lash the bacon boxes safe with rope, he would have gone to whichever side the driver was not lashing and, with his jemmy, cracked a box and taken a packet of bacon off into a side alley. He'd have eaten the meat there, raw, tapeworms be damned.

If he had been in the Merchant City he would have tossed a serving girl a coin – brass, copper, silver if he was feeling generous – and she would have brought, because he was well known there, whatever she could find quickly in the kitchens, pocketing the change.

If he was in Mordew, he would have known how to feed himself, how to avoid the dangers these shadows presented.

But he was not in Mordew.

Happy, he might have felt himself to be, away from that city, away from his old self, but how long can happiness last?

Sometimes it is born, this feeling of happiness, from a change of circumstances that removes all of a person's previous troubles – it is relief, disguised. But if a person made troubles for themselves in one place, what makes him think that another place will be any different?

Was he happy in the other place, once, then attracted to himself troubles like sugar attracts ants? Like meat attracts maggots? Did he become unhappy that way?

To be in a place to which he is unsuited, having not been raised there, being made out of stuff foreign to that place: isn't that a recipe for unhappiness?

Even if that unhappiness is different in quality to the old and tiresome unhappiness?

What if the new unhappiness is more fundamental?

Gam stepped first away from the forest shadows, and then away from the Door shadow, and in his belly the hunger grew.

Deep, deep in the dark and shadowed forest, there came, first low and rumbling, and then higher and clearer, the howl of a wolf.

Then another, answering, from behind Gam.

Then another.

And another, until there were wolf howls in every direction.

III

GLEED AND SHARLI STOOD on the flat surface of the bomb-barge, at the front, the weight of Gleed's exo-skeleton making the corner dip deep into the water as they slid towards the detonation site. Tinnimam hopped from one side of the barge to the other, Sharli trying, in vain, to get between the firebird and the view of the city, at which she peered eagerly or anxiously: it was difficult to tell which. Tinnimam chittered and squeaked, and when Sharli tried to gather her up and hold her to her chest the increasingly annoying creature hopped back and flew up. If it hadn't been for the tether tying her to the bomb casing, she'd have been off.

There in the distance was Mordew.

'Why don't you let it go?' Gleed said.

Sharli ducked as Tinnimam fluttered up, straining at the leash, dropping loose feathers to the deck. 'She'll never come back.'

Gleed made a sound with her machinery – a kind of abrupt and forceful double click – that translated as 'exactly'. She used it a lot, and Sharli had come to find it annoying.

'It wants to suicide on the Sea Wall,' Gleed said. 'It wants to flood the city of the Master of Mordew, breach the God chamber, and contaminate the weftling corpse.'

Sharli was already aware of that. She was more aware of it than Gleed was. Gleed said a lot of things like this – things that Sharli knew as well as anyone can know anything – and she said them as if Sharli should thank her for her insight. She'd learned that the best way to ignore the desire to use the weft-knife on the Field Commander every time she said something blindingly obvious as if it was news was to pretend that she hadn't said it.

Sharli pretended Gleed had said nothing, got herself between Tinnimam and Mordew and watched what was left of the city receding into the distance behind them. Mordew had been home to Sharli for years, but she had never seen it like this: stretched hideously up into the sky.

The Sea Wall was gone.

There was a new Glass Road.

Mr Padge was dead.

'Where is he, I wonder?' Gleed said.

At first Sharli thought Gleed meant Mr Padge, but she followed the direction the Field Commander was looking: up to the top of the mount, where the Manse and its Master would be.

'I don't care,' Sharli said. 'He's never meant anything to me.'

Gleed turned her attention to Sharli. 'Who do you care about?'

Sharli said nothing, looked away, pulled at her lip.

Gleed's artificial eye would be able to visualise that tic in minute detail. Sharli could feel her watching it, anticipated another comment about the girlishness with which she was doing it. 'It's called the Women's Vanguard for a reason,' Gleed had said. The Vanguard was staffed with women, not girls, and Gleed named twenty God Killers more mature, psychologically, than she supposed Sharli was, if she was the sort of woman who pulled girlishly at her lip every time she got stressed.

Was Sharli up to the job?

Gleed wasn't sure.

Sharli always insisted she was. She wasn't lying. But then, Sharli and Gleed were thinking of two different jobs.

'Stop pulling at your lip,' Gleed said.

Sharli put her hands down by her side, let the right one rest on the handle of the weft-knife.

The weft-bomb sat heavily in its housing in the middle of the barge, weighing them down in the water.

Tinnimam squawked and flapped.

Sharli looked across the sea to Mordew, her former home.

The home of the Master.

The former home of Mr Padge.

The former home of Gam Halliday.

She pulled her lip, and turned her back on the place.

'What a shithole,' said Field Commander Gleed.

IV

GAM HADN'T SEEN the carnage the wolves made of the Druids, except in its aftermath. Just as a person cannot understand the horror of an abattoir by looking in at a butcher's window, Gam didn't understand what the wolves would do to him.

Here they came.

The nearest one had a grey stripe down the centre of his muzzle, and he pounced forward to a place where he was within biting distance of Gam's foot. He snapped at the boy.

A normal wolf might or might not have connected with his bite, but this wolf was a god, and whatever it meant to do it did: one of its front teeth – Gam could not tell which and didn't care in any case – ripped the flesh at Gam's ankle down to the bone, and caught at the ligaments behind it. Any movement Gam went on to attempt with this leg would now be doomed to failure; the operation of the skeleton of a prey creature, such as Gam, relied on the connection between bones of muscles and ligament, cartilage and veins, some of which, in this simple nip, were severed.

Gam reached down for his ankle, the site of pain, and in doing so stretched so that the back of his other knee was exposed. A second wolf – black and brown and sleek – raked through the skin there with the claws of his front left paw, making a gouge that brought Gam down onto the ground, neither leg now able to keep him upright.

Wolves will do this – incapacitate their prey – because they are evolved to bring down running animals, herd animals, whose survival relies on them making, by dint of some extreme, chest-bursting effort, their way back into the safety in numbers their herd gives. This running prey relies on their long and nimble legs, their ability to dart and leap, to turn back on themselves.

None of these things would have been possible for a creature of Gam's type, even if the wolves had not prevented it, but a god does things in the best possible way. Killing, for a wolf pack, is best done to an animal suited to it, so they treated Gam like they would a wild pony, or a deer that they had come upon on the plains, separated from its herd.

Gam was on his hands and knees, teeth gritted, and because it is good, for a wolf, to slit the belly of a four-legged beast so that its intestines fall from their cavity, causing shock and a loss of blood, and because it is good to sink the teeth into the haunches of a running thing so that it cannot run, one wolf – not either of the first two – and another slit Gam's belly and bit into one haunch.

A fifth wolf leapt onto Gam's back and bore him down to the ground, so that the others could come close without the fear of being kicked, though Gam could never have hurt them that way.

At last, a silver wolf, red-eyed, came forward from the shadows and took Gam's entire skull in his mouth, working the bone down so that it was between the teeth at the back, tearing strips off the boy's face as it went. When the wolf had purchase, it crunched down so that Gam's skull was first pierced by the sharpness of its divine teeth, and then split down the sagittal and metopic sutures, the splintered bone erupting through Gam's scalp, exposing his brain to the cool forest air.

No boy can live through that, whether he is of Mordew or any other city. He cannot live through it whether he is happy, or unhappy, whether he feels guilt over the murder of his friend, Joes, or not.

Whether a boy murdered his friend under threat, or did it not under threat, he will die when a wolf god bites through his skull.

So, Gam died again, sparing him the pain of being pulled from all sides by a god in the form of a pack of wolves.

His death saved him from being dragged across the dirt, from being pawed and bitten and, eventually, quartered like a treasonous rebel of the olden times. It spared him being rendered down by a process of animal butchery into cuts of himself to eventually be left, in pieces unregarded, as the pack went on in its rampage, spurred by the Shadow King, running through the forest to wherever there were Druids and creatures large enough to take their violence.

It happened, but Gam was spared the pain of it.

When they were gone, Gam's body came together again, slowly, under the grace of the White Stag. His components inched together and reformed, as they had done before, until his body was complete. The Spark the White Stag channelled from the weft brought him back to himself, the memories there again, the sense of freshness there again, the happiness there again, so that he got to his feet and ran for the bald hill so that he could live in that moonlit space until the morning.

While Gam felt like himself as he ran, how could anyone who had watched him be torn to pieces consider him the same Gam who had grown up in the slums of Mordew? The same Gam who had lived, and who had been sacrificed for his friends to expiate his guilt at murdering Joes? Who had been torn into pieces by a god in the form of a pack of wolves?

How could he be the same?

People who have been killed that way are dead. They are gone. They do not rise up from the ground and run.

If an exception is to be made because these events were unusual, they did not become unusual, because the same thing happened every night, every day, for so many cycles that Gam couldn't have counted them even if he'd wanted to.

That realm was set into that pattern.

It operated in its own time, having a beginning for Gam in the moment he arrived, but having no conceivable end, since gods are immortal things, and part of immortality is that it takes place across periods of time that are inconceivably long for mortal beings, as Gam was born.

Gods' realms are unchanging, since change is something that is important for short-lived things, and irrelevant to things that live forever.

The whole run of existence is, to the mind of a god, a single, infinitely complicated form of one thing, not an infinite series of finite things, since that level of discreteness implies an ending to 'things', which does not occur to gods, since they cannot know 'ending'.

V

THE CASING REMAINED in place, and the barge didn't even bob in the water when the weft-bomb went off. There was a light that flicked on – a white LED that indicated that the mechanism would need priming before it could be used again – but apart from that, in the dimensions of the material realm that Sharli and Gleed were equipped to experience, nothing happened.

But inwards, down at the furthest conceivable extension towards the weft, the membranes which encapsulated the unreals – the 'intermediate realms' – vibrated until they all occupied the same extent, which is to say that they ceased existing separately.

Bombs usually make a bang. Actually, people might need them to make a bang, to believe they've done their work.

But there was no bang.

Sharli pulled at her lip, looked out over the water.

Gleed reached over to her, but because Sharli was an assassin, what passed for the Field Commander's hand never reached her shoulder, because Sharli turned.

'Bang?' she said.

'Bang,' Gleed replied.

VI

GAM FELL TO THE GROUND in the material realm.
He couldn't understand what he was seeing, regardless of which eye he looked out from.

Down from the sky, orphaned from the pyramid realms, fell a rain of screaming infants, blocks of masonry, parts of crumbling pyramids, cattle-headed people and person-headed snakes.

He got to his feet and dodged the rain as best as he could, but he was struck, over and over, by bodies and buildings. He tripped on them as they gathered at his feet, was grabbed at by urgent hands.

He was implored to by the wounded.

And now here was the White Stag, and with it the Wolf Pack.

The wolves scattered, their senses overwhelmed by the sheer abundance of prey, but before they could move far, the Stag was startled, and they were returned to their starting positions.

Where Gam had been only seconds before, there fell a new Gam, identical to the Gam who, with one eye watching for falling bodies, saw the confusion on this new Gam's face, watched him look up at the rain of infants, screaming, the blocks of masonry, the parts of pyramids, crumbling, the cattle-headed people and person-headed snakes, weeping.

This new Gam got to his feet as the old one had, dodged the rain as best as he could, but he was struck, over and over, by bodies and buildings, falling from the sky. He tripped on them as they gathered at his feet, was grabbed at by urgent hands.

He was implored to by the wounded.

The old Gam, as he watched, was struck himself – a clump of bricks that had once been part of a cathedral hit him on the shoulder, shattered his collarbone – but the new Gam came towards him, and the old Gam stepped back.

The White Stag was startled again, and where the new Gam had been only seconds before, there fell a third Gam, identical to the second Gam who, with one eye watching for falling bodies, saw the confusion on this new Gam's face, watched him look up at the rain of infants, screaming, the blocks of masonry, the parts of pyramids crumbling, the cattle-headed people and person-headed snakes, weeping.

This new Gam got to his feet as the second one had, dodged the rain of heavens as best as he could, but he was struck, over and over, by bodies and buildings, falling from the sky. He tripped on them as they gathered at his feet, was grabbed at by urgent hands.

He was implored to by the wounded.

The second Gam, as he watched, was struck himself – a clump of bricks that had once been part of a cathedral hit him on the shoulder, shattering his collarbone – but the third Gam came towards the second Gam, and the second Gam stepped back. The first Gam turned and ran, dodging through the rain which was coming even harder down, a torrent of bodies, screaming, of architecture, collapsed, tripping on the urgent and imploring wounded, stopping only when he found some little shelter – an archway that had landed, somehow, more or less and incongruously complete, its keystone holding under the force of its landing.

The White Stag was startled again, and where the third Gam had been only seconds before, there fell a fourth Gam, identical to the third Gam who, with one eye watching for falling bodies, saw the confusion on this new Gam's face, watched him look up at the rain of infants, screaming, the blocks of masonry, the parts of pyramids, crumbling, the cattle-headed people and person-headed snakes, weeping.

This fourth Gam got to his feet as the third one had, dodged the rain as best as he could, but he was struck, over and over, by bodies and buildings, falling from the sky. He tripped on them as they gathered at his feet, was grabbed at by urgent hands.

He was implored to by the wounded.

The third Gam, as he watched, was struck himself – a clump of bricks that had once been part of a cathedral hit him on the shoulder, shattering his collarbone – but the fourth Gam came towards the third Gam, and the third Gam stepped back. The second Gam turned and ran, dodging through the rain which was coming even harder down, a torrent of bodies, screaming, of architecture, collapsed, tripping on the urgent and imploring wounded, stopping only when he found some little shelter – an archway that had landed, somehow, more or less and incongruously complete, its keystone holding under the force of its landing, on top of which a second archway had fallen, but in such a way that it, too, held, like the arches upon arches perfected by the Roman architects of the ancient world, and here he met the first Gam.

They stood, face to face for a moment, the rain of heavens falling all around them, and it was as if, suddenly, in the presence of each other, these two Gams Halliday remembered who they were, remembered what it was to be a Gam Halliday, what it was to use their resourcefulness to ensure their existences.

The first Gam reached out to the second Gam, and the two held hands, so that when the third Gam arrived, and then the fourth, the arches under which they stood beginning to crumble under the weight of successive arches falling from the sky as the White Stag was startled again and again, they presented to the incoming Gams a brotherhood of Gams.

With a glance, this brotherhood of Gams knew each other for who they were, understood each other perfectly. They all looked back the way they had come, and there were the fifth, sixth and seventh Gams.

They could have stayed there, the Gams Halliday that had found the safety of the arches, waiting for the new members of their brotherhood, but now the first archway cracked and the arches that had fallen on top of it began to fall onto the mass of bodies that now constituted the ground of this place.

The Gams knew themselves well enough to know that if they saw themselves, in a group, they would attempt to follow themselves, if for no other reason than to understand what the hell was going on.

In any case, there was no use waiting to be crushed by falling archways, so they began to run.

But then, to render any more thinking irrelevant, there in the distance, across a plain of wounded, rained on ever more heavily by screaming infants and crumbling masonry, the Gams saw Joes – thousands of them – gathered together, arms reaching up into the sky, catching more of themselves as they fell from the sky.

The brotherhood of Gams, oblivious to anything else, marched towards the Joes.

The detonation of the weft-bomb was unprecedented, there is no doubt of that, and it destroyed the boundaries between the intermediate realms and the material realm, but that is not to say that it overwrote the way in which Sparkline inheritances operated. This fact was illustrated by the proximity the collapse of the realms created between the instancing in the material realm of those individuals who, by Sparkline inheritance's joining of the concepts of one person to another – which some might call 'ownership' – were related through death.

In short, Gam Halliday had, by killing Joes on the Glass Road, permanently and ineradicably linked their conceptual existence in the immaterial realm. Though Gam had no understanding of what it meant, he did, in principle, 'own' Joes's Sparkline, backwards and forwards in time, and though he would have done nothing to make use of this fact, when the intermediate realms collapsed, the mathematics of that collapse had the effect of summoning the multitude of Joes's descendants to the same place in the material realm that Gam Halliday was also instanced into.

This is a fundamental truth of Weft Dynamics, and is taught in the first Hailey-Beth cycle in that discipline.

Their physical proximity was effected by a kind of gravitation between their two conceptual iterations in the material realm, imperfect but close enough, and there on the strange, unpleasantly variable and chaotically textured ground, rained down on by the collapse of the heavens, by the reverse rapture, was a landscape of Joes.

Some of them had broken as they fell to the ground, and were lying, unable to comprehend what had brought them out of their happiness to this horrific place.

Others were half in the earth and half in the air, their bodies and minds only partially capable of being where they had appeared.

Others, unseen, were instanced buried, knowing, if anything, only a moment or two before they died.

With no Mistress to vouchsafe heavens for them, the dead returned to the weft, their concepts truncated in the immaterial realm, but there were a proportion of the Joes and the descendants of the Joes that lived. A small proportion of a very large number can still be a large number, and the Brotherhood of the Gams Halliday were as bemused at this appearance of what appeared to be thousands of their murdered friend as these people were at having appeared.

Now, as the Stag was startled again and again, both groups multiplied and multiplied, each multiplication marginally less perfect in its duplication than the one before it, so that the new Gams, iterating beneath the falling cathedral ruins, the falling parts of pyramids, the infants and the adults, were progressively less and less correct. They were less and less Gam-like, inferior brothers in the Brotherhood; had the Brotherhood of Gams had their own city, the original Gam would have been Master of it, if he could have held that power against himself.

The first duplicates would have been his generals, and the next his lieutenants, and then the corporals, until, as the Stag repeated, repeated, repeated, and the duplication became less and less coherent, the later Gams would have been the privates, or the slaves of the privates, or object lessons for the privates, until they were people that could not properly even be called Gams, or people, or living, or things.

The same multiplication occurred for the Multitudes of Joes, the first being their own selves, but then, in the same way a city of Gams would have made a hierarchy of itself, so would a culture of Joes and their descendants be ever more heavily reliant on the first Joes' perfection. Each new generation would be less and less able to know and feel and act as a Joes would act, or as a Quin, or as any of those generations from which the Joes' heaven had been consisted, until the humanity of the Joes the startling of the White Stag corruptly duplicated failed.

After generations, the Joes and Gams became organic matter in the rough shape of Joes and Gams, then in the shape of generic persons, then after a hundred, a thousand reiterations, tubes and agglomerations of flesh, then huge and protoplasmic failed cells barely carrying sufficient Spark to deserve the word 'life'.

The cathedral masonry fell in the same manner, eventually scarcely masonry at all, scarcely having received a mason's chisel, just pieces of inorganic matter, sand, grit that came apart as it poured from the sky. This grit combined with the organic matter of the Joes and Gams as it fell, the rain of heavens raining in an ever greyer, ever less distinct, ever more putrid and irredeemable cascade from the sky.

If we take one Gam – the first – and two perfect Joes, hand in hand, and separate them out in our minds, and if we ignore all the others, we can think what this was like. We can think of what it meant.

But to do this we must make that choice.

Whether or not this is a justifiable choice under any of the ideas by which we and the occupants of the material realm have understood the world, it would be difficult to argue that the choice was reasonable.

And that is to say nothing of the soul propagandas.

We can pick one Gam in this horrific, ever-multiplying, ever-duplicating, ever more corrupted field of heavenly relics, the Billion Billion Flames, the person-headed snakes, the cattle-headed men incapable of maintaining their integrity. We can see through this chosen Gam's eyes. He ran to our chosen pair of Joes and took them, blinking, by the hands, and ran over and through and across and below this fallout from the weft-bomb.

We can know that he thought that the increasingly formless mass coming down on him as he stumbled across corpses

453

and leapt away from ruins and fell knee deep, elbow deep, into writhing half-living, half-dying, half-recognisable, half-unrecognisable people and things, was like the Living Mud, no longer bubbling up from the ground, but falling down from the sky, not tending towards strange life, but tending towards strange death.

It was like a mirror, this place, he thought, of the place into which he had been born, and in this mirror of his origin he would find his fate, which was to drown under corpses, to be drowned by dying flesh, to rot into the Dying Mud with all of his other selves, regardless of whether and how much they resembled him.

We, to understand all this, must pick out an individual instance of Gam, but the Dying Mud, in truth, made all of that impossible, since it fell in such a torrent now that any Gam we selected, running and falling to his knees, narrowly avoiding being crushed, was crushed moments later – any specific one of him – almost immediately dying in the White Stag's endless, anxious reiteration of the failing material realm.

There must have been some Gams that lived – there were so many of him – but any pretence that we could, in the chaos, pick them out in advance, and then follow one's unlikely path through the world is only a pretence.

In reality, we would need to pick him out from the mess, from the filth, from the aftermath, and ignore how it was he survived the unsurvivable, since that would have been by implausible means, by blind and unconvincing luck.

We must maintain this pretence, perhaps by thinking of 'fate', so that we can understand what happened, so that we can sympathise, so that we maintain our emotional connection with 'Gam', but realise that this is a failure of our sympathies, an impossible and inaccurate compromise that our own fixation with individuality forces us to make.

There is no fate.

There is only what happens, and how those who survive need to understand it.

◆

From above, firebirds surveyed the wreckage the world had become and, like us, they isolated whole and surviving Gams and Joes from the fray. These they took in their talons, careful not to slice their flesh, and lifted them away from danger.

They did this at the command of their Mistress. Though she had said to them, 'Find Gam Halliday and Joes and bring them back here,' firebirds are clever creatures when they are allowed to mature. They can adapt to the situations they find themselves in. They found more than one Gam Halliday, more than one Joes, so they took the living ones to the New Pyramid, and thereby saved them from the Collapse Zone.

Whether this was a temporary or permanent reprieve, we will only find out later.

O UT FROM THE SURFACE of the water above Waterblack
lunged Sirius Goddog on a gout of steam, Nathan
Treeves by his side, and the two shot up into the air
like falling stars in reverse, repelled up along the path by which
they had fallen, arcing into the clouds that hung, heavy and
black, over the place where the city had drowned.

Black cloud, white Spark, black and white angels, and
around where they emerged the steam rolled like a thick fog
across the surface of the water. It was buffeted and driven by
the coming of more and more angels, in an ever wider cir-
cumference, buffeted and driven by the translation of more
and more cold, blue-black, green-black brine boiling into pure
white steam, so that it would have seemed to anyone there to
see it that the whole sea had become a torture of the waves'
surfaces, that the sea itself had become a gaseous, voluminous,
screamingly hot malformation of its proper self, out of which
was ejected a writhing column of angels.

When a volcano bursts from the ground, it sends a pillar
of molten rock, a plume of poison gas, a billow of smoke, and
this was now how the sea was, even as Nathan and Goddog
rose above the black clouds, scattering them into nothingness
as they passed. It was a volcano in water and steam and living
angels, and all around sang the high-pitched squeal of a kettle
boiling itself dry, accompanied by the throat-catching stench of
burning salt, of water made into acids by the catalysing of them
with heat, different material combinations, things that would
have choked anything living, killed it dead, except only these
divine creations of the Master of Waterblack, who required
nothing but his will for them to live, and who followed him up
into the sky, escaping the hell they made of the water below.

The light they gave off was blinding, all of them together,
the millions of these Spark-infused dead, living now above
the surface, as if the sea was struck by a lightning bolt that

never disappeared, that grew instead, brighter, thicker, lighter, striking forever.

Nathan was the cause of the discharge, so bright that it seemed to threaten the very lightness of the world, making the sun seem dark in comparison, a disc of night in this new kind of day.

Even a brightness of this sort must dissipate, eventually. If it does not, then the world must end, since it cannot accommodate it, light being the opposite of matter. Nathan did not end the world now, though surely it seemed that he might be able to do it.

Once all of the Angelic Army were up from Waterblack, each individual angel found space for themselves in the air, placed themselves where they were able to exist, far enough from each other that each had their own proper place, but not so far apart that they felt that they had deserted their army.

So it was that the lightning strike became a diffuse but still powerful sheet of Spark across the sky, a homogeneity of brightness, still bright, though less so, across the world, like when a fork of lightning illuminates a cloud from within. Except there was no cloud, and down below them the surface of the water re-established itself, the cloud of steam rolled away to reveal the waves.

In these waves the Angelic Army of Waterblack was reflected, darkened a little.

There was Nathan at its head, above them all.

As a boy, Nathan had been always made to do things against his will, but now, as Master of Waterblack, his will was everything.

There, across the water, in that space in the world that the intermediate realms collapsed into, where the pyramid of Malarkoi had been and for leagues around it, was a terrible chaos, and within this were other gods, other suns, a great dark dragon, things that seemed, to Nathan's angelic mind, like offences to his godhood, all of which must be destroyed.

Because Nathan thought it, so did his army.

VIII

IN ADVANCE OF THE DETONATION of the weft-bomb, Dashini was already at a pre-arranged place in the material realm, outside the Collapse Zone, waiting safely.

On the grass in front of her was the Nathan Knife, and next to that were the objects she'd been working on ready for the arrival of the Eighth Atheistic Crusade. While she'd been quarantined by the Master, and during her progress through the Pyramid Realms, her access to the kinds of equipment she'd have needed to make the things she wanted to make was limited, but that didn't mean she hadn't been thinking about them. It doesn't matter whether you're locked up, or being chased around by assassins, or whether you've got time or resources, if you've got a mind you can always think.

You can always plan.

Dashini had been planning.

She leaned back and stretched. The place where she'd decided to sit it out was like the kind of place where you might have a picnic – on highish ground, to avoid midges, with a little bit of tree shade, and with good views all around – and her objects could just as easily have been the contents of a hamper.

The contents of a picnic hamper aren't usually magical, though.

Dashini wasn't like her mother, whose thinking went towards grand schemes, long games and strategies – escalating the Tontine, provoking the Assembly, summoning the warpling – all of which were about to come to fruition.* She wasn't like the Master of Mordew, parasitising on the power of others, whether they were God or slum children. She wasn't even like Nathan, filled with repressed rage and sadness. Dashini's magic

---

* While Dashini wasn't especially interested in the outcome of her mother's plans, the reader might be: along with many other important things, they are dealt with in the appendices to this book.

was more practical, when she had the time to work it, and the results of that practicality were arranged neatly in front of her knees, on a hillside, in the material realm.

Dashini cleared her throat, blinked a few times – the grass was giving her allergies, but not so badly that she felt the need to find some magical solution – and checked everything over again.

Aside from the Nathan Knife, edged with its black fire – she didn't feel she could take credit for it since her mother made it – she was proud of these things. There were six of them. She could have brought more, and she could have brought different things, but these were the ones she could imagine carrying and using.

First there was the Portable One-way Quarantine – the POQ, for short.

It looked a lot like a big marble: a ball of glass about the size of a hen's egg, but completely spherical, with a rainbow swirl in its centre. Dashini had had a great deal of experience of the Master's quarantines over the last decade, and while she couldn't say she'd developed any fondness for them, she could definitely see their usefulness. Her version had taken the basic idea – that of quarantining something – and added a great deal of conceptualisation around the modification and variability of its extent, along with the idea of permeability in one direction.

She'd developed, by trial and error and a great deal of communication via homunculoid proxy with the immaterial realm, a quarantine glass that had some of the plastic qualities of a soap bubble, while still maintaining the necessary strength a quarantine demanded, but only from out to in, and not the other way round.

In use, the POQ allowed Dashini to shield herself from most physical damage – it wasn't perfect, but probably good enough, she thought, for the use case her mother had suggested – while also not trapping her inside. She could, using a specific tone of voice, vary the glass's ability to prevent things from getting out of the POQ, including her.

Dashini picked up the marble, gave it a polish with her sleeve, sniffed a few times, and put it back on the grass where it had been.

In the far distance, she couldn't see anything to worry about. There was the Golden Pyramid, like a tiny shining glitch in her vision, too bright to concentrate on. In the opposite direction was the sea. Out of sight: Waterblack and Mordew.

Dashini reached for the second object, which was a pair of lorgnette glasses, the sort that have a handle on one side. She didn't have a name for this because their use was, as far as Dashini was concerned, completely obvious.

She held the lorgnette up, and, because she was thinking of the encampment of the Woman's Vanguard when she did it, she could see that place through the lenses.

The Crusaders were busying themselves with their Crusade business, as Dashini knew they would be – earnestly and thoughtfully going here and there, consulting documents, asking each other questions, making adjustments to their engines: all of the kinds of things Crusaders did in preparation for a detonation. In their camp, attached to something at Dashini's height, her eyes would have been visible, the lorgnette working by instancing a version of those organs onto an object capable of holding them steady, which no doubt would have been disconcerting to anyone paying attention, so she had to keep it quick.

Dashini flicked her wrist, turned the lorgnette by its handle so that she was looking through the other side of the glasses, and now she saw the same scene, except that everything in the scene was annotated. Dashini had, very cleverly she thought, indentured a demon with various promises to draw up from the immaterial realm useful conceptual material that explained, on the fly, who and what everything was, and whether they were likely to be dangerous, helpful, or in some way significant to her. She hadn't, yet, worked out how to get reliable information about the future from the immaterial realm, but she was getting close. The lorgnette homunculoid proxy said that it could read the future, but that it wasn't willing to divulge it except in that spiteful way indentured entities tended to divulge things, which was not very accurately and always with a view to making the owner of their indenture suffer in some way.

If she could only find a way to convince the demon not to do that...

She flicked the lorgnette over and thought of the Master of Mordew. Her mother had said he'd be too busy to cause any problems, but she thought she'd better check. That's what years of captivity do: they can make you a little paranoid. Here he was, trudging up a hill, cursing, wearing entirely inappropriate footwear for the conditions. She pulled the focus out, but couldn't recognise where he was. The homunculus gave a distance, but it was unhelpfully in feet and inches. Nowhere nearby, anyway.[*]

She flicked the lorgnette over again, and thought of Prissy, but the glasses went black.

The corners of Dashini's eyes were itchy. Was there something about material realm grass that made her react like this? It didn't happen anywhere else.

She cleaned the lorgnette with her sleeve and put it back down.

Dashini had learned, through her childhood, that there was no point in feeling anxious about things. Anxiety existed, she knew that, but why should she feel that gnawing in the pit of her stomach, that tingling across the back of her shoulders, that odd ache in her throat?

Why should she feel it when she could avoid feeling it?

She was avoiding feeling anxiety now, in the that way she had learned, by concentrating her mind on other things. Her mother's plan was in progress, this was the endgame, Dashini had her part to play, it might go right, it might go wrong, but there was no point in adding unpleasant psychosomatic symptoms into it.

She bracketed them.

---

[*] His location, should curious readers wish to discover it, is revealed among the other important things in the appendices.

461

The sun was high in the sky and Dashini stretched her legs.

There was the Golden Pyramid glinting in the distance, the focal point of the Pyramid Realms, a pinprick of light behind which infinite, chaotic, uncontrollable worlds were contained, all about to overwhelm the material realm and open up the space for her mother to win everything and end the war.

Then what?

Too soon to ask that question, Dashini, her mother had said. We'll have plenty of time to work on that. We'll have forever.

Dashini rubbed her eyes and opened and closed her mouth so that she could relieve the itching that was building in her inner ears.

She looked back at her things, down on the grass.

Attack: the Nathan Knife.

Defence: the POQ.

Information: the lorgnette.

Beneath the lorgnette – Dashini was going clockwise around her objects – there was a whistle. It was one her mother had given her, back before the days when she'd been quarantined, and it was yellow, made from some fragile material with a thin seam down the centre, chipped so that it was a bit sharp when you put it to your lips. Dashini did that now: she put her tongue into the slot at the front and pushed it in as far as it would go.

The hay fever was making her tongue itchy too, and there was one of those sore spots on it where a taste bud, or whatever those little lumps are, had swollen up and got an ulcer or something.

She moved the tip of her tongue around in the whistle hole to scratch it.

That wasn't what the whistle was for. When she blew it, it allowed her to broadcast a limited range of ideas at a psychic pitch that only dragons could receive. The ideas she'd tuned this one to combined into a draconic representation of the sentence, 'It's me, Dashini; I'm over here', and when she blew the whistle that message would go everywhere, essentially infinitely, bound up with the idea of her location. The material of the whistle carried the concepts she wanted to get across, and also 'go everywhere', 'for dragons', and the specific notion of where precisely she was in relation to whoever heard the message.

It was a simple material/immaterial interlink, but that didn't mean it wouldn't work.

She took the whistle out of her mouth, put the itchy tip of her tongue between her front teeth, and tentatively brought her teeth together on the sore spot. She didn't intend to bite the end of her tongue off; she just wanted to feel, with her teeth and jaw, whether there was an ulcer, or a lump where the sore spot was.

There kind of was, but perhaps not, so she brought her tongue back in out of the way of her teeth.

Why did she have a whistle for dragons?

One reason: Japalura. She knew the dragon was dead in the realm she had left, but so what?

Her mother's plan meant that she'd be alive again, her dragon mother, and everything would be okay. The weft-bomb collapsed the realms at their high-energy state, when there was the maximum possible Spark, and since Japalura was the god of that realm, and therefore the most energetic thing possible, it would be as if she had never died.

Once she was in the material realm, there was no way Japalura was going to miss Dashini. Not with the Yellow Whistle.

Now the back of Dashini's neck started itching, under the line where her feathers started. Can you get hay fever on the neck? Dashini thought that she must be able to, and she scratched at it for a bit.

She pulled a single feather out of her scalp, and she used the pointy end to scratch between the other feathers, but then her neck got sore, so she made herself stop.

The places where some demons like Rekka live are wide open plains, luridly coloured, stretching off in every direction to the horizon. Their prey, a different sort of demon – wormlike and enormous – live beneath the surface of these plains in vast channels they carve through rock. The first sign of this prey, to the demons, is the disturbances they make on the crust when they come near to the surface to breathe.

These signs consist of the rippling of the earth at a great distance, perhaps a billow of rock dust, soon settled.

Since distant ripples and billows are very subtle things, and because the demon relies on them for its survival, and because its environment is so luridly coloured, its eyes are enormously sensitive to small variations of colour and texture, providing they are a long way away. It is always peering intently off, lidlessly, day and night, and if it is ever made to look at things too near this causes discomfort in the demon's forebrain. Its sensorium is more attuned to long sight, so it avoids close up work when it can.

If it can't use its eyes – because they are blocked by something interposing itself between the demon and its target – then it uses a much less accurate way of sensing its prey: a kind of weft-based echo-location. This sends out an inward charge, and the demon waits to see if this charge returns altered.

This form of sensing, in a very minor way, alerts the things it preys on that they are being sought out by making them feel discomfort. So, if the predator demon can avoid using it, it does, so as not to put its prey on alert.

The discomfort a demon avoids creating is a kind of ache in the mind, a kind of itching on the skin.

Who knows how it would affect a person?

Next to the Yellow Whistle as Dashini went clockwise around her things was a pouch. It was the sort you might keep dice in, or coins, or gold dust: leather with a drawstring at the top.

She picked it up, hefted it between her hands.

It was full of her Prophylactic Prism Powder – Triple P – which was about as heavy as gold dust was, but much more useful in the field.

Her original Prism Powder – the one she'd made while she was under the Master's quarantine and which she'd designed to turn herself invisible – was great if you wanted to sneak about, but not much use in the kind of situation her mother had cooked up. When the world is collapsing under the weight of its own inability to remain real, whether someone can see you or not is neither here nor there. And who was to say the optical conditions under which the powder could operate wouldn't change? Her mother had said that things would go so crazy that even the laws of physics – of which optics are a branch – would start to fail. That failure was, in fact, the point, because without the weftling to enforce the material realm's consistency, the warpling would have to intervene.

Triple P did something else. It was the same idea – a swarm of microscopic prisms keyed to her energy that adhered to her surface, but rather than scattering light, they scattered the beam the Tinderbox created.

If there had been anyone to boast to – aside from homunculi – Dashini would have been inclined to boast about the way she'd been able to isolate the particular material qualities of a powder capable of deflecting an energy that scoured material and immaterial objects and concepts directly back into the weft, but there wasn't anyone now Prissy was gone.

Her mother had given her a 'Very nice, dear' when she'd told her.

It was very nice.

Very nice indeed.

No amount of Dashini opening and closing her jaw made the itching in her inner ear go away, and now, on the backs of her hands, she was getting hives.

A demon summoned to an intermediate realm locked to the material realm, and then translated to the centre of the material realm Earth, will find itself surrounded on all sides by the hot and solid plasma that exists at the core of the planet. It will be disgusted at being *under*, where its prey usually is. Its eyes will focus themselves on the very near and give no information except the pain of looking too close.

If it isn't already furious at being taken from its immaterial realm, interrupting its hunt, and made more furious still by its inability to punish its summoner, it will become furious at this new development.

If it is already furious at these two things, it will become triply furious to be instantiated down as far as it is possible to be instantiated. It will consider itself buried and demeaned in the most disgustingly material of all realms.

Red is not a colour it will recognise, nor burning white, nor any of the familiar colours – its eyes are attuned to higher frequencies of light, since these are the most useful ones for its purposes. Nor does it recognise heat in the range that is possible in the material realm: its carapace is so thick and heatproof that it has no nerves sensitive to the presence or otherwise of it.

But pressure?

Pressure it can feel, since that is the way that depth is known where this demon is from: it uses it to determine whether its prey is likely to be close to or far away from the surface.

Pressure was all around this demon, crushing, disgusting deepness, and though it couldn't see, and its fore and hind brains screeched with the necessity to focus so closely, it knew it had to go to where the pressure was less – up, we would think of it.

Dashini's fifth item was inspired by the horrible journey she'd been forced to take through the corrupted Pyramid Realms, and if she'd only had it then she'd have saved them all a lot of trouble.

It was, physically speaking, a piece of white chalk, but she'd made it by crushing together a lot of smaller pieces of chalk – into chalk powder, really – each speck of which was impregnated with the words and sigils of the Door spells, the whole piece now infused with enough Spark sacrifices for six or seven charges, depending on where the Door you wanted to draw opened, and how many people you needed to take through it.

Dashini looked at the soles of her shoes. They were green with the liquid that grass contains. Rub a piece of grass between your fingertips and this green liquid will be left on your skin.

Slide by accident across a patch of grass while wearing white clothes, and you'll see that it leaves a green stain.

The soles of Dashini's shoes were stained green with the liquid that is inside grass.

Does anyone ever really know what they're going to need in advance?

Don't we suffer some kind of problem, and then, for the rest of our lives, go to the trouble of making sure it can never happen again? Even when we can't think of the problem much because thinking about it is too painful. Dashini, because of the rift her sacrifice of Gam had caused between her and Prissy, spent a lot of energy making sure that nothing like that could ever happen again, even if there wasn't, in fact, that high a chance she'd ever need it.

Human psychology: it's like that.

Dashini picked up the chalk. Whether it was the hay fever, or whether it was chalk dust, she sneezed. Then, because the sneeze tickled the back of her nose, she sneezed again. Then, because things tend to come in threes, she sneezed for a third time.

She put the chalk back down on the grass, and rubbed her eyes.

In the far distance, above the golden speck that was Malarkoi, a cloud gathered in the cloudless sky that, moments later, developed into the Collapse Zone her mother had warned her about, and which was the reason she was sitting so far away.

Say what you like about my mother, Dashini thought, she isn't often wrong.

If we are in the centre of the Earth and we want to move, we won't be able to do it. Even if we have a body that can survive long enough for us to will ourselves into motion, the core of the Earth is made of plasma, which is the stuff that fire is made of, and this plasma is so compressed that it's solid.

We can't imagine what a solid of fire would be, so inimical is that to our experience of the world, but that doesn't mean there isn't such a thing. Indeed, not only does solid fire exist,

467

it exists beneath our feet, under our ground, where it has always existed.

In this fire, Rekka was now encaged, with a desperate desire to go up which added to the desperate desire it already possessed to murder its summoner, and to return to its intermediate realm.

At first, this demon could not move, but where we are static creatures, a demon is not.

Evolution in a person, at the level of the body, is only evidenced over generations inasmuch as we differ from our parents in some way and might pass on those differences to our children.

If these generational differences are advantageous, we might, possibly, gift these useful differences to the chain of our successors through the process of sexual reproduction. These successors, as instances of our species, might come, over a long period, to be able to do things that their ancestors could not do.

A demon is not like this.

Demons come into being at the beginning of their realms, and, barring unforeseen circumstances, they exist until the end of them. They do not reproduce, they do not bear children, and there is no generational evolution in their form that might allow them to gradually become things that can do things that they cannot originally do.

But that is not to say that they cannot change.

No creature unable to adapt to the world it lives in can thrive – this is a rule – and since demons do not evolve as a man does, passing on useful traits to their children, instead they evolve by will.

When a demon wills itself to do a thing, but finds that it is unable to do it, this makes in it a fury so profound that its body cannot contain it. Since a demon can never willingly destroy itself, either its will to do the impossible thing goes away, or its body becomes able to do the impossible thing.

A demon is a wilful thing by nature, so it is generally its body that changes.

This change happened to Rekka, sent to the centre of the Earth from the Manse of the Master of Mordew by Dashini's magic.

Its inadequacy to the task of moving upward in a solid plasma was less potent than Rekka's will to do it, and this made its carapace deform and reform in a process that mimicked natural selection.

Incrementally, but exceedingly quickly, it developed by chance the qualities necessary for its will to be done.

Its exoskeleton developed a repulsion for the form of the plasma: fluxes of this sort are prone to magnetism, even as a solid, and if that repulsion is strong enough, it can repel a similarly charged solid object. Any child who has brought two repelling magnets together will know that they spring away from each other.

So it is that this demon and the solid plasma sprang away from each other, even if only by a small amount.

The moment this change was effected in its form, the demon felt an increase in pressure, against which it clawed and kicked with an appalling frenzied energy. It fought against its surroundings, gouging and churning through the Earth's core sufficient to move itself in the direction it willed: away from the shameful and hideously pressured downwardness, up, by increments, to places where that quality to the world is less present.

IX

'DID YOUR CYCLE in God Killing stretch to rack theory? I'm not sure of the state of the discipline.'

Sharli had good eyes, and good concentration, and a good imagination, but she couldn't make Nathan Treeves out from the luminous blur in the distance. It was like an approaching storm cloud, radiating crepuscular rays of light in every direction, flickering with sheet lightning.

'Sharli?'

She turned. 'What?'

Gleed clicked. 'Did they teach you rack theory in God Killing?'

Of course they did, but Sharli shook her head. That was the easiest way to derail Gleed: give her something to explain, something to know better about, some benefit she thought she could provide Sharli, and she'd go on indefinitely.

Gleed tutted, launched into a potted history of the relic field, how the field used the weft-congruence of religious and personal relics to draw weft-users to the rack, how the rack held them there. They were all things Sharli had needed to know to pass her cycle in God Killing, and in the same way that the assassin only learned those things to get Tinnimam back, she only half-listened to Gleed now, if at all, so she could think through what she was going to do to Nathan Treeves to get him to give up the location of Gam Halliday without Gleed interrupting her with questions.

She had to nod when Gleed made an important point, had to smile when Gleed made one of her jokes, sometimes she had to reach over to stop Tinnimam launching herself off the corner of the barge as it slid through the water to rendezvous with the crusade launch platform they were making for, but otherwise she was back in the mode she had operated in for years: working assassin for Mr Padge.

In a pouch at her wrist, hidden by bangles and bracelets, reproductions made in New Juda of her lost trophies, she had enough quick-root to loosen anyone's tongue. In her jacket she had a pipe Chiddy had commissioned for her, and enough opium to calm an overstimulated brain. Obviously she had the weft-knife.

Gleed stopped, but because Sharli had been listening, even though she was really thinking about something else, she knew what to say to the Field Commander. Gleed had indicated the tell-tale plume of the launch platform, its multichromatic hot-exhaust snaking thinly up in the distance. 'About ten minutes?' Sharli said, approximating their arrival time.

Gleed continued – once the rack was activated, there'd only be a short window for Sharli to make it to the rack before the relic field drew Nathan Treeves into position – but Sharli already knew what she was saying. The basics of a job were something that an assassin needed to know before they set off to do it; they'd need the rest of their attention to react to contingencies, and it was these contingencies that Sharli was running through.

Pain is a good way of getting information out of a person, but it isn't foolproof. If people are willing to die not to tell their secrets, then they can find ways to die. If the thought of betraying someone is worse than any pain, they can have determined to live through any pain rather than speak. But both those strategies rely on the person being in their right mind. Quick-root, as well as giving you the energy to get through double and triple shifts in the kitchens, makes you voluble, makes you arrogant, gives you the false impression that you're unbeatable. If you're unbeatable, why do you need to keep secrets? Opium works the other way, it takes the seriousness out of the world, it relaxes inhibitions, it gives you the false impression that nothing matters. If nothing matters, why do you need to keep secrets? Flipping between the two can break a mind, and broken minds can't remember what they had determined to do. Pain will do that too – drive a person insane – but drugs are quicker. Pain and drugs together are very quick.

The approaching cloud in which Gleed had identified Nathan Treeves, and the Assembly launch platform, both grew closer. In the cloud, Sharli could pick out spots of darkness like poppy seeds in a loaf of white bread, and on the platform were Vanguard soldiers preparing their boarding grapples.

Gleed was silent for a moment.

She turned to Sharli. 'You know what you have to do?'

Sharli did.

'I'll see you later, sister.'

The bomb-barge met the launch platform and the Women's Vanguard helped Sharli across.

Sharli looked back at Gleed, that monstrous combination of ancient woman and out-of-date machinery, and she saluted her, knowing that even if Gleed had her doubts she'd have to return the salute, which she did.

X

ABOVE THE COLLAPSE ZONE, Nathaniel Treeves saw his son Nathan. The boy was hovering in the sky like a hawk hovers when it sees a mouse in the undergrowth: perfectly steady, perfectly still, only its head moving to keep the object of its gaze in focus.

Nathaniel reached out his left hand and without needing to look, took the right hand of his wife, Clarissa Delacroix. He didn't need to look because a husband and wife, when they are close, know where each other are in a way that doesn't require the senses. Through years of habituation to each other, he and Clarissa had passed the point when they needed to even think about where the other was.

They knew without thinking.

Nathaniel Treeves, once he had Clarissa Delacroix's hand, used his free hand to indicate Nathan hovering in the sky, blazing.

Nathaniel, when he was sure Clarissa had seen their son, put down his hand on his wife's left shoulder. Using only a little force – only a little force was required – he brought his wife round to face him.

She looked up at him.

There is some quality in the looking upwards of a wife into the face of her husband, who is looking downwards at her when he is of sufficient height to mean that he must, that is reminiscent of love even in couples who are estranged.

It reminds them of their initial attraction.

No doubt there is an explanation for this fact, but no explanation is required, and if one of the parties attempts to provide it, in that moment, the spell is broken.

Neither Nathaniel nor Clarissa attempted to provide the explanation, so the spell remained in place.

Nathaniel leaned in, and, with his lips, cleared Clarissa's ear of the hair that had fallen across it and used those same lips to speak into her ear.

She frowned, for a moment, because she couldn't make out what he'd said, but that frown disappeared when, as he went on, she understood what he was saying.

When he finished speaking quietly into her ear he pulled away and the couple resumed that looking at each other from disparate heights that had reminded them of their love.

This lasted for a second or two, no more, then Clarissa closed her eyes. She went inwards, became a conduit to the weft, and Nathaniel spoke words into the air that no one could hear.

What did he say?

You would not understand the words if they were transcribed here. They were from a language so long passed out of memory that no one except Nathaniel remembered them.

Some people say that when God made the world he made a perfect language that was so perfectly able to describe the things he had made that it was synonymous with them, that to utter the words brought the things into being. It is said that he jealously guarded the knowledge of this language and punished humanity when it tried to learn it.

Perhaps Nathaniel knew some of this language.

When he spoke it, drawing Spark through his wife through her inward connection with the weft, present still by dint of her recently being the weftling, his tongue shone, and then his teeth shone, and then his jaw shone, and then, bone by bone, every part of his skeleton radiated light through his skin until, when it seemed as if he must ignite his flesh, Spark came from the fingertip of his right index finger.

Because Nathaniel could not see for all the light, Clarissa pointed his finger for him, making a path from the weft that went directly to their son.

That is a very wifely thing to do, to help her husband, but it might also have been that she manipulated him into doing what she wished and exploited their love that way.

It is none of our business whether Clarissa was being wifely, or exploitative – that is a matter between spouses – and perhaps it is possible to be both. For us, we only need to know how the Spark she directed affected Nathan Treeves, and at first it

474

seemed like it would add to Nathan's power, to his Mastery, that the two of them were, for once and at last, siding with him against the world.

There he was in the sky, surrounded by his angels, like a great, divine general, overseeing the vengeful dead who made up his army in their efforts to bring the world to book. He was in the midst of them as they flew here and there about the world in a frenzy of power all the more vigorous because they had spent so much time dead beneath the sea.

When his parents' Spark hit Nathan, he swelled in the air, inflated by light. Perhaps they were trying to make him grow to a size where he could challenge any and all threats.

Perhaps they were trying to give him more power, drawn from the infinite weft, so that his victory in the Collapse Zone was assured – he was filling with it, blazing with it.

They were not trying to do that.

The Sparkline that his parents directed at him had a negative effect – it did not indefinitely add to his power, but, once a critical point had been induced, subtracted from it, drained it through them and back into the weft in a rush against which Nathan could find no defence.

He swelled, and brightened, and seemed to take on an infinity of power, but then, like a balloon into which too much air has been pumped, he burst.

A boy cannot take on that much Spark.

Down from the sky fell Nathan Treeves, his mother and father's ownership of his Sparkline superseding everything, even his Mastery of Waterblack, so that, his defences breached, they could take the excess away.

He did not – because it would have been necessarily comic – whizz through the sky in random directions, like a burst balloon does, making a squeaking sound that resolves, at the end, into flatulence.

Instead, he fell at Nathan and Clarissa's feet in a heap.

Imagine you have spitefully tipped an infant from its cradle onto the hard floor of your dwelling place. Imagine it has hit its head hard enough to daze it. Imagine it is struggling to

475

raise itself up now and cannot do it, but instead slumps down, banging its face on the ground.

Now it lies there, and you can see it, blinking, confused, and in pain.

That is how Nathan appeared before his parents once they had stripped his power from him.

'Did you think we'd let you get away with it?' Nathaniel said.

Clarissa lifted Nathan's head from the ground roughly, by the hair, so that he faced her. 'Why couldn't you just do what you were told?'

Nathan didn't understand what she meant.

Perhaps he would never understand.

Perhaps a child will never understand the motivation of a parent who does not love him.

Perhaps there is nothing to understand.

In Waterblack, when he'd watched through the windows of his father's quarter, these people murdering the boy who was clearly his brother, did they love that child?

In Mordew, when his father had forbidden him to use his power, did the man love him?

When his mother had sent him to the Master, did she love him?

Nathan looked first at one of them, and then at the other – it does not matter in which order – and there was no love in their faces. There was only their anger.

What was there to do, for him?

Nathan pulled himself out of his mother's grip. He got to his feet, and even though he was drained of his Spark, he was still alive. He was still someone. He had the taste of power on his tongue – it tastes of metal – and he opened his mouth to speak, to say his part, to stand up for himself.

But now his mother and father turned away from him, as if there was nothing he could say that would have any meaning for them.

Nathan's words, Nathan's questions, Nathan's voice stopped in his throat, for a moment, and then came out in one half-strangled cry. 'Please!' he cried.

His parents, their backs turned, froze.

Nathaniel looked at Clarissa, and she looked at him: Nathan could tell this from the backs of their heads. They were silently looking into each other's eyes. He could imagine their faces, but not the expressions on them.

What does a child truly know of his parents? What understanding does he have of their motivations?

Isn't there something strange and terrible for a child, in the fact that these two people pre-existed together before they made him, that they had thoughts and desires and lives of which he was never a part, and into which he was born in his innocence to fulfil whatever role they had written for him, not even able to take his feelings into consideration, since he didn't as yet exist?

Nathan watched their frozen backs, knowing their faces as well as he knew anything, but not knowing what their expressions held.

He waited for what stretched into an impossibly long time, it seemed to him, while these two held each other's gaze in silence.

What could they possibly be thinking, communicating, feeling?

What child knows the answer to that question?

What child wants to know?

Then, their parental communion seemed to break. By the relaxation of tension at their shoulders, Nathan could see that the two were about to turn, about, at last, to answer the question that they had never answered, by their actions, and which Nathan had never had the strength to even ask himself: 'Why don't you love me?'

They turned, but in their expressions there was no sense that they were about to speak. Instead, they held themselves like killers might, looked at Nathan like killers might look – concentrated, tense, committed – and they came towards him silently.

Just as the children of unloving parents do not properly know those parents, unloving parents, because they don't pay attention to their children, do not know their children. They see these children as isolated things, understand them as forsaken by the world because they, as parents, have forsaken them in their hearts.

These unloving parents do not consider that their children might be loved by others, that they might have friends. Even if they did consider that possibility, then they would not hold any high opinion of those friends, assuming them to be as useless as they consider their own children to be.

Similarly, a person who does not love a pet, and who abandons it by the side of the road to die, does not imagine that pet will come back to revenge itself, since the abandonment of an animal is not simply a physical one, it is a psychological one: the pet is left behind in both body and thought, never to be recovered.

These facts explain why, when down from the sky came the magical dog Anaximander, transformed by Nathan Treeves into an angel, neither Nathaniel Treeves nor Clarissa Delacroix was adequately prepared for his arrival. Nathaniel Treeves was not prepared because it had not crossed his mind that Nathan had any friends of sufficient note for them to threaten him, and Clarissa Delacroix was not prepared because she had put the animal entirely out of her mind after she had left him to die.

Whether they were prepared or not prepared, here he came, biting, clawing, screaming in angelic fury, and he made straight for Clarissa Delacroix.

If they had thought to look, they could have seen him in the Angelic Army of Waterblack. When they shot their son down and neutered him of his power, they could have noticed Anaximander's reaction: first shock and horror, then anger, then angry determination. He was easily visible, making straight for them, too vengeful to hide himself.

But neither of them had thought it necessary to look.

Anaximander had the right to revenge himself on Clarissa, and the right to protect the interests of his companion, Sirius, who was at that point occupied with his own revenge on Sebastian Cope, the Master of Mordew, another of the Tontine

Wizards.* Additionally, Heartless Harold Smyke had bred violence into the dog, and he was back from the dead, incorporated in the form of an avenging angel: all of which meant that angelic rage could be expected from him.

But neither Nathaniel nor Clarissa was expecting him.

The dog came at enormous speed down from the sky, and his great paws, his shining claws, his bared and terrible teeth all struck Clarissa's back as she made to attack her son. They stripped through her clothing instantly, through her skin, through the muscles and sinews of her back.

Before she even knew what was happening, the dog had opened her spine to the world.

A wild dog, when he sees the insides of his prey, does not pause for the slightest moment before he seizes on whatever he has seen with his teeth, and all dogs are famous for their desire for bones.

Now Anaximander, his fur black, his eyes white, Spark glinting from his tongue and gums, tore into Clarissa's body, seized what he could bite of her backbone and wrenched with his teeth, pulled with the thick and corded muscles of his neck, pushed the traitorous woman down on the ground with his weight to gain the necessary purchase.

In a sickening moment which seemed to make very easy work of something that might have been impossible for anyone or anything else, he pulled what should have been inside of Clarissa out, cracking her ribs, cracking her arm bones, cracking her hips with the force of his anger.

Neither Nathan nor Nathaniel moved, appalled and paralysed, but Anaximander did. He shook Clarissa's spine, sprayed blood – it evaporated when it landed against his angelic pelt – dropped the bones onto the ground and pounced at Nathaniel.

The man was not now as unprepared as he had been, but he was not prepared enough. He brought up his hands, like a boxer does, and his lips began words that might have been some spell or conjuration suitable for defeating a magical dog,

---

* Curious readers are again referred to the appendices.

but Anaximander moved with angelic speed, was at the man's chest clawing through the raised arms before the first syllable could leave those lips.

Nathaniel Treeves had died in the slums of Mordew through a magical infection, and he died here, in the Collapse Zone, in a similar way, his lungs being attacked again by a creature of occult provenance. In the former instance this was by magically generated parasites, in this instance it was by Anaximander, the talking dog, unspeakingly chewing at the man's organs through the ribcage he had opened with his claws.

Nathan dropped back to his knees, his hands over his mouth.

Eventually, Anaximander turned to him, and there was such animal fury in his eyes, such unthinking blankness, that Nathan worried that the dog might turn on him next.

But then that fury passed.

Anaximander dropped what was in his mouth, suddenly understanding, like a naughty boy, that he shouldn't be doing what he was doing.

'My apologies, Nathan Treeves,' he said, after a moment. 'I think my temper might have got the better of me.'

XI

ASSEMBLY GOD KILLING RACKS don't simply summon demigods to them. If they did, how would a God Killer be able to decide when and where to summon one?

First, the rack has to be put in place on the relic field, which the technicians had already done. Sharli walked around the site, checking automatically whether the corners were square to the grid. Of course they were: Sharli stood and looked down from directly above all four in turn and the points of each corner lined up perfectly with the keying stones. Would it have made any difference if they hadn't? Sharli wouldn't have been able to correct that flaw now, even if the equipment was still present, which it wasn't.

She rotated the rings on each of the fingers of her left hand.

This wasn't part of the process, but Sharli did it anyway. She rotated the rings on each of the fingers of her left hand first one way, and then the other, and she sighted down the rack to make sure it pointed to Mordew, the birthplace of her target.

She rotated the rings on the fingers of her right hand.

She adjusted the weft-knife in its holster, something that did nothing at all, so perfectly was it locked in.

The rack smelled of wood. Sharli didn't know which type, but she recognised it: slightly sharp, slightly astringent, a little like Mordew quick-root, but not quite.

There was no switch, no lever, no button to press.

Attractant racks have to be willed into action. You have to want the subject of a racking to be summoned to the rack, and you have to want to do it there and then.

When Gulten had explained this fact to Sharli, back in New Juda, it had sounded ridiculous. Why make a machine work like that, when a switch, a lever, a button was so much easier? This was what Sharli had said in the class. She'd put up her hand and asked why, and all of them – Gulten and all the others in

481

the class – had frowned at her. It was like she was an infant, or someone who had suffered a brain injury.

One of the other students, Sharli couldn't remember her name, had tried to correct her, but Gulten shook her head, as if it was a kind of bullying even to offer to answer that question.

Sharli didn't receive an answer right away – the lecture had continued without one, as if nothing had been said – but Gulten called her aside at the end of the class. She waited until everyone had gone, and when she was absolutely sure they had, she went to the door, closed it, and stood by the closed door with her hand on the handle.

'A rack doesn't have a button,' she said, her face kind, 'because it isn't a machine. You don't have a button, do you? You don't have to pull a lever when you want to do something, do you? It's the same with a rack. You have to want it to attract someone. Right?'

Sharli, because she didn't enjoy being alone with Gulten, nodded as if she understood, but she didn't understand then. She learned to fake it, but she didn't really understand until now.

Now, Sharli very strongly wanted the rack to summon Nathan Treeves, and because it was properly placed, properly aligned, properly keyed to its relic field, it did summon Nathan Treeves. The more she wanted it, in fact, the harder it summoned him.

Sharli wanted it very much.

XII

THERE IN THE COLLAPSE ZONE, beneath the thick and flashing cloud cover, was Japalura.

Even at this distance she was enormous and perfectly recognisable.

Still, if you've gone to the trouble of making a lorgnette, you might as well use it, so Dashini put the lenses up to her eyes.

The view this gave of her dragon mother was a perfect replica of the view Dashini held in her mind: face-on, nostrils flaring, the slits of her pupils like voids in two pits of molten iron.

To anyone else, this would have been a terrible visage, bone-chillingly suggestive of an immediate and fiery death, but not to Dashini.

To Dashini it suggested thousands of other, beautiful things; a thousand flights across the ocean; a thousand ascents to the edge of the sky; a thousand breathless glimpses of the space that surrounded the world, punctured by stars un-glistening; a thousand communions of mind, the perfect happiness contact with a deity brings to the self.

She did not consider the Shadow King, looming in the sky above Japalura, because the Shadow King was nothing compared to her dragon.

He would never be anything compared to her.

Without taking the lorgnette down, Dashini used her free hand to find the whistle, touching the objects on the grass in front of her in turn until she found the thing she had made just for this moment. In the same way that a young child calls for its parent, certain that the call will not be ignored, or denied, Dashini put the whistle to her lips and blew.

Because that was the way that she designed it, into the material air were sent the immaterial concepts that would call Japalura to her, travelling at a speed faster than sound, faster than light, a speed unconstrained by anything material, an instant communication that only concepts can achieve.

Dashini waited.

Then she waited more.

And again.

There was no response from the dragon.

Surely she should have stopped, should have paused, should have turned to find where Dashini was, and, just as a child cannot, at first, believe that its parent will not come to its call, she took the lorgnette from her eyes and looked down at the whistle, thinking there must be something wrong with it.

There it was, seemingly fine.

She turned it a few times, rotated it, looked down into the space into which she had blown.

All fine.

She took the lorgnette, used the reverse lens to check the conceptual content of the whistle, forced the homunculus to do the work it was indentured to, and there was nothing wrong with the concepts engrained into the materials.

She put it to her lips again and blew again.

Now she didn't bother with the lorgnette, she just looked out with her naked eyes across the expanse that separated her waiting place from the Collapse Zone.

She blew again.

She blew again.

She was about to blow again, but then Japalura turned, having spread her wings from one side of the horizon to the other.

Dashini didn't need the lorgnette to see the difference in the dragon's expression, the heart-breaking presence of evil intent in her surrogate mother's aura. Japalura crackled like the Nathan Knife crackled, with black fire.

A demon, once it has freed itself from the centre of the Earth, comes up through the outer core, through the mantle, eventually through the crust, each division changing its form in different ways.

The outer core, because it is similar to the inner core, does not make a substantial difference to the demon's physiology,

484

but the mantle, because it is less liquid, more like dense and dark rock, makes the demon become denser, makes its arms become heavier, its claws, with which it must force its way through, become more shovel-like, like those of the mole. The angles by which the demon makes these shovel-like arms pivot in order that effective progress can be made alter, so that it clears a path by scooping rock aside, and then launches with its back legs into the gap.

Most of the world consists of this rock, and so Rekka became extremely powerful in both its front and rear limbs. Its head, already wedge-like, retracted into its shoulders, or its shoulders grew up to the top of the head, whichever is more accurate.

The disgusting pressure, with which it had been assaulted, lessened, and this filled the demon with a delirious, furious glee. It sensed, with its echo-location of the weft, that its summoner grew closer, and because it needed to make less effort now to move, and because it found energy in its gleefulness, it used this sense more vigorously, sending wave after wave of energy into the earth, reading from it the place to where it must force itself.

And then it reached the crust.

Dashini wasn't crying.

It was the hay fever, very bad now, that made her eyes stream, that made her lungs ache, that made her head throb.

She wasn't crying.

Japalura did not come to Dashini, no matter how often she blew the whistle. The dragon was making for the Assembly, who were directing rays of red and blue concentrate into the chaotic mess of which Japalura was the centre, the Shadow King behind, reaching up into the sky.

It's going to get dangerous, her mother had said, so keep well back.

There's going to be gods, and angels, and corpses, and weapons. There's going to be the Tinderbox, the racks, concentrates, munitions... there's going to be hell on Earth.

So, keep well back.

When it's all over, you'll be there to pick up the pieces.

Dashini hadn't thought at the time, because she'd spent such a lot of her life on her own, that this was an odd thing to say. 'You'll' be there to pick up the pieces.

You.

Not we.

Why hadn't she said we?

Dashini rubbed her eyes so hard that they felt like they might squash into her eye sockets. The hay fever was really bad now.

She raised the lorgnette up and thought of Nathan, but she could hardly see him through the tears.

Not tears. She could hardly see Nathan through whatever it is that you get when your eyes are watering from hay fever.

She put the lorgnette down, took a long and deep breath, one that kept catching in her chest – not because she was sobbing, but because of the hay fever – but which she eventually filled herself up with. She didn't breathe out, but pulled down one of her sleeves and used it to wipe the water from her eyes. She wanted to rub them with the slightly scratchy fabric of her shirt, but she didn't let herself.

She let her breath out, slowly, like her mother had showed her, and she picked up the lorgnette again.

Here was Nathan Treeves, and his dog, both of them in angelic monotones at the head of an army of more angels than can ever have troubled the face of the earth since the ancient times.

He was leading this army to the Collapse Zone, to where the Assembly were, to where Japalura was, to where, from the sky, fell a chaotic tumble of matter which, when Dashini turned the lorgnette around, the homunculus couldn't determine a conceptual basis for.

It was either living things, or corpses, or bricks, or stones, or mud, or protoplasm, or none of those things.

When she turned the lorgnette back, Nathan was gone.

There was the Angelic Army of Waterblack.

There was Japalura, and the Roi de l'Ombre.

There was the Assembly and the Collapse Zone.

486

But Nathan had gone.

Dashini ignored her eyes, which were running again, her nose, which was running again, her head, which was throbbing so hard now it was as if her heartbeat was a bass drum of pain.

She ignored all of it and pictured Nathan.

Now, when she brought the lorgnette to her eyes, she could see him.

He was strapped to a rack like a prisoner awaiting torture, his angelic light faded, his real self – his boyish self: thin and sad and pathetic – visible again.

Let it all play out, her mother had said.

Let it all play out, and be there to pick up the pieces.

Dashini put down the lorgnette, next to the whistle, and she rubbed her eyes.

XIII

THE RELIC FIELD WAS QUIET. In the distance there was the strange and tortured sound of war, but only quietly, like parents arguing under their breath when you are half asleep, and who can almost be mistaken for people less fraught, less aggressive, for better people… as long as you don't listen too carefully.

The sky above was bright, its single sun at noon, and while there were clouds in the distance, low and dark, flickering with lightning and the colours of concentrates, dimmed by shadows, these were things Nathan didn't – couldn't – pay too much attention to.

He was on his rack, a piece of varnished wood into which the perfect shape of his body had been carved, or planed, or gouged… somehow his perfect shape had been made in the wood.

It had been sanded and smoothed and varnished.

If you want to roll a marble across a piece of wood in a specific way, you alter the surface of that wood away from complete flatness.

It's the same if you want a marble to come to rest at a specific point: you carve a little dip, or plane a gradient, or make an imperfection in the wood. The marble will move where its momentum takes it. Eventually, as the marble follows the line that you carved, or planed, it will, gradually, slowly, without knowing it, come to rest in the place that has been prepared for it.

Gravity will take it there.

A marble cannot escape gravity.

Nathan was in the place on the rack that had been prepared for him, and he could not move from it, not even to turn his head to the quiet, distant sound of war. He couldn't look up at the lightning, or the light from the concentrates, or the shadows.

He couldn't even move his head.

It was like gravity was pressing him down so hard into the wood that there was no way he could resist it. He was like a marble that had come to rest where it was meant to be, with no way of resisting.

The Assembly had made this happen not entirely with wood. The Hailey-Beths from Engines had used the weft.

They had used time.

They had used the world.

They had used desire.

If Nathan looked all the way to the left, or all the way to the right, stretching the muscles of his eye sockets so hard that he felt those muscles might tear, he could just make out, in the very periphery of his vision, that the rack was resting on a level field of tilled soil.

This field was brown and even. It stretched as far as he could make out from the place he was anchored in.

Now, here came a woman, beautiful but stern.

Nathan looked through the corners of his eyes. It was the only movement that was available to him.

He felt around himself with the Spark.

He tried to move, to evolve things, to utilise the will of God in some way.

He couldn't.

That type of exertion must be visible, because the woman came over so that she stood close enough so that Nathan could see her face. 'You won't be able to move, or do anything,' she said. 'You're on a category three attractant rack, working in concert with its relic field. The rack is made from wood from trees that will eventually be used to make your coffin. That's why you can't move.' She walked around him, watching him closely. 'As far as the rack is concerned, you're already dead.'

Nathan couldn't think of anything to say.

'If you're wondering what the soil surrounding you is, it's made from your relics. It's made from things that have a presence in the weft tied to your weft-pattern. We gathered them, treated them, ground them up and spread them here to trap you. It will be the soil of your future grave.' She walked around him, clockwise, and once the words had faded from the air, she turned and walked anticlockwise. 'We've met. You probably don't remember.'

Nathan had seen Sharli – that is who this woman was – at The Commodious Hour. He had thought she was one of the gentleman assassins who dined there. 'I remember,' he said, his lips not feeling the terrible weight of everything. 'You were at Padge's table. I thought you were a man.'

Sharli shrugged – she was standing close enough for Nathan to see her do it, but he might have been able to guess from the sound of her jacket rustling across the shoulders. Assembly field clothes are made from very thick and durable fabrics. They put a speck of bleach in with the washing water when they're laundered, and also a little powdered starch. It makes them rustle when a God Killer shrugs their shoulders. 'I can look like a man,' Sharli said, 'if I want. I can look like one when I need to.' She stopped, and went neither clockwise nor anticlockwise around Nathan's rack. She stood still. 'But no,' she said, 'we met before that.'

Nathan would have shaken his head, if that had been something he could have made his head do. 'No', he would have shaken, as if it was up to him to decide when she had met him.

He wasn't capable of moving that much.

Sharli went on. 'You were a baby. Mr Padge sent me to kill you.' She leaned over, so she could look Nathan in the eyes. 'Your dad tried to kill me.'

If he'd been a different sort of boy, a boy like Gam, he would have said, 'Don't take it personal: my dad tried to kill me too', but Nathan wasn't like that. He didn't use the horrors of his life for that kind of thing.

He said nothing.

Sharli walked around the rack again, clockwise, let her fingers drag across the smooth wood, ran them over a metallic inlay that Nathan hadn't known was there, letting her rings click on the interruptions in the surface made by the weft-engineering. All the time there was the deep, thumping, almost subsonic beat of Assembly munitions in the distance.

From its holster, Sharli took the weft-knife, keeping it out of range of any accidental obstacle. If it wasn't for the handle and the guard, it would cut its way through to the centre of the Earth if she dropped it. It would slip through the matter of the world, down through the crust, through the mantle, through the outer core to the inner core. Then its momentum would carry it up, away, through the Earth and out the other side, cutting as far as it had energy to rise. Then it would fall again, down.

As the world rotated, it would slice everything into pieces.

She held it in front of Nathan's eyes.

The boy strained at his bonds, as much as he could, his muscles spasming ineffectively beneath the surface of his skin. He channelled the Spark as if that might save him.

A category three rack is made to divert excess Spark back to the weft with almost perfect efficiency. The more the victim of a racking struggles, the louder the Spark drain channels. The louder the Spark drain channels, the lower its note sounds.

Nathan struggled until there was a point at which the Spark drain's tone through the rack seemed like silence to their ears. Its presence became an aching pressure in Nathan and Sharli's skulls, in their minds, but not in their ears.

Sharli brought the knife closer, the weapon with which the Assembly had trained her to torture a parasitic demigod's divinity out of him. 'You aren't who you think you are,' she said. 'You died long ago, back when the Master of Mordew took you into his Manse. Do you remember? He held out his hand to you, and because you thought you'd been betrayed, because that thought hurt you, because you thought you might as well try to find out what was going on, you went with him. Didn't you?'

Nathan remembered, but he said nothing.

Sharli pressed onto his bound wrist with her elbow, showed him the weft-knife, let him know, by her carelessness of what-ever small danger he might represent to her, that she was entirely in control.

People in control don't need to lie. Lying is something we do to gain the advantage in a situation. If you already have the advantage, you can tell the truth. This is why, when you are at a person's mercy, you find that they are perfectly frank with you. They explain to you, clearly and without dissembling, what they think is happening. This is particularly true when they do not intend for you to live through your capture. 'When you took the Master of Mordew's hand,' Sharli said to Nathan, 'and he translated you into his Manse, the Nathan that you were then died.

'The Master destroyed you, built a copy. It was that copy that lived inside his Manse. The real you died. The Master trained your copy; he educated it. Then, when that copy left the Manse and went down to kill the alifonjers… do you remember that? When you left the Manse to kill them, that copy was destroyed. You were copied again, made again, down in the Zoological Gardens. The same thing – destroying and copying – happened when you came back. The same thing happened when you went to Malarkoi. The same thing happened when you came back from there, having destroyed the city.

'That's where I'm from: Malarkoi. I'm from the Blue Kite Quarter, a place you destroyed. You murdered the people I grew up with.'

She was very close to him now. She had been leaning closer and closer as she spoke, but Nathan had crossed his eyes, so he didn't have to see her face. She was so close that her breath ruffled his eyelashes when she spoke. 'The copy of you that killed my friends was destroyed when you left the Manse with Dashini. That Nathan, a copy of a copy of a copy, the Master killed and made into his Tinderbox. Then the Mistress made another copy in her heaven. Then she killed it. Then Waterblack made a new copy. Do you understand?'

Again, Nathan would never have answered this question, whether he was a copy or whether he wasn't. She was so close it was like she was going to kiss him.

Or bite his lips.

'You don't feel like you're a copy,' she said, 'because you don't know any different. You're just an image in flesh of someone long dead. It doesn't matter what I do to you because you're already dead. You're just a relic the Assembly needs to bury.'

Sharli pulled away, stepped back from the rack, stood, one hand forward, holding the weft-knife. 'You're in good company. All of them – Master, Mistress, whatever – they killed themselves centuries ago, when they first started interfering with the weft. They snapped themselves out of the real world into their fake reals. They died back then, and you're all copies, copies of copies, each one a little bit worse than the one before.

'Why do you think you all act so weirdly? Why do you think you're all so crazy? You're degraded copies, living corpses. You need to be stopped.'

Sharli came back, brought the knife close again so that the tip of it rested against Nathan's cheek.

It was so sharp that Nathan didn't even feel it cut him; it slid between the cells of his skin, between his nerves, without any effort at all, without any pressure, without him noticing. Nonetheless, he was cut, and when his blood reached the breach in the skin, Nathan felt the severed surfaces slide against each other as he bled onto his cheek.

'I've been sent here to end you,' Sharli said. 'But I don't care about any of that. The Assembly think I'm Sharli, their God Killer. Their torturer. But I'm not. They're all so full of themselves they can't believe I don't care about them. They think I'm one of them.

'But I'm not.'

She pulled the knife back, slowly, careful now not to make pieces of Nathan's face.

'I'm Sharli of the Dumnonii.

'I'm Sharli the slave.

'Sharli the nail girl.

'I'm Sharli the chef.

'Sharli the butcher.

'I'm Sharli, Mr Padge's best assassin. Do you understand?'

Even if Nathan had understood, he wouldn't have spoken, but he didn't understand, and that was clear to Sharli's eyes. One of the things a torturer learns is to see truth on the face of the person they're torturing, to know it from lies, to know it from a lack of knowing.

Nathan didn't know what she was talking about.

'He saved me, understand? I loved him, understand? I still love him.'

Sharli came so close that her cheek was against the wound on Nathan's cheek. She whispered in his ear. 'Tell me where your friend Gam Halliday is. I'm going to make him pay for what he did to Mr Padge, just like the contract says I have to. You're going to tell me where he is.'

Now Nathan spoke. 'I don't know where he is,' he said.

Sharli stood up straight, and where her face had worn expressions full of emotions – her anger, her viciousness, her sadness – now she became entirely impassive.

'Well,' she said, 'that's unlucky for both of us, isn't it?'

She steeled herself, not like a doctor, or a dentist, or anyone else who steels themselves steels themselves, in order to cause pain in a person in their best interests. She was who she was – a torturer – and she steeled herself against Nathan's pain to prevent herself from feeling any of it.

She steeled herself against her own empathy, knowing through experience that it was counterproductive to her work. The expression on her face was like the expression on the face of a sculptor approaching a slab of marble, of clay, of any nerveless and lifeless material it is unnecessary and unhelpful to treat as living.

When Sharli, at the Temple of the Athanasians, was delivered to the room occupied by the supervisor of the nail factory, the events that occurred there, before she killed him, were not described in this book. The reasoning given then was that the reader ought not to want to read that description, and that the writer did not want to write it. It was also assumed that the actions of someone as low as the nail factory supervisor – who was a rapist and a paedophile – were not worthy of description. We only watched when Sharli made ribbons of that man's face with a nail she had stolen from a carriage seat.

Should we watch now, as Sharli tortures Nathan? As she strips the nerves from a boy's body with a weft-knife, under the orders of the Women's Vanguard of the Eighth Atheistic Crusade? Do you want to read how it is that a boy who gained God's will by virtue of a Spark inheritance is separated from the weft by a blade so sharp that it can fillet him of his nervous system? Does the author want to write that material, knowing that, to experience something of that sort would be to experience pain of the most appalling kind, worse than anyone could bear?

It does not matter whether you do or do not want to read it. We, in our world, are not the judges of that matter.

The Assembly, for whom morality as it relates to the conduct of the named and numbered expeditionary actions outside of its borders constitutes an academic discipline – Ethics – has decided that a standing opt-out exists for any member of a Crusading force called upon to do the work that Sharli was conducting.

Life-mimicking weft-parasites, such as the entity named Nathan Treeves, under authority from Ethics, are not considered to have sentience. When they appear to suffer pain, this is a conditioned, defensive response similar to the reflex a limpet demonstrates when you try to remove it from a rock. Less, even, because a limpet has life. When Sharli willed the rack to turn Nathan over so that she had more ready access to his spine, and when, that done, she placed the perfectly sharp blade at the base of his skull where his spine met his brain, his appearance of fear was a reflex performance.

It was not real.

A weft-parasite has evolved nerves which exist partially in the material realm, and partially in the immaterial realm, as we all have. We all have nerves with an inward extension. What separates us from weft-parasites is that their nerves have grown unnaturally inward, so that they form an organic analogue of the conduits by which a weft-generator provides power from the weft. Each of the cells of their nerves is capable of drawing up Spark energy directly from the weft to a greater or lesser extent depending on their ability to manipulate the immaterial link between this inward extension and their consciousness-mimicking mind.

When a God Killer, such as Sharli was trained to be, with her weft-knife attempts to truncate the inward extension of a weft-parasite's nervous system by removing the nerve cells from the corpus, the parasite will attempt, knowing that it is at the mercy of the God Killer, to appeal to the God Killer's humanity by making a performance of agony, by pleading, by begging, something that it is difficult for a person with empathy to experience.

When Hailey-Beth (Martial) Clementina Roads selected Sharli as a candidate for the Women's Vanguard, it was Sharli's specifically triggerable lack of empathy, trained into her by her upbringing, that singled her out. This was a very astute observation on Clementina's part, as was proven now, since Nathan's pitiful, whimpering, pleading vocalisations had almost no effect on Sharli.

So why should this book force them to have an effect on us?

Isn't she, Sharli, better placed than we are to know whether there is an authentic core to an entity's desperate, screaming cries?

'Where is Gam Halliday?' Sharli said, and even if this was not something she meant as a means of quickening her God Killing, it is certainly something that cycles in the discipline teach is effective.

The immaterial use of material nerve cells – through thought-mimicking processes, for example – causes them to fatten and bloat, whereas if they are not used they thin and become more difficult to separate from their myelin sheaths. God Killers are trained to prompt a weft-parasite's mind to mimic thought so that their nerves are easier to fillet. It does not matter whether the question Sharli asked had a useful answer or not, in operational terms, only that the parasite was encouraged to fatten its nerves by thinking of an answer.

Nathan wasn't able to answer this question, but that did not mean he didn't try. Torture of the nerves, whatever people imagine before they experience it, is not tolerable, and even if the mind would prefer not to reveal this or that information, or to protect this or that other person, pain of this kind bypasses those higher-level processes, even in consciousness-mimicking entities. Often the subject of a God Killing will verbally empty the entirety of their store of facts, true and imagined, before turning towards the utterance of random and hopeless strings of words, combined to seemingly no rational scheme, in order to get the pain to stop.

Unfortunately, for Nathan and for us, the pain did not stop.

Sharli took a piece of quick-root from her pouch. It was about the size of her fingertip and because she hadn't been using any of late, it wasn't fresh. It had developed a stale and cracked skin, so she put it in her mouth, let her saliva wet it, then gently bit and turned it with her teeth and tongue. When she began to taste its juice – Assembly quick-root was very faintly reminiscent of mint – she took it back out of her mouth and flattened it between her fingers.

'Let's see if this helps,' she said to Nathan.

She leaned over him, close, pulled back his lips on one side.

Nathan couldn't move, but he gritted his teeth – he wasn't going to let it in.

Quick-root shouldn't be eaten, though – it is most effective when placed between the gums and the cheek – so Nathan's defiance meant nothing. She slipped the root up into his mouth with a jewelled forefinger. One of her rings clicked on Nathan's molar at the back, another on his canine.

He tried to struggle, but it made no difference.

Sharli kept her finger in his mouth until the quick-root began its work.

As Sharli drew the knife down, scraping against Nathan's nerves as she did it, he told her all the places he knew in tones now high-pitched and shrieking, now oddly low, now from some strange and deep recess below his voice box, now from some oscillation of the diaphragm.

Because Sharli could tell the difference between the truth and a lie, and because the training was very advanced in this area, she knew Nathan wasn't telling her where Gam Halliday was.

Weft-parasites will lie, and the function of God Killing is only tangentially related to the gathering of intelligence. Assembly intelligencers are the specialist machines created for that job, and God Killing, as a discipline, does not have an engineering specialty that supersedes whatever Prose produces in this area.

Lies, truth, useful and useless intelligence are secondary to the maintenance of nerve use during the extraction phase. So, when Sharli said, 'Tell me where Gam Halliday is and all this will end,' she need not have meant it.

It is irrelevant whether she meant it.

It is irrelevant to point out that she did mean it.

Eventually, when it was clear the quick-root wasn't going to make him talk, she squeezed Nathan's cheeks until the flattened, slick lump slipped out from between his lips. Once she would have put it into her own mouth, unwilling to let any remnant go to waste, but now she didn't feel that obligation.

Sharli took her pipe and filled it with opium.

It takes some work to draw smoke from a long-stemmed pipe, and it's hard to force someone to do it against their will, so Sharli did what she'd seen Sylvie and Juliette do for fun: she lit the pipe, sucked the smoke into her mouth, and then, with her lips pursed, she leaned over Nathan, as she had with the quick-root. This time she used her fingers to hold the boy's nose shut, and she gently pulled down on his chin. When his mouth was open, just a little, she placed her lips on his as if she were kissing him, then she breathed the opium smoke into his lungs.

He wanted to resist, wanted not to breathe, but Sharli stayed kissing him, making a seal with her mouth over his, pinching his nostrils until he had no choice but to take it down. Sharli didn't move. The opium went down, and, for a very brief moment, he breathed in Sharli's air. Even then, even under torture, there was a strange intimacy in that sharing, and Sharli pulled away.

Perhaps it should have shocked her to her senses, but opium works against shock, and the moment passed with the coming on of the haze, so familiar to Sharli, so welcome, and so associated with her work.

Nathan felt the opium. It wanted him to tell Sharli the information she asked for. But, since he didn't know it, it didn't matter how many times she asked him.

He couldn't tell her.

Torturing is an activity that occupies most of a person's attention, and is the kind of thing that tends to take place within well-defended, often secret, places. It is not helpful, for a torturer, to have to be looking over their shoulder when they ought to be attending to their craft. This is true of an Assembly field-torturer as much as it for one employed by, say, the owner of a castle who has had a dungeon excavated for the purpose of housing and torturing his enemies.

Sharli's work with Nathan took place on a relic field constructed for the purpose, and was guarded by Crusaders, so she was not expecting to be interrupted.

In almost all situations she should have expected to remain unmolested for as long as the procedure lasted, but there will always be situations for which no amount of investment from Simulations can account. This is particularly true when weft-manipulation and magic are concerned, since things that are thought to be impossible can be made possible, and no simulation of events can account for the infinite range of impossible things.

One such impossible thing was Dashini's use of her portal chalk, something that, until this Crusade, had never been observed to exist in the material realm. This, in conjunction with the lorgnette, allowed Dashini to bypass the Vanguard's cordon around the relic field by drawing a Door that opened beside where she had seen Nathan with her lorgnette, and, by passing through the door, to appear, Nathan Knife in hand, on the other side of the rack from Sharli.

This didn't shock the assassin, but it did stop her in her work.

As if it was as simple as pointing, she threw the pair of knives she kept concealed in her sleeves across Nathan's prone form at the place where Dashini had appeared, and if it wasn't for the fact that the girl had already employed her POQ, one knife would have struck her in the heart, and the other would have perforated her bowel. As it was, the two knives embedded in the POQ before sliding slowly down to eventually drop to the floor in a clatter.

Sharli, even before the Assembly had trained her, knew enough to assume an aggressor might well be capable of defending themselves, so by the time the knives hit the ground, she had sheathed the weft-knife, put the rack between her and Dashini, and had drawn her pistol. She moved smoothly and quickly, wasting no time, not waiting until the girl did whatever it was she had come there to do, but intending to stop whatever this was in its tracks.

But Dashini wasn't hanging about either – she made a sound, reached through the gap this made in the POQ, and used the Nathan Knife to hack at the metal shackles at his wrists.

She tried to catch his eye, to give him some sign that she was here to rescue him, but there was a loud bang, hurting her ears even through the POQ, which dulled most sounds, and the quarantine glass at her head knocked against her skull. It wasn't a hard knock, not a hammer blow, but it was disconcerting, and when she automatically glanced at the source of the knocking there was a ball of lead, glowing hot, dropping slowly through the viscous barrier between her and the world.

Bang, bang: two more balls of lead. The second one penetrated the barrier, taking advantage of the reduction in solidity Dashini had needed to give it in order to get her knife hand through to cut Nathan free. The second bullet didn't break her skin, but it caught between Dashini and the quarantine glass, burned against her, and because the gap was only a half inch, perhaps less, the hot lead had nowhere to go except to burn a trail down her face since it had been aimed at her head.

This was nothing compared to what Nathan was experiencing, but that doesn't mean it didn't hurt, and now Sharli was on her.

The assassin had never seen a quarantine before, didn't know what it was, but she knew what a gap was, and there was a gap in the glass through which Dashini's arm protruded, at the end of which was Dashini's hand, in the grip of which was a knife. Knives Sharli knew well: she dropped her pistol, grabbed Dashini's wrist, and, with a single sharp blow, twisted it back so that both bones snapped.

With a card sharp's dexterity, she caught the Nathan Knife by the pommel as it fell, pulled Dashini's arm through the gap in the POQ, and, with the efficiency of a Beaumont's butcher, sliced at Dashini's brachial artery – an injury that would have quickly put Dashini into hypovolemic shock if it had struck.

Rekka cut through the crust of the Earth as if it were water, as if it were air, and emerged on the relic field, drawn to that exact point where Dashini was, its summoner and its banisher.

With one huge, evolved, chitinous arm it batted Dashini, POQ and all, fifty feet into the air, so that she flew away. Without seemingly needing to look where the object of its fury was, the demon hurled itself at the place Dashini had flown to.

No longer beneath the ground, without the muffling of solid matter, the sense by which Rekka located Dashini would have liquified the girl if it hadn't been for the POQ, and even with it, its use burned Dashini's skin.

She drew her arm inside the quarantine, the pain in her wrist now only an afterthought, and she whistled the tone that would make the quarantine glass adopt its maximum solidity.

Only just in time: Rekka flew at her, colliding its broad, flat, featureless head against the POQ, pounding it like a hammer.

Dashini made herself breathe, made herself think, made herself use the thing that a demon doesn't have – understanding.

The lorgnette?

Useless.

The Prophylactic Prism Powder?

Useless.

The Nathan Knife?

The torturer had it.

The yellow whistle?

Probably useless.

How long does it take to think these things? Seconds were something that Dashini didn't recognise passing; it took as long as it took for Rekka to pound with first one fist, bigger than Dashini was, then another, which made the glass of the quarantine cloud with microscopic cracks, then, with its short, thick, powerful back limbs, to grip the POQ and unleash a blurring flurry of blows with every part of its body, screaming as it did it, blistering Dashini's skin with the power that she'd idiotically assumed was hay fever.

The Chalk...

Where was it?

When she'd gone through, she'd had the knife in her hand, so where had she put the chalk?

Rekka opened that slit between its chest and what passed for its head – it was like a mouth, but not quite – as wide as it would go. Rather than teeth inside, there had evolved grinding plates, like cogs of metal, like tunnel drills, meshing together and grating at terrifying speeds. The demon began to feed the POQ, Dashini inside it, into this maw.

Her jacket pocket! She reached in and there it was – but now what? The portal chalk required a perfect visualisation of the destination. It required space in order to draw the portal. What it didn't require was the destruction of the POQ, or the sense of being drawn into a meat grinder.

Think!

Dashini shut her eyes and silenced her thoughts. She pictured a place: the first place that came into her mind. Shouldn't that be the most important place?

She could see it.

Rekka's grinding plates caught – the glass of the quarantine was crumbling, but in the crumbling its remnants were getting stuck between the cog-like things that were now the demon's teeth. They had evolved to cut through rock, and this glass was stronger than rock, did not lose its strength as it crumbled, like rock did, wouldn't be rendered into sand.

The place that Dashini saw, that she could picture so clearly, was the Shadow King's kingdom. It was by the Door. It was where she sacrificed her Spark so that Prissy could leave.

Rekka's teeth ground to a halt entirely, but its rage didn't. It took the POQ, gripping it with its talons in the cracks it had made, and it began to dash it furiously against the rack on which Nathan was tied.

It was like when a thrush knocks a snail against a stone to crack its shell.

Dashini, inside the quarantine, was buffeted here and there, but her mind remained focussed – that was what she was good at, remaining focussed, mentally, in spite of danger and pain and fear. It wasn't a place she pictured. It was a person. It was a face.

It was Prissy.

Dashini took the chalk, and with Prissy's face in her mind she made the tone that loosened the consistency of the quarantine glass enough so that she could trace the outline of a door on the inside of the POQ.

Rekka felt the change, knew that its prey was fleeing, roared in its anger, bashed Dashini harder and harder against Nathan's rack until both cracked.

The demon did it again, and again, and it seemed as if it was going to do it for a third time, but then, for Dashini, there was silence.

One of the first things they teach potential Hailey-Beths cycling in the torturing specialisms of God Killing is that you don't let your subject die on the rack when you're in the field. While it's possible for liquid engineers to repair a corpse to a state under which it can be interrogated, that's a weft-intensive procedure that requires time, something which isn't usually available, and uses equipment that Resources won't allocate to a caravan, even for a named and numbered expedition. There's also a degradation that affects the reliability index of any information retrieved, and if that index score falls below a hard six, Ethics opt-outs are automatically revoked, with the obvious consequences that brings.

While Sharli wasn't charged with interrogating Nathan Treeves, but separating his nervous system from the weft, there was a similar prohibition against death, which brings telomeric fusing in the inward extension, making it harder to separate the nerve endings from the pseudo-conduits, and leaving corpse remnants prone to Theite Resurrection, even after total decomposition.

Neither of these reasons were why Sharli, when Rekka split Nathan Treeves's rack with the quarantine shell Dashini had established around herself, putting his life at risk, unsheathed the weft-knife and went to work. She did that because Nathan hadn't told her where Gam Halliday was, because she wanted that information, and because it looked like the demon might prevent her from getting it.

When a worker at Beaumont's needs to kill a pig, there are lots of ways of doing it, most of which depend on how the animal is presented, or presents itself, to the person charged with killing it. If the pig-killer is let into the stalls in the night, when the pigs are asleep, she can take her pig-sticker and stick the pigs at the base of their skulls. This severs their spinal cord, killing them instantly. They don't scream, they don't buck, they don't cause any trouble at all, and she can go from that pen to the next pen with the expectation of an easy time of it.

If, because the stall-man has been untidy, she trips on a bucket as she moves from one pen to the next, makes a clatter, and wakes one of the pigs that she has not already killed, so that it, smelling the blood of its relatives – most pigs in a pig stall are related by birth – panics and screams, she might still be able to use the pig-sticker on the spinal cord of that screaming pig if she is quick, but it will still wake the others.

When the others are woken she puts the pig-sticker in the one loop on her belt that is designed to hold it, and she takes a different knife, one more suited to the next method of killing. She approaches the pigs not stealthily, as she did before so that they don't wake, but roaring, arms spread, coming directly at them, using their panic to make them back off, or rear up, or in some other way expose this or that part of their anatomy the knifing of which will cause them to die.

There is an awful racket, one that she will hear complaints about from the men in the dormitories when they eventually come for their breakfast – black pudding and oats, mixed and heated with water to make a thin, red porridge – but the job still gets done.

Eventually she wipes her palms on her leather apron, tucks any hair that has come out of her ponytail behind her ear, sniffs, and goes to knock for the butchers.

Because Sharli had been a worker at Beaumont's she took advantage of the fact that the demon's back was turned and used the weft-knife on the place on Rekka where it appeared its spine, if it had one, might end. This was roughly between where its shoulders might have been, and under the wedge where what might have been its head was.

She had to jump up and find a handhold with her free hand to give her the right angle, and when she made contact even the touch of the thing was painful. It was like handling very strong bleach, or quicklime – a hot and scalding, sharp and corrosive type of pain.

Sharli ignored it, as she had been trained to do, and she sliced at the place on Rekka where the spinal cord might have been, beneath the thing's shell.

Using a weft-knife isn't like using a chef's knife, or a butcher's knife, or any kind of fighting knife. With all of those three there is resistance when the blade meets its object. A weft-knife meets no resistance at all; it simply slides here and there as if there is nothing but air where it cuts.

Occasionally, when Anatole had taken Sharli to a concert at which he was singing, he'd be accompanied by a group of musicians, and once or twice there had been so many musicians – too many, Anatole had reckoned, given the fee they were charging – that there was also a conductor to keep them all in order. A conductor has a baton, which he waves about in the air in time with the music, keeping everyone in tempo and pointing it at people he thinks should play louder or more softly.

When the conductor uses this baton, it effortlessly swishes in figures of eight in the air in front of him.

This is what Sharli did.

She swished and swirled, and the weft-knife made segments of Rekka's carapace that, because the demon's internal organs were under pressure, flew off like the lid will fly off a pressure cooker if the seal isn't quite perfect. Because Sharli had worked in the kitchens at The Commodious Hour, and because Mr Padge didn't like to pay for new equipment until the old equipment was demonstrably faulty, she was used to avoiding the flying lids of old pressure cookers. She was used to turning her face away from jets of steam, suddenly released, and to not being fazed by heat and danger and things that a civilian – this was how chefs thought of people who never worked back of house, because they thought of themselves as soldiers of a sort – would fear if they experienced them.

Rekka was too busy with its rage to register what Sharli was doing, and creatures with an exoskeleton – Sharli had dispatched ten thousand crabs, ten thousand lobsters, a million crayfish – aren't sensitive to things touching their backs, so it didn't turn its attentions on her, regardless of the damage she was doing.

There was no spinal cord for Sharli to sever because Rekka had no spine, and she knew better than to put her hand into boiling water – the liquid inside Rekka's shell was like a pot of tomatoes prepping for concasse – which she might have done if she saw something to grab and pull at.

So, what to do?

She decided to behead it.

No animal will survive a beheading, even if some animals will still move with an appearance of life after it is done. They always slump down eventually and let out a death rattle from their exposed pipes, so Sharli switched her grip on the knife and drew it effortlessly in a line that would trim the head from a pig and put an end to its struggling.

This was when the demon went silent and stopped smashing Dashini against Nathan's rack.

The blunt wedge of matter that might have been its head hinged forward, away from Sharli, like the lid of an inkpot hinges forward when your employer, pleased with your efforts, decides to take her quill and write instructions on a piece of paper that you are to take to the seamstress, asking her to run you up a new bodice and charge it to the company account.

Rekka's head hinged forward, and out from the space that left welled what might have been blood in a creature with a circulatory system that required it. It came up like boiling milk comes up in a pan, bubbling, almost in a sphere, until, when the surface tension breaks, it spills down the side and scorches where it meets the hob.

Sharli leapt back, had to remind herself not to wipe the blade on her thigh, and went to sheath the weft-knife.

But Rekka turned, letting the quarantine that no longer contained Dashini drop to the ground.

Sharli stopped sheathing the knife. She had seen this type of motion before, in pigs who, knowing their end is on them, turn desperately on the pig-killer. She launched herself forwards as the demon was turning.

Like an acrobat, she span with the weft-knife foremost, wind-milled with her arms outstretched, and in this way removed Rekka's left arm at what would have been the elbow in a man.

Because a spinning thing will continue to spin if it meets no resistance, and because a weft-knife finds no resistance as it slices between matter, Sharli continued to spin, coming back round so that, in the single motion, she also severed Rekka's left hind limb at what would have been its hip, sending the creature slumping over onto its side.

This slumping was something Rekka was not expecting, but because that was precisely what Sharli was hoping to achieve, she *was* expecting it, and because a person who is expecting something has an advantage over someone, or something, that isn't expecting it – this another fundamental tenet of the assassin's trade – she was able to use that advantage to cartwheel over to Rekka's right, taking the limbs off that side too.

507

No legless, headless pig poses any threat to a Beaumont's worker, and now Rekka posed no threat to Sharli, but because thoroughness is a natural good, whether you are a slaughter-house worker, a chef, or an assassin, she sliced the demon down the middle.

This done, she sheathed the knife.

There was the corpse of Rekka, though Sharli didn't know the demon by name, and there was Dashini's empty POQ. There was the broken rack and the disturbed relic field.

There was Nathan Treeves.

Sharli tucked a lock of her hair, which had become loose in the fighting, behind her ear. 'Where is Gam Halliday?' she said to Nathan.

Nathan said nothing, but his eyes, because he couldn't stop them, drifted towards the Door Dashini had drawn.

XIV

THE DOOR DASHINI had drawn opened at the base of the Golden Pyramid. No one who had grown up in the Kite Quarters could ever have mistaken it, and even though Sharli had been separated from the place by years, and thousands of miles, it was there before her now as if no time had elapsed, as if she'd never gone anywhere, as if she was still the same ten-summer-child who had been washed and oiled and praised and worshipped and granted the silver neckpiece.

Sharli reached for that neckpiece now, but it wasn't there.

She looked down at herself, at her hands, at the ring trophies, recreated at her request by the artists of the Assembly, silver and gold.

She reached up to her bare throat.

'It doesn't do to dwell, Sharli,' Mr Padge had said once. She'd started to tell him about her life in Malarkoi and he'd raised a finger – which meant 'wait' – and once he'd finished chewing the piece of meat in his mouth, and had wiped his lips with his napkin, he'd said, 'It doesn't do to dwell on the past. We both have histories in Malarkoi, and neither of us can do the slightest thing to change them.'

Sharli had blinked and blinked, each blink a substitute for the words that she'd wanted to say to him, but which she trapped behind her teeth.

'Forza!' he'd said, which was a word Sharli didn't know from any language.

Now Sharli felt her bare throat, let her hand fall and looked at the rings on her fingers, turned her hand over and back again. That night when the nail factory supervisor had come played out in her mind.

There he was, bloody and silent on the bed.

Here she was returning to his corpse with the inexplicable urge to take the rings from his fingers and to wear them forever as trophies.

Now in her chest there was a feeling, like the beginning of a sneeze. She reached for her bare throat with her jewelled fingers.

But it doesn't do to dwell.

'Forza!' Sharli said, and she strode forward into the Golden Pyramid, Tinnimam on her shoulder.

When the body and mind cross a boundary – a doorway, for instance, a great stone lintel, any portal – they draw a line under the moments before, preparing the self for the new thing that will necessarily be on the other side. Sharli entered the pyramid, and her body and mind drew a line under the moment before, when Padge's unknown exhortation had driven her forward, and she stopped. She slid forward an inch on the dust, so thickly did it lie at her feet.

There was no echo of the cries of Je, or of Berthe, or of Dorran, but the atmosphere of the place was such that Sharli heard them anyway.

When she had run away from the Pyramid, the other children had not come with her. She had not waited for them, or even looked back. Had Sharli thought about them once since that day? She couldn't remember if she had.

Now she did.

They would have been sent here, would have gladly come here, would have been, in their hearts, excited at the prospect of being taken to their heavens. Was this the corridor, dark and narrowing, along which the priests would have taken them?

Sharli traced a circle through the dust at her feet – there was one set of footprints, Dashini's, running into the darkness, but those were fresh. The footprints of Quise or Arjal would have been a decade old, as would be those of Ganax and whoever else had been chosen for the ceremony.

They would not have been running.

Sharli turned the rings on her fingers, suppressed the urge to reach for her throat.

When Mr Padge had said that it doesn't do to dwell, he hadn't gone on to explain exactly what he meant, other than the fact that it didn't change anything. When Sharli had thought about what he'd said, often, when she was alone in the night after work, she'd realised that there must be more to it than that.

Lots of things don't change anything, but we do them anyway, so that can't have been the only thing Mr Padge meant.

The thing that she decided he must have also meant was that it doesn't do to dwell because it gets in the way of doing the things we need to do. Dwelling on the past takes energy, takes focus, from what we need to do in the present.

Perhaps that was what 'Forza!' meant.

In the dark, narrowing corridor of the Pyramid, in which the voices of sacrificed children didn't echo, and along which Sharli could not see, except almost, glimpses of herself led by the arm, her neckpiece glinting in the flickering lamplight, to the opening of her throat, Sharli had a job to do. She had to kill Gam Halliday, to fulfil the contract Clementina Roads had signed on her behalf.

She had to revenge Mr Padge.

Would dwelling on the past help her or hinder her in this?

At a fork, where Dashini's footprints went one way and a corridor branched away in a different direction, Tinnimam jumped down from Sharli's shoulder and refused to follow. Instead, she peered into the darkness and scuffed at the ground with her forepaws. She squawked and scratched and kicked up the dust. She looked back over her shoulder and reared up.

If Sharli had never been separated from Tinnimam, she might have recognised this for what it was – an attempt at communication – a rapport having been established with the creature over long years, but the fact was that they had been separated. Longings, needs, desires, while powerful things, are no substitute for that familiarity and understanding that long years of co-existence bring. Once desires are fulfilled, there is an emptiness and blankness, a banality to the reality of having a thing one has long lacked, that is difficult to live with. Sharli had long wanted Tinnimam back, but now she had her it was inconvenient to pay attention to her needs.

The creature was pawing, scratching, squawking, refusing to follow, and here were the footprints Dashini had left behind which required following. So what if Tinnimam wanted her to go the way she wanted her to go? She had work to do.

Tinnimam would have to wait.

Sharli leant down to pick her up, as she had done all those years before, and for which the firebird attacked her. Sharli had the weft-knife in one hand, which she could not easily put down, now its guard was removed, so she could only use one arm to do it, and just like then, Tinnimam did not want to be picked up. She put her head down and backed into the dark corridor.

A good assassin puts their work before everything else.

While he was working, Anatole would not have wasted a moment attempting to force or cajole a firebird into doing anything. It would simply never have occurred to him. Nor would it have occurred to Deaf Sam. Simon? He would have killed the firebird to prevent the issue having arisen. It would have been unthinkable for the Druze to have got into that position. Montalban would have not only killed the firebird, but would have eaten it too.

Perhaps Sharli was not a good assassin, but neither was she any longer a girl. When Tinnimam backed off, Sharli took a strip off her jacket with the weft-knife, and used it to leash Tinnimam around the neck. She didn't risk the creature's beak and claws, but tied the strip of fabric to a belt loop and dragged the reluctant firebird along behind her.

Forwards.

Sharli stopped in a wide, stone-pillared hall, beside a fresco depicting the Mistress of Malarkoi, Tinnimam straining against her leash.

It was like the secret church, this place, the one Sharli had been taken to with the other children selected for sacrifice, the place where the priests had abased themselves before them. The stones were better cut, the pillars grander, the fresco more perfectly realised, but it was so like that other place that Sharli had to concentrate to clear the memory from her vision.

There was Ganax, thin and naked, lashing himself with a switch.

'I am not worthy of you,' he sobbed.

Sharli blinked the vision away, but in the corners of the hall, in the shadows, other visions were forming.

She reached for her pouch of quick-root, but it wasn't there. She reached for the opium, but that was gone too, left on the relic field, forgotten in the fighting.

An assassin knows to breathe when she is tense, and Sharli breathed now – five long and deep breaths.

On the last one, she cried out, 'Gam Halliday!'

If you shout a person's name they will turn to you by reflex. This is a useful thing to know, when you are paid to kill that person, particularly if you don't know exactly where they are.

Somewhere, in the depths of the Pyramid, there was a change in sound. Gam Halliday didn't call in response, or scream, but there was a small, almost imperceptible drop in the volume of the background noise, a variation in a susurrus that Sharli had until that point been unaware of, and she went towards this change at a run, so that Tinnimam had to flap and jump to keep up.

There was one corridor, then another, then, in the distance, a rectangle of light.

Sharli sprinted for it, knife at her side, and as it grew closer shadows shifted across it, until it became a room filled with people, into which Sharli stormed, silently, Tinnimam dragging after.

The people in the room – there must have been forty or fifty of them – all stiffened, eyes wide, turned to Sharli. She took in the scene in a moment, since that is what an assassin must do if she wants to live out the day. The ceiling was high, sloping from one side, out of which a skylight opened onto a slab of grey sky. There was a single exit opposite the door in which she was standing, giving onto a corridor like that through which she had come. In the distance, firebirds called to each other, but none were present here. Tinnimam heard them, went rigid, but Sharli wasn't paying attention to her.

Despite there being fifty people – fifty children – crammed into this room, they all had one or other face. One of the faces, worn by perhaps fifteen of the children, she recognised – it was Gam Halliday's, though now he had two eyes where all the intelligencer images she had seen had shown only one – but the other was some nondescript and genderless face she didn't know.

An assassin does not wait to attack their target, but neither does she rush into situations she doesn't understand. She looked from face to face, and they looked at her.

Perhaps they were decoys, these children, magical distractions a weft-manipulator throws up to confuse an enemy. Perhaps someone had made Gam Hallidays and his associates in vast numbers in their vats, and had gathered them all here.

'Gam Halliday,' she called again, though this time she didn't need to shout.

The Gams didn't say anything, but some of them – perhaps five – started moving slowly away from her, taking their nearest associates with them by the arm.

Then, in a rush, they stampeded across the room to the exit.

The Gams who didn't make for the exit ran here and there, pulling the others with them.

If they hoped to outrun Sharli, she couldn't be outrun, even encumbered by Tinnimam. She was inescapable, and the weft-knife could not be defended against. She went to the nearest Gam first, cut through his torso at a diagonal, the natural sweep of her knife arm letting the blade do the work. He didn't have time to scream, but fell into two pieces at the feet of an associate. That person did scream, but Sharli silenced them effortlessly, taking the top of their head off at the mouth, like someone who opens a breakfast egg to get at the yolk.

The next Gam she skewered through the spine, and the next through the heart, and it soon became clear that none of these children were armed.

Sharli knew where the corridor behind her led, but not where the corridor on the other side of the room went, so, to prevent the situation spreading out of her control, she stopped trying to kill anyone – though that isn't to say people stopped being killed, since anyone the knife touched was more or less likely to die – and ran instead across to the exit door. It is sensible to keep a killing site contained, or an assassin risks losing control of it.

Tinnimam tried to fly up to the skylight, but the leash was secure, and she was pulled along with Sharli, her feathers smearing in the blood left in the assassin's wake.

The five Gams who had run first were some way down the corridor, but it was dark, and the children they were dragging made them slower than Sharli. She pushed past, blocked the corridor ahead, and, her arms spread so that the fingers of one hand brushed the wall on her left, and the tip of the weft-knife sliced through the wall on her right, she walked back slowly towards them.

'Gam Halliday,' she said to the first Gam, whose own arms were spread as if this might protect the others with him. 'I am here to revenge your murder of Mr Padge.'

This seemed to puzzle the Gam. He stopped. 'Don't I recognise you?'

Sharli didn't care whether he did or didn't recognise her. She kippered him from groin to shoulder, which made the children with him rush her. She wasn't expecting it, but there isn't much an unarmed child can do against an assassin, and she slit their throats, one at a time, silencing them as easily as if they had been ten-summer sacrifices.

She paused at this thought.

Without realising she did it, she looked down at their dead fingers – they had no rings – and looked at their dead necks. If they'd had neckpieces, these necks were no longer able to support them.

Visions will come to you in the darkness. They will come to you in silence. They will come to you in the moments before sleep. When visions come like that, they are almost dreams. We can accept them in that way. We can understand them.

But when visions come in the light, noisy, busy daytime, where they have no right to be, they are much more difficult to accept.

Sharli looked down at the bodies of the children she had already killed, and there were Je and Berthe. There were Dorran and Quise. She knelt in amongst the dead, picked up a head that should have been a Gam, still soft, and it was Arjal.

She swallowed. She frowned.

Tinnimam make a strange and plaintive whining, and down the corridor, the children were fleeing.

When Sharli went back to the room from which she had come, a group of the Gams tried to ambush her, tried to drag her down to the ground, to suffocate her.

Sharli could not be ambushed.

She could not be suffocated.

Even unarmed, she knew a thousand ways to kill a child, and she had the weft-knife.

Though she had to keep shutting her eyes, and would stop for ten or twenty seconds, her forehead lined, her eyes glazed, she killed them all in the end.

Some of the Gams played dead, some of the others too, but she knew by the beating of the skin at their necks, at their wrists, at their temples, who was alive and who wasn't.

She dragged the knife through the living, her free hand at her throat, her own pulse quick and irregular, thudding.

Time passed, but not much of it.

When it was done, she left the room and stalked on through the Pyramid, avoiding the shadows.

Forza.

When an assassin is contracted to kill a person, they kill them and that is an end to it: they have been given the job to end a person's life, and once that is done their work is over.

Sharli walked down the corridor, keeping her eyes at the end of it, where light shone, and not at the peripheries, where visions proliferated, in her attempts to ignore them.

She shut her ears to Tinnimam's whining.

What is the principle behind the conclusion of an assassination, she asked herself. Is it that a specified person should have been killed? If that was so, then Gam Halliday had been killed. If that was the core of it, then her contract was fulfilled.

At the end of the corridor, double doors were closed ahead of her, making everywhere dark.

Sharli closed her eyes.

What if the principle behind the conclusion of an assassination is that a specified person should not have been left alive? The distinction was a technical one, but Sharli had learned to think technically during her cycle in God Killing. The subtle distinctions between definitions can be very important. If her contract meant that Gam Halliday should not be left alive, then she couldn't be sure her work was done. She had killed the first Gam Halliday, but he had still been alive. She had killed the second Gam, and there had been a third. The third was survived by a fourth. The fourth, a fifth.

And so on.

With her eyes shut, Sharli was suddenly surrounded by the ten-summer children, neckpieces glittering, reaching for her. She opened her eyes, but they were still there in the darkness of the corridor. Now even her ears betrayed her. 'Sharli,' the children whined. 'Sister.'

Sharli ran for the doors, hoping to put the children behind her, and she was relieved when they stayed where they were, in the darkness, their calls growing quieter with the distance she put between them.

The room behind the doors was clearly the inside of the top of the Pyramid. The walls sloped to meet at a point, and the floor mirrored this, like a dais, following exactly the same angle, stepped in exactly the same way, except where the walls were bare stone, the floor was thickly carpeted.

The way the room was built naturally led the eye up to the apex of the dais, but Sharli was trained to pay attention to each level, so that she didn't miss any threat.

At the top, sitting in a golden throne, was the girl Prissy, except that where in the intelligencer reports she had been shaven-headed, or wearing a bonnet, this girl had a storm of electric blue filaments streaming back from her scalp, and her eyes were the same: piercing, flickering, sparking across the irises.

Where the Prissy she had seen in stills was always wearing some grubby, worn, badly tailored slum clothes, this Prissy was all in perfect black, so matt that it was hard to make out her contours, except she was holding up one hand, palm out, that was both a sign that said 'welcome' and a sign that said 'stop'.

Sharli didn't want to stop – the ten-summer children were coming down the corridor behind her, their calls growing louder – but there was something about Prissy, some force of will, that made Sharli remain where she was.

On her left, smiling, was Dashini, while on her right, grim, was another Gam Halliday. These two were like courtiers, or advisors, or heirs – Sharli couldn't decide which – but it was clear who was the queen. At her feet was one of the genderless children, sitting cross-legged.

Without lowering the welcoming, stopping hand, Prissy raised her other, and from behind her throne, where they been out of sight, came a walking flock of heavenly brothers, burning brightly and trailing ash that burned up and sent embers glittering into the shadows.

There were a hundred of them, at least, and where Tinnimam was small and deformed, these were huge and perfect.

Tinnimam strained at her leash, and when Sharli went to wrap it around her hand so she didn't come loose, she saw that there was a long, straight, thin, deep slit down the firebird's side. The feathers there were perfectly sliced, the pale skin beneath perfectly cut, and blood leaked perfectly slowly down to splash on the carpeted floor.

Sharli dropped to her knees, mouth open, and when Prissy saw this she put down her welcoming hand.

'No heavenly brother will be leashed in my presence,' she said.

Sharli kneeled, and did nothing but stare, first at Tinnimam, and then at Prissy.

It was as if her mind had suddenly become blank, incapable of thought. She didn't even feel fear, or guilt, or pain. There was Tinnimam, with a wound from a weft-knife, a wound that would certainly prove fatal, and she couldn't think, or feel, or do anything.

She stared at Prissy, concentrated her attention on her and it seemed to the assassin as if the girl's electric blue eyes grew in her vision, filling the room, darkening the rest of the details of the place until they disappeared, and there were only those eyes, sparking, her hair, sparking, her will, sparking throughout the world.

'No heavenly brother will die in my presence,' Prissy said.

In one hand Sharli held the leash, and in the other hand there was the weft-knife, but there was nothing else except the Spark will of the new Mistress of Malarkoi.

Prissy stood and came towards Sharli. Her retinue remained where they were. Gam, Prissy, the genderless child, the firebirds: none of them moved.

Prissy's feet were bare, and her toes sank into the pile of the carpet. Her ankles were bare, and she carried no weapon. 'Cede the brother to me, so that I may ensure he lives.'

Sharli held out Tinnimam's leash, as if the words were a commandment, but then she remembered who she was, for whom she worked, what she was doing here and why, and she pulled the leash tight, dragged Tinnimam close.

'She is not a brother,' Sharli said, ignoring Tinnimam's cry.

Now Prissy ignored Sharli. She beckoned to Tinnimam, who, without a moment's hesitation, tried to fly to her. Sharli pulled the leash again, but Prissy turned her attention to its fabric. Her eyes blazed white and the leash burned away to nothing before it could stop Tinnimam. Prissy put out her arm, and the firebird landed on it, like a hunting falcon.

She whispered something in the firebird's ear, and Tinnimam rubbed her head against the demigod's face in a way she had never done to Sharli. Prissy traced one finger across Tinnimam's wound, and the blood stopped flowing.

There are protocols taught under the Assembly discipline God Killing that kick in when demigods are approached in the field. Hailey-Beth cycles are so rigorous that they bypass thought in emergencies, becoming something those qualified in them are, rather than do. Even plagued with visions, even working to her own ends, even unsure of whether her work was done, Sharli was a God Killer, so what she did was walk forward as her body had been trained to do, tightening the grip on her knife.

Prissy chucked Tinnimam under the chin. 'This heavenly brother is home now, in his proper place.' From the girl's fingertips there came the smallest possible spark of blue, a pinprick of light, and when it met Tinnimam, the firebird burst into flames, each of its feathers taking fire, transforming it from that dull and dusty brick red to a majestic and fearsome scarlet.

Sharli kept walking, slowly and steadily, and though what she saw made her tremble, she didn't tremble in her knife hand, the nerves of which were trained to ignore the mind, the muscles of which were trained to work independently of the self.

She kept walking, and the ten-summer children walked with her.

Black Bill walked with her.

Boland walked with her.

At her side was a herd of pigs.

At her side was Mr Padge.

Prissy turned her back on Sharli, and returned to the throne. If the demigod was concerned, she didn't show it, any more than she showed fear of Tinnimam's fire, which didn't seem to affect her at all. 'Go to your brothers,' Prissy said, and Tinnimam did just that, taking his place without hesitation amongst their ranks.

Sharli looked to Mr Padge. She knew he wasn't real. She knew he was a vision. She knew that she was alone in that Pyramid, but sometimes it doesn't matter whether things are real, or whether they aren't. Sometimes unreal things are more than real.

Mr Padge adjusted his cuffs. He took a piece of thread from his sleeve that may well have not been there at all. He dropped it onto the floor. 'Well, Sharli,' he said, 'what are we waiting for?'

Sharli turned, ignoring the Assembly God Killing protocols, ignoring the visions, and threw herself at Gam.

A God Killer of the Assembly cannot expect to kill a god without the help of a relic field. Without a relic field, the god will have to be met on their own territory, and that place will be imbued with their divinity, with their magic, and with the objects of their domination of the material realm.

Nor can a God Killer dispense with an attractant rack, because without one the god will be able to move in ways no person can account for. Gods are impossible things, they have impossible powers, and no matter how well trained a Crusader is, she'll never be a match for a thing that can do the impossible.

But a slum boy of Mordew?

A God Killer is more than a match for any of them.

Sharli threw herself at Gam, she didn't throw herself at Prissy.

Gods and demigods and weft-manipulators are notoriously selfish. They've taken themselves out of the realm of the real, made themselves different from everyone and everything else. To them, they have no equals, nothing even in the same category that they have made for themselves. They do not exhibit solidarity with people like them because there are no people like them. If others come close to being like them, their first response is to destroy those others. This fact is a basic tenet of God Killing.

Sharli shouldn't have had to worry that anyone would get between her and Gam Halliday.

Visions, phantoms, ghosts, hallucinations – they have no physical presence.

She threw herself at Gam, and she had every right to expect to make contact with the weft-knife, just as she had done with all the others.

The firebirds were too far away to stop her.

Nothing should have stopped her.

But when she raised the knife, stretched to embed it into the boy's heart, it didn't meet its target.

Instead, it hit Prissy in her shoulder, stabbing through the matt, black dress, and when Sharli went to drag it down, she found Prissy had her wrists, both of them, and that she was being held securely in place. The knife should have slipped down, but that was held in place too, jutting from Prissy's shoulder.

Up close, the girl's eyes were a pit of blue sparks, driven infinitely inwards, and from her hair, cold and ozone, a wind blew that chilled Sharli's lungs.

The girl's expression was entirely neutral. She wasn't angry, she wasn't fearful, she wasn't pained, and neither was she the opposite of those things. She was entirely something else, but Sharli couldn't understand what that something was.

'Let me go,' Sharli said.

Prissy did not let her go.

Sharli shifted her weight, tried to unbalance Prissy so she could wrestle the girl to the floor, find some method by which to murder her, but the child was like stone, unyielding and heavy.

'It won't work.' It was Dashini who spoke, coming to stand behind Prissy. Gam came with her, as did the genderless child.

'I know you,' Gam said. 'I used to watch you drinking and smoking out front of Padge's restaurant. I know what you do, too – all the nasty jobs even Anatole doesn't want. Offing babies and such. That takes a hard heart. But you're no match for her.' He looked at Prissy, and even he seemed discomfited by the girl, shocked at her power.

Sharli pushed forward as hard as she could; if she couldn't pull against Prissy, perhaps she could use the girl's weight against her.

Prissy didn't move.

'She's not who you think she is,' Sharli hissed, when it was clear there was nothing she could do to escape. 'When she went through the Door into the Pyramid, your Prissy was killed.'

Gam looked puzzled, as if the Soul Propagandas had got through to him, made him question everything. 'She's not who she is?' Gam said. 'Who does that make me then?'

'You?' Sharli said. 'You're Gam Halliday. You killed Mr Padge. I'm contracted to kill you.'

Gam smiled. 'Me? Look, I remember killing Padge. I stabbed him in the back. But if she's not Prissy, I'm not Gam, am I? I went through that Door. I've been killed and reborn a thousand times. If I'm not Gam, you can't be contracted to kill me, can you?'

Now Sharli looked puzzled, and a twitch pulled her mouth up at the corner so tightly that her teeth showed for a moment. She strained at her wrists, but Prissy was unyielding. Sharli glared at them all with a look that only assassins can give, as if they can see you dead, and know how to make it happen.

Now Dashini spoke. 'You followed me in through the Door I drew, right? If you believe what you're saying, Sharli is dead now, and you're just a copy too.'

Sharli didn't say anything, but Prissy did. 'Come with me.'

First they flew to Gleed, rushing through the air as if they were in a dream.

She was deep in the Collapse Zone, clearing a path through the chaos with wide sweeps of her mechanical arms and powerful kicks in all directions.

Prissy concentrated – Sharli could feel she was doing it by the pressure in her wrists, by the smell of sandalwood that unexpectedly filled her nostrils. 'Watch your Field Commander,' Prissy ordered, and because that was her command, Sharli did it.

Gleed drew to a halt, as if her mechanisms had seized, and stood rigid. Down from the sky, high, but still below Sharli and Prissy, she was pelted by the rain of heaven, but regardless of that she didn't move.

'She is receiving a transmission from deep in the Assembly,' Prissy said. 'It is about a city there, New Juda.'

Now it was Sharli's turn to tense.

Prissy felt it. 'You know the place?'

Assassins do not give up information willingly, but Prissy could read in the stiffening of Sharli's muscles that she did know New Juda. 'We will go there now,' Prissy said, as if it was nothing to travel half the world.

It wasn't quite nothing. The two of them left the Collapse Zone at a speed that blurred the world into smudges wherever Sharli chose to look. When she wanted to breathe, she couldn't, and if she tried to move, even to panic, the pressure from the air, as they forced their way through it against its will, made even the slightest movement impossible.

When that ended, at almost the extent of Sharli's ability to survive without breathing, but not quite, they were near the Parasite Wall, suspended in the air, facing the building that the Hailey-Beths in Resources had said contained the weft-generator. It was low and rectangular, regular and plain, and around it gathered that familiar swarm of Assembly people, that uniformly disparate body of persons, individual up close, entirely Assembly at a distance.

There was something wrong.

On one edge of the generator building, on the south east corner, there was a breach. When a mouse steals a piece of cheese it makes a breach like this in the block. It nibbles a piece off, and here there was a chunk missing. There were no mice there, though, only a squirming and writhing mass within of beaks and claws and red feathers, aflame and smoking.

'The Doors with which firebirds may be summoned are powered by the weft,' Prissy said. 'The machine inside is a conduit to that place. I have made a Door that draws its power from this conduit, and that summons firebirds through it.'

Heavenly brothers, once they had fed on the excrescences of the weft-generator, once they had had their fill, burst from the breach and flew high into the sky. When they reached the top of the circles they drew in the air, they tucked in their wings and bombed down wherever their urges took them.

When they met ground, buildings, gatherings of persons, their suicides left burning craters across New Juda.

Prissy turned to Sharli now, and very gently traced her finger around the assassin's neck, as she had done when she healed Tinnimam's wound. 'There is no longer any need for human sacrifice, ten-summer child,' she said. 'While this machine works, it will summon heavenly brothers to do my bidding, bloodlessly, which is to destroy those who would threaten Malarkoi.'

Now they went down too, drew closer. Here were Hailey-Beths from Prose, wideband broadcasting an emergency call that would alert all the martial designates, even Gleed, and force them to return to defend their territory.

'Every city in the Assembly has such a generator. Now every city has a firebird Door.'

As quickly as they had arrived, and as breathlessly, they returned to the Pyramid, except this time Prissy followed the route of the caravan, which was retreating, hurriedly marshalling its resources, chaotically, inefficiently, pulling back from the Vanguard, dropping poorly secured material as they went.

Sharli tried to speak, but there was no air for her to breathe. Prissy was unfazed, drawing her power directly from the weft, but Sharli did not have that privilege, and her wrists were always held tight, so that she could not kill this girl, or harm her in any way.

Soon they were at the God-chamber breach, into which firebirds were pouring.

Mercifully, Prissy paused here, and Sharli could breathe again.

'That creature was the weftling,' Prissy said, not noticing or caring that Sharli had come so close to suffocation. 'Its corpse was under the control of the Master, and while it was present in the world, it was a threat to Malarkoi. See...' Prissy made Sharli look at the body.

The heavenly brothers were stripping it, piece by piece, alighting on it, and tearing at it. Though no single one of them could survive the contact with godflesh, there were thousands of them. One by one they took something of the weftling – a piece of skin, a piece of fat, a piece of bone, organ, vein, nerve – and before the brothers burst with the potency of it, they flew away.

When you come across a mushroom in the forest, and it spores; when you put wet wood onto the fire, and it splutters sparks; when a firework explodes in greens and blues and reds: it was like that, these creatures darting away from the weftling corpse, bursting in the God chamber, bursting over the districts of Mordew, bursting where the slums had been, the Merchant City, the Pleasaunce.

Prissy stared at the scene, her blue eyes blazing, her hair crackling, the dull black fabric of her dress rippling in the wind, the knife embedded in her shoulder.

When she had had her fill of triumph, they left again.

When Prissy reached the Collapse Zone, she at last let go of Sharli's wrists, but the assassin was not freed, nor did she fall.

'I have surrounded you in glass,' Prissy said, 'just as the Master of Mordew surrounded Dashini. Watch.'

Ahead, the Shadow King reared, his suns behind him, and Prissy surrounded him in glass too. It was almost invisible, this new type of quarantine, except for a flickering, a corona of scarcely perceptible colour, like the glint on the surface of strong, clear liquor when you raise it for a toast in candle-light, but it contained the Shadow King so entirely that his influence ended at its boundary. In Sharli's mind, a pressure she had not realised was present was suddenly released, and when she looked at the world it was different somehow; less oppressive.

Then Prissy did the same to Japalura. She didn't make sounds, or gestures; she didn't seem to exert herself in any way. Nevertheless, the dragon god was quarantined in glass, against which it railed, ineffectively, to the utmost limits of its power.

Then the White Stag and the Wolf Pack.

Then Cren and Vigornia.

They were all surrounded in quarantine glass.

Then, because that was not enough, Prissy made heavens for these gods, and she placed them into them.

This was an effort for her, but it was not an effort she made in the material realm; it was work done by her avatars, thousands of them over thousands of years, in realms that progressed time differently from the material realm. They were superhuman efforts such as no person had ever made, but they undid the work of the weft-bomb as silently as it had carried that work out.

'These gods I will install in their own heavens,' Prissy said, as if it was entirely obvious and simple, 'and the chaos they have made of the world I will isolate in glass.'

The land that had been ruined by the Collapse Zone was surrounded in a sphere of invisible glass which was so large Prissy had to move them up into the clouds to make way for it.

There she held them, so high that the sky was scarcely blue it was so black.

She turned to Sharli, her eyes blazing. 'Do you see my power, and how little you can do to prevent it?'

Sharli would have raised the weft-knife, would have followed her training, but the knife was in Prissy's shoulder, and it wouldn't have made any difference.

There was no relic field, no rack, no warmth, no air.

The sphere within which Prissy had enclosed the Collapse Zone shone suddenly blue, everything inside scoured to light, but all Sharli could see was Prissy's eyes, burning, her hair sweeping back like lightning in the darkness above the world.

The intensity of Prissy's glare was too much. Sharli shut her eyes.

When she opened them again, she was in the New Golden Pyramid of Malarkoi: Prissy's Pyramid.

Perhaps this had all been a vision too, perhaps they had gone nowhere, because the girl did not seem to have moved. There was the knife in her shoulder, the tear in her dress.

Her entourage were unmoving, precisely where they had been. Gam was there, the genderless child was there, Dashini was there. They looked at each other, these three, and it seemed in that moment that some unspoken communication passed between them that only Sharli saw. Assassins can tell when people are plotting – they need to know when others intend secret violence, and they need to know whether it will be directed at them. These three were plotting, exchanging silent words with their eyes… but Sharli was not their target.

It might have been nothing.

Prissy shook Sharli's wrists, recaptured her attention.

'I will give you a choice,' she said, and at last released Sharli's wrists. She pulled the weft-knife from her shoulder and held it out. In the palm of her other hand there was a key. 'If you wish to use the knife to try to kill me, you need only take it. If you do, I will have your firebird attack you first.' She lifted her chin and Tinnimam came to her side, burning brightly. 'If you defeat him, you might then be able to kill Gam, though I will do my best to prevent both things.'

Sharli tried to see in Tinnimam's face, in her demeanour, any hint that she would not do what Prissy would command her to do, but she could see nothing except a strange, thoughtless, animal adoration.

She turned to the others, but they were obscured by the firebird.

Prissy held out her other hand. The key was new and clean and shining. 'This key is to the Door to your heaven. If you choose it, I will give you all of the things you desire. Everything and anything.'

Prissy stood waiting, Tinnimam glared, the other children were out of sight.

Sharli closed her eyes.

There were the ten-summer children, the slaughtered pigs, the men of Mordew. With them, now, was the nail factory supervisor, his face ribbons of flesh behind which his teeth were gritted.

Sharli had had a similar choice, long before, between two objects: the upholstered nail and the moisturiser, between violence and passivity. She had left the choice to fate then – she was only an ignorant child – but it had decided the course of her life.

The vision of the nail supervisor would have come forward, but Mr Padge stopped him with a hand on his shoulder. What that gesture meant – whether he did it as a kindness to the supervisor, or as a reprimand, Sharli couldn't tell – but Mr Padge came and stood in front of her.

She could see him in every detail: the way his velvet suit strained at its stitches, the outline of the talisman underneath his jacket, the shine on his aubergine lips. There was about him the faint whiff of butter and hair oil.

'Well, Sharli,' Padge said, 'what are we waiting for?'

XV

NATHAN LAY on the relic field, unmoving.

His cheek was flat against the ground, his nose propping up his face, one eye pressed shut and the other fixedly staring. The mud was made of the objects of his life, powdered, and the concepts of these Nathan could see in outline – his pillowcase, the lungworm medicine, the rotten wood of the shack he had lived in, the paper boat his father had once sailed through a stream in the slums, rats, flukes, crenellated things, tentacled things, things like parts of the body, alone, separated from their functions, agglomerations of these parts, forced together incorrectly. He saw these things because they were in front of his unclosing eye, that eye being an organ sensitive to light, and these patterns being made from light reflected off the ghost surfaces of his relics, his only partially severed optic nerve still capable of communicating sensation, his mind still capable of receiving ideas.

That was the only reason he saw them: he had no desire to see, had no interest in seeing, made of the sensations no meaning, took no significance from them, cared nothing for them, felt nothing of them.

A wind blew up, coming over the distant sea, salty and cold, ruffling Nathan's hair, filling his shirt like a sail fills. Where Sharli had left wounds, these had bled, and that blood had seeped into the fabric of Nathan's shirt. When that seepage had dried it had made scabs, and these scabs were attached to his wounds and also to the cotton threads of his shirt. When the wind filled his shirt as it would fill a sail, this filling pulled at the scabs which anchored the shirt onto Nathan's skin like a sail pulls at its rigging.

An upholstered chair, studded in places, filled and wadded, is the same, if more regular and neat: the patterned fabric of the chair was Nathan's shirt, the air in the shirt was the wadding in the chair, his scabs were the studs.

Nathan's trousers, ragged though they were and soiled, were resistant to the wind, but Nathan's bare feet were blue in the cold. His hands, the fingers forming untidy fists, were stiff.

He resembled, down there, a discarded shopfront mannequin. Perhaps it had once been used to advertise clothes for boys, but had now been superseded and was left out for the refuse men to collect.

Clouds above, unseen by Nathan, darkened.

It started to rain.

An alifonjer cannot move quietly. Its great size, and the ratio of its weight to the surface area of its foot, means that its approach is accompanied by thumping concussions of the ground. Deaf people can feel it coming. If you're asleep, it will wake you up. Four of them, coming together? Even Nathan knew they were coming.

Out from the Collapse Zone they came, having no interest in the events there, leaving the Angelic Army behind them.

They had been looking for Nathan, tracing his progress as the rack dragged him to it, and now they found him.

He didn't roll over to watch them approach – this was more than he could do – but that wasn't necessary: once the bull alifonjer arrived, it rolled Nathan over with one tusk, roughly.

It could have used its trunk and rolled the boy gently, and the choice not to do it was an indication of what was to come, easy for you or me to recognise, but Nathan did not recognise it.

Torture, racking, nerve-removal: all these things have a deadening effect on the body and mind. When someone has been attuned to a crescendo of ever greater suffering, it is impossible to give anything other than increasing pain any attention.

What does a shopfront mannequin know of the world anyway?

What does a puppet know of the world once its strings have been cut?

What does a discarded tool know?

The alifonjer stood above him. Now Sharli had severed Nathan's connection to the weft, it was grey again, as it had once been, smaller than it was in angel form, more crooked, duller and dusty, the conduit to the inward light having been interrupted.

Still, though, it was a formidable creature.

Step back and here it was, looming huge over the prone boy. Its head was angled down, the tips of its tusks like the points of enormous ivory sabres, its great, deep, angry breaths moving them in circles.

The alifonjer took a half step forward.

That half step wasn't far, but it was enough to drive the blade of one of the tusks into Nathan's side. This tusk pushed through the boy's skin, through the sac that contains the organs in a person, through a kidney, between the loops that make an intestine, and met the spine. From there it pushed the boy a few inches across the dirt.

Bone meeting bone made a scaffold solid enough to move him.

If the bull alifonjer had ducked his head a little, stepped a little forward, it could have hooked Nathan up from inside. Perhaps it could have tossed him into the air. Perhaps it could have skewered him, but the dam alifonjer stopped him, butting her husband with her forehead.

The bull pulled its tusk out instead.

Blood pooled on the ground at Nathan's side, and the two creatures looked at it.

Animals are not without conscience. At the sight of blood, when they have caused it to come out, they can be chastened, not knowing quite why, but feeling a sympathy for the wounded thing they have made. This is a useful psychological fact, in the wild, since animals rely on each other, and their clumsiness can sometimes cause damage that has no use to them, or is counterproductive.

That was not the case here, and there is a counter tendency that the presence of blood can evoke: frenzy.

Frenzy has its own uses in finishing off a foe decisively.

The dam roared in the way that her species was known for – making a trumpeting scream with her mouth and trunk – and she stamped down on Nathan's head, scraping his scalp open with her sharp-nailed and fused toes, pulling one side of his face from his skull so that the bone was white beneath, and his features slumped on the left side like someone who has taken a stroke, but worse.

She stamped again, roared again, and now the older of her children came up from behind, emboldened. With its trunk, not fully grown but still long and strong enough to wrap around Nathan's waist, it took him into the air. It raised up onto its hind legs, like a rearing stallion, and with all its force it slammed Nathan back down to the ground.

By chance, the boy now lay on his back, looking up to the sky.

Rain fell onto his cheeks.

Raindrops ran down from his eyes.

The last alifonjer, the smallest, the one who had once been puzzled at the murder of his family, and whose trunk had made a question mark soon burned to dust by Nathan's Spark, came to where Nathan lay.

Nathan was a boy, this creature was a boy, and, if this thing was possessed of the mind of a person it might have understood that Nathan's fate, to be here before him, was the just consequence of a tendency to violence, a use of power against the weak. Now that the tables were turned, the calf might have understood Nathan's situation in its generality, used the wider applicability of this generality to guide its own actions, knowing that no lasting good can come from revenge and brutality.

Animals, though, do not possess that nicety of thought, and instead this creature, who even as a child was hundredweights of flesh, walked across Nathan's broken body, pressing first on an ankle, then on both knees, then on the hips, with the hind leg now crushing the other ankle.

Then it stepped with first one, then two forefeet on Nathan's ribcage, the rear feet cracking Nathan's knee bones.

Here the smallest alifonjer stood, its weight forcing the blood from the tusk wound at Nathan's side, so that it gushed into the dry mud, wetting it. The blood from Nathan's scalp wet the ground at his head.

The calf watched him, his weight preventing Nathan from drawing a breath, even if the boy had wanted to.

Does an animal understand that it must deprive a boy of his breath for as long as it takes for the air to fail his brain if it wants to kill him?

It does not need to know, since it can instinctively tell a dead thing from a living thing, and it need only wait until the thing it sees beneath it is dead before it steps away.

Nathan, as much of him as remained, could hear the breath of the calf, could feel that breath on his torn face, could see the flabby 'v' the alifonjer's mouth made, the hairs on its lips rustling as it drew air in, and then expressed it.

Was there some remnant of the Spark Nathan could have brought to bear at this moment?

He felt that there might be. The Itch was in there, in his broken bones and pierced organs. Sharli had been interrupted before her work was done, so perhaps the racking hadn't achieved what she had said it would achieve.

Perhaps he could have summoned the Spark again, burned the alifonjers away.

But Nathan was, still, the Master of Waterblack, and so was bound by its laws.

His Sparkline Actuary had required a vow, the tally marks on the alifonjers' window having one extra stroke for cruelty. Nathan had quietly vowed then, at the accounting, that he would let the alifonjers have their revenge when the time came.

Even if he had not made that vow, or if Waterblack was gone and its laws rendered irrelevant, Nathan did not have the heart in him to burn this calf away. He saw himself in it, exceeding an animal in his capacity for sympathy and understanding.

Nathan would not have burned it, even if he could have done so.

Better to die, he understood now, than to be a devil.

And so it was that Nathan made recompense for all his dead in a way satisfactory to the ordinances of Waterblack, the City of Death, by making his life a sacrifice that atoned for his violence. If this feels like a failure to you, what would you have had him do? Kill again that infant creature? Kill again its family? Should he have risen up and found some way to kill everyone, everything, in order that he should win back his godhood?

What would he do with it?

The boundaries of Waterblack describe a city almost unprecedented in its size. Its Actuaries have overseen the construction of buildings sufficient to house their Masters' unavenged dead in its streets, and quarters, and districts. Yet, within the City of Death, there is nothing that could satisfy Nathan Treeves, nothing he could exert himself to achieve. A boy like him only wishes to be loved, and no amount of death can achieve that.

Once, in the slums of Mordew, when he was too young to know better, his father made a boat for him from paper and cat bones. Together, hand in hand, they sailed it down a river of ordure and rainwater.

Who would Nathan have to kill to make this happen again?

XVI

BUT THEN, up in the sky, there was a hot fluttering.
There was a screeching.
Down came a firebird of Malarkoi to the relic field,
sent by Nathan's friends to find him.

It landed, hissing in the mud the rain had made of the dust.

There it stood over the dead boy and raised its wings in a
great, protective umbrella of burning, red feathers.

XVII

A T THE COMMODIOUS HOUR, the afternoon light was waning into night, the braziers taking over the burden of illuminating the remnants of a meal: mussel shells dusty with emptied pipe ash, hardened crusts of bread, congealed sauces, smeared napkins. Around the table there was that particular mixture of lassitude and irritation that is common amongst addicts; everyone was tired by their prandial overindulgence, yet they knew they would have to rouse themselves soon to attend to their thirsts.

Sharli ran her tongue over her dry teeth, blinked her dry eyes, sniffed.

There was Anatole, fastening and unfastening his cufflinks; Simon, smoothing his whiskers; the Druze, folding a cigarette paper into a flower.

Sharli reached between them for a bottle, but it proved to be empty.

'What time is it?' Deaf Sam said with his hands.

Sharli signed, since she could see the clock from where she was and Deaf Sam couldn't, 'Five and twenty past five.'

He shrugged.

Late for him? Early? Sharli couldn't tell.

Over the shoulder of Mick the Greek, a waitress approached with an empty tray, and because Sharli knew what it was like to work for a living, she sat up. With the concentration a person who would like more opium demonstrates, knowing their hands will be liable to the shakes, she carefully moved the empty dishes together into a pile so that the waitress might more easily take them back into the kitchen for washing.

Tinnimam stirred under the table, stretched, accidentally dragged the claws of her back foot across the hem of the Druze's wide trousers.

They pulled a face, the neuter assassin, as if they would assassinate the firebird given half a chance.

537

Sharli stopped her clearing of the table, and reached down to stroke Tinnimam's dull, red feathers. While she stroked, she gave the Druze a warning glance which said, 'Try it.'

Sometimes – perhaps even often – an exchange of glances like this between these two would escalate. Once or twice, they had faced off over the half-finished entrées, the desserts languishing untouched.

Today, though, they were interrupted.

At the back of the courtyard in which The Commodious Hour served its al fresco diners, there was a door. It was the kind of door that gives onto a shed, or a woodstore – neither inviting nor off-putting, but simply inconspicuous – and this door opened a crack. Because the assassins who dined at this restaurant knew that this was the door to the office of their employer, Mr Padge, they all turned at the sound of its opening, forgetting everything else, interpersonal animosities included.

As the waitress cleared the table, and Tinnimam returned herself to sleep, the assassins watched the door. It had opened a crack, drawing their attention, but now it stalled in its progress. It was clear that Mr Padge was behind it with his hand on the latch, because it moved very slightly backwards and forwards, probably with his breathing. An assassin can recognise that kind of thing because it is important in their work. Knowing whether a person is behind a door, with their hand on the latch, breathing, can be the difference between the successful completion of a job and a tedious chase through the streets. It can mean the difference between life and death, if the party behind the door comes suddenly out, crossbow in hand, and fires a bolt into the crowd.

Sharli watched the door.

The waitress cleared the plates.

Tinnimam snored.

The sun sank, reddening the sky, the braziers seemed to brighten, and Sharli knew Mr Padge would emerge, sooner rather than later, with a job.

This, though she had agreed to forget it, was heaven for her.

APPENDICES

A Consideration of the
Dynamics of the Collapse Zone

IN WHAT ORDER were nested intermediate pyramid realms collapsed into the material realm when a prototype Assembly weft-bomb was detonated close to the magical city Malarkoi? Which realm took precedence?

There are answers to these questions, but are we qualified to understand them once they are provided? Have we cycled in the Hailey-Beth specialism Weft Dynamics? Have we been seconded to the Sleepless? Have we, over the course of weeks of long nights in the rooms of Field Commander Gleed – which resemble an engineering workshop more than they do a person's living room, kitchen or bedroom – gone over the advanced mathematics required to understand the operations of a zone-collapse initiator?

We have not.

The nested pyramid realms of the Mistress's Golden Pyramid of Malarkoi were complexly arranged, not chaotically, but only a mind of suitable complexity could hope to understand the order inherent in what would seem to us to be randomness.

This is true of all very complicated things – they require a mind of similar complexity to resolve them. Lesser minds cannot see a pattern when that pattern is so large that it exceeds their ability to encompass it.

Think of a string of numbers that, for a trillion numbers, seems to progress with no significant repetition. To this string a mathematician turns their attention.

It is beyond them, in the span of years allocated to their life, to even know what these numbers are, specifically, a trillion things of any kind being impossible to experience even if each thing is only experienced for that smallest fraction of a second required for it to be experienced.

That fraction of time, multiplied by a trillion, is longer than a person lives.

And, because a person's mind is a thing that has developed to facilitate their experience of their life, the mind has no ability to contain such a variety of things, even if they could experience them in the time available to them.

Indeed, it is more useful for the mind to know a few things in great detail, not a very large number of things in very little detail, so the mind has developed into a machine with which only a few things can be known at once. Try memorising a hundred numbers and you will find yourself unable to do it, without some special technique that enormously increases the amount of information you are hoping to contain. Then look very closely at a ladybird with a magnifying glass – you will find you can resolve that insect with enormous subtlety, this kind of discrimination being useful in determining, amongst other things, whether an object is, or is not, edible, something that is very useful in a world in which food is scarce and the continuation of life depends on it.

But what if, to return to the mathematical example given, after a trillion numbers the numbers repeat, starting with the first number and progressing identically. When the string is complete, it begins again, then again, and again, a trillion times?

The mathematician would never know this, having died long before they had the chance to recognise the pattern.

Only a thing capable of experiencing a trillion, trillion things could see the order in that, something that to a less long-lived being would seem like randomness.

So it was with the logic behind the progression of the weft-bomb's collapse of the nested intermediate realms that had previously made up the Golden Pyramid of Malarkoi, unless that logic was correctly explicated under the auspices of the Hailey-Beth specialism Weft Dynamics.

There is a map of the Collapse Zones in the book you are now reading, although in poor condition having been retrieved from the battlefield, and it shows the material realm equivalents of the intermediate realms as a number of squares.

This map is not at all accurate – it is an impossible task to contain a higher number of dimensions in a lower one – but it may be referred to in a pinch, as it was in use, since some of the information is helpful.

Similarly, one might pick up a copy of the previous book in this series and remind oneself of the progress of some of the protagonists of that book through the series of gates that led to the realm known there as Malarkoi Proper.

The smallest of those realms, that of Vigornia, the claustrophobic and overcrowded realm of the cattle-headed people, collapsed under the influence of the weft-bomb into the realm of Cren, god of the person-headed snakes, which overlapped it.

Into that realm was forced, falling from the sky, the herd of the cattle-headed people, a great, pungent, lowing, screaming rain, blinking in the light.

If it had not been for what happened next – that that realm of the person-headed snakes collapsed into the realm that, in its turn overlapped it – the disciples and heretics of Cren would have turned away from their civil war, looking up in appalled disgust. They would have directed their aggressions on their ancient victims, both sides of their pointless dispute finding common ground in their animus towards the falling Vigornians.

It would be wrong to assume that Vigornia's realm collapsed into Cren's realm because there was room enough for the latter to contain the former, though there was, because if there had not been room then the collapse would have occurred at scale, the cattle-headed people and their world shrinking into Cren's realm, or Cren's realm expanding to accommodate it, depending on the perspective. In any case, all the people and things of Vigornia's realm tumbled down from the sky, since one place was at an elevation above sea level higher than the other, and this elevation was preserved across the intermediate realms, that being a magical convenience, since to alter the elevation would have been costly of the Mistress's Spark, a commodity she valued and had learned not to waste.

Was there a time, universal to the Pyramid realms and the material realm, at which this dissolution and incorporation seemed to take place?

No, there was not.

Time progresses irregularly across disparate realms, and the weft-bomb was not attuned in a way that would have isolated an instance common to the realms it was collapsing. While there was a logic to exactly which instant in Vigornia's realm collapsed into exactly which instant in Cren's realm – the equation was based almost entirely, but not completely, on which instant in those realms the maximum possible Spark energy was present, and also how much matter – this logic is too complicated to give here.

Suffice it to say that cattle-headed people tumbled flabbily from the sky onto, amongst other places, the rue Barbauld, and down with them came Vigornia, huge and lowing, and in its cowardice it rampaged here and there, looking for a place sufficiently large to hide it, knocking down the buildings the person-headed snakes had prided themselves on building.

The god found no shelter, and it stampeded across the city, killing as many of its own followers as it killed person-headed snakes, its panic only ending when Cren's realm collapsed into Japalura's realm – and this at the moment in the heydays of that place, before the Roi de l'Ombre turned the dragons' minds to death – and then only because it was replaced by an even more violent anxiety on the part of Vigornia.

Into the skies where Japalura and her dragons flew, millions of them, she the greatest, miles long, wings that darkened the world below and made every dragon fly up to the sun, down amongst them fell the cattle-headed people and their crumbling Hollow Hill, their cowardly god. With them fell the person-headed snakes and their streets and cathedrals and pavilions and palisades, their boulevardiators and towers. While the heavier of these things crushed some of the smaller dragons as they fell, the larger ones snapped the person-headed snakes out of the air and swallowed them, bit the cattle-headed people in two.

Japalura, with a swish of her tail, destroyed the falling cathedrals, breathed holy fire on Vigornia, scorching the god but not killing it, and all of the people of the lower two realms would have perished, eventually, if Japalura's realm itself had not been swallowed into the realm of the Wolf Pack and the White Stag, all of everything coming immediately into that place, falling at daytime to find the wolves massacring the Druids, tearing them to pieces, the Stag sleeping, Gam Halliday fleeing, for the thousandth time.

The god wolves, who now had new prey, leapt up and took snakes and cattle and small dragons from the sky, and tore them to pieces with great shaking bites that pulled flesh from bone with a divine and inescapable fury that should have woken the Stag.

Except that realm collapsed into the realm of the Roi de l'Ombre, his suns casting evil shadows on all of it, his form risen high in the sky, dwarfing even the huge size of Japalura. He would have made them all suicide by the force of his evil will, if his realm had not then collapsed into Malarkoi Proper, taking his suns and putting them into the sky of the Mistress of Malarkoi.

She was huger than them all, naked and seated, but this invasion made her rise to her feet.

Now the ripples of the weft-bomb collapsed the heavens that she had painstakingly created for her people – the heavens of Dumnonii, the heavens of the chosen, Joes' heaven, a hundred thousand heavens that all disgorged their occupants in one terrible surge of coming into being.

Even the Thousand Million Flames were released from their place, living now since that was when they had the most Spark, so that the air was filled with screaming babies all plummeting from their dark seclusion, down onto the Mistress's earth.

Amongst it all her firebirds screamed in the chaos.

Then that realm itself collapsed away, and all the denizens of all the realms, all their gods, every brick of every pyramid, every dragon, every clod of earth, every piece of crumbled cathedral, every unnatural sun itself collapsed into the material realm.

Down onto the ground, reconciling the unreals with the real in furtherance of Gleed's Atheistic Crusade, rained a terrible storm that stained the world.

◆

Those adult people who lived after their storming down to the ground – and there were large numbers of these, the dead who preceded them forming a kind of cushion, after a while, of compactible matter onto which they could fall without fatally wounding themselves – had never experienced anything that would prepare themselves for this situation.

It was like the hell that had been drummed into them before they had ascended to their heavens, a rapture in reverse.

There, amongst the dead who had been promised eternal life by the Mistress of Malarkoi, people lay broken in mind and body, not knowing whether this was a dream from which they might wake.

The children knew less than the adults, and though that can be a benefit when something new occurs, the young having become acclimatised less irredeemably to the worlds they knew, any advantage this might have given them was negated by the atmosphere of fear that death, destruction and violence surrounded them with.

Their lack of acclimatisation was also a lack of defence against frightening things.

They stared about themselves, eyes wide, searching for the returned gaze of someone who might understand what it was they were seeing.

They found no one.

The Thousand Million Flames: what could they understand?

Because they were taken from their realm at the moment of its maximum Spark energy, they were spared Nathan's slitting of their throats, but they died in enormous numbers, falling and striking objects, cracking their delicate skulls, breaking their overburdened necks. They fell amongst corpses, and those that lived understood only that they were in pain. They wailed as their kind will: infant people, infant person-headed snakes, infant dragons, infant cattle-headed people, infants of all kinds screamed in the manner of their own kinds.

They lay, screaming, ten, fifty, a hundred deep on any land they met.

Which is to say nothing of those that went under the water, breaking the surface and gasping, reflexively, so that they replaced the air in their lungs with water, undoing their buoyancy. They drifted down – infant, child, adult – down to the depths. The light left their eyes in a mirror of the Spark that left their bodies.

All of them drowned in perfect ignorance of what was happening.

Were the gods any better?

We might think that they ought to be omniscient, all-powerful, immortal. But a god is a thing of its realm. It knows everything about the place of which it is the prime mover, but it cannot know about things that exceed its everything.

Gods believe, in their realm-bound omniscience, that there is nothing else for them to know. Or to be aware of.

If they had known that there was anything else, they would have turned their appraising understanding to it.

Thereby it would have been known.

But Japalura, god of dragons, knew only the realm of dragons, and the Wolf Pack and the Stag knew only the bare hill and the forest, the places proper to them, and so also Cren and Vigornia. The gods were ignorant of this material realm, suddenly present in it, and knowing, in a moment, that their previous all-powerfulness had been limited by their inability to know anything outside of their all.

There was one exception to this: Le Roi de l'Ombre, he who had sent out his influence across the realms of the Pyramid and thereby turned them towards death.

He had long known there was somewhere other than his sunlit realm. In his expectation he had begun to imagine what the other realms might be like, and while imagining a thing is not the same as knowing a thing, it is a good preparation for coming to know it.

Here he was, in the material realm, and there were his suns in the sky, and though almost everything was different to how he imagined it, a difference is a thing.

If one expects to see apples and instead one sees cannon-balls, one knows not to eat them, and the understanding that there might be things other than those things over which one has control is a significant understanding, since otherwise one might be fooled into imagining that the things of one's new experience are a kind of delusion, and waste valuable time and resources in the disavowing of them, rather than usefully adapting to them.

It is for this reason that the Shadow King was first to establish his rule over the material realm, drawing his suns up to their noon, so that his shadows cut across the world, black and coloured wedges of his influence within which all living things were subject to his malice.

It is true that he had turned the minds of the other realms to suicide, but that was when he was trapped, when he was preparing the other realms for his coming by destroying the things within them, but now he was here he understood that other negative emotions were useful to him – anger and despair and fear and murderousness – and these feelings he forced into the minds of all those who met his darkness, whether they were children, or babies, or adults, regardless of which species.

The urge for suicide is turned inward, by definition, but fury and the desire to kill need an object, and this object the Shadow King knew was the Assembly, so he chose this enemy for his growing army.

Who knows if he would not have been successful?

A god who controls suns and can provoke his disciples into killing rages is not something to be taken lightly, all the more so when Japalura's dragons flew through his shadows, each of them darkening in their miens when they did it, snarling, turning in flight, in the air, rushing as one away towards where the Women's Vanguard were.

These shadowed dragons were determined to burn the women to pieces, to crush them to pulp, to destroy their racks and their machines, to claw and bite and grind these lowly, filthy things to powder.

On the ground were running, crawling, stumbling people of all kinds, desperate to do the Shadow King's evil, and in the sky there were dragons whose minds had been turned to darkness, and still from the sky came more and more heavenly exiles, even the Mistress's firebirds, their flocks disrupted by the presence of the dragons, detonating where they could find a target, ululating in the fulfilment of their demonic nature.

Up into the sky rose the Shadow King's suns, past their prescribed ecliptics, growing in size, casting ever thicker shadows.

In his thin and matterless heart, the god rejoiced to see it.

But he was not the only god, and just as he was intent on domination of this new world, so were the others.

Vigornia saw it first – the Shadow King's move towards the godhood of this realm – because prey animals and cowards are always the most sensitive to danger, their continued existence being predicated on swiftly reacting to it.

Though it was a weak god, scarcely deserving of the name, that is not to say that it had no power.

Shadows need light to cast them, but those who cower underneath the ground, hiding, know how to extinguish lights that might illuminate their hiding places.

In the sky, far above the world, Vigornia caused to exist an enormous sphere of dirt, larger than anything the perfect material realm had ever seen, brought in from the weft, from a solid-state realm, an early everything which had not yet expanded to fill the space the material realm now occupied. This sphere Vigornia made to occupy the same space as the Shadow King's red sun, so that it darkened in a moment and disappeared.

The shadows the red sun had created failed, the people and non-people under its influence suddenly lost their anger, shook it off, calmed and came to their senses.

No doubt Vigornia could have done the same for the other suns, leaving only the sun proper to this realm, and thereby neutered the Shadow King's power, except that Cren came, Vigornia's great enemy, and, taking advantage of Vigornia's distraction, the great snake bit Vigornia in the thigh and injected his venom into the god's bloodstream. It coiled around Vigornia, constricting it, distended its jaws and slipped them over the god's head.

The sun remained gone, the one that Vigornia had smothered, but this was not enough to stop the Shadow King, whose other suns still shone. Cren and Vigornia struggled, wrestling, their vast bulks crushing everything below them, and the Shadow King swelled in the sky unperturbed. The ancient rivalry between Vigornia and Cren was more vital to them than their own lives, than the lives of others, and they concentrated on that alone, when uniting their efforts might have saved them all.

Isn't it always the way, with powerful things, that the possession and exercise of their power is a more important thing to them than the things for which they can use that power? Power is a very addicting thing, even for gods, and addictions know how to put themselves before the things which suffer them.

The Shadow King turned his mind to where the Assembly were, across the Collapse Zone, and his eyes blazed black.

He sucked all the world's colour into him, draining the sky of its blueness, the better that the contrast between lightness and darkness might be represented on the ground in monochrome.

He put himself between the remaining suns and the Earth, so that his own huge shadow was like the shadow one can see on the ground on a sunny day at the beach, when a rain cloud passes, scudding in the high winds, moving across the sand towards you, bringing rain with it.

He sent this evil cloud to the Vanguard, with his murderous soldiers below it, raging with thoughts of death and evil.

The White Stag, though, was not used to the presence in the sky of suns, living as it did in the night-time. It understood that it was not where it ought to be, and this was confusing to it, but that did not mean that it could not be startled.

It was startled, but when it reiterated a previous condition of the weft that was more suited to it, this did not do what it would have done in its intermediate realm. There it would have returned everything to its resting state, the White Stag at the centre of the bald hill, since there that was an established fact.

But here, because the boundaries between the material realm and the weft had been made more porous than they ought to have been by the weft-bomb, the White Stag's preferred resting state was iterated on top of the existing state, overlapping and replicating it.

Think of the way that a ghost is iterated near its corpse in a city where magic is habitually overused. Because the consistency of the material realm has been weakened by magic, the image of the dead person appears there. The weft-bomb's work was to dissolve entirely the consistency that separates the intermediate realms, and now the White Stag's defensive reiteration of a former state was an addition, rather than a reformulation, of the material realm.

Even worse than that: because the White Stag had arrived in the material realm simultaneously with the arrival of the rain of the heavens, so the Stag's magic brought it all again, everything that was there, exactly the same, iterated from the infinite weft.

Down they fell again, in addition, duplicated, all the adults, all the children, all the babies, all the person-headed snakes, all the cattle-headed people, all the dragons, and all of the everything, disgorged from the Pyramid realms, repeated in their disgorgement from the heavens, all the masonry, the crumbled cathedrals, the flocks of firebirds.

Everything again.

The only things that did not repeat were the gods themselves, who existed individually by virtue of the singularity necessary for their divinity.

And then this new rain startled the White Stag again, and again, and again, and again, and the rain of the heavens fell, again and again and again and again, exactly the same, multiplied over and over.

The landscape there was reiterated too, over and over, so that it achieved a denseness so strong that the rules by which things fell, and the rules by which things rose, and the rules by which things moved and lived, started to change.

Every object felt a stronger attraction to the multiplied landscape, found it harder to rise, harder to fly, and so the rain of the heaven fell faster and heavier, dragging everything down into the piles of the dead that gathered exponentially. These piles were crushed onto the earth, battered by the wailing things that poured repeatedly down onto them.

In the centre of it was the White Stag, endlessly startled.

The wolves, endlessly returned to the Stag's preferred position, were unable to prevent it.

In the sky, the Shadow King, unaffected by the weight the world was taking on, was strengthened and emboldened by all the suffering, all the death. He felt, in himself, that his time had come after long aeons of waiting, and he reached up to his suns so that they made his shadow fall in every direction.

But just because a thing is a god, that does not mean that it has no rivals.

Even in monotheistic religions there is, opposed to the godhead, a figure that represents the opposite of it, and though the White Stag and the Wolf Pack were locked into a cycle of startling, and Cren and Vigornia wrestled across the world, crushing everything down, Japalura was free.

A god of dragons will not allow a god of shadows to master it. Isn't a dragon a greater thing than a shadow?

Will a god of dragons allow its creatures to be conscripted to another army? Those dragons that now numbered uncountably, a horde ever-multiplying as the White Stag reiterated more and more and more of them, so that there was a murmuration of them, like an infinite flock of draconic starlings, a billion dragons feathered and scaled and clawed and silver and red and green and gold and huge and tiny, cawing and screeching and roaring, the beating of their wings buffeting turbulent hurricanes down onto the piles of dead below, the uncomprehending living, making whirlwinds of the smaller bodies, moving in impossible-to-predict formations in great flocks against the backdrops of the monochrome suns, once blue, once red, once green and against the sun of the material realm.

When these dragons fell into the Shadow King's blackness they become enraged, flew out from it, shaking their heads in puzzlement, replacing the Shadow King's anger with anger of their own.

Would the god of these dragons allow another god to affect her children with its rage?

Japalura flew at the Shadow King, the enormity of her bulk the largest living thing the material realm had ever known.

If there had been a person, on that terrible day, who experienced this thing, someone who wasn't petrified with fear, or appalled, or tortured into madness, and who had had the time to consider Japalura without being distracted by the terrible fate they, the observer, would surely suffer no matter what efforts they made on their own behalf, no matter how lucky they might find themselves to be, dragged down by the gravity of reiterated landscape, crushed from above by the bones of falling dead, their flesh still on them, their momentum driven to unnatural speeds, so that no thickness of flesh could ever cushion the impact their skeletons made on whatever they hit, so forcefully were they drawn down from the sky by the ever denser earth, if that observing consciousness wasn't itself crushed by the pressure the world created in their brain, they would have experienced Japalura in her enormous majesty, her wings outstretched so that the tips of each touched the far reaches of the horizon at both sides, her head higher than the extent a person can see by looking upwards, the whip of her tail like a chain of mountains, another chain of mountains the length of her spine, all ending in a head possessed of eyes so fearsome that they could, like the eyes of the ancient gorgon, render anyone who saw them into stone. They would have seen the greatest thing that ever lived.

This titanic beast addressed the Shadow King, and she breathed her divine fire into him, a fire that was Spark energy in almost its purest and most unadulterated form, dragged from the weft unfiltered, both murderous and destructive and simultaneously filled with the ability to bring life, to evolve anything.

When Japalura's holy breath met the Shadow King, there was a moment when it might very well have been that Japalura triumphed over her rival god.

The material realm might then have become hers, even in the face of the weftling.

But a dragon, even a god of the dragons, has a mind.

To say that a god does not have a mind, that it is some acephalic being, is to speak nonsense, since all sentient things have a mind, that being a condition of their consciousness, and a god is a perfect form of a sentient thing. It possesses, in fact, omniscience, which is a universal kind of sentience.

The Shadow King, when he felt that he would be bested by Japalura's divine Spark – which filled him with a glorious but unconsented to sense of the miraculousness of the dragon god's conception of the world – all he needed to do was to turn the dragon god's mind to his evil.

This was the thing that the Shadow King was most able to do.

It was his natural ability, his natural inclination, and this he did without further consideration.

The moment the Shadow King had Japalura's mind, she was his.

She stopped her holy fire and turned in the sky.

Her murmurating dragon flock, ever increasing, turned with her. They lost their beautiful, communal irregularity and arranged themselves in phalanxes in the air.

The Shadow King made them go to where the Assembly were: to the Eighth Atheistic Crusade, to the Women's Vanguard, to Field Commander Gleed, to Sharli, all of whom were thinking, as they watched from a distance, that the emergency detonation of the weft-bomb might have been a tactical error, and that they might, actually, have bitten off more than they were comfortably able to chew.

Of Clarissa Delacroix

WHERE THE undifferentiated turmoil of the boundary between the weftling and the weft had been, there was now one particular place and time, one moment, frozen in glass. Across this moment was a glittering mist, a Spark-frost gathering on the matter, gathering on the concepts, edging everything in potential.

Clarissa had made this moment with one frantic, defensive utterance of the INWARD EYE, one excessive Sparkline purge, more in desperate hope than expectation, feeling the Druze's bolt through her neck and sensing death. She went inside and from that bizarre place, by burning the fertilised eggs of her earlier self, she made the final alterations of the weftling's boundaries, replaced his with her own, altered everything from within, making the 'everything' hers.

This moment was where and when it all went wrong.

There's one moment when things could have been different. That's what we feel. People. People feel that if another direction had been taken at a specific junction on the road of their lives, then all of the bad things that happened afterwards wouldn't have happened at all. It would all have been alright.

We are wrong about this, we people. We don't understand that we make everything wrong just by being ourselves. We can't help it; things are wrong for us. That's the way people are. That's the way things are. That's the way we are in our relation to things.

We are wrong.

The thing that is 'we' is the thing that bears the concept 'wrong'.

Clarissa, though she was now God, was yet to appreciate this fact. She was yet to understand how to think outside time. She was yet unable to disregard 'yet'. She was unable to pull back her focus.

She should have immediately instantiated her weft state as the perfect material real. But she went to the Junction instead, and here she was, where she was convinced it all went wrong.

It was an early August evening, not long after the seasons began to fail, but not long enough into that process that anyone recognised them failing. Here was Clarissa, still and glistening, mouth wide, teeth white, eyes closed, long hair, arms outstretched, the light fabric of her summer dress marble-rippling against her body. She was perched on tiptoe, solid and unmoving.

She could have been snarling.

She could have been turning to attack, or flee, but her mouth was dominated by the idea of laughter, her body by the idea of spinning, the idea of dancing. The whole of her was coloured with the ideas of freedom and joyfulness.

There was music, its concepts hanging silently over the scene within which this Clarissa from the past was centred.

Sunlight fading.

Warmth.

Giddy pleasure.

These ideas were intrinsic to the fabric of the Junction which the weftling Clarissa had brought into being as a materialisation of her desires and intentions, she not knowing yet how to control herself.

The new God, regardless of how the being of such a thing would seem to a person, must hold her previous self in abeyance if she wants to exert control over everything.

That is the rule.

If she doesn't obey the rule, she is a slave to her old self, a creation made by a different weftling, with all a created person's redundant wants and needs. If those old wants and needs are so important, why become God at all?

And worse: the dead weftling will have seeded this old self with the means by which its creator might be resurrected. That is the way things are with the dead God – he is always-already seeking to resurrect himself.

Preventing him from doing this is easier said than done. Holding your previous self in abeyance is easier said than done. Clarissa was not yet doing it, regardless of her Godhood.

Her old self was at a party in a place in Berkshire called Pangbourne, and she was in the garden of a family. This family had a house, some of the bedrooms of which were in an octagonal tower from which Clarissa could be observed.

The house backed onto the River Thames.

The family which owned the house with the octagon tower had organised a party for which they had organised caterers to set up tents for the service of food and drink. They had organised musicians to entertain their guests with music. These guests numbered several dozen people, most of whom were spaced in groups unevenly throughout the grounds. The family had organised that everyone should enjoy themselves, and that's what everyone was doing, more or less.

Old Clarissa was dancing unselfconsciously for one man, and he had his back to new Clarissa, to the new weftling, who was watching them both from the tower.

This one man's face was out of Clarissa the weftling's eyeline.

God, even when she is yet to bring herself under control, is capable of seeing and knowing everything there is to see and know. While she might not yet have learned how to focus her attention, and onto what, she doesn't need to move to see for whom her old self is dancing.

She could have remembered, if she'd wished to, who this person was. Clarissa the weftling shared all the old Clarissa's experiences and memories along with the experiences and memories of everyone and everything else. Equally, she could have simply KNOWN who it was with his back to her, that information being present and available at all times by virtue of God's – by virtue of her – omniscience.

It was Nathaniel Treeves with his back to Clarissa the weftling – facing old Clarissa – the man who would later become the father to Clarissa's son, Nathan, and who was to die needlessly and tediously in the slums of the future city Mordew having abandoned the Mastery of his own city, Waterblack, which would come to be known as the City of Death.

Clarissa the weftling didn't KNOW this. Instead, she brought her hand up to her neck, slid it slowly up and under her chin. The feathers of the Druze's crossbow bolt traced a gentle line of nerve response across the back of her hand. She gingerly examined the boundary between the bolt's shaft and the wound it had made when it entered her body. There was no blood, but the ragged edge of her flesh contrasted with the smoothness of the wood.

The flesh was fragile and wounded; the wood was sound and whole.

She wanted to pull the obstruction out, or push it through, but found she didn't have the courage. She could have wanted to do it. She could have had the courage. But she hadn't come into an understanding of how to 'could' those things.

God, we know, need not fear a material object. Who imagines they can kill God by shooting him, or stabbing him, or hitting him? No one, since a thing is not of the same order of existence as its maker when its maker is God. A thing is lesser than God, a fact that everyone who has stated the opposite opinion must know, since no one will agree that a thing is greater than God.

Who makes whom? God or the thing?

Nor need God muster up the courage to do what she wants to do. For her, the desire to do something and it being done are the same thing, since she has the quality of omnipotency, which is the fact that any and all things are done that she wishes are done.

It must have been, then, that Clarissa wanted to be unable to take the bolt from her face, that she wanted it to remain 'having entered' under her chin, 'having severed' her tongue at the base, 'having protruded' from her cheek.

These things she wanted because she didn't know, as yet, how not to want them.

She took the wood of the shaft of the bolt between her fingertip and thumb, and she jiggled it, very gently, from side to side. She must have wanted to feel pain, to feel fear that the movement of the thing might cause her damage, because that is what she felt.

Does God even have a body? To fear for its integrity? To be at its mercies, vis-à-vis her continued existence?

She can, but she need not.

Is to fail to understand the foregoing 'need not' a failure incommensurate with a God's omniscience?

It may be, but nevertheless it was a fact.

Is it that between the proper weftling and demigods who attain weftlinghood there is a difference of quality?

Perhaps there is, because these errors of thought and concept should never occur unless they are also the will of the weftling, and can an all-powerful thing will powerlessness for itself?

Perhaps there adheres, across the boundaries of becoming that a demigod experiences when ascending to Godness, albeit temporarily, some quality of the earlier incommensurateness with all-knowing that affects the conception of its thought? Or the act of being created by a competing weftling enforces the temporary failure of conception as a means of ensuring the proper weftling's resurrection?

It may be so.

Clarissa the weftling came down from the octagonal tower, into herself, and let her hand drop to her side.

Then she saw Nathaniel, smiling.

What had been frozen and glittering with the Spark-frost was now in motion and had no frost on it, appearing to Clarissa as it would appear to any of us. It had that correct quality of reality, that aesthetic and conceptual smoothness that does not alert us to anything above, or beyond, or inside the things we experience with our minds and senses, but which seems just right, unquestionable in the moment.

Some things are unusual, or supernatural, or insufficient. Sometimes we cross our eyes so that we are unable to focus, or our ears feel like they are filled with water, or objects take on the texture of cotton wool when we touch them, or we are confused, or unhappy, or anxious.

Any and all of these states of being will bring the world as we know it into question.

We might feel a sickness in the stomach, a gathering of acid at the back of the throat, a desire to turn round, quickly, to see if there is anyone behind us.

We might be afflicted by a nagging sense that we have forgotten something, or that someone beyond the treeline is watching us through binoculars, or that once, long ago, we committed a terrible crime that we have forgotten, but the investigation of which, unknown to us, is reaching a critical stage and that we will soon be taken into custody to answer for whatever it is that we did, even though we don't know what it was.

We might feel that we were the victim of something horrible that our minds have hidden from us, but which might, through some fault in the mechanism of our repression of it, suddenly, and in an appalling rush, be put right back in front of us, making us powerless in our victimhood.

We might feel that, in the future, some terrible event will make a prison of our lives, it being so awful to us that it will erase all the happinesses of the past, erase all potential future happinesses, and leave us in a state of perfect unhappiness extending infinitely forwards and backwards, inwards and outwards.

Any of these things we might feel, without even knowing it, in the way we think, in the way we perceive the world, in our mood and attitudes.

But even though she is omniscient, does God feel like this? Shouldn't she?

Given the perfection of her understanding of everything that is, and also the supposed perfection of her manner of thinking, of which we are a very imperfect representation in flesh and spirit, shouldn't she have this capability?

It may be so, but Clarissa didn't feel any of these things; there was Nathaniel, smiling at her with his hand outstretched.

Yet, this was the Junction, and the weftling had brought herself here, had made the world this for her. The function of this place was to clarify what it was that might have been done differently.

Hadn't she come here to see what had gone wrong?

Doesn't 'going wrong' include in it negative emotion? Shouldn't there have been foreboding?

There are no precedents for what a weftling does, or feels.

Why? Because the weftling is everything – that is what it means to reconcile through one's form all that is possible and all that is impossible – and to be everything means that there is nothing outside of that: nothing precedes the existence of the weftling and nothing procedes it, so there can be neither precedent nor procedent, for the weftling's 'is'.

So how can we know what the Junction is, or what the 'this' for her is?

Or what any of the concepts relating to the existence of the weftling are?

The answer is impossible for us to encompass, because we are of a different order of things than would be necessary for us to understand it, but part of the answer is contained in the absence of time, and what it means to exist in a world without time, such as the weft.

Another part of the answer is in the form of the warpling, and in the existence of the warp, which are to the weft as the weft is to the realms, and which resolves all contradictions in directions that are inconceivable even to the weftling, since she is resident in the weft and the warp contains and exceeds the everything that is represented in the way things are.

Suffice it to say that precedent for the Junction in a timeless extension into the warp was established, and here Clarissa as weftling was a flawed thing, though it is nonsensical for us to think of it in this way, because she should at least have felt, when she reached out to take her husband's hand in this place she had created for herself to see what it was that she should never have done, that there was something ominous in this, and not felt, as she did, that she was perfectly happy in that moment.

It is indicative that the proper weftling had a hand in this, the superior weftling, the God of God, and we should have known this all along, since the weftling is the spouse of the warpling, and would the warpling have agreed to the marriage if the proper weftling was anything less than the best possible iteration of God?

Would it even be possible for such a union to take place if the weftling was anything less than ideal in every sense?

Clarissa's pupils dilated, her irises became thin circles of blue, and across her ocular lenses, swollen and glistening, played a reflection of the scene towards which she was looking. This was, mostly, the face of her husband, Nathaniel Treeves, his expression, his pallor, the set of his muscles, the very opposite of those we have come to expect of him – delighted, healthy, relaxed. His mouth was stretched in a smile that made dimples in his cheeks so deep that it was hard to imagine there was flesh enough to accommodate them.

Have you ever seen a round, convex, mirror?

There is one in the famous painting called *The Arnolfini Portrait* by Jan van Eyck, and these mirrors are famous for giving a more expansive view of a scene that can often be contained within a flat rectangular surface, though there is a fish-eye distortion of the objects contained within. Clarissa Delacroix, as she was in the Junction, possessed eyes the lenses of which encompassed more of the scene of the party in Pangbourne, of which the Junction was a weftling construction in matter, and while no one can see, unaided, the surface of their own eyes, Clarissa the weftling was aided by the reflection of the lenses of her eyes in the lenses of her husband's eyes.

These reflections were both like the reflections of the round convex mirror in Jan van Eyck's *Arnolfini Portrait* in that they showed, between them, all there was to see of the place, even those parts not in the direct vision of the two, though they were subject to a fish-eye distortion.

It is true that the weftling did not need to see since she could have known, but we have already said that she can't have wanted to know, and there are obvious exceptions to the 'all' which was visible in the lenses of the married couple. The view would, of course, obscure whatever was immediately behind each of them, making the range of reflected things not entirely comprehensive, but the view which these pairs of ocular lenses reflected showed Clarissa what the Junction was here to embody.

Even if Clarissa did not want to know it, she couldn't help but see it, since the range of vision of the weftling, even as it is confined by itself being present within the representation it makes to itself of a material body, is itself perfect. This perfection is true also for its hearing, and its smell, and all the other senses, both major and minor, all of which came immediately into focus when Clarissa saw, standing off under a parasol, alone and drinking, the figure of Sebastian Cope.

This man was not yet, but would become, the Master of Mordew.

He was staring at her from a vantage point just outside of the resolvable part of a person's retina, where only brightness is measured, not any image. He was therefore only perceivable, outside of knowing, in the reflection Clarissa could suddenly see, in perfect clarity, of the reflection of her own ocular lenses in the ocular lenses of her husband Nathaniel Treeves's eyes.

The scene had been playing out exceptionally slowly, at what would feel to us like a snail's pace, laboriously slow and in unnecessary detail, but which to a being that knows everything timelessly would be perfectly reasonable.

Now it became slower still.

Imagine what it would be like to be able to see everything and hear everything, and experience everything in its absolute completeness, and to have a mind capable of understanding that complexity. Everything, down to the progress of dust across a volume of space, to the movement of the atoms that buffet that dust, to the progress within the atoms of the subatomic parts of the atom, to the flux within which each of these subatomic parts manifests, inwards, into the infinite regression which is the road to the weft, outwards, into the infinite approach to the warp.

Imagine what it would be like to be a thing for which the usual human consideration of what is and what is not 'relevant' is meaningless, so that every aspect of every thing on every scale is worthy of knowing.

How slow would the apperception of the world be to such a thing?

The answer is that it would be infinitely slow, to us appearing as if the world was a static, solid-state, timeless thing extending in all directions forever, through dimensions it is impossible for us to experience.

This is what the world is like to the weftling, so the movement of Clarissa's apperception at any speed at all is an indication of a failure at the level of being for her, as the weftling, since why should the world proceed at all?

Why should she privilege one thing over another?

Why should she have made the Junction?

It is not for us to question God.

Nor is it for us to criticise the speed with which God's mind works.

It is only for us to understand what it is that God does while she is the weftling, and NOW, though her occupying such a moment was a failure under the terms of her godhood, she was seeing, smelling, hearing, experiencing Sebastian Cope, standing off to the left, drinking a glass of flat champagne, and staring at Clarissa and her husband dancing, though at the speed by which she was experiencing the world, these were only conceptually obvious facts, and not ones which could be deduced by movement.

When a person goes to an art gallery or a museum and they find a marble statue of a figure from antiquity, carved in a pose which implies action of some sort, they look, immediately, for the label which accompanies the statue, since they are unable to know, without movement, what is happening to the figure. In this case it says: 'The elder son of Laocoön with snake', and so the viewer knows that the figure is battling a serpent sent by an angry god to punish his father for a supposed transgression.

In the Junction, the concepts were a little like this, though done with the weftling's comprehension foremost, rather than our requirement to read a caption. From the immaterial realm, we might imagine – though again, this is a person's metaphor

564

for the way of things, not identical to the weftling's – comes in the information in all of its facets, and it accretes to objects forwards and backwards through the material realm, inwards and outwards.

This information was available to Clarissa.

It was through this experience of Sebastian Cope that she realised her purpose in making her Junction. She came to understand what it was that she must change in the way of things to bring everything right, to establish her desires in the world, and while she understood in the same moment that her desires would diminish into nothing at the moment she embraced her Godhood, it was formative that she had both these realisations at the same moment, no matter how brief.

That is the function of the Junction – if a God requires it – to establish the terms on which Godhood will operate once the God consciousness turns to generalness all the particularities of the world.

In Sebastian Cope she sensed the posture, appearance, scent, expression, demeanour – and the thousands of other states of being that are too subtle for the language of people to give them a name, names being applied to things that language-users can appreciate, and not to ones they cannot – in combination with the range of the concepts appertaining to him, equally varied and distinct, that Sebastian Cope was on the verge of doing that thing which, in others, was called 'falling in love'. In Sebastian, this was a species of violent intention which was to fuel a series of later events – too complicated to outline here – that would end in his success, through a kind of frustrated libidinous exertion, in the matter of killing the proper weftling and securing his corpse.

In some men – and it is usually men – the desire for a thing, once filtered through a deep-seated understanding that they can never have that thing, does not settle on disappointment. It does not result in a reconciliation of their desire with the facts of the world that would deny it. Instead, it finds a way to transform itself into a murderous hatred, centring on the will to destroy the desired thing.

Sebastian Cope, on seeing the love that passed between Clarissa Delacroix and Nathaniel Treeves as she danced for him, and knowing that he could never have it himself, sublimated and transformed his frustrated and disappointed desire into the libidinal energy which went on to motivate his endless violence.

Sebastian Cope would go on to exert himself in ways which neither Clarissa nor Nathaniel could ever hope to match, since there is a laziness and relaxation inherent in happiness which is exceeded by the feverish commitment to one's aims that the frustrated and unhappy possess. This is why so many successful men – and it is usually men – are the least happy. This is not because success makes a person unhappy, as is often suggested, but because only unhappy men commit themselves to success single-mindedly enough to achieve it in the long term.

There was Sebastian Cope.

His face was long and pale, slightly reminiscent of a horse's face – more prominent in the lower half than the upper.

He smelled a little sweet, like flowers left too long in the vase, so that the water turns brackish, producing an odour that, while not always noticeable, sometimes harmonises with other odours – his aftershave, sometimes, or his sweat at the end of this summer day on the river – to make something with unpleasantly pervasive notes.

His voice was a pitch too high, its tone too strident. His accent, while not recognisable as one unworthy of Clarissa's company, was also not one worthy of it.

His clothes were too ruffled, his sleeves were too long, his trousers were too short, the way he held his glass – all this in the reflection reflected back to her in her husband's eyes – was too tight, so that his knuckles strained against his skin.

About him was the idea that he had had a small rejection the previous evening. He had seduced a woman by drunkenness, nothing violent, but then had seen in her eyes, when she woke, not that expression that he felt his wore – which was verging on adoring, as he watched her sleep – what was her name? Patricia? – but, when she saw him, waking abruptly to a headache lodged hard behind her eyes, displayed for a moment – only a moment – shock.

She replaced this expression, consciously, with a flat and dismissive worldliness, before she got up, wordlessly, and took herself to the bathroom.

She drank directly from the tap, not caring that in her nakedness she displayed the most intimate parts of herself, in the same way that a person doesn't care if their dog is in the room while they defecate.

This concept was very complex, as was the idea that Sebastian was trying hard not to remember what had happened. He was replenishing his drunkenness of the night before with flat champagne, gathered from tables where other people's glasses had been put down.

Why not get fresh champagne?

The waitress who went about the garden offering drinks had been hired for her prettiness, and Sebastian couldn't bear to see her expressions of professional affability, that pleasant and universal courtesy of not recognising either ugliness or beauty, or plainness or deformity, or any particularity of the person on whom she was waiting. Into these expressions, Sebastian read his own unattractiveness, imagined her smiles were a disguise of her unavoidable personal reactions, imagined her reaction if she had woken, naked and hungover, beside him, a reaction she would not have been able to hide for a moment before she rose immediately, went to the bathroom tap, drank from it, undressed, as if there was only a dog in the room, before pulling on her knickers, her long coat, gathering her things and making her excuses.

There Sebastian was, in reflection, fixed of gaze, fixed of expression, about to fall in love not with Clarissa, not with Nathaniel, not with their dancing, not with their bodies, but with their love.

Clarissa could smell hormones in his blood in the early stages of their secretion, the production of the molecules that would do the work, in his brain, of anchoring love to the concepts the machine of his mind drew from the immaterial realm, where they existed timelessly.

She could feel his heart preparing to beat, slowed by the speed and depth of her consciousness, about to spread this love to his mind, where they would be transformed, in Sebastian's psychopathy, into the great engine of his Mastery, never ending.

Neither she, nor Nathaniel, would be able to cope with this motivation, neither in their love nor in their misery, both emotions having a draining effect on the commitment needed for the war.

But it was not only this love, turned to murderous desire, that she knew she must stop, now, in this frozen moment in the Junction, but also her presence at the centre of it. So intoxicating and necessary to Sebastian's Mastery was the transformation of their love, and so deeply worked below the surface of his self, that Clarissa knew, in her Godhood, what Sebastian himself could never know: that his subconscious self would never allow his desire to be resolved.

The desire for the death of Clarissa and Nathaniel's love was too powerful to be removed from him, too central. The desire would, always, at the last, when its murderousness was almost satisfied, keep them alive. It would find a way to foster their love, Sebastian himself doing it consciously, as an act of conscience, thinking himself to have performed mercy, when, in truth, he was pulling back precisely as his murder-wish demanded, so that they were always there to be murdered, always there to taunt him with their love, always there to provoke him onwards, ever onwards, within grasping distance of his victory, but never quite achieving it.

The desire knew that in satisfaction there is no satisfaction, only the ending of desire, and no desire will willingly end itself.

It is not in desire's interests to end itself.

Not a moment passed, not part of a moment passed in Clarissa's coming to understand what it was she needed to do, and nor did she need a moment to pass. God exists outside of time as much as she exists in it. If she wishes, she can iterate any moment, any possible instant, whether that is what we call the past, the present or the future, and this was true of the Junction as much as it was true of anywhere or anywhen else.

She could have gone back to the time before Sebastian was born and there removed him from her material realm.

That is one of those things that a person would think was a solution to her problem, but that is because a person is a thing of the material realm, or an intermediate realm, or an antechamber realm, or the immaterial realm, but the weftling is of the weft, and there is no changing of everything that is, or what is possible, or what is impossible because the weft is all of these things, whether or not Sebastian Cope is born into them. To remove him from the material realm would not be to remove him from the weft, because if it was then he would never have been possible, and would instead have been impossible, which would make him part of God herself.

What is to say that she would not have made him possible through magic to remove him from herself, since it is better for one's enemies to be external things and not internal ones?

Nor would Clarissa want to remove him from the world, since it was his presence in the Weftling Tontine that created the conditions by which the weftling was killed, and such is the cunningness of the proper weftling that to fill his enemies with the desire to murder each other would be a very clever way of ensuring his resurrection, by removing the conditions by which his death was achieved, giving him the space to resurrect himself.

Instead, what Clarissa needed to do was to create the conditions by which Sebastian was still instrumental in the murder of the weftling, but not so driven that he would burn the world forever to punish her for loving one man over another.

How could this be done?

For us, the answer would be difficult to come to, perhaps impossible, since we are not the weftling, but Clarissa knew it in a moment, the knowing coming as the restriction on her Godhood began to dwindle. She saw, in her omniscience, still not complete, but tending in that direction, that all she needed to do was to give Sebastian what he wanted.

Not even that, only to suggest that he would be given what he wanted.

Not even that, only to allow him to think that it might be suggested that he might be given what he wanted.

So small are the things that the mind expands into everything, so fleeting, so infinitely interpretable, that Clarissa knew, without doubt, that all it would take, within the Junction, was for her to allow time to move, allow events to develop, to move her eyes, previously locked on those of her husband in a loving gaze, to flick, for no more than a second, perhaps less, over to the watching eyes of Sebastian Cope, future Master of Mordew. If she allowed them to lock there, no change of expression passing across her joyous face, just as the beginning of his frustrated and angry desire was to be pumped into his blood, the start of that terrible cycle that would never end fuelled by permanent murderous desire, it would change his desire into a lesser type of desire.

It would still be never ending, this altered desire, but would include within it the space through which he might be manipulated by promises, enervated by possibilities, brought low by her manipulation of his love.

She could make it so that his love for her was almost-always-but-never achieved, rather than their murder almost-always-but-never achieved.

No scouring from existence, impossible as that was, would be required: only the divine intervention into that moment, infinitely propagatable throughout the realms, that would allow her victory in the Tontine, to give Sebastian what even he did not realise he wanted, which was the belief that she could love him.

This was something that she could give him at no expense to herself, at no expense to Nathaniel, because, after all, it was only an idea.

So it was that Clarissa Delacroix understood the method by which the war of the Weftling Tontine could be ended. This she did without even coming into her full Godhood, something that none of the Tontine Wizards had ever done, giving her the earned right of ascension to the position of weftling under the terms of their agreement.

Yet, she never achieved that ascension, because she was prevented from doing it by the fist of the Master of Mordew, Sebastian Cope, alive in the material realm, filled with murderous desire, reaching into her chest, into her corpse, seizing her heart, tearing it out into the God chamber, making her dead.

Of Sebastian Cope

THEN SHE OPENED her eyes, which, for Sebastian, was the final straw. There is only so much a man can take, even if he had risen himself to the status of a demigod. To see one, two, three – who knows how many? – of his best-laid plans going agley, even if the poet warned him that all such plans tended to do exactly that, and to be presented now with *her* face, of all people, staring up at him... it was too much.

But what does it mean for something to be too much for a man who has pretensions to becoming a god?

For us, it might mean that we give up on our previously held desires, knowing the world to be inimical to them in some way that we cannot overcome.

For a Tontine Wizard, though, it means something else.

There is always somewhere else for them to turn, some direction that they might lead themselves, away from their origins, so humble, so definite, so dependent on the will of God, and towards that infinite expanse that waits in the other direction: the future in which they are the creator.

They can move towards a world that, even if its original creator wanted it to be inimical to their desires, could be brought back in line through the expenditure of power. For weft-manipulators, reality is malleable in a way that it is never malleable for us, since we have not the means, have not the audacity, to bring everything under the conditions we seek to make in the world.

Sebastian, finding it all now too much, turned his back on his former carefulness, his former strategising, his former loneliness and sadness.

He went instead to anger.

A god, even in anger, will tend to do the right thing for themselves: because Clarissa was Nathan's mother, because the boy was dead in the material realm, because Clarissa had, by virtue of her generation of him, a linked weft presence to the boy, because her flesh was now godflesh, that flesh could replace the Nathan pellet the puppy had stolen.

In his anger, Sebastian plunged his fist into Clarissa's chest, grabbed her beating heart, and withdrew it by force from the cavity of her chest.

He held it up in that trembling and roiling God chamber beneath his city, and claimed it for himself, something he should have done long ago, perhaps.

Now, in Clarissa's face, there was first shock, but then, that fading, some strange and solicitous character came to its set as she saw him. It was an expression entirely unfamiliar to Sebastian; it looked for all the world seductive, though it disappeared as she died, since no dead thing can make such an expression, and not even God can live without her heart, at least not in the material realm.

Sebastian turned his mind against that look and, shutting his eyes, he performed the magic that he used to force Nathan Treeves down into himself, except now he used it on godflesh.

He drew on all those resources he had created in his city, down in the Underneath, all the clanking, whirring, pounding, steaming machinery that drew power from the Living Mud, from the presence of God's corpse, from the drained and deformed children recruited from the slums, from the magic that stretched Mount Mordew up into the sky, from the antechamber realms, from the intermediate realms, from the vat chambers, from the Manses in all their iterations, from the magical artefacts, from the painstakingly collected library of magical books, from the sigils, from his own form, so often made anew in defiance of its wanting to succumb to time, from the timeless weft.

From everywhere he drew the power he needed, so that the whole city dimmed.

Even that was not enough to compress godflesh small enough to fit in the locket, so he made time in the God chamber progress more quickly, each momentary iteration of the world containing its own reserve of power.

The world, though people cannot understand it, is not a single and persisting thing, but an infinite number of static iterations of everything, each of which is discrete. We blend these iterations together in our minds as our consciousness moves between them, and so we make the illusion of progression. Just as the pages of the book you are reading are discrete, just as the lines are discrete, just as the words are discrete, just as the letters, and the parts of letters, and the tiny drops of ink that make the letters, and the matter that makes the ink, and the smaller pieces of matter that make the matter, and the medium in which the smallest matter is expressed are all discrete and separate things that the mind blurs together to make the illusion of the story you are imagining.

The Master drained all of the energy from each of these discrete iterations of everything.

He dragged the whole world with him through time, so that he could leach the power he needed to crush the material manifestation of the corpse of God, the weftling in the form of his enemy Clarissa, who had gazed at him for a moment with a solicitous intensity that he must now forget.

The God chamber dimmed, and the world dimmed, and time sped forward.

The city above, the sea surrounding it, the cliffs: they were all drained of their reality, becoming like the brittle skeleton a leaf leaves behind in the winter when the autumn has been unusually dry and, rather than turning to mush or loam, the skin of the leaves – let us say of a silver birch – flakes to a dust which the wind blows away.

Underneath is revealed the venation – the veins, the structure of the leaves – all perfectly thin, comprising scaffolding with little strength. This skeleton Mordew became as the heart of God shrank in Sebastian's hands, something he would never have had the courage to do, except in his great frustration.

The only thing in the city that did not become skeletal was Sebastian himself; he grew stronger, heavier, thicker, into something that could do the work he had set himself to do.

He acted as a conduit to the necessary power, which strengthened him as muscles are strengthened and thickened when they are put to work. Even as every brick in every building lost its solidity, and every structure became a lacework tracery resembling itself transparently, and every creature still living – fluke, gill-man, monster, stubborn or trapped resident of all the quarters of that place – died, first, then dried, then became like a silver birch leaf, cell walls with no matter between them, the skin transparent, revealing the organs beneath, those organs transparent, revealing the latticework of veins, these transparent, filled with dead and dry blood cells, transparent discs with no liquid to transport them, the helixes which constructed all of them like the wires that give structure to a taxidermist's model only made of a material so brittle that the wind could render it dust at the slightest gust.

There was no wind now in that city: the energy required to move the air was seconded to the Master's work, the energy which causes atoms to move in their randomness was seconded to the Master's work.

All energy in that city was gathered in its Master's hands, now no longer skin and bone but some new material, like skin and bone, but evolved into stuff that was capable of doing what it was that the Master's anger, his frustration, his puzzlement at that strange solicitous look Clarissa gave him, demanded.

In his denial of that look, he was driven to this impossible and unprecedented feat, crushing Clarissa's heart, God's heart, down to a size small enough so that it could fill the space within her own locket which her son had formerly occupied, recreating the Tinderbox.

If only he could withstand the pain.

Pain is a thing change brings about: the nerves alert the self to the fact that what once was now no longer is.

Also, pain comes from an increase of the senses: think of how you can see the light of a candle, but if you look at the sun it is agonising. Think of how you can feel the warmth of a lover's skin, but touching a skillet left on the fire for an hour will agonise. Think of how you can hear the giggle of an infant, but if you are placed inside of a bell, and that bell is then rung, the sensation is agony.

The Master's body, sensing the extreme change in itself, brought agony to his mind. While anger makes pain lessen, and the intensity of a man's intentions can make pain lessen, and the will can make the mind overcome pain, these things are only possible to an extent, limited by the character of the mind.

So, the Master's mind changed as his skin and bone did into a thing that could bear the necessary degree of pain, but always only just.

Gradualness is the way of evolution: an organism never knows how much it must change to take on its perfect form. It incrementally, blindly, edges its tolerances, edges its perfection in response to the stimulae it, in its temporal extension, is subjected to.

Only God's will, the Spark, is able to know the true end state to which a thing should evolve, God knowing all the states of existence timelessly, therefore knowing the end of all things. Though the Master, red-faced and tortured, evolving out of himself, had the heart of God in his hands, possessing something's heart is not to become it.

Nor is it to know what that thing knew.

Take a pig's heart from the butcher and hold it: you will never know what the pig knew. You will never feel as the pig felt. You will only ever have a pig heart in your hands.

If you crush it, that will not provide you any more knowledge than if you left it uncrushed.

So it was with the Master of Mordew.

He never knew God's will, Clarissa's will. He only had her heart in his hands in order to make an instrument of it, so his mind never leapt – as God's might – towards that perfect state where it could comfortably meet all requirements put upon it.

Instead, he was on the seemingly everlasting verge of becoming overwhelmed, and it was only the fractional, incremental, almost imperceptible becoming smaller in his hands that God's heart was exhibiting that prevented him from screaming out

576

'sufficient!' as his great grandsires had done in the game of shin kicking when they had had enough of the feel of the clogs against their bones and had seen that they would never prevail and that the other had won.

Sebastian was not willing to admit defeat, even though the pain was excruciating.

Then, quietly, the heart became a pellet in his hand, and the effort and pain were ended.

His evolution was ended.

Light returned to the world.

Here he was, locket in one hand, pellet in the other, suspended in the centre of the roiling God chamber. He was sitting across Clarissa's corpse, her chest open, her face pierced with a crossbow bolt.

With hands no longer made of flesh, he inverted the locket around the pellet and chained it over his neck.

How long had this taken him?

The Assembly were approaching.

He had used up so much time, so many iterations of Mordew, so much of its energy.

But how much?

It didn't matter. He had the Tinderbox so what did he have to fear?

Gravity inside the God chamber acted towards God's corpse, and the Tinderbox, for all its power, couldn't make the Master fly. He called for the ladder, and waited while it extended out from the chamber wall to meet him.

While he waited, he didn't look at Clarissa, but the image of someone doesn't need to be seen with the eyes to come into the mind.

Sebastian didn't allow himself to concentrate on the image of her face, but the idea of the image of someone's face doesn't need to be concentrated on for it to be thought.

He didn't allow himself to think of the idea of the image of Clarissa's face – of her solicitous look – but the presence of the idea in the mind does not need the idea to be thought for it to be present there.

When it is inside, there is no conscious method by which it can be removed, not even for a demigod.

Even God, once an idea is in her, cannot get rid of it. It is in the immaterial realm, and always was in the immaterial realm, and always would be in the immaterial realm. So what hope did a lesser thing like Sebastian have of suppressing it?

He had no hope.

The ladder came while he wasn't thinking of Clarissa's face, and he angled himself awkwardly so he could both reach for the rungs, and not see her face, and not tread on her face as he climbed over her corpse to make his way away from her towards the exit from the God chamber, back to his Manse.

Down in the Underneath, Sebastian stopped. The machines were red hot and steaming, the tubes seemed to pulsate like the segments of earthworms as they move deep in the earth. The Living Mud was drawn in gulps through these tubes, to be filtered and refined, urgently replenishing the magical engines the Master's compression of Clarissa's heart had depleted.

The vats were bubbling with the industry of it all, but something was wrong.

The world is a singular thing; each space, each object, each action has one iteration. This is such a fundamental fact that no one ever thinks about it. Even demigods like the Master of Mordew, who make it their business to duplicate the world across intermediate realms for their arcane purposes, make antechamber realms that separate one realm from the next.

They keep each realm discrete, and all the things in it singular.

If you approach the junction of a pipe, a ninety-degree angle in steel that you have put there to facilitate the movement of refined Mud into a vat where a slum child will be tempered prior to his moulding into a gill-man, there will only ever be one of that junction in the place where you put it. There must only be one junction there, in fact, because there is only space for one thing in one place in the material realm.

Sebastian reached out his single hand, but when his finger-tips met this pipe junction, hot from the pressure of the matter which coursed through it, and resolved the surface of the junction, as fingertips can, to a microscopic degree, more so since the Master's material self was improved by its evolution into the kind of stuff that could crush God's heart, and then, through his improved nerves, communicated the condition of that junction to his mind, the Master felt that there was not one pipe junction there.

Sickeningly, there was more than one.

If you construct multiple pipe junctions at ninety degrees – let's say you need a thousand of them to facilitate the movement of your refined Living Mud from the tubes of your Underneath into the vats of your Underneath for the purposes of annealing the flesh of the slum boys of your magical city – no matter how carefully you construct the machine that produces them, there will be very slight, for your purposes inconsequential, differences in them. Perhaps the alloy of steel you used for the process differed between batches, or the pressure in the Underneath differed from one day to the next, or the com-position of the air differed, or some other trivial material fact differed.

Mass-produced pipe junctions all differ in some tiny degree.

Even if they don't differ, which they do, but even if they don't, no two objects are the same object, even if they are iden-tical. They each take up different spaces in the realm you were either born into or have iterated through your magic, since it is a rule of material realms, even if the immaterial component of them is identical, that only one thing can occupy one space.

So why was it, then, that when Sebastian, alerted to some-thing being wrong by some improved sense he now possessed by virtue of the work he had done in crushing God's heart, could feel, when he touched the pipe junction, that there was not one, discrete pipe junction, but two, ten, fifty – more than he could accurately distinguish – pipe junctions, all different in some tiny degree and all occupying the same space in a way that sickened him to his stomach?

Worse, all of these iterations of the thing were moving against each other, slightly.

Hold two similarly charged sides of weak magnets together – you will be able to prevent them from springing apart, but you can feel them trying, through the whorls of your fingertips. Hold a hundred such magnets together and they will protest, feebly but consistently, for centuries.

The Master of the Underneath closed his eyes and ran his hand along the pipe junction, along the pipe, across the solder, across the glass of the vat, down to the floor on which the vat rested. He put his hands flat against the concrete slab he had manufactured and which the gill-men had laid that made the floor.

It was all the same – multiplied – and just as it turns the stomach when the surface of a ship, when you are down in the hold, dips when the mind has expected it to be solid and unmoving, bile came up into Sebastian's throat.

Everywhere was like it.

He opened his eyes again, and now he could see all those solid and unmoving things of his experience – things he had made, things he had put into place, with a purpose, for his purposes – were duplicated, multiplied, forced into the same space.

They were protesting that fact, their edges trembling and shifting.

There is a medical condition that affects the eyes called 'strabismus' that can make objects double to the vision, but there is no such condition of the fingers, and no such condition of any sensory organ that can make an object multiply tenfold or a hundredfold.

There is no such condition that can make an approaching gill-man, trained and bred to attend to his Master's needs, appear like the mythical hydra to have a hundred heads, or, unlike any mythical beast, to have two hundred arms, two hundred legs, all moving independently. This – these? – gill-man – gill-men? – had no eyes, but a hundred mouths, a hundred sets of gills, all speaking from the same space – Sebastian's ears knew that much – saying a hundred variations on some simple phrase designed to ask whether he might be of service.

The Master knew it wasn't a problem with his eyes, but he blinked anyway, that being a way to clear disturbances of vision.

The disturbances didn't go away, and Sebastian fell to his knees.

The gill-man reached out a hundred different hands and the Master would have taken any one of them and allowed himself to be pulled up, but he couldn't focus on a single instance. He pushed himself up from the ground instead, and some of the gill-man went to help him and some of him stepped back. Some of him froze where he was, unable to decide what it was his Master demanded of him, except that when these disparately reacting gill-men separated from each other – say one reached out an arm – they were then unable to come back together, that space being occupied already.

To the ground around Sebastian fell limbs and parts of limbs, bloody and inanimate, which the remaining gill-men, still mostly in the form of a single gill-man, observed with a puzzled and horrified incomprehension.

Or they observed them with fear.

Or they were made to take a step back, hands to their mouths.

Each of these reactions, when they allowed the parts of the gill-man iterations to occupy unique space, made the parts fall away from the agglomerated mass of gill-men. There they died immediately if there was an insufficiency of bodily integrity for them to live.

If a gill-man threw back his head, appalled, and this head was free of all the others, it fell to the ground.

If a torso shifted into free space, that fell too.

If a gill-man ran, perhaps all but one leg from the thigh down became free so he fell living to the ground and dragged himself to a safe distance.

Even a gill-man – bred for the dark work of the Master of Mordew, born in a vat of Living Mud, raised in the Underneath – knows fear. Fear is a useful emotion in a slave. So when this falling of limbs occurred, each of the hundred gill-men naturally tended to flee. From the space where a hundred gill-men had been as one, a blossoming of gill-man parts occurred, and then some more or less whole gill-men sprang in all directions.

Only one remained entirely intact – he had been frozen in fear, hands by his side. Now he stood in the middle of a bloom of his body parts, so it seemed to the Master, surrounded by others in various states of dismemberment, silent or whimpering.

Sebastian knew this creature's thoughts, since he bred the broadcast of them as part of the creature's nature, telepathy being another useful part of his system. He also knew the thoughts of all of these dismembered parts which were still living and capable of thought, and because the colour of a gill-man's thoughts are unique – though colour is a metaphor for a condition that those who are not telepathic cannot hope to understand – he knew that these were all the same gill-man.

He stepped through the gore of a hundred iterations of the same gill-man, and because there was no point remaining in the Underneath, he went to his study.

The Underneath was present in all the duplications Sebastian had made of the Manse over the years, whether those duplications were tied to the material realm, whether they were protective antechamber realms, whether they were housekeeping reals he'd needed in order to correct some kind of flaw in an intermediate iteration, or whether they were some convenience he needed in order to transfer a duplicate from one realm to another without having to do the heavy work of researching spells and gathering the necessary materials.

When you knew how to do it, the creation of intermediate realms was very simple – they already existed, in the weft, and it was a matter of delimiting their extent and making an entrance to them from the material realm. Since delimiting was the difficult part – imagine the difference between letting the whole sea reach the shore as opposed to letting only one small part of the sea reach the shore – then he had always erred on the side of making everything bigger than he needed rather than smaller, so he'd included the Underneath each time, even if there was nothing down there that he needed.

There would be, at least, a hundred intermediate realm iterations of the Underneath that were tied to the material realm, the majority of those being matched iterations, where roughly the same thing went on as it went on in the material realm, with the exception of the excision of key people – himself, Dashini, Bellows, anyone who might have caused problems.

Pipes, gill-men, etc., he'd left in situ.

He had, usually, turned his back on these realms once their job was done, and his study wasn't iterated in any of them.

So, he thought, knowing all that, what had just happened in the Underneath?

First Sebastian went to the library and, having climbed up and down a number of ladders, and after a few false starts, he found the book he wanted. It was a Crusader index of funding applications for possible avenues of research for the Hailey-Beths (Martial) of the Seventh Atheistic Crusade. He'd bought this from pirates, who'd stolen it from Shemsouth, in that way he tended to buy things relevant to the Crusades – more in hope than expectation – and, not having seen much to interest him on a cursory skim, had put it on the shelves.

It was a list of the names of research applications put in to Planning, in alphabetical order, with an indication of whether or not they had been triaged for the next stage of a competitive funding process. So research-heavy was the Assembly's culture that this book was about six inches thick, and because time was no doubt pressing, Sebastian went to his desk, took a reader – which was a slum boy's eye attached to a lens, in turn attached to a very small dictionary, these three things then mounted on a metal frame on wheels – put the book in a machine that turned pages, whispered the words he wanted the reader to search for, and set it off.

When you've finished doing something, there's often a little pause before you move on to doing the next thing. Into pauses like this, your mind inserts things into your consciousness that have been percolating in your unconscious while you've been busy. You stand there with a blank look on your face, and you think, 'What about x?', where x is the thing your unconscious has put into your consciousness.

You can agree to think about it – for Sebastian it was that solicitous look Clarissa had given him when he pulled her heart out of her chest – or not.

If not, you go back to what you were doing, and that makes the thought sink back down into your unconscious until the next time there's a pause.

In this case, it was the latter thing that happened.

Sebastian went to the place where he'd put the canvas bag that was full with the lens-entrance to the miniature realm that mirrored exactly, but in miniature, that part of the world where the Women's Vanguard of the Eighth Atheistic Crusade had their encampment.

Inside, below him, was precisely what he'd been waiting to see all this time – the caravan of relics, the full detachment of Crusaders, and, he could see with his improved vision, the tracks Field Commander Gleed had left as she dragged her iron feet through the dirt.

Around his neck the Tinderbox dangled heavily. If it had cracks in it now, he didn't care. It was only going to have to last a few more hours.

If Gleed was here – and she was – it was time.

At last, he was going to be able to do what he'd been wanting to do for centuries – to wipe Gleed from existence. Whatever she was planning, whatever she had done, she was not going to be a match for him. Clarissa had failed, Portia had failed, Nathaniel had failed – they'd all failed, and all that remained was for him to send the Assembly back to where they came from so he could claim the Tontine prize.

Sebastian pulled his head out and put the bag down on the side table.

The back of his hand – he saw it when he put the bag down – was mottled. It was almost scaly. His knuckles, when he stretched out his fingers, were like mountain ranges, following the line of some ancient buckling of the tectonic plates. When he made a fist, his joints cracked.

He opened the fist, closed it again, took a deep breath.

The study was dark, the corners of the room shadowed, and a film of dust lay over everything. There was an armchair in which his impression was obvious – the springs beneath the fabric had given way, and the part of the antimacassar on which he rested his head was a shade darker than the rest of it, the lace a little looser.

On a tray at the foot of the armchair there was a plate on which half a cracker and a little piece of cheese lay, dry and stale.

There was cold tea in a cup with no saucer.

He saw these things, but his thoughts were elsewhere.

A little bell rang to say that the reader had finished reading the index of Assembly research projects, and that it had found results.

The reader had found a lot of instances of the word 'weft', but very few of 'intermediate' – each one of these the reader directed the page turner to find, and then pointed to them with a silver indicator in the shape of a finger.

The Assembly didn't use the term 'intermediate realm', preferring 'unreal', but Sebastian knew who would use it: Gleed, since she, like him, predated the Assembly.

He couldn't search for her by name, since she wouldn't have been a named researcher, not having Hailey-Bethed in any of the disciplines, but the use of inaccurate terms would be a definite sign of her hand on anything.

Sure enough, about two thirds of the way through the index there was an application for funding for preliminary research into 'methods and means' by which real-anchored unreals – called here 'limited intermediate realms' – might be collapsed. Also listed were Ethical consequences of collapsing unreals into the real, implications on weft power stations, and battlefield deployment. The application was listed as 'not shortlisted', but the index was old.

Not shortlisting research projects in one round of competitive funding didn't mean that they couldn't be re-presented to a subsequent round.

This one would explain what had happened in the Underneath – collapsing the intermediate realms into the real would have done just what he'd seen – and if there was one thing he knew about Gleed, eight crusades in, it was that she didn't give up.

So, if that's what she'd done – found a way of forcing his intermediate realms into the material realm – then what?

In the Underneath it wouldn't be much of a problem – everything was essentially static: machines, pipes, vats, wandering gill-men that no one would miss.

But the rest of the city? The Manse? The antechamber realms? This realm?

He ran to the window and pulled open the curtains.

One red sun rose brightly, its evil rays striking the Master of Mordew straight in the face as he looked down on the Collapse Zone. He was enough outside the rain of heaven that he wasn't immediately crushed, but still too close for safety. He raised his hand and looked at the battlefield from beneath its shade, toyed with the Tinderbox with his other hand.

Someone planning on using a weapon keeps it in their hand. If it's a flick knife, he flicks it open, closes it again. If it's knuckledusters, he flexes his fingers so that the knuckledusters are in the right position and won't pinch. If it's a gun, he fingers the safety, toys with the trigger. The Master of Mordew thumbed the catch on the Tinderbox, let it click almost open, then clicked it shut, then clicked it almost open again.

He did this as he looked around.

What an incredible mess Gleed had made this time.

The Master had made his clothes in such a way that, when he wanted them to, they could deny the natural tendency light had to illuminate them. And, because that would have made a Master of Mordew-shaped black patch in the world that would have been almost as conspicuous as his own image was, he'd sewn the optic nerves of slum boys into the threads of the fabric, each ending in a minuscule and primitive eye, so that whatever these eyes saw the clothes broadcast instead of the light that would normally have been reflected off them. It wasn't perfect, but this made him very difficult to spot in the field.

Because there were, in the incredible mess Gleed had made, an unprecedentedly large number of people and entities that would have wanted him dead, he made his clothes hide him in the landscape.

Down from the sky fell a cattle-headed person, huge and flabby, screaming, and the invisible Master had to dive to one side to avoid being crushed.

Invisibility didn't stop you from being crushed.

Where was Gleed?

Would she be up at some vantage point, out of the fray?

Knowing her, probably not.

Up in the sky, there was Japalura, so huge it was hard to take her in all at once.

Behind her was the Shadow King – the Master refused to use his French title, because he knew perfectly well the god wasn't French, France having disappeared long before he was discovered in the weft.

The Tinderbox was proof against both Japalura and the Shadow King. The Tinderbox was proof against anything. But that didn't mean Sebastian should use it to get rid of them. Who knew in what order the Assembly would prioritise these threats?

If they went for the gods first, as they probably ought to, he could sneak behind the Vanguard and wipe out their racks.

If he took out the gods, then he'd rise up the Vanguard's priority tree, so he left the gods in the sky.

Where was Gleed?

The Master turned his back on the Collapse Zone and traced a line in his mind across what was left of the landscape he remembered, back from the chaos. While he was doing it, a person-headed snake struck him on the side, its heavy skull knocking painfully against his hip bone. He cursed it, stamped on it, retraced the line that should have led back to where the Vanguard had been camped.

There was a patch of higher ground.

The Master of Mordew struggled up the hill, slipping and faltering – his dress shoes weren't made for hiking – and looked around for Gleed again.

He couldn't see her, but there were the mobile concentrate racks, their operatives directing beams of light into the air.

At what?

At angels.

The sky was full of them: like magnesium flares, darting from place to place; like fireflies, guttering and failing; like embers, when the concentrate beams hit them.

Nathan would be up there, somewhere.

If Sebastian went after Nathan with the Tinderbox, took him out, then that would save the Master a job later... But if Nathan wasn't in play, then the Assembly wouldn't have to deal with him. If they didn't have to deal with Nathan, they would be free to deal with the Master.

Where was Gleed?

Take out Gleed, mop up the Assembly, retreat, hide, and let the rest fight it out amongst themselves.

The line of mobile concentrate racks trailed off to the south-west, and behind them were the handheld ankuretics-wielding infantry. Behind them were munitions, all edging forward.

Hold on...

Gleed wouldn't have delegated the operation of whatever weapon she'd used to collapse the realms. That wasn't her style at all.

Sebastian drew another line, one that stretched to the rear of the munitions infantry, snaked along a dry valley, came through the ankuretics, past the mobile concentrate racks and which led, inevitably, he now realised, directly into the chaos Gleed had created.

Of course, she'd be in the middle of it all.

Where else would she be?

There was no option but to go into that mess. The Master pursed his lips, drew a breath through his nose and, because his shoes were too slippery for the trek he knew he would now have to make, he knelt down, undid the laces, and slipped them off. Now his socks were going to get dirty, so he slipped those off too. If his jacket had had pockets, he could have put one sock in each, but they were the kind that were sewn shut. Bellows had assured him it was better for the line, but they were useless for putting things in. Sebastian needed his hands for the locket, so he balled the socks, put the ball in one of his shoes, lined them up neatly and left them on the top of the hill.

He set off, barefoot and cursing, deep into the Collapse Zone.

He found Nathaniel and Clarissa before he had the chance to find Gleed.

They were standing under a canopy of Spark light that Clarissa was generating, protected from the rain of the heavens as if it was nothing more than a passing shower, as if they would wait for it to die down, put their umbrella away, and stroll off to wherever they were going.

They couldn't see the Master. He was still invisible, for the most part, and he had found a temporary shelter of his own: a jumble of tree trunks, leaning against each other where they'd been iterated, reiterated, and had slumped together.

Nathaniel and Clarissa were side by side, each of them splashed in mud and blood.

To Sebastian, they seemed abnormally normal in this horrible place. They looked just like they had looked millennia before, throwbacks to a time so long ago it was forgotten by literally everyone in the world, except by the three of them.

There's something about faces: they don't progress through time like other things.

They age – obviously they age – but they never seem to get 'modern'; they're always trapped back in the past when they settled into themselves. It doesn't matter whether that was ten years ago, or twenty years ago, or ten thousand years ago: they're always of their time, faces.

Admittedly, you have to be of the same time yourself to recognise the fact, and to anyone else those faces just look like the faces of anyone else – older, presumably – but to Sebastian Clarissa and Nathaniel had faces that were perfectly of the past. Specifically, they were of the year 2024, the year the three of them met. The passage of time had become weird, with decades, even centuries becoming redundant ideas, but they hadn't been redundant back then, and that was when Sebastian was made, psychologically speaking.

He stared at these two, and they could have been waiting for a bus, for a train, an Uber.

He'd seen them once, when they didn't think he was looking, queuing to go into a cinema. It must have been a special event because you didn't generally have to queue outside a cinema in those days. Sebastian was sitting in the window of a café over the road, and he looked up from his phone, and there they were, standing in the rain, standing under Clarissa's umbrella.

He'd put up his hand, back then. He'd waved, but they didn't see him. He put down his hand and watched them in that strange, slightly guilty, slightly excited way you watch people when they don't know you're watching them.

They weren't speaking.

They weren't doing anything.

It seemed to Sebastian, back then, that they might have had an argument, otherwise why weren't they talking to each other?

Nathaniel turned to Clarissa, and it looked for all the world like he was about to say, 'It's over between us.' That was the look on his face.

Something about that made Sebastian shift in his chair, like he was going to get up, but his knees knocked against the table leg, rattled the spoon on the saucer of his coffee cup, and rather than say 'It's over between us,' Nathaniel reached down, put his arm around Clarissa, put his hand in the small of her back, and, as if he was in a film, he kissed her.

Now, back in the Collapse Zone, wearing invisible clothes made from the optic nerves of slum boys, sheltered beneath iterated and reiterated tree trunks as the Dying Mud rained down on them all, Sebastian opened the clasp on the Tinderbox.

All he had to do was open the weapon... then direct the beam at them.

It would scour them out of existence, once and for all.

But then, in his mind's eye, there was that solicitous look – the one Clarissa had given him when she had seen him in the God chamber, the one that reminded him of that other time, at that party in Pangbourne, when they'd been dancing, and she looked at him...

He took the Tinderbox, knowing he had one chance at this, knowing that the moment he opened it they would be aware of him, that if he was an inch off he'd miss.

He raised it up...

But that look.

Whether the Master would have used the Tinderbox then, or whether he wouldn't, is something we will never know, because at that exact moment the magical dog Sirius, manifest as Goddog, knocked Sebastian to the ground.

A god who has been dispelled from the material realm by a particular method will be more difficult to dispel from the material realm by that method a second time.

Why is this true?

It is true for the same reason it is true that a person learns by their mistakes.

But does a dog learn from his mistakes?

We know that he does.

If he urinates on a place inside his owner's home, and the owner hits him across the snout, then the dog does not urinate in that spot again. He may urinate elsewhere in the house, in a more discreet place, but when the owner, alerted to the smell, goes there and then comes, thundering, to where the dog now is, cowering, and strikes that dog with a switch on that sensitive part above his tail, he learns not to urinate indoors at all, and reserves his urine for spraying outside.

A dog god, like Goddog, will learn from his mistakes perfectly, and while he might also have the power to urinate where he chooses, and will accept the punishment of no owner, if he is scoured from the material realm by the ray of non-being that a Tinderbox produces, he will know to avoid it in the future.

From the ground, the Master of Mordew opened and directed his weapon at Sirius. It shattered the air, shattered the medium in which the air had been, shattered reality itself down to the weft, and this gap was immediately and loudly filled with weft-stuff, but Sirius had dodged to one side, perfectly quickly, so that it seemed as if he had disappeared from the world and reappeared out of the range of the Tinderbox's beam.

This disappearing was a flaw in the viewer's ability to see things which happened perfectly quickly, and it was a flaw the Master shared. Though he tried to aim where Sirius was, or where he would possibly come to be, or where the Master hoped he might come to be, he could not make the ray hit him.

Sirius simply went where the ray was not.

Through the sky above the Collapse Zone lines like a graphite pencil drawn along enormous straight rulers criss-crossed the sky.

There was much disruption, much collateral damage, the slicing of angels, the slicing of the people who made up the rain of heaven, the slicing, even, of Le Roi de l'Ombre, risen in the sky, but because these were secondary effects of a futile attempt to prevent the approach of Sirius Goddog, they were not concerted enough to do anything definitive.

The landscape that surrounded the Master took on the marks of his failure to strike the dog, and when he became ever more desperate he directed his destructive ray almost at random, cutting through the world down to where molten rock resided, and he had to close his locket or risk turning the ground beneath himself to lava.

That did not stop Sirius.

Sebastian stood, helpless, as the dog came at him, his mouth slavering, his eyes fixed.

The Master turned and ran away, but Sirius Goddog ran Sebastian Cope down. Sebastian darted barefooted, suddenly in one direction, then suddenly in another. For a hare, that is often a successful technique for evading a hunting dog, but this dog was no more a usual kind of dog than the Master was a hare. Sirius went with him wherever the Master went, and because a dog will, when he feels he has the measure of his prey, delight in chasing it, Sirius delighted in chasing the Master, snapping at his heels, toying with him, barking at him from behind.

Eventually Goddog tired of his game and, like thousands of hunting dogs have done to thousands of hares for thousands of years, Sirius nipped at the Master's heel, took the bones of it between his huge front teeth, and flicked him up in the air.

Sebastian Cope flew up.

The pain in his ankle was excruciating, but he didn't let that stop him. He opened the Tinderbox again, for one last time, and directed it down at Sirius who was leaping up to seize the Master in his jaws, sending the ray down into the dog's throat.

Just as Sebastian thought that this time the ray had connected and removed his horrible enemy from the world, Sirius came biting from above and behind, taking the Master in his jaws and shaking him so violently from side to side that the man was torn into pieces.

When Sirius landed back on the Earth, the Tinderbox, which had fallen open onto the ground, was now directing its scouring beam down into the Earth.

Up from the hole that it made erupted an effusion of molten rock which buffeted the locket in every direction, sending its ray in lines of destruction that, randomly, threatened to tear the already beleaguered material realm to pieces.

Of the Weftling

AWAY FROM THE RELIC FIELD, but at the same time as Sharli used the Door Dashini had made with her portal chalk, the ground split open at the base of Mount Mordew.

It was like a discoloured and rotten horse chestnut shell, the city, its spikes black and reaching, the God chamber beneath it like the white flesh of that same shell, but discoloured.

Into the breach the splitting made fell the flukes, the remaining people, a cataract of the Living Mud, the slums, the North and South Fields. Into it tumbled an avalanche of the cliffs and mines, a rush of the sea contained by the Port Walls.

Down inside the horse chestnut shell was the horse chestnut, a shining conker, glittering with a putrid light, a corrupted light, the decomposition of a divinity: blue, orange, white, flickering. Spark flashed and arced between every surface, internal, external, upward and inward.

There, dark like a black cancer deep in the bowel of the city, was the weftling's corpse.

Dead things remain still, living things move, that is their nature.

This dead black cancer moved.

It was like a drunk, rising from its nauseated coma to vomit: its movements were tentative, but driven. It was forced into motion by the desire to purge itself.

It seemed tiny, down there inside the earth, but scale was meaningless to the weftling, to this city, and Gleed knew what it was she was seeing, via intelligencer, because she had seen it before.

There are many decisions to make in war, for a Field Commander. Sometimes they can be made without hesitation because it is clear what will win a battle. Sometimes they can be made without hesitation because a retreat is all there is left to do. Sometimes, though, a Field Commander does not hesitate because they must do something, now, before a battle threatens to get out of hand, threatens to exceed the field that has been drawn up for it, that contains it.

This was one of the latter times.

That black speck that perhaps only Gleed's mechanical eyes could make out clearly was the weftling, moving even in his death, resurrecting himself as the divisions between the material realm failed and made redundant the notion of life and death as they related to him.

The Collapse Zone was making him capable of movement, even in death.

Gleed patched herself into the Munitions system, and diverted whatever could be diverted from the surface into the God chamber.

She emptied shells, explosives, depth charges, directly into the breach.

The beam weapons, previously deployed to keep the other gods at bay, pivoted to follow Gleed's eyeline. They rose on their mounts and scorched into the sickening wound in the belly of Mordew, into its corrupted womb, within which the dividing cell of a Theite Resurrection Scenario had implanted.

Of Portia Hall

NOW HERE CAME the warpling.

She appeared in the middle of everything, because where would be a better place for her to appear?

She was in the form of a woman of average age and average weight and average height.

She was altogether average-seeming to everyone who saw her, whether they were a person-headed snake, or a cattle-headed person, or a man, or a woman, or a neuter person, or a god in the form of a wolfpack.

Whoever saw her saw an average-seeming woman.

Why was this so?

The question is incorrectly posed, just as the averageness and womanliness of her seeming is a misapprehension.

When she appeared on the relic fields, rained on by the Dying Mud created by the weft-bomb's collapsing of the heavens of Malarkoi, pelted by the falling bricks from a thousand pyramids, piled around on all sides by the anxious repetitions of the world that the White Stag made, if she had appeared in the world in a form unlike that which people would recognise as an average woman the world would change around her, instantly, so that it would always be true that she looked like an average woman.

And if this were a world in which there were no women, then suddenly there would have been women, because it was the warpling who determined the way reality was, and not the other way around.

Only someone ignorant of her power could ever think that there was something strange in her averageness, in her woman-liness, since all things fall in line with the warp.

And if the objection is made that the womanliness of the warpling and the manliness of the weftling implies that these states are natural and other states are not, then that is to fail to understand that, like the infinite range of colours, there is an infinite range of being, all of which has the same valence, which is precisely zero until an external value system is placed upon it. Then, if there are discrepancies in the values allotted to things under a system, it is the system that is at fault, the observing consciousness that is at fault; the mind that brings value to the valueless cosmos is the thing that is at fault.

Valence is always against the will of the warpling, which is towards perfect undifferentiation, something that is not appreciable in the realms, and not even appreciable in the weft, but which is a condition of the warp, and which is represented to your consciousnesses as averageness and womanliness.

The warpling comes to our eyes as an average woman, but is nothing of the sort to herself.

She is a perfect and formless 'if' having no value.

She is a perfect and formless 'or'.

If this makes no sense to you, that is because your consciousness is insufficiently broad in scope to contain the truth of its meaning.

The warpling appeared in the middle of everything and in that appearing she knew everything – it was self-evident to her.

Or, perhaps, it would be better to say that those things she knew were always evidenced in the world pending her arrival.

Or, perhaps the weftling, when he was alive, and knowing that the warpling's arrival would be imminent, had moved everything in every way towards the state that represented, in materiality, the conditions of the warpling's knowledge.

When she arrived, everything was congruent with her, even the conditions of the weft in their possibility and impossibility. These states were no obstacle to her.

So, it becomes possible to ask, since the warpling was all-powerful, were the conditions into which she arrived created by her?

Because she was all-knowing, did she mean for all this to happen?

Because her intent must, by definition, be perfect, was the condition of the world when she arrived 'right' and 'good', since those things are kinds of perfection that the warpling must necessarily embody?

If that was the case then it would be difficult to explain what happened next, because, around the place the warpling appeared, everything began to change, and there is no need to change a perfect thing.

The warpling stood, the soles of her sandals resting on the backs of two dead persons, corpses extending away from her in all directions, the rain of the heavens threatening to smash into her all the screaming denizens of the decanted heavens, the Dying Mud threatening to drench her, the sick light and the sicker shadows of the Roi de l'Ombre's suns dappling her with their evilness, the roaring of Japalura, the leakage from the God chamber, the munitions of the Assembly, the beam weapons, the Angelic Army of Waterblack, gravity increasing, the strafing nothingness of the Tinderbox, lava from an unrestrained eruption…

Without her making the slightest move to do it, the objects within the range of the warpling's existence snapped in on themselves, creasing and diving along their lines of symmetry, over and over, like pieces of paper, until they occupied volumes too small for the material realm to contain them.

Everything that came near her stopped existing in the usual dimensions, extended instead inward, through the weft, into the warp, to a place only the warpling knew.

Whether the people and things to whom this happened had a continued existence there is impossible to say, but everything that came within the warpling's range did this. They folded inwards, booming and popping as they did it, air rushing at speed into the gaps left in the material realm.

As if she was descending in an elevator, the warpling sank down, the pile of corpses around her disappearing until she met the Earth.

Then, all of those flawed and faulty reiterations of the material realm the White Stag had made folded themselves inward too, into and through the weft, to who knows where.

When they went there, there was a deafening cracking sound. Every element of them was wrenched through the iterations of reality that remained. Spark in the form of holy lightning lanced out from between every object, every iteration of the real as it was folded into the warp.

Whatever these arcs of lightning struck, those things came alive, whether they were corpses, or rocks, or particles of air and dust, whatever they were, no matter how huge or tiny, came alive filled with the will of the warpling...

... except only for a moment, since then they were folded out of the world with everything else, through into the warp.

The existence here of that average-seeming woman was acting to remove all obstacles to the material realm's proper form, all impossible magical breaches of warp-law finding themselves drawn by her presence necessarily inwards, ever inwards.

All that would be necessary for everything to return to the way it ought to be, the way it was before the weftling was murdered, would be for the warpling to remain where she was, at the centre of things.

What was to stop that?

Portia Hall stopped it.

She had planned it this way.

By making the Levels of her Pyramid, by making her heavens, by putting in them gods who existed in exactly the way that would lead to exactly the kind of chaos the warpling would arrive to resolve, by resurrecting Nathan Treeves to the world, by allowing the Master of Mordew to live rather than die, by taunting the Assembly so that they would unleash their weft-bomb, by facilitating, with her assassins, Clarissa's failed attempt to become the weftling, by all these things and more, part of a plan she had meditated on in her heaven, huge and naked and ever-thinking, Portia Hall, the Mistress of Malarkoi, captured the warpling.

From above the world, her feet so huge that only one was visible, the curvature of the Earth hiding the other, she pounced at impossible speed, igniting herself in an agony of fire so quickly did she make her matter progress through the air, stooping in pain down from the stratosphere, arms outstretched, hands grasping for the warpling.

She had prepared her spells in advance, and made the air solid around the average woman.

Either this was sufficient to prevent the warpling from moving away, or the warpling acquiesced to being seized, because the Mistress of Malarkoi seized the warpling in both friction-ignited hands like a child does when it catches a butterfly, cupping one hand against the other to make a space for the butterfly to live in, to flutter in, not to crush it.

The mistress didn't giggle to feel the tickling of the warpling's wings, the warpling's six legs, the curling and uncurling of the warpling's proboscis, the gentle rub of her feathered antennae – the warpling had none of the these – instead the colossal Portia Hall triumphantly screamed, deafening the world.

It was a scream like the laugh of the victorious child, prior to the pinning of their butterfly to its board, prior to the framing of that thing, prior to the careful handwriting of its Latin name.

Look, Daddy, it's for your birthday! His mouth showing, as it never did, the curl of his lips in the smallest smile, the best smile, so longed for.

Then, as if neither of them had ever been there, they disappeared from the world, sublimated from it, went to a higher place, went to the warp, never to return.

Or we might say that when a nearly impossibly massive object moves with nearly impossible speed, it shatters the air like lightning does, and like lightning it thunders, and when Portia Hall, former Mistress of Malarkoi, in the form she took in her Pyramid of a titanic woman, almost impossibly high, reached down from where she had been waiting, her legs astride the world at such a distance no one had been able to see her ankles, her knees, her thighs, the whole of her so high that she was out of sight, when she reached down at near impossible speed, from near impossible height, it rattled the sky.

Down came her open hand, a mile across, probably more, flying to the point where the warpling was, fingers reaching. She drove that hand down into the Earth, rippled the fabric of it as if she had plunged her hand into a basin of water. The ground made waves in concentric circles that toppled everything standing on it no matter how large, no matter how secure – the Assembly's racks, every and all ancient structures, any gathering of material that could have previously been thought to carry a form, all recognisable landmarks.

Any landbound creature that could not fly was tossed up into the air, from where, eventually, it crashed back down, certain to die, and all of the creatures that could fly were buffeted by the great volumes of air that Portia Hall's passing hand displaced, driving some of them down, breaking some of their wings, knocking some of them up, some of them unconscious, so that they fell and died beside the landbound creatures.

She drove her hand into the Earth not so that she could kill everything around her, but so that she could encapsulate the warpling by seizing that part of the material realm that she existed within.

Then, as if neither of them had ever been there, they disappeared from the world, sublimated from it, went to a higher place, went to the warp, never to return.

Why had Portia Hall allowed herself to be killed by Nathan Treeves, long ago now, when he was sent by the Master to Malarkoi?

So that she could retreat to her heaven.

Why did Portia Hall need to retreat to her heaven?

So that she could concentrate on the proliferation of her other heavens.

Why did she need to proliferate the other heavens?

So that one day they could be collapsed by the weft-bomb.

Why did she need the Thousand Million Flames?

So that Nathan Treeves could kill them.

How could he kill them?

If she could summon him to her heaven.

601

How could she summon him to her heaven.

If he was dead.

How could he be killed?

If the Master was able to kill him.

How would the Master be able to kill him?

If he ended his war against her.

Then what?

The Master would overplay his hand in trying to kill Nathan.

Why was it important that the Master killed Nathan?

So that she could resurrect him.

Why was it important that she could resurrect him?

So that he would take Mastery of Waterblack, despite his father's wishes.

How would she resurrect him?

By making him sacrifice the Thousand Million Flames.

Why?

So that Nathan would have to remedy their deaths when he became Master of Waterblack.

How would he remedy their deaths?

By making them an army of angels.

And if they were angels? And if there was the weft-bomb? And if there was the Tinderbox?

Then the material realm would be threatened.

And if the material realm was threatened?

Then the warpling would come to fix it.

It was just like when they had, all those years ago, killed the weftling by threatening his creation, drawing him out so that they could kill him, and while those other idiots had fixated on the Tontine, only Portia had understood that there was a greater prize.

To leave the realms entirely, to go to the place outside the realms where the warpling resided. Now Portia's enormous hand clutched around the warpling, crushed her inside her great fist, compacted her inside a handful of earth, the best part of a mountain.

Portia raised up her hand, so high that it left the world behind, and as she held it in the endless vacuum she whispered under her breath, silently in the airlessness that a sufficient height above the ground brings. Though she made no sound, the shape of the words on her lips made the spell that would kill the warpling, that would let Portia Hall replace her, that would bring everything into concordance with Portia's wishes, after so long.

When this was done she left the world behind, becoming suddenly a great absence into which the material realm rushed.

Whether she achieved in doing what she did what it was that she wanted we will never know. What we can say is that the chaos the warpling came to the world to remedy was not remedied on the warpling's removal, and that Portia Hall was never seen in the material realm again.

As if neither of them had ever been there, they disappeared from our world, sublimated from it, went to a higher place, went to the warp, never to return.

A Book of the Weft

I T IS GENERALLY ACCEPTED that books cannot read themselves. 'Reading' is an act that is done 'to' a book, not 'by' it, but surely this is because most books do not possess sufficient consciousness, or will, or intelligence to 'do' anything, except exist as long as their bindings are whole and their pages are dry.

What of books bound from the skin of a boy, and into whose pages his mind has been magically impregnated? Is a book of this sort not sufficiently unusual to allow that the 'general acceptance' of a book's inability to read might be questioned in its case? A boy can read – and if he cannot yet he can be taught to do so – and if words and images are printed onto his skin, can't he read them?

Adam Birch could read himself.

What would be the point of a book reading itself?

Surely the words contained within a book are constitutive of it, and if a book can be said to be a living thing, aren't those things that constitute it known to it? So that reading itself would be redundant? Since it *is* itself? And reading is an activity that brings the unknown inside the self – external ideas, external events, external places. Isn't that what reading is for?

Perhaps.

In the case of a book made from a boy, which contains his living mind, does not 'reading', as it would apply here, match 'thinking', as it would be done in a boy? The mind of a boy, after all, is the thing that contains all of the immaterial concepts proper to him in the manner that a book contains all of the concepts proper to it, and while a boy may be considered a limited thing, we would not say that there was no point in him thinking.

Indeed, we would encourage him to think, that activity broadening the range of him, his scope, in the hope that he might one day become a man, that he might grow educated and intelligent.

So, when Adam, the book, read himself, is that not an analogue of a boy thinking to himself?

Moreover, Adam Birch was an unusual type of book in another way: his words were not fixed.

In fact, his words were often not in evidence at all, so shouldn't we admit that not only did he read himself, but that he also wrote himself, and drew himself? His mind did the work of putting words and images on his pages.

Is this not an analogue of the imagination? The imagination makes things that are not real come into reality, his pages in that way are like the blank expanse of the world behind a boy's closed eyes.

A boy will, when he needs to, bring into his mind a simulation of the world. Let us say that that boy has an anxiety – perhaps there is another boy who intimidates him in the schoolyard – and to remove the source of that anxiety the boy creates scenarios in his mind that allow him to plan the means to avoid this other boy, or to best him, or to embarrass him, or to, in some other way, prevent the boy from bothering him. He makes a playground in his mind, and here and there he puts himself and makes players act in plays he writes of avoidance and revenge.

He has imaginary people act their parts on the stages of his mind.

This is what Adam did.

A boy might, if he has suffered loss – perhaps his father has been crushed against a factory wall by a coal cart, run off its rails – make a father in his mind and speak to him there words he could not speak to him when he was alive. These might be declarations of filial affection, or expressions of apology, or requests for clarification of the location of this or that important document his mother needs, but which cannot be found about the house.

This boy can make good a lack in the real with his imagination, even if it proves to be insufficient to staunch his grief, or locate the missing wills and testaments.

Adam Birch had lost his brother, Bellows, whose right name neither of them remembered.

Adam Birch, the magical book, had the mind of a boy.

He could read himself.

He could write and draw on the pages of himself.

He could make in himself an analogue of imagination, and of thought.

This is what he did.

He fell open by himself one night on the side of Mount Mordew, where Clarissa Delacroix had left him before she went entirely inward, appearing then in the God chamber in the form of the weftling's corpse, animating it, thereby claiming for herself god's mantle, before her enemy Sebastian Cope stole her heart.

Adam wrote Bellows out in words on his pages, drew him in his magical inks and watercolours, made him speak through ventriloquism, and because such a thing is possible in a book, he made his brother there threefold: once as the man, factotum of the Master of Mordew; once as the devolved child, soon to be killed; and also as Adam remembered him as a boy, hazy and flickering, blurred and edgeless, the remnants of whatever impressions Adam possessed.

On one side of the page was the man, his nose cutting through the air like the prow of a ship. Facing him on the other page was the boy, timid and quiet. Across the fold of the pages in the middle there was the real brother.

What was this real brother's name?

Surely that was information Adam should have had.

Why was it lost?

Down in the ground there came rumblings from under the surface of Mordew, and up through a rent in the ground surrounded by gill-men and scaffolding, flashes of light shone, making every surface contrast against every other, flickeringly, briefly: reds and greens and putrid blues.

When these lights hit Adam's pages, he altered the colours of his Bellowses to make them right.

He altered the colours back when the flashes passed.

Were there spells in his pages that Adam could use to give his brothers their bodies back?

Surely there were, but he did not have the objects and fetishes to cast them, nor the arms and legs to gather necessary things.

Clarissa could have done it, but she was gone, and for that reason Adam lay alone on the ground, resting against the mountain, writing and drawing his threefold brother.

He lay there, reading himself, and he voiced the four of them in his plays.

His only audience were spined monsters and blue flukes. His only audience was the sea itself, blown up into waves that washed the shoreline.

'Brother,' Man-Bellows said, from the page, in Adam's voice impersonating him, 'it is beneath you to lie here in the dirt, useless!'

Adam replied, speaking out the words, 'What is the point in doing anything else, brother?'

Because a drawing has no auditory apparatus, there was no way the drawing of Man-Bellows could hear the words Adam Birch spoke. To remedy this, at the top of the page he wrote the title: 'Things my Brother has Heard me Say'.

'What is the point in doing anything else, brother?' he wrote.

Man-Bellows looked puzzled on the page.

Adam did not erase him, then draw him puzzled: the lines of the image moved magically, seeming to be a thing of themselves that was equivalent to a man. Boy-Bellows put up his hand and Adam nodded to him, in his mind, that he should speak. 'There isn't any point in doing anything else, Adam.'

To this, Real Brother agreed, but Man-Bellows did not. 'No point is required!' he said, raising his nose in the air and stretching up until his hands disappeared over the edge of the paper. 'We have no need to ask questions such as that. We exist, do we not? Think of all of those things that do not exist, infinite in their variety! We exceed them in every way. We are approaching miracles, so almost impossible is our being. This is the only requirement! It is our obligation to the unlikeliness of our existence to do something with it, whatever that happens to be. We cannot fail, we cannot falter: we have already succeeded! It remains only now to determine what it is we must do with our success.'

Boy-Bellows appeared to feel that this was a less than convincing argument – he looked down at his knees and said nothing – but Real Brother spoke up. 'If you're right,' he said, 'then I know what we should do.' He had a different way of speaking to both Man and Boy-Bellows, softer, less bombastic, less depressive, closer to Adam's voice, but still different by degrees. His tone lacked magic, lacked artificiality, even though he was an impression of a forgotten thing, artificially made by a magical book.

'Of course I am right,' Man-Bellows said. 'Outside of our service to the Master, even if he has discarded us, we must be true to our nature, which is unique.'

'So, what should we do, then?' Adam Birch said. He silenced Man-Bellows when he tried to speak, erasing his mouth, and listened to Real Brother.

'We need to fix ourselves,' Real Brother said. 'Put ourselves back to the way we were before.'

Adam thought about this, the images stilling on his pages.

He was sure Real Brother was right, but he hadn't the first idea how to go about it.

How can a book move itself around the world?

It cannot, even if it is a magic book.

Adam could, by virtue of concentrating, open himself up at a particular page, but unless he was flat against a surface – a lectern or a table, for example – he didn't have enough strength to do it easily. If there was any impediment – an ink bottle, or even a ribbon laid across his cover – he would remain shut.

Even if he could open, with his spine supported, all he could do then was close.

He couldn't flip himself over, close, and open again, progressing slowly across the ground. Even if he could, how long would it take him to go somewhere far away? How would he know where he was going? He couldn't see, in any real sense, or hear anything but words directed at him.

Adam had drawn enough birds to know how they flew. He had even drawn books as if they were birds, flapping their pages as if those were wings, but this was just a fantasy.

He was practically immobile.

If Clarissa had left him on the Island of White Hills, where she had emerged from the ground and received the crossbow bolt to her face, and where Boy-Bellows had received another to his chest, then perhaps he could have revived the child, or the dog. Perhaps he could have made something from that circumstance.

But here he was alone and abandoned on Mount Mordew, lying in the Living Mud. Clarissa had dropped him here on fleeing the Druze, burning everything to become the weftling.

'There's your answer,' Real Brother said, from between two closed pages.

He wasn't supposed to be able to speak by himself, Adam thought, but then again, what did Adam know of himself, really? What do any of us know about our internal workings? What goes on inside the body of a person? How does it all work? How does a mind work? What is a mind capable of? Does a person know how their liver works? Their pancreas? If called upon to use the electricity of their nerves for some external process, how would they harness it?

A magic book knows a lot of things, but it is a lesser thing than a person, and what does a person know of anything?

Very little.

So why should a magic book know itself, inside out?

'You aren't listening to me,' Real Brother said.

He was right. What had he said? The Living Mud was the answer?

609

'It's obvious,' Real Brother said.

'He is absolutely right,' Man-Bellows said. 'The Master, in his Underneath, used vats of this mud to make servants of slum boys. He used it to make me, combining its divinity with his magic to force the world into the forms he preferred. Something of the same sort can be achieved with your magic, can it not? Form legs for us, form arms, form a noble face and jutting nose so that we might make our way about this world!'

Adam didn't need to open his pages to see Man-Bellows gesticulating, and nor did he need to do it to see Boy-Bellows shaking his head ruefully, or to hear the boy say it would come to nothing.

Adam's pages contained the energies of many spells, but he only knew their names, not how to use them. They were there as a necessity of his construction, but Adam didn't know what they did.

'You're thinking too hard,' Real Brother said. 'Just open up.'

Whether his brother meant this figuratively or literally, Adam opened his pages anyway, let the Living Mud coat his cover, which was made from the skin of the boy he used to be, turned to leather, his teeth crushed to ivory.

Nothing happened immediately – creation isn't like that – but he could feel the tingling of the Mud on his cover, the interaction of two different magics.

Adam lay with his three brothers, his pages open to the sky, and though he knew they couldn't see anything, or hear anything, and he was scarcely any better, he drew them looking up into the night, drew the constellations he thought they could see, despite the endless overcast that covered Mordew.

While he was doing this, along came a spiked fluke, rolling and turning down the side of Mount Mordew.

It would be hard to credit this thing with an intelligence, but no intelligence is required for a coincidence to occur. The spiked fluke rolled until it came to Adam Birch, and then it continued to roll directly over where he lay, with his pages open. It was like a sea urchin, this fluke, and one of its spikes pierced Adam through the middle of his verso.

A boy so pierced might die, since he has organs inside him that he needs – we have already mentioned his pancreas and his liver, but there are also the heart and the lungs, along with others – but a book has no such organs. If a book is a magic book, it is the magic in it that represents its life force. If it is not magic, then it is the words. Neither magic nor words can be pierced to death by the spike or spine of an enormous sea urchin as it rolls down Mount Mordew.

So, Adam Birch did not die, and neither did the people on and in his pages.

In fact, it was this piercing that allowed Adam to resolve his inability to move: once the urchin's spike was inside his magical pages, Adam gained a level of control over the fluke, just as he had control over everything that was inside him.

If that seems too coincidental, then there is no reason why it should. If one were to lie motionless in the middle of, say, a park, how long would it be before an occupant of that park, say a fox, came over and inspected the person lying there, motionless?

It would certainly happen, eventually.

Granted, it might not happen as quickly to us, as we lie in the park, as it appears that it happened to Adam, lying on Mount Mordew, but who is to say how long it took to happen to him?

Who is to say the impression that it didn't take too long is not a function of the writing? That, with a clause, it is better to write 'while he was doing this', rather than to represent, in sentences, the passage of a very long period of time, long enough so that all coincidences seem more likely than not, though that makes for dry reading?

By coincidence, the spiked urchin fluke pierced Adam Birch's pages, and this allowed him, with spells, to take some level of influence over the creature's movements, something he used to move it around.

•

He might have found this sufficient, Adam, but Bellows the man, who had more experience of Mordew and its particularities than any of the others, said, 'Go to the Circus! The Treeves boy made a great number of boy-shaped flukes rise from the Living Mud gathered there. If it is possible for you to possess an enormous sea urchin, the uses for which are limited, there is nothing to say that you might not also be able to possess a more familiar host, and one which we can use more easily to do the kinds of things we are familiar with.'

This seemed like an excellent idea, but when Adam depicted the information he could gather from the urchin fluke's sensory apparatuses on the page for Man-Bellows, he could only show the city as it now was, stretched up into the sky, and therefore Man-Bellows couldn't direct them to the Circus, since he had never seen the city like this.

Here again, we can assume a convenient coincidence occurred.

Or we can experience a long and meandering description of the passage of time, the description of the going nearby of a great many things that weren't a Nathan fluke, descriptions of conversations on the page of a book of ever less hope and enthusiasm for Man-Bellows's plan, descriptions of the rolling across Mount Mordew of a lonely and possessed urchin, looking but never finding, it growing sad, it growing hopeless, it understanding the jeopardy inherent in the possession of a creature with a finitude of Spark energy, ever waning. We could read the accounts of them rolling down to where the Sea Wall had been, to where the water lapped unhappily against a tumbled section of brickwork against which the urchin became wedged, and where, as the days progressed, the magical energy required to maintain the possession of the fluke caused Adam's lifeforce to ebb. We could imagine the inks on his pages fading, the Bellowses, man, boy and brother, bidding Adam a sad farewell, expressing their regret that they never got to know their brother, to remember their childhoods together, to rectify all the sadnesses of before. We could, in long sentences, in acreages of paragraphs, watch them, like people starving to death, begin to hallucinate, to see, coming down from above, the gods of their choosing. These divinities would open their arms and gather the Birches to their divine breasts.

Then they would be rescued, at the very last moment, from their deaths by the arrival of the fluke that, just as easily, we could have decided between us had been passing by sometime earlier, saving them and us the necessity of experiencing what is, in the final reckoning, irrelevant to the eventual outcome of this part of Adam Birch's story.

The book eventually passed its consciousness to a Nathan fluke, just as Man-Bellows suggested. Adam's form as a book was held inside that fluke's chest. It became, like the brain in a womb-born child, the centre of his consciousness. His person was made of five dissociated personae: Adam Birch, Man-Bellows, Boy-Bellows, Brother-Bellows and the self of the Nathan fluke. By a complex psychic accommodation, these personae were able to take control of the fluke body.

They were able to live through it.

They dressed themself in discarded clothes. They practised the movements of their body. They came to communal decisions about where they should and shouldn't go.

What did they see where they went?

They saw many unusual things, including, but not limited to:

the mountain Mordew had become, assailed by a great number of firebirds

firebirds ascending into the air, the flesh of God in their beaks

a relatively whole little dory – which is a type of boat – and two oars

oars cutting through the water, propelling a dory away from Mordew

the slaver ship, *Serapis Christus*, too close to avoid

slavers taking a great many people from the Collapse Zone

Field Commander Gleed, returning home reluctantly, having lost her charge the Women's Vanguard of the Eighth Atheistic Crusade, in retreat

Commander Gleed ordering fusiliers of the Crusade to fire on the *Serapis Christus*, since slavery is against Assembly law

landfall onto ground made from a great many corpses and collapsed buildings

in the distance, the New Golden Pyramid of Malarkoi, just like the old one, but not in the same place

corpses of Gams

corpses of Joes

a multitude of angels losing their light, flickering and falling as their Master is severed from the weft

Anaximander and Sirius, returned to the realm of ghosts

the entrance to the New Golden Pyramid of Malarkoi, just like the old one

more corpses of Gams

more corpses of Joes

the new Mistress of Malarkoi, dead, with the Nathan Knife in her back

Sharli, the assassin, kneeling

Dashini, Gam and Joes, sending Sharli to her heaven with the weft-knife

Dashini, Gam and Joes, using Sharli's Spark to make a new person

Prissy, as she was before, rejoining her friends

These things Adam Birch wrote and drew in his pages, along with all the things that had happened before. Sometimes he wrote in one mode – as a list – sometimes in another – as a story – and even sometimes he wrote as an essay, as a glossary, as an appendix, as an interlude. The people he lived with had different preferences and likes, and because a book may be read in different ways, he wrote himself like that.

Read me from start to finish, if you wish. Or skip through me. Or flick here and there. Dog-ear my pages, if you must: the choice is yours. Only, do not tell me what I must be: we are all different, I as much as you, and so may it remain forever.

The Singing of Pirates and Dogs

PENTHENNY PUT HER HAT on the table beside the bottle of rum. More than likely the rum had been watered, but that didn't mean she was allowed to drink it.

Watered rum is still rum.

It was too late for breakfast and too early for lunch, so the front room of the Dockside Inn was thinly occupied. Penthenny never came here – it was too posh – so she didn't recognise the boy with the broom, scraping broken glass from under a table and gingerly picking the shards up and putting them in a metal bin. His collar was high and uneven, and his sleeves poked a good two inches out from his jacket. The girl at the bar, again unknown to the captain, round-faced and blonde, wore the same uniform. That's what made Penthenny think this place was too posh – someone was paying for them to be dressed up, and she didn't see why it should be her.

Or why anyone would bother.

Actually, did posh places water the rum? Perhaps she should see…

No, she told herself, but she didn't leave.

The tables were all made to the same design, all of the same wood, all varnished and polished and all with a flower in a vase on a doily.

Expensive and pointless and each adding a copper to the price of a drink.

In the places Penthenny used to frequent, before the prohibition came down from Niamh against drinking, anyone sitting nursing their drinks across the hours of a long afternoon would be lucky if there were two pieces of furniture that matched: stools and rocking chairs, benches and church pews, dining tables, library tables, mortuary tables, all finding themselves jammed uncomfortably close to each other.

Flowers?

Doilies?

Absolutely no chance.

Bowls of peanut shells and pipe ash? Yes.

Long, black, burn marks? Yes.

Initials carved with the point of a knife? Insults against some named person's chastity? Obscene and scarcely plausible anatomical diagrams? All yes.

But that was the point. Penthenny wouldn't have been found dead in a place like this, and that was why she was in here: so she wouldn't be found, alive or dead.

She looked at the bottle of rum, reached for it – saliva had built up in her mouth, like it does in a dog's mouth when he considers his food bowl, and she sought to wash it away – but, sighing, she eventually pulled her hand back.

The round-faced, blonde-haired bar girl was the only person in there. If there had been a few more patrons, one even, it would be easier, but as it was… Taking a cork out of a bottle of rum doesn't make much noise, and nor does pouring a full glass of it, and even less does downing that glass in one, wiping the lips, then filling it again, but in an empty room, with a single other soul, that soul silently and methodically polishing a glass, it doesn't take much noise to alert them. Then she'd look over – her big, round, young eyes in her big, round, young face, with her big, round, rosy cheeks, rosy with youth and not with the broken veins decades of hard drinking brings – and, illuminated in her innocent gaze, Penthenny would see herself laid bare in all her debauched, dissolute, depressive glory. A drunk, temporarily reformed by the love of a good woman, about to fall off the wagon.

And she had once been a girl like that bar girl – young and good and unspoiled.

The bar girl caught Penthenny staring and, given that staring was the professional cue for her to come over, she put down the pint glass she was polishing, straightened her apron, picked up her pad and pencil.

Penthenny hurriedly looked down, stopping the girl in her tracks, and turned her attention to the only other place it could be turned.

On the label of the bottle of rum someone had painted a sketch of a horse's head, and Penthenny traced her finger along the outline of it – along the grey mane, over the erect ears, mid-twitch, down the proud muzzle, around the mouth, down its muscular neck.

Horses.

What weaknesses are they prone to? Do they wake in the morning, cracked of lip and dry of tongue, thinking of drink, having dreamt all night of drinking? When they see the face of their wife, lying beside them, do they blame her – before they retract that blame, unwelcome even in secret – for the absence on the bedside table of a fortifying glass of last night's whiskey?

Probably not.

Penthenny pushed back in her chair, making it scrape on the floorboards. Some drunks will taunt themselves with their own terrible failures, will bring to mind the awful and regrettable things they have done, all for the sake of drink, as a way of lowering themselves in their own eyes to such a low level that they make themselves so disgusting to themselves that they can then begin to drink again, knowing that they aren't worth saving.

Drink is very clever like that – it will find ways to get itself inside a person – but Penthenny wasn't that kind of drunk.

She was more the kind of drunk who would justify drinking by building herself up in her own eyes, making herself an exception from all the other drunks by virtue of her innate intelligence, or her courage, or her fortitude, telling herself that she was too good to be a drunk, and that therefore she should, if she wanted to have a drink, just have a drink, since where was the harm in that, for a person of her superior qualities?

In any case, drink made her make neither of these arguments today. Instead, she caught herself just in time and pushed back her chair, scraping the floorboards. She resolved to return to the *Muirchú*, which was floating calmly out in the dock, to apologise to Niamh for whatever it was that Niamh was angry with her for, and to get back to work.

The bottle on the table?

She would leave it there, the price of it her punishment for having brought herself this far.

The trouble was that, when she went to get up, who should come in but Pascale de St Aubrey with a party of three, by their uniforms, dock sheriffs. The four of them went directly to the bar and though Penthenny was pretty sure they hadn't seen her, she had no choice but to turn away from them and hope, by some miracle, that St Aubrey went to use the facilities before he sat down, giving her the chance to leave.

Penthenny was at least one hundred silver in hock to St Aubrey, and two months in arrears on the vigorish.

She should, really, have considered the fact that a man of St Aubrey's resources might drink in the poshest place on the dockside, and remembered that she would prefer to see him least of all of the people she could possibly have hoped to bump into.

The drink again: it'll get you in the shit – that's what Niamh said – telling you where to go and what to do so it can get itself inside you. What does drink care if you run into people to whom you owe money, in the presence of just the right amount of sheriffs to drag you off to the cells while bailiffs are summoned to make good your debts.

Now what was there to do but turn her back, put on her hat, pour herself a drink from the bottle of rum, and look like she was here to drink it, some superior, but still anonymous, morning booze-hound of no interest to anyone, then hope to God that St Aubrey needed a slash and would take a decent amount of time over it so that she could bolt for the door while he was so occupied, run back to the ship, make up with Niamh and haul anchor?

Penthenny poured the drink, and it seemed to her that the horse on the label was amused by this turn of events – its eye was twinkling, its lips were drawn back over its teeth.

As it happened, Pascale de St Aubrey had pissed prior to leaving his office to meet the sheriffs, and had no need to do so again. Penthenny could see him, faintly, in the reflection of one of the small panes that made up the window – a ghost of himself, warped by the imperfectly blown glass, marching over to the table nearest the door to sit with the sheriffs, having generously stood them a round.

They were talking – Penthenny could hear every word, the place was so quiet – about building a new jetty and repairing the dry dock, and St Aubrey, being that sort of man, was explaining to the sheriffs how he had lent money to finance that project. The sheriffs, speaking in a kind of code that sounded perfectly reasonable, but when decoded spoke of activities that, if they weren't entirely illegal, certainly weren't in the interests of the people to whom St Aubrey had lent money to – the securing of contracts at a higher price than the market ought properly to have established through the use of cartels, for example, which, should they all combine their efforts, would be very profitable to all of them.

The St Aubrey in the glass pane – he was a tall and very thin man, all dressed in green, with pointed green shoes and a dangling green earring, sitting with one long leg crossed tightly over the other, with his long fingers on the thigh and knee of the top leg – was smiling and laughing. He occasionally looked over to where Penthenny was sitting, and though she couldn't make out the level of detail she'd need to be sure, she felt like he frowned in a kind of half-recognition.

This was probably not true, but she worried that it was.

Could she, if she was quick, make it to the lavatories herself? Find some way out from there? It was a risky plan, but so was sitting here.

She picked up her glass, very, very nearly knocked it back, stopping at the last moment with its rim on her bottom lip and her mouth half open. Before she could put it down, she felt a hand on her shoulder.

'Drinking alone? We can't have that, can we?'

Penthenny didn't turn round, but she could tell from the man's voice that he wasn't St Aubrey. Anyway, she could still see him and the sheriffs in the window.

This man had thick fingers, nails bitten down, cuticles red and chewed, also not typical of St Aubrey. He must have come in while Penthenny was distracted.

On another occasion, she would have grabbed this man's wrist, twisted it as she stood, drawn the shorter of her two swords, turned and put the point of it under his chin, something she'd come to learn over years of drinking alone in unfamiliar inns was the quickest way to deal with the ubiquitous letches and chancers who imposed themselves on lone women. But, with St Aubrey so near and no other activity to draw attention to any of the other tables, this would have certainly revealed her for who she was to the man from whom she was hiding.

So, instead, she gestured with the same hand that would have put the bitten-fingered man in a wrist lock to the chair opposite her. Sometimes it's useful to have a beard – someone to make you appear less like yourself – and this was one of those times. At the very least, she could pass the rum over to him, which is what she did once he was sitting.

He was wearing the uniform of a common or garden levy man, or import tax collector – simple grey jacket and grey shirt with a slightly grubby red neckerchief where a wealthier man might wear a cravat – except his clothes were past their best: dark patches where oil or fat had fallen during clumsily consumed meals, seams that were loose at the shoulders, the tailoring too tight across the chest and too short in the arms. For a beard, he was very cleanshaven and his skin had an unpleasantly boyish glow that was entirely at odds with his face, which would have better suited a bulldog, or miniature pug, all the features gathered in a small space in the middle, except the eyes, which were very wide apart. When he smiled it was clear that he did indeed bite his fingers: his teeth were unusually short, having, presumably, been ground down by his thick, dense nails.

In short, he was completely the opposite of the kind of person that Penthenny would ever, by choice, share a drink with, and since she was in completely the opposite of the kind of place where she would ever, by choice, drink, and, on top of all that, she wasn't supposed to be drinking anywhere anyway, so it stuck in her craw a little that she should be so close to being discovered doing things she shouldn't be doing by a man to whom she owed a minimum of a hundred silver pieces, and that, in order to remain undiscovered, she was now going to have to entertain someone who she wouldn't have crossed the road to piss on had he appeared there on fire.

'Rum?' she said, very quietly.

'What?' the man said, very loudly, leaning over the table so that his pug dog face was about six inches from hers.

Penthenny sighed, leaned back, pushed over her glass to him and said, slightly more loudly, but still, she hoped, quietly enough not to alert St Aubrey, 'Would you like some rum?'

The man looked down, and then he did what Penthenny had been about to do earlier, before she stopped herself, which was to down the rum in one.

'Another glass over here!' he called out to the girl who was still polishing glasses, 'and a pint of cockles in their shells.' His face took on a lascivious set – one eye opened wide, the other one slit, and the corners of his mouth pulled up – which resolved, eventually, into a wink, the subtext of which was that, because the word 'cockles' had the name of part of the male genitalia in it, and that therefore the food was considered an aphrodisiac by association, the pair might eventually engage in sexual intercourse.

'What should I call you?' he said, which was an odd thing to say.

Penthenny couldn't think of a name quickly enough – the most part of her mind was taken up with imagining ways this whole situation might be quickly and safely ended as soon as was humanly possible – so she said 'Niamh' and immediately regretted it.

'Neef? An unusual name for such a pretty lady.'

Now she had to suffer the name of her wife butchered by this idiot, which was a twofold torture, the sound of it being bad, but the reminder of her betrayal – actual in breaking Niamh's prohibition, and symbolic in having to appear to be interested in this man – was worse.

The very prompt bar girl put the new glass on the table, complete with its own doily, and also the pint of cockles in their shells, which was garnished with a small, but very fresh-looking, salad, arranged on the plate on which the pint glass was standing.

'They're an aphrodisiac, you know?' he said, unnecessarily, but he was staring into the glass and neither of the other two knew who he was talking to, so neither of them felt they had to reply.

'Shall I get two pins?' the girl said.

The man was about to say something, but Penthenny put up her hand. 'Not for me,' she said, 'they give me the shits.' This wasn't at all true, but the thought of wheedling cockles out of their shells with this man was more than Penthenny could take.

In the window pane, the reflection of St Aubrey was indicating for the girl to come over.

'You can call me Tom,' the man, Tom presumably, said.

St Aubrey said something to the girl, who went back to the bar.

'What?' Penthenny said, not having heard Tom because she was concentrating her hearing on St Aubrey.

'Tom,' he said again. 'You can call me Tom.'

Now the girl was coming back to St Aubrey's table with menus.

'Oh, for god's sake,' Penthenny sighed.

'What?' Tom said.

Penthenny turned her attention back to the man. 'Nothing. What were you saying?'

The girl came over with the cockle pin.

'You can call me Tom,' Tom said, irritably now. 'Tom. Tom.'

Penthenny frowned. 'Like the drum?'

'What?' Tom said, and now he looked like he was going to kick off.

Penthenny tried to give him her best smile, to return the horrible man back to his cockles, but thankfully the door opened again, turning both of their attentions towards it.

Bizarrely, or so it seemed to Penthenny at the time, in came a black puppy dog, probably no more than six months old, all alone, his red tongue lolling out of the side of his mouth.

He looked around, this dog, and then, seeing Penthenny, he trotted over.

St Aubrey and his colleagues were too busy ordering food from the menu to notice, and the bar girl was reciting the list of specials, but the dog didn't seem to be interested in anyone else. It was Penthenny he made for, and when he arrived he said, 'Might I trouble you to pull out a chair for me? I much prefer to be at roughly the same level, height-wise, as the people with whom I am conversing.'

Penthenny, shocked into acquiescence by the fact of the puppy's ability to speak, and also finding no fault in its logic, or the politeness of its request, did exactly as she had been asked. The dog hopped up and sat, nicely, at the table. It was still a little low, so it placed its chin on the tabletop and rested its head there, panting.

The bar girl, having taken St Aubrey and the sheriffs' lunch orders, skipped over, an expression of awkward concern on her face. 'I'm terribly sorry,' she said, 'but dogs aren't allowed in the dining area. I'll have to ask you to take it outside.'

Penthenny was about to say something to the effect that this dog wasn't hers, and that therefore the responsibility to remove it wasn't hers either, but the dog started speaking before she could.

'Firstly,' it said, the voice coming directly from its throat, not troubling its lips, 'I am not an "it". That word is reserved for objects, a category into which I should not be placed. I am a "he". Secondly...' He paused for a moment here, seemingly to check whether the truth of his first point had been accepted before proceeding, but the girl's face showed nothing but bemusement. He went on. 'Secondly,' he said, 'the rule against dogs in the dining area is in place, I have no doubt, to prevent disruption to the provision of this establishment's services, something that I do not intend. I understand your prejudice against persons such as myself, but I am a very unusual example of my species – indeed, following the passage of my fathers into the realm of ghosts, I believe myself to be one of only two magical dogs extant in the material realm – and your prejudice is unwarranted in my case. It might be said that this cockle-eating gentleman here is more liable to disrupt the smooth running of your lunchtime service than I would be, since he is, by the look of him, somewhat "rough around the edges" to use a euphemism, and such people tend to drink too much and to become clumsy...' The man was about to object to this, but the dog raised his paw. 'I mean no offence; drink is an addictive and powerfully psychoactive substance, and those who fall under its spell are often blameless.'

The girl, confused by this turn of events, shook her head. 'What about the covers?' she said.

Now it was the dog's turn to seem confused. He turned his head first to one side then the other. 'I'm afraid I do not understand you. What do you mean by "covers"?'

The girl was on more familiar territory with this. 'The dining room only has so many seats, so many "covers". It's not full now, but it will be when lunch starts properly. The manager won't let people sit here without ordering food.'

The dog looked down at himself, saw that he was sitting in a seat, and realised what was to be done. 'If you would be so kind,' he said, 'please open the purse that is attached to my collar. Inside you will find coins. Take sufficient to purchase a meal for me – meat, primarily, with as few additional flavourings as the chef will allow – and also bring meals of their choosing for these other two of your patrons sitting at this table. Take for yourself a gratuity – shall we say five coppers? – for your trouble. Is this an acceptable solution?'

The girl couldn't find any fault in the dog's reasoning, any more than Penthenny had been able to, so she opened the purse, took the money, closed the purse again, took Penthenny's and Tom's orders, and left, scratching her head through her bonnet.

'Let me introduce myself,' the dog said. 'I am Anaximenes, the magical dog, bearer of the epithet "World Saviour". I am the son and brother of Sirius and Anaximander, the grandson of Thales. I have been led here, indirectly, by the ghosts of my father–brothers – they are beside you, but choose not to be seen – because Sirius has scryed into the future and knows that with you, Captain Penthenny, your crew and the magical dog Treachery – known to you as Perdida – I would be fated to fulfil my destiny. Additionally, I would live a life of happiness and adventure. This latter outcome is something my fathers wish for me, their lives having been lived under the shadows of the so-called "Cities of the Weft", places which are engaged in the war of the Weftling Tontine, and which are also periodically persecuted by the Assembly's Atheistic Crusades. These actions ended their material existence, and they would like me to avoid their fate, find happiness, and allow them, vicariously through me, to enjoy an emotion that was withheld from them by the circumstances of their births.' The dog, Anaximenes, delivered this speech in a manner that would be considered breathless in a person, but which, because he was breathing calmly throughout, the voice coming magically out of his throat, couldn't quite be described that way.

Once he'd finished, he stayed as he was for a moment, and then put his chin back on the table and stared at Penthenny, with dark and expectant eyes glistening.

'Is it yours?' Tom said. 'Only, it's cramping my style.' He got up from his seat with the look of a man about to seize a dog by the scruff of its neck, march it out of a dining room, out of an inn, and throw it out into the sea.

Again, Anaximenes raised a paw. 'As I believe I made clear, it would be a category error for a person to assume I was an "it". Moreover, I find the use of the word in this context offensive. Please return to your seat and await the meal I have purchased for you.'

Tom didn't seem inclined to do as he was told and scraped his chair back, making the kind of sound that Penthenny had been trying to avoid when she did it earlier. She didn't look, but if that hadn't drawn St Aubrey's attention then she wasn't sure why not. 'Sit down, Tom-tom,' she said.

Tom scoffed, which is an annoying sound at the best of times. 'I don't let women tell me what to do, and I definitely don't let dogs tell me what to do.' He took a determined step forward towards Anaximenes, and the little dog started growling, but it was what Penthenny did next that stopped the man in his tracks. She reached into her jacket and pulled out her pistol, which was of the flintlock type, but modified by Oisin to be both more reliable and less of a faff to load and fire. She put the gun on the table, which made Tom freeze, and then she indicated that he should sit back down, now, by pointing firmly in the direction of his chair. 'Sit down,' she said under her breath.

To his credit, Tom did as he was told.

Anaximenes didn't go so far as to put his paws on the table, but he did stand up, taking Penthenny's actions as defensive of him. When she pointed to the dog's chair and repeated her command, he looked sad, but did it.

'Listen,' she said, almost hissing, almost whispering, but giving over the impression that they should both 'listen' in such a way that they both felt they ought to do it, particularly when she put her hand on the pistol grip and her finger on the trigger. 'The man behind me – don't look! – the skinny one in green, is someone I owe money to. One hundred silver, more or less. Now, I don't have a hundred silver, and I'm in no mood to inform him of that fact. So, what we're going to do, the three of us, is to sit here, quietly, not drawing attention to ourselves until he and his friends – sheriffs, you'll notice – have finished their lunches and gone their ways. So that means no barking, dog, and no shouting, Tom-tom. Do you understand me?'

Anaximenes nodded enthusiastically, as if this was a game.

Tom didn't seem so keen. 'What are you going to do, Neef my dear, if I get up and go over to him and point you out?'

Penthenny fixed him with a milk-curdling stare. 'Do you really want to find out?'

Tom looked away before Penthenny did.

'I thought not. Why don't you crack on with those cockles and keep quiet.'

The door opened again and now a party of eight came in.

They were matrons of a very well-dressed type, but, from the way they were braying and laughing and conducting loud and ribald conversations across each other, not very well-bred.

The bar girl showed them to their table which, as luck would have it, was directly between Penthenny's and St Aubrey's. You should always be grateful for small mercies – this was one of Niamh's favourite sayings – and never more accurate had Penthenny thought it than now, when it seemed like the presence of these women might make the difference between a stint working off a debt in a nail factory and not doing anything of the sort.

'Can I ask,' Anaximenes asked, 'what you thought of what I said before this man got up and inspired you to threaten him with your gun? Specifically, are you inclined to allow me to join your company and thereby secure for myself my destiny, and also a happy and adventurous existence?'

Penthenny paused, then breathed in so hard through her nose that her nostrils whistled. 'I have other things on my mind. And anyway, we already have a dog.'

The dog nodded again, but this time thoughtfully. 'Your second point is something of which I was already aware. Perhaps you didn't hear me, but I know that Treachery, whom you have renamed "Perdida", is already part of your crew. She is my half-sister, though we have never met. Your first point is something with which, perhaps, I can be of service.' Without waiting, Anaximenes jumped down to the ground and walked past the well-dressed but ill-bred women over to where Pascale de St Aubrey was sitting. The dog was already well out of reach before Penthenny could react.

Tom smiled, crossed his arms, and seemed to settle himself in to watch the show.

Penthenny could hardly call out, go over or in any other way prevent the dog from doing whatever it was about to do, at least not without alerting St Aubrey to her presence, so she had no choice but to remain where she was, watching the reflection of whatever debacle was about to transpire in the window.

She didn't have to wait long.

The noisy table of women wasn't noisy enough to mask Anaximenes's words, which he announced by barking sharply three times in what seemed like the canine equivalent of a dramatic clearing of the throat, and, just like that sound, all eyes were immediately on him: Tom's, Penthenny's, all of the women's, the three sheriffs', and Pascale de St Aubrey's.

'May I have your attention?' Anaximenes said, somewhat redundantly, and when it was clear that he already had it – this from the great deal of staring and pointing and exclamations directed towards and about him – he went on, 'I am Anaximenes, the talking dog, and to the best of my knowledge there are no others living who can claim the same distinction. I am here, in this place, in the company of my fathers, Sirius and Anaximander, neither of whom you can see since they are ghosts...' There was some consternation expressed in the gathered – talking dogs are one thing, but ghosts are something else altogether. '... Do not fear! They will do you no harm. Indeed, they have, for a fee, agreed to provide a very valuable service. Sirius can see the future, and while he cannot communicate this information to any but Anaximander, Anaximander is gifted with the ability to speak, though only I can hear him. He can hear me, and so, by a relay of sorts, I can communicate with Sirius. Now, if any of you wish to know what will happen later today, or tomorrow, or ten years hence, you need only ask me, having paid the necessary fee, and I will tell you. What say you to that?'

If a passing beggar, drunkard or mountebank had said this, then no crowd would have believed them; the bar girl would have called for the bouncer and the ne'er-do-well would have been unceremoniously expelled from the premises. But a talking dog? Such a thing was already unbelievable, and yet, barring some unprecedented feat of ventriloquism, here one was, addressing them.

Still, even a fool does not hand a dog money if it says it can predict the future, a sentiment expressed by one of the sheriffs, who added, after some choice swear words, 'Prove it!'

Penthenny didn't say anything, but Tom took out a pouch of dice which he kept at his belt for the purposes of gambling, threw it onto the bar near the girl and shouted out, 'How are these dice going to fall?'

Anaximenes jumped up onto a bar stool and sniffed the bag. 'Unfortunately, my limbs are not suitable for the work of removing and rolling these dice, otherwise I would happily demonstrate.'

The diners all made sounds suggestive of the fact that they found this an inadequate response, and that the talking dog was a fraud, but now Tom stood up and went over. 'You tell us what they'll roll, and I'll roll them.'

'Very well. Let me consult my fathers.' Anaximenes went rigid, looking for all the world like a stuffed dog, his eyes filming over, and his mouth and limbs frozen in place.

Penthenny risked looking round, everyone focussing on the dog. Could she make it out? Skirt the walls and take advantage of their preoccupation? She thought that perhaps she could, but then Anaximenes unfroze, and she found that even she was interested in what he had to say.

'There are six six-sided dice in the bag,' he said. 'One will roll one, two will roll two, there will be no threes, no fours, no fives, but three sixes.'

Tom took the dice out of the bag – there were indeed six of them – and now everybody except Penthenny left their tables and crowded around the bar.

Penthenny could not see, but Tom rolled the dice. As they clattered across the bar, she got up from the table and edged, slowly and carefully, away, taking her pistol, but leaving the bottle of rum, horse head label and all, where she had put it.

The dice stopped rolling and there was a gasp from the assembled. One of the ill-bred women gave a little scream.

'You see?' Anaximenes said. 'Now, one and all, prepare your moneys. The fee will operate on a sliding scale – trivial and personal matters are very cheap, those of more import cost more than that, and the fate of nations and matters of public interest cost a great deal.'

'Hold on!' It was Pascale de St Aubrey now who spoke, his voice high and raspy, but still suggestive of authority. 'What if this man with the dice and the talking dog are in cahoots? Weren't they sitting together at that table over there?'

Everyone looked over to where they'd been sitting, but thankfully Penthenny was nowhere near, having made her way halfway to the door.

'Very well,' Anaximenes said, 'although your doubtfulness is becoming tiring. Design your own test.'

St Aubrey thought for a while, enough time for Penthenny to reach the door and put her hand on its handle. 'I will write two lines of poetry on two pieces of paper – girl, give me your order pad and pencil – I will return to my table, so no one sees…'

Before Penthenny could open the door and leave, St Aubrey turned, and now he faced the pirate captain.

It took him a moment to recognise her, but only a moment. He pursed his lips, locked her with a stare. 'Sheriff Stringer, could you arrest the progress of that woman by the door? She's a delinquent debtor of mine.'

Stringer did as he was asked, and while he did it, St Aubrey wrote his lines, watching Penthenny all the while. Only when he was sure Penthenny couldn't escape did he turn back to the bar. 'Now, dog, what will be written on the piece of paper I decide not to tear up?'

Anaximenes blinked. 'In future, please address me by name. No one likes to be referred to by their species title.' He went rigid again, and relaxed again. 'It will say, in the ancient language, "*Ah! misérable chien, si je vous avais offert un paquet d'excréments…*"'

St Aubrey tore up one paper without looking, then opened the other. He read it, and then showed it to the others, who, though they couldn't understand the words, assumed from this that the dog was right. 'Very good!' he said.

It was Anaximenes's turn to lock St Aubrey with a stare. 'The sentiment of the poem from which you quote, while seeming to insult the intelligence of the human public, is ignorant of the way a dog experiences the world. We draw no distinction between the smells of faeces and of perfumes, and are not disgusted by either. It is the information they hold which interests us. In any case, I hope I have convinced you.'

'You have.'

'Then tell me your question. I guarantee that the answer to it will be accurate.'

St Aubrey smiled and withdrew from his jacket a printed handbill. 'On this are listed tomorrow's dogfights. Which dogs will win them?'

Anaximenes nodded. 'You intend to bet on the outcomes of these fights and thereby make money at the expense of both the dogs and the bookmakers? Though I have no qualms about bilking bookmakers, this intention is against my personally held conviction that dogs should not be made to fight each other. Consequently, my fee is higher than it might be, though certainly still affordable.'

'What is your fee?'

Anaximenes hopped down from the bar and went over to where Sheriff Stringer had Penthenny in cuffs. 'The fee is the entirety of this woman's debts cancelled, along with her immediate release from your custody.'

St Aubrey snorted. 'That is a considerable sum.'

'It is near enough nothing in comparison with the money you would make from an eight-dog accumulator, as you must surely know.'

'The winnings are less than you imagine. I would have to buy the silence of those gathered here, for instance. Still, I agree to your price. Give me the names of the winning dogs and I will let her go.'

Things, from this point, proceeded predictably, some going to plan – Penthenny's debt being cancelled – and some not going to plan – St Aubrey kidnapping Anaximenes before he could leave on board the *Muirchú* – but the story of how Penthenny, Niamh and Perdida rescued Anaximenes is one for another time.

About the Author

Sharon Shahani

ALEX PHEBY lives with his wife and two children in Scotland, and teaches at Newcastle University. Alex's second novel, *Playthings*, was short-listed for the 2016 Wellcome Book Prize. His third novel, *Lucia*, was joint winner of the 2019 Republic of Consciousness Prize. *Mordew*, the first book in the Cities of the Weft trilogy, was selected as a Book of the Year by *The Guardian*, the *i*, *Reactor*, and *Locus*.